"Glen Cook single-handedly chan
something a lot of people didn't notice, and maybe still don't.
Reading his stuff is like reading Vietnam War fiction on Peyote."
—Steven Erikson, author of the Malazan Book of the Fallen series

"Over the past 25 years, Cook has carved out a place for himself
among the preeminent fantasy writers of his generation. . . . His
work is unrelentingly real, complex, and honest. The sense of place
that permeates his narrative and characters gives his 'fantasies' more
gravitas and grit than most fictions set in the here-and-now."
—*New York Times* bestselling author Jeff VanderMeer

"A master realist of the imagination."
—*Locus*

"Glen writes a mean book."
—Jim Butcher, author of The Dresden Files

"These books, like so many of Cook's series, are epic in scale but
intimate in focus . . . Cook is a brilliant writer."
—*The Green Man Review*, on *A Fortress in Shadow*

"One of the defining fantasy series ever written. Glen Cook's writing
is a great flood that washes fantasy tropes and clichés away and in
their place we are given three novels that make us reflect on what it
means to be human. . . . On more than one occasion I found chills
running down my spine. Words don't do these novels justice."
—*The Ostentatious Ogre* on *A Cruel Wind*

"Glen Cook is the author of some of my hands-down favorite
books. I hold out his *Black Company* series as arguably the best
military fantasy ever written. The early Garrett books set a
standard for the blending of fantasy and hardboiled fiction."
—*Black Gate*

THE BEST OF GLEN COOK

Books by Glen Cook

The Heirs of Babylon
The Swordbearer
A Matter of Time
The Dragon Never Sleeps
The Tower of Fear
Sung in Blood

Dread Empire

A Cruel Wind (Omnibus):
    A Shadow of All Night Falling
    October's Baby
    All Darkness Met
A Fortress in Shadow (Omnibus):
    The Fire in His Hands
    With Mercy Toward None
Wrath of Kings (Omnibus):
    Reap the East Wind
    An Ill Fate Marshalling
    A Path to Coldness of Heart
An Empire Unacquainted with
    Defeat

The Starfishers Trilogy (Omnibus):
    Shadowline
    Starfishers
    Stars' End

Passage at Arms

Darkwar

Doomstalker
Warlock
Ceremony

The Black Company

The Black Company
Shadows Linger
The White Rose
The Silver Spike
Shadow Games
Dreams of Steel
Bleak Seasons
She Is the Darkness
Water Sleeps
Soldiers Live
Port of Shadows

The Garrett Files

Sweet Silver Blues
Bitter Gold Hearts
Cold Copper Tears
Old Tin Sorrows
Dread Brass Shadows
Red Iron Nights
Deadly Quicksilver Lies
Petty Pewter Gods
Faded Steel Heat
Angry Lead Skies
Whispering Nickel Idols
Cruel Zinc Melodies
Gilded Latten Bones
Wicked Bronze Ambition

Instrumentalities of the Night

The Tyranny of the Night
Lord of the Silent Kingdom
Surrender to the Will of the Night
Working Gods' Mischief

THE BEST OF

GLEN COOK

18 STORIES FROM THE AUTHOR OF
THE BLACK COMPANY AND THE DREAD EMPIRE

GLEN COOK

NIGHT SHADE BOOKS

NEW YORK

TABLE OF CONTENTS

Sunrise... 1

The Devil's Tooth... 21

In the Wind... 53

Quiet Sea... 88

Ghost Stalk... 114

Call for the Dead.. 146

Soldier of an Empire Unacquainted with Defeat...................... 193

Filed Teeth... 256

Darkwar... 298

Enemy Territory... 322

The Waiting Sea... 338

Severed Heads... 348

Winter's Dreams.. 379

The Good Magician... 396

Shadow Thieves... 426

Shaggy Dog Bridge.. 455

Bone Eaters.. 479

Chasing Midnight.. 501

A lot of people can't believe that I, as a writer, may have forgotten details of a story I wrote before they were born. They reckon that I should recall every spoken word and twist, every minor character's secret middle name . . . But I don't. I'm sorry. It doesn't work that way for me.

When I revisit my earlier writing I find, usually, that I don't remember much at all. My novels, especially, are never anything like the romances that I think I remember writing. I tend to end up reading something that I consider to be pretty good stuff from somebody who isn't me now and who maybe never was.

—Glen Cook, 2019

SUNRISE

I liked this story on re-reading but I don't remember anything about it other than that it is set in the same future history as most of my science fiction and that it is a precursor to the novel Shadowline, *first volume in the Starfishers Trilogy. It is included here because I thought it was cool when I reread it.*

1

Kim the Piper, pale and thin, walked the silent streets of a judgement morning—a morning which was, of course, no morning at all but merely the beginning of another day-called period etched on an endless night. Never in all his eighteen hundred years, nor she in her ten thousand, had Edgeward City seen sunrise breaking the darkness besieging her protective dome. Blackworld was a one-face planet, lifeless and boiling on Brightside, frozen on Darkside, where were built the cities of men.

City of men, Kim told himself as he reached Dome Street, which encircled the City just inside the massive glassteel shield. The Star Fathers had made one small error in creating the world. They'd left it with a little spin. It rotated once every twenty-five thousand years, a mile a year, nearly fifteen feet each day. In a sacrilegious moment, Kim questioned the omnipotence of the Star Fathers. They'd been sloppy planet builders, not taking into account the long-term effects of the world's spin.

Ancient books placed Edgeward City near the western terminator, in a vest, steep-walled meteor crater behind the Thunder Mountains. That morning, as Kim climbed stairs to an observation chamber thirty feet up, inside the glassteel of the dome itself, the eastern terminator lay fifty miles away, about to break over the White Mountains which hugged the crater's eastern lip. A first real dawn, and doom, was creeping steadily closer.

Kim entered the chamber, seated himself in an ancient chair, wondered at the need for observation. There was so very little to see. Night, forever on. Stars immobile, untwinkling; frozen constellations. A hint of dark landscape, poorly illuminated by the stars. A dull red glow at the foot of the driftwall (which kept dust from the crater wall from engulfing the base of the dome) where the conical and hemispherical tractor and presser fields of the meteor screens were generated. A ghost image of the White Mountains, starlight reflected off fields of oxygen and nitrogen snow.

There was a hint of coruscation outlining the peaks of the mountains, barely discernable, gaseous matter and stripped ions fleeing to Darkside from the sun-burned plains beyond, reflecting the sun's electro-magnetic field and particular radiations. The matter solidified again this side of the mountains. Gradually, over the decades as sunrise drew nearer, the white snowfields darkened, the dust against the driftwell deepened . . .

The conical tractor field glowed pinkly, the pressor hemisphere glared into golden flame, the City shuddered on its foundations, grumbled. "Meteor," Kim whispered to himself. "Big one." High in the night above the City somewhere the meteor's course was changed, directed away from the dome. Kim saw it, white hot from the heat energy gained during the sudden change, smash into the crater wall some miles away. The explosion was almost atomic in proportions. Dust boiled up, the City shivered, glowing bits of shattered rock streaked toward the White Mountains like a thousand tiny rockets.

"Magnificent!" he whispered. For the first time in a year, he was glad to be alive. Lately, he had been thinking much of voluntary termination, but this vindicated his reluctance. There was always one more new thing to be seen, if one could endure the overpowering boredom between happenings. Two new things, perhaps.

He was nearly blinded by the sudden spear of light exploding upward from somewhere in the White Mountains. Like a long and dissipating arm of fire, it reached toward the City. "Flame tongue." He was awed. It was the first time he had seen this most spectacular of Blackworld's few weather phenomena, the result of the sun's rays falling suddenly on a patch of gas snow, converting it from the solid to gaseous states in microseconds. Sunlight reflected off the dust carried upward by the expanding vapors made the flame tongue.

Kim considered both manifestations with something like religious awe. They were omens, harbingers of the fiery doom the sun promised the City.

So said the Disciple of the Sun Cultists, whose word was presently law, both religious and temporal (conveniently ignoring the fact that the meteors were present only because Blackworld had entered their cometary orbits as they came in from deep space, as happened every nine hundred years; and sunrise was an event expected for millennia). Edgeward was the last of the great dome cities of Blackworld, farthest from the sun when the world was created (or colonized, as a small, atheist faction would have it), last to be destroyed as the world turned, her agony prolonged because, according to Sun Cult dogma, the Sun God had known she was the city to sink deepest into iniquity. For her wickedness and belief in the heresy of the Star Fathers, the jealous god would slay her with spears of light. One day soon the sun would rise above the White Mountains, The tractor and pressor screens would be as nothing before the sudden storm of radiant energies. The top of the dome would melt, the City's atmospheric temperature would soar three thousand degrees, and molten glassteel would be hurled into a burning sky.

So said the Disciple of the Sun, and Kim knew most of it was true. He had watched the destruction of The City of Night fifteen hundred years earlier, and had talked to men who had seen Darkside Landing die . . .

He sighed, tried to turn his thoughts to more pleasant subjects, could not. Well, thank the Star Fathers, the end, when it finally came would be swift. A lance of sunlight, a boom, and the structures of Edgeward City would like waxen images melt into a vast and bubbling pool—a lake of fire. The Disciple made much of that lake of fire.

A few structures would remain standing—skeletal grotesqueries with melting temperatures above those induced by Blackworld's fierce little pre-nova sun.

Another shudder ran through the dome's foundations. Meteor? He saw no evidence. Probably caused by tectonic activity in the White Mountains. Perhaps there should be some changes in old names. The Thunder Mountains were now silent and white with gas snows while the White

Mountains were dirty and rumbling with the expansion effects of the sun's heat. Once it had been the other way around.

The clicking open of the chamber door drew Kim's mind from the sword extended over Edgeward City. But he did not turn. This was his private place, the place where an immortal could escape the crowds of anciently familiar faces, the place where he could be alone with his thoughts. He would recognize no intrusions.

"Kim?" Soft, feminine, a voice he knew well, a voice which was part of the laughter and tears of his recent past, a voice not entirely unexpected. A voice from the days—before the rise of the Disciple—when a Piper had been allowed to pipe, and a Dancer to dance. Illian Gey, a Dancer. Still a mortal, only twenty, undecided as to when she would begin taking the drugs—as if they mattered now. He and she had nearly been a couple once, when joy and entertainment had been unforbidden.

"Kim?" There was pleading in her voice this time, a soft little cry for support. "Did you hear? The Disciple sentenced my brother to the fire."

He had no need to look to picture her face as it must be, surrounded by disheveled hair, her eye- and cheek-paints smeared by hands and tears. Thus she had appeared an hour earlier when, at the Temple, the Disciple had ordered the stake for her brother, guilty of trying to flee the doomed City. Kim had watched Illian from across the chamber. He remembered the sudden pallor, the sudden shriek, the struggle with Heaven's Guard . . .

"Kim?" This time there was desperation.

"I know," he replied, still not turning. "I saw a flame tongue this morning. My first."

"How nice for you." Her sarcasm overrode her sorrow. Soon she would be angry. Kim smiled at the night before him.

"What're we going to do?" she asked. "My father won't help. You're all I have."

"I'll watch the execution, perhaps," Kim replied. "I've never seen one. I should before the end. One vision of all things . . ."

"You hate him!"

Smiling again, Kim said, "And not without reason. What did Walther the Dancer deny Kim the Musician, without cause?"

"Dancers don't couple with Musicians!" she retorted. But her words had that ring of rote Kim remembered all too well. She had said those words before, and had denied them by her actions until her brother and father had threatened to stop her dancing—all pointless now, with the Disciple in power, entertainment denied, and sunrise but days away.

"Nor do devil worshippers, sun worshippers, cultists rule the City," he replied. "If *that* tradition can be broken, how little meaning have the customs of Artists?"

"He didn't do anything!"

"He denied me you." Kim wished she would go away now. Her sorrow and self-pity had been replaced by anger. Fine. He had given all he was willing. Now let her take her problem to her own kind.

"That's not what I meant. His crime. All he did was try to leave the City, to join the Nomads. They're a people who'd appreciate him. He committed no crime."

Kim frowned. This was growing tedious. Yet he answered her, "But he did. He tried to deny the Sun God retribution for his unbelief. As the Disciple said, he has to be given to the flames early, lest he escape punishment. It's simple, Illian. Surely even you can understand." His frown deepened. He had spoken her name, He had vowed never to do so again.

He did not believe his words. Sun Cultists were mad mortals, their religion insane. Enough, Illian, go away. He had no time for the frenzied affairs of mortals.

No time? He had had ages of leisure, ages of boredom, Edgeward City was automated to the nth degree. What work there was was play, with waiting lists hundreds of names long. Art was the reason most people lived. Music, sculpture, painting, dancing, writing, and each immortal Artist had an eternity in which to do nothing but polish his art.

Had, Kim reminded himself. No more. The sun was close. Works centuries in the creation were being savagely whipped to completion. His own *Dying Star* a vast, epic overture two centuries in the composition, had been claiming all his attention of late. Working under pressure, he had almost regained the urgency of Man the Mortal. Until he had gone this morning to see Illian's brother's judgement . . .

"Kim, I need help."

His anger grew. Would she not leave? He had already tolerated more than he would have from anyone else. "Go to your Dancers!" he snapped as he turned in his seat. "Or your mortals."

He stopped. Looking at her was a mistake. Behind him, she was a disembodied voice. Now she was Illian, the woman with whom he had almost coupled. A woman he loved still, though he refused to admit it, even to himself. To look at her was to see her, in dimension up into the past, to the happy days and beyond, and all along the line downward to the present misery.

"They say Musicians can be crueler than priests," she murmured.

Harsh words, marshalled at his lips, were stifled. Her point told. He stared at her there, silhouetted against the lights of the City behind and below her, a woman-shape without the features painted in.

"There's nothing I can do," he said at last, "so there's nothing I'll try to do. Your brother, like most mortals, is a fool. There's no escape." Inside, although he would not admit it, this disturbed him. "I've no love for the Sun Cult, yet I'll die here in the City where I was born and have lived. To join the Nomads and become Homeless . . . that would be worse, I think."

She moved up beside his chair. The light through the glassteel behind her did little to illuminate her. "Are you sure *he's* the fool?" she asked softly. Kim shivered. Her voice . . . So many memories . . . "Father says we have a week. Seven days, then sunrise—" the word came out like a curse which had to be forced—"will come through the Teeth—" she pointed to a pair of tall, conical mountains with a deep cleft between them, clearly defined by the coruscation—"and hit the dome. Don't you want to live?"

After a moment of silence, Kim replied, "Yes. But not in a Nomad tractor."

"Isn't that better than being dead?"

"No." Did he really believe that? He wanted to think about it, but she gave him no time.

"There's a city . . ."

"Illian, Illian, don't be silly. Rumors, legends. Barrow-Beneath-the-Mountain? That's nonsense. And you know it. The Nomads haven't the art. They're mortals. They don't live long enough to build cities. And, even if the fairy tale were true, the sun will reach the Thunder Mountains before the end of the century. Here or there, where would my death be more important?"

2

Illian stamped the floor beside him, looked down angrily. Part of the anger, she realized, was because he refused to look at her again. "Why?

Why're immortals determined to die? Why won't you save yourselves?" She knew one answer, though it was hard to accept. The immortality drug. One paid in lost emotion and initiative for the banishment of death. Some of the oldest immortals had grown lethargic almost to the point of catatonia—there was so little to *do* with all the time gained. Which, when considered with the imminent death of the City, was why she had not as yet taken the drugs. She felt that if she must die, she should do so as a whole human.

But, she admitted to herself, if the sun were no threat, she would have taken the drugs. Twenty years old was a perfect age to be forever, for a woman. Looking into the night above Kim's head, she tried to picture the extinction of death (she could not accept the afterlives of the Sun Cult or the Church of the Star Fathers). Not even stars to break the eternal darkness—if even that could be experienced.

She was suddenly aware that he was trying to answer her questions. "This is the last city on a graveyard world. What future have we? What cosmic difference if we die now, next year, or next century? We're an old race, Illian, pale and tired. There're no frontiers anymore. To lie down, to rest, to steal a few moments of peace, these are the only things that interest us. There's no reason to live. You, your brother, your mortal friends, you're anachronisms, throwbacks, relics from a time so far in the past that, were you not human, you'd be considered rare artifacts. Take the drugs. You'll soon understand." He paused, sighed wearily. "You've heard my thoughts. May I be alone?" He turned his eyes back to the landscape outside, leaned back in his chair, closed his eyes.

Pique. "We're the anachronisms?" she asked softly, staring down, almost laughing. "Us? Throwbacks? Kim, that's funny. You're what? Ten, twenty centuries older than me? You Old Ones are the ones who want to die . . ." Suddenly she was frightened, terribly frightened. She did not want to die.

Didn't he remember the death of The City of Night, fifteen hundred years ago, and the destruction of Darkside Landing a century before that? Did he want that for himself? Wasn't he afraid too? Why were the Old Ones so little interested in surviving? Because they were so old death was unreal? Many were older than Kim and had watched their world dying for millennia. Perhaps it was because the drugs left them no will.

Something caught her eye. "Oh, look!"

"Now what?" Kim grumbled. But he opened his eyes. "Oh. Another flame tongue."

She'd not noticed it. "No, no," pointing, "there by the driftwall."

"A Nomad tractor," he said. "So? They're not uncommon."

"Well, what's it doing there?"

She could have slapped him for his unconcern. He just shrugged, said, "I don't know. Wasn't there a while ago," and closed his eyes again.

She stamped her foot again, anger rising because she could not understand his lack of emotion. While he had been courting her, she had been so flattered at receiving the attentions of an immortal that she had overlooked his flatness. But now she saw him for what he was. Just a name, ambulatory. Hardly a person, different from other Musicians only in his choice of instrument. A nothing.

The flame tongue faded, the Nomad tractor flickered into invisibility. It occurred to her that the tractor might be there to pick up refugees. The Nomads were descendants of refugees from other domes. Suddenly excited, she revealed the true reason she had come. "Kim, I've got to know the key-code for the gate locks." He was old enough to remember. No one had gone out of the City for centuries, and the verbal opening code was almost forgotten, but Kim knew it. If only her brother had not tried to open them by trial and error . . .

Kim's head, almost invisible in the renewed darkness, shook slowly. He lifted his pipe to his lips, ran up and down a scale, then began playing experimentally. She recognized a passage from his *Dying Star*. A flat, gloomy work, like Kim himself, and as lifeless. She doubted it would be proclaimed a masterwork, for, of all Musicians, Kim was the only one who did not know he had no talent.

He offered no hope—for the moment. She turned, eased out the door, left him to contemplate the City's last days of night.

Illian Gey was a sad young woman striding angrily, returning home. The young of Edgeward City, except those of the Sun Cult, were all sad or angry—cultists were merely mad. It was something youth was born to, something they outgrew when they began taking immortality capsules. For the drug, like most, exacted a price. It polished off the edges and corners, wore the hollows, of a user's emotions. It pulled the teeth of curiosity and clipped the claws of the competitive drive. In the eyes of Illian, it left one less than human.

She slowed, considering the immortals' lack of passion in the face of sunrise. Above, serpents of light wriggled across the inner surface of the dome, masking the forever darkness beyond. Like intellect, she thought, which helped mask the forever darkness beyond life. Let either flicker for an instant and the endless black gulf rolled quickly in upon one.

She feared death. Was terrified. Though dawn had approached as inexorably, she had not feared before the rise of the Sun Cult. There had been no need, men had evaded death for millennia. It was an accidental thing, involving only the incautious. It was no personal danger, no, never, for there were the drugs and, certainly, *she'd* never be careless. And when sunrise drew near, one could go live with the Nomads.

She had not anticipated the difficulty of escaping the City. Nor had she expected the rise of the Sun Cult. Suddenly, death was at hand.

She shivered as she walked The Street of a Thousand mirrors where her reflection was presented in a thousand distortions, like her self-image on a thousand different days. This, she thought, was Edgeward City's one truly great work of art. Here the Artist's message was simplicity itself, you cannot know all your own faces.

She neared home. Music came forth, and laughter. Her friends, mortal Artists, mocking death the unreal. They could not believe that doom crouched behind the White Mountains. It would leap upon them, and they would die not believing.

She passed a man of the Sun Cult who made no secret of watching her house. Stanwin, a childhood friend of Walther's. How did he dare appear here, after the morning's trial? She wanted to scream, to claw—no, no sense following Walther's deadly lead. Stanwin would report her if given reason. A child, trying to hurt in return for the hurt of rejection . . .

She entered the house and a dozen gay couples surrounded her, grew silent in the face of her depression. She looked at their faces, saw disbelief—and the underlying fear and resignation. Were they beaten? After only one defeat? Or did they truly disbelieve? Why the laughter? Forced cheer to banish thoughts of night?

Pale laughter forcedly resumed.

"Illian?"

She turned. Markel Gay, a cousin. Not a favorite. The sort who would've been a cultist had he been allowed to run things. A man of machinations, totally self-centered, often unconsciously cruel, uncaring if aware. "He'd scarcely talk to me."

"Hard feeling still?"

She nodded. "And he doesn't care. None of them do. It's the drug."

"Yes." He was a handsome young man, easily able to project an unreal "rightness" that made people want him to have his way. Illian sometimes wished he wasn't a relative. She knew him well enough to see the monster behind the public mask. But fear had begun to crack that mask. "Can we talk?"

In those three words, Illian knew, he expressed his contempt for the partiers' intellect. Leave them. They were unworthy of inclusion. Sometimes she hated Markel. At that moment she wondered if she was a cut above the partiers only because she was a link with Kim and the key-code.

"Father's bedroom. It's the only room not filled."

They went.

"There's a notion that's been in my head all morning," said Markel. "Hand me a life capsule."

She took one from a container on a table near her, tossed it.

"These can be opened." He demonstrated, pulling the halves apart and dumping immortality drug onto her palm. "Suppose we replace Kim's drug with powdered sugar? Five days without won't hurt him, and should release his emotions."

"And?" She did not like the risks, yet the alternative was to do as Kim did—sit and wait.

"He'll get scared. Scared enough, maybe, to want out. Can you get into his room?"

"Yes." Unless his door key-code had changed, Unlikely. Immortals changed nothing. She bit her lower lip, feeling guilty. As with Kim, the love spark within her died hard.

"Oh," she said, remembering, "there's a cultist across the street. Watching us."

"I know. Stanwin. I'll take care of him." She moved away, suddenly frightened. That look on his face . . . But she had to listen. He was leader, now that Walther was gone. She distracted herself by saying, "There's a Nomad tractor outside the east gate, by the driftwall."

Markel mulled this over before saying, "Good. What kind?"

"I don't know. Big, though, like some of the mining machines in the museum."

"Could carry a lot of people, Wait a few minutes while I take care of Stanwin. Then go to Kim's." He left.

Illian dropped to her father's bed, wondered if she was doing right. To keep the drug from Kim was dangerous. If the concentration in his tissues grew too small, he would begin aging again. Rapidly. He could die.

But everyone would die soon if something weren't done! The fear came on like a tall breaker, crushing . . . So terrible to know one's allotted time and have to sit counting the minutes . . . She had to do something, anything, to keep from thinking. Kim. The capsules. A hope. A hope that endangered someone else; better than nothing . . .

The logical, survival, and moral parts of her mind fought, and, as they will, yielded a compromise favorable to herself. She'd change the capsules and risk Kim, but would stay close to see that nothing bad happened. Just because of an old feeling for an immortal Musician.

She got powdered sugar from the kitchen, made hasty explanations to curious partiers who watched her go out with uncertain frowns.

Stanwin wasn't in the street.

Kim's apartment. She knocked. No answer. She spoke the words that opened his door. As expected, they were unchanged. She found his capsules, replaced the drug of the dozen in the container.

She was shaking when she finished, again uncertain of the rightness of it. But fear knew no morality, paid no service to scruples.

She had to get out before he returned. Her presence would be too suspicious . . .

The door opened as she approached it.

3

Kim was uneasy as he walked The Street of a Thousand Mirrors. Here and there he paused to examine his distorted image, as if he might find the cause of his malaise hidden in his reflection. It was getting worse fast. Now there were nightmares—how long since he had dreamed? So many centuries he had lost count. Since the destruction of The City of Night. Destruction. Perhaps that was it. The discomfiture had begun with Illian's visit, and had grown steadily since.

He glanced toward the east end of the street, saw nothing but dome, blackness overlaid by squirming serpents of light. The same above.

The City shuddered underfoot. Another omen. They were increasingly common, caused by almost constant tectonic activity in the thawing White Mountains.

There were executions, too. A dozen in the past four days as the Disciple made certain his Sun God went uncheated. Mortals of all stripes were growing increasingly frightened—Illian among them.

Illian. He'd found her in his apartment, terrified, and she'd fallen into his arms weeping, begging him to help her brother. He'd been defensive, thinking she was after the key-code again, yet had been touched by her concern for Walther. Of course, nothing could save the man, but her emotions were impressive (familial bonds were tenuous among immortals—Kim had a sister he'd not seen in centuries). Today he fought a vague guilt—in addition to the ghosts of other unfamiliar emotions—at not being able to help Illian.

He paused, piped a tentative arpeggio for *Dying Star*. It sounded sour. The entire work was sour. In a fit of frustration, last night, he'd thrown away two decades' work, begun an entire movement anew. Illian had been there—she was at his apartment often, which disturbed him not a little—and had been shocked.

He stared at himself in a mirror, portrayed with a head shrunken by two-thirds. What had happened to the easy comfort of his life? He knew death would claim him sometime, despite the drugs, and had thought his peace was made—until the past few days he'd never worried about his final event. His head seemed bigger now, with sudden room for all the fears of mortal man.

Mortal man. Ages had passed since he'd become immortal. And now he felt as he had before taking the first capsules. And he was tired, feeling old. Did a known hour of death do that? He'd noticed no distress in his fellows.

He piped another arpeggio. Better. Perhaps he should return to work. He had forty-six hours to complete *Dying Star* . . . He hurled the pipe at a mirror. Neither was damaged, but his heart was broken. He'd suddenly and clearly seen his creation for what it was. Hackwork. He was no composer. Anyone honest could have told him *Dying Star*, grand as it was in conception, was mediocre. Bad. Passage moved into passage jerkily; some of the movements, if orchestrated, would prove sheer cacophony. He remembered the forced smiles and shaking heads he wasn't supposed to see, that he hadn't noticed even when looking, and realized how patronizingly he had been treated. He could pipe another's music, but could create nothing significant himself. His heart was shattered. In self-realization he was left with nothing, save, perhaps, a pale anger.

Suddenly, there was no more solace in music. He felt alone, abandoned. A mere technician. Less than a machine, for a machine could perform and never make a mistake. Less than a machine.

He had been bound to Music Hall for premier and final performances, to hear the epitaph compositions of friends; but, no, not now, they might laugh. In these last few hours, with no future to concern them, they could freely laugh at the little incompetent with his simple pipe—the only instrument he could master. No, he could not face that. He must go home. Illian would be there. Poor, sad Illian. They could comfort one another. Too bad that only imminent death had been able to bring them together.

As he walked, he met several people he knew. They smiled pleasantly and bowed and made small talk and asked if he had seen Regev's superb *Requiem—A Sonata in B flat Major*, and he had to say no, he'd been working, and they all went away with little shakes of the head, hiding condescension behind modest little smiles, Meaningless smiles, mocking smiles for the village idiot. They went about their business, smiling as if the sun would never rise.

What was wrong? The more time passed, the more he thought mortally, and the older he felt, His emotions, too long dull, were raging like storms. Soon, if they continued to grow, they would be explosive as sunrise.

Sunrise. For the first time in memory, it frightened him. Just a mild fear, nothing to set him running like a mortal, but a fear all the same. Until that moment, sunrise had been just another event in the orderly progression of his life. More important than most, true, because of its magnitude . . . Suddenly, he panicked. He ran for the safe, warm womb of home.

Illian was out. Where was she? The panic grew. She was all he had. He gulped an immortality capsule and glass of water, rushed back into the street. Her house. She must be there. He ran again, and ignored the amazed glances of fellow immortals. Some were shocked.

His lungs were bags of fire when he reached the street where she lived. No athlete, he was unaccustomed to such activity—still, he shouldn't have been so tired. He was growing old while regaining the wild emotionalism of his youth.

A mortal in Sun Cult dress lounged opposite Illian's tiny house. The boy's eyebrows rose slightly. Kim ignored him, knocked.

Her father answered. His face clouded, angry as ever an immortal's grew. "Go away," he said.

Kim's fear evaporated. A new emotion formed. A hard, cold emotion. It grew in him like a sword—a two-edged sword, he quickly saw. And didn't care.

"Where's Illian?"

"Go away, Musician." Contempt dripped from his last word. Dancers saw Musicians as an evil necessary to their art, but of no importance in the general scheme. Musicians thought Dancers mere leeches . . .

The sword within grew hard and long. Eighteen hundred years long, Kim thought. "Move aside, Dancer." He surprised himself with the hardness of his voice. And Illian's father, Kim found his expression a delight. But the man would not move. Kim swung.

It was a clumsy blow, delivered with no forethought and no idea of target. It hit the man's chest. He gasped, staggered back. Kim moved forward for another. Here, on this man, he could vent all his anger, all his frustrations, could show all Edgeward City he was not a dull child to be patronized . . .

"Kim!"

He stopped. Illian, distraught, got between them, flashed him an angry look, then maneuvered her bewildered father into another room. Soon she returned, more collected.

"What's the matter? You're acting like a savage."

He wanted to say something pithy, something shocking, but when he started, his distress poured out: the fear, loneliness, sorrow, love, hurt. Especially the fear. It grew rapidly, approaching real terror. He wanted to, had to get away . . .

"We can, Kim, we can," Illian whispered. She glanced at the door to her father's bedroom. "You know the key-code, remember? We can get out . . ."

And all his earlier arguments against that raced mockingly across his mind. Nomad life no longer seemed so terrible, Barrow-Beneath-the-mountain was an incredible legend no more. "Outside?" he murmured, aware of yet another fear. "Outside? I haven't been outside for . . . since The City of Night . . ."

4

Illian rose, went to the door, opened it a crack, peeped into the street. As she feared, the watcher was gone. A small knife of terror pinked her heart.

She'd call Markel. He'd know what to do. "Excuse me a minute, Kim." He nodded. But his face said he'd rather she didn't. Fear. She had never seen its like in an immortal.

She entered her bedroom hoping her father would stay out of the way, made the call. "Markel? He's here, I think he's ready."

Questions.

"The watcher's gone," she replied.

"They'll be suspicious," said his faint voice. "You'd better hide till we're ready."

"Where?"

"Hydroponics plant. Meet me in thirty hours at the west gate dressing station."

"My father . . ." He cut her off. An old argument. There were too few suits, and, anyway, the old man wouldn't go. Illian broke the connection. Despite Markel's logic, she hated leaving her father to die. She glanced at the time, forty-two hours to sunrise. She and Kim must hide for thirty. Bad, bad. Men hunting men to kill when death for all was less than two days away . . .

Why hadn't she done her father's capsules the same as Kim's? She started in horror. She could have saved him, if only she'd thought . . . Tears came with self-accusation, but there was no time . . .

She had to hurry. No telling when the cultists would arrive with questions she dared not answer. Quickly she added personal items to a bagful already gathered. One small bag, all of her life she would carry into the new world.

She'd not learn about vacuum damage until too late.

"Kim," she said on returning to the sitting room, "we've got to run. The cultists will be looking for us."

He seemed startled; surprised the Disciple's people might be interested in him. Then he nodded wearily. "The gates. All right, Illian, you win, I'll open them, I can't stay here."

He seemed so old, so tired. His capsules. He would have to start the drug again soon. "Let's go to your apartment," she suggested. "You'll want some things." Especially capsules. *Murderess!* a voice screamed inside.

Through inattentiveness she was killing her father, and for her own survival, possibly, Kim.

5

Kim gulped his daily pill. Eight hours till meeting time, at the fall of Edgeward City's last official night. In twenty hours the true, long night would end. Just twenty hours the City would live, and the people were still unconcerned, He could not now comprehend his own past disinterest. He was so frightened by sunrise, now, that he had been unable to sleep since going into hiding, although weary to collapse.

Illian stirred under his right arm, woke. "You let me sleep too long," she complained. "You have to rest too."

He shook his head, surveyed the quietly busy machines of the hydroponics plant. "Couldn't." He couldn't say that thoughts of his own mediocrity, along with fear, had made sleep impossible.

She took his pipe from him, pushed his head down onto her bag of belongings. "Try." He felt her lips against his forehead.

And then she was shaking him. "Time," she said. "There was a patrol through, but they weren't looking very hard. Come on. It's time." Her words were taut. A sudden tenseness of his own made it a sharing. Time. Half an hour till the meeting. Twelve and a half till sunrise. Close. Time was suddenly a torrent, rushing past, time that had been an ally for eighteen centuries, time he'd thought would never run out.

It was a short walk to the rendezvous, the ancient "dressing station" at the west gate. There the suits for outside work were stored, unused for generations. Sudden new fear. Suppose none were operable? Suppose the cultists had destroyed them?

There were too many fears already. The new suffered anonymity in the crowd. His prime fear of the moment was Sun Cultists. Surely, they would be searching . . .

They were. Three patrols crossed their path along the way. But each they avoided easily. The searchers were not very concerned about escapes. Kim soon saw why. At least a dozen cultists held the gate. No problem, Kim told himself. A man in suit, with a suit's servos and protection, could easily walk through them.

There were eight people at the dressing station, Markel and two mortal men, two mortal women, and three cultists. The cultists had been bound and gagged and tossed in a corner like yesterday's forgotten underwear.

"Ah, Illian," said Markel. "I was beginning to worry. You'd better get your suits on." He and the others were in the process of dressing.

Two suits lay on a table. Kim glanced at them, at Markel. "These all?" He saw no others.

"The others weren't functional," Markel said blithely. He gestured at a darkness-hidden pile. An arm here, a leg there. The non-functionality had been helped along. No one would follow to bring them back to the City.

Kim looked at the pair again. He felt a little twinge of uncertainty, of new fear. The larger suit, obviously his, was not functional either. Fifteen hundred years had passed, but Kim knew a weak suit when he saw one. It would, where little cracks appeared at seams, break open as the gate lock decompressed.

"The suit's no good." And he knew he should have kept silent. Though Markel hid it quickly, he had smiled. A suspicion formed. Kim stepped to the table, looked closer. The cracks were no cracks at all. They were tiny cuts. A clumsy, though sinister, attempt. He looked at each of the others, at all the frightened young Dancers—especially Illian. He reserved judgement.

"What's the key-code?" Markel asked. It sounded casual. Kim felt it was anything but.

"Listen when I open the gate," said Kim. Through narrowed eyes, he studied the mortals. Markel was dressing as if nothing was to happen. The others were tense, frightened—except Illian.

"I guess I will," said Markel. He turned with a wicked smile. "Do hurry, Illian."

"The suit's no good," Kim repeated, "Damaged." Into that one word went all the hatred that had built during the past few days. Markel's eyes widened a fraction. "I'll need another." That steely sword he'd felt growing at Illian's made itself felt anew, harder and sharper than ever, obliterating a rising fear.

"There aren't any," Markel replied. "If you refuse this; you'll have to tell me the key-code." There was a hint of condescension, of mockery behind his words. He looked away, unable to meet Kim's angry eyes.

Perhaps Markel meant the cuts to be seen. Perhaps he meant to bluff Kim into staying behind. Perhaps . . .

Kim's fear suddenly returned. It came in a huge wave, left beads of perspiration standing out on his forehead and throat, then went, left the sword within him tempered.

No, Markel probably hadn't intended a murder. There was zero personal violence in Edgeward City. Was.

"Markel . . ." said Illian. Her voice was like a distant child's cry. Kim saw she had realized what her cousin was doing.

Markel smiled. "Won't you tell us the key-code? For Illian's sake?"

The rage came suddenly, explosively. Kim jumped at Markel, swung his pipe at the man's astonished face. Violence had returned to Edgeward City (the Disciple's executions were, of course, sanctioned by law). Markel staggered, grunting in surprise, raised his hands to protect his eyes. Kim hit him again. Again. The pipe bent in his hands. He struck repeatedly, repaying days of fear, anger, and frustration.

Markel was no villain. Night was, darkness, death, the oblivion of mediocrity—one's self being a nothing before all these things. Markel was no villain, yet Kim used him as one. Kim made him an enemy with a face. He let the rage roar through him and enjoyed it. Markel fell to his knees, shielding his head with his arms, Kim kicked, and a part of him stood separate, amazed by his savagery. So great, his fear and frustration. Markel collapsed, panting, nose bleeding.

A light touch at his arm. He looked down into Illian's frightened face. The pleading in her eyes shattered the mad anger. The others were staring at him, stunned. He regained some calmness—though it was exterior only. His mind, his body, were riot with the juices and emotions of battle.

He stripped Markel before Illian's frightened eyes, donned the man's suit himself. "He meant to kill me." And, although it was true, even to him it sounded a weak excuse for the madness he had shown. *He tried to kill me . . . tried to kill me . . .* That expression, worn by Markel now crawling for a corner of darkness to be alone with his fear and pain; how long would it haunt him?

"Let's go. Just push through the guards at the gate."

6

While he practised self-mortification of the mind, the Nomad tractor whined and growled around him, an ancient iron leviathan clawing through shadows up the sides of the Thunder Mountains. Illian and the mortals were scattered about the passenger chamber, silent, though in the passing hours they seemed to have forgiven him his outburst.

The tractor whined louder, slowed, backed, turned, came to a stop. A lean, cadaverous, smiling young man thrust his head through the pilot room hatch. "We're at the top. Fifteen minutes. Anyone want to look?" One by one, the mortals shook their heads. Kim thought a moment, remembering The City of Night—perhaps seeing the truth might lay Markel's ghost.

He went forward, surprised that Illian changed her mind and followed. They were given seats where they could watch through polarized glass, in the safety of a long-shadowed pass thirty miles from Edgeward City.

Spears of light already probed through slots in the wall of the White Mountains, passed above Edgeward and her deep crater, and caressed the snow-clad flanks of the Thunder Mountains, as the world slowly turned, the heads and shafts of the spears crept nearer the City . . . That which came through the Teeth reached the crater ringwall. Ten minutes.

The White Mountains were outlined by a brilliance almost eye-searing. Beyond, the pre-nova white dwarf consumed itself in incandescent fury, blasting its only daughter. Here, gas, steam, dust, boiled up from a worse-than-lunar, mad landscape. Sunbeams played among the gasses and dust, setting them aflame with reflected light—flame tongues on a grand scale, like a fire among forests of insane rock spires. The Thunder Mountains were thunderous once more. Heat expansion caused a constant grumbling beneath the tractor.

Illian, face averted from visions of a world gone mad, whispered, "I'm not a Dancer anymore, Kim. You're not a Musician . . ."

Her way of saying the past was dead and there was a future they could build upon their might-have-beens. She had forgiven him. His heartbeat increased. He shivered. His hand found hers in the darkness.

The first of Edgeward City's screens flared brilliantly as it was touched by a storm of solar radiation, died as it burned itself out. The second quickly followed. The City lay open to the flood of charged particles. Five minutes.

"You should hate me," he said softly. "Markel . . ."

"Please," she murmured. "I can't. Let it be. We've got forever to forget."

Silence, except for the grumbling of the mountains. The Nomad crewmen watched the City with ghoulish interest. They were the mortals of their society, knew the destruction of cities only through the stories of their fathers.

Forever. The Nomads had given them capsules already. Kim smiled. Forever. He and Illian. One small success for the incompetent little Musician. Forever. Around the world running with the Nomads, always one step ahead of the demon sun, until it finally went nova in its efforts to kill the lice on the corpse of its child.

Perhaps there would be an escape from that, too.

No minutes.

Sun God's spear touched the top of the City's dome.

THE DEVIL'S TOOTH

"The Devil's Tooth" was the first story in a planned cycle of Dying Earth-type stories that featured a character named Fastenrath-by-the-Sword, a wanderer who kept stumbling into weird and interesting situations. This was the only one of his several adventures ever actually published.

1

A man with long arms and legs, thin waist and barrel chest, a long hatchet face, clothed in knee-length kilt and a true-steel sword scabbarded across his back, stopped carving the small wooden doll that had been in his hands for hours and became as motionless as the weathered old idols beside the dusty road. He could have been a statue himself but for lacking the dull greyness of skin.

The man's cold eyes, bright as the violet sky, watched a three-inch gallowglass beetle venture near, its imposing mandibles clacking ravenously. Its antennae twitched toward him, sensing meat, then toward its fellows, hundreds of thousands strong, crossing the road in a dark, glistening river a hundred yards wide and miles long, heading south in an unbroken flow. If so tiny a monster had a mind, this one must have spent that moment of antennae-dancing trying to decide whether to rejoin its fellows or investigate the attracting aroma of flesh. The decision was: feast first.

The man's hand scarcely moved, yet the true-steel knife with which he had been whittling transfixed the hungry beetle. A wan smile tugged at the already uptilted corners of his mouth. White teeth sparkled for a moment. A flick of the wrist and one less insect blocked his path.

Violet eyes rose beneath coppery brows, studying the cluster of squalid ochre buildings huddled between two small hills a few miles southwest, the city to which he was bound but which remained unattainable until the beetles were passed.

His eyes fell to the earth again. A half-dozen large pale blue executioner ants, which always hung about the edges of gallowglass armies, were marching toward the still living knife-stricken insect. They surrounded it with military efficiency, carefully avoiding the poisonous mandibles, and quickly closed in. Audible, chitinous snip! snip! in the right places, and the gallowglass ceased writhing. There came a brief waft of sour odor; the executioners' victory scent.

A new party of ants hurried from the purple-black, shining grass beside the road. These were smaller, dully-colored, slaves of the executioners. They began opening the exoskeleton of the gallowglass and chopping its muscle tissue into portable pieces. The blue executioners, which were equipped with poisons much more deadly than those of the beetles, formed a skirmish line between man and insect corpse.

The man smiled again, with respect, and a touch of smugness. He had not tried to recover his knife because he had expected the deadly ants.

His name was Fastenrath-by-the-Sword and, in this final age of Earth when no one dared stand alone, he was that rarest kind of man: a lone wandering free-sword. He came from a town called Sidikih in Draugenstarke country, born of an unwed woman scarcely a decade older than himself, Judi-with-the-Bells-on.

Again, Fastenrath examined the upstream end of the insect horde. Far up the low hill, in an area stripped to bare earth, he saw the glistening backs of the last beetles. Soon he could proceed along the dusty yellow road, to his appointment in Kristengrin. His eyes darted to the sun, to check the time. It was ancient, that sun; bloated, its dull red face blemished by a dozen leprous black sunspots. It hung overhead like a vast, bloody balloon, apparently close enough to touch, nearly ready to collapse in upon itself. It was ancient and tired, like the Earth it sullenly warmed.

There would be time to reach his destination before sundown, unless he miscalculated the beetles' speed. Leaning far forward, he both recovered his true-steel knife and re-read the legend on the stone he sat upon: three miles to the Kristengrin gates. But how much further to the house among many that he sought, on the corner of Metal Street and Music Lane, where artists and artisans mixed? All he had was that address, and a name; the name of a man of many memories. The possessor of that name might have the answer to the question that nagged at his brain since he first heard of a now forgotten land called Moon.

His first knowledge of that land came from a crumbling manuscript scribed in Old High Lothman that he found in the hands of a skeleton occupying the blackest depths of a crypt that superstition had saved from thieves, until he had come. He had squinted in the light of his hand—held torch, deciphering the ancient script which hinted at strange things and used words that had no counterparts in modern tongues, and just when he was in the grip of intrigue, the page ended. Fastenrath reached for the manuscript, anxious to turn the page and resolve the mysteries the first page hinted at. To his greatest frustration, the millennia-undisturbed bones and manuscript alike powdered at his touch. Now to find his answers he had to seek the knowledge of this learned one, who some said was immortal and knew all and some said was a sorcerer with three mirrors that one each saw into the past and present and future. There was only one thing about him that offered no difference of opinion; that he was evil and parted with his knowledge only at high prices. This Fastenrath was willing to face, for he suffered a curiosity unfashionable for his time and would not sleep well until that strange word that rolled strangely off his tongue was given meaning: Moon.

The gallowglass beetles had almost passed, down to the stragglers. Soon he could move on, but in the meantime he would work some more on the piece of hardwood he had been whittling.

The gathering shadows of evening were bizarre, distorted; shifting like the play of light and darkness at the bottom of an underwater garden. Kristengrin was not pleasant without sunlight. It was not a pleasant city at any time. Dark and Deadly were its names. But there was little pleasure anywhere in the world anymore. The dark and deadly lurked everywhere.

Fastenrath-by-the-Sword walked the shadowed streets boldly, silently, seldom letting his eyes probe the clots of darkness around him. His air of casual self-confidence was his best protection.

And there was that long-bladed, gold-damascened, shining true-steel sword hanging across his back, over his brown leather shirt, and the true-steel knife on his hip, over his ragged kilt, also with gold-inlaid spells of omnipotence. But he did not entirely trust the protection of the magic in those blades. After all, they had done little enough to save the man he had slain to obtain them.

Sounds of toenails on worn flagstones. A rat scuttled out of his path. Then came a wolf-like growl.

A large, hairless dog with blood-red eyes was challenging his passage. His orange boot flickered forward with casual swiftness. The dog could only whine once the metal toe had crushed its windpipe. Fastenrath stepped around the thrashing body.

He reached the crossing of Metal and Music, considered a moment, then selected the large, dark blood house behind the wall on the southeast corner. The windows were unlit, but it looked like the place he had heard described. There dwelt the man.

He smiled. The soft feet that had been following him did not resume their stalk when he started toward the house. In fact, his choice elicited a startled gasp.

There was no knocker on the gate, but it stood open a crack, as if in invitation. That in itself was a warning. Peeping through, Fastenrath saw a strange garden; quiet, peaceful, and deadly. Just behind the gate grew a dancing sabers, a sword-leafed plant that would stab at anything warm, and which carried an anti-coagulant drug on the hard tips of its leaves.

Beyond the dancing sabers stood a skull-bell tree with its white, skull-shaped blossoms twirling in the evening breeze. The fruit of that tree, pleasing to the eye and nose, if eaten, caused an instant paralysis. As he watched, a rodent tested a fallen fruit, shuddered, twitched, froze. Hair-fine rootlets rose from the earth and sank into the unfortunate animal, drawing nourishment.

There were other dark plants, all adapted to depleted soil conditions. The dancing sabers enriched the earth around it with blood, the skull-bell with corpses. And yonder butterfly tree, with the gaudy, scented butterfly blossoms, lured unsuspecting lepidoptera, trapped their feet in sticky gums, and planted its seeds in their living bodies, which were later allowed to fall to earth.

A strange, deadly garden, but no more deadly than the world at large; just more concentrated. Fastenrath-by-the-Sword surveyed it, trying to determine a safe path to the house.

Did he really want to continue his quest, into this place? He looked up, at the scattered red dots forming a bloody belt in the sky. The ancient manuscript had posed a mystery, saying that those crimson droplets came from Moon. Moon? Where, or what, had the place been? Curiosity, which had already earned him more scars than he cared to count, demanded that he find the answer. The search could not be abandoned now, not after a month of inquiry which had done no more than yield an address, and the name Valdur of Kristengrin. Valdur would know, he had been told. Valdur knew everything. He was Valdur the Eye.

The doorbell was a serpent's head with open jaws that formed the handles of a small bellows. Unusual. Fastenrath examined it for several minutes, making certain it was no trap. He squeezed the handles, was startled by a honking cry from behind the door. It echoed, as if the room within were vast and empty.

Nothing happened. After a reasonable wait he slapped the serpent's ruby eyes. Another honk died away with mocking echoes. Then came a shuffling sound. And the heavy bronze door swung slowly inward. Fastenrath found himself staring into cold, glowing blue eyes. He could see nothing else, just those disembodied eyes.

His own eyes adjusted to the greater darkness. He made out the form of a man bundled in heavy robes, distinguishable only because they were of a darkness even deeper than that which seemed to flow from the interior of the house. The face in the cowl, too, was black, glossy like polished ebony. He could not make out the features, save those remarkable blue eyes.

"Valdur the Eye?" he asked.

"I am he," said the dark one.

"I have a question."

"Of course. None come for any other reason. You can pay?"

"Perhaps. I have yet to hear the price."

"And I the question."

Fastenrath took a breath, and had a strange thought: what if he really were talking to a hole shaped like a man, so dark and substanceless was he. A rent in darkness, with two blue candles shining in what appeared to be a cowl. He shook off the dreadful notion and stated his inquiry, "What, or where, is, or was, Moon? This thing I must know to banish the demon curiosity."

The voice called through the man-shaped hole with a bemused tone. "A strange question in these times. What do you know of it already?"

"That it may be a far country, a fallen empire. There was a manuscript in a Lothman tomb, ancient beyond reckoning, that crumbled as I finished the first page."

"You are a man of attainments. Those who read the Lothman are not common. A true seeker I see you to be, so you will have your answer."

"Ah?"

The shadow figure moved slightly, nodding. "But still there is the matter of price."

"My ears remain open."

"In the west there is a city called Warasdin, on the River Bryne, near a sea. And west of the city is a mountain, Arcelin, overlooking both city and sea. People there say it is the tallest mountain in the world, though you and I know otherwise."

"Ah. And?"

"Atop the mountain is a monastery. It is occupied by the last devotees of the most ancient religion in the world. It is called the Monastery of the Moon."

"This is my answer? Moon is a monastery?"

"No. I merely lay grounds for discussing price. Inside the central cathedral—which was once the heart of a great city and empire that antedated the Lothman by a millennium of millennia—stands a statue of a god. There is a large, fang-shaped ruby in the statue's mouth. The Devil's Tooth."

"And you want this ruby?"

"In exchange for your answer."

"I have heard of Warasdin. A dark city dying and evil."

"Everything is dying. It is in the nature of a created universe that all things shall die in time. And all creation is innately evil."

"Perhaps. I will collect your jewel."

The heavy bronze door began to close slowly, as if loath to shut out the night. Fastenrath shivered, disturbed by the implied nature of the interior of Valdur's home, darkness thick as treacle. His curiosity was sparked. How did the man, if man he was, live in such a place? He fought that curiosity, intuitively knowing that to enter the house was to leave the rest of the world forever.

The curiosity, the curiosity, something would have to be done about it. Someday he would have a magician exorcise it, lest it be the death of him. This dark earth with its billion deadly traps had no room for the inquisitive. Curiosity was an atavism, survival of an age when the world was friendlier and sticking one's nose in was not a contra-survival trait.

He turned, surveyed the sinister garden, picked a path among the deadly plants. But, as he started to leave, the door groaned open behind him and Valdur's ghostly voice said, "A moment."

Fastenrath turned. "Yes?"

"I'd beg a favor. That you deliver a package to a colleague in Warasdin." Dark from the darkness, a robed arm reached out, a glossy black hand proffered a small brown packet tightly wrapped in some thin skin. Fastenrath tried not to consider from whence that skin had come.

"A colleague?"

"One called Ghul. Deal carefully with him. He has the soul of a spider, though his word is good." Valdur quickly described the home of his correspondent, added, "Arrive at sundown. Ghul will give you honest shelter. But beware once you leave his house. Warasdiners take pleasure in the Wild Hunt."

"A tale I have heard told," Fastenrath nodded indifferently, though inwardly the fact revolted him. The Wild Hunt was the hunting of men for sport and, considering the reputation of Warasdin, for dark usage. "As for my answer?"

"When next we meet, you will have had your answer," the ebony, featureless face assured mysteriously. Then the door groaned shut. Fastenrath considered a moment, fingering the skin-wrapped package, finding the wrapper smoother and thinner than pig-skin. He shrugged, then took his first step toward the distant Monastery of the Moon.

Fastenrath-by-the-sword paused on the last low ridge lying between himself and Warasdin. His eyes, tracing the ill-marked trail before him, found a metal and silica-leafed forest downhill to the right of the road. Tree trunks stood like dark glass sculptures. The wind set up a song like the tinkling of windchimes. His thoughts raced back over all the long roads of his memories and lingered over a tavern conversation of years before. He had heard a tale then, about the deadly woodland view ahead. This, he knew, was the Tinsel Forest;

twisted willows hung with razored leaves. Its deadliness would be obvious to a fool, but the road that skirted it did not take passers close enough to cause a real problem. So Fastenrath was at a loss to surmise the real danger, and that half-remembered tavern-tale tugged at his memory like a mouse trying to ring a temple bell. What was it? What was it?

He looked around. A hundred yards below, to the left of the road, stood a lone weeping pine. Out of season, the tree could not drip the poison that killed on contact. He strode thither, kicked a dog-sized skeleton out of the shade, sat down and leaned against the trunk and stared at the strange forest while he searched his memory. He would not move on till he knew the form of his danger.

For a long space of time, nothing came, and he roughly carved the hard block, shaping it more and more into a small, rotund human form, all the while trying to recall the threat imposed by the Tinsel Forest. Occasionally he looked up and yonder where the sharp edges of glass leaves and iron trees reflected the reds and purples in the light of the dying sun. Not until he heard the sound of distant singing rise above the accompaniment of the tinkling music of wind-danced leaves did Fastenrath cease his slow, careful carving and recall the peril that lay at hand.

Within that forest lived an immortal and, as usual, immortality was predicated on death. The undying female who lurked in the Tinsel Forest—somehow protected from the flesh rending foliage—was a dryad; death in a most attractive package. He pocketed his doll, rose, strode down the road, kept his eyes off the forest.

The voice sang out sweetly. Despite himself, Fastenrath looked for the source, saw naked female flesh flickering behind the deadly leaves. Danger! He turned his eyes away, chanted a Lothman marching tune to drown temptation, and lengthened his stride. Women were another of his weaknesses. The creature in the woods sang back to him, pursued him down the boundary of the lethal forest. Hers was a siren call, almost irresistible, yet by hurrying, and occasionally pricking his palm with the knife of true-steel, he succeeded in passing the beautiful snare.

Past one danger, he looked ahead to the next: Warasdin brooding beyond the Bryne, a grey city crumbling, where old men behind moldering walls amused themselves with evil while waiting out the last of the world's days. There, once upon a time, Yeshudi the Wise had held court, and from the city had ruled the ruins of the Lothman Empire. But now the city was fallen, physically and morally, the victim of no enemy but Time, and had become a lurking place for all the darkness haunting the human soul.

Fastenrath found his eyes caught by the upward sweep of the mountain behind the city; up, up, to where ancient structures perched like a broken crown atop its bald head. The Monastery of the Moon, his goal, atop Mount Arcelin. He closed his violet eyes and shivered.

He picked a path to the river carefully, for this was a country where dragon's teeth grew in great profusion. The grass-related plant lay hidden in sandy places until triggered by a footfall. Then long, toothlike spikes shot up to stab feet. At the least, the plant drew blood nourishment. If its victim were not quick, the poisons on the spikes would cause unconsciousness and collapse, allowing more spikes the opportunity to kill.

The sun was moving westward, a bloated, blood colored fruit marred by sunspots like black wormholes. How long till the end, he wondered. In his lifetime? It dropped behind that marred mount and left a thick violet twilight that deepened rapidly toward indigo. Fastenrath reached the river bank wondering if there would be any tomorrow.

The ferryman was a surly, misshapen fellow, as much gorilla as man, who wore a cunning expression and more than once tried to sidle behind his fare. Fastenrath did not turn his back till he was safely across the river.

Darkness came, indigo evening giving way to night with no noteworthy display. The first stars appeared. A belt of tiny asteroids stretched like falling blood droplets across the sky, hurrying to some rendezvous beyond the western horizon. Fastenrath began walking the last mile.

Something passed overhead, high up, like a shadow against the blood drops. In shape it resembled a bat, yet was larger than any Fastenrath had ever seen. But this was a strange land with unfamiliar horrors, and its night beasts might be quite unusual. Nothing in this world was cause for surprise. It trailed a muted chuckle.

The fallen gates and moldering walls of Warasdin loomed ahead. He trotted forward eager to be out of the night, yet moved with more than normal caution. Remembered rumors and travelers' tales weighed upon his mind, sending chills along his spine.

Yet nothing stirred behind the shattered gates, which sometime in the deep past had been opened by force and never repaired. The dark city streets were empty. Not even the usual rodents moved about. He did not like it. Normal city night-dangers being absent implied much greater perils. He thumped his purse, wondering. Should he deliver Valdur's package? His thin fingers strayed upward to the hilt of the sword hung over his shoulder; to make certain that his coppery hair was firmly held by his headband, out of his eyes.

Playing confident, as in Kristengrin, he strode into the city, followed streets between ranks of crumbling buildings, moving toward the shadowy black silhouette of the structure that fulfilled Valdur's description of Ghul's abode. But he could not muster the bravado to stray from the deeper shadows.

Something was deadly wrong. The smells of death, decay, and evil surrounded him.

But no dangers he found.

Ghul's door was ancient wood, rotted, worm-eaten. It looked past due collapse. All the grey city round was overripe. An ordinary brass knocker hung to one side. He used it.

The door quickly opened as if—and surely he had—the little cripple there had been waiting. "Yes?"

"Ghul?"

"Indeed."

"I have a package from Valdur of . . ."

"Yes, yes, I've been waiting. Do come in." The dwarfed, misshapen man (his right arm and side were withered into near-immobility) stepped aside.

Fastenrath paused, wondering if he dared enter.

"Safety here," said the dwarf, around a chuckle. "Warasdin is honorable about one thing: guest right. I owe you for the delivery. All my power will stand between you and disaster as long as you remain in my house. Outside, I promise nothing."

Fastenrath thought a moment. Yes, the fat little merchant he had met on the road yesterday, and with whom he had shared a fire last night, had spoken of Warasdin's guest-right. And Valdur had said Ghul would keep his word. He stepped into a chamber where spiders had for generations made their homes undisturbed. Little Ghul himself looked like a creature that should properly be lurking in the corners of webs.

The dwarf had red eyes and drooping, heavy mustachios—facial hair was rare these days—that looked like mandibles. "A moment," said Ghul, and hustled off, opening the package from Kristengrin as he went. Somewhere, shortly, he began shouting and soon he was back, saying, "A meal is being set out. If you'll follow me?"

Fastenrath was led to a room where a table had been hastily set so fast that he wondered about Ghul's unseen servants. Hearing strange, unpleasant noises, he decided to ask no questions.

"Take a seat, take a seat," said Ghul, offering a choice of two. "Here's hot food, fresh from the kitchen, the finest in all Warasdin."

Warily, Fastenrath took a seat. The dwarf scrambled into the other, snatched a fork with his good hand, began. Around a mouthful he asked, "Well. Another of Valdur's thieves, eh? The Devil's Tooth again?"

Fastenrath started slightly as he lifted his first forkful, but made no comment.

"Yes, I see it, it's the Devil's Tooth again. They come and they come to steal it, to sate Valdur's lust for life, and they never go home." Was there a malicious glee behind the dwarf's bland expression? Fastenrath could not be sure. Shadows had gathered like cobwebs about him, a cloak to hide expressions.

"Yes, they come and they come, and they go up Arcelin to steal Valdur's immortality, and we never see them again. And the Tooth remains in the Devil's mouth. Warasdin has its reputation," and here the dwarf paused, as if waiting for confirmation, "but they don't come back from Arcelin to tell damning tales." He stopped, though Fastenrath felt there was something more he had been about to say.

Still the wanderer did not speak. He ate, watched Ghul through narrowed eyes, and waited.

"The Devil's Tooth. You know what it is?" Ghul waited for an answer, visibly irked by Fastenrath's endless unresponsiveness. Finally, he went on, "It's not just a jewel, it's a cusp; not just a bauble in a stone idol but a channel and broadcast point for all the power of life that keeps the monks alive eons beyond their time. For as long as there has been a mountain called Arcelin they have been there, and they'll remain till the death of the sun or the theft of the Tooth, a deed that has been tried hundreds of times since Valdur first began to covet immortality." Ghul fell silent, stared into his empty mug, awaited comment.

When it became apparent that again none was forthcoming, he continued, "The Tooth is Life. Valdur is ancient beyond your reckoning, but the monks are to him as a grandfather to a new-born babe. And even his extended span will soon end—unless he can seize some greater talisman than he owns. The Tooth . . ."

Fastenrath questioned a lust for immortality in a world so dark and obviously doomed. He shook his head. There were too many questions. His curiosity threatened him with passage through the gates of hell. "It's been a weary journey, and dangerous."

"Ah, to be sure," said Ghul, sparklingly, as if glad of a change of subjects. "A safe, comfortable room should be ready by now. Follow me."

Fastenrath followed through dusty halls draped with tapestries bearing Ghul's crest: a giant bloodhawk standing with feet on the backs of a pair of huge spiders. Moments later and a floor higher, he was standing inside the door of a bedroom—as grey and dusty and moldering as the rest of the house—waiting for Ghul's chatter to end. Finally the dwarf tired of his unresponsive audience, said, "The guest-rule is inviolable," and hurried away. Displeased by the grim little smile he had last seen, Fastenrath braced the door shut and checked the walls for hidden means of entry. He found nothing.

After dousing the lamp, he lay on the bed for a long time, hands behind his longish head, staring out the room's single small window. The blood-drop asteroids still chased one another across the night. They were quite like himself, he thought, always in pursuit but never quite overtaking their quarry.

The question of aspiration had begun to bother him. Where was he going? What did he want? Why? His progression from bastard child to orphan to beggar and thief, to wanderer and adventurer, had seemed to suit him for many years, but now the life had begun to pale. His three years in service to Frey Levchescu of Gormflaith, when he had been taught so much—the reading, writing, and speaking of many languages, kindness, art appreciation, and the belief that every man should be an artist (the Frey had started him carving dolls of blocks of wood)—and had learned so little, had spoiled the joys of aimlessness for him. Perhaps it was Levchescu's fault, perhaps his own. In any case, that period had been the only in his life when he had really *belonged*. And he had destroyed that. Perhaps his problem was guilt. Like a fanged and clawed animal brought from the wild as a kitten, there had come a day when he had turned on his benefactor, for the sake of possessing a true-steel sword and dagger pair with magical gold damascening. Whatever the cause, now his life was pale.

The Frey had almost pressed him into a new mold.

Now, always, his adventures began with questions. Damn Levchescu for starting that! He was no scholar, no wandering truth-seeker and do-gooder like the Frey. He was a wanderer, a sword-for-hire, a thief. He did not want to be a student, a slave of his own curiosity. He wanted to return to the life he had always lived.

Yet here he was, in a black, lethal corner of the world, about to hazard a darkness and death, and all for a worthless bit of knowledge!

Gradually, he grew angrier, both with himself and Frey Levchescu, until a single large tear slipped from the corner of one large violet eye and trailed hotly down over his angular cheekbone. Then he sealed out the vision of the perverse, hurtling blood drops in the sky, rolled onto his stomach, and forced himself into a troubled, shallow sleep.

2

While tightening the belt of his kilt and settling the sword more comfortably across his shoulder, he listened. The ancient house was silent. He listened again before opening the door, then, after a deep breath, slipped out.

The halls were dark, lighted only by small lamps at great intervals which did little to conquer the shadows. They were navigating lights, no more. Fastenrath started off with his right hand held high, near his sword.

No opposition did he meet, and all his caution seemed wasted. Through the house and downstairs he went, to the door he had entered by, and saw no one, heard nothing. Perhaps Ghul did not care if he left.

Relieved, he lifted the bar from the door. A lean smile played across his thin lips. So much for the horrors of Warasdin.

"Ghul!" the door screamed, from no mouth that Fastenrath could detect, "Ghul!" The cry echoed through the decayed halls, "Ghul-ghul-ghul-ghul."

Fastenrath broke the rigidness which had seized him when the door first screamed. He dashed out, picked the street that he thought led to the gate, and trotted off. A mile separated him from that safety.

There were shouts in the house behind him, laughter, and Ghul's voice raised in exultation. They had been waiting for him to leave. Fastenrath caught the words, "Blue hounds." He lengthened his stride and silently, angrily cursed himself for being a fool. Would it all end this pointlessly?

Elsewhere, at that moment, bells began ringing. He glanced back. High in the truncated tower of another mansion, men were a-scurry, gesturing toward him. Their cruel laughter came lightly on the breeze, maniacally gleeful.

The Wild Hunt was on. All Warasdin had been waiting for him.

Levchescu had brought him to this. What subtle revenge.

Somewhere, something bayed long and dolefully, with a lust for blood, like the cry of a banshee. Those were the voices of the blue hounds, dogs bred for hunting men.

He was on a long, straight avenue with a quarter mile to go when first he saw the hounds, as far behind as he had to go to reach freedom. And his human pursuers were behind the hounds, some afoot, some in sedan chairs. Two sedans vied for the lead, one of which had curtains emblazoned with the crest Fastenrath had seen on the hangings at Ghul's home.

The hounds were closing fast, though not running all out. They moved at a fast lope, certain of their prey. But Fastenrath, with huge chest and long legs, was a born runner. He suddenly stretched himself in a wind-sprint that took him along almost as fast as the hounds, fast enough to take him out the shattered gates a step ahead of snapping teeth. There, momentarily safe, he slowed to a brisk walk, panting, feeling he had somehow cheated fate.

For the blue hounds had stopped, waiting for instructions from their slower masters. Then Fastenrath, too, stopped and spat in the direction of the tall, lean, whippetlike hunters. All travelers' tales he had heard said that the hounds never left the city.

But Ghul and his followers were close now, and presented another danger. Fastenrath gulped air and began to trot up Arcelin, toward the Monastery of the Moon. If the place was as terrible as Ghul had claimed, there would be no pursuit.

After climbing a half mile of naked slope, Fastenrath paused at the edge of a thick stand of skull bells. Looking back, he saw men and hounds milling behind Warasdin's gate. An argument seemed to be in progress, perhaps over whether or not he ought to be pursued, or, more probably, to whom the right of pursuit belonged. He shrugged, entered the deadly wood, carefully avoided a bone-strewn patch of sand which obviously harbored dragon's teeth. A flock of small, stupid birds had visited the wood lately, to eat the fruit of the skull bells. Feathers and tiny bones littered the forest floor. Carrion-eating insects were thick, picking at the decaying flesh, and in their turn were being trapped and eaten by bat's wings, a breed of pitcher plant which exuded a carrion smell. The plant had wings like a bat's, night black, which closed over the mouth of the pitcher.

A place of danger and death, that wood, but safe enough for a careful man. He need only beware the dragon's teeth and have the good sense not to eat skull bell fruit.

Fastenrath made it through easily and sat down on the bank of a shallow gully above. There he took out his true-steel knife and a block of wood, whittled while he studied the Monastery of the Moon still high above. A partially fallen wall lay scattered down a hundred yards of slope toward him. Something grey to white lay scattered among the stones. Behind the wall stood a half dozen buildings in poor repair. All but one were small grey stone things. The larger structure was time-worn gothic, all the frills scrubbed away by age. The gargoyles had become blind, featureless, lump-headed monsters, fading in their endless vigil. The monastery as a whole could have room for no more than two dozen monks. He whittled, and wondered how those monks supported themselves. He saw no fields, nor chattel, nor orchards, unless they were on the seaward side of Arcelin.

He sat there for twenty minutes, the doll almost unconsciously taking shape in his hands as he tried to reason out how that innocuous-looking structure could contain all the horror Ghul had proposed the night before. Not that he disbelieved the dwarf. Masks of innocence often hid the faces of the world's blackest terrors.

Terror. Surely nothing else lay ahead. He began to question his presence on Arcelin, to question the driving curiosity that had taken him first to Valdur the Eye, then to Ghul, and now here. It was going to get him killed. Ghul had hinted darkly when speaking of the Monastery. If Warasdiners feared the place . . .

There was a gruff bark, a shuffling, and a yelp of pain in the wood behind him. Someone growled a curse at the clumsiness of blue hounds.

Fastenrath leapt to his feet, silently cursing himself for assuming the Warasdiners would not pursue him this far up the mountain. Now his decision was being forced upon him. He would have to go on. Down the bank of the gully he scrambled, and up the far side with a yelp and a bound high into the air that carried him to naked rock ten feet from his jumping point.

There he paused to suck the poison from the puncture where the dragon's teeth spike had pierced his left palm. Only his quick leap had saved his feet and, perhaps, his life. He looked at the flood of little brown spikes washing against the rock. He could jump over or pick a path through. He decided on the latter course, knowing that a second patch might be triggered if he leapt to the sand beyond the limits of the patch he knew.

Carefully he moved, placing his orange boots between spikes until he reached the limits of the dragon's teeth. Yes, another patch nestled against this.

Behind him, in the wood, his pursuers drew noisily closer. He triggered the second patch with a stone. It was the last. Once through he could run.

Halfway between the wood and tumbled stone monastery wall he paused. Sounds from the cathedral, the larger building, had reached him: a distant, deep, weird chanting. He listened, pulled his hair back out of his eyes, for the first time considered the white and grey detritus scattered among the rocks from the shattered wall.

Bones! Thousands and tens of thousands of bones. Human, it seemed, all stripped of flesh, the larger ones cracked as if something had been after the marrow. The thousand broken skulls leered at him with empty eye-sockets, their broken jaws spoke—not with words for none were needed—of peril above.

Fastenrath once more thought of abandoning his quest. For these were not just dead men decayed where they had fallen. These had been butchered and eaten and their bones tossed away when the flesh was gone.

He glanced back. Nothing could be seen, but his enemies were making noise near the verge of the wood. There was no escape downward. They could intercept him in all directions. So up the mountain he continued, into the field of stones and bones, avoiding several patches of dragon's teeth—he had never seen that deadly plant so ubiquitous—and, from the cover of a large block of stone, in the company of skulls, watched his pursuers come from the wood and cross the gully.

Ghul had won some argument below. His was the only sedan chair coming up, carried by four armed men. Bowmen with arrows ready walked before and behind the chair, calling encouragement to the hounds. Only two of these were in evidence and they, after taking one look up the mountain, began to drop to the rear.

The gaudy sedan chair came winding up among the patches of dragon's teeth with all the stateliness of a coronation processional. Ghul's ugly face peeped out once, grinning evilly. Fastenrath, on all fours, scurried toward the monastery wall. A shout informed him that he had been seen.

Angrily, he asked himself why the dwarf was so persistent. Ah. Perhaps because of his eyes. It would not be the first time someone had coveted his strange violet eyes.

He paused just inside the shattered wall and looked back. The chanting in the cathedral went on, chillingly, like an invocation of some unspeakable god. Ghul's men were drawing close to the bone field now and the cripple leaned from behind his curtains to exhort them onward. The six refused to approach the monastery any closer. The two blue hounds had begun slinking down the mountain like whipped pups.

Ghul's porters dropped the sedan to earth and stepped back. Ghul held the curtains aside, shouted angered orders, but the six hunters cowed and did not obey. Fastenrath watched his enemy and carried on a silent argument with the guilt-ghost of the kind old man he had slain a year before. The chanting in the cathedral at his back went endlessly on, utterly depressing in its sameness.

The curtains of Ghul's sedan snapped shut and his shame-faced men stood in expectation. Nothing happened for a spell and Fastenrath nearly lost interest. Then a sudden agonized shriek rose from the sedan that snapped Fastenrath to attention. The curtains were being fluttered and buffeted as though the occupant were having some sort of a fit. Then, after another shriek, those curtains burst open and a huge red bloodhawk hurtled out, took flight, and climbed into the sky. It ascended staggeringly because one wing was deformed to a point where it was only barely of use. Fastenrath goggled.

The six footmen did not seem startled by events. But one was forced to leap out of the path of the bird and, unable to watch where he was going, set foot in a patch of dragon's teeth. And tripped. His still living body was pierced by hundreds of spikes, profusely providing scarlet sustenance for the subterranean plant.

Fastenrath watched the hawk, noted that it always wheeled the same direction above, always favoring the bad wing.

The tenor of the chant from the cathedral changed. It became excited and seemed to be approaching culmination. Fastenrath slipped off his rock, bounded down a safe path he had already selected, and concealed himself in a shadow lying thick between a wall and a fallen pillar. Squatting, sword across his lap, he watched the door of the cathedral.

As were the five hunters. They stood with terror on their faces, as if petrified, staring up the mountain.

One by one, the monks of the monastery came forth. Tall, taller even than Fastenrath-by-the-Sword, and so thin that their heavy brown robes seemed supported by stick frames, were they. They bent forward slightly as they walked so it seemed that their weight was supported by the long, thin, carven black staffs they bore in their left hands. Their progress was slow, as if hasty movement was dangerous.

One of the men of Warasdin moaned, ran. A monk's staff came up, pointed down the slope, and the man stopped moving. He fell. The others remained frozen by terror.

There were seven of those iniquitous priests. They paused just where Fastenrath had entered the monastery, considering the Warasdiners. Staffs rose, men below fell. Eagerly, then, the priests hurried forward.

And, suddenly, Fastenrath was painfully aware of whom it was that had gnawed and broken all those bones below the wall. Why did immortality always cost so horribly? It depended on cannibalism here; vampirism on the part of that dryad beyond the river Bryne. In other places, at other times, he had encountered other creatures equally depraved, all plunged into degradation and horror because of their lust to escape the claws of the great inescapable. Valdur the Eye, of Kristengrin, was trying to obtain the Devil's Tooth with full awareness that it would lead him along the same dark path being followed by these seven brown-clad priests. Was death that terrible?

The priests. They were now gathered like thin vultures among the Warasdiners, cackling shrilly to one another in an unknown tongue. What better time to enter the cathedral and snatch the Tooth from the Devil's jaw? For he had decided that it would give him a strong bargaining position when he tried to get back out.

Staying low, darting from cover to cover, with his true-steel sword in hand for the first time since starting this adventure, Fastenrath hurried toward the gothic arch of the cathedral door. Were there more priests inside? He hoped not.

A shadow passed. He threw himself against a block of stone, looked up. The huge, deformed bloodhawk was diving, its wings folded, but not at him. Its talons hit the cowl of one of the priests, ripped the robe away, and sent the priest tumbling. A wailing stick figure that seemed hardly a man at all, naked, rose and staggered several steps, fell again, and moaned. Ray sunlight, even of this bloated, dying sun, was too much for him. The other priests forgot their prey, gathered round their brother, chattered shrilly while they shielded him with their shadows.

And then the bloodhawk was coming down the sky again, wobbling in flight as staffs came up to point threateningly. As it neared the priests it seemed to decide that further attack was too dangerous. It broke its plunge and hurried off toward Warasdin. Fastenrath wasted no more time watching. He sprinted into the cathedral, looked for the idol. It was not easy to overlook.

The huge black Buddha-fat, many-armed and ugly thing squatted in the shadows at the far end of the nave, the Tooth in its mouth burning a sullen red with a life of its own. It looked as though it had been freshly dipped in blood. In all the vastness of the place Fastenrath saw nothing else of note. Time had ruined everything not made of stone.

He hurried toward the stone monster thinking surely it had been patterned after nothing that had ever lived. No one, nothing stood in his way. He reached it, climbed into its lap, cocked his arm back for a smashing blow with the pommel of his sword. The Tooth looked like it would pop right out.

Shrill voices raised angrily, preceded by long shadows across the cathedral door. Murmuring a curse, Fastenrath leaped from the Devil's lap and scrambled behind the idol. There he found a narrow crack opening on a hollow interior. He used it immediately. Only a man as thin as himself, or one of the priests, could have done so.

He found himself inside a tiny chamber containing a desk and chair carved of the idol's stone. There were eye-level peepholes for a seated man which looked out through the Devil's mouth. The red light of the Tooth filtered through them. Here, he decided, priests of the past had given the Devil a voice, using the desk to support a heavy book from which they read responses to a litany. The desk held such a book now, an ancient, dust-encrusted thing.

Through the peepholes Fastenrath watched the seven thin priests make their entry, two carrying the one who had fallen, the other four carrying two of the stricken Warasdiners. They came down the nave, laid their fallen comrade and victims before the idol, began chanting pleadingly. Idly, Fastenrath wondered if they remembered the importance of the Tooth, or if they thought its power was that of the god the idol represented. He turned away when sacrificial knives came out to carve up a gory offering. Blood they caught in cups and splashed on the Tooth. Fastenrath could have sworn that it hummed softly after the soaking.

He shifted his attention to the book, which he opened as delicately as possible. But it was not the fragile thing he had expected. Its contents were engraved on incredibly thin sheets of an unfamiliar silvery metal and the crumbling expected was limited to the binding, which appeared to have been changed many times. The writing within, on wide pages, existed in three narrow columns per page, Fastenrath had little difficulty reading what appeared to be the most recent version, which was in Old High Lothman, still used as a liturgical tongue though it was tens of thousands of years old.

It was a holy book of a not unusual sort, a copy of a copy of a copy that began with the beginning and recounted the events of millennia on every page. But the viewpoint was unfamiliar, as was much of the earliest mythology. Fastenrath oh'd and ah'd silently, and soon lost himself in chronicles of times and nations ancient beyond anything he had ever before encountered. He nearly forgot the chanting priests, almost gave himself away when he happened on the long-sought answer to his question concerning "Moon." Only years of self-discipline damped an explosion of joy.

Moon, he discovered, was no far and forgotten country, but a celestial orb like the sun; one which millennia past had come too near the earth and had been torn apart by tidal forces in its crust. The earth, too, had suffered terribly. The manuscript mentioned upheavals Fastenrath was sure had to be grossly exaggerated: nations and continents had been utterly destroyed, mountain ranges had risen and fallen, whole new lands had emerged from beneath the sea. Very few men had survived.

All this was covered on a single page, then abandoned as the forgotten historian went on to describe other disasters attributable to his dark god.

Fastenrath became aware that shadows were gathering thickly in the nave, as if it were growing late, and that the six hale priests had departed with the meatier portions of their sacrifices. The seventh priest still lay before the idol, motionless, apparently dead. Time to move.

But first there was a question he must answer to his own satisfaction. Did he owe Valdur of Kristengrin a service for this serendipitous answer to his question about Moon? Had the man foreseen this? Perhaps. Rumor had it that Valdur the Eye saw everything, even, at times, the future.

A little squeaking mouse of suspicion scampered through the back hallways of his mind, a suspicion that had first arisen while he had been listening to Ghul's monologue the night before. Was Valdur already an immortal of sorts, buying exposure to the power of the Devil's Tooth by sending victims to the seven dark priests? Ghul, it seemed, had suggested the possibility.

He would steal the Devil's Tooth. It should be raped away from the human monsters who dwelt here. The question was, could he, or should he, keep it from Valdur the Eye? He was morally certain that he should not be responsible for removing the horror of Arcelin to Kristengrin.

No. He decided. No Tooth for Valdur.

He must move out. The priests might be back soon, and the longer he lingered the more he risked discovery. After binding the old holy book across his back so he could carry it and still have free hands—it would be of tremendous value in certain markets—he left the idol's interior, slipped around its flank, stepped over the stricken priest, climbed over the pile of gore and human parts which had been placed in the god's lap, clung to the idol's lower lip with one hand while he drew his sword with the other. He dealt the glowing ruby a blow with the pommel.

It barely wiggled. He struck again, again, seven times in all before the thing broke loose, fell, and came to rest on the idol's tongue.

Then came a shriek of horror as he was about to sheath his blade. He whirled, found the injured priest risen from the altar, his skull-face a sallow mask of fear, his hands reaching like a pair of giant spiders. Fastenrath seized the Tooth from the idol's tongue as cold, claw-like hands closed on his throat. The sword was too long to operate at close quarters, so he dropped it purposely as he fell into the gore, the priest atop him. His wind was going fast as he struggled with the amazingly strong skeletal figure whose fingers crimped his wind-pipes. Using the Tooth as a dagger, he stabbed and stabbed and stabbed. The world began to grow black. Unconsciousness was closing in.

The Tooth hummed in his hand as he struck with it, pulling as if desirous of more blood. The priest's shrieks took on a new and even more desperate note, slowly dying away, and Fastenrath was certain there would be more than one corpse left in the idol's lap.

Something had begun to happen to him just as he was on the verge of blacking out. New strength was flowing up his arm. He suddenly felt able to fight thousands. He clawed the priest's hand free of his throat with one hand while continuing to stab with the Tooth. At long last his attacker suffered a series of spasms, relaxed. Fastenrath's stomach churned sickly. For a certainty he knew that the Tooth had raped the man's strength and soul and transferred his vital forces to himself. He felt ages younger. Was this the path to immortality, the will-o'-the-wisp so many pursued?

Sounds of excitement and anger reached his ears. The other priests, aroused by the uproar, were returning to the cathedral. He had to run. Could he avoid the power of their staffs and the horror of death on their altar?

He grabbed his sword, sheathed it, thrust the Tooth into his purse, and sprinted down the nave and out the cathedral door. Shouts followed. The other priests had seen him.

He immediately went down on his hands and knees, scrambling along trying to keep fallen blocks between them and himself. The tenor of their outcry changed, from outrage to terror. They had sensed the theft of the Tooth. He was raping away their immortality. And their shouts were drawing closer, though they still could not see him where he crept. Fear, not a familiar passion, made him quiver and sweat. Soon they would cut off his retreat.

A shadow passed near him and Fastenrath looked up, seeing something slanting down the purple sky of twilight. It struck the nearest priest, soared up, circled for altitude; circled left because one wing did not function well. The sudden reappearance of the bloodhawk Ghul caused massive confusion among the already upset priests.

No less confused, but grateful for the diversion, Fastenrath scrambled out of the monastery into the boneyard before the fallen wall.

Down came the bloodhawk again, shrieking, but this time it did not make a direct attack. Instead, it dropped something round and the size of a clenched fist. Fastenrath watched it tumble down, heard it hit stone with a tinkle of breakage, saw sudden clouds of gas flare up, saw the priests begin staggering and coughing in the vapor. The bloodhawk squealed triumphantly. Fastenrath resumed running, keeping low, one eye always on the sky.

What cunning plan, he wondered, had Ghul put into motion? He certainly had one or he would not have returned with the globe of gas. And unquestionably there was some selfish reason for Ghul coming to the aid of the violet-eyed adventurer and seeker.

Then he knew. Below the bonefield, shadowed in the twilight, were many armed men and sedan chairs; likely all the lords of Warasdin and their retainers. So. An alliance of thieves come up after the immortality in his purse.

Out of the pan, into the fire. How had he ever come to this pass? That Frey Levchescu . . .

Ghul wheeled above him, shrieking triumphantly. How long before the bloodhawk came down to pinpoint his position for the lords on the ground?

The twilight thickened. Fastenrath, clinging to the deepest shadows, moved to his left in an effort to slip around the Warasdiners' right flank, anchored where the skull bell wood came nearest the monastery. But the bloodhawk spotted him, circled overhead, shrieked. Below, men moved to prevent his escape. When he turned to go in the other direction the bloodhawk shrieked again and again men moved to intercept. And, emboldened by Ghul's victory over the monks, the men on the ground began moving uphill through the bone field, the ends of their line swinging to encircle. Fastenrath considered retreating into the monastery and trying to escape down the seaward side of the mountain, but he soon saw that Ghul's attack on the monks had served a double purpose. The gas that had defeated the priests also made withdrawal impossible for him. So this was the end to which his unconquerable curiosity had brought him. Wishing he had a bow, he drew his sword. Perhaps if he charged suddenly they would be surprised enough to kill him quickly, rather than at leisure later in Warasdin.

Another something appeared in the gathering night of the sky, coming from the seaward side of Arcelin. It appeared to be the same creature he had seen after crossing the River Bryne the previous evening; the laughing bat-thing. With a much clearer view this time, he saw its great black wings and polished-ebony body. Valdur, surely, here to reap his profit.

As the bat-thing wheeled past the bloodhawk, circling right in counter to the instability imposed by the crippled wing, Fastenrath stared and wondered. The bat flickered back and forth as agilely as its smaller relatives, sailed along the line of armed men approaching. There were cries of fear. Someone shouted something about vampires. The line broke. Men ran down the slopes so carelessly that they did not beware of dragon's teeth. There were shrieks of agony as the dark traps sprung. The outcry shattered the nerves of those who had not as yet broken. Before long the slope below Fastenrath was naked of all human life.

Above, the bloodhawk screamed angrily and clumsily flapped after the laughing bat-thing. It seemed unafraid. The bat scrambled for altitude, the bloodhawk struggling upward close behind. The darkness of falling night was by then almost complete. Under its cover Fastenrath moved down Arcelin as fast as he dared, more cautiously than the Warasdiners, but fast. His immediate goal was the skull bell wood. There the victor of the aerial battle would have great difficulty reaching him.

He attained the wood without difficulty or mishap, as often as not avoiding the dragon's teeth by circling the dead men who marked the patches. The traps were otherwise hard to see by the wan blood-light of the Moon-droplets racing above. He wished the great reflecting body of Moon was still extant, in all the glory described in the book tied to his back.

The battle above, it became obvious, would come to no fast conclusion, for both were-creatures continued shrieking endless challenges above the night. Fastenrath could occasionally spot one or the other as its vast wings obscured a star or hurtling fragment of Moon.

A thought came to him. He took the Devil's Tooth from his pouch. Yes, it cast sufficient light for his needs. Moving ahead with great care, he made his way through the thousand snares of the wood, taking a good two hours reaching its lower verge.

3

Fastenrath crouched in a cluster of sawgrass, least of the dangers of Arcelin, and studied the gates of Warasdin. Excited and fearful men, restraining a pack of blue hounds, waited there with torches, crowding close together as if to reassure one another against the night. Their talk was low, frightened, reached Fastenrath only as a constant low grumble. He could imagine what they were discussing: the chances of being killed by one snare or another as weighed against the certainty of immortality if only they were able to capture the Devil's Tooth.

Renewed shrieks broke out above. Dimly, Fastenrath saw a bat shape hurtle overhead pursued by a limping bloodhawk. So that battle endured still. No wonder the Warasdiners yet waited within their gates. They would not venture out till Ghul had a certain victory.

Fastenrath considered. His hopes of survival lay in getting out of the area quickly, and in not leaving a trail indicating whence he had gone. Yet he was a remarkable man physically and would be remembered wherever he passed. Bad. And he needed to be rid of the Devil's Tooth soon, before it got a firm hold on him. (The thought of giving up the immortality it promised already hurt a little, yet he knew that there would always be those, like the thousands whose bones littered the slopes of Arcelin, who would hunt him as long as he possessed the Tooth.) It had to be put away somewhere where it would be unattainable. Such a place had come to him as he passed through the skull bells, though he was more hesitant to risk its dangers than he had been to face those of the Monastery of the Moon.

But first he must escape the environs of Warasdin, had to reach and cross the River Bryne, which meant crossing miles of open fields without light. To use the glow of the Tooth would mean revealing himself to both those who waited at Warasdin's gates and the embattled creatures in the sky. By daylight he could make the crossing in half an hour. By night it was possible he wouldn't make it at all.

He dropped to his hands and knees and began creeping along, using his long true-steel blade to probe for danger. In the back of his mind lurked the names of all the strangely adapted night-creatures that might waylay him. In this age no sane man risked the night alone. But, hopefully, all the uproar of the evening would have frightened the night-haunters away. The dangers he met were those of the earth, primarily the ubiquitous dragon's teeth. Many times his probing blade rang softly to the strike of upthrusting spikes.

Near dawn, and with a half mile still separating him from the ferry, Fastenrath paused. There had been silence above and behind him for a long time now, as if the battle in the air had stopped. Yet he had heard no cry of victory nor any scream of defeat. It occurred to him that, perhaps because they had been unable to fight to any conclusion, Ghul and Valdur could have come to some accommodation. A frightening possibility. Perhaps they now lurked above on silent wings, stalking. Involuntarily he glanced at the sky. There was nothing to see.

There was dawnlight sufficient to sketch in Warasdin's grey distant walls by the time Fastenrath reached and pounded upon the ferryman's door. He got no answer. Angry at being thwarted this late in the game, he dealt the door a savage kick. Unlocked, it opened easily.

The ferryman had crossed his last river. He lay sprawled across his filthy cot, his throat ripped out. But there was no blood to be seen anywhere. Vampire. Fastenrath immediately pictured a great bat-thing coming during the night, sating a wicked thirst while sealing one avenue of escape. So. They would see.

Outside again. Yes, as he had expected, the ferryboat had been sunk. But its bronze guiding chain still hung in a long curve above the turgid water. Fastenrath looked about him, wondering if a guard had been posted. Ah, yes, he saw the fellow now. But he would never give an alarm.

The night-creatures had not all been idle. Something huge, slimy, and hungry had come from the river and returned, leaving bones, clothes, weapons, alarm horn, and bits of flesh scattered near the watchman's hiding place a hundred yards upstream from the ferryman's home. As he made certain that his weapons, the ancient book, and the contents of his purse would not be lost in the crossing, Fastenrath prayed that the creature had had enough to eat.

Hanging like a sloth he inched out along the chain, finally dropped to earth on the far bank after what had seemed an eternity of exposure. He wrung out his kilt where it had dragged in the water, then rubbed at his legs, where the chain had caused abrasions, to ease the sting.

He considered Warasdin. Nothing seemed to be happening there. Then he turned toward the vale whence he had come yesterday. Very faintly, he thought he heard the dryad of the Tinsel Forest singing. He started off at a trot.

A half hour later he had reached his immediate goal, a low hummock topped by a bit of bald rock just off the trail, close beside the deadly Tinsel Forest. From up the vale a short distance he could hear the singing of the dryad. She had not as yet noticed him, apparently expecting travelers from the opposite direction. Well. He took a seat on the boulder, tried to decide whether he should read the religious book or should carve again at his doll. He decided on the latter. It wouldn't command his attention to the point where he would forget to watch for danger. And it might become useful later. Frey Levchescu may have taught him something of value after all.

Frey Levchescu. His thoughts returned to that charming, chubby, foolish old man, to those brief three years during which the blind (metaphorically) old teacher had tried to shape an image of his own idealism in already hardened clay. For the first time Fastenrath caught glimmerings of the true motives behind the old man's having taken him in. Without having come into contact with Ghul and Valdur, he might never have made the discovery. But the Frey had been seeking an immortality of his own, by stamping his values on the heart and mind of a pupil. It wasn't a cruel form of immortality, yet, in its way, it was as selfish as the methods selected by the rival magicians.

His eyes sought the decrepit sun. What form did his own search for foreverness take? With present death so constantly flaunted by that scarlet, leprous orb, every man sought some way to stamp his memory upon every moment. Was this the cause of his own early wanderlust? A need to carve his immortality with a blade? With a stolen blade?

The old guilt returned. Frey Levchescu had never treated him other than well. Perhaps the inner man was now trying to repay the crime of the outer and this was the cause of the curiosity that kept pulling him into impossible adventures. Sure, he owed the Frey something, for Levchescu had given him much more than a pair of extremely rare true-steel magical blades. He stared at his hands.

Under his expert touch the image of a fat baby grew quickly more humanoid. The sun rose above the eastern hills and bathed the vale with its bloody light. Suddenly Fastenrath turned to discover the source of a long shadow that had come stretching down toward him. It was cast by the fat merchant with whom he had spent the night a few days earlier. He was leading his slow fat burro, heavily laden, toward Warasdin. Merchants, of all people, had little to fear at the hands of their own kind. Even the worst bandits and murderers and magicians treated them with a respect bordering on the religious. They did not need to fear traveling alone if they were wise in the traps of nature.

The fat man was moving at an unseemly pace, possibly from gallowglass beetles. Fastenrath did not like that possibility. Gallowglass beetles could bar his path when flight was critical. He began to consider revisions of his plan, but inasmuch as the original plan had not taken clear form it was hard to make sensible changes. Yet there was the glimmer of a plan, a foolish one perhaps, and a river of marching beetles could well ruin his chances.

The distant dryad's voice rose in a sudden song of exultation. Fastenrath watched the fat merchant stop as if instantly petrified. He pitied the man— he had shown him kindness when it was unnecessary—but made no move to go to his aid. He needed all his will to fight the song of the dryad himself.

The merchant was unable to fight it successfully, perhaps because he was unaccustomed to facing dangers from human sources. It was not long before he started walking toward the source.

A sudden outbreak of excited speech behind and below him caught his attention. Ah. He smiled. Here came armed men from Warasdin, with blue hounds. Ghul and Valdur were sure to be somewhere nearby. Though he disliked seeing the merchant condemned, there could have been no better time for his demise.

A shadow passed Fastenrath's resting place. Above him he discovered a giant bloodhawk soaring on one good and one crippled wing. Nearby, a black bat-thing which defied visual examination was having extreme difficulty operating in sunlight. Both were dropping down toward him, one cutting his path to the ridge top, the other escape across the vale to his right. The Warasdiners were hurrying to prevent any escape in the direction of the river. No sane man would willingly enter the Tinsel Forest, so that route was left clear.

Fastenrath rose, surveyed the land one last time, carefully arranged a mental photograph, then burst into a hard run. Far down the vale he had pictured the glistening purple flood of encroaching insects. Animals—predators and prey alike—were scattering quickly. From the width of the coming flood, Fastenrath judged it would prove the biggest army of gallowglasses he had ever seen. The presence of that deadly flow could prove beneficial after all, he reasoned as his plan became a bit clearer, complete with the revisions necessitated by the beetles. He could only hope those insects would not enter the Forest, as that might spoil the plan after all, and he would have enough to reckon with when his swift legs had brought him to those boundaries.

This he took in the instant before he broke into his speedy retreat, doll and knife in hand. Ghul and Valdur shrieked in the voices of the shapes they wore and adjusted their flight to cut him off. He was pretending to try for the top of the hill, but when Ghul was almost upon him he stopped, took two careful steps to his left, and was in the Tinsel Forest, amongst the razor-edged, metal and silica leaves. Those leaves tinkled maddeningly around him, reflected a thousand shades and hues of reds and purples. Behind him, Ghul flew into a loud rage. At the very least he and Valdur would have to resume human shapes before they dared pursuit. If they dared at all.

Fastenrath was no more than a dozen careful steps into the Forest when he encountered the dryad, a beautiful nude, just then lifting her bloody mouth from the throat of the fat merchant. Her satiated eyes were a dull blue, glazed, and took nearly a minute to fully focus on him. She was blonde, lithe, and lovely, and it was easy to see how a man could fall into her deadly hands even if she were unarmed with songs of compulsion.

Carefully Fastenrath sat down facing her, crossed his lank legs, and exchanged stares over the corpse. He prayed that her lusts were sated. Here, as with the Devil's Tooth, was another ancient experiment in immortality; one that had yielded the woman endless life but at the cost of almost everything else that was human. Was life really so dear?

Warily, but without fear, the woman watched as he resumed carving his doll. He was a quick worker when he concentrated, able to fulfill a pattern with the deft speed that comes of long practice. Her blue eyes never left his moving hands. She seemed mesmerized by his creation. She was beauty, he, art. And between them lay a warm corpse with an arm slowly moving as dead muscles contracted.

There were shrieks and thrashings beyond the edge of the weird Forest. The shape-changing process was, apparently, extremely painful. Fastenrath smiled grimly, hoping he had time.

Red sunlight broke through the tinkling leaves overhead, got caught amidst the golden hair of the woman, hung there like splashes of blood. She was unaware of her own grimness, completely innocent of either good or evil, childlike in her rapture with his carving. It was curious that such innocence and deadliness should be found in one being. Yet many of the ancient immortals were like that, Fastenrath knew. They did not remember what they had been, did not understand what they had become, had even lost much of their ability to reason. Most interacted with the world in rote manner dictated by long ages of experience, not by using the minds that had developed the immortality processes. In some ways they had regressed to the purely animal plane.

He finished the doll, looked into her eyes once more while holding it up for display. A small, childish flash of greedy hope crossed her face. He offered the doll. She stared at him in disbelief, slowly extending a hand, then grabbed, held the doll in closely folded hands while studying it, crushed it to her breasts and crooned softly. Fastenrath sighed in relief. He had guessed right when he had decided to try playing on her long-denied attribute of Mother. She might not remember babies, but her instincts did.

Minutes passed. Eventually something moving tinkled the leaves behind him. He shivered. The moment of decision was almost at hand. He thrust a hand into his purse, brought forth the Tooth, slowly extended it toward the woman.

Her eyes rose from the doll, saw the glowing ruby, widened with a childish interest. It was a pretty bauble, that could not be denied. Slowly, uncertainly, she reached for it.

Then she was crushing both doll and ruby to her breasts, one in each hand. While she was thus bemused, Fastenrath rose carefully and made his cautious way deeper into the Forest. Despite all his care, his bare arms and legs became badly lacerated; his shirt, kilt, and boots were slashed to ribbons by the leaves. At least they did not actively oppose his passage as would have been the case if the woman had considered him an enemy.

He soon found a suitable hiding place, and from it continued to observe the woman. She continued crooning to her doll and ruby. He congratulated himself on the success of his ploy. It was a long chance he had taken, betting his life on the naivete and denied instincts of this unhuman creature.

He had been successful up till then, but he wasn't out of his difficulties yet. Key parts of his plan were still to unfold and could easily go wrong.

Already there was a feeling of terrible loss and a growing temptation. Could he wait his plan out, recover the Tooth from the dryad when it was complete, and with its promise of immortality escape her anger? The Tooth had gotten a hold on him, such power it had to shape and warp the mind. He shuddered with horror at his own thoughts. He had seen and done many black things during his years—the murder of Frey Levchescu weighed ever more heavily on his mind—but this temptation was almost too much for reason. His one taste of the Tooth's power, when he had slain the priest, had become as haunting and attractive as a draught of Night's Dream, a spicy narcotic wine made of the de-poisoned juices of skull bell fruit. He felt both fear and horror of the Tooth even while his mind kept trying to find ways to steal it back. A temptation altogether too attractive, this immortality.

Events helped defeat the devils of his mind. The sounds he had heard before ridding himself of the Tooth now came from quite near the enthralled dryad, approaching. Ghul appeared, stared down at the corpse, at the woman, at the treasures in her hands. He glanced behind him, perhaps to ascertain the nearness of his unwanted partner. Fastenrath smiled. He could see what was in Ghul's mind. He was considering seizing the jewel, hiding it, and allowing Valdur to think that it was still in Fastenrath's possession.

The dwarf took the first step, snatched the Tooth.

The dryad looked up, surprised, then sprang with the suddenness of a cat. The tinkling of the Forest changed from a soft merry note to an angry one. The branches of the metal trees began to stir. The woman's nails went for Ghul's eyes, her teeth for his throat, and she had both in a death-grip before he could utter his first startled cry. Fastenrath watched unsmiling. The dwarf would struggle a bit, but he was as good as dead. With teeth in his throat he could neither call for help nor utter the words of a defensive spell. The trap was nicely sprung; Ghul's greed had brought him to a form of suicide. Fastenrath's estimates of the woman's behavior had come off even better than he had hoped.

As Ghul twitched his last, one dying hand vainly clutching that of the merchant already dead, Valdur of Kristengrin stepped into the tiny clearing. Man and clothes, though the latter had been savaged by angry leaves, were so deeply black that Fastenrath's eyes kept slipping off to more substantial objects. Looking at Valdur was like staring into a hole in nothingness.

Chuckling, Valdur snatched the Tooth from dying Ghul's hand and ran.

The dryad rose angrily, but too late to attack. Fastenrath cursed softly. He had brought the Tooth here because he had thought it would be unattainable once in her care.

The woman sang something. Valdur froze for an instant, then resumed his flight. The woman sang again. All around the man the Tinsel Forest, already writhing, sprang into insanely lashing life, the razor-edged leaves and steely-whip branches reaching for his body. Stripes of scarlet began to mar his perfect blackness. One of his arms seemed nearly severed. He shrieked, dropped the Tooth from a hand that could no longer grip, and hurled himself at the last writhing barrier to his freedom. He made it through.

Fastenrath cursed again. Valdur had escaped. The trap had worked less than perfectly. But, at least, the Tooth would now be even more unattainable than it had been in the Monastery of the Moon, though Valdur would know its new location and would continue trying to get it.

The woman recovered her new bauble, returned to the clearing and resumed crooning. Fastenrath tried to make out the subject being discussed by the excited voices arguing beyond the Forest edge. At last he got it. Valdur was demanding, unsuccessfully, that Ghul's retainers break him a path through the dangerous leaves. Moving with the utmost caution, Fastenrath eased away from the dryad and his hiding place and made for the uphill end of the Forest. Leaves continued cutting him, but not maliciously. He endured.

He stepped from the Forest an hour later, just above where the flood of gallowglass beetles washed against its flank and turned away, moving toward the River Bryne. No enemies did he see anywhere, and even were they near, he had come out of the Forest on the opposite side of the vast living river of beetles. Likely, seeing themselves foiled, they were already on their way to Warasdin, grey and brooding in the distance.

A man's skeleton lay in the gallowglass stream. He wondered if it could be Valdur, struck down by Ghul's angry retainers. But that seemed to be too much to hope. More likely it was that of a man who had angered the sorcerer. Fastenrath shrugged, smiled crookedly. Well, enough of wizardry for a while. He was off to find a buyer for the ancient book.

And to lay at peace the ghost which would otherwise haunt him all his life. He set his course for Gormflaith.

IN THE WIND

Early on my plan was to create a vast sprawl of related stories set in two major realms: science-fictionally, a future history, while, fantastically, there would be in the world of the Dread Empire, which empire would itself seldom be on stage. The future history remained fairly consistent, most of the stories fitting without conflicting even though they did not relate to one another. "In the Wind" was one such, although I think the principal fighter pilot might have gotten a mention, somehow in passing, in the Starfishers Trilogy.

1

It's quiet up there, riding the ups and downs over Ginnunga Gap. Even in combat there's no slightest clamor, only a faint scratch and whoosh of strikers tapping igniters and rockets smoking away. The rest of the time, just a sleepy whisper of air caressing your canopy. On patrol it's hard to stay alert and wary.

If the aurora hadn't been so wild behind the hunched backs of the Harridans, painting glaciers and snowfields in ropes of varicolored fire, sequinning snow-catches in the weathered natural castles of the Gap with momentary reflections, I might have dozed at the stick the morning I became von Drachau's wingman. The windwhales were herding in the mountains, thinking migration, and we were flying five or six missions per day. The strain was almost unbearable.

But the auroral display kept me alert. It was the strongest I'd ever seen. A ferocious magnetic storm was developing. Lightning grumbled between the Harridans' copper peaks, sometimes even speared down and danced among the spires in the Gap. We'd all be grounded soon. The rising winds, cold but moisture-heavy, promised weather even whales couldn't ride.

Winter was about to break out of the north, furiously, a winter of a Great Migration. Planets, moons and sun were right, oracles and omens predicting imminent Armageddon. Twelve years had ticked into the ashcan of time. All the whale species again were herding. Soon the fighting would be hard and hopeless.

There are four species of windwhale on the planet Camelot, the most numerous being the Harkness whale, which migrates from its north arctic and north temperate feeding ranges to equatorial mating grounds every other year. Before beginning their migration they, as do all whales, form herds—which, because the beasts are total omnivores, utterly strip the earth in their passage south. The lesser species, in both size and numbers, are Okumura's First, which mates each three winters, Rosenberg's, mating every fourth, and the rare Okumura's Second, which travels only once every six years. Unfortunately . . .

It takes no mathematical genius to see the factors of twelve. And every twelve years the migrations do coincide. In the Great Migrations the massed whales leave tens of thousands of square kilometers of devastation in their wake, devastation from which, because of following lesser migrations, the routes barely recover before the next Great Migration. Erosion is phenomenal. The monsters, subject to no natural control other than that apparently exacted by creatures we called mantas, were destroying the continent on which our employers operated.

Ubichi Corporation had been on Camelot twenty-five years. The original exploitation force, though equipped to face the world's physical peculiarities, hadn't been prepared for whale migrations. They'd been lost to a man, whale supper, because the Corporation's pre-exploitation studies had been so cursory. Next Great Migration another team, though they'd dug in, hadn't fared much better. Ubichi still hadn't done its scientific investigation. In fact, its only action was a determination that the whales had to go.

Simple enough, viewed from a board room at Geneva. But practical implementation was a nightmare under Camelot's technically stifling conditions. And the mantas recomplicated everything.

My flight leader's wagging wings directed my attention south. From a hill a dozen kilometers down the cable came flashing light, Clonninger Station reporting safe arrival of a convoy from Derry. For the next few hours we'd have to be especially alert.

It would take the zeppelins that long to beat north against the wind, and all the while they would be vulnerable to mantas from over the Gap. Mantas, as far as we could see at the time, couldn't tell the difference between dirigibles and whales. More air cover should be coming up . . .

Von Drachau came to Jaeger Gruppe XIII (Corporation Armed Action Command's unsubtle title for our Hunter Wing, which they used as a dump for problem employees) with that convoy, reassigned from JG IV, a unit still engaged in an insane effort to annihilate the Sickle Islands whale herds by means of glider attacks carried out over forty-five kilometers of quiet seas. We'd all heard of him (most JG XIII personnel had come from the Sickle Islands operation), the clumsiest, or luckiest incompetent, pilot flying for Ubichi. While scoring only four kills he'd been bolted down seven times—and had survived without a scratch. He was the son of Jupp von Drachau, the Confederation Navy officer who had directed the planet-busting strike against the Sangaree homeworld, a brash, sometimes pompous, always self-important nineteen year old who thought that the flame of his father's success should illuminate him equally—and yet resented even a mention of the man. He was a dilettante, come to Camelot only to fly. Unlike the rest of us, Old Earthers struggling to buy out of the poverty bequeathed us by prodigal ancestors, he had no driving need to give performance for pay.

An admonition immediately in order: I'm not here to praise von Drachau, but to bury him. To let him bury himself. Aerial combat fans, who have never seen Camelot, who have read only corporate propaganda, have made of him a contemporary "hero," a flying do-no-wrong competitor for the pewter crown already contested by such antiques as von Richtoffen, Hartmann and Galland. Yet these Archaicists can't, because they need one, make a platinum bar from a turd, nor a socio-psychological fulfillment from a scatterbrain kid . . . *

Most of the stories about him are apocryphal accretions generated to give him depth in his later, "heroic" aspect. Time and storytellers increase his stature, as they have that of Norse gods, who might've been people who lived in preliterate times. For those who knew him (and no one is closer than a wingman), though some of us might like to believe the legends, he was just a selfish, headstrong, tantrum-throwing manchild—albeit a fighter of supernatural ability. In the three months he spent with us, during the Great Migration, his peculiar talents and shortcomings made of him a creature larger than life. Unpleasant a person as he was, he became *the* phenom pilot.

> *This paragraph is an editorial insertion from a private letter by Salvador del Gado. Dogfight believes it clarifies del Gado's personal feelings toward his former wingman. His tale, taken separately, while unsympathetic, strives for an objectivity free of his real jealousies. It is significant that he mentions Hartmann and Galland together with von Richtoffen; undoubtedly they, as he when compared with von Drachau, were flyers better than the Red Knight, yet they, and del Gado, lack the essential charisma of the flying immortals. Also, von Richtoffen and von Drachau died at the stick; Hartmann and Galland went on to more prosaic things, becoming administrators, commanders of the Luftwaffe. Indications are that del Gado's fate with Ubichi Corporation's Armed Action Command will be much the same.*
>
> *—Dogfight*

2

The signals from Clonninger came before dawn, while only two small moons and the aurora lighted the sky. But sunrise followed quickly. By the time the convoy neared Beadle Station (us), Camelot's erratic, blotchy-faced sun had cleared the eastern horizon. The reserve squadron began catapulting into the Gap's frenetic drafts. The four of us on close patrol descended toward the dirigibles.

The lightning in the Harridans had grown into a Ypres cannonade. A net of jagged blue laced together the tips of the copper towers in the Gap. An elephant stampede of angry clouds rumbled above the mountains. The winds approached the edge of being too vicious for flight.

Flashing light from ground control, searchlight fingers stabbing north and east, pulsating. Mantas sighted. We waggle-winged acknowledgment, turned for the Gap and updrafts. My eyes had been on the verge of rebellion, demanding sleep, but in the possibility of combat weariness temporarily faded.

Black specks were coming south low against the daytime verdigris of the Gap, a male-female pair in search of a whale. It was obvious how they'd been named. Anyone familiar with Old Earth's sea creatures could see a remarkable resemblance to the manta ray—though these had ten meter bodies, fifteen meter wingspans, and ten meter tails tipped by devil's spades of rudders. From a distance they appeared black, but at attack range could be seen as deep, uneven green on top and lighter, near olive beneath. They had ferocious habits.

More signals from the ground. Reserve ships would take the mantas. Again we turned, overflew the convoy.

It was the biggest ever sent north, fifteen dirigibles, one fifty meters and larger, dragging the line from Clonninger at half kilometer intervals, riding long reaches of running cable as their sailmen struggled to tack them into a facing wind. The tall glasteel pylons supporting the cable track were ruby towers linked by a single silver strand of spider silk running straight to Clonninger's hills.

We circled wide and slow at two thousand meters, gradually dropping lower. When we got down to five hundred we were replaced by a flight from the reserve squadron while we scooted to the Gap for an updraft. Below us ground crews pumped extra hydrogen to the barrage balloons, lifting Beadle's vast protective net another hundred meters so the convoy could slide beneath. Switchmen and winchmen hustled about with glass and plastic tools in a dance of confusion. We didn't have facilities for receiving more than a half dozen zeppelins—though these, fighting the wind, might come up slowly enough to be handled.

More signals. More manta activity over the Gap, the reserve squadron's squabble turning into a brawl. The rest of my squadron had come back from the Harridans at a run, a dozen mantas in pursuit. Later I learned our ships had found a small windwhale herd and while one flight busied their mantas the other had destroyed the whales. Then, ammunition gone, they ran for home, arriving just in time to complicate traffic problems.

I didn't get time to worry it. The mantas, incompletely fed, spotted the convoy. They don't distinguish between whale and balloon. They went for the zeppelins.

What followed becomes dulled in memory, so swiftly did it happen and so little attention did I have to spare. The air filled with mantas and lightning, gliders, smoking rockets, explosions. The brawl spread till every ship in the wing was involved. Armorers and catapult crews worked to exhaustion trying to keep everything up. Ground batteries seared one another with backblast keeping a rocket screen between the mantas and stalled convoy—which couldn't warp in while the entrance to the defense net was tied up by fighting craft (a problem unforeseen but later corrected by the addition of emergency entryways). They winched their running cables in to short stay and waited it out. Ground people managed to get barrage balloons with tangle tails out to make the mantas' flying difficult.

Several of the dirigibles fought back. Stupid, I thought. Their lifting gas was hydrogen, screamingly dangerous. To arm them seemed an exercise in self-destruction. So it proved. Most of our casualties came when a ship loaded with ground troops blew up, leaking gas ignited by its own rockets. One hundred eighty-three men burned or fell to their deaths. Losses to mantas were six pilots and the twelve-man crew of a freighter.

3

Von Drachau made his entry into JG XIII history just as I dropped from my sailship to the packed earth parking apron. His zepp was the first in and, having vented gas, had been towed to the apron to clear the docking winches. I'd done three sorties during the fighting, after the six of regular patrol. I'd seen my wingman crash into a dragline pylon, was exhausted, and possessed by an utterly foul mood. Von Drachau hit dirt long-haired, unkempt, and complaining, and I was there to greet him. "What do you want to be when you grow up, von Drachau?"

Not original, but it caught him off guard. He was used to criticism by administrators, but pilots avoid antagonism. One never knows when a past slight might mean hesitation at the trigger ring and failure to blow a manta off one's tail. Von Drachau's hatchet face opened and closed, goldfish-like, and one skeletal hand came up to an accusatory point, but he couldn't come back.

We'd had no real contact during the Sickle Islands campaign. Considering his self-involvement, I doubted he knew who I was—and didn't care if he did. I stepped past and greeted acquaintances from my old squadron, made promises to get together to reminisce, then retreated to barracks. If there were any justice at all, I'd get five or six hours for surviving the morning.

I managed four, a record for the week, then received a summons to the office of Commander McClennon, a retired Navy man exiled to command of JG XIII because he'd been so outspoken about Corporation policy.

(The policy that irked us all, and which was the root of countless difficulties, was Ubichi's secret purpose on Camelot. Ubichi deals in unique commodities. It was sure that Camelot operations were recovering one such, but fewer than a hundred of a half million employees knew what. The rest were there just to keep the windwhales from interfering. Even we mercenaries from Old Earth didn't like fighting for a total unknown.)

Commander McClennon's outer office was packed, old faces from the wing and new from the convoy. Shortly, McClennon appeared and announced that the wing had been assigned some gliders with new armaments, low velocity glass barrel gas pressure cannon, pod of four in the nose of a ship designed to carry the weapon system . . . immediate interest. Hitherto we'd flown sport gliders jury-rigged to carry crude rockets, the effectiveness of which lay in the cyanide shell surrounding the warhead. Reliability, poor; accuracy, erratic. A pilot was nearly as likely to kill himself as a whale.

But what could you do when you couldn't use the smallest scrap of metal? Even a silver filling could kill you there. The wildly oscillating and unpredictable magnetic ambience could induce sudden, violent electrical charges. The only metal risked inside Camelot's van Allens was that in the lighters running to and from the surface station at the south magnetic pole, where few lines of force were cut and magnetic weather was reasonably predictable.

Fifty thousand years ago the system passed through the warped space surrounding a black hole. Theory says that's the reason for its eccentricities, but I wonder. Maybe it explains why all bodies in the system have magnetic fields offset from the body centers, the distance off an apparent function of size, mass and rate of rotation, but it doesn't tell me why the fields exist (planetary magnetism is uncommon), nor why they pulsate randomly.

But I digress, and into areas where I have no competence. I should explain what physicists don't understand? We were in the Commander's office and he was selecting pilots for the new ships. Everyone wanted one. Chances for survival appeared that much better.

McClennon's assignments seemed indisputable, the best flyers to the new craft, four flights of four, though those left with old ships were disappointed.

I suffered disappointment myself. A blockbuster dropped at the end, after I'd resigned myself to continuing in an old craft.

"Von Drachau, Horst-Johann," said McClennon, peering at his roster through antique spectacles, one of his affectations, "attack pilot. Del Gado, Salvador Martin, wingman."

Me? With von Drachau? I'd thought the old man liked me, thought he had a good opinion of my ability . . . why'd he want to waste me? Von Drachau's wingman? Murder.

I was so stunned I couldn't yell *let me out!*

"Familiarization begins this afternoon, on Strip Three. First flight checkouts in the morning." A few more words, tired exhortations to do our best, all that crap that's been poured on men at the front from day one, then dismissal. Puzzled and upset, I started for the door.

"Del Gado. Von Drachau." The executive officer. "Stay a minute. The Commander wants to talk to you."

4

My puzzlement thickened as we entered McClennon's inner office, a Victorian-appointed, crowded yet comfortable room I hadn't seen since I'd paid my first day respects. There were bits of a stamp collection scattered, a desk becluttered, presentation holographs of Navy officers that seemed familiar, another of a woman of the pale thin martyr type, a model of a High Seiner spaceship looking like it'd been cobbled together from plastic tubing and children's blocks. McClennon had been the Naval officer responsible for bringing the Seiners into Confederation in time for the Three Races War. His retirement had been a protest against the way the annexation was handled. Upset as I was I had little attention for surroundings, nor cared what made the Old Man tick.

Once alone with us, he became a man who failed to fit my conception of a commanding officer. His face, which usually seemed about to slide off his skull bones with the weight of responsibility, spread a warm smile. "Johnny!" He thrust a wrinkled hand at von Drachau.

He knew the kid?

My new partner's reaction was a surprise, too. He seemed awed and deferential as he extended his own hand. "Uncle Tom."

McClennon turned. "I've known Johnny since the night he wet himself on my dress blacks just before the Grand Admiral's Ball. Good old days at Luna Command, before the last war." He chuckled. Von Drachau blushed. And I frowned in renewed surprise. I hadn't known von Drachau well, but had never seen or heard anything to suggest he was capable of being impressed by anyone but himself.

"His father and I were Academy classmates. Then served in the same ships before I went into intelligence. Later we worked together in operations against the Sangaree."

Von Drachau didn't sit down till invited. Even though McClennon, in those few minutes, exposed more of himself than anyone in the wing had hitherto seen, I was more interested in the kid. His respectful, almost cowed attitude was completely out of character.

"Johnny," said McClennon, leaning back behind his desk and slowly turning a drink in his hand, "you don't come with recommendations. Not positive, anyway. We going to go through that up here?"

Von Drachau stared at the carpet, shrugged, reminded me of myself as a seven year old called to explain some specially noxious misdeed to my creche-father. It became increasingly obvious that McClennon was a man with whom von Drachau was unwilling to play games. I'd heard gruesome stories of his behavior with the CO JG IV.

"You've heard the lecture already, so I won't give it. I do understand, a bit. Anyway, discipline here, compared to Derry or the Islands, is almost nonexistent. Do your job and you won't have it bad. But don't push. I won't let you endanger lives. Something to think about. This morning's scrap left me with extra pilots. I can ground people who irritate me. Could be a blow to a man who loved flying."

Von Drachau locked gazes with the Commander. Rebellion stirred but he only nodded.

McClennon turned again. "You don't like this assignment." Not a question. My face must've been a giveaway. "Suicidal, you think? You were in JG IV a while. Heard all about Johnny. But you don't know him. I do, well enough to say he's got potential—if we can get him to realize aerial fighting's a team game. By which I mean his first consideration must be bringing himself, his wingman, and his ship home intact." Von Drachau grew red. He'd not only lost seven sailships during the Sickle Islands offensive, he'd lost three wingmen. Dead. "It's hard to remember you're part of a team while attacking. You know that yourself, del Gado. So be patient. Help me make something out of Johnny."

I tried to control my face, failed.

"Why me, eh? Because you're the best flyer I've got. You can stay with him if anyone can.

"I know, favoritism. I'm taking special care. And that's wrong. You're correct, right down the line. But I can't help myself. Don't think you could either, in my position. Enough explanation. That's the way it's going to be. If you can't handle it, let me know. I'll find someone who can, or I'll ground him. One thing I mean to do: send him home alive." Von Drachau vainly tried to conceal his embarrassment and anger. I felt for him. Wouldn't like being talked about that way myself—though McClennon was doing the right thing, putting his motives on display, up front, so there'd be no surprises later on, and establishing for von Drachau the parameters allowed him. The Commander was an Old Earther himself, and on that battleground had learned that honesty is a weapon as powerful as any in the arsenal of deceit.

"I'll try," I replied, though with silent reservations. I'd have to do some handy self-examination before I bought the whole trick bag.

"That's all I ask. You can go, then. Johnny and I have some catching up to do."

I returned to barracks in a daze. There I received condolences from squadron mates motivated, I suppose, by relief at having escaped the draft themselves.

Tired though I was, I couldn't sleep till I'd thought everything through.

In the end, of course, I decided the Old Man had earned a favor. (This's a digression from von Drachau's story except insofar as it reflects the thoughts that led me to help bring into being the one really outstanding story in Ubichi's Camelot operation.) McClennon was an almost archetypically remote, secretive, Odin/Christ figure, an embastioned lion quietly licking private wounds in the citadel of his office, sharing his pain and privation with no one. But personal facts that had come flitting on the wings of rumor made it certain he was a rare old gentleman who'd paid his dues and asked little in return. He'd bought off for hundreds of Old Earthers, usually by pulling wires to Service connections. And, assuming the stories are true, the price he paid to bring the Starfishers into Confederation, at a time when they held the sole means by which the Three Races War could be won, was the destruction of a deep relationship with the only woman he'd ever loved, the pale Seiner girl whose holo portrait sat like an icon on his desk. Treason and betrayal. Earthman who spoke with forked tongue. She might've been the mother of the son he was trying to find in Horst-Johann. But his Isaac never came back from the altar of the needs of the race. Yes, he'd paid his dues, and at usurious rates.

He had something coming. I'd give him the chance he wanted for the boy ... Somewhere during those hours my Old Earther's pragmatism lapsed. Old Number One, survival, took a temporary vacation.

It felt good.

5

Getting along with von Drachau didn't prove as difficult as expected. During the following week I was the cause of more friction than he. I kept reacting to the image of the man rumor and prejudice had built in my mind, not to the man in whose presence I was. He was much less arrogant and abrasive than I'd heard—though gritty with the usual outworlder's contempt for the driving need to accomplish characteristic of Old Earthers. But I'd become accustomed to that, even understood. Outworlders had never endured the hopelessness and privation of life on the motherworld. They'd never understand what buying off really meant. Nor did any care to learn.

There're just two kinds of people on Old Earth, butchers and bovines. No one starves, no one freezes, but those are the only positives of life in the Social Insurance warrens. Twenty billion unemployed sardines. The high point of many lives is a visit to Confederation Zone (old Switzerland), where government and corporations maintain their on-planet offices and estates and allow small bands of citizens to come nose the candy store window and look at the lifestyle of the outworlds ... then send them home with apathy overcome by renewed desperation.

All Old Earth is a slum/ghetto surrounding one small, stoutly de-fended bastion of wealth and privilege. That says it all, except that getting out is harder than from any historical ghetto.

It's not really what Old Earth outworlders think of when they dust off the racial warm heart and talk about the mother-world. What they're thinking of is Luna Command, Old Earth's moon and the seat of Confederation government. All they have for Old Earth itself is a little shame-faced under-the-table welfare money . . . bitter. The only resource left is human life, the cheapest of all. The outworlds have little use for Terrans save for work like that on Camelot. So bitter. I shouldn't be. I've bought off. Not my problem anymore.

Horst (his preference) and I got on well, quickly advanced to first names. After familiarizing ourselves with the new equipment, we returned to regular patrols. Horst scattered no grit in the machinery. He performed his tasks-within-mission with clockwork precision, never straying beyond the borders of discipline.

He confessed, as we paused at the lip of Ginnunga Gap one morning, while walking to the catapults for launch, that he feared being grounded more than losing individuality to military conformity. Flying was the only thing his father hadn't programmed for him (the Commander had gotten him started), and he'd become totally enamored of the sport. Signing on with Ubichi had been the only way to stick with it after his father had managed his appointment to Academy; he'd refused, and been banished from paternal grace. He *had* to fly. Without that he'd have nothing. The Commander, he added, had meant what he said.

I think that was the first time I realized a man could be raised outworld and still be deprived. We Old Earthers take a perverse, chauvinistic pride in our poverty and persecution—like, as the Commander once observed, Jews of Marrakech. (An allusion I spent months dredging: he'd read some obscure and ancient writers.) Our goals are so wholly materialistic that we can scarcely comprehend poverty of the spirit. That von Drachau, with wealth and social position, could feel he had less than I, was a stunning notion.

For him flying was an end, for me a means. Though I enjoyed it, each time I sat at catapult head credit signs danced in my head; so much base, plus per mission and per kill. If I did well I'd salvage some family, too. Horst's pay meant nothing. He wasted it fast as it came—I think to show contempt for the wealth from which he sprang. Though that had been honest money, prize and coup money from his father's successes against the Sangaree.

Steam pressure drove a glasteel piston along forty meters of glasteel cylinder; twenty seconds behind von Drachau I catapulted into the ink of the Gap and began feeling for the ups. For brief instants I could see him outlined against the aurora, flashing in and out of vision as he searched and circled. I spied him climbing, immediately turned to catch the same riser. Behind me came the rest of the squadron. Up we went in a spiral like moths playing tag in the night while reaching for the moons. Von Drachau found altitude and slipped from the up. I followed. At three thousand meters, with moonlight and aurora, it wasn't hard to see him. The four craft of my flight circled at ninety degree points while the rest of the squadron went north across the Gap. We'd slowly drop a thousand meters, then catch another up to the top. We'd stay in the air two hours (or we ran out of ammunition), then go down for an hour break. Five missions minimum.

First launch came an hour before dawn, long before the night fighters went down. Mornings were crowded. But by sunrise we seemed terribly alone while we circled down or climbed, watched the Gap for whales leaving the Harridans or the mantas that'd grown so numerous.

Daytimes almost every ship concentrated on keeping the whales north of the Gap. That grew more difficult as the density of their population neared the migratory. It'd be a while yet, maybe a month, but numbers and instinct would eventually overcome the fear our weapons had instilled. I couldn't believe we'd be able to stop them. The smaller herds of the 'tween years, yes, but not the lemming rivers that would come with winter. A Corporation imbued with any human charity would've been busy sealing mines and evacuating personnel. But Ubichi had none. In terms of financial costs, equipment losses, it was cheaper to fight, sacrificing inexpensive lives to salvage material made almost priceless by interstellar shipment.

6

Signals from the ground, a searchlight fingering the earth and flashing three times rapidly. Rim sentries had spotted a whale in the direction the finger pointed. Von Drachau and I were front. We began circling down.

We'd dropped just five hundred meters when he wag-winged visual contact. I saw nothing but the darkness that almost always clogged the canyon. As wide as Old Earth's Grand Canyon and three times as deep, it was well lighted only around noon.

That was the first time I noticed his phenomenal vision. In following months he was to amaze me repeatedly. I honestly believe I was the better pilot, capable of outflying any manta, but his ability to find targets made him the better combat flyer.

The moment I wagged back he broke circle and dove. I'd've circled lower. If the whale was down in the Gap itself that might mean a three thousand meter fall. Pulling out would overstrain one's wings. Sailplanes, even the jackboot jobs we flew, are fragile machines never intended for stunt flying.

But I was wingman, responsible for protecting the attack pilot's rear. I winged over and followed, maintaining a constant five hundred meters between us. Light and shadow from clouds and mountains played over his ship, alternately lighting and darkening the personal devices he'd painted on. A death's-head grinned and winked . . .

I spied the whale. It was working directly toward Beadle. Size and coloring of the gasbag (oblate spheroid sixty meters long, patched in shades from pink to scarlet and spotted with odd other colors at organ sites) indicated a juvenile of the Harkness species, that with the greatest potential for destruction. Triangular vanes protruding ten meters from muscle rings on the bag twitched and quivered as the monster strove to maintain a steady course. Atop it in a thin Mohawk swath swayed a copse of treelike organs believed to serve both plantlike and animal digestive and metabolic functions. Some may have been sensory. Beneath it sensory tentacles trailed, stirring fretfully like dreaming snakes on the head of Medusa. If any found food (and anything organic was provender for a Harkness), it'd anchor itself immediately. Hundreds more tentacles would descend and begin lifting edibles to mouths in a tiny head-body tight against the underside of the gasbag. There'd be a drizzling organic rainfall as the monster dumped ballast/waste. Migrating whale herds could devastate great swaths of countryside. Fortunately for Ubichi's operations, the mating seasons were infrequent.

The Harkness swelled ahead. Horst would be fingering his trigger ring, worrying his sights. I stopped watching for mantas and adjusted my dive so Horst wouldn't be in line when I fired . . .

Flashing lights, hasty, almost panicky. I read, then glanced out right and up, spied the manta pair. From high above the Harridans they arrowed toward the whale, tips and trailing edges of their wings rippling as they adjusted dive to each vagary of canyon air. But they were a kilometer above and would be no worry till we'd completed our pass. And the other two ships of our flight would be after them, to engage while Horst and I completed the primary mission.

The relationship between mantas and whales had never, to that time, been clearly defined. The mantas seemed to feed among the growths on whale backs, to attach themselves in mated pairs to particular adults, which they fiercely defended, and upon which they were apparently dependent. But nothing seemed to come the other way. The whales utterly ignored them, even as food. Whales ignored everything in the air, though, enduring our attacks as if they weren't happening. If not for the mantas, the extermination program would've been a cakewalk.

But mantas fought at every encounter, almost as if they knew what we were doing. A year earlier they'd been little problem. Then we'd been sending single flights after lone wandering whales, but as migratory pressures built the manta population had increased till we were forced to fight three or four battles to each whale attack—of which maybe one in twenty resulted in a confirmed kill. Frustrating business, especially since self-defense distracted so from our primary mission.

Luckily, the mantas had only one inefficient, if spectacular, weapon, the lightning they hurled.

That fool von Drachau dropped flaps to give himself more firing time. Because I began overtaking him, I had to follow suit. My glider shuddered, groaned, and an ominous snap came from my right wing. But nothing fell apart.

Fog formed before Horst's craft, whipped back. He'd begun firing. His shells painted a tight bright pattern in the forest on the whale's back. Stupidly, I shifted aim to the same target. Von Drachau pulled out, flaps suddenly up, used his momentum to hurl himself up toward the diving manta pair, putting them in a pincer.

A jagged bite of lightning flashed toward von Drachau. I cursed. We'd plunged into a trap. Mantas had been feeding in the shelter of the whale's back organs. They were coming up to fight.

I'd begun firing an instant before the flash, putting my shells in behind Horst's. Before the water vapor from my cannon gas fogged my canopy I saw explosions digging into the gasbag. I started to stick back and fire at the mantas, but saw telltale ripples of blue fire beneath the yellow of my shells. The bag was going to blow.

When the hydrogen went there'd be one hell of an explosion. Following Horst meant suicide.

The prime purpose of the explosives was to drive cyanide fragments into whale flesh, but sometimes, as then, a too tight pattern breached the main bag—and hydrogen is as dangerous on Camelot as elsewhere.

I took my only option, dove. With luck the whale's mass would shadow me from the initial blast.

It did. But the tip of my right wing, that'd made such a grim noise earlier, brushed one of the monster's sensory tentacles. The jerk snapped it at the root. I found myself spinning down.

I rode it a while, both because I was stunned (I'd never been downed before, accidentally or otherwise) and because I wanted the craft to protect me from downblast.

The sun had risen sufficiently to illuminate the tips of the spires in the gap. They wheeled, jerked, reached up like angry claws, drawing rapidly closer. Despite the ongoing explosion, already shaking me, blistering the paint on my fuselage, I had to get out.

Canopy cooperated. In the old gliders they'd been notoriously sticky, costing many lives. This popped easily. I closed my eyes and jumped, jerking my ripcord as I did. Heat didn't bother me. My remaining wing took a cut at me, a last effort of fate to erase my life-tape, then the chute jerked my shoulders. I began to sway.

It was cold and lonely up there, and there was nothing I could do. I was no longer master of my fate. You would have to be an Old Earther near buying off to really feel the impact of that. Panicky, I peered up at the southern rim of the Gap—and saw what I'd hoped to see, the rescue balloon already on its way. It was a hot air job that rode safety lines played out from winches at the edge. If I could be salvaged, it'd be managed. I patted my chest pockets to make sure I had my flares.

Only then did I rock my chute away so I could see what'd happened to von Drachau.

He was into it with three mantas, one badly wounded (the survivor of the pair from the Harkness—the other had died in the explosion). He got the wounded one and did a flap trick to turn inside the others. His shells went into the belly of one. It folded and fell. Then the rest of our flight was pursuing the survivor toward the Harridans.

I worried as burning pieces of whale fell past. Suppose one hit my chute?

But none did. I landed in snow deep in the Gap, after a cruel slide down an almost vertical rock face, then set out my first flare. While I tried to stay warm, I thought about von Drachau.

I'd gone along with his attack because I'd had neither choice, nor time to think, nor any way to caution him. But that precipitous assault had been the sort that'd earned him his reputation. And it'd cost again. Me.

Didn't make me feel any better to realize I'd been as stupid in my target selection.

A rational, unimpetuous attack would've gone in level with the whale, from behind, running along its side. Thus Horst could've stayed out of sight of the mantas riding it, and I could've avoided the explosion resulting from a tight fire pattern in the thin flesh of the back. Shells laid along the whale's flanks would've spread enough cyanide to insure a kill.

Part my fault, but when the rescue balloon arrived I was so mad at Horst I couldn't talk.

7

Von Drachau met the rescue balloon, more concerned and contrite than I'd've credited. I piled out steaming, with every intention of denting his head, but he ran to me like a happy puppy, bubbling apologies, saying he'd never had a chance at a whale . . . righteous outrage became grumpiness. He was only nineteen, emotionally ten.

There were reports to be filed but I was in no mood. I headed for barracks and something alcoholic.

Von Drachau followed. "Sal," he said with beer in his mustache, "I mean it. I'm sorry. Wish I could look at it like you. Like this's just a job . . ."

"Uhm." I made a grudging peace. "So can it." But he kept on. Something was biting him, something he wanted coaxed out.

"The mantas," he said. "What do we know about them?"

"They get in the way."

"Why? Territorial imperative? Sal, I been thinking. Was today a set-up? If people was working the other side, they couldn't've set a better trap. In the old ships both of us would've gone down."

"Watch your imagination, kid. Things're different in the Islands, but not that different. We've run into feeding mantas before. You just attacked from the wrong angle." I tossed off my third double. The Gap bottom cold began leaking from my bones. I felt a bit more charitable. But not enough to discuss idiot theories of manta intelligence.

We already knew many odd forms of intelligence. Outworlders have a curious sensitivity to it, a near reverence puzzling to Old Earthers. They go around looking for it, especially in adversity. Like savages imputing powers to storms and stones, they can't accept disasters at face value. There has to be a malignant mover.

"I guess you're right," he said. But his doubt was plain. He *wanted* to believe we were fighting a war, not exterminating noxious animals.

Got me thinking, though. Curious how persistent the rumor was, even though there was no evidence to support it. But a lot of young people (sic!—I was twenty-eight) are credulous. A pilot, dogfighting a manta pair, might come away with the notion. They're foxy. But intelligence, to me, means communication and cooperation. Mantas managed a little of each, but only among mates. When several pairs got involved in a squabble with us, we often won by maneuvering pairs into interfering with one another.

The matter dropped and, after a few more drinks, was forgotten. And banished utterly when we were summoned to the Commander's office.

The interview was predictable. McClennon was determined to ground von Drachau. I don't know why I defended him. Labor united against management, maybe. Guess Horst wasn't used to having a friend at court. When we left he thanked me, but seemed puzzled, seemed to be wrestling something inside.

Never did find out what, for sure—Old Earthers are tight-lipped, but von Drachau had the best of us beaten—but there was a marked improvement in his attitude. By the end of the month he was on speaking terms with everyone, even men he'd grossly alienated at JG IV.

That month I also witnessed a dramatic improvement in Horst's shooting. His kills in the Sickle Islands had been almost accidental. Changing from rockets to cannons seemed to bring out his talent. He scored kill after kill, attacking with a reckless abandon (but always with a care to keep me well positioned). He'd scream in on a manta, drop flaps suddenly, put himself into a stall just beyond the range of the manta's bolt, then flaps up and fall beneath the monster when he'd drawn it, nose up and trigger a burst into its belly. Meanwhile, I would fend off the other till he was free. My kill score mounted, too.

His was astonishing. Our first four weeks together he downed thirty-six mantas. I downed fourteen, and two whales. I'd had fifty-seven and twelve for four years' work when he arrived, best in the wing. It was obvious that, if he stayed alive, he'd soon pass not only me but Aultmann Zeisler, the CO JG I, a ten year veteran with ninety-one manta kills.

Horst did have an advantage we older pilots hadn't. Target availability. Before, except during the lesser migrations, the wing had been lucky to make a dozen sightings per month. Now we piled kills at an incredible rate.

Piled, but the tilt of the mountain remained against us. Already stations farther south were reporting sightings of small herds that had gotten past us.

It was coming to the point where we were kept busy by mantas. Opportunities to strike against whales grew rare. When the main migratory wave broke we'd be swamped.

Everyone knew it. But Derry, despite sending reinforcements, seemed oblivious to the gravity of the situation. Or didn't care. A sour tale began the rounds. The Corporation had written us off. The whales would remove us from the debit ledger. That facilities at Clonninger and stations farther down the cable were being expanded to handle our withdrawal didn't dent the rumors. We Old Earthers always look on the bleak side.

In early winter, after a severe snowstorm, as we were digging out, we encountered a frightening phenomenon. Cooperation among large numbers of mantas.

8

It came with sunrise. Horst and I were in the air, among two dozen new fighters. The wing had been reinforced to triple strength, one hundred fifty gliders and a dozen armed zeppelins, but those of us up were all the ground personnel had been able to dig out and launch.

Signals from ground. Against the aurora and white of the Harridans I had no trouble spotting the Harkness whales, full adults, leaving a branch canyon opposite Beadle. Close to a hundred, I guessed, the biggest lot yet to assault the Gap. We went to meet them, one squadron circling down. My own squadron, now made up of men who'd shown exceptional skill against mantas, stayed high to cover. We no longer bothered with whales, served only as cover for the other squadron.

I watched for mantas. Had no trouble finding them. They came boiling 'round the flank of an ivory mountain, cloud of black on cliff of white, a mob like bats leaving a cave at sunset. Hundreds of them.

My heart sank. It'd be thick, grim, and there was no point even thinking about attack formations. All a man could do was keep away and grab a shot at opportunity. But we'd take losses. One couldn't watch every way at once.

A few mantas peeled off and dove for the ships attacking the whales. The bulk came on, following a line that'd cross the base.

We met. There were gliders, mantas, shells and lightning bolts thicker than I'd ever seen. Time stood still. Mantas passed before me, I pulled trigger rings. Horst's death's-head devices whipped across my vision. Sometimes parts of gliders or mantas went tumbling by. Lower and lower we dropped, both sides trading altitude for speed.

Nose up. Manta belly before me, meters away. Jerk the rings. Fog across the canopy face, but no explosions against dark flesh. We struggled to avoid collision, passed so close we staggered one another with our slip-streams. For a moment I stared into two of the four eyes mounted round the thing's bullet head. They seemed to drive an electric line of hatred deep into my brain. For an instant I believed the intelligence hypothesis. Then shuddered as I sticked down and began a rabbit run for home, to replace my ammunition.

A dozen mantas came after me. Horst, alone, went after them. I later learned that, throwing his craft about with complete abandon, he knocked nine of those twelve down before his own ammunition ran out. It was an almost implausible performance, though one that need not be dwelt upon. It's one of the mainstays of his legend, his first ten-kill day, and every student of the fighting on Camelot knows of it.

The runway still had a half meter of snow on it. The three mantas followed me in, ignoring the counterfire of our ground batteries. I was so worried about evading their bolts that I went in poorly, one wing down, and ended up spinning into a deep drift. As a consequence I spent two hours grounded.

What I missed was sheer hell. The mantas, as if according to some plan, clamped down on our landing and launching gates, taking their toll while our craft were at their most vulnerable. In the early going some tried to blast through the overhead netting. That only cost them lives. Our ground batteries ate them up. Then they tried the barrage balloons, to no better effect.

Then the whales arrived. We'd been able to do nothing to stop them, so busy had the mantas kept us. They, sensing food beneath the net, began trying to break in. Our ground batteries fired into the dangling forests of their tentacles, wrecking those but doing little damage to the beasts themselves. Gigantic creaks and groans came from the net anchor points.

For pilots and ground crews there was little to do but prepare for a launch when circumstances permitted. I got my ship out, rearmed, and dragged to catapult head. Then for a time I stood observer, using binoculars to watch those of our craft still up.

In all, the deaths of a hundred fourteen mantas (four mine, ten Horst's) and twenty-two whales were confirmed for the first two hours of fighting. But we would've gone under without help from down the cable.

When the desperation of our position became obvious the Commander signalled Clonninger. Its sailcraft came north, jumped the mantas from above. They broke siege. We launched, cats hurling ships into the Gap as fast as steam could be built. Horst and I went in the first wave.

Help had come just in time. The whales had managed several small breaches in the netting and were pushing tentacles through after our ground people.

Even with help the situation remained desperate. I didn't think it'd take long for the mantas, of which more had come across, to clamp down again. When they did it'd only be a matter of time till the whales wrecked the net. I pictured the base destroyed, littered with bones.

Before we launched, the Commander, ancient with the strain, spoke with each pilot. Don't know what he said to the others, but I imagine it was much what he told me: if I judged the battle lost, to run south rather than return here. The sailcraft had to be salvaged for future fighting. If we were overrun the fighting would move to Clonninger.

And in my ear a few words about taking care of von Drachau. I said I would.

But we survived. I won't say we won because even though we managed to break the attack, we ourselves were decimated. JG XIII's effectiveness was ruined for the next week. For days we could barely manage regular patrols. Had we been hit again we'd've been obliterated.

That week McClennon three times requested permission to evacuate nonessential ground troops, received three refusals. Still, it seemed pointless for us to stay when our blocking screen had been riddled. Small herds were passing daily. Clonninger was under as much pressure as we and had more trouble handling it. Their defenses weren't meant to stand against whales. Their sailplanes often had to flee. Ground personnel crouched in deep bunkers and prayed the whales weren't so hungry they'd dig them out.

Whale numbers north of the Harridans were estimated at ten thousand and mantas at ten to twenty. Not vast, but overwhelming in concentration. Populations for the whole continent were about double those, with the only other concentrations in the Sickle Islands. By the end of that week our experts believed a third of the Harridan whales had slipped past us. We'd downed about ten percent of those trying and about twenty-five percent of the mantas.

9

A fog of despair enveloped Beadle. Derry had informed McClennon that there'd be no more reinforcements. They were needed further south. Permission to withdraw? Denied again. We had only one hundred twelve effective sailcraft. Ammunition was short. And the main blow was yet to fall.

It's hard to capture the dulled sense of doom that clung so thick. It wasn't a verbal or a visible thing, though faces steadily lengthened. There was no defeatist talk. The men kept their thoughts to themselves—but couldn't help expressing them through actions, by digging deeper shelters, in a lack of crisp efficiency. Things less definable. Most hadn't looked for desperate stands when they signed on. And Camelot hadn't prepared them to face one. Till recently they'd experienced only a lazy, vacation sort of action, loafing and laughter with a faint bouquet of battle.

One evening Horst and I stood watching lightning shoot among the near pure copper peaks of the Harridans. "D'you ever look one in the eye?" he asked.

Memory of the manta I'd missed. I shuddered, nodded.

"And you don't believe they're intelligent?"

"I don't care. A burst in the guts is all that matters. That's cash money, genius or retard."

"Your conscience doesn't bother you?"

Something was bothering him, though I couldn't understand why. He wouldn't worry bending human beings, so why aliens? Especially when the pay's right and you're the son of a man who'd become rich by doing the same? But his reluctance wasn't unique. So many people consider alien intelligence sacred—without any rational basis. It's a crippling emotional weakness that has wormed its way into Confederation law. You can't exploit a world with intelligent natives . . .

But conscience may've had nothing to do with it. Seems, in hindsight, his reluctance might've been a rationalized facet of his revolt against his father and authority.

Understandably, Ubichi was sensitive to speculations about manta intelligence. Severe fines were laid on men caught discussing the possibility—which, human nature being what it is, made the talk more persistent. Several pilots, Horst included, had appealed to McClennon. He'd been sympathetic, but what could he have done?

And I kept wondering why anyone cared. I agreed with the Corporation. That may have been a defect in me.*

*If this thought truly occurred to del Gado at the time, it clearly made no lasting moral impression. News buffs will remember that he was one of several Ubichi mercenaries named in Confederation genocide indictments stemming from illegal exploitation on Bonaventure, though he was not convicted.

—Dogfight

As soon as we recovered from attack, for morale purposes we launched our last offensive, a pre-emptive strike against a developing manta concentration. Everything, including armed zeppelins, went. The mission was partially successful. Kept another attack from hitting Beadle for a week, but it cost. None of the airships returned. Morale sagged instead of rising. We'd planned to use the zepps in our withdrawal—if ever authorized.

In line of seniority I took command of my squadron after a manta made the position available. But I remained von Drachau's wingman. That made him less impetuous. Still addicted to the flying, he avoided offending a man who could ground him. I was tempted. His eye was still deadly, but his concern over the intelligence of mantas had begun affecting his performance.

At first it was a barely noticeable hesitance in attack that more than once left blistered paint on his ship. With his timing a hair off he sometimes stalled close enough for a manta's bolt to caress his craft. My admonitions had little effect. His flying continued to deteriorate.

And still I couldn't understand.

10

His performance improved dramatically six days after our strike into the Harridans, a day when he had no time to think, when the wing's survival was on the line and maximum effort was a must. (He always performed best under pressure. He never could explain how he'd brushed those nine mantas off me that day. He'd torn through them with the cold efficiency of a military robot, but later couldn't remember. It was as if another personality had taken control. I saw him go through three such possessions and he couldn't remember after any.) It was a battle in which we all flew inspired—and earned a Pyrrhic victory . . . the back of the wing was broken, but again Beadle survived.

The mantas came at dawn, as before, and brought a whale herd with them. There'd been snow, but this time a hard night's work had cleared the catapults and sailships. We were up and waiting. They walked—or flew—into it. And kept coming. And kept coming.

And by weight of numbers drove us to ground. And once we'd lost the air the whales moved in.

McClennon again called for aid from Clonninger. It came. We broke out. And soon were forced to ground again. The mantas refused to be dismayed. A river came across the Gap to replace losses.

Clonninger signalled us for help. From Beadle we watched endless columns of whales, varicolored as species mixed, move down the dragline south. We could do nothing. Clonninger was on its own.

McClennon ordered a hot air balloon loaded with phosphorous bombs, sent it out and blew it amidst the mantas crowding our launch gate. Horst and I jumped into their smoke. That entire mission we ignored mantas and concentrated on the whales, who seemed likely to destroy the net.

Before ammunition ran out we forced them to rejoin the migration. But the mantas didn't leave till dark.

Our ground batteries ran out of rockets. Half our ships were destroyed or permanently grounded. From frostbite as much as manta action (the day's high was −23° C.), a third of our people became casualties. Fourteen pilots found permanent homes in the bottom of Ginnunga Gap. Rescue balloons couldn't go after them.

Paradoxically, permission to withdraw came just before we lost contact with Clonninger.

We began our wound-licking retreat at midnight, scabby remnants of squadrons launching into the ink of the Gap, grabbing the ups, then slanting down toward Clonninger. Balloons began dragging the line.

Clonninger was what we'd feared for Beadle: churned earth and bones ethereally grim by dawn light. The whales had broken its defenses without difficulty. Appetites whetted, they'd moved on. From three thousand meters the borders of the earth-brown river of devastation seemed to sweep the horizons. The silvery drag cable sketched a bright centerline for that death-path.

We were patrolling when the first airships came south. The skies were utterly empty, the ground naked, silence total. Once snow covered the route only memory would mark recent events . . .

Days passed. The Clonninger story repeated itself down the cable, station after station, though occasionally we found salvageable survivors or equipment. Operations seemed ended for our ground units. But for us pilots it went on. We followed the line till we overtook straggler whales, returned to work.

As the migration approached Derry corporate defenses stiffened. Though we'd lost contact, it seemed our function at the Gap had been to buy time. True, as I later learned. A string of Beadle-like fortress-bases were thrown across the northern and Sickle Islands routes. But even they weren't strong enough. As the mantas learned (even I found myself accepting the intelligence proposition), they became more proficient at besieging and destroying bases. The whales grew less fearful, more driven by their mating urge. Mantas would herd them to a base; they'd wreck it despite the most furious defense. Both whales and mantas abandoned fear, ignored their own losses.

JG XIII was out of the main action, of course, but we persevered—if only because we knew we'd never get off planet if Derry fell. But we flew with little enthusiasm. Each additional destroyed base or mine (whatever Ubichi was after had to be unearthed) reassured us of the inevitability of failure.

When a man goes mercenary in hopes of buying off, he undergoes special training. Most have a paramilitary orientation. (I use "mercenary" loosely.) Historical studies puzzled me. Why had men so often fought on when defeat was inevitable? Why had they in fact given more of themselves in a hopeless cause? I was living it then and still didn't understand. JG XIII performed miracles with what it had, slaughtered whales and mantas by the hundreds, and that after everyone had abandoned hope . . .

Horst reached the one fifty mark. I reached one hundred twenty. Almost every surviving pilot surpassed fifty kills. There were just thirty-three of us left.

11

On the spur of the moment one day, based on two considerations, I made my first command decision: good winds during patrol and a grave shortage of supplies. For a month the wing had been living and fighting off the remnants of stations destroyed by migrating whales. Rations were a single pale meal each day. Our remaining ammunition was all with us on patrol.

When I began this I meant to tell about myself and Horst-Johann von Drachau. Glancing back, I see I've sketched a story of myself and JG XIII. Still, it's almost impossible to extricate the forms—especially since there's so little concrete to say about the man. My attempts to characterize him fail, so robotlike was he even with me. Mostly I've speculated, drawn on rumor and used what I learned from Commander McClennon. The few times Horst opened at all he didn't reveal much, usually only expressing an increasing concern about the mantas. Without my speculations he'd read like an excerpt from a service file.

The above is an admonition to myself: don't digress into the heroism and privation of the month the wing operated independently. That wasn't a story about von Drachau. He endured it without comment. Yet sleeping in crude wooden shelters and eating downed manta without complaining might say something about the man behind the facade, or something about changes that had occurred there. Hard to say. He may've ignored privation simply because it didn't impinge on his personal problems.

We were in the air, making the last patrol we could reasonably mount. I had command. In a wild moment, inspired by good ups and winds, I decided to try breaking through to Derry territory. Without knowing how far it'd be to the nearest extant station—we hadn't seen outsiders since borrowing the Clonninger squadrons. That Derry still held I could guess only from the fact that we were still to its north and in contact with mantas and whales.

The inspiration hit, I wag-winged *follow me* and went into a long shallow glide. Derry itself lay over two hundred kilometers away, a long fly possible only if we flitted from up to up. Much longer flights had been made—though not against opposition.

It took twelve hours and cost eight sailcraft, but we made it. It was an ace day for everyone. There seemed to be a Horst-like despair about the mantas that left them sluggish in action. We littered the barren earth with their corpses. Horst, with seven kills, had our lowest score. Because I was behind him all the while I noticed he wasn't trying, shot only when a pilot was endangered. This had been growing during the month. He was as sluggish as the mantas.

Our appearance at Derry generated mixed reactions. Employees got a big lift, perhaps because our survival presented an example. But management seemed unsettled, especially by our kill claims, our complaints, and the fact that there were survivors they were obligated to rescue. All they wanted was to hold on and keep the mines working. But aid to JG XIII became an instant cause *célèbre*. It was obvious there'd be employee rebellion if our survivors were written off.

I spent days being grilled, the price of arrogating command. The others were supposed to remain quarantined for debriefing, but evaded their watchers. They did the public relations job. Someone spread the tales that were the base for von Drachau's legend.

I tried to stop that, but to do so was beating my head against a wall. Those people in the shrinking Derry holding needed a hero—even if they had to make him up, to fill in, pad, chop off rough corners so he'd meet their needs. It developed quickly. I wonder how Horst would've reacted had he been around for deep exposure. I think it might've broken his shell, but would've gone to his head too. Well, no matter now.

Myself, I'd nominate Commander McClennon as the real hero of JG XIII. His was the determination and spirit that brought us through. But he was an administrator.

Much could be told about our stay at Derry, which lasted through winter and spring, till long after the manta processes of intellection ponderously ground to the conclusion that we humans couldn't be smashed and eaten this time. The fighting, of course, continued, and would till Confederation intervened, but it stayed at a modest level. They stopped coming to us. Morale soared. Yet things were really no better. The mating whales still cut us off from the south polar spaceport.

But the tale is dedicated to Horst-Johann von Drachau. It lasts only another week.

12

Once free of interrogation, I began preparing the wing to return to action. For years I'd been geared to fighting; administration wasn't easy. I grew short-tempered, began hunting excuses to evade responsibility. Cursed myself for making the decision that'd brought me inside—even though that'd meant volunteer crews taking zepps north with stores.

An early official action was an interview with Horst. He came to my cubby-office sullen and dispirited, but cheered up when I said, "I'm taking you off attack. You'll be my wingman."

"Good."

"It means that much?"

"What?"

"This stuff about manta intelligence."

"Yeah. But you wouldn't understand, Sal. Nobody does."

I began my "what difference does it make?" speech. He interrupted.

"You know I can't explain. It's something like this: we're not fighting a war. In war you try to demonstrate superiority of arms, to convince the other side it's cheaper to submit. We're trying for extermination here. Like with the Sangaree."

The Sangaree. The race his father had destroyed. "No big loss."

"Wrong. They were nasty, but posed no real threat. They could've been handled with a treaty. We had the power."

"No tears were shed . . ."

"Wrong again. But the gut reaction isn't over. You wait. When men like my father and Admiral Beckhart and Commander McClennon and the other militarists who control Luna Command fade away, you'll start seeing a reaction . . . a whole race, Sal, a whole culture, independently evolved, with all it might've taught us . . ."

It had to be rationalization, something he'd built for himself to mask a deeper unhappiness. "McClennon? You don't approve of him?"

"Well, yeah, he's all right. I guess. But even when he disagreed, he went along. In fact, my father never could've found the Sangaree homeworld without him. If he'd revolted then, instead of later when his actions turned and bit back . . . well, the Sangaree would be alive and he'd be off starfishing with Amy."

I couldn't get through. Neither could he. The speeches on the table were masks for deeper things. There's no way to talk about one thing and communicate something else. "Going along," I said. "What've you been doing? How about the kid who squawks but goes along because he wants to fly? That's what we're all doing here, Horst. Think I'd be here if I could buy off any other way? Life is compromise. No exceptions. And you're old enough to know it."*

Shouldn't've said that. But I was irritable, unconcerned about what he'd think. He stared a moment, then stalked out, considering his own compromises.

Two days later my ships were ordered up for the first time since our arrival. Command had had trouble deciding what to do with us. I think we weren't employed because the brass were afraid we were as good as we claimed, which meant (by the same illogical process that built legends around Horst and the wing) that our survival wasn't just a miracle, that we'd really been written off but had refused to die. Such accusations were going around and Command was sensitive to them.

We went up as air cover for the rescue convoy bringing our survivors in from up the cable. We wouldn't've been used if another unit had been available. But the mantas had a big push on, their last major and only night offensive.

*Del Gado may indeed have said something of the sort at the time, and have felt it, but again, once the pressure was off, he forgot. He has been bought off for years, yet remains with Ubichi's Armed Action Command. He must enjoy his work.

—Dogfight

Winds at Derry are sluggish, the ups are weak, and that night there was an overcast masking the moons. The aurora is insignificant that far south. Seeing was by lightning, a rough way to go.

We launched shortly after nightfall, spent almost an hour creeping to altitude, then clawed north above the cable. Flares were out to mark it, but those failed us when we passed the last outpost. After that it was twenty-five ships navigating by guesswork, maintaining contact by staying headache-making alert during lightning flashes.

But it was also relaxing. I was doing something I understood. The whisper of air over my canopy lulled me, washed the week's aggravations away.

Occasionally I checked my mirrors. Horst maintained perfect position on my right quarter. The others spread around in ragged formation, yielding compactness and precision to safety. The night threatened collisions.

We found the convoy one hundred twenty kilometers up the line, past midnight, running slowly into the breeze and flashing signals so we'd locate them. I dropped down, signalled back with a bioluminescent lantern, then clawed some altitude, put the men into wide patrol patterns. Everything went well through the night. The mantas weren't up in that sector.

Dawn brought them, about fifty in a flying circus they'd adopted from us. We condensed formation and began slugging it out.

They'd learned. They still operated in pairs, but no longer got in one another's way. And they strove to break our pairs to take advantage of numbers. But when a pair latched onto a sailplane it became their entire universe. We, however, shot at anything, whether or not it was a manta against which we were directly engaged.

They'd overadopted our tactics. I learned that within minutes. When someone got half a pair, the other would slide out of action and stay out till it found a single manta of opposite sex. Curious. (Shortly I'll comment on the findings of the government investigators, who dug far deeper than Ubichi's exobiologists. But one notion then current, just rumor as the sentience hypothesis became accepted, was that manta intelligence changed cyclically, as a function of the mating cycle.)

We held our own. All of us were alive because we were good. Dodging bolts was instinctual, getting shells into manta guts second nature. We lost only two craft, total. One pilot. Two thirds of the mantas went down.

Horst and I flew as if attached to ends of a metal bar. Book perfect. But the mantas forced us away from the main fray, as many as twenty concentrating on us. (I think they recognized our devices and decided to destroy us. If it were possible for humans to be known to mantas, they'd've been Horst and I.) I went into a robotlike mood like Horst's on his high-kill days. Manta after manta tumbled away. My shooting was flawless. Brief bursts, maybe a dozen shells, were all I used. I seldom missed.

As sometimes happened in such a brawl, Horst and I found our stations reversed. A savage maneuver that left my glider creaking put me in the wingman slot. During it Horst scored his hundred fifty-eighth kill, clearing a manta off my back. Far as I know that was the only time he fired.

The arrangement was fine with me. He was the better shot; let him clear the mess while I protected his back. We'd resume proper positions when a break in the fighting came.

A moment later Horst was in firing position beneath a female who'd expended her bolt (it then took several minutes to build a charge). He bored in, passed so close their wings nearly brushed. But he didn't fire. I took her out as I came up behind.

The eyes. Again I saw them closely. Puzzlement and pain(?) as she folded and fell . . .

Three times that scene repeated itself. Horst wouldn't shoot. Behind him I cursed, threatened, promised, feared. Tried to get shells into his targets, but missed. He maneuvered so I was in poor position on each pass.

Then the mantas broke. They'd lost. The rest of the squadron pursued, losing ground because the monsters were better equipped to grab altitude.

Horst went high. At first I didn't understand, just continued cursing. Then I saw a manta, an old male circling alone, and thought he'd gotten back in track, was going after a kill.

He wasn't. He circled in close and for a seeming eternity they flew wingtip to wingtip, eyeballing one another. Two creatures alone, unable to communicate. But something passed between them. Nobody believes me (since it doesn't fit the von Drachau legend), but I think they made a suicide pact.

Flash. Bolt. Horst's ship staggered, began smoking. The death's-head had disappeared from his fuselage. He started down.

I put everything in my magazines into that old male. The explosions tore him to shreds.

I caught Horst a thousand meters down, pulled up wingtip to wingtip.

He still had control, but poorly. Smoke filled his cockpit. Little flames peeped out where his emblem had been. The canvas was ripping from his airframe. By hand signals I tried to get him to bail out.

He signalled he couldn't, that his canopy was stuck. Maybe it was, but when McClennon and I returned a month later, after the migration had passed south, I had no trouble lifting it away.

Maybe he wanted to die.

Or maybe it was because of his legs. When we collected his remains we found that the manta bolt had jagged through his cockpit and cooked his legs below the knees. There'd've been no saving him.

Yet he kept control most of the way down, losing it only in the last five hundred meters. He stalled, spun, dove. Then he recovered and managed a low angle crash. He rolled nose over tail, then burned. Finis. No more Horst-Johann.

I still don't understand.*

*Hawkins, you keep harping on the 'meaning' of Horst's death. Christ, man, that's my point: it had no meaning. In my terms. By those he utterly wasted his life; his voluntary termination didn't alter the military situation one iota. Even in terms your readers understand it had little meaning. They're vicarious fighters; their outlooks aren't much different than mine—except they want my skin for taking a bite from their sacred cow. Horst was a self-appointed Christ-figure. Only in martyr's terms does his death have meaning, and then only to those who believe any intelligence is holy, to be cherished, defended, and allowed to follow its own course utterly free of external influence. What he and his ilk fail to understand is that it's right down deep-streamed fundamental to the nature of our intelligence to interfere, overpower, exploit and obliterate. We did it to one another before First Expansion; we've done it to Toke, Ulantonid and Sangaree; we'll continue doing it. "In terms of accomplishment, yes, he bought something with his life, An injunction against Ubichi operations on Camelot. There's your meaning, but one that makes sense only in an ethical framework most people won't comprehend. Believe me, I've tried. But I'm incapable of seeing the universe and its contents in other than tool-cattle terms. Now have the balls to tell me I'm in the minority."

From a private letter by Salvador del Gado.

—Dogfight

13

According to the latest, the relationship between Manta and whale is far more complex than anyone at Ubichi ever guessed. (Guessed—Ubichi never cared. Irked even me that at the height of Corporate operations, Ubichi had only one exobiologist on planet—a virologist-bacteriologist charged with finding some disease with which to infect the whales. Even I could appreciate the possible advantages in accumulation of knowledge.) At best, we thought, when the intelligence theory had gained common currency, the whales served as cattle for the mantas.

Not so, say Confederation's researchers. The mantas only *appear* to herd and control the whales. The whales are the true masters. The mantas are their equivalent of dogs, fleet-winged servants for the ponderous and poorly maneuverable. Their very slow growth of ability to cope with our aerial tactics wasn't a function of a cyclic increase in intelligence, it was a reflection of the difficulty the whales had projecting their defensive needs into our much faster and more maneuverable frame of reference. By means of severely limited control.

At the time it seemed a perfectly logical assumption that the mantas were upset with us because we were destroying their food sources. (They live on a mouse-sized parasite common amongst the forest of organs on a whale's back.) It seemed much more unlikely, even unreasonable, that the whales themselves were the ones upset and were sending mantas against us, because those were better able to cope, if a little too dull to do it well. The whales always carried out the attacks on our ground facilities, but we missed the hint there.

It seems the manta was originally domesticated to defend whales from a pterodactyl-like flying predator, one which mantas and whales had hunted almost to extinction by the time Ubichi arrived on Camelot. As humans and dogs once did with wolves. Until the government report we were only vaguely aware of the creatures. They never bothered us, so we didn't bother them.

The relationship between whales and mantas is an ancient one, one which domestication doesn't adequately describe. Nor does symbiosis, effectively. Evolution has forced upon both an incredibly complex and clumsy reproductive process that leaves them inextricably bound together.

In order to go into estrus the female manta must be exposed to prolonged equatorial temperatures. She mates in the air, in a dance as complex and strange as that of earthly bees, but only with her chosen mate. Somewhat like Terran marsupials, she soon gives birth to unformed young. But now it gets weird. The marsupial pouch (if such I may call it for argument's sake) is a specially developed semi-womb atop the back of a *male* whale. While instinct compels her to deposit her young there, the male whale envelopes the she-manta in a clutch of frondlike organs, which caress her body and leave a whitish dust—his "sperm." Once her young have been transferred, the female manta goes into a kind of travel-frenzy, like a bee flitting from flower to flower visiting all nearby whales. Any receptive female she visits will, with organs not unlike those of the male, stroke the "sperm" from her body.

Incredibly complicated and clumsy. And unromantic. But it works.

We never would've learned of it but for Horst—who, I think, had nothing of the sort in mind when he let that old manta bolt him down.

And that's about all there is to say. It's a puzzle story. Why did von Drachau do it? I don't know—or don't want to know—but I work under severe handicaps. I'm an Old Earther. I never had a father to play push-me pull-you with my life. I never learned to care much about anything outside myself. A meager loyalty to companions in action is the best I've ever mustered. But enough of excuses.

The fighting with mantas continued four years after Horst's death, through several lesser migrations that never reached the mating grounds. Then a government inquiry board finally stepped in—after Commander McClennon and Fleet Admiral von Drachau had spent three years knocking on doors at Luna Command (Ubichi's wealth has its power to blind). Their investigations still aren't complete, but it seems they'll rule Camelot permanently off limits. So Horst did buy something with his life. Had he not died, I doubt the Commander would've gotten angry enough to act.

That he did so doesn't entirely please me, of course. I inherited his position. Though I pulled down a handsome income as JG XIII's wing leader and on-going top killer, I loathed the administrative donkey work. Still, I admire the courage he showed.

I also admire Horst, despite his shortcomings, despite myself. But he wasn't a hero, no matter what people want to hear me say. He was a snot-nosed kid used to getting his own way who threw a suicidal tantrum when he saw there was no other way to achieve his ends.

And that's it, the rolling down of the socks to expose the feet of clay. Believe the stories or believe his wingman. It's all the same to me. I've got mine in and don't need your approval.*

*Not true, in your editor's opinion. Especially in his private communications, del Gado seems very much interested in finding approval of things he has done. Perhaps he has a conscience after all. He certainly seems desperate to find justification for his life.

—Dogfight

QUIET SEA

"Quiet Sea" is another fragment from my future history. Most of those have not been included here, in part because so many never saw print. This one, however, was a cover story for The Magazine of Fantasy & Science Fiction.

With dawn a hundred doves unfurled their varicolored wings upon the quiet sea, fluttering nervously. The waves ran gentle now, but during the night the earth beneath the deep had groaned and shaken like a brunwhal in its death throes. Ahead lay deep blue water, cool Fenaja water from the arctic, but Rickli sensed no danger. They would reach the Pimental Bank before noon. Meanwhile, he would mend sail, ignoring the aches in his heart and leg, and daydream of mountains, forests, and snow. Maybe later, when they got ready to put the seines over the side and he would only be in the way, he would limp down to the galley and swap lies with the Shipwrecked Earthman and help sharpen scaling knives.

Such were the thoughts of Rickli Manlove at dawn on the Ninth of Eel in the year 866 of the local reckoning. The Shipwrecked Earthman preferred 3060. He had lost count of his months and days. After a few years he had given up trying.

Rickli, too, had given up. It had been a year since the Fenaja harpoon had shattered his knee. For months he had hoped, but, finally, he'd had to accept the truth: never again would he ride the bowsprit of a racing chaser and, with the salty spray stinging his eyes and soaking his beard, plant his harpoon in the glistening back of a fleeing brunwhal. Nor would he ever trade insults and harpoons with the cruel Fenaja.

Once the crew had named him Left Hand Sea Terror. Now he was only The Crippled Sailmaker. So it went. So it went. He bore the Fenaja no special malice. They had done what they'd had to do, as did Man. When the grunling weren't running, the blackfin were.

He wet a finger, held it up, sniffed, and considered the bow of the sails. The breeze was barely sufficient to keep way on. An inauspicious sign at dawn. The fleet could become becalmed. The Fenaja would be hard pressed to resist such temptation.

But there was no feeling of danger in the deep blue water. Perhaps the Fenaja were elsewhere.

Far over the quiet sea, shell horns winded. A chaser's mainsail fat-bellied in the breeze. Throughout the fleet youngsters scrambled into the rigging to watch. The brunwhal were the most valuable, and most cunning, creatures of the deep. The Children of the Sky used everything but the name.

The Shipwrecked Earthman had been amazed that they remembered their offworld origins after so many centuries. But many things had amazed him here, their survival most of all.

Rickli and the Earthman were almost friends, close enough that the Earthman had confided that he wasn't an Old Earther at all but a colonial from a world called Bronwen. The distinction seemed important to him.

They hadn't always been friendly. There had been a time, before the big fight off LaFata Bank, when Rickli had joined his peers in mocking the man for his incompetence. But a harpoon through the knee, the Earthman's ministrations, and a year of mending sail had given him a new perspective. The Earthman was no longer sailing his native sea, was almost as helpless as one of the bottom creatures the divers brought up and threw on deck. In the Earthman's water, Rickli suspected, he would be more helpless than was the Earthman here.

The youngsters drifted down from the rigging. Rickli chuckled. Even at the winding of the shells he had known there wasn't enough breeze for the chaser to overhaul the brunwhal. He carefully inserted his tools into their brunwhal-hide case, reached for his carved cane of spearfish ivory. The ship grew quiet around him. Soon there were no sounds but the soughing of the wind in the rigging, the sea whispering along the hull, and the creak of the vessel's planks and frame. Those sounds, in the deeps of the nightwatches, could leave a man terribly lonely. He added the thump of his cane as he hobbled aft.

There were times when Rickli cursed his leg for what it denied him, but as often he remembered that he was lucky to have it at all. Had it not been for the Shipwrecked Earthman, he might never have survived. As the augurs reminded them, when the grunling weren't running, the blackfin were.

"Thomas?" he called down into the galley.

"Here, Rickli." The man came to help him down the ladder.

Thomas Hakim, the Shipwrecked Earthman, was a small, dusky, dark-eyed man who had only recently developed the habit of wearing his hair long and tied back in a tail, though he still kept his beard carefully trimmed in a "space." It had taken years to break the habit of regular haircuts. On his ships, he had said, short hair had been mandatory.

The people of Quiet Sea all wore theirs long. Hair became rope and twine. On Quiet Sea all available resources were exploited.

"Looks like a peaceful crossing."

"Good. Good." The Earthman returned to his scaling knives. "A pity we can't make peace with the Fenaja."

It was, Rickli thought, one of the Earthman's favorite themes, one whose futility the man recognized. Natural competition made peace and cooperation impossible.

"The augurs say we'll do well here. No one's been to Pimental Bank for years. The sandweg should be tall."

The Earthman was ever a devil's advocate. "So? And what then? We build another ship. For what?"

Rickli chuckled, playing the game. "Why, so we can gather sandweg faster and build another ship sooner. Someday we'll have the biggest fleet on Quiet Sea."

"You already have it. One of those days you'll all listen to me, say the hell with it, and sail off the edge of the world."

"That's what I like about you, Thomas. Always a cheery outlook."

"Christ!" But he smiled. The manner was a pose, Rickli had learned after having been thrown into Hakim's constant company by the Fenaja harpoon. "What were the horns about?" Though he had been with the fleet for years, Hakim still couldn't read signals.

"Brunwhal. They didn't get him."

"So it goes."

"When the grunling aren't running, the blackfin are. You need any help?"

"No. I'm almost done. Nothing till the salting starts. Checkers?"

The game had made the Shipwrecked Earthman famous across Quiet Sea. Before his falling-star arrival, all games had had to do with the sea. Checkers had caught on as a simple alternative to tradition. Hakim had tried teaching other games as well, especially chess, but the Children of the Sky had rejected them as too complicated. Their culture, Hakim had told Rickli, was too tight and changeless, with never-varying, simple goals, to accept unnecessary complexity.

The Children, though, enjoyed it when he told fortunes with a now ragged deck of tarot cards, though the augurs frowned at his treading on their heels. The Earthman thought that it was the pictures which seized their attention, not the patter. Pictures were almost unknown on Quiet Sea.

With Hakim's aid, Rickli returned to the maindeck. They set up the board atop a cargo hatch. People not otherwise occupied came over to watch. They were the best players on board.

"So tell me about Outside," Rickli said after a few moves. Hakim never lost his zest for reminiscing. Rickli didn't believe a tenth of what he said, nor did anyone else, but his tales were always entertaining. Also, they distracted him from his game.

"Did I tell you about the Iron Legion and the war with Richard Hawksblood in the Shadowline on Blackworld?" Hakim scanned his listeners, responded to their headshakes with: "It started centuries ago, before the Ulantonid War, but the high game, the endgame, was played out on Blackworld . . ."

The crowd grew till Dymon Tipsword, captain of *Rifkin's Dream*, came round growling at people off their watch stations. It was one of the Earthman's best stories. He got into it so deeply that Rickli beat him three straight.

Despite his crankiness and inability to master the simplest skills of seamanship, the Earthman was well liked. Aboard *Rifkin's Dream*, at least as a storyteller, he had become an honored institution.

"Pale water!" a lookout shouted from the maintop.

"The bank," Rickli said. All aboard relaxed slightly. The Fenaja shunned shallow, warm water.

Hakim gathered the checkers. "Even in paradise there's work for the sinful," he muttered. Rickli had become accustomed to such cryptic remarks, remarks Hakim seldom explained.

For the hundredth time Rickli wondered what twist of fate had brought Thomas to Quiet Sea. Though Hakim willingly chattered about himself, he refused to explain how he had come to be in a small ship, alone, near this long-forgotten world, nor would he tell what had led him to crash. His sole recorded remark on the affair was an observation that he had been lucky to set down near the fleet.

Rickli remembered the day well. He had been a rigging boy then, a maintop boy, when the morning sky had shown sudden, short-lived, unknown stars, and it had been during his masthead watch, later, that the sky had opened up and a shooting star, throwing off blinding-bright fragments of itself, had come roaring down with thunders worse than those of any storm. The main body had hit the water beyond the horizon. A great column of steam had risen to mark the site.

The augurs, versed in the old lore, had turned the fleet that way, though the object had splashed down in Fenaja water.

Thousands of dead sea creatures had floated round a burned and twisted object wallowing deep in the waves. It had been huge, frighteningly so, and made of metal . . . That had brought awe into the eyes of everyone who had not yet made the pilgrimage to Landing, where the remains of the Ship still lay.

When the strange object had cooled enough to be touched, every person who could had set about scavenging metal, much of which had proven unworkable later. On Quiet Sea, where there was no land at all and smelters consisted of charcoal hearths in the galleys of ships where handfuls of bottom nodes, recovered by lucky divers, were worked, that much refined metal seemed an unbelievable fortune.

Then they had broken through the outer skin and had found the unconscious man hanging in the curious strapping. He had been a dark, angry little man whose features had borne the stamp of intense concentration and fear. Though fearful, the augurs had brought him out and had done their best to mend his health. In the meantime, his vessel had been looted. Many of the Children still wore bits of glass and plastic for jewelry.

In the early days there had been a communications problem. Hakim hadn't spoken a language anything like their own, which had evolved through the centuries into one whose primary concern was the sea, its colors, deeps, moods, denizens, and the ships that sailed upon it. There were language difficulties even between the older fleets, though the augurs did their best to discourage diversion.

The Earthman's ancestors, and Rickli's, hadn't spoken the same language as contemporaries on Old Earth. And Hakim's people had followed a far different road since then.

But he had been a fast study. Perhaps a hint of why could be found in his tales of adventures on many worlds.

Though it had been obvious he would be a long time becoming productive, every ship in the fleet had vied for possession of the castaway. The augurs had spread the news that he had come from the semi-mythical world of their origin. The Children of the Sky had been hungry for news and knowledge.

The competition had become so intense that the augurs, fearing violence, had ordered a lottery.

Rifkin's Dream had won.

And had never been sorry, though at first the young people, Rickli included, had resented his presence because he had been granted so much unearned privilege.

But when he had come to understand the tongue and culture, he had done his best to pull his weight. Often over Dymon Tipsword's objections. The captain had sensed from the first that his new man would never make a sailor.

Thomas Hakim had never seen a sailing ship before Quiet Sea. He could only admire the complex relationships between the maze of booms, yards, rigging, masts, and sails, not begin to understand. The youngsters, who had grown up on the ships, sometimes thought him retarded.

Where and when, the Earthman did what he could. He had settled into the galley because cooking was what, it proved, he best understood.

Signals sounded over the water as the lead vessels entered the shallows. Orders shouted by dozens of captains carried over the quiet sea, sometimes resulting in confusion. Sails came in with whines and shrieks of tackle. In places the Pimental was so shallow that the larger vessels might run aground. The Bank was rich, but had to be exploited carefully. One dared not risk losing the vessel that was one's only home.

Quiet Sea was a calm, peaceful, relatively friendly world which supported its human population comfortably, in almost Polynesian ease, but there were pragmatic realities to be faced even in Eden. Worst was the lack of living space. The ships were all they had, were difficult to build for lack of land, and were always populated to their supportive limits. Humanity being fecund, stringent measures were required to control population.

In Rickli's fleet this took its simplest form. Crews were segregated by sex. Male children were allowed to remain with their mothers only during their first two years. In other fleets other methods, often harsher methods, were employed, including drowning of unwanted newborns, the old and halt. No technology of contraception existed.

The sexual mores of the society had been hard on the Shipwrecked Earthman. His great goal, he had once told Rickli, was to make it possible to mate without breeding. He had shown Manlove one of his ideas, a sheath of finest grunling gut carefully scraped and cured. Rickli had understood the technical aspect, but not the emotional. He had simply remarked that the material could be put to better use as sausage casing.

The fleet began to disperse. Some, like *Rifkin's Dream*, would seine. Chasers would range out in search of brunwhal, which hugged the food-rich banks. Others would send divers below for shellfish, useful bottom plants, sand, and stone, the latter for potential ore, ballast use, and transport to the centuries-old project to create, at Landing, what Quiet Sea lacked naturally: dry land. Specialized vessels would harvest sandweg, a huge bottom plant that could be cut into lumber. The stands were rich on Pimental, often rising five meters above sea level.

Hakim and Rickli, with everyone else not otherwise occupied, helped clean and salt the catch.

"Mixed catch," said Rickli, puzzled, dragging a thrashing blackfin from a lively pile and stilling it with one quick jab of the butt of his knife.

Hakim took a smaller, more easily cleaned grunling. "Not a good sign," he agreed. When the species mixed in the shallows, it was because the blackfin felt threatened by something in the deeps. Blackfin preferred the cooler, deeper waters on the faces of the banks. The grunling preferred the warmer shallows. "Fenaja?"

"Probably not. There would've been some sign."

Dymon Tipsword, too, was concerned. He had a caution pennant bent to a halyard and run to the maintruck. Here and there, similar pennons ran to other mains.

"Whatever, we'll find out first," said Rickli. *Rifkin's Dream* was seining on the extreme left of the fleet, nearest the deep water.

"Probably just the temblor last night."

"Maybe." But a feeling of wrongness had begun growing on Rickli. Why hadn't there been any Fenaja sign during the crossing? They didn't attack often, but when ships entered their waters, they always came up to watch, their ugly, whiskered snouts trailing Vs on the surface as they dared the humans to start something. Sometimes they would lift their dun, scaly foreparts from the waves and croak insults learned from other men. But as long as there were no bone-tipped harpoons in sight, their intentions remained peaceful. Their attacks, generally, came in waters where one of their occasional, sudden, inexplicable population explosions had left the blackfin schools depleted.

The winchmen hauled a bulging net aboard, scattering the sand-covered deck with flopping fish. The youngsters, wearing brunwhalskin chaps and gloves, began heaving the smallest and females over the side. Neither grunling nor blackfin had dangerous teeth, but their scales could rasp the skin off a man with one caress. Dried blackfin hide was used to sand the decks. During fishing those decks were covered two centimeters deep with sand from ballast meant to absorb spilled blood and entrails.

"Uhn!" Hakim grunted. "There's your Fenaja."

Rickli stood, ignoring the sudden sharp pain in his knee. "Part of one." He hobbled forward, helped others pull the mangled corpse from the pile of fish. "Dymon!"

Tipsword came down from the helm, spent a long minute staring at the remains. "All right. Back to work. We've got a hold to fill. You three, put it back over the side. Its people will be looking for it." As activity resumed, the captain stalked back to his station. A new set of pennons ran to the main. The ship's armorer began making the round of battle stations, setting out harpoons, axes, swords.

Rickli resumed his seat, said nothing for a long time.

"What is it?" Hakim asked.

"Half the body had been eaten. It still had a broken harpoon in its hand."

Hand was a misnomer. From the Fenaja's forward end, near what might pass for shoulders were it accustomed to going upright, a specialized pair of tentacles grew; the ends of these had modified into three finger-length sub-tentacles. The quasi-intelligent creatures used them as a man used hands.

"Meaning he maybe died fighting something that was eating him?"

"Uhm." Naturally enough, the monsters of the legends and folklore of the Children of the Sky were all creatures from the deep and, though Hakim had never encountered a man who had seen one, the sea people believed in their existence as devoutly as their ancestors had believed in dragons and trolls.

The only known enemies of the Fenaja were human. But the Children of the Sky had little real knowledge of what lived at the bottom of the deeps. Their interest was the banks, an ecological cycle into which their ancestors had inserted themselves.

The seining, cleaning, and salting went on, though wary eyes kept glancing toward deep water. Yet the crew trusted Tipsword's judgment. Had he believed real danger existed, he would have had the nets hauled in and stored.

The tension bothered the Earthman. "Think I'll go get Esmeralda," he said, putting his knife aside.

Rickli nodded, reached for another blackfin. The thing the Earthman called Esmeralda had been one of the few possessions he had reclaimed after the looting of his ship. To Rickli it looked like an ornate mutation of a shipfitter's mallet, except that Hakim always handled it backwards. Manlove suspected it was some sort of Outside talisman. Hakim brought it out each time *Rifkin's Dream* sailed into danger, but Rickli had yet to see the man do anything with it.

Just as Thomas returned, flying fish began skipping across the sea. Tipsword judged their numbers and the length of their jumps, shouted, "Ship the nets! Forget the fish! Bring them in!"

It wasn't necessary to tell the cleaners and salters to clear the decks. Every man able began pitching fish over the side. New signals rose to the main; hornmen stood by.

The sea began boiling two hundred meters off the port bow.

"Cut it!" Tipsword thundered at the netmen. "Now! Move it!" Men shuddered. A good seine costs hundreds of man-hours to make. But, if they were lucky, they could come about and recover it later. Bladders made of brunwhal stomachs would keep it afloat. Someone began wielding an ax. The trouble horns screamed across the water. Nearby ships became furious with activity.

"Hard right rudder!" Tipsword ordered. "Stand by to shift sail."

The rigging boys were already aloft.

Rifkin's Dream was the long-dead shipbuilder Rifkin's attempt to combine the best of two types of rigging in one of the fleet's largest vessels. She was square-rigged on her forward and topmainmasts, schooner-rigged on her main and mizzen. Sharp course changes could result in mass confusion.

There was little of that this time. Everyone was too frightened to make a mistake.

"Oh!" said Rickli. Nothing else would come.

"Jesus," said the Shipwrecked Earthman, softly. "What the hell is it?"

"Grossfenaja. The deepdark-devil."

Rifkin's Dream slowly heeled over as her rudder took hold and she took the wind on her beam. The stern slid sideways toward the thing rising from the deep. The nearest seining ship winded its own horns and cut its net lines too.

A shout from the masthead directed their attention forward. Half a kilometer ahead, another one was rising. Then another, off the port quarter.

"Never heard of anything like this!" Rickli shouted. The nearest beast was still surfacing, more and more tentacles slapping the water, some reaching for *Rifkin's Dream*. Dymon Tipsword shouted for the younger boys to get below.

"Must have been the earthquake," Hakim muttered. "Christ! Another one."

The main body of the nearest broke water. It was over sixty meters long and serpentine, like a fat Midgard serpent whose tail had turned into a kraken. The head was at the end opposite the main mass of tentacles, with just two five-meter Fenaja-type limbs nearby.

Regaining his composure, Rickli said, "Any of the other old monsters I would've believed, but this . . ."

The creature writhed in an effort to direct its head toward the ship, but it seemed Tipsword had acted in time and the vessel would slip away.

"Sandweg!" the forward lookout cried. A moment later he hurtled into the sea as the vessel plowed into a dense young stand, the tops of which hadn't yet broken water. The bows rose high, *Rifkin's Dream* shuddered, then lurched forward as her momentum snapped or uprooted the plants.

But she hadn't enough way on to carry her through. Her stern and rudder hung up. In moments she was dead in the water.

"Battle stations!" Tipsword bellowed. "You boys below, see if she's sprung any leaks. Spearsong, get a boat over. Winchmen, stand by to kedge her. Thomas, get coals from the galley."

Hakim ran. Rickli, trying to stay out of the way, wondered how their puny weapons, even fire, could stave off the predator. He glanced at the rest of the fleet. No help there. Panic and confusion were the supreme admirals of the moment. And running for shallower water seemed no real solution. The creature that had surfaced immediately ahead was already dragging itself through water just four meters deep. Speed seemed the only escape.

He noted a racked harpoon with an ornate grip of brunwhal ivory. His own, that the crew had given him when he had been Left Hand Sea Terror, best chaser spritman in the fleet. He hobbled over and exchanged it for his cane. There was comfort in the familiar grip. He would die with his old companion in hand.

The decks and tops seemed utter chaos, yet the frenetic activity had its purposes. But for the thing bearing down, it might have been the last moment before an ordinary Fenaja fight. There had been more panic and confusion at LaFata. Rickli stayed out of the way, gradually drifted forward.

The sword, ax, and harpoon men all seemed so young, just boys. Where were the longbeards, the grizzled old men who had manned the rail at LaFata? Dead, of course. Still there, consigned to the deep. Not many had been as lucky as he. Half this crew had transferred aboard after that battle.

"Jesus," he murmured, borrowing from the Shipwrecked Earthman. The thing's head was scarred with a mouth large enough to take a man or Fenaja at a gulp.

Twenty meters from *Dream*, it plunged beneath the water, torpedoing into the sandweg wrack left by the ship's passage. Rickli shouted a warning to Spearsong, but too late. The head rose and destroyed the longboat with a single snap of huge jaws. The foretentacles snatched men from the water.

The thing's rear smashed into the port side. The vessel jumped, shook, groaned in protest. Everyone went tumbling. Rigging boys rained from above, smashing into deck or sea with terrified screams. Rickli lost the harpoon.

Tipsword thunderously ordered everyone back to the rail. Then a tentacle whipped over and snatched him away from the wheel. He went over the side, into the sea, hacking with a rare metal sword.

Though they numbered only twenty and were no thicker than a man's arm, the monster's rear tentacles seemed to fall in a deadly rain. Against them harpoons were useless. The sword and ax men managed to damage a few, but the beast seemed oblivious to pain. Its head reared high to starboard and observed critically while its tail worked murder to port.

Dead men speckled the sea. Tentacles began reaching through hatches and snaking out the boys below. Terrified, pathetic screams echoed below decks.

Rickli suddenly understood that they were fighting the wrong end. Its normal prey probably never realized that. He tried to tell someone, but with Dymon gone there was no one to make them listen. He glanced to starboard. The creature was casually nibbling on a boatman. He bent, picked up a harpoon, cast it.

His knee betrayed him. He collapsed on bloody sand, almost cried when the harpoon whispered past the thing's trunk, a meter below his target. He had to get closer.

It had to be out the bowsprit. From nowhere else could he be certain of being close enough to overcome his knee. He grabbed another harpoon and started.

There wasn't much thought in the journey, that seemed an endless pilgrimage to keep a rendezvous with death. There was pain such as he hadn't known since the Fenaja harpoon had struck. Tentacles whipped about with Rickli Manlove seemingly their special target. One seized him round the bad knee, pulled and squeezed, but fate placed a level-headed axman nearby. He went on, crawling, dragging the re-injured leg. Something had gone in the knee. He had heard and felt it.

Three meters out the bowsprit, he collapsed, unable to go on.

Salt spray stung his eyes. Or was it tears? Failed again . . . He wasn't sure where he was, on a chaser racing after the humping brown back of a brunwhal, or lying half-dead after LaFata . . . His will returned. Then his strength. Just enough. He made it to the leadsman's platform, dragged himself upright, gripped his harpoon, threw.

And sagged in defeat. Low again. It buried itself deep, but a meter below the huge yellow eye for which he had aimed.

"Rickli! Rickli Manlove!" The Earthman's curious, harshly accented voice seemed to come from years and kilometers away. Slowly, he turned.

The Earthman stood at the foot of the bowsprit, harpoon in one hand, his talisman in the other. A tentacle had him round the waist.

Rickli reached a futile hand . . .

The Earthman put the harpoon in the air. It slapped his palm.

He felt familiar ivory, the old, comfortable grip of his high years.

He turned. He aimed. He cast.

He collapsed, but only after he had seen his old companion buried grip-deep in the yellow eye.

Rickli lay unconscious for days. He came round to find *Rifkin's Dream*, with help from other ships, trying to keep afloat during repairs to her hull and rigging. Some vessels worked the beast's remains. Masts crowded the battle site. Through them he could see a similar cluster in the distance.

The Shipwrecked Earthman lay beside him, drugged, his waist a mass of ripped skin and ugly bruises. His guts must have been churned good. His talisman remained gripped in his left hand.

"Good afternoon, Captain."

"Ilyana Wildhaber. What're you doing here?"

"Keeping this tub off the bottom." She was captain of *Replete*, a repair and stores vessel. "It's a jinx."

"Have Weatherhead change our station."

"There'll be changes. This made LaFata look like a christening party."

"Tell me."

"There were six of them. Several ships weren't as lucky as *Dream*. Three were dragged into the deep. Six more went down in the shallows. Two we'll refloat. Most everyone got involved."

"Guess there'll be work for a crippled sailmaker, then." Rickli's greatest fear was that the crew would vote him supernumerary, a fear that had begun while the Fenaja harpoon still quivered in his knee. No such vote had been taken in living memory, even against incorrigibles, but Rickli felt he was a child of fate. A malevolent fate.

"Didn't you hear? You're captain now."

"No."

"Yes. They voted. You'll replace Dymon. If you live."

Rickli at last found the nerve to look down. "A one-legged man?"

She shrugged. "Got to go. You lie still, don't get it infected. They'd take it off at the neck next time."

Rickli stared at the battered masts and rigging, pondering the odd course of fate. A harpoon man in good condition grew old in his job, usually perishing when age tricked him into fatal error. But as a sailmaker who could fight, he had with one cast of a harpoon won the hearts of a crew.

Such as it might be. His elevation might be a mockery. Losses had been heavy when he had made his throw.

Rijkin's Dream did not weigh anchor for six weeks and then moved only a kilometer. Rickli and the Earthman were both off their backs but not in good health. Hakim couldn't handle solid food.

Rickli drilled his crew mercilessly, trying to meld a scattering of veterans and dozens of transfers into a new ship's company.

"What do you think?" he asked the Earthman one day.

"They'll cope. They always do. Why worry?"

"I want them to look sharp. We're going on pilgrimage."

"Landing?" The Shipwrecked Earthman had never visited the site of Man's first touchdown on Quiet Sea. During his tenure individual ships or squadrons had felt the need and made the hadj, but *Rifkin's Dream* had sailed on, remaining with the fleet as it crawled from bank to bank. It had been twenty-five years since the vessel had gone.

"The whole fleet. We need the luck. Two disasters in one year . . . It's time."

Landing's special significance hadn't attained religious standing but some superstition had attached itself, encouraged by the augurs. To maintain their birthluck, all Children of the Sky were encouraged to visit the Ship every few years.

The reason, the Earthman had suggested, was so the augurs at the Ship could gather information from scattered sources, collate it, and disseminate it again.

The Earthman, Rickli reflected, had a lot of strange ideas about the Children of the Sky. He supposed that was the alien viewpoint. Whatever, Thomas was eager to reach Landing.

If anything, the encounter with Grossfenaja had ripened and mellowed their relationship. The Earthman now shared more of his alien thoughts.

While crossing the Finneran Bank, the traditional boundary between seas well-known and the frontier waters the fleet generally cruised, just a week's fast sail from Landing, Rickli said, "Thomas, you've never told us why you're here. Something must've brought you."

The sun had set an hour before. The bright jewels of the galaxy winked down as they began their migration toward dawn. *Rifkin's Dream* had settled into the long, lonely silence of night, whispering and creaking to herself, but telling few stories to listening ears. The passage of ships excited bioluminescent plankton in the shallows, scrawling pale stripes across the quiet sea. Hakim stared at the stars, at the constellation the sea people called the Spiderfish, for a long time.

"I don't know, Rickli," he said at last. "Why *does* a man leave home? I thought I knew then. Somehow, from here, it doesn't seem all that important."

"Was it so wicked a thing?" Rickli knew he had touched a nerve with the initial question. When Thomas stayed awake to watch the Spiderfish, he was feeling homesick. That much Rickli knew for sure about the Earthman.

Hakim frowned to him, his expression barely visible in the starlight. Afraid he had overstepped, Rickli turned to survey the running lights of nearby ships. Night sailing could be tricky.

"Some thought so. You wouldn't comprehend. The survival imperatives are different. Here, you all live in the same environment and culture." He pointed upward. "There's a fleet, the greatest of them all. Every ship is as far from its neighbor as we are from any of them. Some are big, some small, some strong, some weak. Like the fishes of the sea. Here, there're warm shallows where the living is easy and the fish get along, then the cold deeps, and in them things that get hungry, that sometimes surface, like Grossfenaja ..."

Rickli wasn't sure he followed, unless the Earthman meant that some of his people preyed on others. "You mean like the pirate ship in the Saga of Wilga Stone-cipher?"

"Eh? Oh. Yes, I suppose so. In any case, men Outside sometimes go after other men the way chasers pursue brunwhal."

He went silent, continued staring at the Spiderfish.

Rickli knew he had pushed as far as he dared, yet couldn't resist asking, "Would you go back now? If you had the chance?"

Hakim studied him a moment, looked back to the sky, said nothing. Rickli shrugged, surveyed the fleet again.

Thomas had been thinking about it, he knew. The man couldn't help it, no more than he could help thinking about serving in chasers, despite LaFata. The Earthman was crippled too. It just wasn't anything as obvious as a missing leg. Perhaps it could be called a broken heartline home.

Landing, for those who had never seen it, appeared on the horizon as the most outstanding anomaly of the sea, a great hump rising from the water like the back of some mythologically huge brunwhal.

"That's the Ship," Rickli told the Shipwrecked Earthman, when the thing finally became visible from helm level. Excited crewmen had been scampering up and down the rigging for hours. But not Hakim. He had a positive terror of heights.

Strange, for a man who flew between the stars.

"Jesus, how'd they bring her down in one piece?"

"They didn't, really." Rickli scanned the fleet. By now, every vessel had hoisted at least one black sail. Some looked like the dark birds of death Hakim had called them. The chaser crews were getting impatient, waiting for Weatherhead's permission to begin their race to the ancient wreck. "That's why we're still here."

The vessel had been built at the close of Old Earth's Twenty-second Century, equipped with crude hyper generators, to take out certain political favorites before an anticipated collapse of civilization. Almost two kilometers long, she had never been meant to enter atmosphere. Rickli was unsure of the circumstances that had brought her to, and had forced her landing upon, Quiet Sea. Only the augurs knew. He cared only that it had been managed and that his ancestors had survived.

Thomas cared, mostly from curiosity, but could get no more from Rickli.

"Ask the augurs when we get there," Manlove kept telling him. "They'll spend a month talking to anyone willing to listen."

He thought he understood Thomas's interest. The Ship was the nearest a connection Outside as existed on Quiet Sea. A hopeless, centuries-out-of-date connection but certainly something more concrete than shared specieshood.

Outsiders, judging by Hakim, set great store by artifacts and possessions. The Earthman still, at times, mourned some small item lost when his ship had been looted.

Rickli had spread the word among the captains, but little had turned up. Everything convertible had long since been made into something useful.

Weatherhead released the chasers. With a strong following breeze they were soon dwindling in their race to the hump.

"You really miss it that much?" the Earthman asked.

Rickli smiled. "It shows? I think it's just not being able. It was my life, you know."

"I understand." Thomas glanced at the sky. "Those old-timers had guts. People out there nowadays, in their shoes, would just give up."

"It was a chosen crew. They knew they couldn't go back before they started."

"A definite advantage. None of us can, but few of us realize it." After a pause: "You know, I think what I miss most, more than land, is birds. They were always a symbol of freedom." His expression became faraway. Rickli reached out and, for an instant, let his hand rest lightly on the Earthman's shoulder.

Thomas had told him a dozen times that his fellows would not be coming to rescue him. They had had no idea where to look.

It was almost dark when *Rifkin's Dream* dropped her stone anchors. In the morning she would move to one of the stone quays whiskering the dry land the Children of the Sky had built around their Ship.

"Seems to me," said the Earthman, gazing at the island that had taken centuries to create, "that it would've been easier to poulder. More land for less fill."

Rickli had to have it explained. Thomas told him about dikes and sub-sea-level land recovery.

"Suggest it to the augurs. They might be interested."

"I'm not sure I want to go anymore." Hakim nervously caressed his talisman. Since his narrow escape, he had kept it with him always.

Rickli smiled. Of course he would go, just as he himself would visit a chaser if invited. Every man tried to mend his heartlines.

"They've made a lot of headway since I was here last," Rickli said the following morning, as *Rifkin's Dream* warped in to a low stone pier. "They've doubled the land area. They didn't used to work that hard at it."

The Earthman observed without comment. Several vessels were already off-loading ballast to be added to the fill. The Ship itself was completely surrounded. Curious sea people were looking it over, some lining up at an open hatchway for an interior tour.

"Rickli, it sounds defeatist, but why bother? You seem to have adapted."

"We did without for centuries. It was just a dream thing. Ships would come on pilgrimage and everyone would bring a stone as a symbolic gift. They piled up. Then the augurs built a little sawmill on the pile. It made cutting sandweg so much easier that people started thinking it might be handy to have an island just for that. So they started bringing bigger loads of stone. Didn't push it, though, because they were used to doing things the old way. Then the augurs built a bigger sawmill, that handled about half the sandweg used in the fleets, and a smelter where they turned out almost a tonne of metal a month."

He took out the knife that, with the captaincy, he had inherited from Dymon Tipsword. "This's a genuine Wintermantel. Better than anything they make here, but it took the man a month, sometimes, to make one blade."

Hakim laughed sourly. "The glories of industrialization."

"It's so bad? Look there. Places where they can take a ship out of the water for repairs. And ways where they can build a ship in a tenth the time it takes at sea, with a quarter of the men."

"No. I'm a cynic. What're those buildings down there? Beyond the dry-docks and shipyard."

"I don't know. They're new. Must be important, though. That's a lot of sandweg to hold out of ship construction."

"Uhm. Curious."

It wasn't till later that Rickli realized he had missed the specific that had caught the Earthman's eye. The buildings had glass windows. Hundreds of them, especially on top.

Partial starts on other buildings lay scattered over the manmade island. The augurs seemed to have a big program in mind. Rickli frowned. Providing the materials cost the fleets time and materials they could use themselves. He didn't understand. Unless there were rewards worth the cost, as with the sawmill and smelters.

Thomas didn't know what he wanted. Sometimes he would start for the pier, then would pace, then would return to wait till Rickli had fulfilled his duties. Then he would grow impatient again, only to repeat the cycle.

At last Rickli felt able to go. He left the ship to the duty section and, with Thomas's help, slowly advanced up the pier. He felt uncomfortable, naked, defenseless, so wide had the world expanded. And he felt dizzy. For the first time in a decade he was on footing that did not sway and roll with the restlessness of the sea.

"This isn't going to cut it," said Thomas. "I'm going to make those crutches."

They had argued about it before. Rickli didn't want them. But practicality began to alter his mindset.

"Where're you going?" he asked. Hakim was turning right, away from the rusty mountain of the Ship.

"I want to look at something." But they never reached the windowed buildings. Rickli's leg bothered him too much. At his request they paused to rest in the shade of an oddly designed hull in the last stages of construction.

The Earthman studied it, finally asked, "How much glass do they make here, Rickli?"

He shrugged. "Things have changed. Used to be just a little, from bottom sand, for special bottles and trinkets."

"Hand-blown?" Thomas ran his fingers over the smooth seamless hull.

"Never saw it done any other way." He, too, studied the strange vessel. So much metal had gone into its construction. Surely the augurs wouldn't be so wasteful. "Is something wrong?"

"I don't know. This isn't my native sea. But there's something odd here, something that makes me feel the way I did just before the Grossfenaja surfaced." He caressed his talisman, which protruded from the waistband of his trousers. Perhaps because he was in a suggestible mood, or because he was uncomfortable ashore, Rickli began to feel it too. "Let's go back to the ship. You make those crutches, and we'll poke around later."

"Crutches? Oh, yes." He helped Rickli up, saying, "Maybe you should think about a wooden leg."

"A *what?*"

By way of explanation, Thomas told him a decidedly fishy tale about an ancient seaman named Long John Silver. The idea intrigued Rickli. Though the notion wasn't unique, it hadn't occurred to him in relation to himself. He had encountered few men who'd had to cope with being an amputee. The state of medicine was such that few men ever survived such operations.

Returning, they encountered acquaintances from *Replete*, who, in good humor, offered to carry Rickli back to *Rifkin's Dream*, although the ship was out of their way. It seemed they hoped his luck would rub off. Though it hurt his pride, he accepted. His remaining leg hurt more.

As they moved down the pier, Hakim asked one of the women, "May I see your knife?" A shiny new fishknife protruded from her waistband.

Grinning, "Sure. The augurs are trading them for sandweg." Less cheerfully: "After Pimental, we're overstocked."

Rickli thought the Earthman would never stop turning the blade, examining its grip, thumbing its edge. Finally: "Rickli, can I see yours?"

The sailors, now puzzled, released him so he could hand Thomas the knife. It was one of only a dozen iron blades to be found aboard *Rifkin's Dream*. "Forged by Aulgur Wintermantel himself," he told the others. The smith, though a century dead, was still a legend.

The Earthman placed Rickli's knife back down on pier stone, suddenly swung the other so that their edges met sharply.

"Thomas!"

Ilyana's women growled angrily.

Hakim held the blades up for all to see. Rickli's had been deeply notched, the other nicked imperceptibly.

"A genuine Wintermantel?" the new blade's owner asked, her anger fading as she saw the quality of her knife. "Really?"

"Yes." Rickli was dumfounded. His edge should have damaged the other.

As the sailors drifted away, talking excitedly of further trades, Hakim said, "You may get an answer to the question you asked the other night." He didn't apologize for damaging the Wintermantel. He seemed terribly upset.

Rickli let it ride till they were comfortably back aboard, observing ship and Ship from the captain's station. The Earthman stared into the distance and caressed his talisman.

"What is it, Thomas? What's wrong?"

"I'm not sure. The knife. The finish on that hull. The glass-topped buildings. But especially the knife."

"Why? It was a good one."

"Exactly. Too good, don't care what the augurs have been doing, they couldn't have made that knife. That was a machined blade, an Outside blade. The question is, did it come with the Ship?" After a glance toward the strange buildings, "I'm afraid of the answer."

Rickli made the intuitive leap. "You think the augurs are in touch with your people?"

"Not mine, Rickli. Not mine."

"Ah, so. The enemy. Your Fenaja."

Hakim took the talisman from his waistband, peered down its long axis. "Grossfenaja." One word. But still he wouldn't elaborate.

"Your enemies are mine. Twice you've honored my life."

"So it goes," Hakim murmured to himself, the ancient acceptance of fate characteristic of Children of the Sky. "No. They're merciless. They'd destroy you all if I dragged you in. If they're really here."

Now Rickli said, "So it goes. If they're that kind of people, then they *should* be enemies."

"Stay out of it, Rickli. Stay out. I'll try to avoid them. Yes. That's best. If they don't know I'm here, they won't bother anybody. I'll just stay aboard till you put to sea again. I'll decide what to do when you're ready to cast off."

But the wills of Fate and the Shipwrecked Earthman weren't in concert. Shortly, Rickli said, "What's this?" indicating a group coming down the pier. "Ship augurs."

A youth ran up, announced, "Augurs Blackcraft and Homewood request permission to board, sir."

"Granted." To Thomas, "The top people. Must've heard about the Grossfenaja."

"Uhm." Hakim was not convinced.

The augurs were old, and some disabled. The lore mastery was reserved to those no longer able to cope with the sea. Though the whole party boarded, only Blackcraft and Homewood, male and female, approached the captain's station. Both eyed the Earthman.

"Greetings," said Homewood, her voice surprisingly youthful. "It's been long since Landing was honored by *Rifkin's Dream.*

"And longer since *Dream* was graced by the presence of an elder augur." Rickli decided he should try to put them on the defensive.

Their eyes kept drifting to Thomas.

"We hear some strange things have befallen in the interim." Blackcraft seemed strangely wary. "The years drift past, the ships come in, and sailors tell their tales. Some were hard to credit."

"No doubt. The young embellish with drama. A Saga grows from ordinary events."

"So it goes."

"Yet these tales seemed no rigging boy's daydream," said Homewood, looking directly at the Earthman.

"How can we judge the truth of sea stories?"

"Never mind the fencing, Rickli," said Hakim. To the augurs: "What do you want?"

"You're the Shipwrecked Earthman?"

"What do you want?"

"Are you the man called Thomas Hakim?"

"What do you want?"

"You must come with us."

"No," said Rickli. "Thomas is restricted to ship."

They were growing irritated. Blackcraft grumbled, "Captain, these are matters beyond you. And I remind you, you're no longer at sea."

"An oversight that can be corrected with a word."

"Tell your masters," said the Earthman, "that if they want me, they'll have to come see me themselves."

"Masters?"

"The Outsiders. The Sangaree. The people who sent you here. The people who have been giving you Outside goods in return for use of Landing. You probably think they've done well by you. But you've been cheated. Terribly. You don't know them, don't know what they are. Tell them that if they want Thomas Hakim, they'll have to meet him before the Children of the Sky. You'll learn."

They could see Thomas was immovable. Homewood bowed slightly. "So it goes." She and Blackwood rejoined their deputation. Soon one of the lesser augurs was hurrying up the pier.

"Ah." The Earthman chuckled nervously. "I was right. But I was only guessing."

"What's it all about, Thomas?" Rickli asked.

"My enemies are here. But they're not sure who I am." After a time: "You should have stayed out of it."

Rickli shrugged. "You're my friend. You were my right hand at Pimental." From the captain's equipment rack he took a shell-horn. "You're one of our own now." He blew recall.

Stunned silence settled over Landing. Then sea people were everywhere, running. Before the Earthman could protest, Rickli had had danger pennons run to the main and had instructed the armorer to fill the weapons racks. By ones, twos, and threes, crewmen came running aboard, battering the augurs in their haste to reach their stations.

"You're a fool, Rickli Manlove. This isn't your fight." But the Earthman wore a smile.

"Maybe. Stay out of the way till I get muster."

Other vessels, too, began readying weapons and sail. The chaos on Landing diminished as crews found their ways to their ships.

Through the confusion came a wedge of five tall men in outlandish clothing. Rickli stared. They were heavier than his people, more muscular. Even from a distance he could see that there was no humor in their faces.

"These are your enemies?" he asked.

"Some of them. Watch the little one. The one who seems the least. He's their leader, Gaab w'Telle. There're blood debts between us. I'll keep out of sight." He slipped down into the galley.

Rickli called his armorer.

The five came aboard as if they owned *Rifkin's Dream*. Their not having asked permission aggravated Rickli's predisposition to dislike them. The light one spoke with Homewood and Blackcraft, then came aft. All five had hard, dark eyes. Fenaja eyes.

"Where is he?" Telle asked. He glanced speculatively at Rickli's stump. Quiet as death, with an expression as grim, Thomas slipped from the galley, his talisman in hand. He nodded.

"Right behind you," Rickli replied.

They turned. The leader went pale. "You!"

"Of course. I take some killing. How's the universe been treating you, Telle? Not well, I hope."

"But . . ."

"As a writer once said, the reports of my death were exaggerated. You didn't send enough shooters."

So, thought Rickli, this was the man who had tried to kill Thomas. He signaled his armorer. Crewmen began selecting weapons.

Men of Quiet Sea almost never used weapons against one another. Rickli doubted his men could now. But maybe the Outsiders wouldn't recognize the bluff.

"I'll make sure this time. This's one operation you're not going to wreck." He didn't seem impressed by the martial display.

Thomas pointed his talisman.

The leader laughed. "Bluffing with a dead lasepistol, von Rhor? Six years old? Gotta. Take him."

One man took one step.

There was a dazzling flash. The man fell, steam twisting from a small black hole in his back.

Pandemonium. Crewmen scattered. The augurs fled to the bows. The tableau of confrontation remained a tense pocket of false calm amidst the confusion.

Telle and his men seemed stricken. And Thomas, too, as though he could neither believe what he had done nor that his weapon had actually functioned.

Rickli took his ivory-gripped harpoon from the captain's equipment rack. A great calm, like that of the last moment before the cast from a racing chaser's sprit, descended upon him. The sight of one man killing another had not shaken him as much as he thought it should. Maybe he would react later, after the tension had passed.

"Six years, Telle. Six years I've sailed the quiet sea, without a hope, yet cherishing this thing. My only regret had been that you were still alive, that I'd failed and you were still peddling your death dust.

"I don't expect to live through this. I tried to avoid it because it'll cost these good people. The augurs think you're benefactors; yet you're raising the drug right in their front yard. When I die, you'll carry the candle to light my way into Hell."

"Spoken like a true hero," Telle sneered. But most of his arrogance had faded.

"Rickli," said the Earthman. "A favor."

"Anything, Thomas."

"Have them stripped. Move the shooters forward."

"Thomas?" Telle asked. "What happened to Nicholas von Rhor?"

"Don't mean anything here, Telle. And just between us, that's not it either." The bodyguards moved away. "Actually, it's Soren Deatherage."

"The Hell Stars!"

"Yes."

Rickli did not understand the exchange, but the winds of hatred blowing between the men made it clear they had hurt one another deeply and often. Maybe Thomas would explain later. But he doubted it. He had learned more about Hakim in the past ten minutes than in all the years before.

Thomas handed his talisman to the armorer, began shedding his own clothing.

Rickli had never seen Thomas unclothed. Now he frowned. The Earthman was older than he had suspected. His body hair was heavily salted with grey.

"In the fleets we settle personal disputes by wrestling," said Hakim. "Man to man, Telle. I'll be thinking about what you did to my wife."

A smile ghosted across Telle's thin lips. "Then I'll remember Karamar and the Hell Stars." With a swiftness that stunned Rickli, he attacked.

Thomas was lighter, shorter. All the disadvantages seemed his. Yet he held his own.

He moved as suddenly as Telle, throwing an open-handed finger punch Rickli was unable to follow. Telle blocked with a forearm as he whipped past, flicked a kick at Hakim's groin. Thomas took it on his thigh, unleashed a kick of his own that connected with the back of Telle's pivotal knee as he turned. Telle went down. As he did, he caught Thomas's foot and dragged the smaller man with him. They rolled across the deck, kneeing, gouging, biting, then bounced up, and squared off. They traded feints and counterfeints, almost too subtle for Rickli to follow.

This, he thought, was another new facet of Hakim. The style of fighting was quick and deadly. He was glad Thomas hadn't lost his temper under the heavy needling of his first few years aboard. He might not be able to work ship, but he could kill.

The fighters came together in a flurry of punches and kicks. Then Hakim was on the deck, bleeding from one cheek. Telle circled him warily while Thomas awaited a chance to regain his feet.

Thomas seemed less practiced and clearly had less stamina than his opponent. Rickli worried.

Hakim suddenly seemed to do three things at once, reversing their positions. Now he circled cautiously while Telle awaited a chance to rise.

It went on and on, time weighing ever more heavily on the Earth-man. He was getting slower. Telle began moving with more confidence.

The larger man suddenly moved in, forcing a contest of strength. For long minutes the two strained in one another's grasp; then there was a loud crack. Thomas gasped. His left arm went slack. Telle stepped back with a look of satisfaction—and Thomas loosed a kick that destroyed his knee as thoroughly as the Fenaja harpoon had destroyed Rickli's.

Telle went down with an expression of pained surprise.

Holding his broken arm with his good hand, Thomas circled, waiting to kick again.

Telle seized an ax from a nearby weapons rack, threw. Thomas dodged, but not fast enough. The blade opened a gash on the outside of his left thigh. He fell, his blood staining the deck. He tried to rise, groaned, fell back, dragged himself to the mizzenmast, placed his back to it.

Telle pulled a sword from the rack, crawled toward the Earthman.

"Thomas! Thomas Hakim!" The Shipwrecked Earth looked Rickli's way. Manlove threw the ivory-gripped harpoon.

It slapped Thomas's hand. He held on.

Crossing the Finneran Bank by night again, Rickli Manlove peered at the Spiderfish. Unnatural stars had been blooming there since before sundown. Thomas's people had come searching for their enemies. Hakim's message, sent on Telle's Landing equipment, had gotten through.

Quiet Sea would never be the same.

Rickli thought of Hakim's talisman, of the battle, and of Outside as Thomas had described it. *Rifkin's Dream* had departed Landing. He wondered if, knowing of those things, the augurs would have pulled the Earthman from the sea six years ago.

Too late now.

"So it goes," he murmured, surveying the running lights of the fleet. "When the grunling aren't running, the blackfin are."

Changes due or no, there was work to be done. Fish to be caught, sandweg to be harvested, Fenaja to be fought, stone to be transported to Landing. He had enough to concern him here on the quiet sea.

GHOST STALK

This story appeared in the May 1978 issue of The Magazine of Fantasy & Science Fiction. *It was the first of a series of novelettes about the crew of* Vengeful Dragon. *At one time I attempted to cobble them together into a fix-up novel but there were no takers. The story was well-received critically and garnered a number of Nebula Award recommendations.*

I

It seemed we had been aboard the *Vengeful D.* forever, madly galloping the coasts from Simballawein to The Tongues of Fire. We looked toward land with the lust of stallions for mares beyond a twelve-foot fence. But our barrier was far less visible. It consisted solely of Colgrave's will.

"Going to the Clouds of Heaven next time I hit Portsmouth," said Little Mica, bending over his needle. He was forever patching sail. "Best damned cathouse on the coast. Best damned cats. Going to make them think Old Goat God himself has arrived." He giggled.

It was Subject Number One with Little Mica. It was with most of us. I had never met a sailor who was not drunk or horny. He would be both if he had his feet on dry land

"Runt like you couldn't satisfy a dwarf's grandmother," Student remarked from behind the inevitable book. They dueled with insults awhile. There was little else to do. We were running before a steady breeze.

During the exchange Student's eyes never left his book.

It was one we had taken off a Daimiellian two-master months earlier. We were due to take another vessel soon. (Maybe The One. I hoped. I prayed.

Colgrave had vowed to remain at sea till he found her.) Our stores were running low. There was mold down to the heart of the bread. Maggots were growing in the salt pork, which had gotten wet in a recent storm. There was no fruit to fight the scurvy. And we were down to our last barrel of grog. One lousy barrel would not last me long.

I had no stomach for a beach raid just there, much as I wanted to feel earth and grass beneath my soles. We were a half-dozen leagues north of Cape Blood, off Itaskian coasts. Those were shores Trolledyngjans habitually plundered. And it was their season for hell raising. Coast watchers were, likely, considering us with cold, hard eyes at that moment.

"Sail ho!"

Men scrambled, clearing the decks. I glanced up. As usual, Lank Tor, our chief boatswain, was in the crow's nest. He was as crazy as the Old Man.

Colgrave stalked from his cabin. As always, he was armed and clothed as if about to present himself at court. The boatswain's cry, like a warlock's incantation, had conjured him to the weather decks. "Where away?" He would not go below till we had caught her. Or she shook us. *That* seldom happened.

I peered to seaward. There were always squalls off Cape Blood. That day was no exception, though the storm was playing coy, lying on the horizon instead of embracing the coast. Prey ships liked to duck in to escape. The rocky shoreline offered no hope better than drowning amidst wreckage and thundering surf.

"On the bow!" Tor shouted. "Just round the point and making the landward tack."

"Ah-ha-ha-ha," the Old Man roared, slapping his good thigh.

His face had been destroyed by fire. The whole left side was a grotesque lava flow of scar tissue. His left cheekbone showed an inch-square iceberg tip of bare bone.

"We've got her. Had her before we ever saw her."

Cape Blood was a long, jagged, desolate finger of rock diddling the ocean across the paths of cold northern and warm southern currents. If the ship *were* round the point and on a landward tack, she was almost certainly caught. We had a strong breeze astern. She would have to shift sail for a long seaward tack, coming toward us, piling onto the rocks round the headland. That turn, and bending on sail, would take time too.

"Shift your course a point to starboard," Colgrave roared at the helmsman. Toke, our First Officer, so summarily relieved of his watch, shrugged and went to watch Hengis and Fat Poppo, who had the chip log over the side.

"Making eight knots," he announced a moment later. The Old Man eyed the sails. But there was no way we could spread more canvas. With a breeze like the one we had we always ran hell-bent, hoping to catch somebody napping.

"She's seen us," Tor shouted. "Starting to come around. Oh! A three-master. Caravel-rigged." We were a caravel ourselves, a stubby, pot-bellied vessel high in the bows and stern.

The Old Man's face brightened. Glowed. The ship we were hunting was a caravel. Maybe this was The One.

That was what we called her aboard *Vengeful Dragon*. No one knew her true name, though she had several given her by other sailors. *The Ghost Ship. The Hell Ship. The Phantom Reaver.* Like that.

"What colors?" Colgrave demanded.

Tor did not answer. We were not that close. Colgrave realized it and did not ask again.

I did not know if the phantom were real or not. The story had run the western coast almost since the beginning of sea trade, changing to fit the times. It told of a ghost ship crewed by dead men damned to sail forever, pirating, never to set foot on land, never to see Heaven or Hell, till they had redeemed themselves for especially hideous crimes. The nature of their sins had never been defined.

We had been hunting her for a long time, pirating ourselves while we pursued the search. Someday we would find her. Colgrave was too stubborn to quit till he had settled his old score. Or till we, like so many other crews who had met her, fed the fish while she went on to her next kill.

The Old Man's grievance involved the fire that had ruined his face, withered his left arm, and left him with a rolling limp, like a fat galleon in a heavy ground swell. The phantom, like so many pirates, always fired her prey when she finished with them. Colgrave, somehow, had survived such a burning.

His entire family, though, had gone down with the vessel.

The Captain, apparently, had been a rich man. Swearing he would find The One, he had purchased the *Vengeful Dragon*. Or so the story went, as it had been told to us.

None of us knew how he had gotten rich in the first place. All we knew about him was that he had a terrible temper, that he compensated for his disfigurement by dressing richly, that he was a genius as a pirate, and that he was absolutely insane.

How long had we been prowling those coasts? It seemed an age to me. But they had not caught us yet, not the Itaskian Navy, or the witch-mastered corsairs of the Red Isles, or the longshipmen of Trolledyngja, nor the warships of the many coastal city-states. No. We caught them, like spiders who hunted spiders. And we continued our endless hunt.

Always we hunted. For the three-master caravel with the deadman crew.

II

"Steward!" Colgrave called. "Half pint for all hands." The Old Man seldom spoke at less than a bellow.

Old Barley flashed a sloppy salute and went looking for the key to the grog locker. That was my cue. Grog had been scarce lately. I shuffled off to be first in line.

From behind his book Student remarked to Little Mica, "Must be rough to be a wino on the *Vengeful D.*"

I threw him a daggers look. He did not glance up. He never did. He was not interested in observing the results of his razor-tongued comments.

As always, Priest fell in behind me, tin cup in hand. Service aboard *Vengeful Dragon* and a taste for alcohol were all we had in common. I suppose, though, that that made him closer to me than to anybody else. He was universally, thoroughly hated. He was always trying to save our souls, to renounce sin and this mad quest for a phantom killer little more evil than we.

Priest was strange. He was blue-assed hell in a boarding party. He went in like he meant to cutlass his devil right back to Hell.

The Kid and my friend Whaleboats jockeyed for the third position, till the Old Man turned his one ice-blue eye their way. The Kid did a fast fade. He was supposed to be on watch.

Kid had not been with us long. We had picked him up off a penteconter in the Scarlotti Gulf. We had taken her in full view of Dunno Scuttari's wharves. Their little navy had been too scared to come out after us.

Kid was crazy-wild, would do anything to get attention. He and I did not get along. I reminded him of the headmaster of the orphanage he had been fleeing when he had stowed away aboard the penteconter.

I had heard that that headmaster had been murdered, and arson, that had taken a score of lives, had been committed on the orphanage. The Kid would not say anything one way or the other

We kept our sins to ourselves.

Few of us got along. *Dragon* remained taut to her main truck with anger and hatred.

Ah. A life on the rolling wave, a cruise of the *Vengeful D.,* buccaneering with sixty-eight lunatics commanded by the maddest captain on the western ocean. . . . Sometimes it was Hell. Sheer, screaming Hell.

Old Barley was having trouble finding the key. The old coot never could remember where he had put it so he would not miss it next time he needed it.

"Shake a leg down there, buzzard bait. Or I'll bend you to the bowsprit for the gulls."

That would get him moving. Barley was a coward. Scared of his own shadow. You told him something like that, and he thought you were serious, he would carve you into pieces too small for fish bait. He was the only man aboard meaner than Colgrave and deadlier than Priest.

Curious what fear could do to a man.

Little Mica, leaning on the rail, said, "I can see her tops."

"So who cares?" Whaleboats replied. "We'll see all we want in an hour." He had been through the stalking dance so often it was all a dreadful bore for him now.

Whaleboats had picked up his nickname long ago, in an action where, when we had been becalmed half a mile from a prospective victim, he had suggested we storm her from whaleboats. It had been a good idea, except that it had not worked. They had brought up their ballast stones and dropped them through the bottoms of our boats. Then the breeze had freshened. We had had to swim back to *Dragon* while they sailed off. That vessel was one of the few that had gotten away.

Mica persisted. "Why's she running already? She can't know who we are."

"What difference does it make?" Whaleboats growled. "Barley, if you're not up here in ten seconds. . . ."

"Ask Student," I suggested. "He's got all the answers." But some he would not tell, like how to retire from the crew.

She was running because she had to. Anyone beating round Cape Blood who encountered a vessel running before the wind did so. Nine times out of ten, the second vessel was a pirate who had been lying in ambush behind the headland. I had never understood why the Itaskian Navy did not keep a squadron on station there, to protect their shipping. Maybe it was because the weather was always rotten. That day's fairness was unusual in the extreme.

Nervously, I glanced at the squall line. Had it moved closer? I hated rough weather. Made me sick. Grog only made it worse.

Old Barley showed up with the bucket he had tapped off the barrel. There had better be some on the three-master, I thought. Doing without made me mean.

The Old Man stood behind Barley, beaming at us like a proud father. For that moment you would have thought he had completely forgotten his prey in his concern for his crew.

Dragonfeathers. The hunt was all that ever mattered to him.

He would sacrifice everyone and everything, even himself, to fulfill his quest. And we all knew it.

I thought, I could reach out with my fish knife . . . *schlock-schlock*, and spill his guts on the deck. End it all right now.

I would have to remind Tor to get sand up from ballast before we closed with the caravel. To absorb the blood. He never remembered. He forgot a lot from day to day, remembering only his name and trade. He came to every battle with the eagerness of a male virgin.

It would have been easy to have gotten Colgrave. He was so vulnerable. Crippled as he was, he was no infighter. But I did not try. None of us ever did, though we all thought about it. I could see the speculation on a dozen faces then.

So easy. Kill the crazy bastard, run *Dragon* aground, and forget hunting spook ships.

You'll never do it, never do it, echoed through my mind.

Any other crew on any other ship would have strangled the insane sonofabitch ages earlier.

III

"I can see her mainsail," said Little Mica. "She's shifting sail again."

"Speed it up, Barley," said the Old Man. He put that cold eye on me as

I tried to sneak my cup in again. A half pint was barely enough to warm the throat.

Better be hogsheads full on that three-master, I thought.

"Looks like she's trying for the squall," Tor called down. "I make her a Freylander. She was showing personal colors but got them in before I could read them."

Ah. That meant there was someone important aboard. They thought maybe we would not try as hard if we did not know.

Freyland lay west of Cape Blood, a dozen leagues to seaward where it came nearest the mainland. The caravel must have been making the run from Portsmouth to Songer or Ringerike, an overnight journey.

We seldom prowled the coasts of the island kingdom because the ghost ship seldom appeared there. We left Freyland to our competitors, the Trolledyngjans.

Colgrave's expression—what could be read through the scars—was deflated. Not The One. Again. Then he reconsidered. The flight and flirting with colors could be a ploy. He had done the same himself, to lull a Red Islander or Itaskian.

"Shift your heading another point to starboard," he ordered. "Bosun, come down and prepare the decks."

Lank Tor descended as agilely as an ape. Only the Kid scrambled through the rigging more quickly. But Kid sometimes fell.

A loud thump on the main deck, waking you in the night, told you he had been showing off again.

As Tor hit the deck he began growling orders through a grin of anticipation.

He enjoyed these bloodlettings. They were the only times he felt alive. The boring interim periods were the devil's price he paid for his moments of bloody ecstasy. The lulls were not bad for him, though. His memory was so weak it seldom reached back to our last conquest.

One of his mates began issuing weapons. I took a cutlass, went below for the bow and arrows I kept by my hammock, then repaired to my station on the forecastle deck. I was the best archer aboard. My job was to take out their helmsman and officers.

"I'd shoot a lot straighter with a little more grog in me," I grumbled to Whaleboats, who had charge of the forward grappling hooks.

"Couldn't we all. Couldn't we all." He laughed. "Talk about your straight shooting. I ever tell you about the thirteen-year-old I had in Sacuescu? Don't know where she learned, but she came well trained. Positive nympho. Male relatives didn't approve, though." He drew back his left sleeve to expose a long jagged scar on the roll of muscle outside the shoulder socket. "Two hundred fifty yards, and me running at the time."

I daydreamed while pretending interest. He had told the story a hundred times. Without improving it, the way most of us did. I don't think he remembered having told it before.

No imagination, Whaleboats. The sea ran in long, yard-tall, polished jade swells. Not a fleck of white. No depth. I could not see in. It must have been calm for days. There was none of the drifting seaweed usually torn up by the Cape's frequent storms.

The next one would be bad. They always were when they saved their energies that way.

The ship's pitch and roll were magnified on the forecastle deck, which was twenty feet above the main. My stomach began to protest. I should have saved the damned grog for later.

But then there would have been less room for spirits from the caravel.

The wind was rising, shifting. We were nearing the squall. Little rills scampered over the larger swells.

We were getting nearer Cape Blood, too. I could hear the muted growling of the surf, could make out the geysers thrown up when a breaker crashed in between rocks, shattered, and hurled itself into the sky.

The caravel was less than a mile away. She was showing her stern now, but we had her. Just a matter of patience.

Barley and Priest came up, leading several of the best fighters. It looked like Colgrave planned to board forecastle to stern castle. That was all right by me. It was all over but the killing, once we seized their helm.

Whaleboats spit over the rail. He was so unkempt he was disreputable even among us. "Maybe there'll be women," he mused. "Been a long time since we took one with women."

"Save one for the Virgin." I chuckled. That was the Kid's other name. It got used mostly when somebody was baiting him.

Whaleboats laughed too. "But of course. First honors, even." Then his face darkened. "One of these days we're going to catch another wizard."

They had tried it before.

It was our one great fear. Battles we could win when they were man against man and blade against blade. We were the meanest fighters on the western ocean. We had proven it a hundred times. But against sorcery we had no protection save the grace of the gods.

"Itaskia. We've hurt them most. They'll send out a bait ship with a first-rate witch-man aboard. Then what good our luck?"

"We managed before."

"But never again. I might take Student up on it." He did not say what.

The pirates of the Red Isles had tried it. It had been a close thing. We had been lucky, that time, that Colgrave was too crazy to run. Barley had gotten the sorcerer an instant before he could unleash a demon that would have scattered *Dragon* over half the western ocean.

Our competitors in the islands were not fond of us at all. We showed their vessels the same mercy we gave any others.

Each man of us prayed that we would find The One before some eldritch sea-fate found us.

I could make out faces on the caravel. Time to get ready. I opened their waterproof case and carefully considered my arrows. They were the best, as was my bow. Worth a year's hire for most men. Time was, I had made their price hiring them, and myself, out for a month.

I studied, I touched, I dithered. I finally selected the gray shaft with the two red bands.

Whaleboats observed the ritual with amusement, having failed to entice anyone into a wager on which I would choose. I always took the same one in the end. It was my luckiest shaft. I had never missed with it.

Someday I would exchange arrows with the archer aboard the phantom. They said he was sure death inside three hundred yards. I did not believe he could possibly be as deadly as I as long as I had the banded lady.

It would be interesting, if dangerous, meeting him.

The caravel was trying to trim her canvas. One of the cutlass men guffawed and shouted, "Fart in them! That'll give you all the wind you need."

I wondered what it was like to look over your taffrail and see certain death bearing down. And know there was not a thing you could do but wait for it.

IV

The caravel ran straight away, under full canvas. But the gap narrowed steadily. I could make out details of weapons and armor. "They've got soldiers aboard!"

"Uhm. A lot of them." That was Tor, who had the sharpest eyes on *Vengeful D.* He had known for some time, then.

I turned. The Old Man had clambered up to the poop, stood there looking like some dandified refugee from Hell.

"'Bout close enough for you to do your stuff," said the boatswain, tapping my shoulder.

"Yeah?" It was a long, long shot. Difficult even with the banded arrow. Pitch, roll, yaw. Two ships. And the breeze playing what devil's games in between? I took my bow from its case.

It was worth a year's pay to most men. A magnificent instrument of death. It had been designed solely for the killing of men and custom-crafted to my hands and muscles. I ran my fingertips lightly over its length. For a long time the weapon had been my only love.

I had had a woman once, but she had lost out to the bow.

I bent it, strung it, took out the banded arrow.

They were making it difficult over there, holding up shields to protect their helmsman. They had recognized us.

The banded lady never missed. This time was no exception. At the perfect instant she lightninged through a momentary gap between shields.

The caravel heeled over as she went out of control. She slowed as her sails spilled wind. Panic swept her poop. We raced in.

Colgrave bellowed subtle course changes at our own helmsman. Our sails came in as we swept up.

One by one, I sped my next eleven shafts. Only two failed finding their mark. One was the treacherous blue and white I had threatened to break and burn, it seemed, a thousand times.

The Old Man brought our bows alongside their stern with a touch so deft the hulls barely kissed, as Barley, Priest, and their party leapt over. The shambles I had made of the other poop left no contest. We controlled her immediately.

Sails cracked and groaned as both vessels took them in. Our bows crept past the Freylander's waist.

Whaleboats threw his grapnel. I helped heave on the line.

Screaming, our men poured over the main deck rail to assault the mob awaiting them. They were regular soldiers, Freylander troops tempered in a hundred skirmishes with Trolledyngjan raiders. Once Whaleboats made fast, I resumed plying my bow, using scavenged Freylander arrows.

Crude things, they were unfit to caress a weapon like mine. No wonder they had not harmed any of us.

I dropped a score into the melee, probing for officers and sergeants, then took out a bothersome pair of snipers in the caravel's rigging. They had been plinking at the Old Man, who stood like a gnarled tree defying a storm, laughing as arrows streaked around him

He would be some match for the dead captain of the phantom.

The caravel's poop was clear. Barley and Priest were holding the ladders against counterattacks from below. The men with them threw things at the crowd on the main deck. I decided to recover my arrows before some idiot trampled them, went aft.

The uproar was overwhelming. Shouts. Clanging weapons. Shrieks of pain. Officers and sergeants thundering contradictory orders. The sides of the vessels ground together as the seas rolled on beneath them. And the Old Man still laughed crazily on the poop. He and I were the only ones who remained aboard.

He nodded. "As always, well done."

I gave him an "it was nothing" shrug. When the stern castles rolled together, I jumped across.

My feet came down in a pool of blood, skidded away. Down I went, my head bounding off the rail.

Colgrave laughed again.

It was nearly over by the time I came around. A handful of soldiers were defending a hatchway forward. Most of our men were pitching corpses overboard. They were eying that hatchway hungrily. Feminine wailing came from behind it. Priest and Barley were getting ready for the final rush.

I staggered up, planning to help with a few well-placed arrows.

Damn! My head! And the Freylander seemed to be rolling badly.

It was not my imagination. The squall was closer. It would arrive in a few hours.

That was time enough for recreation. And to find the grog.

U

It had been another of those good battles. I sipped from a quart tankard I had found in the Freylander captain's cabin. No serious injuries for our boys. Lots of cuts and scratches, a bashed head here and a broken finger there. Nothing permanent. The gods must, as Colgrave claimed, have favored our mission. They seldom allowed any of us to come to harm.

The men were having a grand time down on the main deck. Twelve women. A genuine princess and her ladies-in-waiting. What Whaleboats called a jackpot ship. The Virgin, I saw, was not anymore. He abandoned his conquest, scrambled into the Freylander's rigging, began dancing on a yardarm. He was naked from the waist down.

His sureness in the tops, his fearlessness, was his great talent. He showed it off too much.

Whaleboats, a keg of priceless Daimiellian brandy under one arm, a woman's satin bolster under the other, joined me on the poop. "Another master stroke." He nodded toward Colgrave, who still stalked *Dragon*'s poop, muttering, cursing the luck that kept him from finding The One.

Student joined us, glancing at Whaleboats questioningly. Whaleboats shrugged.

Student had found himself some new books. "Squall's moving in," he observed. The water had become a bluish gray showing freckles and stripes of white. The seas were running closer together.

"Going to be a blue-assed bitch of a storm," I prophesied. "The way it's taking its time."

Little Mica was the next of the clique to arrive. He was half-naked, sweat-wet. "The chunky one's not bad." He grinned. His performance had been up to brags.

He was carrying several pounds of gold and silver. We had collected a lot in our time. So much we used it for ballast. Once we found and destroyed The One, we planned to return landside rich as princes.

"That fool Kid's gonna break his neck yet."

He was hopping on one foot, on the tip of the yard, while hosing spurts of piss into the gap between ships.

He suddenly yelled wildly, threw up an arm, bounced his butt off the yard and plunged seaward, limbs flailing. The seamen roared as he did a perfect belly-buster. The ships nudged together. Everyone not otherwise occupied manned the rail.

"I told you. . . ."

"Hold it." The Old Man was peering intently with his one eye. I saw it, too, then. Coming out of an arm of the squall that had reached landward north of us. "Two of them. Longships. Trolledyngjans."

They were no more than three miles away. Their sails were fat with wind and distinct as they spotted us and altered course. One was a black sail bearing a scarlet wolf's head. The other was a yellow-red striped one bearing a black ax.

They were coming after us. Already they were putting their shields on their gunwales and taking in their sails so they could unstep their masts. They looked quick and practiced. Old hands.

Gloating, no doubt, about having caught a competitor with his pants down.

The Old Man bellowed, bellowed, bellowed. Not much sense came through, but the men, drunk though they were, reacted. A storm of booty flew from vessel to vessel. Fat Poppo chucked the naked princess over. She screeched as she landed on her shapely little derriere. Lank Tor, laughing, planted a slobbery, wine-dark kiss on her tender young lips, tossed her back. He clouted Poppo when the fat man protested.

"Fire time," said Student. He looked at Whaleboats in a way that must have had meaning. My friend hurried down the ladder after him.

In moments cutlasses were chopping at lines. Bow and arrows in one hand, half-empty tankard in the other, I watched the deck force make sail. They kept tripping over plunder.

When the proper combination of rolls arrived, I casually stepped from rail to rail without losing a drop of my drink.

"Fo'c'sle," Colgrave growled. I nodded. "Wolf's Head first." I was not so far gone that I could not remember which had been which before they had gotten their sails in.

The Old Man was going to fight. Of course. He always fought. He would fight if the whole damned Itaskian Navy were coming down. He believed in his mission and that he was invincible because the gods were on his side.

The northmen were just a mile away when we finally got under way. Their oars worked with the swift precision of a centipede's legs.

Old hands. They needed no drummer to keep the cadence. They would be tough fighters.

Smoke poured from the Freylander. Naked women reached out to us, pleading.

"She's not burning right," said Mica, who had followed me to the forecastle.

As we drew away, the women abandoned the rail, began scurrying around with buckets.

"Student and Whaleboats better stay out of the Old Man's way," I replied. Colgrave would not be pleased.

He set a course angling seaward, squallward, across the bows of the Trolledyngjans. Any fugitive would have done the same, hoping to evade their first rush and get into the weather before they could come round and overhaul. The ax ship sheered to cut us off and to maneuver so they could board us over both rails. Less than half a mile separated us.

Old hands, yes, but they did not know us. They must have been used to working the coasts of Freyland. Seemed to me there was a good chance they had come over specifically to take the fish we had caught already. There was a big king at Songer, and a scattered gaggle of smaller ones who, nominally, owed him allegiance. The little kings plotted against the big one, and one another, constantly. They were not above tipping the Trolledyngjans to an opportunity to plunder their rivals.

Politics is one specialized field of sin I haven't the wit to comprehend.

A quarter mile. I caressed the banded arrow. Except for Mica, she and I were alone this time. Any fighting would take place on the main deck because the longships had such low freeboard. And it would involve only the ax ship. I kissed the arrow. After all our time together, I thought, we were finally going to part.

Time. The Old Man threw the helm over hard. *Dragon* staggered. The sails rumbled and cracked as they spilled wind.

I sent the banded arrow on her final flight. Ever faithful, as that slut of a wife in Itaskia could not be, she sped to the northern helmsman's heart. He sagged against his rudder arm. Wolf's Head heeled and bucked.

We took her directly amidships, our bows surging up and over, grinding and crunching her into driftwood and halves. Her mast, which had been shipped lengthwise atop her deck thwarts, levered up, speared through, and tangled in our sprit rigging. As we ploughed the wreckage, we staggered and shuddered like a fat lady donning a corset.

Little Mica yipped. A huge, incredibly hairy barbarian with mad blue eyes came up the mast one-handed, lugging an immense battle-ax. He sprang over the rail, howled. While he chased Mica, I dug up a boathook, then smacked him behind the ear. He was so huge it took both of us to dump him overboard. The water revived him. He splashed, cursed. The last I saw of him, he was swimming strongly toward the Freylander.

Our turn brought us round on a southerly course once more. We ploughed through the wreckage. I stared down at bearded warriors busy drowning, clinging to debris, calling for help. The other Trolledyngjan had turned to pick up survivors but had second thoughts now that we were coming back.

They surely thought we were berserkers then, mad killers. Losing some of the precision they had shown earlier, they stepped their mast, made sail, and fled toward the squall.

I groaned, rubbed my stomach in anticipation. Colgrave would not turn loose. No matter that we were shipping water forward and a dozen men had to go to the pumps. No matter that we were drunk on our asses and exhausted from a battle already fought. He had been challenged. He would respond if it meant chasing the Trolledyngjan off the edge of the world.

UI

The waves stood taller and taller, the sea became leadish gray with ever more white running the ridges and faces of the swells. Spray salted my lips even there on the forecastle deck. *Dragon* bucked and rolled, her timbers protesting. Splatters of rain beaded on the decks. The air grew cooler. The Trolledyngjan entered the squall and gradually faded from visibility.

This was more her sort of weather. Her high, curved bows, broad beam, and shallow draft made it possible for her to ride up and down even the most awesome waves—as long as she met them bow on. With her low freeboard she could ship a lot of water fast. I suspected she would put out a sea anchor once she was safely concealed in the storm.

Dragon's altitude, fore and aft, had not been designed with waves in mind. The castles were meant to provide an advantage in battle. They made us a tad top-heavy and wind-vulnerable. In rough weather they existed solely to compound my misery.

There was a lot of wind in that squall. And Colgrave had reduced sail only as much as absolutely compelled by the need to keep *Dragon* from being torn apart. The rigging cracked, screamed, groaned, as if a hundred demons were partying there. A topsail tore with a *sh-whack!* like the fist of a giant whooshing into a stone wall, began popping and cracking in the gale. Only ribbons remained by the time they got it in.

The Kid was up there, helping cut parts free. Some thoughtful soul had remembered to fish him out as we were getting under way. He was a lucky little bastard.

I was rather pleased. Though he had little use for me, I liked him. As much as I liked anyone. He reminded me of myself when I was a lot younger.

He knew that he had been lucky. He was not clowning anymore. He was even using a safety harness.

I collected my weapons and cases. I had to take them below and care for them. Moisture and salt could ruin them forever. Colgrave did not protest. Everyone else, cook included, had to drop everything to work ship, but I was exempted. I was the thunderbolt, the swift, deadly lightning, that determined the course of battles the moment they were joined. Colgrave did not value me as a human being, but he did value my skills and weapons.

The seas were thirty feet tall and gray-black when I dragged myself back topside. My guts were flooding back and forth between my toes and ears. But I had to help with the work. We had reached a point where we were not only pursuing our mad captain's mission, we were fighting to survive.

Every man had found some way to rope himself to his station. Floods raged round the tossing decks, threatening anyone not securely tied. It was a long, watery walk home.

A caravel was not designed to endure that.

I staggered, splashed around, lost a stomach full, snagged the rail in time to save myself. Fat Poppo handed me a safety line. I joined the men trying to control the canvas the Old Man insisted we show.

Lank Tor, the crazy bastard, was in the crow's nest, watching for the Trolledyngjan. He should have been down on the main deck showing off his sea wisdom, not up there proving he had a pig-iron gut. My stomach revolted just at the thought of being up where the mast's height magnified motion horrendously.

We did not regain contact till the weak light began fading from the gray, thick storm. In the interim I found too much time to think and remember, to be haunted by the woman in Itaskia.

She had not been bad, as wives went, but had been short on understanding. And too willful. The conclusion of the El Murid Wars had made jobs for bowmen scarce. You had needed to be related to someone. I had not been. And had not known anything else but farming. I had had enough of that as a boy. She had nagged about the money. It had been good in the war years and she had developed tastes to suit. So I had done a spot of work for Duke Greyfells. Some men had died. She had sensed their blood on my hands. That had led to more nagging, of course. There is just no pleasing them. Whatever you try, it's wrong. It had gotten so bad that I had started spending more time at the Red Hart than in our tenement room.

In alcohol I had found surcease, though more from a critical self than from a wife who, despite making her points in the most abrasive manner possible, had been right. But a man can't shake the pain he carries around inside him. All he can do is try deadening it. In my case that just made the wife situation worse.

There had come an evening when I arrived home early—or late, considering I had been gone three days—and had learned how she had been able to maintain our standard of living, how she had been obtaining the silver I stole to maintain my alcoholic tranquility.

It had been a double blow. A gut-wrecked and a rabbit punch. Your wife is seeing someone else. That is a decker, but you can get up and learn to live with it. But when you find out that there has been a parade, and you're living off the proceeds. . . .

I swear by the Holy Stones, for all our troubles, I never laid a hand on that woman before, not even when roaring drunk. Not once, even provoked.

A couple of men died, and the woman, and I went on the run, bitter, never quite sure just what had come over me, why, or what it had all been about. Not long afterward, Colgrave had scavenged me off a ship he had taken and shanghaied me as replacement for a man who had been washed overboard earlier.

There were sixty-eight stories as shameful, or worse, lurking aboard the *Vengeful D*. Few of us talked about them. The Old Man's tale, if he had one, was his alone. All we knew was the story about the fire.

Student, though, thought he had guessed it. And claimed he knew how to get off *Dragon*, to where he wanted to be. He caused a lot of frowns and nervous questions when he talked like that.

He never would elaborate.

VII

The men were grumbling seditious by the time we spied the Trolledyngjan again. For hours we had been pushing westward, either into the heart of the ocean or onto the rocky coasts of southern Freyland. We had left the waters we knew far behind. Though not one of us had been ashore in a long time, we liked it handy just in case. We were not deep-water sailors. Losing all touch seemed a nightmare.

Colgrave stood on the poop like a statue, staring straight ahead, as if he could see through the spray and waves and rain. Reports of cracked planking, broken frames, and water gushing in as fast as the pumpers could bail, bothered him not at all. He persevered. That, if any one word ever did, encapsulated him perfectly. He persevered.

Dragon larked about on the shoulders of seas as huge as leviathans.

"I see her!" Lank Tor cried. How? I wondered. I could barely see *him*. But it was my cue. I recovered my weapons, repaired to the forecastle deck.

I could see her from there. She was a specter fading in and out almost dead ahead.

The problem was the size of the seas. She swooped down one side like a gull diving, vanished in a trough, then staggered up the next wave like an old man in an uphill race. Her sail had been torn to tatters. Her crew had been unable to unstep their mast. Now they huddled on their oar benches, trying to keep their bows into the waves. They had no protection from Mother Ocean's worst. They were brave, hardy men. What would they do if she swamped?

I never had much use for Priest. But when he clambered up to join me he looked so puzzled and pathetic that I could not ignore him. "What's up?"

"Whaleboats and Student. They're gone

"Gone? What do you mean, gone?" Whaleboats. My only friend. He could not abandon me.

Where the hell could he go? *Dragon*'s rails were the edge of our world.

"Over the side, I guess. Nobody's seen them since they fished the Kid out." He paused, stared at the sea with the look that usually presaged a sermon. Awe, I think you could call it. "The Old Man wanted to talk to them. About why the Freylander didn't burn. One-Hand Nedo says he saw them dump most of the oil into the drink instead of on the deck."

"Whaleboats?" Student, maybe. He had been spooky, unpredictable. But not the biggest woman-hater on the *Vengeful D.* The screams of a tormented female had been like the voices of harps to Whaleboats.

"Yes."

"Strange. Very strange." The man who had fished the Kid out of the drink at Dunno Scuttari had also gone over the side in a few hours. Was the Kid a jinx? I did not think so. Losing someone was unusual, but not unprecedented. In fact, the Old Man had kept the Kid mostly because we had lost another man a week earlier.

And the rebellion? Their failure to fire a captured vessel? That was beyond my comprehension.

"Whaleboats? Really?"

There had to have been more there than met the eye. I could feel it. It was something outside the normal ken, something almost supernatural. The same something that had gotten Priest into such a state.

I could sense some terribly important revelation hovering on the marches of realization, teasing, taunting, a butterfly of truth on gossamer wings. Gods were trying to touch me, to teach me. I pictured Student's dusky face, peeping over the inevitable book. His eyes were merry with the mockery he had always shown when he hinted around his secret.

Maybe he *had* known the way home. But miles at sea, amidst a storm, seemed a strange place and time to start the journey. There was nothing off *Dragon* but drowning and the teeth of fishes.

Or had they swum to the Freylander? They could have expected no mercy from possible rescuers.

Nobody died on the *Vengeful D.* Not in my memory, anyway, though that gets cloudier as it goes back toward my coming aboard. The battles might be fierce, gruesome, and bloody. The decks might become scarlet and slippery. Toke, who doubled as our surgeon (a profession he once had pursued), might stay busy for days sewing wounds, cauterizing, and setting bones, but none of us passed into the hands of Priest for burial with the fishes. All his prayers he had to save for the souls of our enemies.

We, like *Dragon* herself, wore a thousand exotic scars, but, as Colgrave said, the gods themselves guarded us. Only restless, treacherous Mother Ocean could steal a soul from *Vengeful D*.

It was no wonder the Old Man could hurl ship and crew against odds that would have assured mutiny on the most disciplined Itaskian man-o'-war. We believed ourselves immortal. Excepting Old Barley, we dreaded only the completion of our quest and the wizard trap that someone, someday, surely would spring.

What would become of our band of cutthroats if we found The One, or if the gods withdrew their favor?

We closed with the Trolledyngjan. Descending darkness, more than the storm, obscured her now. Still, when we were both at wave crest, I could see the pale faces of their chieftains. They showed fear, but also the dogged determination to die fighting that animates all northmen. We could expect them to turn on us soon.

A *creak-clump* sound drew my attention. The Old Man had come forward. How he had managed, I could not guess. He leaned on the rail while we ran up and down several watery mountains. The ship's motion did not discomfit him at all.

My guts were so knotted that it had become impossible for me to keep heaving them up.

"Can you do it?" he finally asked. "The helmsman?"

I shrugged. "In this? I don't know. I can try." Anything to end the chase and get *Dragon* out of that gray sea hell. He would not break off till we had made our kill.

"Wait for my signal." In a journey that was almost an epic, he returned to the poop. As darkness thickened, he brought *Dragon* more and more abreast of the Trolledyngjan.

She crested. He signaled. I sped my second-best shaft.

She was not the banded lady. She wobbled in the gale, failed the clean kill.

The helmsman had to drown with the others.

Out of control, the Trolledyngjan turned sideways as she slid into a trough, broached.

She survived one wave, but the next swamped her.

One arrow. One deadly shaft well sped, and our part was over. The terrible, terrible sea would do the rest.

Now we could concentrate on surviving. And I could look forward to respite from that constant roar and plunge.

UIII

Smooth sailing was a long time coming. We had to wait for a lull before putting about, lest we share the northman's fate. Then we drove back into it, the wind an enemy as vicious as the waves. We made headway only slowly. Three torturous days groaned past before we staggered through a rainy curtain and saw land and quieter seas once more.

The Old Man's dead reckoning was uncanny. He brought us back just two leagues south of Cape Blood.

But the caravel, that we had halfway hoped to find still adrift, had vanished. We would get no chance to finish plundering her.

Colgrave growled, "Tor, up top. Quick now." He surveyed the sea suspiciously.

Someone had come along. There was no other explanation. The caravel was not on the rocks. And those women, courtiers all, would never have worked ship well enough to have sailed her away. Itaskians summoned by the coast watchers? Probably.

They could be hanging around.

The work began. *Dragon* had taken a vicious pounding. She was leaking at a hundred seams. We had cracked planks forward from the ramming of the Trolledyngjan. Their condition had been worsened by days of slamming into heavy seas. The rigging looked like something woven in a mad war between armies of drunken spiders. Dangling cables, torn sheets, broken spars were everywhere aloft. We needed to pull the mizzenmast and step a spare, and to replace the missing foretopmast. We had enough replacements on board, but would have to plunder new spares off our next victim.

And stores. We had not gotten much off the Freylander. What had become of the keg Whaleboats had plundered, I wondered. I doubted that he had taken it over the side with him.

That was a good sign. I do not worry about alcohol when I'm seasick.

We had the mizzen half pulled, the foretop cleared, sails scattered everywhere for Mica's attention, and half the lines and cables down.

It was the perfect time.

And the enemy came.

As always, Lank Tor saw her first. She came out of the foul weather hugging the cape. Matter-of-factly, he announced, "Galleon, ho. Two hundred fifty tonner, Itaskian naval ensign."

Equally calmly, Colgrave replied, "Prepare for action, Bosun. Keep the repair materials on deck." He climbed to the poop. "And watch for more."

It was my turn. "Signals ashore. Mirrors, looks like." There were flashes all along the coast.

"Coast watchers. They'll be calling everything out of Portsmouth." Colgrave resumed his laborious climb.

We wasted no time trying to run. In our state it was hopeless. We had to fight, and count on our fabulous luck.

"Could be three, four hundred men on one of those," Barley muttered as he stalked past with the grog bucket. He was so damned scared I expected him to wipe them out single-handedly.

"Sail!" someone cried.

A little slooplike vessel, long, low, lateen-rigged, had put out from a masked cove. No threat.

"Messenger boat," said Fat Poppo, who had been in the Itaskian Navy at one time. "She'll log the action and carry the report to the Admiralty."

We did not like one another much, we followers of the mad captain's dream, but we were a team. We made ready with time to spare.

The Itaskian came on as if she intended ramming.

She did! She was making a suicide run with the messenger standing by, if needed, to collect survivors.

The Old Man bent on a main topsail and a storm spritsail, just enough to give us steerage way. At precisely the appropriate instant, he dodged.

The galleon rolled past so closely we could have jumped to her decks. She was crammed with marines. The snipers in her rigging showered me with crossbow bolts.

I leaned back and roared with laughter. Their best effort had but creased my right sea boot.

Each of my shafts took out a Crown officer. Our men drew blood with a storm of javelins.

To ram had been their whole plan. Going away in failure, they seemed at a loss.

Wigwag signals came from the sloop. They were in a cipher Poppo could not read.

"They'll be back," Priest predicted. It was no great feat of divination.

Already they were taking in sail, preparing to come about. This time they would not roar past like a mad bull.

"Find me some arrows!" I demanded. "Tor. . . ."

"On the way," the boatswain promised, gaze fixed on the Itaskian.

I touched the hilt of my cutlass. It had been a long time since I had had to use one. I expected to this time, though. We had to take that galleon so I could recover my arrows. And get at their grog. Itaskians always carried a stock.

Our luck had held that far. There was but one casualty during the first pass. The Kid. He had fallen out of the rigging again. He was just dazed and winded. He would be all right.

The crazy little bastard should have broken every bone in his body.

The moment the Itaskian was clear, Tor put everyone to work.

Colgrave was crazier than I thought. He meant to try dodging till we completed repairs.

They let us get away with it one more time. They had little choice, really. We had the wind. I put down as many officer-killing shafts as I could. But they were prepared for me. Their decision-makers remained hidden while they were in range.

The repair parties succeeded in one thing: freeing most of the men from the pumps. We needed them.

Third time past, the Itaskian sent over a storm of grappling hooks. Despite flailing axes and busy swords and my carefully targeted arrows, they pulled us in, made us fast.

It began in earnest.

How long had it been since we had had to fight on our own decks? I could not remember the last time. But Itaskian marines overran the rail, swarmed aboard, coming and coming over the piles of their own dead. My god, I thought, how many of them are there? The galleon had them packed in like cattle.

I expected them to drive for our castles, to take out Colgrave and myself, but they disappointed me. The point of their assault was the mainmast.

I soon saw why. A squad of sailors with axes went to work on it.

The Old Man thundered at Barley and Priest. They went after the ax men. But the Itaskian marines kept ramparts of flesh in their path.

It was up to me. Ignoring the endless sniper fire, I sped arrow after arrow. That eventually did the trick, but not before they had injured the mainmast grievously.

A grappling hook whined past my nose. What now?

The Itaskian sailors still aboard the galleon were throwing line after line in our rigging.

It was insane. Suicidally insane. No ship, knowing us, tried to make it impossible for us to get away. No. Even the proudest, the strongest, made sure *they* could escape. At least two hundred dead men littered *Dragon*'s decks. Blood poured from our scuppers. And still the Royal Marines clambered over the hills of their fallen.

What drove them so?

The assault's direction shifted from the mainmast to the forecastle. Despite vigorous resistance, the Itaskians broke through to the ladders. I downed as many snipers as I could before, putting my bow carefully out of harm's way, I drew my cutlass and began slashing at helmeted heads.

It had been a long time, but my hand and arm still knew the rhythms. Parry, thrust, parry, cut. No fancy fencing. Riposte was for the rapier, a gentleman's weapon. There were no gentlemen on the *Vengeful D.* Just damned efficient killers.

The Itaskian captain sent the remnants of his sailors in after the marines. And, a grueling hour later, he came over himself, with everyone left aboard.

IX

As always, we won. As always, we left no survivors, though in the end we had to hunt a few through the bowels of their ship. An enraged Barley had charge of that detail.

The long miracle had persisted. Once those of us who were able had thrown the Itaskians to the fishes, it became apparent that not one man had perished. But several wished that they had.

I paused by Fat Poppo, who was begging for someone to kill him. There was not an inch of him that was not bloody, that had not been slashed by Itaskian blades. His guts were lying in his lap.

Instead of finishing him, I fetched him a cup of brandy. I had found Whaleboats's keg. Then, accompanied by Little Mica, who did not look much better than Poppo, I crossed to the galleon.

I wanted to find a clue to the cause of their madness. And a chance to be first at their grog.

Priest had had the same idea. He was wrecking the galley as we passed through.

Screams came from up forward. Barley had found a survivor.

We found the brig.

"Damned," said Mica. "Ain't he a tough one?"

Behind bars was the Trolledyngjan we had thrown overboard. Must be important, I thought, or he would be sleeping with the fishes. Probably some chieftain who had made himself especially obnoxious.

My banded arrow lay in his lap.

I gaped. She had found ways to come home before, but never by such an exotic route.

Mica was impressed too. He knew what that arrow meant to me. "A sign. We'd better take him to the Old Man."

The Trolledyngjan had been eying us warily. He jumped up laughing. "Yes. Let's go see the mad captain."

Colgrave listened to what I had to say, considered. "Give him Whaleboats's berth." He turned away, eye burning a hole in the southern seascape. The messenger vessel still lay there, watching.

I returned to the Itaskian for the banded arrow's sisters.

Ordinarily I did not do much but speed the deadly shafts. I was a privileged specialist, did not have to do anything unless the urge hit me. But now everyone had to cover for those too sliced up to rise, yet too god-protected to die. Not being much use in the rigging, I manned a swab.

They had caught us good, had tangled us thoroughly. It would take all night to get free, and another day to replace the masts. The main, now, would have to go too.

"They'll be here before we're ready," said Mica, passing on some errand.

He was right. All logic said we had sailed into a trap, and even now the ladies of Portsmouth were watching the men-o'-war glide ponderously down the Silverbind Estuary.

The Old Man knew. That was why he kept glaring southward. He was thinking, no doubt, that now he would never catch The One.

Me? All I wanted was to get away alive.

I hoped Colgrave still had a trick or two up his elegant sleeve.

Poppo waved weakly. I abandoned my swab to fetch him another brandy.

"Thanks," he gasped. Grinning, "I know now."

"What's that?"

"The secret. Student's secret,"

"So?"

"But I can't tell you. That's part of it. You've got to figure it out yourself."

"Not Whaleboats."

"Smarter than he looked, maybe. Back to your mopping. And think about it."

I thought. But I could not get anything to click. It was a good secret. I could not even define its limits, let alone make out details.

It had caused Whaleboats and Student to do something completely out of character: fake the fire aboard the Freylander.

Darkness closed in. It was the most unpromising night I had ever seen. Signal fires blazed along the coast. The messenger moved closer, to keep better track of us.

Those of us who were able kept on working. By first light we had stripped the Itaskian of everything useful and had freed *Dragon*. The Old Man spread the fore mainsail and, creeping, we made for the storm.

"There they are."

This time I paid attention to Mica. This time it was important.

Lank Tor and the Old Man, of course, had known for some time.

There were sails on the horizon. Topsails. Those of seven warships, each the equal of the one we had taken. No doubt there were smaller, faster vessels convoying them.

The messenger stayed with us, marking our slow retreat.

The gods were not entirely with us anymore. The squall line retreated as we approached, remaining tantalizingly out of reach. Soon it broke free of Cape Blood and began drifting seaward.

"We could try for Freyland. . . ." I started to say, but Mica silenced me with a gesture.

There was a second squadron north of the Cape. Three fat galleons eager to make our acquaintance.

"We're had. What's that?"

Something bobbed on the waves ahead. Low, dark. Gulls squawked and flapped away as we drew nearer.

It was a harbinger of what Itaskia's Navy planned for us.

Trolledyngjans from Wolf's Head had managed to assemble a raft and start paddling for land. They had not made it. Itaskian arrows protruded from each corpse. The gulls had been at their faces and eyes.

"Always the eyes first," said Mica. He glanced at the wheeling birds, shivered.

"That," I said, "is the only ghost ship we're ever going to see."

The repairs went on and on. The Old Man stood the poop as stiffly as if this were just another plundering-to-be. Not till after they had drawn the noose tight did he act. And then he merely went below to change into fresher, dandier clothing.

Ten to one, and all of them bigger. How much can the gods help? But they took no chances. They surrounded us carefully, then slowly tightened their circle.

When it was almost time, I paused to speak to my banded arrow. This time, I told her, we were going to do a deed that would re-echo for decades. It would be our only immortality.

But they gave me no opportunity to employ her.

Two fat galleons moved in on our sides. We killed and killed and killed, till the sea itself turned scarlet and frothed with the surging to and fro of maddened sharks. They cut us up one by one till, like Fat Poppo, we could do nothing but squat in our own gore and watch the destruction of our shipmates.

The first pair of vessels eventually pulled away so another pair could put their marines aboard. And so on. And so on. Such determination. That Freylander must have been far more important than we had thought.

There came a time when I was alone on the forecastle, Colgrave was alone on the poop, and the Kid was alone in the rigging. Then even we had been cut down.

The Itaskians cleared their countless dead while, unable to interfere, we lay in our own blood. Would they fire us, as we had done to so many victims? No. Gangs of sailors came over and took up the repair work we had started.

I supposed they were planning to take us into Portsmouth. Our trials and executions would make a huge spectacle.

It would be the events of the decade.

✕

The Itaskians worked a day and a night. Dawn proved my pain-fogged speculations unfounded.

The messenger ship then drew alongside. Just one man came aboard. He wore the regalia of a master sorcerer of the Brotherhood.

This was the man we had feared so long, the one against whom we had no defense. His was the mind, no doubt, which had engineered our destruction. He had been subtle. Not till now had we suspected the presence of a magical hand. Knowing he was there, Colgrave might have gone another way.

He surveyed *Dragon* with a pleased look, then went aft to begin a closer inspection. He started with the Old Man.

One by one, working his way forward, he paused over each man. Finally, he climbed the forecastle ladder and bent over me.

"So, Archer," he murmured. I clutched the banded arrow beneath my broken leg and wished I had the strength to drive her into his chest. I had not felt so much rage, so much hatred, since the night that I had killed my wife. "Your long journey is almost done. You're almost there. In just a few hours you'll have your heart's desire. You'll meet your ghost ship after all."

He must have said the same thing to the others. *Dragon* fairly quivered with anger and hatred. Mine was so strong I half sat up before I collapsed from pain and the weight of the spells he had spun about us.

"Farewell, then," he chuckled. "Farewell all!" A minute later he was aboard his sloop. Her crew cast off. By then the galleons had fled beyond the southern horizon.

I could still hear his voice, singing, as the sloop pulled away. At first I thought it imagination. But it was not. He was chanting up some new sorcery. The old began to relax.

My anger broke that enchantment's limits. I rolled. I found my bow. Ignoring nerves shrieking with the pain in my leg, I surged upward.

Three hundred yards. He had his back to me, his arms raised in an appeal to the sky. "This's the flight for which you were made." I kissed the banded lady good-by.

I fell as she left the bow, cursing because I would be unable to follow her final flight.

She was faithful to the last.

The skull-pounding chant became an endless tortured scream.

All the thunders of the universe descended at once.

I had let fly seconds too late.

The first thing I noticed was the gentle whisper of the ship moving slowly through quiet seas. Then the damp fog. I rolled onto my back. The mist was so dense I could barely make out the albatross perched on the fore truck. I sat up.

There was no pain. Not even the ache of muscles tormented by the exertions of combat. I rubbed my leg. It was whole. But I had not imagined the break. There was a lump, no longer tender, at the fracture site. My cuts, scrapes, and bruises had all healed, their only memorial a few new scars.

It takes months for bones to knit, I thought.

I stood, tottered to the rail overlooking the main deck. The bone held.

My shipmates, as puzzled as I, were patting themselves, looking around, and murmuring questions. Fat Poppo kept lifting his shirt, fingering the line across his belly, then flipping his shirt down and glancing around in embarrassed disbelief. Lank Tor stared upward, mouthing a silent "How?" over and over.

The sails were aloft and pregnant with wind.

I turned slowly, surveying the miracle. Maybe we *were* beloved of the gods, I thought.

The fog seemed less dense ahead. Light filtered through.

The Old Man sensed it too. He began clumping round the poop in suspicious curiosity, leaning on the rails, the stern sheets, trying to garner some hint of what had happened.

He paused, stared past me.

In a voice that was but a ghost of his usual thunder, he called Toke and Lank Tor, conferred. In minutes, quietly, they were about their work. He called to me to keep a sharp lookout.

The boatswain and First Officer took in sail.

XI

And now we drift, barely making steerage. Every man remains self-involved in the mystery of our survival.

The fog *is* thinning. I can see the water now, like polished jade, an algae-rich soup in which the only ripples are those made by *Dragon*'s cutwater.

Yet there is a breeze up top. Curious.

A dozen birds are perched in the tops, silently watching us, moving only when the Kid or another topman pushes by. Spooky.

The Old Man is as much at a loss as anyone. He is ready for anything, expects nothing good. He sends one of Tor's mates round to make sure we are all fully armed.

The fog gradually breaks into patchlets. But the low sky remains solidly overcast. It is no more than two hundred feet up. It is so thick, the light is so diffuse, that there is no telling exactly where the sun stands. Sometimes the cloud dips down, and the maintop ploughs through, swirling it like a spoon does cream in a cup of tea.

I check my arrows, mourn my banded lady. She was a truer love than any I have ever known, was faithful to the end. Not like this blue and white. She is as fickle as that bitch I killed in Itaskia.

Heart's desire. The dead sorcerer promised. Then what am I doing here, sailing to a rendezvous with the ghost ship? A queasiness not of wind or wave stampedes through my stomach. I will face a grim opponent, if the wizard did not lie. And without my deadly lady. The bowman there, they say, is at least as good as I.

This is my desire? Then I have fooled myself more thoroughly than anyone else.

I wish I could talk to Colgrave, to make sure there aren't any last-minute changes in plan.

Like a chess opening thoroughly planned beforehand, our initial moves will go by rote. We have discussed them a hundred times. We have taken a score of vessels in dress rehearsal.

I am the Old Man's key piece, his queen. He relies on me heavily. Perhaps too heavily.

I am supposed to take out that legendary bowman first. Before he can get me. Then I take the dead captain, the helmsman, anyone taking their places, and, as we go hand to hand, their deadliest fighters.

Dragon's prow slices through a final cloud.

I see her! A caravel emerging from a fog bank directly ahead, bearing down on us. I wave to Colgrave.

It's Her. The One. The Phantom. I can smell it, taste it. Its taste is fear. The sorcerer did not lie. Even from here I can see the bowman on her forecastle deck, glaring our way.

The butterflies grow larger

Colgrave shifts our heading a bit to starboard. The reaver immediately does the same. We have barely got steerage way, but it seems we are rushing toward one another at the breakneck speed of tilting knights. I glance at Colgrave. He shrugs. How and when I act is up to me.

I take my second-best arrow and lay it across my bow. "Now, if you ever aspired to greatness, is the time to fly true," I whisper. My hands are cold, moist, shaky.

We proceed in near silence, each man awed by what we are about to attempt. The ghost makes not a sound as she bears down, evidently intending a firing pass similar to our own. Even the birds, usually so raucous, are still. Colgrave stands tall and stiff, refusing to make himself a difficult target. He has complete confidence in my skill and the protection of the gods.

He is positively aglow. This is the end to which he has dedicated his life.

Momentarily, I wonder what we will really do if by some chance we are the victors in this encounter. Will we beach the *Vengeful D.* and haul our treasures ashore as we have always said? But where? We must be known and wanted in every kingdom and city-state fronting the western ocean.

Four hundred yards. The phantom seems a little hazy, a little undefined. For a moment I suspect my eyes. But, no. It's true. There is an aura of the enchanted about her.

There would be, wouldn't there?

Three fifty. Three hundred yards. I could let fly now, but it does not feel right.

There is something strange about the reaver, something I cannot put my finger on.

Two-fifty. The crew are getting nervous. All eyes are on me now. Two hundred. I cannot wait any longer. He won't

I loose.

As does he, at virtually the same instant.

His shaft moans past my ear, nicking it, drawing a drop of blood. I stoop for another, cursing. I missed too.

The butterflies have grown as big as falcons. I send a second arrow, and so does he. And we both miss, by a wider margin.

Does he have the shakes too? He is supposed to be above that, is supposed to be far better than he has shown. The Phantom has never met a foe she needed fear.

But she has never met us. Perhaps fear is why we have never been able to track her down. Perhaps she has heard how terrible her stalkers can be.

One-fifty. I miss twice more. Now it has become a matter of pride. He can miss forever, so far as I'm concerned, but I've got a reputation to uphold and a nervous crew to reassure.

Another miss. And another. Damned! What is wrong with me?

Student's mocking grin comes haunting. I frown. Why now?

One hundred yards. Toe-to-toe. And I'm down to just one arrow. Might as well kiss it all good-by. We have lost. This feckless blue and white will miss by a mile.

But a dead calm comes over me. Disregarding my opponent, who, I suppose, has been toying with me, I ready the shot with tournament care.

It goes.

A thunderbolt strikes me in the chest. The bow slides from my fingers. The crew moan. I clutch the arrow. . . .

A blue and white arrow.

I can hear Student laughing now. And, with blood dribbling from the corners of my mouth, I grin back. So that's his secret.

It's a good one. A cosmic joke. The sort that sets the gods laughing till their bellies ache and then, ever after, when they remember, is good for a snicker.

My opponent falls as I fall. I wind up seated with my back against the rail, watching as the grapnels fly, as the ships come together, as the faces of the men portray a Hell's gallery of reactions.

I suppose we'll drift at the heart of this circular mile forever, tied to ourselves, to our sins.

It's too late for redemption now.

CALL FOR THE DEAD

This was the second Vengeful Dragon *story. It appeared in* The Magazine of Fantasy & Science Fiction *for July 1980. It proved that few endings are irrevocably final. It received numerous excellent reviews, many Nebula Award recommendations, and was a finalist on the Balrog Awards ballot for best short fantasy of 1980.*

I

The figure wore scarlet.

It had a small, hairless skull. Its face was as delicate as that of a beautiful woman. A rouge colored its lips. Kohl shadowed its eyes. Zodiacal pendants hung from its earlobes. Yet no observer could have sworn to its sex.

Its eyes were closed. Its mouth was open.

It sang.

Its song was terror. It was evil. Its voice stunk with its own fear.

Its lips did not move while the words came forth.

A dark basaltic throne served as its chair. A pentagram marked the floor surrounding it. That Stygian surface seemed to slope away into infinity. The arms of the pentagram, and the cabalistic signs filling them, had been sketched in brilliant reds and blues, yellows and greens. The colors rippled and changed to the tempo of the song. They surrendered to momentary flashes of silver, lilac, and gold.

Perspiration dribbled down the satin-smooth effeminate face. Veins stood out darkly at its temples. Neck and shoulder muscles became knots and cords. Small, slim, delicate hands clawed at the arms of the throne. The fingernails were long, curved, sharp, and painted the color of fresh blood.

Torches surmounting the throne's tall back flickered, growing weaker and weaker.

The song faltered. . . .

The figure surged, drew upon some final bastion of inner resource. A scream ripped from its throat.

The darkness gradually withdrew.

The figure slowly stood, arms rising. Its song/scream transmuted into a cry of triumph.

Its eyes opened. They were an incredible cerulean blue, almost shining. And they were incalculably malevolent.

Then the darkness struck. A finger came from behind, swiftly, coiling round its victim like a python of night. Tendrils of the tentacle thrust into the sorcerer's nostrils and open mouth.

II

The caravel revolved slowly in an imperceptible current. The sea was cool and quiet, a plain of polished jade. Neither fin nor wind rippled its lifeless surface. It looked as unyielding as a serpentine floor.

I stared as I had for ages. It was there, but I no longer saw it.

Fog domed the place where *Vengeful Dragon* lay becalmed. It made granite walls where it met the quiet sea, but overhead it thinned. Daylight leaked through.

How many times had the sun come and gone since the gods had abandoned us to the spite of that Itaskian sorcerer? I had not counted.

Sometimes, when I tried hard enough, I drifted away from my body. Not far. The spells that bound us were of the highest order.

It pleased me that I had slain the spell-caster. If ever I escaped this pocket hell and encountered him in the afterworld, I would attack him again.

I could get free just enough to survey the scabby remnants of my drifting coffin.

Emerald moss clung to her sides. It crept a foot up from her waterline. Colorful fungi gnawed at her rotting timbers. Her rigging dangled like strands of a broken spider's web. Her sails were tatters. Their canvas was old and brittle and would crumble at the first caress of wind.

The decks were littered with fallen men.

Arrows protruded from backs and chests. Limbs lay twisted at odd, painful angles. Bowels lay spilled upon the slimy planks. Gaping wounds marked every body, including mine.

Yet there was no blood. Nor any corruption.

Not of the biological kind. Morally, *Dragon* had been the cesspool of the world.

Sixty-seven pairs of eyes stared at the gray walls of our tiny, changeless universe.

Twelve black birds perched in the savaged tops. They were as dark as the bottom of a freshly filled grave. There was no sheen to their feathers. Only the movement of their pupilless eyes betrayed their claim to life.

They knew neither impatience, nor hunger, nor boredom. They were sentinels standing guard over the resting place of old evil.

They watched the ship of the dead. They would do so forever.

They had arrived the moment our fate had overtaken us.

Suddenly, as one, twelve heads jerked. Yellow eyes peered into the thinner fog overhead. One short screech filled the heavy air. Dark pinions drummed a frightened bass tattoo. The birds fled clumsily into the granite fog.

I had never seen them fly. Never.

A shadow, as of vast wings, occluded the sky without actually blocking the light.

I suffered my first spate of emotion in ages. It was pure terror.

III

The caravel no longer revolved. Its battered prow pointed an unerring north-northeast. A tiny swale of jade bowed around her cutwater. A shallow depression bordered her stern.

Vengeful D. was moving.

Dark avians wheeled round her splintered masts, retreated in consternation.

Our captain lay on the caravel's high poop, beneath the helm, clad in rags. Once they had been noble finery. He still clutched a broken sword. He was Colgrave, the mad pirate.

Not all Colgrave's wounds had come in our last battle. One leg had been crippled for years. Half his face had been so badly burned that a knoll of bone lay exposed on his left cheek.

Colgrave had been the worst of us. He had been the cruelest, the most wicked of men.

Our fell commander had collapsed atop several men. His eyes still stared in fiery hatred, burning like the lamps of Hell. For Colgrave, Death was a temporary lover. A woman he would betray when his time came.

Colgrave was convinced of his immortality, of his mission.

Stretched on the high forecastle deck, in rags as dark as the loss of hope, lay another man. A blue and white arrow protruded from his chest. His head and shoulders lay propped against the vessel's side. His hating eyes stared through a break in the railing opposite him. His face was shadowed by ghosts of madness.

He was me.

I hardly recognized him anymore. He seemed more alien than any of my shipmates.

I remembered him as a grinning young soldier, a cheerful boy, a hero of the El Murid Wars. He had been the kind you wanted your daughters to meet. That man on the forecastle deck, beyond his obvious injuries, had wounds to the bones of his soul. Their scars could be seen by anyone. He looked like he had endured centuries of hurt.

He had dealt more than he had received in his thirty-four years.

He was hard, bitter, petty, vicious. I could see it, know it, and admit it when looking at him from my drifting place amidst the rigging. I could not from inside.

He was not unique. His shipmates were all hating, soul-crippled men. They hated one another more than anything else. Except themselves.

A seven-legged spider limped down my right shoulder, across my throat, and out along my left arm. The arachnid was the last living creature aboard *Dragon*. She was weakening in her relentless quest for one more victim.

The spider's odyssey took her out onto the pale white of a hand still gripping a powerful bow. My bowstring had parted long ago, victim of rot and irresistible tension.

I felt her. . . ! My skin twitched beneath her feet.

The spider scuttled into a crack between planks and observed with cold, hungry eyes.

My eyes itched. I blinked.

Colgrave shuddered. One spindly arm rose deliberately. Colorless fingers brushed the helm. Then his hand fell, stirred feebly in the slime covering the deck.

I tried moving. I could not. What a will Colgrave had!

It had driven us for years, compelling us when no other force in Heaven or Hell could move us.

A shadow with saffron eyes wheeled above us. It uttered short, sharp cries of dismay.

Tendrils of the darkness that could not be seen were weaving new evils on the loom of wickedness of our accursed ship. And the watchers could do nothing. The sorcerer who had summoned them, who had commanded them and who had charged them with watching and bearing tidings, was no more.

I had silenced his magical songs forever with a last desperate shaft from my bow.

The birds could fly to no one with their fearful news. Nor could anyone liberate them from their bondage.

One by one my shipmates stirred the slightest, then returned to their long rests.

Sometimes in darkness, sometimes in light, the caravel glided northward. The shadow-weaver ran its shuttle too and fro. No foul weather came to nag at our ragged floating Hell. The fog surrounding us neither advanced nor receded, nor did the water we sailed ever change. It always resembled polished jade.

My shipmates did not move again.

Then darkness descended upon me, the oblivion for which I had longed since my realization that *Vengeful Dragon* was not just another pirate but a seagoing purgatory manned by the blackest souls of the western world. . . .

And while I slept in the embrace of the Dark Lady, the weaver weaved. The ship changed. So did her crew. And the watchbirds followed in dismay.

IV

A dense fog gently bumped Itaskia's South Coast. It did not cross the shoreline. The light of a three-quarters moon gleamed off its low-lying upper surface. It looked like an army of cotton balls come to besiege the land.

A ship's main truck and a single spar cut the fog's surface like a shark's fin, moving north.

The moon set. The sun rose. The fog dissipated gradually, revealing a pretty caravel. She had a new but plain look, like a miser's beautiful wife clothed in homespun.

The fog dwindled to a single irreducible cloud. That refused to disperse. It drifted round the ship's decks. Black birds dipped in and out.

I began to itch all over. My skin twitched. Awareness returned. Straining, I opened my eyes.

The sun blazed in. I decided to roll over instead.

It was the hardest thing I had ever done. A physical prodigy.

Battered old Colgrave staggered to his feet. He leaned on the helm and scanned the gentle sea. He wore a bewildered frown.

Here, there, my shipmates stirred. Who would the survivors be? Priest, the obnoxious religious hypocrite? The Kid, whose young soul had been blackened by more murders than most of us older men? My almost-friend, Little Mica, whose sins I had never discovered? Lank Tor? Toke? Fat Poppo? The Trolledyngjan? There were not many I would miss if they did not make it.

I climbed my bow like a pole. I could feel the expression graven on my face. It was wonder. It tingled through me right down to my toenails.

We had no business being anywhere but perpetually buried in that sorcerer's trap.

I scanned the horizon suspiciously, checked the main deck, then met my Captain's eye. There was no love between us, but we respected one another. We were the best at what we were.

He shrugged. He, too, was ignorant of what was happening.

I had wondered if he had not brought the resurrection about by sheer force of will.

I bent and collected an oiled leather case. Inside lay twelve arrows, labeled, and several new bowstrings. My bow, which had been exposed for so long, had been restored by careful oiling and rubbing. I strung and tested it. It remained as powerful as ever. I did not then have the strength to bend it completely.

A dozen men were afoot. They searched themselves for wounds that had disappeared during the darkness.

I wondered how many had shared my vigil of impotent awareness, denied even the escape of madness.

They started checking each other.

I looked for Mica. I spotted the little guy studying himself in a copper mirror. He ran fingers over a face that had been half torn away.

Everyone was recovering.

I descended to the main deck and strolled aft. *Dragon* was in the best shape I had ever seen. She had been *renewed*. . . .

I walked stiffly. The others moved jerkily, like marionettes manipulated by a novice. I reached the ladder to the poop as vanguard of a committee. Our First Officer and Boatswain, Toke and Lank Tor, had joined me. Old Barley tagged along, hoping the Old Man would order a ration of rum.

Barley was one of the alcoholic in-group. Priest was another. He was watching Barley closely. Barley always did the doling.

Rum! My mouth watered. Only Priest could outdrink me.

Colgrave shooed his deck watch down the starboard ladder.

Why hadn't our mysterious benefactors done a full repair job on the Captain? I looked round. Several men had not been restored completely. We were as we had been the day we had stumbled into the Itaskian sorcerer's trap.

Colgrave was first to speak. He said, "Something happened." Not an ingenious deduction.

My response was no more brilliant. "We've been called back."

Colgrave's voice had a remote, sepulchral timbre. It seemed to reach us after a journey up a long, cold, furniture-crowded hallway. There was no force in it. It had no volume, and very little inflection

"Tell me something I don't know, Bowman," Colgrave growled.

The lack of love between us was not unique. This crew had shipped together, and fought together, by condemnation of the gods. We cooperated only because survival demanded it.

"Who did? Why?" I demanded. Again I scanned the horizons.

I was not a lone watcher. We had powerful enemies along these coasts. Dread enemies, they had at their disposal the aid of men like the one who had banished us to that enchanted sea.

"We don't have time to worry about it." Colgrave threw a spidery hand at the coast. "That's Itaskia, gentlemen. We're only eight leagues south of the Silverbind Estuary."

The Itaskian Navy had sent that sorcerer after us. Itaskians hated us. Especially Itaskian merchants. We had plundered them so often that we used gold and silver for ballast.

We had preyed on them for ages, slaughtering their crews and burning their ships during our relentless search for what, in the end, had proven to be ourselves.

The great naval base at Portsmouth lay just inside the mouth of the Estuary.

"Coast watchers have spotted us by now," Colgrave continued. "The news will have reached Portsmouth. The fleet will be coming out."

It did not occur to us that we could have been forgotten. Or that we might not be recognized. But we did not know how long we had been gone, nor did *Dragon* look the same.

"We better get this bastard headed out to sea," Tor said. "Head for the nether coast of Freyland. Hole up in a cove till we know what's happening. Some timbre entered the boatswain's voice. It smelled of fear.

We had never been well-known in the island kingdoms. Seldom had we plundered there.

"We'll do that. Meantime, check out this tub from stem to stern. Check the men. Tor, take a look round from the tops. They could be after us already."

Tor had the best eyes of any man I've ever known.

The crew milled below, touching each other, speculating in soft tones. Their voices, too, sounded remote. I do not know why that was. It soon corrected itself.

"First watch," Tor called. "Rigging. Prepare to shift sail for the seaward tack."

They moved slowly, stiffly, but sorted themselves out. Some clambered into the rigging. Lank Tor said, "Ready to shift course, Captain."

Colgrave spun the wheel. Tor bellowed to the topmen.

Nothing happened.

Colgrave tried again. And again. But *Vengeful D.* would not respond.

We just stood round staring at one another till Kid called down, "Sail ho!"

U

"Boatswain, see to the weapons," Colgrave ordered.

I looked at him narrowly. A fire was building within him. Action imminent. The old Colgrave flared through, despite what we had endured, despite what we had learned about ourselves. "See that sand is scattered on the decks. Barley! One cup for all hands. Bowman. Take yours first. Go to the forecastle."

Our gazes locked. I had had my fill of killing. At least for this madman.

But the compulsion was still there. The fire that forced a man to adapt his will to Colgrave's. I looked down like a kid who had just been scolded. I descended to the main deck.

Mica caught up with me. "Bowman. What's going on? What happened to us?"

He called me Bowman because he did not know my name. None of them did, unless Colgrave had penetrated the secret. It was one I could no longer answer myself.

Vengeful Dragon had a way of stealing memories. I could not remember coming aboard. I did remember murdering my wife and her lovers before I did. But what was her name...?

The curse of the gods lies heavy. To remember my crime, to remember the love and hate and pain that had gone into and pursued it, and yet to forget the very name of the woman I had killed.... And, worse, to have forgotten my own, so that the very cornerstone of my identity was denied me.... They award their penalties in cruel and ingenious ways, do the gods.

Some of the others remembered their names but had forgotten why they had committed their sins. That, too, was torture.

None of us remembered much of our life aboard *Vengeful Dragon*.

Colgrave and I had the murder of our families in common. That was not much of a foundation for friendship.

"I don't know, Mica. No more than you."

"I thought maybe the Old Man.... It scares me, Bowman. To be recalled...."

"I know. Think of the Power involved. The evils unleashed.... Come up to the forecastle with me, Mica."

He did not have anything else to do. He was our sail maker. Our sails were in chandler's shop condition.

We leaned against the rail, staring over the quiet green water at the tops of a pair of triangular sails.

"That's no Itaskian galleon," Mica observed.

"No." I debated for several seconds before I hinted at my suspicion. "Maybe the gods are tinkering with us, Mica." A gull glided across our bows. For a moment I marveled at its graceful flight. A shadow followed. One of the black birds.

"Suppose they're giving us another chance?"

He watched the black bird for several seconds. "How patient are they, Bowman? We had our chances in life. We had them in limbo, while we harried the coasts. And we didn't even recognize them."

"And maybe we couldn't. This ship. . . . We forget things. We stop thinking. We get like Lank Tor, who can't remember yesterday. Remember Student and Whaleboats?"

They had been friends of ours. They had disappeared during a terrible storm shortly before the sorcerer had caught us.

"Uhm."

We had never talked about it, but the suspicion could not be denied. There was a chance that Student and Whaleboats had found redemption. There was a connection between righteous deeds and disappearances from *Dragon*. It *had* to be more than coincidence. Our memories were reliable only back to the time Kid had come aboard, but since then several men had vanished. Each had been guilty of doing something truly *good* shortly before.

How Colgrave had screamed and cussed at Student and Whaleboats for not setting fire to that shipload of women. . . .

"Student claimed there was a way out. Fat Poppo told me he figured it out too. I think there is. I think they found it. And I think I know what it is, now."

Mica did not say anything for at least a minute. Then, "Did you die at that place, Bowman?"

"What?" For some reason I did not want to tell him. "What place?"

"The foggy sea, dummy. Where we met ourselves and lost the battle."

Colgrave's habit was to destroy every vessel we encountered. We had entered that quiet place out of a deep fog, with a sorcerer's grim promise still ringing in our ears. Black birds had roosted in our tops and another ship had been headed our way. Colgrave, mad Colgrave, had ordered the attack. And when we had come to grips with the caravel, who had we found manning her but doppelgangers of ourselves. . . ?

"Were you aware the whole time?"

"Yeah." The grunt liked to choke me getting out. "Every damned second. I couldn't sleep. I couldn't even go crazy."

He raised an eyebrow.

"All right. Crazier than I already am."

Mica grinned. "Sometimes, Bowman, I wonder if we're not just a little less wicked than we think. Or maybe it's pretend. We're great pretenders, the crew of the *Vengeful D.*"

"Mica, you ain't no philosopher."

"How do you know what I am? I don't. I don't remember. But what I'm saying, man, is I think we all knew what was going on. Every minute. Even the Old Man."

"What's the point?"

"The sun rose and set a lot of times, Bowman. I didn't sleep either. That's a lot of time to think. And maybe change."

I turned my back to the rail. The crew were about ship's work. They were quieter than I remembered. Thoughtful. They moved less jerkily now.

How long had it been? Years?

"We don't look any different." Colgrave was the same old specter of terror there on the poop. He had changed clothing. He was clad in regal finery now. Clothes were his compensation for his deformity.

When he dressed this well, and kept to the poop instead of lurking in his cabin, he meant to spill blood.

"I mean different inside." He considered Colgrave too. "Maybe some of us can't change. Maybe there's nothing else in there."

"Or maybe we just don't understand." I suffered an insight. "The Old Man's scared."

"He should be. These are Itaskian waters. Look what they did already."

"Not just afraid of what they'll do if they catch us. We had that hanging over us before. It didn't bother anybody. Won't now. I mean scared like Barley. Of everything and nothing."

Old Barley was our resident coward. He was also the meanest fighter on the *Vengeful D.* His fear drove him to prodigies in battle.

"Maybe. And maybe he's changed, too."

"I haven't. Not that I can see."

"Look at your right hand."

I did. It was my hand, fore and middle fingers calloused from drawing bowstrings. "So?"

"Every guy here can tell you two things about your hands. If there's a ship in sight, your left will be holding a bow. And your right, when

Colgrave lets you, will be hanging on to a cup of rum like it was your first-born child."

I looked at Mica. He smiled. I looked at my hand. It was naked. I looked down at the main deck, that I had crossed without thinking of rum. Barley was almost finished issuing the grog ration.

The craving hit me hard. I must have staggered. Mica caught my arm.

"Try to let it go, Bowman. Just this once."

I waved at Barley.

"Just to see if you can do it."

Why didn't he mind his own business? Gods, I needed a drink.

Then Priest caught my eye. Priest, the king of us alkies. The man who peddled salvation to the rest of us and remained incapable of saving himself.

Priest did not have a tin cup either. He leaned over the starboard rail. His expression said that his guts were tearing him apart. His need for a drink was devouring him. But he was not drinking. His back was to Barley.

"Look at Priest," I murmured.

"I see him, Bowman. And I see you."

The cramps started then. They pissed me off. I whirled and planted myself against the rail, mimicking Priest, overlooking the bowsprit. I tried to shut out the world.

"No way that pervert is going to outlast me," I declared.

Our bow began rising and falling gently. The water was assuming the character of a normal sea. Our resurrection was about finished.

I did not look forward to its completion. I could get seasick in a rowboat on a lake on a breezy day.

The other vessel was hull up on the horizon and headed our way fast.

I re-examined my bow and arrows. Just in case.

VI

Had we changed? The gods witness, we had. The two-master came in alongside, gently, and we did not swarm over her. We did not cast her screaming crew to the sharks. We did not set her aflame. We did not do anything but hold our weapons ready and wait.

Colgrave did not ask us to do anything more.

Mica and I surveyed our shipmates. I'm sure he saw as much wonder in my face as I saw in his.

We watched Colgrave almost constantly. The Old Man would determine the smaller vessel's fate. Like it or not, if he gave the order, we would attack.

"We're a pack of war dogs," I told Mica. "We might as well be slaves."

He nodded.

Never a word escaped our mad captain's mouth. That astonished him more than the rest of us, I think.

The ship lay bumping against *Dragon* for fifteen minutes. Her strangely clad, silent crewmen studied us. We studied them. Not a one would meet my eye. They knew who and what we were. We could smell the fear in them.

Yet they had come to us, and they stayed. And that was reason for us to fear.

The vessel had a small deckhouse amidships. Its door finally opened. Two more strangers stepped out, stationed themselves to either side. They studied us with startled, frightened eyes.

A person in red came forth, looked up.

"A woman!" Mica swore.

We did not have a reputation for being gallant.

"I don't think so. . . ." But I could not be sure. I had never seen a bald woman. "But. . . . Call it an it."

Its incredible blue eyes stared in slight bewilderment. Unlike its shipmates, it did not fear us. It was confident.

I got the impression that we had been a disappointment. Because we had not conformed to our vicious reputation.

The urge to let an arrow fly was as strong in me as the need for a drink. I did not bend my bow.

One glance into those weird eyes was all I could handle. Incredible Power sparked them. They proclaimed their possessor a sorcerer greater than he who had banished us to fogs and leaden seas.

The creature also had that aura of command that animated Colgrave.

"This's the one who called us back," I whispered.

Mica nodded.

I had myself in control. I tested the draw of my bow.

Black birds wheeled overhead, screeching their consternation. One dove at the figure in red.

The figure raised a palm. It spoke a single word.

Feathers exploded. They spun down toward ships and sea, smoldering as they fell. The stench of burnt feathers assailed the air.

The naked albatross smashed into *Dragon*'s side. It broke its neck. It thrashed in the water briefly, then changed form. In seconds it became a thing like a snake of night. The thing wriggled away through water and air with lightning speed.

Its companions screeched once, then remained silent. They did not cease their endless patrol. They clearly preferred avoiding their comrade's liberation.

The figure in red said something.

Someone shouted orders in a strange language. Sailors threw grappling hooks over *Dragon*'s rail.

I looked at Colgrave. An arrow lay across my bow.

He made a slight negative head gesture.

"He *has* changed," I told Mica. "He says let them come." I looked again. Colgrave was instructing Toke and Lank Tor. They descended to the main deck.

They disposed the men in such fashion that they could attack the boarders from all sides.

We waited.

One of the smaller ship's officers came up. He looked round, saw the lay of things. He was not happy. He glanced at me. I half drew my bow. He cringed.

I laughed. Old Barley giggled. The crew took it up.

We were not kind people. We enjoyed tormenting our captives.

Again Colgrave gave me that little headshake. A nasty grin smeared his face too. He liked my joke.

More of them came. And more, and more.

"Mica, they're all coming over."

"Looks like."

They stood on the main deck, nervously watched Colgrave.

"Slide back and tell the Old Man we can sneak down and knock a hole in their bottom when they're all up here. If he wants."

Mica grinned. "Yeah." It was his kind of dirty trick. He liked sneaking.

I expect his sins involved some fancy sneakiness. He wasn't chicken, mind. Just the kind of guy who sees the advantages of back-stabbing. A low-risk type guy. He could handle himself face-to-face, when the stakes were high. He shoved through the strangers. They twisted away from him like he was a plague carrier.

I watched a grin spread across Colgrave's battered face. It was as lopsided as the altars of Hell. The muscles only worked on one side.

He liked it. My suggestion did not violate his inexplicable armistice with the creature in red.

Mica almost danced back to the forecastle.

The sorcerer boarded last. Its crew surrounded it. It disappeared among them. They were all bigger.

I laughed, catching the creature's attention. I again half drew my bow.

It looked at me with no apparent fear, but I knew better. I knew I could take the sorcerer if just one instant's gap opened through those bodyguards.

We had not been stripped of our defenses. I could get an arrow from here to there quicker than the creature could blink.

It knew too. That was why it had brought its whole crew. In the time it would take us to kill them, it could perform the sorceries needed to save itself.

It, too, concentrated on Colgrave.

The Old Man's eye flicked my way just once, for a tenth of a second.

Mica and I rolled over the rail into the ratlines, transferred to the other vessel's stays, got down to her deck in seconds.

"Bowman, you see about sinking her. I'll go through the cabin."

"Good thinking. But look for something besides loose gold."

He gave me a look.

I looked back. Gold was Mica's weakness. Whenever we took a ship, he spent most of the celebration scrounging gold and silver. He brought it back, and we took it down and put it in ballast, never knowing what we would ever do with it.

That was one tough little ship. It took me twenty minutes to chop a decent hole through her thin planking. By the time I finished I knew she would not sink before the strangers could get back aboard.

I chuckled. That made the joke richer.

I hustled back topside. We were taking too long. "Mica!" I called softly. "Come on. We haven't got all day."

He poked his head out the deckhouse door. "Here. Take some of this crap."

He had gotten some gold, of course. But not much. The rest seemed to be books, papers, and the thing-gobbies sorcerers have to have to be comfortable doing their nasties.

VII

I rolled over *Dragon*'s rail expecting all eyes to be looking my way.

None were. None did. The strangers were crowded against the base of the poop. Colgrave stood above them, a mocking smile on half his face. Everybody stared at him like he was some demon god.

Sometimes I thought he was myself.

The men were impatient. The strangers felt it. Their fear was about to become panic. Only the will of the creature in red kept them from running.

Mica handed up our plunder. I concealed it beneath a spritsail lying on the forecastle deck. Mica rolled over the rail.

Colgrave's glance flicked our way. His smile stretched. He terminated the audience with a shrug and a turned back.

The creature in red started back to its vessel. Its followers surged around it, eager to be gone.

I half drew my bow for the third time.

The creature in red smiled at me.

That made me mad. I would have let fly had Colgrave not shook his head. Nobody mocked the Bowman. . . .

Then they were gone, their vessel turning away and heading back whence it had come. They stood around watching us, as if to make sure we did not change our minds about letting them go.

Their ship was a foot lower in the water already. Soon they would realize that she was not responding properly. They would discover the hole. . . .

I had cut it too big for them to keep afloat by pumping. And I doubted that they would be able to get a good patch on it. I slapped Mica's back. "Let's take the stuff to the Old Man."

It was not a chore that pleased me. Though it was unavoidable, I plain did not like being anywhere near Colgrave. But with Student gone, he was the only reader left aboard.

Anyway, he needed to know what we had. If anything.

He stirred through the pile. Mica's personal plunder he pushed to one side. Mica took it below. The rest Colgrave sorted into three piles. A half-dozen items he just flipped over his shoulder, over the rail, into the sea. Then he examined the piles again. He deep-sixed several more items.

Toke, Tor, and I watched in silence. Colgrave kept dithering, poking. I don't think he knew what he had. But Colgrave was not the kind to admit ignorance.

Finally, I could stand no more. "What did they want?" I demanded.

"The usual," Colgrave replied without looking up. "A little murder. A little terror. With his enemies on the bull's-eye, of course. Not ours."

"His?"

"I think it was a he. You cut a big hole, Bowman?"

"Big enough. It'll stop them." He seemed so damned blasé after what had been done to us. Was he still trusting in divine protection? After the Itaskian sorcerer? If so, he was a fool.

That was one thing that had never been pinned on Colgrave.

"Tor, go to the masthead. Let us know when they go dead in the water. Toke, make sail for Freyland. I think she'll respond now."

I watched while Colgrave examined several books. He seemed awfully undignified, sitting on the deck with his legs crossed. Finally, "Captain, what're we going to do?"

He peered at me with that one evil eye till I thought he was going to have me thrown to the sharks. One did not address Colgrave. Colgrave called one to the presence.

He finally replied, "It would be a raid to belittle anything we've ever tried. Portsmouth itself. Burn the docks. Burn the town. Kill everybody we can."

"Why?"

"I didn't ask, Bowman." His voice was cold and hard. He was tired of my questions. Yet I remained where I was. He *had* changed. He was more open than ever I had seen. "He ordered us. We haven't yet tested the limits of his control. We may not be able to do otherwise."

"And we do have our grievances."

"Yes. We have scores to settle with Portsmouth."

Dragon shifted her heading to north-northeast. We were on course for the island kingdoms.

"The little sail maker must have missed something," Colgrave said. "There's nothing here we can use. All we can do is deny this stuff to him."

"She's taking in sail, Captain," Tor called down. A vast amusement filled his voice.

The story had passed through the crew, spread by Mica. There was a lot of laughter.

I looked north. I could barely make out the other vessel.

Damn, did that Tor have eyes.

Excellent eyes. "Sail ho!" he called a moment later. "She's a big one. War galleon, by her look."

His arm thrust aft. Colgrave and I turned.

We could just make out her maintops. I looked at Colgrave.

I could see the torment in him. The need. . . . He had to have bloodshed the way I had to have rum, had to use my bow.

"She's an Itaskian," Tor called a few minutes later. The bloodlust filled his voice. He, too, needed the killing.

Nervousness and uncertainty washed the main deck. The men no longer had the absolute confidence that had impelled them before our capture.

Dragon had changed indeed. And was changing still.

"Maintain your heading, First Officer," Colgrave finally croaked.

It tore him up to say it, but he did.

A breeze came up. It took us on our port quarter, setting us to landward. The more we turned to seaward, the harder it blew.

The smell of wizardry tainted it.

Colgrave gathered Mica's plunder, took it to his cabin, then returned to the poop. He said nothing more. The stubborn Colgrave of old, he kept *Dragon*'s course inalterably fixed on Freyland.

We passed within three hundred yards of the sorcerer's ship. Its crew were too busy keeping from drowning to pay attention. Several called for help. We sailed on.

Colgrave laughed at them. I'm sure his voice carried that far.

The breeze died soon afterward, as the other ship began going under. I guess the wizard needed to concentrate on surviving.

One round for us.

We took orders from nobody. Not even those who pretended to be our saviors.

That is what Tor said the thing in red claimed when it had spoken to Colgrave. It had wanted to bargain.

To bargain? I thought. Then its hold on us could not be as strong as it would like.

I smiled. And stood on the forecastle looking forward to the coasts of Freyland. It had been a long time since we had sailed them.

The black birds circled overhead. After a time, one by one, they settled into our tops. They seemed less outraged than they had been.

VIII

Spring had only recently conquered the western shores of Freyland. The cove where we anchored was surrounded by low, forested hills blushing green. The afternoons were warm and lazy.

There was nothing to do. For the first time since I had come aboard. *Dragon* was in perfect repair. Half the ship's work being done was stuff Toke and Lank Tor conjured up because they did not have anything to do either. For several days we just plain loafed.

But in the background lurked the nagging questions, the aching doubts. What would Colgrave decide? Would it be the right thing?

"Right thing?" Mica demanded. Pure amazement animated his features. "What the hell kind of question is that, Bowman?"

He and I and Priest had rigged us a couch of folded sail and were lying back staring at cloud castles while dangling fishing lines over the side. Fishing was something I had not done since boyhood.

I could not remember that far back. I just knew that I had liked to fish.

"It's a valid question," Priest insisted. "We have come to the crossroads of righteousness, Sailmaker. We stand at the forking of the way. . . ."

"Oh, knock it off, Priest," I grumbled. "Don't you ever give up?"

"I think I got a bite," he replied.

"Take it easy, Bowman," Mica said. "He's getting better."

That he was, I had to admit. I used to loathe Priest because he insisted on being our conscience while remaining one of the worst sinners himself.

Priest dragged a small fish over the side. "I'll be damned."

"Doubtless. We're all damned. We have been for ages."

"That's debatable. I meant the fish."

It was a little speckled sand shark about sixteen inches long. Not exactly what we were after. I started to smash its head with my heel.

"Why don't you just throw it back?" Mica asked. "It ain't hurting nothing."

Trouble was, the shark did not want to go. Not with our help. Its little jaws kept going chompity-chomp. Its skin sandpapered the hide off my fingers when I tried to hold it so Priest could get his hook back.

It died before we could save it.

"You was talking about doing the right thing," Mica told me. "What made you say that? I've never heard the Bowman talk that way before."

I gave him a look.

Priest took his side. "He's right. Colgrave's the only man here meaner than the Bowman."

I did not agree. At least, I had never thought of it that way. I rated Priest and Old Barley meaner than me any day.

The Kid came up and joined us. He had been keeping a low profile lately. He seemed to be completely tied up inside himself. Ordinarily, he was our number-one showoff, our number-one mouth man.

I was at the end of the sail couch. He sat down beside me.

Amazing.

I kind of liked the Kid. Really. He reminded me of myself when I was younger. But he had no use for me. I never understood, unless it was true that I looked like somebody he had hated before coming aboard.

"Hey, Bowman. What do you think?" he asked.

"Hunh? About what, Kid?" Why was he asking me? Anything.

"About this. About us coming back." He sat up, started making himself a fishing line of his own. He fumbled around. It was obvious that he had never fished in his life. I helped him get it right.

And I asked him why he was asking me.

"Because you're the smart guy now that Student's gone. Toke. Lank Tor. They're just zombies. And the Old Man wouldn't give me the time of day if I begged."

"Kid. Kid. I. . . ." I let it drift off unsaid.

"What?"

I forced it. "I never much cared about anybody. But it hurts me to see you here, so young."

He looked at me strangely, then smiled. That smile was worth a ton of gold. "I earned it, Bowman."

"Didn't we all?" Mica mused.

"That we did," Priest declared. "The sins on our souls. . . ." He shut himself off, said instead, "The question is, are we going to go right on deserving it?"

Mica got a bite. He hauled in another goddamned shark. This one was more cooperative. Or we had gotten better at handling them.

"Kid, I don't know what to think. That's the gospel. I'm lost. I go half crazy worrying about it sometimes."

A body plopped down the other side of Kid. I glanced over. It was the Trolledyngjan, the final addition to our mad crew. We had picked him up off an Itaskian warship we had taken in our next-to-last battle. He had been confined to her brig.

He had a name, Torfin something, but nobody ever used it. He was one long drink of silence. I don't think he had spoken twenty words the whole time he had been aboard. He did not say anything now. He just looked at me and Mica.

We had tried to kill him once. Before he had become part of our crew. Back when we were raiders. We had attacked his ship. He had tried boarding us. Me and Mica had dumped him into the drink.

And then he had turned up aboard the Itaskian, and Colgrave had decided he ought to replace Student or Whaleboats.

A treaty of forgiveness passed between us without words being spoken.

The Trolledyngjan said, "There be tales told in the Fatherland of the *Oskorei*. The Wild Hunt. They be souls of the damned who ride Hell's stallions through the high range hunting the living."

The Kid passed him a hook and some line. He started fiddling with it.

"What're you driving at?" I asked.

"We be the *oskoreien* of the sea." He baited his hook and flipped it over the side. We waited. Finally, he continued. "They tell of the Wild Hunt that they be hating none so much as they be hating one another."

We waited some more. But that was all he had to say.

It was enough. It made me think.

He had stated a truth and posed a question in a characteristically oblique Trolledyngjan manner.

Hatred had always been the one shared, unifying emotion aboard *Dragon*. And we hated each other more than any outsiders.

Only, we were getting along now. More or less.

The others saw it too. Even the Kid. "What's it mean, Bowman?" the boy asked.

"I don't know."

The changes were progressing. I no longer knew myself. If ever I had.

Fat Poppo laboriously clambered to the forecastle deck. His appearance was another declaration of how the crew regarded me.

"Welcome to the philosophy klatch, Poppo," I said. "What brings you dragging your ass all the way up off the main deck?" He seldom moved if he did not have to, so fat and lazy was he.

He dropped to his knees behind me, whispered, "In the trees across the cove. Under the big dead one you guys been calling the hanging tree."

I looked. And I saw what he meant.

There were four of them, and they wore livery. Soldiers.

The honeymoon was over. "Mica, slide down and dig up the Old Man. Tell him to take a gander at what we've got under the hanging tree. Try to keep it casual."

Colgrave had been holed up in his cabin since we had dropped anchor. He was studying the wizard's things. He would not appreciate being disturbed.

But this was important.

Maybe I made a mistake. The rest of us might not have been recognized. We were well-known, but there was nothing really unique about our appearances. Not the way Colgrave's was unique.

I reached for my bow and quietly strung it behind the mask of the railing.

IX

Colgrave strode from his cabin dressed for a day at court. Mica dogged along behind him as he climbed to the poop. He turned his one grim eye on our watchers.

"The dead captain!"

It carried clearly over the water. Brush crackled. I leapt to my feet and pulled an arrow to my ear.

"It's them! That's the Archer!"

"Bowman. Let them run."

I relaxed. Colgrave was right. Wasting arrows had no point. I could not get them all. Not through the trees.

Still, a gesture seemed necessary.

One turned, stared back through a small opening in the foliage. He bore a spade-shaped shield. A griffin rampant was its device. I let fly with a waste arrow, a practice arrow. It pierced the griffin's eye.

I still had it. After however long it had been, my shafts still flew true.

The soldier's jaw dropped. I bowed mockingly.

"That wasn't smart," Priest told me.

"Couldn't help myself. I had to do it."

The black birds above cursed me in their squawky tongue. I glared my defiance.

My archery was my one skill, my one way of defying the universe and its perversity. The gesture had been important to me. It was a statement that the Bowman existed, that he was well, that his aim was still deadly. It was a graffito on the walls of time, screaming I AM!

Colgrave beckoned.

I shook in my sea boots. I was going to catch hell for defying orders. . . .

But he did not mention my shot. Instead, he gathered Toke, Lank Tor, and myself, and told us, "The decision is at hand. Within two days the whole island will know we've returned. They'll know in Portsmouth in three days, in Itaskia in four. They won't endure us anymore. Our return will scare them so much that they'll send out every ship they have. They won't trust warlocks this time. They'll destroy us absolutely, with fire, at whatever cost we demand."

He stared at the western sea, his one good eye gazing on sights the rest of us could never see. He said again, "At whatever cost we demand."

Tor giggled. Fighting was his only love, his only joy. He did not care whether he would win or lose, only that he would be able to swing a blade in another battle. He was the same old Tor. I did not think there was anything in him capable of change. He was a hollow man.

Toke said, "There's no hope, then? We have to depart this plain memorialized by mountains of dead men and seas scattered with burning ships?"

I sighed. "There's nowhere to run, Toke. Destiny's winds have blown us into the narrow channel. We can't do anything but ride the current."

Colgrave looked at me strangely. "That's odd talk from you, Bowman."

"I feel odd, Captain."

"There's still the sorcerer who recalled us," he said. "And we aren't forgotten of the gods. Not completely." He glanced at the black birds.

The creatures strained their necks toward us.

I surveyed my long-time home. Forward, against the base of the forecastle, I could discern a tiny, almost invisible patchlet of dark fog. I had not noticed it since the day the sorcerer had boarded us. I imagined it had always been there, unnoticed because it stayed behind the corner of my vision.

"I'll give my orders in the morning," Colgrave declared. "For today, celebrate. Our final celebration, Tor. See to the arms. Toke, tell Barley to use his keys."

My guts snapped into an agonized knot. Rum. . . !

"We'll sail at dawn," the Old Man told us. "Be ready. I'll tell you our destination then."

He scanned us once with that wicked eye, and it seemed that there was pain and care in his gaze. He left us there, stunned, and returned to his cabin.

Emotion? In Colgrave? It was almost too much to bear.

I returned to the forecastle and plopped my ass down between the Kid and Little Mica. I leaned back and stared at the clouds, at the green hills where four terrified soldiers were racing to unleash the hounds of doom. "Damned!" I muttered. "Damned. Damned. Damned."

The Kid was first to ask, "What did you say, Bowman?"

I glared at the hills as if my gaze could drop those Freylanders in their tracks. "We sail with the morning tide. He hasn't decided where or why."

The Trolledyngjan hooked a sand shark. We went through the routine, dumped it back.

"Think it's the same one?" Priest asked. "It don't look any different."

"Why would it keep coming back?" Mica wanted to know.

The Kid asked me, "What do you think he'll decide, Bowman?"

"To spill blood. He's still Colgrave. He's still the dead captain. He only knows one way. The only question is who he'll go after."

"Oh."

"Give me a line." I baited my hook and flipped it over the rail. "Priest, Barley's passing out grog." I needed a drink something cruel. But I was not going to give in first.

I watched the torment in his face. And he watched it in mine as he replied, "Don't think so, Bowman. Too far to walk. Besides, I'm getting a nibble."

He got the nibble, but I caught the fish. It was the same damned shark. What was the matter with that thing? Couldn't it learn?

Dragon rocked gently on quiet swells. A breeze whispered in the trees surrounding the cove. We kept catching that sand shark and throwing it back, and not saying much, while the sun dribbled down to the horizon behind us.

✗

Toke, Lank Tor, and I clambered up to the poop. The crew gathered on the main deck, their eyes on the Old Man's cabin door. The sun had not yet cleared the hills to the east.

"Tide's going to turn soon," Toke observed.

"Uhm," I grunted.

Lank Tor shuffled nervously. The blood-eagerness in him seemed tempered by something else this morning. Had the changes begun to reach even him?

Colgrave came forth.

The crew gasped.

Tor, Toke, and I leaned over the poop rail to see why.

He wore old, battered, plain clothing. It was the sort a merchant captain down on his luck might wear. There wasn't a bit of color or polish on him.

A new Colgrave confronted us. I was not sure I liked it. It made me uneasy, as if the man's style of dress were the root of our failures and successes.

He ignored everybody till he had reached the poop and surveyed his surroundings. Then, "Make sail, First Officer. North along the coast, two points to seaward. They're watching. Let them think we're bound for North Cape."

Toke and Tor went to get anchor and sails up. I stood beside Colgrave searching the shore for this morning's watchers.

He said, "We'll keep this heading till we're out of sight of land. Then we'll come round and run south. We'll stay in the deep water."

I shuddered. We were not deep-water sailors. Though hardly any of us had set foot on dry land in years, we did not want to let it out of sight. Few of us had been sailors before fate shanghaied us onto this devil ship.

And deep water meant heavier seas. Seas meant seasickness. My stomach was in bad enough shape, having had no rum.

"What then?" I asked.

"Portsmouth, Bowman."

"The wizard wins? *Dragon* runs to his beck? We do his murders for him?"

"I don't know, Bowman. He's the crux. He's the answer. Whatever happens, it'll revolve around him. He's in Portsmouth. We'll take our questions to him."

There was uncertainty in Colgrave's voice. He, the megalithic will round which my universe turned, no longer knew what he was doing. He just knew that something had to be done.

"But Portsmouth? You're sure?"

"He's there. Somewhere. Masquerading as something else. We'll find him." There was no doubt in him now. He had selected a course. Nothing would turn him aside.

I could not fathom Colgrave's thinking. He wanted to take *Dragon* into the very den of our enemies? Just to confront that sorcerer again? It was pure madness.

No one had ever accused Colgrave of being sane. Only the once had he come out a loser.

We sailed north. We turned and ran south once Tor could no longer discern land from the maintop. A steady breeze scooted us along. By nightfall, according to Toke, we had come back south of the southernmost tip of Freyland. But Colgrave did not alter course till next morning. Several hours after dawn he ordered a change to a heading due east.

He shifted course a point this way, a point that as we sailed along. He had Toke and Tor put on or take off canvas.

A plan was shaping in his twisted mind.

Time lumbered along. The sun set, and it rose. Tension built up till we were all ready to snap. Tempers flared. Some of the old hatred returned. We were not very tolerant of one another.

The sun set again.

I had seen Colgrave's matchless dead reckoning before. I was not overwhelmed when he brought *Dragon* into the mouth of the Silverbind Estuary with the same accuracy I showed in speeding a shaft to its target.

We were all dismayed. To a man we had hoped that he would change his mind, or that something would change it for him.

We had not seen one ship during our time at sea.

They had taken our false trail for true. The fleet had cleared Portsmouth only that morning, heading north in hopes of catching us in the wild seas between Freyland and Cape Blood. The only vessels we saw now, as we eased along the nighted Itaskian coast, were fishing boats drawn up on 'the beaches for the night.

Watch fires burned along the Estuary's north shore. They winked at us as if secretly blessing our surreptitious passage.

Those winks conveyed messages. A steady flow were coming from the north. Fat Poppo tried reading them but the Itaskians had changed their codes since he had been in their navy.

No one noticed our little caravel creeping along through the moonless night.

The lights of Portsmouth appeared on our starboard bow. Little bells tinkled over the water ahead. Poppo softly announced that he had spotted the first channel-marker buoy.

Its bell pinged happily in the gentle swell.

Colgrave sent Tor to the forecastle to watch the markers.

He meant to try the impossible. He meant to take *Dragon* up the channel by starlight.

Colgrave's confidence in his destiny was justified. *Dragon* was surely a favored charity of the gods that night. The breeze was absolutely perfect for creeping from one bell buoy to the next. The current did not bother us at all.

We penetrated the harbor basin two hours after midnight. Perfect timing. The city was asleep. Colgrave warped *Dragon* in to a wharf with a precise beauty that only a sailor could appreciate.

Fear had the ship by the guts. I was so rattled that I don't think I could have hit an elephant at ten paces. But there I was on the forecastle, ready to cover the landing party.

Priest, Barley, and the Trolledyngjan jumped to the wharf. They searched the darkness for enemies. Mica and the Kid jumped. Others threw them mooring lines. They made fast in minutes. The gangplank went down for the first time in anyone's memory. Toke and Tor started ushering the men ashore. Tor made sure they were armed.

Some did not want to go.

I was one. I had not set foot on any land in so long that I could not remember what it was like. . . . And this was the country of my birth. This was the land of my crimes. This land loved me no more, nor wanted its sacred soil defiled by the tread of my murderer's feet. . . .

Nor did I want to do any sorcerer's bloodletting.

Colgrave beckoned.

I had to go. I relaxed my grip on my bow, descended to the main deck, crossed to the gangplank.

Only the Old Man and I remained aboard. Toke and Tor were trying to maintain order on the wharf. Some of the men were trying to get back to the ship, to escape stable footing and everything that land meant. Others had fallen to their knees and were kissing the paving stones. Some, like Barley, just stood and shook.

"I don't want to return, either, Bowman," Colgrave whispered. "My very being whines and pules. But I'm going. Now march."

The old fire was in his eyes. I marched.

He had not changed clothing. He still wore rags and tatters. Following me down the gangplank, he looped a piece of cloth across his features the way they do in the deserts of Hammad al Nakir.

Colgrave's presence made the difference. The men forgot their emotions. Toke quickly arranged them in a column of fours.

A late drunk staggered out of the darkness. "Shay. . . ." he mumbled. "What're. . . . Who're. . . ." He almost tripped over me and Colgrave.

He was an old man young. A beggar, by his look, and a cripple. He had only one arm, and one leg barely functioned. He reeked of cheap, sour wine. He stumbled against me again. I caught him.

"Thanks, buddy," he mumbled. His breath was foul.

My god, I thought. This could be me if I keep on the grog. . . . I forced honesty. I was looking at what I had been when I had committed my murders, and most of the time since.

All I could see was ugliness.

The drunk stared at me. His eyes grew larger and larger. He glanced over the crew, peered at the Old Man.

A long, terrified whine, like the plea of a whipped cur, ripped from his throat.

"Priest!" the Old Man snapped.

Priest materialized.

"This man recognizes us. Man, this is Priest. Do you know him, too? You do? Good. I'm going to ask some questions. Answer them. Or I'll let Priest have you."

The drunk became so terrified that for several minutes we could pry no sense from him at all.

He did know us. He had been a sailor aboard one of the warships that had helped bring us to our doom. He had been one of the few lucky survivors. He remembered the battle as if it had taken place yesterday. Eighteen years and a sea of alcohol had done nothing to erase the memories.

Eighteen years! I thought. More than half my lifetime. . . . The life I had lived before boarding *Vengeful D.* The whole world would have changed.

Colgrave persisted with his questions. The old sailor answered willingly. Priest shuffled nervously.

Priest had been the great killer, the great torturer, back when. He had loved it. But the role did not fit him anymore.

Colgrave learned what he wanted. At least, he learned all the drunk had to tell. A moment of decision arrived. The old sailor recognized it before I did. It was the moment when a man should have died, based on our record.

A black bird squeaked somewhere in *Dragon*'s rigging.

"There is a ship at the wharf," Colgrave said. "Barley! The keys." Barley came. Colgrave gave the keys to the drunk. He stared at them as if they fit the locks in the one-way gates of Hell.

"You will board that ship," Colgrave told him. His tone denied even the possibility that his will might be challenged. "You will stay there, drinking the rum behind the lock those keys fit, till I give you leave to go ashore."

The watchbird squawked again. Excited wings punished the night air.

Fog started drifting in from the Estuary. Its first tendrils reached us.

The drunk looked at Colgrave, stunned. His head bobbed. He ran toward *Dragon.*

XI

"Bowman, come," Colgrave said. "You've been to Portsmouth before. You'll have to show me the way to the Torian Hill."

I did not remember ever having been to Portsmouth. I told him so, and suggested that Mica be his guide. Mica was always talking about Portsmouth. Mostly about its famous whorehouses, but sometimes about its people and their strange mores.

"You will remember," Colgrave told me. He used the same tone that he had directed at the drunk.

I remembered. Not much, but enough to show him the way to the Torian Hill, which was the area where the mercantile magnates and high nobility maintained their urban residences.

Dawn launched its assaults upon the eastern horizon, though in the fog we were barely aware of it. We began to encounter early risers. Some instinct made them avoid us.

We passed out of the city proper, into the environs of the rich and powerful. Portsmouth was not a walled city. There were no gates to pass, no guards to answer.

We broke from fog into dawn light halfway up the Torian Hill.

It was not like I remembered it. Mica's expression confirmed my feeling.

"There's been a war pass this way," he said. "Only a couple years ago."

It was obvious. They were still picking up the pieces. "Where are we going?" I asked Colgrave.

"I don't know. This's the Torian Hill?" Mica and I both nodded.

Colgrave dug round inside his rags, produced a gold ring.

"Hey!" Mica complained. "That's. . . ." He shut up.

A glance from Colgrave's eye could chill the hardiest soul.

"What is it?" I asked Mica.

"That's my ring. I took it off the wizard's ship. He said I could have it. I put it down in the ballast with my other things."

"Must've been more than just gold."

"Yeah. Must have been." He eyed Colgrave like a guy trying to figure how best to carve a roast.

He would not *do* anything. We all had those thoughts sometimes. Nobody ever tried.

Colgrave forced the ring onto a bony little finger, closed his eyes.

We waited.

Finally, "That way. The creature is there. It sleeps."

I caught the change from *he* to *it*. What had changed Colgrave's mind? I did not ask. During the climb he had become the mad captain again.

People began to notice us. They did not recognize us, but we were a piratical crew. They got the hell away fast.

Some were women. We had not laid hands on women in ages. . . .

"Sailmaker." Colgrave said it softly. Mica responded as though he had been lashed. He forgot women even existed, let alone the one he had begun stalking.

We came to a mansion. It skulked behind walls that would have done a fortified town proud. The stone was gray, cold limestone still moist from the fog.

"Bowman, you knock." He waved everyone against the wall, out of view of the gateman's peephole.

I pounded. And pounded again.

Feet shuffled behind the heavy gate. The shield over the peephole slid aside. An old man's eye glared through. "What the hell you want?" he demanded sleepily.

Colgrave dropped the cloth concealing his face. "Open the gate." He used the voice that had made Mica forget a skirt, that had driven a drunk aboard *Dragon.*

The old man croaked, "Gah. . . . Gah. . . ."

"Open the gate," Colgrave told him.

For a moment I did not think that he would.

The gate creaked inward an inch.

Colgrave hit it with his shoulder. I lunged through after him, nocking an arrow. Colgrave seized the gateman's shirt, demanded, "Where us he? The thing in red?"

I do not think he knew the answer. But he talked.

Something growled. Barley eased past us and opened the mastiff's skull with a brutal sword stroke. Priest silenced a second growler.

Men charged toward us from behind shrubbery, from behind trees. They had no intention of talking things over. They had blades in their hands and murder on their minds.

Yet it was not an ambush. Ambushers do not pull their pants on as they attack.

"I don't think we be welcome," the Trolledyngjan drawled laconically.

I sped a half-dozen arrows. Men dropped. The crew counter-charged the rest.

"Do it quietly!" Colgrave ordered.

They did. Not a word was spoken. Not a warcry disturbed the morning song birds. Only the clang of blades violated the stillness.

I sped a couple more arrows. But the men did not need my help. They had the defenders outnumbered. I turned to Colgrave.

He had the gatekeeper babbling. Aside, he told me, "Lock the gate." I did.

"Come on, Bowman." Colgrave stalked toward the mansion. He left the gatekeeper lying in a widening lake of blood.

A black bird scolded from the limestone wall.

This was the Colgrave of old. This was the mad captain who killed without thought or remorse, who fed on the agony and fear of his victims. . . .

The creature in red was not going to be pleased with him.

I recovered my spent arrows, running from victim to victim so I could keep up with the Old Man. I recognized some of the dead. They had crewed the sorcerer's ship.

The thing they dreaded had overtaken them after all.

"Where are we headed?" I asked Colgrave.

"Cellars. The thing's got to be hiding under the house somewhere."

"Hey! What's going on?" A sleepy, puzzled, powerfully built gentleman of middle years had come onto the mansion's front porch. He still wore his night clothes. Servants peeped fearfully from the doorway behind him.

I never found out who he was. Somebody important. Somebody who had thought he could get the world by the ass if he allied his money and political pull with the magical might of the creature in red. Somebody driven by greed and addicted to power. Somebody laboring under the false impression that his mere presence would be enough to cow low-life rogues like ourselves. Somebody who did not know that deals with devils never come out.

He was in for a big disappointment quick. Nobody faced Colgrave down.

The Old Man grabbed him exactly the way he had grabbed the gateman. The man lunged, could not break Colgrave's hold. "The thing in your cellar. What is it?"

The man's struggles ceased. He became as pale as a corpse. "You know?" he croaked. "That's impossible. Nobody knows. He said that nobody would ever find out. . . ."

"He did? Who is he? What is he?" Aside, "Tor. Toke. Surround the house. Be ready to fire it if I call."

"No! Don't burn. . . ."

"Colgrave does whatever he damn well pleases. Answer me. Where is he? Why did he call us back. . . ?"

"Colgrave?"

"Colgrave. Yes. That Colgrave."

"My God! What has he done?"

I bowed mockingly. "They call me Bowman. Or the Archer."

He fainted.

The servants scattered. Their screams dwindled into the depths of the house.

"Priest. Barley. Mica. Bowman. Trolledyngjan. Come with me." Colgrave stepped over our host, into the house.

"Catch one of the servants."

Mica came up with one in seconds. She was about sixteen. His leer betrayed his thinking.

"Not now," Colgrave growled.

Mica, too, was reverting.

"Girl," Colgrave said, "show us the way to the cellar."

Whimpering, she led us to the kitchens.

"Barley, you go down first."

Barley took a candle. He was back in a minute. "Wine and turnips, Captain."

"Girl, I'll give you to Mica if. . . ."

Something screeched. Lamps overturned and pottery broke in a room behind us. I whirled. A black bird waddled into the kitchens.

I said, "She probably doesn't know, Captain. It's probably a hidden doorway."

Hatred flamed from Colgrave's eye when he glanced my way. "Uhm. Probably." He fingered the gold ring he had plundered from Mica's hoard. "Ah. This way."

We surged back into the front rooms. Everyone pounded panels. "Here," said Colgrave. "Trolledyngjan."

The northman swung his ax. Three resounding blows shattered the panel.

A dark, descending stairway lay behind it. I seized a lamp.

"Barley goes first," the Old Man said. "I'll carry the lamp. Bowman. I want you behind me with an arrow ready."

It would be tight for drawing, but I had my orders.

XII

The stair consisted of more than a hundred steps. I lost count around eighty. It was darker than the bottom side of a buried coffin.

Then light began seeping up to meet us. It was a pale, spectral light, like the glow that sometimes formed on our mastheads in spooky weather. Colgrave stopped.

I glanced back up. The servant girl stood limned in the hole through the panel. The waddling silhouette of a black bird squeezed past her legs. Another fluttered clumsily behind her, awaiting its turn.

We went on. The stair ended. An open door faced its foot. The pale light came splashing through, making Barley look like a ghost.

He went on. He was shaking all over. There was nothing in the universe more deadly than a terrified Barley.

Colgrave followed him. I followed Colgrave. Priest, Mica, and the Trolledyngjan crowded us. We spread out to receive whatever greeting awaited us. Barley was a step or two ahead.

The creature in red reposed on a dark basaltic throne. The floor surrounding it had been inscribed with a pentagram of live fire. The signs and sigils defining its angles and points wriggled and gleamed. The floor itself seemed darker than a midnight sky.

This was the source of light. The only source. There were torches atop the red thing's throne, but they were not alight.

The creature's eyes were closed. A gentle smile lay upon its delicate lips.

"Kill it?" I whispered to Colgrave. I bent my bow.

"Wait. Move aside a little and be ready."

Barley started forward, blade rising. Colgrave caught his sleeve.

At the same instant one of the black birds flopped past us, positioned itself in Barley's path.

"We're here," Colgrave said softly, to himself. "So what do we do now?"

He had altered again. Once more he was the mellowed Colgrave. The old Colgrave did not know the word *we*.

"You don't know?" I whispered.

"Bowman, I'm a man of action. Action begets action, till resolution. . . . My goal has been to get here. I haven't thought past that. Now I must. For instance, what happens if we do kill this thing? What happens if we don't? To us, I mean. And to everyone else. Those aren't the kinds of things Colgrave usually worries about."

I understood. Tomorrow had never mattered aboard *Dragon*. Life on that devil ship had been a perpetually frozen Now. Looking backward had been a glance at a foggy place where everything quickly became lost. Looking ahead had consisted of waiting for the next battle, the next victim ship, with perhaps hope for a little rape or drunkenness before we fired her and leaned back to enjoy the screams of her crew. Tomorrow had always been beyond our control, entirely in the hands of whimsical gods.

They had taken remarkable care of us for so long, till they slipped us that left-handed one with the Itaskian sorcerer. . . .

Here we stood at a crossroads. We had to decide on a path, and both went down the back side of a hill. We could only guess which was the better.

If we could even glean a hint of what they were. The trails were virtually invisible from this side of the crest.

"Ready your arrows, Bowman," Colgrave told me. "If he needs it, put the first one between his eyes. Or down his throat. Don't give him time to cast a spell."

"What'll your signal be?"

"You make the decision. There won't be time for signals."

We locked gazes. This was a new Colgrave indeed. Technique was my private province, but the decision to shoot had never been mine.

"Think for *Dragon*," he said. And I realized that that was what *he* was trying to do, and had been for the past several days. And Colgrave was unaccustomed to thinking for or about anyone but himself.

As was I. As was I.

A tremor passed through my limbs. Colgrave saw it. His eyebrows rose in question.

"I'll be all right." I nocked a different arrow. The motion was old and familiar. My hands stopped trembling. "You see?"

He nodded once, jerkily, then spun to face the creature in red.

It remained unchanged. It slept, wearing that insouciant smile. "Wake him up," Colgrave ordered.

Barley started forward.

"Don't enter the pentacle!" the Old Man snapped. "Find another way."

The Trolledyngjan took an amulet from round his neck. "This be having no potency here anyway," he said. He flung it at the sleeper.

It coruscated as it flew. It trailed smoke and droplets of flame. It fell into the sorcerer's lap.

The creature jumped as if stung. Its eyes sprang open. I pulled my arrow to my ear.

Mine were the first eyes it met. It looked down the length of my shaft and slowly settled back to its throne, its hand folded over the amulet in its lap. We had dealt it a stunning surprise, but after that first reaction it hid it well. It turned its gaze from me to Colgrave.

They stared at one another. Neither spoke for several minutes. Time stretched into an eternity. Then the thing in red said, "There is no evading fate, Captain. I see what you mean to do. But you cannot redeem yourself by killing me instead of those whom *I* desire slain. In fact, unless I misread you, you have slain to reach me. Wherefore, then, can you expect redemption?"

His lips were parted a quarter inch, still smiling. They never moved while he spoke. And I was never sure whether I was hearing with my ears or brain.

I do not know what was on Colgrave's mind. The sorcerer's remarks did not deflate him. So I presume that he had seen the paradox already.

"Nor can you win redemption simply through performing acts. There must be sincerity." There was no inflection in his voice, but I swear he was mocking us.

I remembered an old friend who had disappeared long ago. Whaleboats had never been very sincere. Unless he had hidden it damned well.

"The damned can be no more damned than they already are," Colgrave countered. A grim rictus of a smile crossed his tortured face. "Perhaps the not-yet-damned can be spared the horror of those who are."

My eyes never left my target, but my mind ran wild and free. This was Colgrave, the mad captain of the ghost ship? The terror of every man who put to sea? I had known him forever, it seemed, and had never sensed this in him.

We all have our mysterious deeps, I guess. I had been learning a lot about my shipmates lately.

"There is life for you in my service," the sorcerer argued. "There is no life in defying me. What I have once called up I can also banish."

"This be no life," the Trolledyngjan muttered. "We be but *oskoreien* of the sea." Priest nodded.

Barley was poised to charge. Colgrave caught his sleeve lightly. Like the faithful old dog he was, Barley relaxed.

I relaxed too, letting my bow slack to quarter pull. It was one of the most powerful ever made. Even I could not hold it at full draw long.

I stopped watching the sorcerer's eyes. There was something hypnotic about them, something aimed specially at me.

His hands caught my attention. They began moving as he argued with Colgrave, and I ignored his words for fear there would be something compelling hidden in his voice. His hands, too, were playing at treacheries.

I whipped my shaft back to my ear.

His hands dropped into his lap. He stopped talking, closed his eyes.

A wave of power inundated me. The creature was terrified of me! Of *me!*

It was the power I had felt as *Dragon*'s second most famous crewman, while standing on her poop as we bore down on a victim, my arrows about to slay her helmsman and officers. It was the power that had made me the second most feared phenomenon of the western seas.

It was the absolute power of life and death.

And in that way, I soon realized, he was using me too.

I had the power, and he did fear me, but he was playing to my weakness for that power, hoping that it would betray me into his hands. In fact, he was counting on using all our weaknesses. . . .

He was a bold, courageous, and subtle one, that creature in red. Whatever the stakes in his game, he was not reluctant to risk losing. Not one man in a million would have faced *Dragon*'s crew for a chance at an empire, let alone have recalled us from our fog-bound grave.

He spoke again. And again he made weapons of his hands, his eyes, his voice. But he no longer directed them my way.

He chose Barley. It made a certain sense. Barley was the most wicked killer of us all. But I held the power of death, and Barley would have to get past Colgrave and Priest to take it away from me.

He whirled and charged. And the Trolledyngjan smacked the back of his head with the flat of his ax. Barley pitched forward. He lay still. Colgrave knelt beside him, his eye burning with the old hatred as he glared at the creature in red.

I nodded to the Trolledyngjan. I was pleased to see that I was not alone in my awareness of what the sorcerer was doing.

"I think you just made a mistake," Colgrave said.

"Perhaps. Perhaps I'll send you back to your waiting place. There are other means to my ends. But they're much slower. . . ."

"You shouldn't ought to have done that," Priest said. "Barley was my friend."

What? I thought. You never had a friend in your life, Priest.

One of the black birds shrieked warningly. Colgrave reached out. . . .

Too late. Priest's left hand blurred. A throwing knife flamed across the space between himself and the creature in red.

The sorcerer writhed aside. The blade slashed his left shoulder. His left hand rose, a finger pointing. He screamed something.

"Wizard!" I snarled.

And loosed my shaft.

It passed through his hand and smoked away into darkness. He looked down the length of my next shaft. His bloody hand dropped into his lap. Pain and rage seethed in him, but he fought for control. He wadded his robe around his hand.

My gaze flicked to Colgrave. We had a stand-off here. And unless the Old Man did something, that wizard would pick us off one by one. Colgrave had to decide which way to jump.

Colgrave had to? But he had told me. . . . But. . . .

XIII

All the black birds had joined us. They were big. I called them albatrosses, but their size was the only thing they had in common. They lined up between us and the wizard. Their pupilless yellow eyes seemed to take in everything at the same time.

They were doing their damnedest to make sure we knew they were there.

I had always been aware of them. For me they had become as much a part of *Dragon* as Colgrave or myself. What were they? Lurkers over carrion? Celestial emissaries? Sometimes, because I sympathized with their plight, I wanted to make them something more that what they were.

Those sentinels posted by a dead man were as trapped as we. Maybe more than we were. Their exit might be even narrower.

Neither Colgrave nor the creature in red paid them any heed. To those two the birds were squawking nuisances left from another time.

Those squawking nuisances had been trying to guide us since our recall. We had seldom heeded them. Maybe we should have.

Why were they trying to intercede? That had to be beyond their original writ. That, surely, had been but to keep their summoner informed of what was happening amongst *things* he could only banish, not destroy.

I suppose his last-second death compelled them to interpret their mission for themselves.

One squawked and threw itself into the pentagram.

There were sorceries upon that bird. It was nothing of this world. The spells shielding the thing in red were less efficacious against it than they had been against arrow, dagger, or amulet.

Nonetheless, it fell before it reached the sorcerer. The stench of smoldering feathers assailed my nostrils. Smoke boiled off the writhing bird. It emitted some of the most pathetic sounds I had ever heard.

Then, like the bird the sorcerer had downed at sea, it became a snake of smoke and slithered off like black lightning, through air and cellar wall. . . . I presumed.

The thing in red had begun some silent enchantment. We now faced it amidst a vast plain, walled by mists instead of limestone.

A second bird threw itself into the pentacle the instant the first changed and hurtled off.

It penetrated a foot farther. Then a third flopped clumsily forward, achieving perhaps fourteen inches more than the second.

Mica's voice echoed eerily from the mist behind us. "Captain. Bowman. Hurry up. There's a big mob in the street. They're armed. We're in trouble if they break in."

Another bird hurled itself at the sorcerer. This one managed to sink a beak into an ankle.

The sorcerer called down a thunderbolt. It scattered flesh and feathers. Another leapt.

The Old Man said, "Have Toke and Tor gather the men behind the house, Sailmaker. If we're not up in ten minutes, go back to *Dragon*. Tell them not to wait for us. They'll have to clear the Estuary before the fleet gets back from Cape Blood."

"Captain!"

I could read Mica's thoughts. What would they do without Colgrave? *Dragon* would become lifeless without the dead captain's will animating it.

"Do as I say, Sailmaker."

Two black birds threw themselves into the pentacle together. The sorcerer got the first in midair. The second landed in his lap, tearing with beak and talons. They *had* to be driven by more than their original assignment. Maybe the gods were interceding. . . .

Barley clambered to his feet with the Old Man's help. He was groggy. Colgrave dithered round him.

The grumble of a crowd working itself up reached the cellar.

We were in trouble.

"Maybe we ought to run for it," Priest suggested.

Colgrave hit him with that one cold eye. "Colgrave doesn't run." Then, "We have an enemy here." He indicated the thing in red. "He's decided to send us back. We have to stop him. Sixty men counting on us. . . . I don't want any of us to go back. It's forever this time."

"I'll buy that," I muttered. It reflected my thinking of the moment. But I was surprised to hear it from the Old Man. It was not his kind of thinking.

It seemed that the black birds had been trying to stop us from compounding our sins. That was all I could get their admonitory squawks to add to. "Sorry, guys," I murmured. A sin or two looked necessary for the greater welfare.

I did not want to see that quiet, fog-bound sea again. Eighteen years was long enough. The others felt the same.

I could see just one way out of it. Kill the sorcerer in red.

Another murder.

What was one more death on my soul? I asked myself. Not a pennyweight.

The last black bird hurled itself into the pentagram.

The sorcerer was covered with blood, reddening its clothing even more. Pain had destroyed the delicacy of its face. And yet a tiny smile began to stretch its lips again.

I drew to my ear and let an arrow fly.

The others had the same idea at the same instant. The Trolledyngjan hurled his ax. Priest and Barley flung themselves against the waning Power of the pentagram. Colgrave drew his blade and followed at a more casual pace. The Trolledyngjan whipped out a dagger and joined him. My arrow and the Trolledyngjan's ax did not survive the smashing fist of a lightning bolt. Both weapons touched the creature in red, but only lightly.

The last bird became another serpent of night and slithered off to wherever they went when they devolved.

The spells protecting the sorcerer gnawed at Priest and Barley. They screamed like souls in torment.

And kept on.

They were Colgrave's favorite hounds, those two. Because nothing stopped them.

They had been the two most dreaded in-fighters on the western sea.

A continual low moan emanated from the Trolledyngjan. Colgrave made no sound at all. He just leaned ahead like a man striding into a gale, his eye fixed on the sorcerer's throat.

Priest and Barley went down. They writhed the way the birds had. But they kept trying to get to the creature in red. Barley's blade struck sparks from the stone beside the wizard's ankle.

Its smile grew larger. It thought it was winning.

I sped three arrows as fast as I could.

The first did no good at all. The second pinked him lightly. It distracted him for an instant.

His attackers surged at him, threatening to bury him.

I sent my third arrow beneath Colgrave's upraised arm. It buried itself in the creature's heart.

The Old Man's blade fell. It sliced the flesh away from one side of that delicate face.

The thing slowly stood. A mournful wail came from between its motionless lips. The sound rose in pitch and grew louder and louder. I dropped my bow and clapped my hands over my ears.

That did not help. The sound battered me till I ached.

The Trolledyngjan was down with Priest and Barley. I did not expect them to rise ever again.

The creature in red touched Colgrave. My captain started to drop too.

He fell slowly, like a mighty kingdom crumbling.

"Go, Bowman," he told me in a voice that was hardly a whisper, yet which I heard through the sorcerer's wail. "Take *Dragon* back to sea. Save the men."

"Captain!" I seized his arm and tried to drag him away. The thing in red touched him. The touch anchored the Old Man.

"Get the hell out of here!" he growled. "I'll handle him."

"But. . . ."

"That's an order, Bowman."

He was my Captain. These were my comrades. My friends.

"Will you get the hell gone?"

He used the old Colgrave's voice. It was strong. Compelling. I could defy it then no more than ever before. I seized my bow and fled.

XIV

The others had needed little urging to make a run for it. Mica and the Kid were the only ones hanging around when I hit the mansion's door. Not counting the owner and half an army of citizens headed our way.

It was your basic mob. A ravening killer monster made up of harmless shopkeepers. An organism without fear because it knew its components were replaceable.

Mica screeched. "Come on, Bowman! You going to wait till they tie you to a burning stake?"

I was not as numb as I looked. I was looking for the thousand-eyed monster's brain cells. I had eight good arrows left.

But Mica was right. The mob did not have a brain. Random fragments had begun vandalizing the grounds.

I took off round the side of the house.

As we loped along, the Kid asked, "What happened down there? Where's Barley and Priest and the Trolledyngjan and the Old Man?"

"Down there. All gone but the Old Man and the sorcerer. The thing is all chopped up, but it's still alive."

"You left him there?"

"He made me, Kid. You ever win an argument with Colgrave?"

He just grinned.

"Hold up for a second, Bowman," Mica panted. We were in the street now and drawing some startled looks. "What happens when they go?"

"What?"

"Colgrave runs us. What do we do without him? And that wizard called us back. What happens when he dies? To his spells?"

"Oh. Man, I don't know." I was no expert on wizardry. Some sorceries devolved with the death of the sorcerer, and some did not. I could not tell him what he wanted to know.

There were shouts behind us. I wheeled. Part of the mob was after us.

"Let's take them," the Kid said.

There were about twenty of them. For a *Dragon* sailor, protected by the Bowman, the odds did not look bad.

The earth started quivering like a bear in restless slumber. The timbers of nearby buildings creaked.

Our pursuers stopped, looked back.

We could see the steep tiled roofs of the mansion. Cracks lightninged across them. They began sagging, as if some huge invisible hand were pressing downward. . . .

The cracks leaked a black fog that looked first cousin to the one that dogged *Vengeful D.* The breeze did nothing to disperse it.

"Let's hike," I said. "While they're distracted. Maybe we can catch the others."

I was afraid Toke and Tor would sail without us.

Could anger be an absolute? The cloud over the mansion said it could be. I felt it from a quarter-mile away.

That shadow was a being. It echoed the feeling I had been given by the creature in red. I now understood our ambiguous reactions to the sorcerer. He or she had no meaning if the thing were not human at all.

It was not alone. A second being held it in a death grip. That being radiated an absoluteness too, an utter refusal to yield to any other will.

"Colgrave," I whispered.

Colgrave had been a man, of that there was no doubt. But he had been larger than life and animated by a determination so unswerving that it had made him a demigod.

"Children of evil." Mica muttered.

We resumed walking toward the waterfront. No one interfered. We were forgotten.

The Torian Hill shook like a volcano about to give birth.

"What?" I asked.

"We are all children of evil," Mica said.

"What're you talking about?" He was off on some sideways line of thought, saying the obvious and not meaning what he was saying. "Keep stepping. I don't think the Old Man will win this one."

"He already has, Bowman. He's forced that thing to take it's natural form. Look, it's fading. It can't stay here that way."

He was right. The thing was evaporating the way a cloud of steam does. So was the thing created by the will of my Captain.

In minutes they were gone.

There were tears in my eyes. Mine. The Bowman's. And I was the deadliest, coldest, most remorseless killer ever to sail the western seas, excepting only the man for whom my tears fell.

I had hated him with a passion as deep and black and cold as the water in the ocean's deepest deeps. Yet I was weeping for him.

I averted my face from the others.

I had not wept since I did not know when. Maybe after I had killed my wife, when I had been alive and still one of the smaller evils plaguing the world.

We reached *Dragon*. They had the mooring lines in but the gangplank still down. The crew manned the rail. Their eyes were on the hills behind the city. Their faces showed relief when we raced onto the wharf. Then dismay when they realized we three were the last.

They had the drunk at the head of the gangplank, holding him like a hostage against Portsmouth's ill-will.

"The others?" Toke asked.

"They won't be coming," I replied.

"What do we do?"

"You're asking me?" He was First Officer. He should have taken charge.

He looked me in the eye. He did not have to speak to tell me that he was no Colgrave, that he was incapable of commanding *Vengeful Dragon*.

I glanced around. Every eye fixed me with that same expectant stare.

I am the Bowman, I thought. Second only to Colgrave. . . . Second to none, now. "All right. Mica. Take the old guy and leave him on the wharf. Healthy. Tor, stand by to make sail."

Some of them looked at me oddly. Letting the drunk go was not *Dragon's* style.

But *Dragon* had changed. We had learned, just a little, the meaning of pity and mercy.

"Give him something to tell his grandkids," I remarked to Tor, whose disappointment was obvious. He was the most bloodthirsty and unchanged member of the crew.

A breeze rose as the gangplank came in. It was a perfect breeze. It would carry us into the channel at just the right speed. I assumed Colgrave's old place on the poop and peered at the sky. "You still with us?" I murmured.

I started. For an instant I thought I saw faces in the racing clouds. Strange, alien faces with eyes of ice, in which no hint of motivation could be read.

Was this what Colgrave had seen? Had he just looked up whenever he wanted to know if the gods were still with us?

I had a lot to learn if I was going to replace the Old Man. . . . I looked at the clouds again. I saw nothing but clouds. Imagination?

I paused to reflect on the fact that I was the only survivor among *Dragon*'s four greatest evils.

Why? What had they done that I had not? Or was it the reverse?

The crew seemed thin. How many had been redeemed? "Toke, take a muster."

"I have, Captain. We lost five besides those you know. One-Hand Nedo. Fat Poppo. . . ."

"Poppo? Really? He said he knew. . . . I'm glad for him. But we'll miss them all."

"We will, Captain."

Mica's "We are all children of evil" returned to me. I think I understood now. He was stating the reason why I could not understand why some had been redeemed and some not. The evil in us was such that we could not recognize facts laid openly before us. It would take a moment of truth, an instant of revelation, to drive the message home.

I remembered sitting with Priest and Mica and the Kid, fishing, pulling in a sand shark that just could not quit hitting our hooks. I glanced at the clouds and wondered if they would quit trying to teach that stupid shark.

XU

The dividing line between the sea and the Silverbind's flood is as sharp as a pen stroke. Turgid brown against slightly choppy jade. The two do not mix till you are out of sight of land.

Dragon is in the brown, straining toward the green. We have bent on every piece of canvas we can find. Lank Tor is up top yelling things nobody wants to hear.

"Another one, Captain. On the starboard quarter."

Their sails crowd the north. They came back in a hurry.

I try to think like Colgrave. What would he do?

Colgrave would fight. Colgrave always fought.

I try to remember his face. I cannot. The forgetfulness of *Dragon* is at work. Before long he, and the others, will be completely forgotten and we'll have a whole new style.

It is necessary. Colgrave was incapable of backing down. But *Dragon* is no longer invincible. These Itaskians' fathers proved how vincible we are. They just have to be willing to pay an extreme price.

I look at the clouds. "You tired of hauling in the same stupid sharks?"

A distant cloud wears a face for an instant. I swear it sticks out its tongue.

The tongue is lightning. It stabs the sea. "Steer for that," I order. The helmsman shifts our heading.

Another bolt falls. Then another and another. The sky grows dark. The wind picks up. *Dragon* fairly dances toward the sudden foul weather. The sails in the north seem to bounce in anger as this slim chance to escape develops.

"Damn you!" I shake a fist at the sky. For an instant I think I hear mocking laughter.

The seasickness is grinding my entrails already. It will be tearing me apart after we hit the storm.

The gods do have senses of humor. But the level seems to be that which ties the tails of cats for draping over clotheslines.

Lightning bolts are falling like the javelins of a celestial army. The helmsman is nervous. He keeps glancing my way, awaiting the order to turn away. Others join him.

Nobody asks questions.

My predecessor trained them well.

Now the bolts are hitting the sea around us. We have never seen anything like this. . . .

"Tor?"

"They're coming after us, Captain."

Those bold, brave fools. They would be. They know the game well now. They know they have to be as determined as we.

The granddaddy bolt of them all hits the mainmast. Tor shrieks. The mast snaps. Topmen scream. The Kid tumbles through the rigging and hits the main deck with a thud I can hear over the roar of wind and sea. The masts, the spars, the lines and stays all begin to glow. *Dragon* crawls with a pale, cold fire that must be visible for miles.

She rides up a mountainous wave and plunges down its nether side.

Darkness comes, sudden and sharp as a sword stroke.

I am striding across the poop when it does, intending to take a look at the Kid.

I trip into the rail when the light returns as suddenly as it went. I catch myself, look around.

We are in a bank of dense fog. The sea is absolutely still. "Damned! No."

The fog thins quickly. I can see my command.

The men are scattered over the decks, motionless, eyes glassy. I know where we are, what has happened. We have returned to the beginning, and Colgrave's sacrifices were in vain.

The jokes of the gods can be damned cruel.

The fog gives way. We glide into the heart of a circle of lifeless jade sea. Lethargy gnaws at me. It takes all my will to take up my bow so I can use it as a prop on which to lean.

I will not go down. I will not fall. I refuse. *They* do not have the Power....

Dragon eases to a stop and begins revolving slowly in the imperceptible current. The featureless face of the fog slides past. The mist overhead is light sometimes, and sometimes dark. It does not make an exciting day. Before long I lose interest in counting the days.

It will not be long before I cease to think at all.

Till then, I must try to find the answer. What did I do wrong?

SOLDIER OF AN EMPIRE UNACQUAINTED WITH DEFEAT

The following novella was the longest of the published short fiction pieces in the Dread Empire world setting. It is a sidelight involving none of the characters from the several novels. Possibly the best received of all my short fiction, this garnered numerous excellent reviews, was on the Locus *recommended reading list, and was chosen one of the five best novellas of 1980 in the* Locus Readers' Poll. *The world of the Dread Empire is, of course, the most important character of the series. It is always there, always on stage, always a stage, but never to be taken for granted.*

I

His name was Tain and he was a man to beware. The lacquered armor of the Dread Empire rode in the packs on his mule.

The pass was narrow, treacherous, and, therefore, little used. The crumbled slate lay loose and deep, clacking underfoot with the ivory-on-ivory sound of punji counters in the senyo game. More threatened momentary avalanche off the precarious slopes. A cautious man, Tain walked. He led the roan gelding. His mule's tether he had knotted to the roan's saddle.

An end to the shale walk came. Tain breathed deeply, relieved. His muscles ached with the strain of maintaining his footing.

A flint-tipped arrow shaved the gray over his right ear.

The black longsword leapt into his right hand, the equally dark shortsword into his left. He vanished among the rocks before the bowstring's echoes died.

Silence.

Not a bird chirped. Not one chipmunk scurried across the slope, pursuing the arcane business of that gentle breed. High above, one lone eagle floated majestically against an intense blue backdrop of cloudless sky. Its shadow skittered down the ragged mountainside like some frenetic daytime ghost. The only scent on the breeze was that of old and brittle stone.

A man's scream butchered the stillness.

Tain wiped his shortsword on his victim's greasy furs. The dark blade's polish appeared oily. It glinted sullen indigoes and purples when the sun hit right.

Similar blades had taught half a world the meaning of fear.

A voice called a name. Another responded with an apparent, "Shut up!" Tain couldn't be sure. The languages of the mountain tribes were mysteries to him.

He remained kneeling, allowing trained senses to roam. A fly landed on the dead man's face. It made nervous patrols in ever-smaller circles till it started exploring the corpse's mouth.

Tain moved.

The next one died without a sound. The third celebrated his passing by plunging downhill in a clatter of pebbles.

Tain knelt again, waiting. There were two more. One wore an aura of Power. A shaman. He might prove difficult.

Another shadow fluttered across the mountainside, Tain smiled thinly. Death's daughters were clinging to her skirts today.

The vulture circled warily, not dropping lower till a dozen sisters had joined its grim pavane.

Tain took a jar from his travel pouch, spooned part of its contents with two fingers. A cinnamon-like smell sweetened the air briefly, to be pursued by an odor as foul as death. He rubbed his hands till they were thoroughly greased. Then he exchanged the jar for a small silver box containing what appeared to be dried peas. He rolled one pea round his palm, stared at it intently. Then he boxed his hands, concentrated on the shaman, and sighed.

The vultures swooped lower. A dog crept onto the trail below, slunk to the corpse there. It sniffed, barked tentatively, then whined. It was a mangy auburn bitch with teats stretched by the suckling of pups.

Tain breathed gently between his thumbs.

A pale cerulean light leaked between his fingers. Its blue quickly grew as intense as that of the topless sky. The glow penetrated his flesh, limning his finger bones.

Tain gasped, opened his hands. A blinding blue ball drifted away.

He wiped his palms on straggles of mountain grass, followed up with a dirt wash. He would need firm grips on his swords.

His gaze never left the bobbing blue ball, nor did his thoughts abandon the shaman.

The ball drifted into a stand of odd, conical rocks. They had a crude, monumental look.

A man started screaming. Tain took up his blades.

The screams were those of a beast in torment. They went on and on and on.

Tain stepped up onto a boulder, looked down. The shaman writhed below him. The blue ball finished consuming his right forearm. It started on the flesh above his elbow. A scabby, wild-haired youth beat the flame with a tattered blanket.

Tain's shadow fell across the shaman. The boy looked up into brown eyes that had never learned pity. Terror drained his face.

A black viper's tongue flicked once, surely.

Tain hesitated before he finished the shaman. The wild wizard wouldn't have shown him the same mercy.

He broke each of the shaman's fetishes. A skull on a lance he saved and planted like a grave marker. The witch-doctor's people couldn't misapprehend that message.

Time had silvered Tain's temples, but he remained a man to beware.

Once he had been an Aspirant. For a decade he had been dedicated to the study of the Power. The Tervola, the sorcerer-lords of his homeland, to whose peerage he had aspired, had proclaimed him a Candidate at three. But he had never shown the cold will necessary, nor had he developed the inalterable discipline needed, to attain Select status. He had recognized, faced, and accepted his shortcomings. Unlike so many others, he had learned to live with the knowledge that he couldn't become one of his motherland's masters.

He had become one of her soldiers instead, and his Aspirant training had served him well.

Thirty years with the legions. And all he had brought away was a superbly trained gelding, a cranky mule, knowledge, and his arms and armor. And his memories. The golden markings on the breastplate in his mule packs declared him a leading centurion of the Demon Guard, and proclaimed the many honors he had won.

But a wild western sorcerer had murdered the Demon Prince. The Guard had no body to protect. Tain had no one to command. . . . And now the Tervola warred among themselves, with the throne of the Dread Empire as prize.

Never before had legion fought legion.

Tain had departed. He was weary of the soldier's life. He had seen too many wars, too many battles, too many pairs of lifeless eyes staring up with "Why?" reflected in their dead pupils. He had done too many evils without questioning, without receiving justification. His limit had come when Shinsan had turned upon herself like a rabid bitch able to find no other victim.

He couldn't be party to the motherland's self-immolation. He couldn't bear consecrated blades against men with whom he had shared honorable fields.

He had deserted rather than do so.

There were many honors upon his breastplate. In thirty years he had done many dread and dire deeds

The soldiers of Shinsan were unacquainted with defeat. They were the world's best, invincible, pitiless, and continuously employed. They were feared far beyond the lands where their boots had trod and their drums had beaten their battle signals.

Tain hoped to begin his new life in a land unfamiliar with that fear.

He continued into the mountains.

One by one, Death's daughters descended to the feast.

II

The ivory candle illuminated a featureless cell. A man in black faced it. He sat in the lotus position on a barren granite floor. Behind a panther mask of hammered gold his eyes remained closed.

He wasn't sleeping. He was listening with a hearing familiar only to masters of the Power.

He had been doing this for months, alternating with a fellow Aspirant. He had begun to grow bored.

He was Tervola Candidate Kai Ling. He was pursuing an assignment which could hasten his elevation to Select. He had been fighting for the promotion for decades, never swerving in his determination to seize what seemed forever beyond his grasp.

His body jerked, then settled into a tense lean. Little temblors stirred his extremities.

"West," he murmured. "Far, far to the west." The part of him that listened extended itself, analyzed, fixed a location.

An hour passed.

Finally, Kai Ling rose. He donned a black cape which hung beside the nearly invisible door. He smiled thinly behind his mask. Poor Chong. Chong wouldn't know which of them had won till he arrived for his turn on watch.

III

Tain rested, observing.

It seemed a calm and peaceful hamlet in a calm and peaceful land. A dozen rude houses crowded an earthen track which meandered on across green swales toward a distant watchtower. The squat stronghold could be discerned only from the highest hilltops. Solitary shepherds' steads lay sprinkled across the countryside, their numbers proclaiming the base for the regional economy.

The mountains Tain had crossed sheltered the land from the east. The ivory teeth of another gigantic range glimmered above the haze to the north. Tain grazed his animals and wondered if this might be the land he sought.

He sat on a hillside studying it. He was in no hurry to penetrate it. Masterless now, with no fixed destination, he felt no need to rush. Too, he was reluctant. Human contact meant finalization of the decision he had reached months ago, in Shinsan.

Intellectually he knew it was too late, but his heart kept saying that he could still change his mind. It would take the imminent encounter to sever his heartlines home.

It was... *scary*... this being on his own.

As a soldier he had often operated alone. But then he had been ordered to go, to do, and always he had had his legion or the Guard waiting. His legion had been home and family. Though the centurion was the keystone of the army, his father-Tervola chose his companions, and made most of his decisions and did most of his thinking for him.

Tain had wrestled with himself for a year before abandoning the Demon Guard.

A tiny smile tugged his lips. All those thousands who wept on hearing the distant mutter of drums—what would they think, learning that a soldier of the Dread Empire suffered fears and uncertainties too?

"You may as well come out," he called gently. A boy was watching him from the brushy brookside down to his right. "I'm not going anywhere for hours."

Tain hoped he had chosen the right language. He wasn't sure where he had exited the Dragon's Teeth. The peaks to the north, he reasoned, should be the Kratchnodians. That meant he would be in the part of Shara butting against East Heatherland. The nomadic Sharans didn't build homes and herd sheep, so these people would be immigrants from the west. They would speak Iwa Skolovdan.

It was one of four western tongues he had mastered when the Demon Prince had looked westward, anticipating Shinsan's expansion thither.

"I haven't eaten a shepherd in years." An unattended flock had betrayed the boy.

The lad left cover fearfully, warily, but with a show of bravado. He carried a ready sling in his right hand. He had well-kempt blond hair, pageboy trimmed, and huge blue eyes. He looked about eight.

Tain cautioned himself: the child was no legion entry embarking upon the years of education, training, and discipline which gradually molded a soldier of Shinsan. He was a westerner, a genuine child, as free as a wild dog and probably as unpredictable.

"Hello, shepherd. My name is Tain. What town would that be?"

"Hello." The boy moved several steps closer. He eyed the gelding uncertainly.

"Watch the mule. She's the mean one."

"You talk funny. Where did you come from? Your skin is funny, too."

Tain grinned. He saw things in reverse. But this was a land of round-eyes. He would be the stranger, the guest. He would have to remember, or suffer a cruel passage.

Arrogant basic assumptions were drilled into the soldiers of Shinsan. Remaining humble under stress might be difficult.

"I came from the east."

"But the hill people. . . . They rob and kill everybody. Papa said." He edged closer, fascinated by Tain's swords.

"Sometimes their luck isn't good. Don't you have a name?"

The boy relented reluctantly. "Steban Kleckla. Are those swords? Real swords?"

"Longsword and shortsword. I used to be a soldier." He winced. It hurt to let go of his past.

"My Uncle Mikla has a sword. He was a soldier. He went all the way to Hellin Daimiel. That was in the El Murid Wars. He was a hero."

"Really? I'll have to meet your uncle."

"Were you a hero when you were a soldier? Did you see any wars?"

"A few. They weren't much fun, Steban." How could he explain to a boy from this remote land, when all his knowledge was second-hand, through an uncle whose tales had grown with the years?

"But you get to go places and see things."

"Places you don't want to go, to see things you don't want to see."

The boy backed a step away. "I'm going to be a soldier," he declared. His lower lip protruded in a stubborn pout.

Wrong tack, Tain thought. Too intense. Too bitter. "Where's your dog? I thought shepherds always had dogs."

"She died."

"I see. I'm sorry. Can you tell me the name of the village? I don't know where I am."

"Wtoctalisz."

"Wtoctalisz." Tain's tongue stumbled over the unfamiliar syllables. He grinned. Steban grinned back. He edged closer, eying Tain's swords.

"Can I see?"

"I'm sorry. No. It's an oath. I can't draw them unless I mean to kill." Would the boy understand if he tried to explain consecrated blades?

"Oh."

"Are there fish in the creek?"

"What? Sure. Trout."

Tain rose. "Let's see if we can catch lunch."

Steban's eyes grew larger. "Gosh! You're as big as Grimnir."

Tain chuckled. He had been the runt of the Demon Guard. "Who's Grimnir?"

The boy's face darkened. "A man. From the Tower. What about your horse?"

"He'll stay."

The roan would do what was expected of him amidst sorcerers' conflicts that made spring storms seem as inconsequential as a child's temper tantrum. And the mule wouldn't stray from the gelding.

Steban was speechless after Tain took the three-pounder with a casual hand-flick, bear fashion. The old soldier was *fast*.

"You make a fire. I'll clean him." Tain glowed at Steban's response. It took mighty deeds to win notice in the Dread Empire. He fought a temptation to show off.

In that there were perils. He might build a falsely founded, over-optimistic self-appraisal. And a potential enemy might get the measure of his abilities.

So he cooked trout, seasoning it with a pinch of spice from the trade goods in his mule packs.

"Gosh, this's good." As Steban relaxed he became ever more the chatterbox. He had asked a hundred questions already and seldom had he given Tain a chance to answer. "Better than Ma or Shirl ever made."

Tain glowed again. His field cooking was a point of pride. "Who's Shirl?"

"She was my sister."

"Was?"

"She's gone now." There was a hard finality to Steban's response. It implied death, not absence.

IU

Steban herded the sheep homeward. Tain followed, stepping carefully. The roan paced him, occasionally cropping grass, keeping an eye on the mule. For the first time Tain felt at ease with his decision to leave home.

It was unlikely that this country would become his new home, but he liked its people already, as he saw them reflected in Steban Kleckla. He and the boy were friends already.

Steban jerked to a stop. His staff fell as he flung a hand to his mouth. The color drained from his face.

That Aspirant's sense-feel for danger tingled Tain's scalp. In thirty years it had never been wrong. With the care of a man avoiding a cobra, he turned to follow Steban's gaze.

A horse and rider stood silhouetted atop a nearby hill, looking like a black paper cutout. Tain could discern little in the dying light. The rider seemed to have horns.

Tain hissed. The roan trotted to his side. He leaned against his saddle, where his weapons hung.

The rider moved out, descending the hill's far side. Steban started the sheep moving at a faster pace. He remained silent till the Kleckla stead came into view.

"Who was that?" Tain hazarded, when he reckoned the proximity of lights and parents would rejuvenate the boy's nerve.

"Who?"

"That rider. On the hill. You seemed frightened."

"Ain't scared of nothing. I killed a wolf last week."

He was evading. This was a tale twice told already, and growing fast. First time Steban had bragged about having driven the predator away. Then he had claimed to have broken the beast's shoulder with a stone from his sling.

"I misunderstood. I'm sorry. Still, there was a rider. And you seemed to know him."

The lights of Steban's home drew nearer. Boy and sheep increased their pace again. They were late. Steban had been too busy wheedling stories from his new friend to watch the time closely.

"Steban? That you, boy?" A lantern bobbed toward them. The man carrying it obviously was Steban's father. Same eyes. Same hair. But worry had etched his forehead with deep lines. In his left hand he bore a wicked oaken quarterstaff.

An equally concerned woman walked beside him.

Once, Tain suspected, she had been beautiful. In a round-eye sort of way. Doubtlessly, life here quickly made crones of girls.

"Ma. Papa. This's my new friend. His name is Tain. He used to be a soldier. Like Uncle Mikla. He came across the mountains. He caught a fish with his hands and his horse can do tricks, but his mule will bite you if you get too close to her. I told him he should come for supper."

Tain inclined his head. "Freeman Kleckla. Freelady. The grace of heaven descend." He didn't know an appropriately formal Iwa Skolovdan greeting. His effort sounded decidedly odd in translation.

Man and wife considered him without warmth.

"A Caydarman watched us," Steban added. He started coaxing the sheep into pens.

The elder Kleckla scanned the surrounding darkness. "An evil day when we catch their eye. Welcome, then, Stranger. We can't offer much but refuge from the night."

"Thank you, Freeman. I'll pay, that your resources be not depleted without chance of replacement." There was a stiffness about Kleckla which made Tain feel the need to distance with formality.

"This is the Zemstvi, Stranger. Titles, even Freeman and Freelady, are meaningless here. They belong to tamed and ordered lands, to Iwa Skolovda and the Home Counties. Call me Toma. My wife is Rula. Come. I'll show you where to bed your animals."

"As you will. . . Toma." He bowed slightly to the woman. "Rula." She frowned slightly, as if unsure how to respond.

This would be harder than he had anticipated. At home everyone had positions and titles and there were complicated, almost ritualized protocols and honorifics to be exchanged on every occasion of personal contact. "They'll need no fodder. They grazed all afternoon."

One bony milk cow occupied Kleckla's rude barn. She wasn't pleased by Tain's mule. The mule didn't deign to acknowledge her existence.

Toma had no other stock save his sheep. But he wasn't poor. Possessing cow and flock, he was richer than most men. Richer, in some ways, than Tain, whose fortune was in metal of changeable value and a few pounds of rare spice. Which would bring more in the marketplace of the heart?

"You'll have to sleep out here," Toma informed him. "There's no room...."

Tain recognized the fear-lie. "I understand." He had been puzzling the word *zemstvi*, which seemed to share roots with *frontier* and *wilderness*. Now he thought he understood.

"Are you a new Caydarman?" Toma blurted. He became contrite immediately. "Forget that. Tell me about the man you saw."

Because Toma was so intent, Tain cut off all exterior distractions and carefully reconstructed the moment in the manner he had been taught. A good scout remembered every detail. "Big man. On a big horse, painted, shaggy. Man bearded. With horns."

"Damned Torfin." Toma sublimated anger by scattering hay. "He didn't have horns. That was his helmet."

There was a lot to learn, Tain thought. This was an odd land, not like the quiet, mercantile Iwa Skolovda he had studied at home.

He considered the little barn. Its builders had possessed no great skill. He doubted that it was two years old, yet it was coming apart.

"Might as well go eat. It isn't much. Boiled mutton with cabbage and leeks."

"Ah. Mutton. I was hoping." Responding to Toma's surprise, "Mutton is rare at home. Only the rich eat it. Us common soldiers made do with grain and pork. Mostly with grain."

"Home? Where would that be?"

"East. Beyond the Dragon's Teeth."

Toma considered the evasion. "We'd better get inside. Rula gets impatient."

"Go ahead. I have a couple of things to do. Don't wait on me. I'll make do with scraps or leftovers."

Toma eyed him, started to speak, changed his mind. "As you will."

Once Toma departed, Tain pursued the Soldier's Evening Ritual, clearing his heart of the day's burdens. He observed the abbreviated Battlefield Ritual rather than the hour of meditation and exercise he pursued under peaceful circumstances. Later he would do it right.

He started for the door.

His neck tingled. He stopped, turned slowly, reached out with an Aspirant's senses.

A man wearing a horned helmet was watching the stead from the grove surrounding the Klecklas' spring. He didn't see Tain.

Tain considered, shrugged. It wasn't his problem. He would tell Toma when they were alone. Let the Freeman decide what ought to be done.

U

The sun was a diameter above the horizon.

Tain released the mule and roan to pasture. He glanced round at the verdant hills. "Beautiful country," he murmured, and wondered what the rest of his journey would bring. He ambled a ways toward the house. Rula was starting breakfast.

These people rose late and started slowly. Already he had performed his Morning Ritual, seen to his travel gear and personal ablutions, and had examined the tracks round the spring. Then he had joined Toma when his host had come to check the sheep.

Toma had first shown relief, then increased concern. He remained steadfastly close-mouthed.

Tain restrained his curiosity. Soldiers learned not to ask questions. "Good morning, Steban."

The boy stood in the door of the sod house, rubbing sleep from his eyes. "Morning, Tain. Ma's cooking oats."

"Oh?"

"A treat," Toma explained. "We get a little honeycomb with it."

"Ah. You keep bees?" He hadn't seen any hives. "I had a friend who kept bees. . . ." He dropped it, preferring not to remember. Kai Ling had been like a brother. They had been Aspirants together. But Ling hadn't been able to believe he hadn't the talent to become Tervola. He was still trying to scale an unscalable height.

"Wild honey," Toma said. "The hill people gather it and trade it to us for workable iron."

"I see." Tain regarded the Kleckla home for the second time that morning. He wasn't impressed. It was a sod structure with an interior just four paces by six. Its construction matched the barn's. Tain had gotten better workmanship out of legion probationers during their first field exercises.

A second, permanent home was under construction nearby. A more ambitious project, every timber proclaimed it a dream house. Last night, after supper, Toma had grown starry-eyed and loquacious while discussing it. It was symbolic of the Grail he had pursued into the Zemstvi.

Its construction was as unskilled as that of the barn.

Rula's eyes had tightened with silent pain while her husband penetrated ever more deeply the shifting paths of his dreams.

Toma had been an accountant for the Perchev syndicate in Iwa Skolovda, a tormented, dreamless man using numbers to describe the movements of furs, wool, wheat, and metal billets. His days had been long and tedious.

During summer, when the barges and caravans moved, he had been permitted no holidays.

That had been before he had been stricken by the cunning infection, the wild hope, the pale dream of the Zemstvi, here expressed rudely, yet in a way that said that a man had tried.

Rula's face said that the old life had been emotional hell, but their apartment had remained warm and the roof hadn't leaked. Life had been predictable and secure.

There were philosophies at war in the Kleckla home, though hers lay mute before the other's traditional right. Accusing in silence.

Toma was Rula's husband. She had had to come to the Zemstvi as the bondservant of his dreams. Or nightmares.

The magic of numbers had shattered the locks on the doors of Toma's soul. It had let the dream light come creeping in. *Freedom*, the intellectual chimera pursued by more of his neighbors, meant nothing to Kleckla. His neighbors had chosen the hazards of colonizing Shara because of the certainties of Crown protection.

Toma, though, burned with the absolute conviction of a balanced equation. Numbers proved it impossible for a sheep-herding, wool-producing community not to prosper in those benign hills.

What Tain saw, and that Toma couldn't recognize, was that numbers wore no faces. Or were too simplistic. They couldn't account the human factors.

The failure had begun with Toma. He had ignored his own ignorance of the skills needed to survive on a frontier. Shara was no-man's-land. Iwa Skolovda had claimed it for centuries, but never had imposed its suzerainty.

Shara abounded with perils unknown to a city-born clerk.

The Tomas, sadly, often ended up as sacrifices to the Zemstvi.

The egg of disaster shared the nest of his dream, and who could say which had been insinuated by the cowbird of Fate?

There were no numbers by which to calculate ignorance, raiders, wolves, or heart-changes aborting vows politicians had sworn in perpetuity. The ciphers for disease and foul weather hadn't yet been enumerated.

Toma's ignorance of essential craft blazed out all over his homestead. And the handful of immigrants who had teamed their dreams with his, and had helped, had had no more knowledge or skill. They, too, had been hungry scriveners and number-mongers, swayed by a wild-eyed false prophet innocent of the realities of opening a new land. All but black sheep Mikla, who had come east to keep Toma from being devoured by his own fuzzy-headedness.

Rula-thinking had prevailed amongst most of Toma's disciples. They had admitted defeat and ventured west again, along paths littered with the parched bones of fleeting hope.

Toma was stubborn. Toma persisted. Toma's bones would lie beside those of his dreams.

All this Tain knew when he said, "If you won't let me pay, then at least let me help with the new house."

Toma regarded him with eyes of iron.

"I learned construction in the army."

Toma's eyes tightened. He was a proud man.

Tain had dealt with stiff-necked superiors for ages. He pursued his offer without showing a hint of criticism. And soon Toma relaxed, responded. "Take a look after breakfast," he suggested. "See what you think. I've been having trouble since Mikla left."

"I'd wondered about that," Tain admitted. "Steban gave the impression that your brother was living here. I didn't want to pry."

"He walked out." Toma stamped toward the house angrily. He calmed himself before they entered. "My fault, I guess. It was a petty argument. The sheep business hasn't been as good as we expected. He wanted to pick up a little extra trading knives and arrowheads to the tribes. They pay in furs. But the Baron banned that when he came here."

Tain didn't respond. Toma shrugged irritably, started back outside. He stopped suddenly, turned. "He's Rula's brother." Softly, "And that wasn't true. I made him leave because I caught him with some arrowheads. I was afraid." He turned again.

"Toma. Wait." Tain spoke softly. "I won't mention it."

Relief flashed across Kleckla's face.

"And you should know. The man with the horns. The. . . Caydarman? He spent part of the night watching the house from the grove."

Toma didn't respond. He seemed distraught. He remained silent throughout breakfast. The visual cues indicated a state of extreme anxiety. He regained his good humor only after he and Tain had worked on the new house for hours, and then his chatter was inconsequential. He wouldn't open up.

Tain asked no questions.

Neither Toma nor Rula mentioned his departure. Toma soured with each building suggestion, then brightened once it had been implemented. Day's end found less of the structure standing, yet the improvement in what remained had Toma bubbling.

VI

Tain accidentally jostled Rula at the hearth. "Excuse me." Then, "Can I help? Cooking is my hobby."

The woman regarded him oddly. She saw a big man, muscled and corded, who moved like a tiger, who gave an impression of massive strength kept under constant constraint. His skin was tracked by a hundred scars. There wasn't an ounce of softness in or on him. Yet his fingers were deft, his touch delicate as he took her knife and pan. "You don't mind?"

"Mind? You're joking. Two years I haven't had a minute's rest, and you want to know if I mind?"

"Ah. There's a secret to that, having too much work and not enough time. It's in the organization, and in putting yourself into the right state of mind before you start. Most people scatter themselves. They try everything at once."

"I'll be damned." Toma, who had been carrying water to the sheep pens, paused to watch over Tain's shoulder.

Turning the browned mutton, Tain said, "I love to cook. This is a chance for me to show off." He tapped a ghost of spice from an envelope. "Rula, if we brown the vegetables instead of stewing them. . . ."

"I'll be damned," Toma said again. He settled to the floor to watch. He pulled a jar of beer to his side.

"One should strive to achieve the widest possible competence," Tain remarked. "One may never *need* a skill, but, again, one can't know the future. Tomorrow holds ambushes for the mightiest necromancers. A new skill is another hedge against Fate's whimsy. What happens when a soldier loses a limb here?"

"They become beggars," Rula replied. "Toma, remember how it was right after the war? You couldn't walk a block. . . ."

"My point made for me. I could become a cook. Or an interpreter. Or a smith, or an armorer, according to my handicap. In that way I was well-served. Where's Steban? I asked him to pick some mushrooms. They'll add the final touch. But don't expect miracles. I've never tried this with mutton. . . . Rula? What is it?"

Toma had bounced up and run outside. She was following him.

"It's Steban. He's worried about Steban."

"Can you tell me?"

"The Caydarmen. . . ." She went blank, losing the animation she had begun showing.

"Who are they?"

"Baron Caydar's men." She would say no more. She just leaned against the door frame and stared into the dusk.

Toma returned a moment later. "It's all right. He's coming. Must have spent the day with the Kosku boy. I see his flock too."

"Toma. . . ." Fear tinged Rula's voice.

"The boy can choose his friends, woman. I'm not so weak that I'll make my children avoid their friends because of my fears."

Tain stirred vegetables and listened, trying to fathom the situation. Toma *was* scared. The timbre of fear inundated his voice.

He and Rula dropped the subject as if pursuing it might bring some dread upon them.

Steban had collected the right mushrooms. That had worried Tain. He never quite trusted anyone who wasn't legion-trained. "Good, Steban. I think we'll all like this."

"You're cooking?"

"I won't poison you. The fish was good, wasn't it?"

Steban seemed unsure. He turned to his father. "Wes said they were fined five sheep, five goats, and ten geese. He said his dad said he's not going to pay."

Dread and worry overcame his parents' faces.

"Toma, there'll be trouble." Rula's hands fluttered like nervous doves.

"They can't afford that," Toma replied. "They wouldn't make it through winter."

"Go talk to him. Ask the neighbors to chip in."

"It's got to end, Rula." He turned to Tain. "The Crown sent Baron Caydar to protect us from the tribes. We had less trouble when we weren't protected."

"Toma!"

"The tribes don't bother anyone, Rula. They never did. Hywel goes out of his way to avoid trouble. Just because those royal busybodies got themselves massacred. . . . They asked for it, trying to make Hywel and Stojan bend the knee."

"Toma, they'll fine us too."

"They have to hear me first."

"They know everything. People tell on each other. You know. . . ."

"Because they're scared. Rula, if the bandits keep pushing, we won't care if we're afraid."

Tain delivered the meal to table. He asked, "Who are the Caydarmen? The one I saw was no Iwa Skolovdan."

"Mercenaries." Toma spat. "Crown wouldn't let Caydar bring regulars. He recruited Trolledyngjans who escaped when the Pretender overthrew the Old House up there. They're a gang of bandits."

"I see." The problem was taking shape. Baron Caydar would be, no doubt, a political exile thrust into an impossible position by his enemies. His assignment here would be calculated to destroy him. And what matter that a few inconsequential colonists suffered?

Tain's motherland was called Dread Empire by its foes. With cause. The Tervola did as they pleased, where and when they pleased, by virtue of sorcery and legions unacquainted with defeat. Shinsan did have its politics and politicians. But never did they treat civilians with contempt.

Tain had studied the strange ways of the west, but he would need time to really grasp their actuality.

After supper he helped Toma haul more water. Toma remarked, "That's the finest eating I've had in years."

"Thank you. I enjoyed preparing it."

"What I wanted to say. I'd appreciate it if you didn't anymore."

Tain considered. Toma sounded as though he expected to share his company for a while.

"Rula. She shouldn't have too much time to worry."

"I see."

"I appreciate the help you're giving me. . . ."

"You could save a lot of water-hauling with a windmill."

"I know. But nobody around here can build one. Anyway. I couldn't pay much. Maybe a share of the sheep. If you'd stay. . . ."

Tain faced the east. The sunset had painted the mountains the color of blood. He hoped that was no omen. But he feared that legionnaires were dying at the hands of legionnaires even now. "All right. For a while. But I'll have to move on soon."

He wondered if he could outrun his past. A friend had told him that a man carried his pain like a tortoise carried his shell. Tain suspected the analogy might be more apt than intended. Men not only carried their pain-shells, they retreated into them if emotionally threatened.

"We need you. You can see that. I've been too stubborn to admit it till now...."

"Stubbornness is a virtue, properly harnessed. Just don't be stubborn against learning."

Steban carried water with them, and seemed impressed. Later, he said, "Tell us about the wars you were in, Tain."

Rula scowled.

"They weren't much. Bloody, sordid little things, Steban. Less fun than sheep-shearing time."

"Oh, come on, Tain. You're always saying things like that."

"Mikla made a glory tale of it," Rula said. "You'd think.... Well.... That there wasn't any better life."

"Maybe that was true for Mikla. But the El Murid Wars were long ago and far away, and, I expect, he was very young. He remembers the good times, and sees only the dullness of today."

"Maybe. He shouldn't fill Steban's head with his nonsense."

So Tain merely wove a tale of cities he had seen, describing strange dress and customs. Rula, he noted, enjoyed it as much as her son.

Later still, after his evening ritual, he spent several hours familiarizing himself with the countryside. A soldier's habits died hard.

Twice he spied roving Caydarmen. Neither noticed him.

Next morning he rose early and took the gelding for a run over the same ground.

VII

Rula visited Tain's makeshift forge the third afternoon. Bringing a jar of chill spring water was her excuse. "You've been hammering for hours, Tain. You'd better drink something."

He smiled as he laid his hammer aside. "Thank you." He accepted the jar, though he wasn't yet thirsty. He was accustomed to enduring long, baking hours in his armor. He sipped while he waited. She had something on her mind.

"I want to thank you."

"Oh?"

"For what you're doing. For what you've done for Toma. And me."

"I haven't done much."

"You've shown Toma that a man can be proud without being pig-headed. When he's wrong. But maybe you don't see it. Tain, I've lived with that man for eighteen years. I know him too well."

"I see." He touched her hand lightly, recognizing a long and emotionally difficult speech from a woman accustomed to keeping her own counsel.

He didn't know how to help her, though. An unmarried soldier's life hadn't prepared him. Not for a woman who moved him more than should be, for reasons he couldn't comprehend. A part of him said that women were people too, and should respond the same as men, but another part saw them as aliens, mysterious, perhaps even creatures of dread. "If I have done good, I have brought honor to the house."

He chuckled at his own ineptitude. Iwa Skolovdan just didn't have the necessary range of tonal nuance.

"You've given me hope for the first time since Shirl. . . ." she blurted. "I mean, I can see where we're getting somewhere now. I can see Toma seeing it.

"Tain, I never wanted to come to the Zemstvi. I hate it. I hated it before I left home. Maybe I hated it so much I made it impossible for Toma to succeed. I drove Shirl away. . . ."

"Yes. I could see it. But don't hate yourself for being what you are."

"His dreams were dying, Tain. And I wouldn't give him anything to replace them. And I have to hate myself for that. But now he's coming alive. He doesn't have to go on being stubborn, just to show me."

"Don't hate anybody, Rula. It's contagious. You end up hating everything, and everybody hates you."

"I can't ever like the Zemstvi. But I love Toma. And with you here, like a rock, he's becoming more like the boy I married. He's started to find his courage again. And his hope. That gives me hope. And that's why I wanted to thank you."

"A rock?"

"Yes. You're there. You don't criticize, you don't argue, you don't judge, you don't fear. You know. You make things possible. . . . Oh, I don't know how to say what I want. I think the fear is the biggest thing. It doesn't control us anymore."

"I don't think it's all my fault, Rula. You've done your part." He was growing unsettled. Even embarrassed.

She touched his arm. "You're strong, Tain. So strong and sure. My brother Mikla. . . . He was sure, but not always strong. He fought with Toma all the time."

Tain glanced south across the green hills. Toma had gone to the village in hopes of obtaining metal that could be used in the windmill Tain was going to build. He had been gone for hours.

A tiny silhouette topped a distant rise. Tain sighed in a mixture of disappointment and relief. He was saved having to face the feelings Rula was stirring.

Toma loved the windmill. He wanted to let the house ride till it was finished. Tain had suggested that they might, with a little ingenuity, provide running water. Rula would like that. It was a luxury only lords and merchant princes enjoyed.

Rula followed his gaze. Embarrassment overtook her. Tain yielded the jar and watched her flee.

Soon Toma called, "I got it, Tain! Bryon had an old wagon. He sold me enough to do the whole thing." He rushed to the forge, unburdened himself of a pack filled with rusty iron.

Tain examined the haul. "Good. More than enough for the bushings. You keep them greased, the windmill will last a lifetime."

Toma's boyish grin faded.

"What happened? You were gone a long time."

"Come on in the house. Share a jar of beer with me."

Tain put his tools away and followed Toma. Glancing eastward, he saw the white stain of Steban's flock dribbling down a distant slope, heading home. Beyond Steban, a little south, stood the grotesque rock formation the locals called the Toad. The Sharans believed it was the home of a malignant god.

Toma passed the beer. "The Caydarmen visited Kosku again. He wouldn't give them the animals."

Tain still didn't understand. He said nothing.

"They won't stand for it," Rula said. "There'll be trouble."

Toma shrugged. "There'll always be trouble. Comes of being alive." He pretended a philosophical nonchalance. Tain read the fear he was hiding. "They'll probably come tonight. . . ."

"You've been drinking," Rula snapped. "You're not going to. . . ."

"Rula, it's got to stop. Somebody has to show them the limits. We've reached ours. Kosku has taken up the mantle. The rest of us can't. . . ."

"Tain, talk to him."

Tain studied them, sensed them. Their fear made the house stink. He said nothing. After meeting her eyes briefly, he handed Toma the beer and ignored her appeal. He returned to his forge, dissipated his energies pumping the bellows and hammering cherry iron. He didn't dare insinuate himself into their argument. It had to remain theirs alone.

Yet he couldn't stop thinking, couldn't stop feeling. He hammered harder, driven by a taint of anger.

His very presence had altered Toma. Rula had said as much. The man wouldn't have considered supporting this Kosku otherwise. Simply by having entered the man's life he was forcing Toma to prove something. To himself? Or to Rula?

Tain hammered till the hills rang. Neutral as he had tried to remain, he had become heir to a responsibility. Toma had to be shielded from the consequences of artificial bravado.

"Tain?"

The hammer's thunder stammered. "Steban? Home so early?"

"It's almost dark."

"Oh. I lost track of time." He glanced at his handiwork. He had come near finishing while roaming his own mind. "What is it?"

"Will you teach me to be a soldier?"

Tain drove the tongs into the coals as if their mound contained the heart of an enemy. "I don't think so. Your mother. . . ."

"She won't care. She's always telling me to learn something."

"Soldiering isn't what she has in mind. She means your father's lessons."

"Tain, writing and ciphers are boring. And what good did they do my dad? Anyway, he's only teaching me because Mother makes him."

What kind of world did Rula live in, there behind the mask of her face? Tain wondered.

It couldn't be a happy world. It had suffered the deaths of too many hopes. Time had beaten her down. She had become an automaton getting through each day with the least fuss possible.

"Boring, but important. What good is a soldier who can't read or write? All he can do is carry a spear."

"Can you read?"

"Six languages. Every soldier in my army learns at least two. To become a soldier in my country is like becoming a priest in yours, Steban."

Rula, he thought. Why do I find you unique when you're just one of a million identical sisters scattered throughout the feudal west? The entire subcontinent lay prostrate beneath the heel of a grinding despair, a ponderous changelessness. It was a tinder-dry philosophical forest. The weakest spark flung off by a hope-bearing messiah would send it up.

"A soldier's training isn't just learning to use a sword, Steban. It's learning a way of life. I could teach you to fence, but you'd never become a master. Not till you learned the discipline, the way of thinking and living you need to. . . ."

"Boy, you going to jabber all night? Get those sheep in the pens."

Toma leaned against the doorframe of the house. A jar of beer hung from his hand. Tain sensed the random anger rushing around inside him. It would be as unpredictable as summer lightning.

"Take care of the sheep, Steban. I'll help water them later."

He cleaned up his forge, then himself, then carried water till Rula called them to supper.

Anger hung over the meal like a cloying fog rolling in off a noisome marsh. Tain was its focus. Rula wanted him to control Toma. Toma wanted his support. And Steban wanted a magical access to the heroic world his uncle had created from the bloodiest, most ineptly fought, and most pointless war of recent memory. Tain ate in silence.

Afterward, he said, "I've nearly finished the bushing and shaft bearings. We can start the tower tomorrow."

Toma grunted.

Tain shrugged. The man's mood would have to take care of itself.

He glanced at Rula. The appeal remained in her eyes. He rose, obtained a jar of beer, broke the seal, sipped. "A toast to the windmill." He passed it to Toma.

"Steban, let's get the rest of that water."

A breeze had come up during supper. Good and moist, it promised rain. Swift clouds were racing toward the mountains, obscuring the stars. Maybe, Tain thought, the weather would give Rula what he could not.

"Mom and Dad are mad at each other, aren't they?"

"I think so."

"Because of the Koskus?"

"Yes." The walk from the spring seemed to grow longer.

"Dad's afraid. Of the Caydarmen." Steban sounded disappointed.

"With good reason, I imagine." Tain hadn't met any of the Baron's mercenaries. He hadn't met any of the neighbors, either. None had come calling. He hadn't done any visiting during his reconnaissances.

"Soldiers aren't ever afraid."

Tain chuckled. "Wrong, Steban. Soldiers are always afraid. We just learn to handle fear. Your Dad didn't have to learn when you lived in the city. He's trying to catch up now."

"I'd show those Caydarmen. Like I showed that wolf."

"There was only one wolf, Steban. There're a lot of Caydarmen."

"Only seven. And the Witch."

"Seven? And a witch?"

"Sure. Torfin. Bodel. Grimnir. Olag. I don't remember the others."

"What about this witch? Who's she?"

Steban wouldn't answer for a while. Then, "She tells them what to do. Dad says the Baron was all right till she went to the Tower."

"Ah." So. Another fragment of puzzle. Who would have thought this quiet green land, so sparsely settled, could be so taut and mysterious?

Tain tried pumping Steban, but the boy clammed up about the Baron.

"Do you think Pa's a coward, Tain?"

"No. He came to the Zemstvi. It takes courage for a man to leave everything just on the chance he might make a better life someplace else."

Steban stopped and stared at him. There had been a lot of emotion in his voice. "Like you did?"

"Yes. Like I did. I thought about it a long time."

"Oh."

"This ought to be enough water. Let's go back to the house." He glanced at the sky.

"Going to rain," he said as they went inside.

"Uhm," Toma grunted. He finished one jar and started another. Tain smiled thinly. Kleckla wouldn't be going out tonight. He turned his smile on Rula.

She smiled back. "Maybe you'd better sleep here. The barn leaks."

"I'll be all right. I patched it some yesterday morning."

"Don't you ever sleep?"

"Old habits die hard. Well, the sheep are watered, I'm going to turn in."

"Tain?"

He paused at the door.

"Thanks."

He ducked into the night. Misty raindrops kissed his cheeks. A rising wind quarreled with itself in the grove.

He performed the Soldier's Ritual, then lay back on the straw pallet he had fashioned. But sleep wouldn't come.

VIII

The roan quivered between his knees as they descended the hill. It wasn't because of the wind and cold rain. The animal sensed the excitement and uncertainty of its rider.

Tain guided the animal into a brushy gully, dismounted, told the horse to wait. He moved fifty yards downslope, sat down against a boulder. So still did he remain that he seemed to become one with the stone.

The Kosku stead looked peaceful to an untrained eye. Just a quiet rural place passing a sleepy night.

But Tain felt the wakefulness there. Someone was watching the night. He could taste their fear and determination.

The Caydarmen came an hour later. There were three of them, bearing torches. They didn't care who saw them. They came down the hill from behind Tain and passed within fifty yards of him. None noticed him.

They were big men. The one with the horn helm, on the paint, Tain recognized as the Torfin he had seen before. The second was much larger than the first. The third, riding between them, was a slight, small figure in black.

The Witch. Tain knew that before she entered his vision. He had sensed her raw, untrained strength minutes earlier. Now he could feel the dread of her companions.

The wild adept needed to be feared. She was like as untrained elephant, ignorant of her own strength. And in her potential for misuse of the Power she was more dangerous to herself than to anyone she threatened.

Tain didn't doubt that fear was her primary control over the Baron and his men. She would cajole, pout, and hurt, like a spoiled child. . . .

She *was* very young. Tain could sense no maturity in her at all.

The man with the horns dismounted and pounded on the Kosku door with the butt of a dagger. "Kosku. Open in the name of Baron Caydar."

"Go to Hell."

Tain almost laughed.

The reply, spoken almost gently, came from the mouth of a man beyond fear. The Caydarmen sensed it, too, and seemed bewildered. That was what amused Tain so.

"Kosku, you've been fined three sheep, three goats, and five geese for talking sedition. We've come to collect."

"The thieves bargain now? You were demanding five, five, and ten the other day."

"Five sheep, five goats, and ten geese, then," Torfin replied, chagrined.

"Get the hell off my land."

"Kosku. . . ."

Assessing the voice. Tain identified Torfin as a decent man trapped by circumstance. Torfin didn't want trouble.

"Produce the animals, Kosku," said the second man. "Or I'll come after them."

This one wasn't a decent sort. His tone shrieked bully and sadist. This one *wanted* Kosku to resist.

"Come ahead, Grimnir. Come ahead." The cabin door flung open. An older man appeared. He leaned on a long, heavy quarterstaff. "Come to me, you Trolledyngjan dog puke. You sniffer at the skirts of whores."

Kosku, Tain decided, was no ex-clerk. He was old, but the hardness of a man of action glimmered through the gray. His muscles were taut and strong. He would know how to handle his staff.

Grimnir wasn't inclined to test him immediately.

The Witch urged her mount forward.

"You don't frighten me, little slut. I know you. I won't appease your greed."

Her hands rose before her, black-gloved fingers writhing like snakes. Sudden emerald sparks leapt from tip to tip.

Kosku laughed.

His staff darted too swiftly for the eye to follow. Its iron-shod tip struck the Witch's horse between the nostrils.

It shrieked, reared. The woman tumbled into the mud. Green sparks zig-zagged over her dark clothing. She spewed curses like a broken oath-sack.

Torfin swung his torch at the old man.

The staff's tip caught him squarely in the forehead. He sagged.

"Kosku, you shouldn't have done that," Grimnir snarled. He dismounted, drew his sword. The old man fled, slammed his door.

Grimnir recovered Torfin's torch, tossed it onto the thatch of Kosku's home. He helped the Witch and Torfin mount, then tossed his own torch.

Tain was inclined to aid the old man, but didn't move. He had left his weapons behind in case he encountered this urge.

He didn't need weapons to fight and kill, but he suspected, considering Kosku's reaction, that Grimnir was good with a sword. It didn't seem likely that an unarmed man could take him.

And there was the Witch, whose self-taught skill he couldn't estimate.

She had had enough. Despite Grimnir's protests, she started back the way they had come.

Tain watched them pass. The Witch's eyes jerked his way, as if she were startled, but she saw nothing. She relaxed. Tain listened to them over the ridge before moving.

The wet thatch didn't burn well, but it burned. Tain strode down, filled a bucket from a sheep trough, tossed water onto the blaze. A half-dozen throws finished it.

The rainfall was picking up. Tain returned to the roan conscious that eyes were watching him go.

He swung onto the gelding, whispered. The horse began stalking the Caydarmen.

They weren't hurrying. It was two hours before Tain discerned the deeper darkness of the Tower through the rain. His quarry passed inside without his having learned anything. He circled the structure once.

The squat, square tower was only slightly taller than it was wide. It was very old, antedating Iwa Skolovda. Tain assumed that it had been erected by Imperial engineers when Ilkazar had ruled Shara. A watchtower to support patrols in the borderlands.

Shara had always been a frontier.

Similar structures dotted the west. Ilkazar's advance could be chronicled by their architectural styles.

IX

Toma was in a foul mood next morning. Toma was suffering from more than a hangover. Come mid-morning he abandoned his tools, donned a jacket and collected his staff. He strode off toward the village.

He had hardly vanished when Rula joined Tain. "Thanks for last night," she said.

Tain spread his hands in an "it was nothing" gesture. "I don't think you had to worry."

"What?"

"Nothing." He averted his gaze shyly.

"He's gone to find out what happened."

"I know. He feels responsible."

"He's not responsible for Kosku's sins."

"We're all responsible to one another, Rula. His feelings are genuine. My opinion is, he wants to do the right thing for the wrong reasons."

"What reasons?"

"I think he wants to prove something. I'm not sure why. Or to whom. Maybe to himself."

"Just because they blame him...." Her gaze snapped up and away, toward the spring. Tain turned slowly.

A Caydarman on a painted horse was descending the slope. "Torfin?" Today he wore no helmet.

"Oh!" Rula gasped. "Toma must have said something yesterday."

Tain could sense the unreasoning fear in her. It refused to let the Caydarman be anything but evil. "You go inside. I'll handle him."

She ran.

Tain set his tools aside, wiped his hands, ambled toward the spring. The Caydarman had entered the grove. He was watering his mount.

"Good morning."

The Caydarman looked up. "Good morning."

He's young, Tain thought. Nineteen or twenty. But he had scars.

The youth took in Tain's size and catlike movements.

Tain noted the Caydarman's pale blue eyes and long blond hair, and the strength pent in his rather average-appearing body. He was tall, but not massive like Grimnir.

"Torfin Hakesson," the youth offered. "The Baron's man."

"Tain. My father's name I don't know."

A slight smile crossed Torfin's lips. "You're new here."

"Just passing through. Kleckla needed help with his house. I have the skills. He asked me to stay on for a while."

Torfin nodded. "You're the man with the big roan? I saw you the other day."

Tain smiled. "And I you. Several times. Why're you so far from home?"

"My father chose a losing cause. I drifted. The Baron offered me work. I came to the Zemstvi."

"I've heard that Trolledyngjans are terse. Never have I heard a life so simply sketched."

"And you?"

"Much the same. Leaving unhappiness behind, pursuing something that probably doesn't exist."

"The Baron might take you on."

"No. Our thinking diverges on too many things."

"I thought so myself, once. I still do, in a way. But you don't have many choices when your only talent is sword work."

"A sad truth. Did you want something in particular?"

"No. Just patrolling. Watering the horse. Them." He jerked his head toward the house. "They're well?"

"Yes."

"Good." The youth eyed the stead. "Looks like you've gotten things moving."

"Some. Toma needed help."

"Yes. He hasn't made much headway since Mikla left. Well, good-day, Tain. Till we meet again."

"Good-day, Torfin. And may the grace of heaven guide you."

Torfin regarded him with one raised eyebrow as he mounted. "You have an odd way of putting things," he replied. He wheeled and angled off across the hillside. Tain watched till the youth crossed the low ridge.

He found Rula hunkered by the cookfire, losing herself in making their noonday meal.

"What did he want?" she demanded.

"To water his horse."

"That's all?"

"That and to look at me, I suppose. Why?"

"He's the dangerous one. Grimnir is big and loud and mean. The others are bullies too. But Torfin. . . . He's quiet and quick. He once killed three of Stojan's warriors when they tried to steal horses from the Tower corrals."

"Has he given you any trouble?"

She hesitated. Tain knew she would hide something.

"No. To hardly anybody. But he's always around. Around and watching. Listening. Then the others come with their fines that aren't anything but excuses to rob people."

So much fear in her. He wanted to hold her, to tell her everything would be all right. "I have to get to work. I should finish the framework today. If Toma remembers to look for lumber, we might start the tank tomorrow." He ducked out before he did anything foolish.

He didn't understand. He was Tain, a leading centurion of the Demon Guard. He was a thirty-year veteran. He should be past juvenile temptation. Especially involving a woman of Rula's age and wear. . . .

He worked hard, but it did no good. The feelings, the urges, remained. He kept his eyes averted during lunch.

"Tain. . . ." she started once

"Yes?"

"Nothing."

He glanced up. She had turned toward the Tower, her gaze far away.

Afterward, he saddled the roan and led out the mule and took them on a short patrol. Once he spied Torfin in the distance, on a hilltop, watching something beyond. Tain turned and rode a few miles westward, till the Tower loomed ahead. He turned again, for home, following a looping course past the Kosku stead. Someone was repairing the thatch.

Rula was waiting, and highly nervous. "Where have you been?" she demanded.

"Exercising the animals. What happened?"

"Nothing. Oh, nothing. I just hate it when I have to be alone."

"I'm sorry. That was thoughtless."

"No. Not really. What claim do I have on your time?" She settled down. "I'm just a worrier."

"I'll wait till Toma's home next time." He unsaddled the roan and began rubbing him down. The mule wandered away, grazing. Rula watched without speaking.

He was acutely conscious of her gaze. After ten minutes, she asked, "Where did you come from, Tain? Who are you?"

"I came from nowhere and I'm going nowhere, Rula. I'm just an ex-soldier wandering because I don't know anything else."

"Nothing else? You seem to know something about everything."

"I've had a lot of years to learn."

"Tell me about the places you've been. I've never been anywhere but home and the Zemstvi."

Tain smiled a thin, sad smile. There was that same awe and hunger that he heard from Steban.

"I saw Escalon once, before it was destroyed. It was a beautiful country." He described that beauty without revealing his part in its destruction. He worked on the windmill while he reminisced.

"Ah. I'd better start supper," Rula said later. "Toma's coming. He's got somebody with him."

Tain watched her walk away and again chastised himself for unworthy thoughts.

She had been beautiful once, and would be still but for the meanness of her life.

Toma arrived wearing an odd look. Tain feared the man had divined his thoughts. But, "The Caydarmen went after Kosku last night. The old coot actually chased them off."

"Heh?" Tain snorted. "Good for him. You going to be busy?" He glanced at the second man. "Or can you help me mount these bearings?"

"Sure. In a couple minutes. Tain, this is my brother-in-law."

"Mikla?" Tain extended his hand. "Good to meet you. I've heard a lot about you."

"None of it good, I'm sure." Laughter wrinkled the corners of Mikla's eyes. He was a lean, leathery man, accustomed to facing hard weather.

"More good than bad. Steban will be glad to see you."

Rula stuck her head out the door. Then she came flying, skirts a-swirl. "Mikla!" She threw her arms around her brother. "Where *have* you been? I've been worried sick."

"Consorting with the enemy. Staying with Stojan and trying to convince him that we're not all Caydarmen."

"Even Caydarmen don't all seem to be Caydarmen," Tain remarked as he hoisted a timber into position.

Mikla watched the ease with which he lifted. "Maybe not. But when the arrows are flying, who wonders about the spirit in which they're sped?"

"Ah. That's right. Steban said you were a veteran."

A whisper of defensiveness passed through Mikla's stance. "Steban exaggerates what I've already exaggerated silly."

"An honest man. Rare these days. Toma. You said Kosku chased the Caydarmen away? Will that make more trouble?"

"Damned right it will," Mikla growled. "That's why I came back. When the word gets around, everybody in the Zemstvi will have his back up. And those folks at the Tower are going to do their damnedest to stop it."

"Kind of leaves me with mixed feelings. I've been saying we ought to do something ever since the Witch turned the Baron's head. But now I wonder if it'll be worth the trouble. It'll cause more than beatings and judicial robberies. Somebody'll get killed. Probably Kosku."

"I really didn't think it would go this far," Toma murmured. Tain couldn't fathom the pain in Kleckla. "I thought she'd see where she was heading. . . ."

"Enough of this raven-cawing," Mikla shouted. He swept Rula into a savage embrace. "What's for supper, little sister?"

"Same as every night. Mutton stew. What did you expect?"

"That's a good-looking mule over there. She wouldn't miss a flank steak or two."

Rula startled them with a pert, "You'll get your head kicked in for just thinking about it. That's the orneriest animal I ever saw. She could give mean lessons to Grimnir. But maybe you could talk Tain into fixing supper. He did the other day. It was great."

Tain thought he saw a glimmer of the girl who had married Toma, of the potential hiding behind the weary mask.

"He cooks, too? Mercy. Toma, maybe you should marry him."

Tain watched for visual cues. How much of Mikla's banter had an ulterior motive? But the man was hard to read.

Rula bounced off to the house with a parting shot about having to poison the stew.

"That story of Kosku's is spreading like the pox," Toma observed. He reassumed the odd look he had worn on arriving.

So, Tain thought. Kosku is talking about the mystery man who doused the fire in his thatch. Was that what had brought Torfin?

"A Caydarman stopped by," he told Kleckla. "Torfin. He watered his horse. We talked."

"What'd he want?"

"Nothing, far as I could tell. Unless he was checking on me. Seemed a pleasant lad."

"He's the one to watch," Mikla declared. "Quiet and deadly. Like a viper."

"Rula told me about Stojan's men."

"Them? They got what they asked for. Stojan didn't like it, but what could he do? Torfin cut them down inside the Baron's corral. He let a couple get away just so they could carry the warning."

"With only seven men in his way I wouldn't think Stojan would care how things looked."

"Neither Stojan's nor Hywel's clans amount to much. They had smallpox bad the year before we came out. Stojan can't get twenty warriors together."

"Steban must have heard the news," Tain observed. "He's coming home early."

The boy outdistanced his flock. Toma hurried to meet him.

Tain and Mikla strolled along behind. "What army were you in?" the latter asked.

Tain had faced the question since arriving. But no one had phrased it quite this directly. He had to tell the truth, or lie. A vague reply would be suspicious. "Necremnen." He hoped Mikla was unfamiliar with the nations of the Roë basin.

"Ah." Mikla kept asking pointed questions. Several tight minutes passed before Tain realized that he wasn't fishing for something. The man just had the curiosities.

"Your sister. She's not happy here."

"I know." Mikla shrugged. "I do what I can for her. But she's Toma's wife."

And that, thought Tain, told a whole tale about the west. Not that the women of his own nation had life much easier. But their subjugation was cosmeticized and sweetened.

Toma reached Steban. He flung his arms around wildly. Mikla started trotting.

Tain kept walking. He wanted to study Mikla when the man wasn't conscious of being observed.

He was a masculine edition of Rula. Same lean bone structure, same dark brown hair, same angular head. Mikla would be several years older. Say thirty-six. Rula wouldn't be more than thirty-three, despite having been married so long.

The world takes us hard and fast, Tain thought. Suddenly he felt old.

Toma and Mikla came running. "Steban saw smoke," Toma gasped. "Toward Kosku's place. We're going over there." They ran on to the house.

Tain walked after them.

He arrived to find Toma brandishing his quarterstaff. Mikla was scraping clots of earth off a sword he had dug out of the floor.

✗

Sorrow invaded Tain's soul. He couldn't repulse it. It persisted while he helped Steban water the sheep, and worsened while he sat with Rula, waiting for the men to return. Hours passed before he identified its root cause. Homesickness.

"I'm exhausted," he muttered. "Better turn in."

Rula sped him a look of mute appeal. He ignored it. He didn't dare wait with her. Not anymore. Not with these unsoldierly feelings threatening to betray all honor.

The Soldier's Rituals did no good. They only reminded him of the life he had abandoned. He was a soldier no more. He had chosen a different path, a different life.

A part of life lay inside the sod house, perhaps his for the asking.

"I'm a man of honor," he mumbled. Desperation choked his voice.

And again his heart leaned to his motherland.

Sighing, he broke into his mule packs. He found his armorer's kit, began oiling his weapons.

But his mind kept flitting, taunting him like a black butterfly. Home. Rula. Home. Rula again.

Piece by piece, with exaggerated care, he oiled his armor. It was overdue. Lacquerwork needed constant, loving care. He had let it slide so he wouldn't risk giving himself away.

He worked with the unhappy devotion of a recruit forewarned of a surprise inspection. It required concentration. The distractions slid into the recesses of his mind.

He was cleaning the eyepieces of his mask when he heard the startled gasp.

He looked up. Rula had come to the barn.

He hadn't heard her light tread.

She stared at the mask. Fascination and horror alternated on her face. Her lips worked. No sound came forth.

Tain didn't move.

This is the end, he thought. She knows what the mask means. . . .

"I. . . . Steban fell asleep. . . . I thought. . . ." She couldn't tear her gaze away from that hideous metal visage.

She yielded to the impulse to flee, took several steps. Then something drew her back.

Fatalistically, Tain polished the thin traceries of inlaid gold.

"Are you?. . . Is that real?"

"Yes, Rula." He reattached the mask to his helmet. "I was a leading centurion of the Demon Guard. The Demon Prince's personal bodyguard." He returned mask and helmet to his mule packs, started collecting the rest of his armor.

He had to go.

"How?. . . How can that be? You're not. . . ."

"We're just men, Rula. Not devils." He guided the mule to the packs, threw a pad across her back. "We have our weaknesses and fears too." He threw the first pack on and adjusted it.

"What are you doing?"

"I can't stay now. You know what I was. That changes everything."

"Oh."

She watched till he finished. But when he called the roan, and began saddling him, she whispered, "Tain?"

He turned.

She wasn't two feet away.

"Tain. It doesn't matter. I won't tell anyone. Stay."

One of his former master's familiar spirits reached into his guts and, with bloody talons, slowly twisted his intestines. It took no experience to read the offer in her eyes.

"Please stay. I. . . . We need you here."

One treacherous hand overcame his will. He caressed her cheek. She shivered under his touch, hugging herself as if it were cold. She pressed her cheek against his fingers.

He tried to harden his eyes. "Oh, no. Not now. More than ever."

"Tain. Don't. You can't." Her gaze fell to the straw. Savage quaking conquered her.

She moved toward him. Her arms enveloped his neck. She buried her face in his chest. He felt the warm moistness of tears through his clothing.

He couldn't push her away. "No," he said, and she understood that he meant he wouldn't go.

He separated himself gently and began unloading the mule. He avoided Rula's eyes, and she his whenever he succumbed.

He turned to the roan. Then Mikla's voice, cursing, came from toward Kosku's.

"Better go inside. I'll be there in a minute."

Disappointment, pain, anger, fear, played tag across Rula's face. "Yes. All right."

Slowly, going to the Rituals briefly, Tain finished. Maybe later. During the night, when she wouldn't be here to block his path. . . .

Liar, he thought. It's too late now.

He went to the house.

Toma and Mikla had arrived. They were opening jars of beer.

"It was Kosku's place," Toma said. Hate and anger had him shaking. He was ready to do something foolish.

"He got away," Mikla added. "They're hunting him now. Like an animal. They'll murder him."

"He'll go to Palikov's," Toma said; Mikla nodded. "They're old friends. Palikov is as stubborn as he is."

"They can figure the same as us. The Witch. . . ." Mikla glanced at Tain. "She'll tell them." He finished his beer, seized another jar. Toma matched his consumption.

"We could get there first," Toma guessed.

"It's a long way. Six miles." Mikla downed his jar, grabbed another. Tain glanced into the wall pantry. The beer supply was dwindling fast. And it was a strong drink, brewed by the nomads from grain and honey. They traded it for sheepskins and mutton.

"Palikov," said Tain. "He's the one that lives out by the Toad?"

"That's him." Mikla didn't pay Tain much heed. Toma gave him a look that asked why he wanted to know.

"We can't let them get away with it," Kleckla growled. "Not with murder. Enough is enough. This morning they beat the Arimkov girl half to death."

"Oh!" Rula gasped. "She always was jealous of Lari. Over that boy Lief."

"Rula."

"I'm sorry, Toma."

Tain considered the man. They were angry and scared. They had decided to do a deed, didn't know if they could, and felt they had talked too much to back down.

A lot more beer would go down before they marched.

Tain stepped backward into the night, leaving.

XI

He spent fifteen minutes probing the smoldering remnants of Kosku's home and barn. He found something Toma and Mikla had overlooked.

The child's body was so badly burned he couldn't tell its sex.

He had seen worse. He had been a soldier of the Dread Empire. The gruesome corpse moved him less than did the horror of the sheep pens.

The animals had been used for target practice. The raiders hadn't bothered finishing the injured.

Tain did what had to be done. He understood Toma and Mikla better after cutting the throats of lambs and kids.

There was no excuse for wanton destruction. Though the accusation sometimes flew, the legions never killed or destroyed for pleasure.

A beast had left its mark here.

He swung onto the roan and headed toward the Toad.

A wall collapsed behind him. The fire returned to life, splashing the slope with dull red light. Tain's shadow reached ahead, flickering like an uncertain black ghost.

Distance fled. About a mile east of the Kleckla house he detected other night travelers.

Toma and Mikla were walking slowly, steering a wobbly course, pausing frequently to relieve their bladders. They had brought beer with them.

Tain gave them a wide berth. They weren't aware of his passing.

They had guessed wrong in predicting that they would beat the Caydarmen to Palikov's.

Grimnir and four others had accompanied the Witch. Tain didn't see Torfin among them.

The raiders had their heads together. They had tried a torching and had failed. A horse lay between house and nightriders, moaning, with an arrow in its side. A muted Kosku kept cursing the Witch and Caydarmen.

Tain left the roan. He moved downhill to a shadow near the raiders. He squatted, waited.

This time he bore his weapons.

The Toad loomed behind the Palikov home. Its evil god aspect felt believable. It seemed to chuckle over this petty human drama.

Tain touched the hilt of his longsword. He was tempted. Yet. . . . He wanted no deaths. Not now. Not here. This confrontation had to be neutralized, if only to keep Toma and Mikla from stumbling into a situation they couldn't handle.

Maybe he could stop it without bloodshed.

He took flint and steel from his travel pouch. He sealed his eyes, let his chin fall to his chest. He whispered.

He didn't understand the words. They weren't in his childhood tongue. They had been taught him when he was young, during his Aspirant training.

His world shrank till he was alone in it. He no longer felt the breeze, nor the earth beneath his toes. He heard nothing, nor did the light of torches seep through the flesh of his eyelids. The smell of fetid torch smoke faded from his consciousness.

He floated.

He reached out, locating his enemies, visualizing them from a slight elevation. His lips continued to work.

He struck flint against steel, caught the spark with his mind.

Six pairs of eyes jerked his way.

A luminous something grew round the spark, which seemed frozen in time, neither waxing nor dying. The luminosity spread diaphanous wings, floated upward. Soon it looked like a gigantic, glowing moth.

The Witch shrieked. Fear and rage drenched her voice.

Tain willed the moth.

Its wings fluttered like silk falling. The Witch flailed with her hands, could touch nothing. The moth's clawed feet pierced her hood, seized her hair.

Flames sprang up.

The woman screamed.

The moth ascended lightly, fluttered toward Grimnir.

The Caydarman remained immobile, stunned, till his hair caught fire. Then he squealed and ran for his horse.

The others broke a moment later. Tain burned one more, then recalled the elemental.

It was a minor magick, hardly more than a trick, but effective enough as a surprise. And no one died.

One Caydarman came close.

They were a horse short, and too interested in running to share with the man who came up short.

Whooping, old man Kosku stormed from the house. He let an arrow fly. It struck the Caydarman in the shoulder. Kosku would have killed him had Tain not threatened him with the moth.

Tain recalled the spark again. This time it settled to the point it had occupied when the moth had come to life. The elemental faded. The spark fell, dying before it hit ground.

Tain withdrew from his trance. He returned flint and steel to his pouch, rose. "Good," he whispered. "It's done."

He was tired. He hadn't the mental or emotional muscle to sustain extended use of the Power. He wasn't sure he could make it home.

But he had been a soldier of the Dread Empire. He did not yield to weariness.

XII

The fire's smoke hung motionless in the heavy air. Little more than embers remained. The ashes beneath were deep. The little light remaining stirred spooky shadows against the odd, conical rocks.

Kai Ling slept soundly. He had made his bed there for so long that his body knew every sharp edge beneath it.

The hillmen sentinels watched without relaxing. They knew this bane too well. They bothered him no more. All they wanted of him was warning time, so their women and children could flee.

Kai Ling sat bolt upright. He listened. His gaze turned west. His head thrust forward. His nose twitched like that of a hound on point. A smile toyed with his lips. He donned his golden panther mask.

The sentinels ran to tell their people that the man-of-death was moving.

XIII

Toma and Mikla slept half the day. Tain labored on the windmill, then the house. He joined Rula for lunch. She followed him when he returned to work.

"What happened to them?" he asked.

"It was almost sunup when they came home. They didn't say anything."

"They weren't hurt?"

"It was over before they got there." The fear edged her voice again, but now she had it under control.

I'm building a mountain of responsibility, Tain thought.

She watched him work a while, admiring the deft way he pegged timbers into place.

He clambered up to check the work Toma had done on the headers. Out of habit he scanned the horizon.

A hill away, a horseman watched the stead. Tain balanced on the header. The rider waved. Tain responded.

Someone began cursing inside the sod house. Rula hurried that way. Tain sighed. He wouldn't have to explain a greeting to the enemy.

Minutes later Mikla came outside. He had a hangover. A jar of beer hung from his left hand.

"Good afternoon," Tain called.

"The hell it is." Mikla came over, leaned against a stud. "Where were you last night?"

"What? Asleep in the barn. Why?"

"Not sure. Toma!"

Toma came outside. He looked worse than his brother-in-law. "What?"

"What'd old man Kosku say?"

"I don't know. Old coot talked all night. I quit listening to him last year."

"About the prowler who ran the Caydarmen off."

"Ah. I don't remember. A black giant sorcerer? He's been seeing things for years. I don't think he's ever sober."

"He was sober last night. And he told the same story the first time they tried burning him out."

Toma shrugged. "Believe what you want. He's just crazy." But Toma considered Tain speculatively.

"Someone coming," Tain said. The runner was coming from the direction of the Kosku stead. Soon Toma and Mikla could see him too.

"That's Wes. Kosku's youngest," Toma said. "What's happened now?"

When the boy reached the men, he gasped, "It's Dad. He's gone after Olag."

"Calm down," Mikla told him. "Catch your breath first."

The boy didn't wait long. "We went back to the house. To see if we could save anything. We found Mari. We thought she ran to Jeski's. . . . She was all burned. Then Ivon Pilsuski came by. He said Olag was in town. He was bragging about teaching Dad a lesson. So Dad went to town. To kill him."

Tain sighed. It seemed unstoppable now. There was blood in it.

Toma looked at Mikla. Mikla stared back. "Well?" said Toma.

"It's probably too late."

"Are you going?"

Mikla rubbed his forehead, pushed his hair out of his eyes. "Yes. All right." He went to the house. Toma followed.

The two came back. Mikla had his sword. Toma had his staff. They walked round the corner of the house, toward the village, without speaking.

Rula flew outside. "Tain! Stop them! They'll get killed."

He seized her shoulders, held her at arm's length. "I can't."

"Yes, you can. You're. . . . You mean you won't." Something had broken within her. Her fear had returned. The raid had affected her the way the Caydarmen wanted it to affect the entire Zemstvi.

"I mean I can't. I've done what I could. There's blood in it now. It'll take blood to finish it."

"Then go with them. Don't let anything happen to them."

Tain shook his head sadly. He had gotten himself cornered here.

He had to go. To protect a man who claimed the woman he wanted. If he didn't, and Toma were killed, he would forever be asking himself if he had willed it to happen.

He sealed his eyes briefly, then avoided Rula's by glancing at the sky. Cloudless and blue, it recalled the day when last he had killed a man. There, away toward Kosku's, Death's daughters planed the air, omening more dying.

"All right." He went to the Kosku boy, who sat by the new house, head between his knees.

"Wes. We're going to town. Will you stay with Mrs. Kleckla?"

"Okay." The boy didn't raise his head.

Tain walked toward the barn. "Take care of him, Rula. He needs mothering now."

Toma and Mikla traveled fast. Tain didn't overtake them till they were near the village. He stayed out of sight, riding into town after them. He left the roan near the first house.

There were two horses in the village. Both belonged to Caydarmen. He ignored them.

Kosku and a Caydarman stood in the road, arguing viciously. The whole village watched. Kosku waved a skinning knife.

Tain spotted the other Caydarman. Grimnir leaned against a wall between two houses, grinning. The big man wore a hat to conceal his hairless pate.

Tain strolled his way as Mikla and Toma bore down on Olag.

Olag said something. Kosku hurled himself at the Caydarman. Blades flashed. Kosku fell. Olag kicked him, laughed. The old man moaned.

Mikla and Toma charged.

The Caydarman drew his sword.

Grimnir, still grinning, started to join him.

Tain seized his left bicep. "No."

Grimnir tried to yank away. He failed. He tried punching himself loose. Tain blocked the blow, backhanded Grimnir across the face. "I said no."

Grimnir paused. His eyes grew huge.

"Don't move. Or I'll kill you."

Grimnir tried for his sword.

Tain tightened his grip.

Grimnir almost whimpered.

And in the road Tain's oracle became fact.

Mikla had been a soldier once, but now he was as rusty as his blade. Olag battered his sword aside, nicked him. Toma thrust his staff at the Caydarman's head. Olag brushed it away.

Tain sighed sadly. "Grimnir, walk down the road. Get on your horse. Go back to the Tower. Do it now, or don't expect to see the sun set." He released the man's arm. His hand settled to the pommel of his longsword.

Grimnir believed him. He hurried to his horse, one hand holding his hat.

Olag glanced his way, grinned, shouted, "Hey, join the game, big man." He seemed puzzled when Grimnir galloped away.

Tain started toward Olag. Toma went down with a shoulder wound. Mikla had suffered a dozen cuts. Olag was playing with him. The fear was in him now. His pride had neared its snapping point. In a moment he would run.

"Stop it," Tain ordered.

Olag stepped back, considered him from a red tangle of hair and beard. He licked his lips and smiled. "Another one?"

He buried his blade in Mikla's guts.

Tain's swords sang as they cleared their scabbards. The evening sun played purple and indigo upon their blades.

Olag stopped grinning.

He was good. But the Caydarman had never faced a man doubly armed. He fell within twenty seconds.

The villagers stared, awed. The whispers started, speculating about Kosku's mystery giant. Tain ignored them.

He dropped to one knee.

It was too late for Mikla. Toma, though, would mend. But his shoulder would bother him for the rest of his life.

Tain tended Kleckla's wound, then whistled for the roan. He set Toma in the saddle and laid Mikla behind him. He cleaned his blades on the dead Caydarman.

He started home.

Toma, in shock, stared at the horizon and spoke not a word.

XIV

Rula ran to meet them. How she knew, Tain couldn't fathom.

Darkness had fallen.

Steban was a step behind her, face taut and pallid. He looked at his father and uncle and retreated into an inner realm nothing could assail.

"I'm sorry, Rula. I wasn't quick enough. The man who did it is dead, if that helps." Honest grief moved him. He slid his arm around her waist.

Steban slipped under his other arm. They walked down to the sod house. The roan followed, his nose an inch behind Tain's right shoulder. The old soldier took comfort from the animal's concern.

They placed Mikla on a pallet, and Toma in his own bed. "How bad is he?" Rula asked, moving and talking like one of the living dead.

Tain knew the reaction. The barriers would relax sometime. Grief would demolish her. He touched her hand lightly. "He'll make it. It's a clean wound. Shock is the problem now. Probably more emotional than physical."

Steban watched with wide, sad eyes.

Tain squatted beside Toma, cleansing his wound again. "Needle and thread, Rula. He'll heal quicker."

"You're a surgeon too?"

"I commanded a hundred men. They were my responsibility."

The fire danced suddenly. The blanket closing the doorway whipped. Cold air chased itself round the inside walls. "Rain again," Rula said.

Tain nodded. "A storm, I think. The needle?"

"Oh. Yes."

He accepted needle and thread. "Steban. Come here."

The boy drifted over as if gripped by a narcotic dream.

"Sit. I need your help."

Steban shook his head.

"You wanted to be a soldier. I'll start teaching you now."

Steban lowered himself to the floor.

"The sad lessons are the hardest. And the most important. A soldier has to watch friends die. Put your fingers here, like this. Push. No. Gently. Just enough to keep the wound shut." Tain threaded the needle.

"Uncle Mikla. . . . How did it happen?" Disbelief animated the boy. His uncle could do anything.

"He forgot one of a soldier's commandments. He went after an enemy he didn't know. And he forgot that it's been a long time since he used a sword."

"Oh."

"Hold still, Steban. I'm going to start."

Toma surged up when the needle entered his flesh. A moan ripped from his throat. "Mikla! No!" His reason returned with his memory.

"Toma!" Tain snapped. "Lie down. Rula, help us. He's got to lie still."

Toma struggled. He started bleeding.

Steban gagged.

"Hold on, Steban. Rula, get down here with your knees beside his head. Toma, can you hear me?"

Kleckla stopped struggling. He met Tain's eyes.

"I'm trying to sew you up. You have to hold still."

Rula ran her fingers over Toma's features.

"Good. Try to relax. This won't take a minute. Yes. Good thinking, Steban."

The boy had hurled himself away, heaved, then had taken control. He returned with fists full of wool. Tain used it to sponge blood.

"Hold the wound together, Steban."

The boy's fingers quivered when the blood touched them, but he persevered.

"Good. A soldier's got to do what's got to be done, like it or not. Toma? I'm starting."

"Uhm."

The suturing didn't take a minute. The bandaging took no longer.

"Rula. Make some broth. He'll need lots of it. I'm going to the barn. I'll get something for the pain. Steban. Wash your hands."

The boy was staring at his father's blood on his fingers.

A gust of wind stirred fire and door covering. The wind was cold. Then an avalanche of rain fell. A more solid sound counterpointed the patter of raindrops.

"Hailstones," Rula said.

"I have to get my horse inside. What about the sheep?"

"Steban will take care of them. Steban?"

Thunder rolled across the Zemstvi. Lightning scarred the night. The sheep bleated.

"Steban! Please! Before they panic."

"Another lesson, Steban." Tain guided the boy out the door. "You've got to go on, no matter what."

The rain was cold and hard. It fell in huge drops. The hailstones stung. The thunder and lightning picked up. The wind had claws of ice. It tore at gaps in Tain's clothing. He guided the roan into the rude barn. The gelding's presence calmed the mule and cow. Tain rifled his packs by lightning flashes.

Steban drove the sheep into the barn too. They would be crowded, but sheltered.

Tain went to help.

He saw the rider in the flashes, coming closer in sudden jerks. The man lay against his mount's neck, hiding from the wind. His destination could be nowhere but the stead.

Tain told Steban, "Take this package to your mother. Tell her to wait till I come in."

Steban scampered off.

Tain backed into the lee of the barn. He waited.

The rider passed the spring. "Torfin. Here."

The paint changed direction. The youth swung down beside Tain. "Oh, what a night. What're you doing out in it, friend?"

"Getting the sheep inside."

"All right for a Caydarman to come in out of it?"

"You picked the wrong time, Torfin. But come on. Crowd the horse inside."

Lightning flashed. Thunder rolled. The youth eyed Tain. The ex-soldier still wore his shortsword.

"What happened?"

"You haven't been to the Tower?"

"Not for a couple days."

"Torfin, tell me. Why do you hang around here? How come you're always watching Steban graze sheep?"

"Uh. . . . The Klecklas deserve better."

Tain helped with the saddle. "Better than what?"

"I see. They haven't told you. But they'd hide their shame, wouldn't they?"

"I don't understand."

"The one they call the Witch. She's their daughter Shirl."

"Lords of Darkness!"

"That's why they have no friends."

"But you don't blame them?"

"When the Children of Hell curse someone with the Power, is that a parent's fault? No. I don't blame them. Not for that. For letting her become a petulant, spoiled little thief, yes. I do. The Power-cursed choose the right- or left-hand path according to personality. Not so?"

"It's debatable. They let me think she was dead."

"They pretend that. It's been a little over a year since she cast her spell on the Baron. She thought he'd take her to Iwa Skolovda and make her a great lady. But she doesn't understand politics. The Baron can't go back. And now she can't come home. Now she's trying to buy a future by stealing."

"How old are you, Torfin?"

"Nineteen, I think. Too old."

"You sound older. I think I like you."

"I'm a Caydarman by chance, not inclination."

"I think you've had pain from this too."

A wan smile crossed Torfin's lips. "You make me wonder. Do you read minds? What are you, carrying such a sword?" When Tain didn't respond, he continued bitterly, "Yes, there's pain in it for Torfin Hakesson. I was in love with Shirl. She used me. To get into the Tower."

"That's sad. We'd better go in. Be careful. They're not going to be glad to see you. Caydarmen burned the Kosku place. One of his girls was killed."

"Damn! But it was bound to happen, wasn't it?"

"Yes. And that was just the beginning. Kosku went after Olag and Grimnir. He was killed too."

"Which one did it?"

"Too late. Olag, but he's dead too. He killed Mikla and wounded Toma first, though."

"Help me with the saddle. I can't stay."

"Stay. Maybe together we can stop the bloodshed here."

"I can't face them. They already hate me. Because of Shirl."

"Stay. Tomorrow we'll go to the Tower. We'll see the Baron himself. He can stop it."

"Mikla lived with Stojan's daughter. The old man will want to avenge him."

"All the more reason to stop it here."

Torfin thought again. "All right. You didn't cut me down. Maybe you have a man's heart."

Tain smiled. "I'll guard your back, Trolledyngjan."

XU

Rula and Toma were talking in low, sad tones. Tain pushed through the doorway. Silence descended.

Such hatred! "Torfin will stay the night. We're going to the Tower in the morning. To talk to the Baron." Tain glared, daring opposition.

Toma struggled up. "Not in my house."

"Lie down, damn it. Your pride and fear have caused enough trouble."

Toma said nothing. Rula tensed as if to spring.

"Tain!" Steban whined.

"Torfin has said some hard things about himself. He's almost too eager to take his share of responsibility. He's willing to try to straighten things out.

"In no land I know does a father let his daughter run away and just cry woe. A man is responsible for his children, Toma. You could have gone after her. But it's easier to play like she's dead, and the Witch of the Tower has nothing to do with you. You sit here hating the Baron and refuse to admit your own part in creating the situation. . . ."

He stopped. He had slipped into his drillmaster's voice. Pointless. Recruits had to listen, to respond, to correct. These westerners had no tradition of personal responsibility. They were round-eyes. They blamed their misfortunes on external forces. . . .

Hadn't Toma blamed Mikla? Didn't Rula accuse Toma?

"That's all. I can't do any good shouting. Torfin is spending the night. Rula. Steban gave you a package."

She nodded. She refused to speak.

"Thank you."

For an instant he feared she hadn't understood. But the packet came with a murmured, "It's all right. I'll control my feelings."

"Is the broth ready?" He felt compelled to convince Rula.

She ladled a wooden bowl full. "Tain."

"Uhm."

"Don't expect me to stop feeling."

"I don't. I feel. Too much. I killed a man today. A man I didn't know, for no better reason than because I responded to feelings. I don't like that, Rula."

She looked down, understanding.

Steban chimed, "But you were a soldier. . . ."

"Steban, a soldier is supposed to keep the peace, not start wars." The almost-lie tasted bitter. The Dread Empire interpreted that credo rather obliquely. Yet Tain had believed he was living it while marching to conquest after conquest. Only when Shinsan turned upon itself did he question his commanders.

"Tain. . . ." There was a life's worth of pain in Steban's voice.

"People are going to get killed if we don't stop it, Steban." Tain tapped herbs into Toma's broth. "Your friends. Maybe there are only six Caydarmen. Maybe they could be beaten by shepherds. But what happens when the Baron has to run?" He hoped Toma was paying attention. Steban didn't care about the long run.

Toma's eyes remained hard. But he listened. Tain had won that much respect.

"Governments just won't tolerate rebellion. It doesn't matter if it's justified. Overthrow the Baron and you'll have an army in the Zemstvi."

Toma grunted.

Rula shrieked, "Tain!"

He whirled, disarmed Steban in an eye's blink. Torfin nodded in respect. "Thank you."

"Steban," Toma gasped. "Come here."

"Dad, he's a Caydarman!"

Tain pushed the boy. A soul-searing hatred burned in his young eyes. He glared at Mikla, Torfin, and Tain.

Tain suddenly felt tired and old. What was he doing? Why did he care? It wasn't his battle.

His eyes met Rula's. Through the battle of her soul flickered the feelings she had revealed the day before. He sighed. It *was* his battle.

He had killed a man. There was blood in it. He couldn't run away.

XUI

"I want to see Shirl," Rula declared next morning. "I'm going too."

"Mom!" Steban still didn't understand. He wouldn't talk to Tain, and Torfin he eyed like a butcher considering a carcass.

Tain responded, "First we take care of Mikla. Steban. The sheep. Better pasture them." To Toma, "Going to need sheds. That barn's too crowded."

Toma didn't reply. He did take his breakfast broth without difficulty.

He finally spoke when Steban refused to graze the sheep. "Boy, come here."

Steban went, head bowed.

"Knock it off. You're acting like Shirl. Pasture the sheep. Or I'll paddle your tail all the way out there."

Steban ground his teeth, glared at Tain, and went.

Rula insisted that Mikla lie beside the new home's door. Tain and Torfin took turns digging.

Tain went inside. "We're ready, Toma. You want to go out?"

"I've got to. It's my fault. . . . I have to watch him go down. So I'll remember."

Tain raised an eyebrow questioningly.

"I thought about what you said. I don't like it, but you're right. Four dead are enough."

"Good. Torfin! Help me carry Toma."

It was a quiet burial. Rula wept softly. Toma silently stared his brother-in-law into the ground. Neither Torfin nor Tain spoke. There were no appropriate words.

Tain saddled the roan and threw a pad on the mule. He spoke to her soothingly, reassuringly.

He knelt beside Toma while Torfin readied the paint. "You'll be all right?"

"Just leave me some beer. And some soup and bread."

"All right."

"Tain?"

"Yes?"

"Good luck."

"Thanks, Toma."

The mule accepted Rula's weight, though ungraciously. Tain donned his weapons. Little was said. Tain silently pursued his Morning Ritual. He hadn't had time earlier. Torfin watched. He and Rula couldn't talk. There were too many barriers between them.

The Tower was a growing, squat, dark block filled with frightening promise. A single vermilion banner waved over its ramparts. A feather of smoke curled from an unseen chimney.

"Something's wrong," Torfin remarked. They were a quarter mile away. "I don't see anybody."

Tain studied their surroundings.

Sheep and goats crowded the pens clinging to the Tower's skirts. Chickens and geese ran free. Several scrawny cattle, a mule, and some horses grazed nearby.

No human was visible.

"There should be a few women and children," Torfin said. "Watching the stock."

"Let's stop here."

"Why?" Rula asked.

"Beyond bowshot. Torfin, you go ahead."

The youth nodded. He advanced cautiously. The closer he drew, the lower he hunched in his saddle.

"Rula, stay here." Tain kicked the roan, began trotting round the Tower. Torfin glanced back. He paused at the Tower gate, peered through, dismounted, drew his sword, went it.

"Whoa." The roan stopped. Tain swung down, examined the tracks.

"Six horses," he murmured. "One small." He leapt onto the roan, galloped toward the Tower gate. "Torfin!" He beckoned Rula.

Torfin didn't hear him. Tain dismounted, peered through the gate into a small interior court. Quarters for the garrison had been built against the bailey walls.

"What is it?" Rula asked.

"Six riders left this morning. The Witch and the other five Caydarmen, probably."

Rula's cheek twitched. She wove her fingers together. "What about the people here?"

"Let's find Torfin."

The youth appeared above. "They're up here." He sounded miserable.

Tain guided Rula up the perilous stair. Torfin met them outside a doorway.

"In here. They saw us coming."

Tain heard muted weeping.

"Trouble," Torfin explained. "Bad trouble."

"I saw the tracks."

"Worse than that. She'll be able to cut loose for real. . . ." The youth pushed the door. Frightened faces peered out at Tain.

The three women weren't Trolledyngjan. And their children were too old to have been fathered by the mercenaries.

Tain had seen those faces countless times, in countless camps. Women with children, without husbands, who attached themselves to an occupying soldiery. They were always tired, beaten, frightened creatures.

Mothers and children retreated to one corner of the Spartan room. One woman brandished a carving knife. Tain showed his palms. "Don't be afraid. We came to see Baron Caydar."

Rula tried a smile. Torfin nodded agreement. "It's all right. They mean no harm."

The knife-woman opened a path.

Tain got his first glimpse of Caydar.

The Baron lay on a pallet in the corner. He was a spare, short man, bald, with a scraggly beard. He was old, and he was dying.

This was what Torfin had meant by saying the trouble was big. There would be no brake on the Witch with the Baron gone. "Torfin. Move them. I'll see if I can do anything."

The Baron coughed. It was the first of a wracking series. Blood froth dribbled down his chin.

Torfin gestured. The Tower people sidled like whipped dogs. Tain knelt by the old man. "How long has he been sick?"

"Always. He seldom left this room. How bad is it?"

"Rula. In my left saddle bag. The same leather packet I had when I treated Toma." She left. "He'll probably go before sundown. But I'll do what I can."

"Tain, if he dies. . . . Grimnir and the others. . . . They'd rather take the Witch's orders. Her style suits them better."

Tain checked the Baron's eyes and mouth, dabbed blood, felt his chest. There was little left of Caydar. "Torfin. Anyone else shown these symptoms?"

"I don't think so."

"They will. Probably the girl, if she's been intimate with him."

Rula reappeared. She heard. "What is it?"

"Tuberculosis."

"No. Tain, she's only a child."

"Disease doesn't care. And you could say she's earned it."

"No. That isn't fair."

"Nothing's fair, Rula. Nothing. Torfin. Find out where she went." Tain took the packet from Rula, concentrated on Caydar.

He left the room half an hour later, climbed the ladder to the ramparts. Hands clasped behind him, he stared at the green of the Zemstvi.

A beautiful land, he thought. About to be sullied with blood.

Fate, with a malicious snicker, had squandered the land's last hope.

Torfin followed him. "They're not sure. She just led them out."

"Probably doesn't matter. It's too late. Unless. . . ."

"What?"

"We smash the snake's head."

"What? He's going to die? You can't stop it?"

"No. And that leaves Shirl."

"You saying what I think?"

"She has to die."

Torfin smiled thinly. "Friend, she wouldn't let you do it. And if she couldn't stop you with the Power, I'd have to with the sword."

Tain locked eyes with the youth. Torfin wouldn't look away. "She means a lot to you, eh?"

"I still love her."

"So," Tain murmured. "So. Can you stand up to her? Can you bully the others into behaving themselves."

"I can try."

"Do. I'm into this too deep, lad. If you don't control her, I'll try to stop her the only way I know." He turned to stare across the Zemstvi again.

Though the Tower wasn't tall, it gave a view of the countryside matched only from the Toad. That grim formation was clearly visible. The rain had cleared the air.

Someone was running toward the Tower. Beyond, a fountain of smoke rose against the backdrop formed by the Dragon's Teeth.

A distance-muted thunderclap smote the air.

"That's your place," Torfin said softly.

XVII

A man in black, wearing a golden mask, rounded a knoll. He paused above the Palikov stead. Bloody dawn light leaked round the Toad. It splashed him as he knelt, feeling the earth. It made his mask more hideous. The faceted ruby eyepieces seemed to catch fire.

Thin fingers floated on the air, reaching, till they pointed westward. The man in black rose and started walking. His fingers led him on.

He went slowly, sensing his quarry's trail. It was cold. Occasionally he lost it and had to circle till he caught it again.

The sun scaled the sky. Kai Ling kept walking. A gentle, anticipatory smile played behind his mask.

The feel of the man was getting stronger. He was getting close. It was almost done. In a few hours he would be home. The Tervola would be determining the extent of his reward.

He crossed a low hilltop and paused.

A shepherd's stead lay below. He reached out. . . .

One man, injured, lay within the crude sod house. A second life-spark lurked in the grove surrounding the nearby spring.

And there were six riders coming in from the southwest.

One seized his attention. She coruscated with a stench of wild, untrained Power.

"Lords of Darkness," Kai Ling whispered. "She's almost as strong as the Demon Princess." He crouched, becoming virtually invisible in a patch of gorse.

Five of the riders dismounted. They heaped kindling round the timbers of a partially finished house.

A man staggered from the sod structure. "Shirl!" he screamed. "For god's sake. . . ."

A raider tripped him, slipped a knife into his back as he wriggled on the earth.

Kai Ling stirred slightly as two blasts of emotion exploded below.

A child burst from the grove, shrieking, running toward the killer. And the wild witch lashed the man with a whip. He screamed louder than the boy.

Kai Ling reeled back from the raw surge. She *was* as strong as the Prince's daughter. But extremely young and undisciplined.

He stood.

The tableau froze.

The boy thought quickest. He paused only a second, then whirled and raced away.

The others regarded Kai Ling for half a minute. Then the witch turned her mount toward him. He felt the uncertainty growing within her.

Kai Ling let his Aspirant's senses roam the stead. The barn stood out. That was his man's living place. But he was gone.

Faceted rubies tracked the fleeing boy. Lips smiled behind gold. "Bring him to me, child," he whispered.

The raiders formed a line shielding the woman. Swords appeared. Kai Ling glanced at the boy. He waited.

She felt him now, he knew. She knew there had been sorcery in the Zemstvi. She would be wondering. . . .

A raider wheeled suddenly. Kai Ling could imagine his words.

He had been recognized.

He folded his arms.

What would she try?

The fire gnawed at the new house. Smoke billowed up. Kai Ling glanced westward. The child had disappeared.

The witch's right arm thrust his way. Pale fire sparkled amongst her fingertips.

He murmured into his mask, readying his defenses.

She was a wild witch. Untrained. She had only intuitive control of the Power. Her emotions would affect what little control she had. He remained unworried despite her strength.

Kai Ling underestimated the size of the channel fear could open in her. She hit him with a blast that nearly melted his protection.

He fell to his knees.

He forced his hands together.

Thunder rolled across the Zemstvi. The timbers of the burning house leapt into the air, tumbled down like a lazy rain of torches. The sod house twisted, collapsed. The barn canted dangerously. The cow inside bawled.

The witch toppled from her horse, screaming, clawing her ears. She thrashed and wailed till a raider smacked her unconscious.

The Caydarmen looked uphill. Kai Ling, though unconscious, remained upon his knees. Golden fire burned where his face belonged. They tossed the witch aboard her horse, fled.

Kai Ling eventually fell forward into the gorse, vanishing.

Then only the flames moved on the Kleckla stead, casting dancing color onto the man whose dreams were dying with him.

XVIII

Tain pushed the roan. He met Steban more than a mile from the Tower. The boy was exhausted, but his arms and legs kept pumping.

"Tain!" he called. "Tain, they killed Pa." He spoke in little bursts, between lung-searing gasps.

"You go on to your mother. She's at the Tower. Come on. Go." He kicked the roan to a gallop.

Steban didn't reach the Tower. Rula, having conquered Tain's mule, met him. She pulled him up behind her and continued toward her home.

Tain saw the Caydarmen to the south, but didn't alter course. He would find them when their time came.

It was too late now. Absolutely too late. He had switched allegiance from peace to blood. He would kill them. The Witch would go last. After she saw her protectors stripped away. After she learned the meaning of terror.

He was an angry, unreasoning man. Only craft and cunning remained.

He knew he couldn't face her wild magic armed only with long and shortsword. To do so he had to resume his abandoned identity. He had to become a soldier of the Dread Empire once more. A centurion's armor bore strong protective magicks.

What amazing fear would course through the Zemstvi!

He pulled up when he topped the last hill.

The after-smell of sorcery tainted the air round the stead. The familiar stench of the Dread Empire overrode that of the Witch. . . .

He hurled himself from the horse into the shelter of small bushes. His swords materialized in his hands. His emotions perished like small flames in a sudden deluge. He probed with Aspirant senses.

They had come. Because of the civil war he hadn't believed they would bother. He had fooled himself. They couldn't just let him go, could they? Not a centurion with his background. He could be too great a boon to potential enemies.

The heirs of the Dread Empire, both the Demon Princess and the Dragon Princes, aspired to western conquests.

Tain frowned. Sorceries had met here. The eastern had been victorious. So what had become of the victor?

He waited nearly fifteen minutes, till certain the obvious trap wasn't there. Only then did he enter the yard.

He couldn't get near Toma. The flames were too hot.

Kleckla was beyond worry anyway.

Tain was calm. His reason was at work. He had surprised himself in the jaws of a merciless vice.

One was his determination to rid the Zemstvi of the Witch and her thieves. The other was the hunter from home, who would be a man stronger than he, a highly ranked Candidate or Select.

Where was he? Why didn't he make his move?

Right now, just possibly, he could get away. If he obscured his trail meticulously and avoided using the Power again, he might give his past the slip forever. But if he hazarded the Tower, there would be no chance whatsoever. He would have to use the Power. The hunter would pin him down, and come when he was exhausted. . . .

Life had been easier when he hadn't made his own decisions. Back then it hadn't mattered if a task were perilous or impossible. All he had had to do was follow orders.

He released the old cow, recovered his mule packs. He stared at them a long time, as if he might be able to exhume a decision from their contents.

He heard a noise. His hands flew to his swords.

Rula, Steban, and the mule descended the hill.

Tain relaxed, waited.

Rula surveyed the remains. "This's the cost of conciliation." There was no venom in her voice.

"Yes." He searched her empty face for a clue. He found no help there.

"Rula, they've sent somebody after me. From the east. He's in the Zemstvi now. I don't know where. He was here. He chased the Caydarmen off. I don't know why. I don't know who he is. I don't know how he thinks. But I know what his mission is. To take me home."

Steban said, "I saw him."

"What?"

"A stranger. I saw him. Over there. He was all black. He had this ugly mask on. . . ."

A brief hope flickered in Tain's breast.

"The mask. What did it look like? What were his clothes like?"

Steban pouted. "I only saw him for a second. He scared me. I ran."

"Try to think. It's important. A soldier has to remember things, Steban. Everything."

"I don't think I want to be a soldier anymore."

"Come on. Come on." Tain coaxed him gently, and in a few minutes had drawn out everything Steban knew.

"Kai Ling. Can't be anybody else." His voice was sad.

"You know him?" Rula asked.

"I knew him. He was my best friend. A long, long time ago. When we were Steban's age."

"Then. . . ."

"Nothing. He's still a Tervola Aspirant. He's been given a mission. Nothing will deflect him. He might shed a tear for our childhood afterward. He was always too emotional for his chosen path."

She surveyed his gear while he helped Steban off the mule. "You mean you have to run to have a chance?"

"Yes."

"Then run. Anything you did now would be pointless, anyway."

"No. A soldier's honor is involved. To abandon a task in the face of a secondary danger would be to betray a code which has been my life. I'm a soldier. I can't stop being one. And soldiers of the Dread Empire don't retreat. We don't flee because we face defeat. There may be a purpose in sacrifice. We withdraw only if ordered."

"There's nobody to order you. You could go. You're your own commander now."

"I know. That's why it's so difficult."

"I can't help you, Tain." The weight of Toma's demise had begun to crack her barriers against grief.

"You can. Tell me what you'll do."

"About what?"

He indicated the stead. "You can't stay. Can you?"

She shrugged.

"Will you go with me if I go?"

She shrugged again. The grief was upon her now. She wasn't listening.

Tain massaged his aching temples, then started unpacking his armor.

Piece by piece, he became a leading centurion of the Demon Guard. Steban watched with wide eyes. He recognized the armor. The legions were known far beyond lands that had endured their unstoppable passing.

Tain donned his helmet, his swords and witch kit. He paused with his mask in hand. Rula said nothing. She stared at Toma, remembering.

Tain shook his head, donned the mask, walked to the roan. He started toward the Tower

He didn't look back.

The armor began to feel comfortable. The roan pranced along, glad to be a soldier's steed once more. He felt halfway home. . . .

What he had said penetrated Rula's brain soon after he passed out of view. She glanced around in panic.

The mule remained. As did all Tain's possessions except his weapons and armor. "He left his things!"

Quiet tears dribbled from Steban's eyes. "Ma. I don't think he expects to come back. He thinks he's going to die."

"Steban, we've got to stop him."

XIX

Tain came to the dark tower in the day's last hour. Caydarmen manned its ramparts. An arrow dropped from the sky. It whistled off his armor.

Torfin stood beside the Witch. Tain heard her say, "He's not the same one. He wore robes. And walked."

And Torfin responded, awed, "It's Tain. The man who stayed with your father."

There was no thought in the old soldier. He was a machine come to destroy the Tower. He let decades of combat schooling guide him.

He began with the gate.

From his witch pouch he drew a short, slim rod and a tiny glass vial. He thrust the rod into the vial, making sure the entire shaft was moist. He spoke words he had learned long ago.

Fire exploded in his hand. He hurled a flaming javelin.

It flew perfectly flat, immune to gravity. It struck the gate, made a sound like the beating of a brass gong.

Timbers flew as the gate shattered.

Caydarmen scrambled down from the ramparts.

Tain returned to his pouch. He removed the jar and silver box he had used in the pass. He greased his hands, obtained one of the deadly peas. He concentrated, breathed. The cerulean glow came into being. He hurled a fiery blue ball upward.

It rose slowly, drifted like gossamer toward the ramparts.

The Witch didn't recognize her peril until too late. The ball jumped at her, enveloping her left hand.

She screamed.

Torfin bellowed, followed his confederates downstairs.

Tain dismounted and strode through the gate.

Grimnir met him first. Fear filled the big man's eyes. He fought with desperate genius.

And he died.

As did his comrades, though they tried to team against the man in black.

Trolledyngjans were feared throughout the west. They were deadly fighters. These were amazed by their own ineffectuality. But they had never faced a soldier of the Dread Empire, let alone a leading centurion of the Demon Guard.

The last fell. Tain faced Torfin. "Yield, boy," he said, breaking battle discipline. "You're the one good man in this viper's nest. Go."

"Release her." The youth indicated the ramparts. The girl's screams had declined to moans. She had begun fighting the ball. Tain knew she had the strength to beat it, if she could find and harness it.

He smiled. If she failed, she would die. Even if she succeeded, she would never be the same. No matter what happened to him, he had won something. At her age pain could be a powerful purgative for evil.

Still, he had to try to make the situation absolute. "Stand aside, Torfin. You can't beat me."

"I have to try. I love her, Tain."

"You're no good to her dead."

At the bottom of it, Torfin was Trolledyngjan. Like Tain, he could do nothing but be what he was. Trolledyngjans were stubborn, inflexible, and saw all settlements, finally, in terms of the stronger sword.

Torfin fell into a slight crouch, presenting his blade in a tentative figure eight.

Tain nodded, began murmuring the Battle Ritual. He had to relax, to give his reflexes complete control. Torfin was more skilled than his confederates. He was young and quick.

He shrieked and lunged.

Tain turned his rush in silence. The soldiers of Shinsan fought, and died, without a word or cry. Their silence had unnerved men more experienced than Torfin.

Tain's cool, wordless competence told. Torfin retreated a step, then another and another. Sweat ran down his forehead.

Tain's shortsword flicked across and pinked Torfin's left hand. The dagger flew away. The youth had used the weapon cunningly, wickedly. Its neutralization had been Tain's immediate goal.

Torfin danced away, sucked his wound. He looked into faceted crystal and knew the old soldier had spoken the truth when claiming he couldn't be beaten.

Both glanced upward. Shirl's moans were fading.

Tain advanced, engaging with his longsword while forcing Torfin to give ground to the short. Torfin reached the ladder to the ramparts. He scrambled up.

Tain pursued him mercilessly, despite the disadvantage. The youth was a natural swordsman. Even against two blades he kept his guard almost impenetrable.

Tain pushed. Torfin was relying on youth's stamina, hoping he would tire.

Tain wouldn't. He could still spend a day in his hot armor, matching blows with the enemy. He hadn't survived his legion years by yielding to fatigue.

Tain stepped onto the battlements. Torfin had lost his last advantage. Tain paused to glance at the Witch.

The blue ball had eaten half her arm. But she was getting the best of it. Only a few sparks still gnawed at her mutilated flesh.

She looked extremely young and vulnerable.

Torfin looked, too.

Tain feinted with the longsword, struck with the short.

It was his best move.

Torfin's blade tumbled away into the courtyard. Blood stained both of his hands now.

He backed away quickly, seized a dagger his love carried at her waist.

Tain sighed, broke battle discipline. "Boy, you're just too stubborn." He sheathed his swords, discarded their harness. He removed his helmet, placed it between his blades.

He went to Torfin.

The youth scoured Tain's armor twice before the soldier took the dagger and arced it out into the grass of the Zemstvi.

Torfin still would not yield.

Tain kicked his feet from beneath him, laid the edge of one hand across the side of his neck.

Tain backed away, glanced down. Torfin's dagger had found a chink. Red oozed down the shiny ebony of his breastplate. A brutalized rib began aching.

He recovered his shortsword, went toward the Witch.

In seconds she would complete her conquest of his magick. In seconds she would be able to destroy him.

Yet he hesitated.

He considered her youth, her vulnerability, her beauty, and understood how she had captivated Torfin and the Baron.

She bleated plaintively, "Mother!"

Tain whirled.

Rula stepped onto the ramparts. "Tain. Don't. Please?"

Seconds fled.

Tain sheathed his blade.

Shirl sighed and gave up consciousness.

"Tain, I brought your things. And your mule." Rula pushed past him to her daughter.

"The wound is cauterized. I'll take care of the bone."

"You're wounded. Take care of yourself."

"It can wait."

He finished Shirl's arm ten minutes later. Then he removed his breastplate and let Rula tend to his injury. It was minor. The scar would become lost among its predecessors.

Rula finished. "You'd better go. The hunter. . . ."

"You're staying?" An infinite sadness filled him as he drew his eyes from hers to scan the Zemstvi. Kai Ling was out there somewhere. He could sense nothing, but that had no meaning. His hunter would be more cunning than he. The trap might have closed already.

"She's my daughter. She needs me."

Sadly, Tain collected his possessions and started for the ladder.

Torfin groaned.

Tain laid his things aside, knelt beside the youth. "Ah. She does have this stubborn ass, you know." He gathered his possessions again. This time he descended without pausing.

Soldiers of the Dread Empire seldom surrendered to their emotions.

He had a hand on Steban's shoulder, trying to think of some final word, when Rula came to him. "Tain. I'll go."

He looked into her eyes. Yes, he thought. She would. Dared he?. . .

Sometimes a soldier did surrender. "Steban. Go find you and your mother some horses. Rula, get some things from the Tower. Food. Utensils. Clothes. Whatever you'll need. And hurry." He scanned the horizon.

Where was Kai Ling?

"Old friend, are you coming?" he whispered.

Not even the breeze responded. It giggled round the Tower as if the gathering of Death's daughters were a cosmic joke.

Their shadows scurried impatiently round the old stronghold.

They were a hundred yards along the road to nowhere.

"Tain!"

He whirled the gelding.

Torfin leaned on the battlements, right hand grasping his neck. Then he raised the other. "Good luck, centurion."

Tain waved. He didn't reply. His ribs ached too much for shouting.

The day was dead. He set a night course for the last bit of sunlight. Rula rode to his left, Steban to his right. The mule plodded along behind, snapping at the tails of the newcomers.

He glanced back just once, to eye the destruction he had wrought. Death's daughters had descended to the feast. The corner of his mouth quirked downward.

His name was Tain, and he was still a man to beware.

XX

The wind of dark wings wakened Kai Ling. The daughters of Death circled close. One bold vulture had landed a few feet from his outstretched hand.

He moved.

The vulture took wing.

He rose slowly. Pain gnawed his nerve ends. He surveyed the stead, the smoking ruins, and understood. He had survived his mistake. He was a lucky man.

Slowly, slowly, he turned, feeling the twilight.

There. To the west. The centurion had called on the Power yet again.

FILED TEETH

This story is a collateral sequel to the novel All Darkness Met. *It appeared in the anthology* Dragons of Darkness, *edited by Orson Scott Card, a companion volume to* Dragons of Light. *Michael Whelan produced an absolutely stunning cover painting based upon "Filed Teeth" — which ended up on* Dragons of Light *because the artist doing that cover did not deliver his work on time. Whelan also did a fine interior illo of Lord Hammer, which has appeared on magazine and book covers around the world. And which resides proudly in my library now.*

I

Our first glimpse of the plain was one of Heaven. The snow and treacherous passes had claimed two men and five animals.

Two days later we all wished we were back in the mountains.

The ice storm came by night. An inch covered the ground. And still it came down, stinging my face, frosting the heads and shoulders of my companions. The footing was impossible. We had to finish two broken-legged mules before noon.

Lord Hammer remained unperturbed, unvanquishable. He remained stiffly upright on that red-eyed stallion, implacably drawing us northeastward. Ice clung to his cowl, shoulders, and the tail of his robe where it lay across his beast's rump. Seldom did even Nature break the total blackness of his apparel.

The wind hurtled against us, biting and clawing like a million mocking imps. It burned sliding into the lungs.

The inalterable, horizon-to-horizon bleakness of the world gnawed the roots of our souls. Even Fetch and irrepressible Chenyth dogged Lord Hammer in a desperate silence.

"We're becoming an army of ghosts," I muttered at my brother. "Hammer is rubbing off on us. How're the Harish taking this?" I didn't glance back. My concentration was devoted to taking each next step forward.

Chenyth muttered something I didn't hear. The kid was starting to understand that adventures were more fun when you were looking back and telling tall tales.

A mule slipped. She went down kicking and braying. She caught old Toamas a couple of good ones. He skittered across the ice and down an embankment into a shallow pool not yet frozen.

Lord Hammer stopped. He didn't look back, but he knew exactly what had happened. Fetch fluttered round him nervously. Then she scooted toward Toamas.

"Better help, Will," Chenyth muttered.

I was after him already.

Why Toamas joined Lord Hammer's expedition I don't know. He was over sixty. Men his age are supposed to spend winter telling the grandkids lies about the El Murid, Civil, and Great Eastern Wars. But Toamas was telling *us* his stories and trying to prove something to himself.

He was a tough buzzard. He had taken the Dragon's Teeth more easily than most, and those are the roughest mountains the gods ever raised.

"Toamas. You okay?" I asked. Chenyth hunkered down beside me. Fetch scooted up, laid a hand on each of our shoulders. Brandy and Russ and the other Kaveliners came over, too. Our little army clumped itself into national groups.

"Think it's my ribs, Will. She got me in the ribs." He spoke in little gasps. I checked his mouth.

"No blood. Good. Lungs should be okay."

"You clowns going to talk about it all week?" Fetch snapped. "Help the man, Will."

"You got such a sweet-talking way, Fetch. We should get married. Let's get him up, Chenyth. Maybe he's just winded."

"It's my ribs, Will. They're broke for sure."

"Maybe. Come on, you old woods-runner. Let's try."

"Lord Hammer says carry him if you have to. We've still got to cover eight miles today. More, if the circle isn't alive." Fetch's voice went squeaky and dull, like an old iron hinge that hadn't been oiled for a lifetime. She scurried back to her master.

"I think I'm in love," Chenyth chirped.

"Eight miles," Brandy grumbled. "What the hell? Bastard's trying to kill us."

Chenyth laughed. It was a ghost of his normal tinkle. "You didn't have to sign up, Brandy. He warned us it would be tough."

Brandy wandered away.

"Go easy, Chenyth. He's the kind of guy you got to worry when he stops bitching."

"Wish he'd give it a rest, Will. I haven't heard him say one good word since we met him."

"You meet all kinds in this business. Okay, Toamas?" I asked. We had the old man on his feet. Chenyth brushed water off him. It froze on his hand.

"I'll manage. We got to get moving. I'll freeze." He stumbled toward the column. Chenyth stayed close, ready to catch him if he fell.

The non-Kaveliners watched apathetically. Not that they didn't care. Toamas was a favorite, a confidant, adviser, and teacher to most. They were just too tired to move except when they had to. Men and animals looked vague and slumped through the ice rain.

Brandy gave Toamas a spear to lean on. We lined up. Fetch took her place at Lord Hammer's left stirrup. Our ragged little army of thirty-eight homeless bits of war-flotsam started moving again.

II

Lord Hammer was a little spooky. . . . What am I saying? He scared hell out of us. He was damned near seven feet tall. His stallion was a monster. He never spoke. He had Fetch do all his talking.

The stallion was jet. Even its hooves were black. Lord Hammer dressed to match. His hands remained gloved all the time. None of us ever saw an inch of skin. He wore no trinkets. His very colorlessness inspired dread.

Even his face he kept concealed. Or, perhaps, especially his face. . . .

He always rode point, staring ahead. Opportunities to peek into his cowl were scant. All you would see, anyway, was a blackened iron mask resembling a handsome man with strong features. For all we knew, there was no one inside. The mask had almost imperceptible eye, nose, and mouth slits. You couldn't see a thing through them.

Sometimes the mask broke the colorless boredom of Lord Hammer. Some mornings, before leaving his tent, he or Fetch decorated it. The few designs I saw were never repeated.

Lord Hammer was a mystery. We knew nothing of his origins and were ignorant of his goals. He wouldn't talk, and Fetch wouldn't say. But he paid well, and a lot up front. He took care of us. Our real bitch was the time of year chosen for his journey.

Fetch said winter was the best time. She wouldn't expand.

She claimed Lord Hammer was a mighty, famous sorcerer.

So why hadn't any of us heard of him?

Fetch was a curiosity herself. She was small, cranky, long-haired, homely. She walked more mannish than any man. She was totally devoted to Hammer despite being inclined to curse him constantly. Guessing her age was impossible. For all I could tell, she could have been anywhere between twenty and two hundred.

She wouldn't mess with the men.

By then that little gnome was looking good.

Sigurd Ormson, our half-tame Trolledyngjan, was the only guy who had had nerve enough to really go after her. The rest of us followed his suit with a mixture of shame and hope.

The night Ormson tried his big move Lord Hammer strolled from his tent and just stood behind Fetch. Sigurd seemed to shrink to about half normal size.

You couldn't see Lord Hammer's eyes, but when his gaze turned your way the whole universe ground to a halt. You felt whole new dimensions of cold. They made winter seem balmy.

Trudge. Trudge. Trudge. The wind giggled and bit. Chenyth and I supported Toamas between us. He kept muttering, "It's my ribs, boys. My ribs." Maybe the mule had scrambled his head, too.

"Holy Hagard's Golden Turds!" Sigurd bellowed. The northman had ice in his hair and beard. He looked like one of the frost giants of his native legends.

He thrust an arm eastward.

The rainfall masked them momentarily. But they were coming closer. Nearly two hundred horsemen. The nearer they got, the nastier they looked.

They carried heads on lances. They wore necklaces of human finger bones. They had rings in their ears and noses. Their faces were painted. They looked grimy and mean.

They weren't planning a friendly visit.

Lord Hammer faced them. For the first time that morning I glimpsed his mask paint.

White. Stylized. Undeniably the skullface of death.

He stared. Then, slowly, his stallion paced toward the nomads.

Bellweather, the Itaskian commanding us, started yelling. We grabbed weapons and shields and formed a ragged-assed line. The nomads probably laughed. We were scruffier than they were.

"Gonna go through us like salts through a goose," Toamas complained. He couldn't get his shield up. His spear seemed too heavy. But he took his place in the line.

Fetch and the Harish collected the animals behind us

Lord Hammer plodded toward the nomads, head high, as if there were nothing in the universe he feared. He lifted his left hand, palm toward the riders.

A nimbus formed round him. It was like a shadow cast every way at once.

The nomads reined in abruptly.

I had seen high sorcery during the Great Eastern Wars. I had witnessed both the thaumaturgies of the Brotherhood and the Tervola of Shinsan. Most of us had. Lord Hammer's act didn't overwhelm us. But it did dispel doubts about him being what Fetch claimed.

"Oh!" Chenyth gasped. "Will. Look."

"I see."

Chenyth was disappointed by my reaction. But he was only seventeen. He had spent the Great Eastern Wars with our mother, hiding in the forest while the legions of the Dread Empire rolled across our land. This was his first venture at arms.

The nomads decided not to bother us after all. They milled around briefly, then rode away.

Soon Chenyth asked, "Will, if he can do that, why'd he bring us?"

"Been wondering myself. But you can't do everything with the Power."

We were helping Toamas again. He was getting weaker. He croaked, "Don't get no wrong notions, Chenyth lad. They didn't have to leave. They could've took us slicker than greased owl shit. They just didn't want to pay the price Lord Hammer would've made them pay."

III

Lord Hammer stopped.

We had come to a forest. Scattered, ice-rimed trees stood across our path. They were gnarled, stunted things that looked like old apple trees.

Fetch came down the line, speaking to each little band in its own language. She told us Kaveliners, "Don't ever leave the trail once we pass the first tree. It could be worth your life. This is a fey, fell land." Her dusky little face was as somber as ever I had seen it.

"Why? Where are we? What's happening?" Chenyth asked.

She frowned. Then a smile broke through. "Don't you ever stop asking?" She was almost pretty when she smiled.

"Give him a break," I said. "He's a kid."

She smiled a little at me, then, before turning back to Chenyth. I think she liked the kid. Everybody did. Even the Harish tolerated him. They hardly acknowledged the existence of anyone else but Fetch, and she only as the mouth of the man who paid them.

Fetch was a sorceress in her own right. She knew how to use the magic of her smiles. The genuine article just sort of melted you inside.

"The forest isn't what it seems," she explained. "Those trees haven't died for the winter. They're alive, Chenyth. They're wicked, and they're waiting for you to make a mistake. All you have to do is wander past one and you'll be lost. Unless Lord Hammer can save you. He might let you go. As an object lesson."

"Come on, Fetch. How'd you get that name, anyway? That's not a real name. Look. The trees are fifty feet apart. . . ."

"Chenyth." I tapped his shoulder. He subsided. Lord Hammer was always right. When Fetch gave us a glimmer of fact, we listened.

"Bellweather named me Fetch. Because I run for Lord Hammer. And maybe because he thinks I'm a little spooky. He's clever that way. You couldn't pronounce my real name, anyway."

"Which you'd never reveal," I remarked.

She smiled. "That's right. One man with a hold on me is enough."

"What about Lord Hammer?" Chenyth demanded. When one of his questions was answered, he always found another.

262 — GLEN COOK

"Oh, he chose his own name. It's a joke. But you'll never understand it. You're too young." She moved on down the line.

Chenyth smiled to herself. He had won a little more.

His value to us all was his ability to charm Fetch into revealing just a little more than she had been instructed. Maybe Chenyth could have gotten into her.

His charm came of youth and innocence. He was fourteen years younger than Jamal, child of the Harish and youngest veteran. We were all into our thirties and forties. Soldiering had been our way of life for so long we had forgotten there were others. Some of us had been enemies back when. The Harish bore their defeat like the banner of a holy martyr. . . .

Chenyth had come after the wars. Chenyth was a baby. He had no hatreds, no prejudices. He retained that bubbling, youthful optimism that had been burned from the rest of us in the crucible of war. We both loved and envied him for it, and tried to get a little to rub off. Chenyth was a talisman. One last hope that the world wasn't inalterably cruel.

Fetch returned to Lord Hammer's stirrup. The man in black proceeded. I studied the trees.

There was something repulsive about them. Something frightening. They were so widely spaced it seemed they couldn't stand one another. There were no saplings. Most were half dead, hollow, or down and rotting. They were arranged in neat, long rows, a stark orchard of death. . . .

The day was about to die without a whimper when Lord Hammer halted again.

It hadn't seemed possible that our morale could sink. Not after the mountains and the ice storm. But that weird forest depressed us till we scarcely cared if we lived or died. The band would have disintegrated had it not become so much an extension of Lord Hammer's will.

We massed behind our fell captain.

Before him lay a meadow circumscribed by a tumbled wall of field stone. The wall hadn't been mended in ages. And yet. . . .

It still performed its function.

"Sorcery!" Brandy hissed.

Others took it up.

"What did you expect?" Chenyth countered. He nodded toward Lord Hammer.

It took no training to sense the wizardry.

Ice-free, lush grass crowded the circle of stone. Wildflowers fluttered their petals in the breeze.

We Kaveliners crowded Fetch. Chenyth tickled her sides. She yelped, "Stop it!" She was extremely ticklish. Anyone else she would have slapped silly. She told him, "It's still alive. Lord Hammer was afraid it might have died."

Remarkable. She said nothing conversational to anyone else, ever.

Lord Hammer turned slightly. Fetch devoted her attention to him. He moved an elbow, twitched a finger. I didn't see anything else pass between them.

Fetch turned to us. "Listen up! These are the rules for guys who want to stay healthy. Follow Lord Hammer like his shadow. Don't climb over the wall. Don't even touch it. You'll get dead if you do."

The black horseman circled the ragged wall to a gap where a gate might once have stood. He turned in and rode to the heart of the meadow.

Fetch scampered after him, her big brown eyes locked on him.

How Lord Hammer communicated with her I don't know. A finger-twitch, a slight movement of hand or head, and she would talk-talk-talk. We didn't speculate much aloud. He was a sorcerer. You avoid things that might irritate his kind.

She proclaimed, "We need a tent behind each fire pit. Five on the outer circle, five on the inner. The rest here in the middle. Sentinels will be posted."

"Yeah?" Brandy grumbled. "What the hell do we do for wood? Plant acorns and wait?"

"Out there are two trees that are down. Take wood off them. Pick up any fallen branches this side of the others. It'll be wet, but it's the best we can do. *Do not* go past a live tree. Lord Hammer isn't sure he can project his protection that far."

I didn't pay much attention. Nobody did. It was *warm* there. I shed my pack and flung myself to the ground. I rolled around on the grass, grabbing handfuls and inhaling the newly mown hay scent.

There had to be some dread sorceries animating that circle. Nobody cared. The place was as cozy as journey's end.

There is always a price. That's how magic works.

Old Toamas lay back on his pack and smiled in pure joy. He closed his eyes and slept. And Brandy said nothing about making him do his share.

Lord Hammer let the euphoria bubble for ten minutes.

Fetch started round the troop. "Brandy. You and Russ and Little, put your tent on that point. Will, Chenyth, Toamas, yours goes here. Kelpie. . . ." And so on. When everyone was assigned, she erected her master's black tent. All the while Lord Hammer sat his ruby-eyed stallion and stared northeastward. He showed the intensity of deep concentration. Was he reading the trail?

Nothing seemed to catch him off guard.

Where was he leading us? Why? What for? We didn't know. Not a whit. Maybe even Fetch didn't. Chenyth couldn't charm a hint from her.

We knew two things. Lord Hammer paid well. And, within restrictions known only to himself, he took care of his followers. In a way I can't articulate, he had won our loyalties.

His being what he was was ample proof, yet he had won us to the point where we felt we had a stake in it too. We wanted him to succeed. We wanted to help him succeed.

Odd. Very odd.

I have taken his gold, I thought, briefly remembering a man I had known a long time ago. He had been a member of the White Company of the Mercenaries' Guild. They were a monastic order of soldiers with what, then, I had thought of as the strangest concept of honor. . . .

What made me think of Mikhail? I wondered.

IU

Lord Hammer suddenly dismounted and strode toward Chenyth and me. I thought, thunderhead! Huge, black, irresistible.

I'm no coward. I endured the slaughterhouse battles of the Great Eastern Wars without flinching. I stood fast at Second Baxendala while the Tervola sent the *savan dalage* ravening amongst us night after night. I maintained my courage after Dichiara, which was our worst defeat. And I persevered at Palmisano, though the bodies piled into little mountains and so many men died that the savants later declared there could be no more war for generations. For three years I had faced the majestic, terrible hammer of Shinsan's might without quelling.

But when Lord Hammer bore down on me, that grim death mask coming like an arrowhead engraved with my name, I slunk aside like a whipped dog.

He had that air. You *knew* he was as mighty as any force of Nature, as cruel as Death Herself. Cowering was instinctive.

He looked me in the eye. I couldn't see anything through his mask. But a coldness hit me. It made the cold of that land seem summery.

He looked at Chenyth, too. Baby brother didn't flinch.

I guess he was too innocent. He didn't know when to be scared.

Lord Hammer dropped to one knee beside Toamas.

Gloved hands probed the old man's ribs. Toamas cringed. Then his terror gave way to a beatific smile.

Lord Hammer strode back to where Fetch pursued her regular evening ritual of battling to erect their tent.

"You're a damned idiot, girl," she muttered. "You could've picked something you could handle. But no, you had to have a canvas palace. You knew the boys would just fall in love and stumble all over themselves to help. Then you hired lunks with the chivalry of tomcats. You're a real genius, you are, girl."

The euphoria had reached her too. Usually she was louder and crustier.

Chenyth volunteered. Leaving me to battle with ours.

That little woman could shame or cajole a man into doing anything.

I checked Toamas. He was sleeping. His smile said he was feeling no pain. "Thanks," I threw Lord Hammer's way, softly. No one heard, but he probably knew. Nothing escaped him.

When the tents were up Fetch chose wood-gatherers. I was one of the losers.

"Goddamned, ain't fair, Brandy," I muttered as we hit the ice. "Them sumbitches get to sit on their asses back there...."

He laughed at me. He was that kind of guy. No empathy. And no sympathy even for himself.

Some lessons have to be learned the hard way.

The circle had turned me lazy. Malingering is a fine art among veterans. I decided to get the wood-gathering over with.

What I did was go after a prime-looking dead branch lying just past the first standing tree. I mean, how hard could it be to find your way back when all you had to do was turn around?

I whacked and hacked the branch out of the ice. All the while Brandy and the others were cussing and fussing behind me as they wooled a dead tree.

I turned to go back.

Nothing.

I couldn't see a damned thing but ice, those gnarled old trees, and more ice. No circle. No woodcutters.

The only sound was the ice crackling on branches as the wind teased through the forest.

I yelled.

Chips of ice tinkled off the nearest tree. The damned thing was laughing! I could feel it. It was telling me that it had me, but it was going to play with me awhile.

I even felt the envy of neighboring trees, the hatred of a brother, who had scored. . . .

I didn't panic. I whirled this way and that, moving a few steps each direction, without surrendering to terror. Once a man has faced the legions of the Dread Empire, and has survived nights haunted by the unkillable *savan dalage*, there isn't much left to fear.

I could hear the others perfectly when I turned my back. They were yelling at me, each other, and Lord Hammer. They thought I had gone crazy.

"Will," Brandy called. "How come you're jumping around like that?"

"Tree," I said, "you're going to lose this round."

It laughed in my mind.

I started backing up. Dragging my branch. Feeling for any trace of footsteps I had left coming here.

Good thinking. But not good enough. The tree hadn't exhausted its arsenal.

A branch fell. A big one. I dodged. My feet slipped on the ice. I cracked my head good. I wasn't thinking when I got up. I started walking. Probably the wrong way.

I heard Brandy yelling, "Will, you stupid bastard, stand still!"

And Russ, "Get a rope, somebody. We'll lasso him."

I didn't understand. My feet kept shuffling.

Then came the crackle of flames and stench of oily smoke. It caught my attention. I stopped, turned.

My captor had become a pillar of fire. It screamed in my mind.

Nothing could burn that fast, that hot. Not in that weather. But the damned thing went up like an explosion.

The smell of sorcery fouled the air.

The flames peaked, began dying. I could see through.

The circle and my friends glimmered before me. Facing the tree, a few yards beyond, stood Lord Hammer. He held one arm outstretched, fingers in a King's X.

He stared at me. I peered into his eye slots and felt him calling. I took a step.

It was a long, long journey. I had to round some kink in the corridor of time before I got my feet onto the straight-line path to safety.

I made it.

Still dragging that damned branch.

I stumbled. Lord Hammer's arm fell. He caught me. His touch was as gentle as a lover's caress, yet I felt it to my bones. I had the feeling that there was nothing more absolute.

I got hold of myself. He released me.

His shoulders slumped slightly as he wheeled and stalked back to the circle. It was the first sign of weariness he had ever shown

I glanced back.

That damned tree stood there looking like it hadn't been touched. I felt its bitterness, its rage, its loss. . . . And its siren call.

I scooted back inside the circle like a kid running home after getting caught pulling a prank.

U

"Chenyth, it was on fire. I saw it with my own eyes."

"I saw what happened, Will. Lord Hammer just stood there with his arm out. You stopped acting goofy and came back."

The campfires cast enough light to limn the nearest trees. I glanced at the one that had had me. I shuddered. "Chenyth, I couldn't get back."

"Will. . . ."

"You listen to me. When Lord Hammer says do something, do it. Mom would kill me if I didn't bring you home."

She was going to get nasty anyway. I had taken Chenyth off after she had sworn seven ways from Sunday that he wasn't going to go. It had been a brutal scene. Chenyth pleading, Mom screaming, me ducking epithets and pots.

My mother had had a husband and eight sons. When the dust of the Great Eastern Wars settled, she had me and little Chenyth, and she hadn't seen me but once since then.

Then I had come back with my story about signing on with Lord Hammer. And Chenyth, who had been feeding on her stories about Dad and the rest of us being heroes, decided he wanted to go too.

She told him no, and meant it. It was too late to do anything about me, but her last child wasn't going to be a soldier.

Sometimes I was ashamed of sneaking him out. She would be dying still, in tiny bits each day. But Chenyth had to grow up sometime. . . .

"Hey! Listen up!" Fetch yelled. "Hey! I said knock off the tongue music. Got a little proclamation from the boss."

"Here it comes. All-time ass-chewing for doing a stupid," I said.

She used Itaskian first. Most of us understood it. She changed languages for the Harish and a few others who didn't. We drifted toward the black tent.

From the heart of the meadow I could see the pattern of the fire pits. Each lay in one of the angles of a five-pointed star. A pentagram. This meadow was a live magical symbol.

"It'll only be a couple days till we get where we're heading. Maybe sooner. The boss says it's time to let you know what's happening. Just so you'll stay on your toes. The name of the place is Kammengarn." She grinned, exposing dirty teeth.

It took a while. The legend was old, and didn't get much notice outside Itaskia's northern provinces, where Rainheart is a folk hero.

Bellweather popped first. "You mean like the Kammengarn in the story of Rainheart slaying the Kammengarn Dragon?"

"You got it, Captain."

Most of us just put on stupid looks, the southerners more so than those of us who shared cultural roots with Itaskia. I don't think the Harish ever understood.

"Why? What's there?" Bellweather asked.

Fetch laughed. The sound was hard to describe. A little bit of cackle, of bray, and of tinkle all rolled into one astonishing noise. "The Kammengarn Dragon, idiot. Silcroscuar. Father of All Dragons. The big guy of the dragon world. The one who makes the ones you saw in the wars look like crippled chickens beside eagles."

"You're not making sense," Chenyth responded. "What's there? Bones? Rainheart killed the monster three or four hundred years ago."

Lord Hammer came from his tent. He stood behind Fetch, his arms folded. He remained as still, as lifeless, as a statue in clothes. We became less restive.

He was one spooky character. I felt my arm where he had caught me. It still tingled.

"Rainheart's successes were exaggerated," Fetch told us. She used her sarcastic tone. The one that blistered obstinate rocks and mules. "Mostly by Rainheart. The dragon lives. No mortal man can kill it. The gods willed that it be. It shall be, so long as the world endures. It is the Father of All Dragons. If it perishes, dragons perish. The world must have its dragons."

It was weird. The way she changed while she was talking. All of a sudden she wasn't Fetch anymore. I think we all sneaked peeks at Lord Hammer to see if he were doing some ventriloquist trick.

Maybe he was. He could be doing anything behind that iron mask.

I wasn't sure Lord Hammer was human anymore. He might be some unbanished devil left over from the great thaumaturgy confrontations of the wars.

"Lord Hammer is going to Kammengarn to obtain a cup of the immortal Dragon's blood."

Hammer ducked into his tent. Fetch was right behind him.

"What the hell?" Brandy demanded. "What kind of crap is this?"

"Hammer don't lie," I replied.

"Not that we know of," Chenyth said.

"He's a plainspoken man, even if Fetch does his talking. He says the Kammengarn Dragon is alive, I believe him. He says we're going to kype a cup of its blood, there it is. I reckon we're going to try."

"Will. . . ."

I went and squatted by our fire. I needed a little more warming. The dead wood of the forest burned pretty ordinarily.

The men were quiet for a long time

What was there to say?

We had taken Lord Hammer's gold.

Even professional griper Brandy didn't say much by way of complaint.

Mikhail had been right. You went on even when the cause was a loser. It became a matter of honor.

Ormson killed the silence. His action was a minor thing characteristic of his race, but it divided the journey into different phases, now and then, and inspired the resolution of the rest of us.

He drew his sword, began whetting it.

The stone made a *shing-shing* sound along his blade For an instant it was the only sound to be heard.

We were old warriors. That sound spoke eloquently of battles beyond the dawn. I drew my sword. . . .

I had taken the gold. I was Lord Hammer's man.

UI

A metallic symphony played as stones sharpened swords and spearheads. Men tested bowstrings and thumped weathered shields. Old greaves clanked, leather armor, too long unoiled, squeaked.

Lord Hammer stepped from his tent. His mask bore no paint now. Only chance flickers of firelight revealed the existence of anything within his cowl.

When his gaze met mine I felt I was looking at a man who was smiling.

Chenyth fidgeted with his gear. Then, "I'm going to see what Jamal's doing."

He sheathed the battered sword I had given him and wandered off. He didn't cut much of a figure as a warrior. He was just a skinny blond kid who looked like a gust of wind would blow him away, or a willing woman turn him into jelly.

Eyes followed him. Pain filled some. We had all been there once. Now we were here.

He was our talisman against our mortality.

I started wondering what the Harish were up to myself. I followed Chenyth. They were almost civil while he was around.

They were ships without compasses, those four, more lost than the rest of us. They were religious fanatics who had sworn themselves to a dead cause. They were El Murid's Chosen Ones, his most devoted followers, a dedicated cult of assassins. The Great Eastern Wars had thrown their master into eclipse. His once vast empire had collapsed. Now, according to rumor, El Murid was nothing but a fat, decrepit opium addict commanding a few bandits in the south desert hills of Hammad al Nakir. He spent his days

FILED TEETH — 271

pulling on his pipe and dreaming about an impossible restoration. These four brother assassins were refugees from the vengeance of the new order. . . .

Defeat had left them with nothing but one another and their blades. About what victory had given us.

Harish took no wives. They devoted themselves totally to the mysteries of their brotherhood, and to fulfilling the commands of their master.

No one gave them orders anymore. Yet they had sworn to devote their lives to their master's needs.

They were waiting. And while they waited, they survived by selling what they had given El Murid freely.

Like the rest of us, they were what history had made them. Bladesmen.

They formed a cross, facing their fire. Chenyth knelt beside Jamal. They talked in low tones. The others watched with stony faces partially concealed by thin veils and long, heavy black beards. Foud, the oldest, dyed his to keep the color. They were all solid, tough men. Killers unfamiliar with remorse.

All four held ornate silver daggers.

I stopped, amazed.

They were permitting Chenyth to watch the consecration of Harish kill-daggers. It was one of the high mysteries of their cult.

They sensed my presence, but went on removing the enameled names of their last victims from amidst the engraved symbols on the flats of their blades. Those blades were a quarter-inch thick near the hilt. The flat ran half the twelve-inch length. Each blade was an inch wide at its base.

They seemed heavy, clumsy, but the Harish used them with terrifying efficiency.

One by one, oldest to youngest, they thrust their daggers into the fire to extinguish the last gossamer of past victims' souls still clinging to the deadly engraving. Then they laid their blades across their hearts, beneath the palms of their left hands. Foud spoke a word.

Chenyth later told me the ritual was couched in the language of ancient Ilkazar. It was an odd tongue they used, like nothing else I've heard.

Foud chanted. The others answered.

Fifteen minutes passed. When they finished even a dullard like myself could feel the Power hovering round the Harish fire.

Lord Hammer came out of his tent. He peered our way briefly, then returned.

The four plunged their blades into the fire again.

Then they joined the ritual everyone else had been pursuing. They produced their whetstones.

I considered Foud's blade. Nearly two inches were missing from its length. It had been honed till it had narrowed a quarter. The engraving was almost invisible. He had served El Murid long and effectively.

His gaze met mine. For an instant a smile flickered behind his veil.

This was the first any of them had even admitted my existence.

A moment later Jamal said something to Chenyth. The younger Harish was the only one who admitted to understanding Itaskian, though we all knew the others did too. Chenyth nodded and rose.

"They're going to name their daggers. We have to go."

Times change. Only a few years ago men like these had tried to kill Kavelin's Queen. Now we were allies.

The glint in Foud's eye told me that things might be different now if he had been the man sent then.

The Harish believed. In their master, in themselves. Every assassin who consecrated a blade was as sure of himself as was Foud.

"What're they doing here?" I muttered at Chenyth. I knew. The same as me. Doing what they knew. Surviving the only way they knew. Still. . . .
The Harish revered their Cause, even though it was lost.

They wanted to bring the Disciple's salvation to the whole word, using every means at their disposal.

Toamas was awake and chipper when we got back. "I ever tell about the time I was with King Bragi, during the El Murid Wars, when he was just another blank shield? It was a town in Altea. . . ."

I guess that kept us going, too. Maybe one mercenary in fifty thousand made it big. I guess we all had some core of hope, or belief in ourselves, too.

VII

"All right, you goat-lovers! Drag your dead asses out. We got some hiking to do today."

Fetch had a way with words like no lady I've ever known. I slithered out of my blankets, scuttled to the fire, tumbled some wood on, and slid back into the wool. That circle may have been springish, but there was a nip in the air.

Chenyth rolled over. He muttered something about eyes in the night.

"Come on. Roll out. We got a long walk ahead."

Chenyth sat up. "Phew! One of these days we've got to take time off for baths. Hey. Toamas. Wake up." He shook the old man. "Oh."

"What's the matter?"

"I think he's dead, Will."

"Toamas? Nah. He just don't want to get up." I shook him.

Chenyth was right.

I jumped out of there so fast I knocked the tent down on Chenyth. "Fetch. The old man's dead. Toamas."

She kicked a foot sticking out of another tent, gave me a puzzled look. Then she scurried into the black tent.

I tried to look inside. But there were inside flaps too.

Lord Hammer appeared a moment later. His mask was paintless. His gaze swept the horizon, then the camp. Fetch popped out as he started toward our tent.

Chenyth came up cussing. "Damnit, Will, what the hell you. . . ." His jaw dropped. He scrambled out of Lord Hammer's path.

Fetch whipped past and started hauling tent away. Lord Hammer knelt, hand over Toamas's heart. He moved it to the grass. Then he walked to the gap we thought of as a gate.

"What's he doing?" Chenyth asked.

"Wait," Fetch told him.

Lord Hammer halted, faced left, began pacing the perimeter. He paused several times. We resumed our morning chores. Brandy cussed the gods both on Toamas's behalf and because he faced another miserable breakfast. You couldn't tell which mattered more to him. Brandy bitched about everything equally.

His true feelings surfaced when he was the first to volunteer to dig the old man's grave.

Toamas had saved his life in the mountains.

"We Kaveliners got to stick together," he muttered to me. "Way it's always been. Way it'll always be."

"Yeah."

His family and Toamas's lived in the same area. They had been on opposite sides in the civil war with which Kavelin had amused itself during the interim between the El Murid and Great Eastern Wars.

It was one of the few serious remarks I had ever heard from Brandy.

Lord Hammer chose the grave site. It butted against the wall. Toamas went down sitting upright, facing the forest.

"That's where I saw the thing last night," Chenyth told me.

"What thing?"

"When I had guard duty. All I could see was its eyes." He dropped a handful of dirt into the old man's lap. The others did the same. Except Foud. The Harish Elder dropped onto his belly, placed a small silver dagger under Toamas's folded hands.

We Kaveliners bowed to Foud. This was a major gesture by the Harish. Their second highest honor, given a man who had been their enemy all his life.

I wondered why Foud had done it.

"Why did he die?" Chenyth asked Fetch. "I thought Lord Hammer fixed him."

"He did. Chenyth, the circle took Toamas."

"I don't understand."

"Neither do I."

I wondered some more. Ignorance and Lord Hammer seemed poles apart.

Maybe he had known. But I couldn't hate him. The way Fetch talked, thirty-seven of us were alive because Toamas had died. The circle certainly was more merciful than the forest.

Lord Hammer gestured. Fetch ran to him. Then he ducked into his tent while she talked.

"Get with it. We've got a long way to go. We'll have to travel fast. Lord Hammer doesn't want to spend any more lives. He wants to leave the forest before nightfall."

We moved. Our packs were trailing odds and ends when we started. Our stomachs weren't full. But those were considerations less important than enduring the protection of another circle.

As we were leaving I noticed a flower blooming in the soft earth where we had put Toamas down. There were dozens of flowers along the wall. The few places where they were missing were the spots where Lord Hammer had paused in his circuit of the wall.

What would happen when all the grave sites were full?

Maybe Lord Hammer knew. But Hammer didn't have much to say.

We passed another circle about noon. It was dead.

The day was warmer, the sky clear. The ice began melting. We made good time. Lord Hammer seemed pleased.

I stared straight ahead, at Russ's back, all morning. If I looked at a tree I could hear it calling. The pull was terrifying

Chenyth seized my arm. "Stop!"

I almost trampled Russ. "What's up?" Lord Hammer had stopped.

"I don't know."

Fetch was dancing around like a barefoot burglar on a floor covered with tacks. Lord Hammer and his steed might have been some parkland pigeon roost, so still were they. We shuffled round so we could see without leaving the safety of the trail.

We had come to a clearing. It was a quarter mile across. What looked like a mud-dauber's nest, the kind with just one hole, lay at the middle of the clearing. It was big. Like two hundred yards long, fifty feet wide, and thirty feet high. A sense of immense menace radiated from it.

"What is it?" we asked one another. Neither Lord Hammer nor Fetch answered us.

Lord Hammer slowly raised his left arm till it thrust straight out from his shoulder. He lifted his forearm vertically, turning the edge of a stiffened hand toward the structure. Then he raised his right arm, laying his forearm parallel with his eyeslits. Then he stiffened his hand, facing the structure with its edge.

"Let's go!" Fetch snapped. "Follow me." She started running.

We whipped the mules into a trot, ran. We weren't gentle with the balky ones.

We had to go right along the side of that thing. As we approached, I glanced back. Lord Hammer was coming, his mount pacing slowly. Hammer himself remained frozen in the position he had assumed. He was almost indiscernible inside a black nimbus.

His mask glowed like the sun. The face of an animal seemed to peep through the golden light.

I glanced into the dark entry to that mound. Menace, backed by rage and frustration, slammed into me.

Lord Hammer halted directly in front of the hole. The rest of us raced for the forest behind the barrow.

Fetch was scared, but not scared enough to pass the first tree. She stopped. We waited.

And Lord Hammer came.

Never have I seen a horse run as beautifully, or as fast. It may have been my imagination, or the way the sun hit its breath in the cold, but fire seemed to play round its nostrils. Lord Hammer rode as if he were part of the beast.

The earth shuddered. A basso profundo rumble came from the mound.

Lord Hammer swept past, slowing, and we pursued him. No one thought to look back, to see what the earth brought forth. It was too late once we passed that first tree.

"Will," Chenyth panted. "Did you see that horse run? What kind of horse runs like that, Will?"

What could I tell him? "Sorcerer's horse, Chenyth. Hell horse. But we knew that already, didn't we?"

Some of us did. Chenyth never really believed it till then. He figured we were giving him more war stories.

He never understood that we couldn't exaggerate what had happened during the Great Eastern Wars. That we told toned-down stories because there was so much we wanted to forget.

Chenyth couldn't take anything at face value. He worked his way up the column so he could pump Fetch. He didn't get anything from her, either. Lord Hammer led. We followed. For Fetch that was the natural order of life.

VIII

We passed another dead circle in the afternoon. Lord Hammer glanced at the sun and increased the pace.

An hour later Fetch passed the word that we would have to stop at the next circle—unless it were dead.

Dread sandpapered the ends of our nerves. The men who had stood sentry last night had seen too much of the things that roamed the forest by dark. And Hammer's reluctance to face the night.... It made the price of a circle almost attractive.

Even thirty-seven to one aren't good odds when my life is on the line. I've been risking it since I was Chenyth's age, but I like having some choice, some control. . . .

The next circle was alive.

Darkness was close when we reached it. We could hear big things moving behind us, beyond the trees. Hungry things. We zipped into the circle and pitched camp in record time.

I stood sentry that night. I saw what Chenyth had seen. It didn't bother me much. I was a veteran of the Great Eastern Wars.

I kept reminding myself.

Lord Hammer didn't sleep at all. He spent the night pacing the perimeter. He paused frequently to make cabalistic passes. Sometimes the air glowed where his fingers passed.

He took care of us. Not a man perished. Instead, the circle took a mule.

"Butcher it up," Fetch growled. "Save the good cuts. Couple of you guys dig a hole over there where I left the shovel."

So we had mule for breakfast. It was tough, but good. Our first fresh meat in weeks.

We were about to march when Fetch announced, "We'll be there tomorrow. That means goof-off time's over. Respond to orders instantly if you know what's good for you."

Brandy mumbled and cussed. Chenyth wasn't any happier. "I swear, I'm going to smack him, Will."

"Take it easy. He was in the Breidenbacher Light. I owe him."

"So? They got you out at Lake Turntine. That was then. What's that got to do with today?"

"What it's got to do with is, he'll kick your ass up around your ears."

"Kid wants to duke it out, let him, Will. He's getting on my nerves too."

"Stow it," Fetch snarled. "Save it for the other guys. It's time to start worrying about getting out alive."

"What? Then we'd have to walk all the way back." Brandy cackled.

"Fetch, what's this all about?" Chenyth asked.

"I already told you, question man."

"Not why."

She scowled, shook her head. I asked, "Weren't you ever young, Fetch? Hey! Whoa! I didn't mean it like that."

She settled for the one shin-kick. Everybody laughed. I winked. She grinned nastily.

Brandy and Chenyth forgot their quarrel.

Chenyth hadn't forgotten his question. He pressed.

"All I know is, he wants the blood of the Father of Dragons. We came now because the monster is sluggish during the winter. Now why the hell don't you just jingle the money in your pocket and do what you're told?"

"Where'd you meet him, Fetch? When?"

She shook her head again. "You don't hear so good, do you? Long ago and far away. He's been like a father. Now get your ass ready to hike." She tramped off to her position beside Lord Hammer's stallion.

The woman had the least feminine walk I've ever seen. She took long, rolling steps, and kind of leaned into them.

"You ask too many questions, Chenyth."

"Can it, will you?"

We were getting close. Not knowing, except that we were going to go up against a dragon, frayed tempers. Chenyth's trouble was that he hadn't had enough practice at keeping his mouth shut.

Noon. Another barrow blocked our trail. We repeated our previous performance. The feeling of menace wasn't as strong. The thing in the earth let us pass with only token protest.

The weather grew warmer. The ice melted quickly, turning the trail to mud.

Occasionally, from ridge tops, we saw the land beyond the forest. Mountains lay ahead. Brandy moaned his heart out till Fetch told him our destination lay at their feet. Then he bitched about everything happening too fast.

Several of those peaks trailed dark smoke. There wasn't much snow on their flanks.

"Funny," I remarked to Chenyth. "Heading north into warmer country."

We passed a living circle. It called to us the way the trees called to me.

An end to the weird, wide forest came. We entered grasslands that, within a few hours, gave way to rapidly steepening hills. The peaks loomed higher. The air grew warmer. The hills became taller and more barren. Shadows gathered in the valleys as the sun settled toward the Dragon's Teeth.

Lord Hammer ordered us to pitch camp. He doubled the sentries.

We weren't bothered, but still it was a disturbing night. The earth shuddered. The mountains rumbled. I couldn't help but envision some gargantuan monster resting uneasily beneath the range.

IX

The dawn gods were heaving buckets of blood up over the eastern horizon. Fetch formed us up for a pep talk. "Queen of the dwarves," Brandy mumbled. She *was* comical, so tiny was she when standing before a mounted Lord Hammer.

"Lord Hammer believes we are about three miles from the Gate of Kammengarn. The valley behind me will lead us there. From the Gate those who accompany Lord Hammer will descend into the earth almost a mile. Captain Bellweather and thirty men will stay at the Gate. Six men will accompany Lord Hammer and myself."

Her style had changed radically. I had never seen her so subdued.

Fetch was scared.

"Bellweather, your job will be the hardest. It's almost certain that you will be attacked. The people of these hills believe Kammengarn to be a holy place. They know we're here. They suspect our mission. They'll try to destroy us once we prove we intend to profane their shrine. You'll have to hold them most of the day, without Lord Hammer's help."

"Now we know," Brandy muttered. "Needed us to fight his battles for him."

"Why the hell else did he hire us?" Chenyth demanded.

Lord Hammer's steed pranced impatiently. Hammer's gaze swept over us. It quelled all emotion.

"Lord Hammer has appointed the following men to accompany him. Foud, of the Harish. Aboud, of the Harish. Sigurd Ormson, the Trolledyngjan. Dunklin Hanneker, the Itaskian. Willem Clarig Potter, of Kavelin. Pavlo della Contini-Marcusco, of Dunno Scuttari." She made a small motion with her fingers, like someone folding a piece of paper.

"Fetch!. . ."

"Shut up, Chenyth!" I growled.

Fetch responded, "Lord Hammer has spoken. The men named, please come to the head of the column."

I hoisted my pack, patted Chenyth's shoulder, said, "Do a good job. And stay healthy. I've got to take you back to Mom."

"Will. . . ."

"Hey. You wanted to be a soldier. Be a soldier."

He stared at the ground, kicked a pebble.

"Good luck, Will." Brandy extended a hand. I shook. "We'll look out for him."

"All right. Thanks. Russ. Aral. You guys take care." It was a ritual of parting undertaken before times got rough.

The red-eyed horse started moving. We followed in single file. Fetch walked with Bellweather for a while. After half an hour she scampered forward to her place beside Lord Hammer. She was nervous. She couldn't keep her head or hands still.

I glanced back, past Ormson. "Fight coming," I told the Trolledyngjan. Bellweather was getting ready right now.

"Did you ever doubt it?"

"No. Not really."

The mountains crowded in. The valley narrowed till it became a steep-sided canyon. That led to a place where two canyons collided and became one. It had a flat bottom maybe fifty yards across.

It was the most barren place I had ever seen. The boulders were dark browns. The little soil came in lighter browns. A few tufts of desiccated grass added sere browns. Even the sky took on an ochre hue. . . .

The blackness of a crack in the mountainside ahead relieved the monochromism.

It was a natural cleft, but there were tailings everywhere, several feet deep, as if the cleft had been mined. The tailings had filled the canyon bottom, creating the little flat.

I searched the hillsides. It seemed I could feel eyes boring holes in my back. I looked everywhere but at that cavern mouth.

The darkness it contained seemed the deepest I had ever known.

Lord Hammer rode directly to it.

"Packs off," Fetch ordered. "Weapons ready." She twitched and scratched nervously. "We're going down. Do exactly as I do."

Bellweather brought the others into the flat. He searched the mountainsides too. "They're here," he announced.

War howls responded immediately. Here, there, a painted face flashed amongst the rocks.

Arrows and spears wobbled through the air.

There were a lot of them, I reflected as I got myself between my shield and a boulder. The odds didn't look good at all.

Bellweather shouted. His men vanished behind their shields. . . .

All but my baby brother, who just stood there with a stupefied look.

"Chenyth!" I started toward him.

"Will!" Fetch snapped. She grabbed my arm. "Stay here."

Brandy and Russ took care of him. They exploded from behind their shields, tackled the kid, covered him before he got hurt. That got his attention. He started doing the things I had been teaching the past several months.

An arrow hummed close to me, clattered on rock. Then another. I had been chosen somebody's favorite target. Time to worry about me.

The savages concentrated on Lord Hammer. Their luck was poor. Missiles found him repulsive. In fact, they seemed to loath making contact with any of us.

Not so the arrows of Bellweather's Itaskian bows.

The Itaskian bow and bowman are the best in the world. Bellweather's men wasted no arrows. Virtually every shaft brought a cry of pain.

Then Lord Hammer reached up and caught an arrow in flight.

The canyon fell silent in sheer awe.

Lord Hammer extended an arm. A falling spear became a streak of smoke.

The hillmen didn't give up. Instead, they started rolling boulders down the slopes.

"Eyes down!" Fetch screamed. "Stare at the ground."

Lord Hammer swept first his right hand, then his left, round himself. He clapped them together once.

A sheet of fire, of lightning, obscured the sky. Thunder tortured my ears. My hearing recovered only to be tormented anew by the screams of men in pain.

It had been much nastier above. Dozens of savages were staggering around with hands clasped over their eyes or ears. Several fell down the slope.

Bellweather's archers went to work.

"Let's go." Fetch said. "Remember. Do exactly what I do."

The little woman was scared pale. She didn't want to enter that cavern. But she took her place beside Lord Hammer, who laid a hand atop her disheveled head.

His touch seemed fond. His fingers toyed with her stringy hair. She shivered, looked at the ground, then stalked into that black crack.

He only touched the rest of us for a second. The feeling was similar to that when he had caught me after my run-in with the siren tree. But this time the tingle coursed through my whole body.

He finished with Foud. Once more he swept hands round the mountainsides, clapped. Lightning flashed. Thunder rolled. Bellweather's archers plied their bows.

The savages were determined not to be intimidated.

Lord Hammer dismounted, strode into the darkness. The red-eyed stallion turned round, backed in after us, stopped only when its bulk nearly blocked the narrow passage. Hammer wound his way through our press, proceeded into darkness.

Fetch followed. Single file, we did the same.

✕

"Holy Hagard's Golden Turds!" Sigurd exploded. "They're on fire."

Lord Hammer and Fetch glowed. They shed enough light to reveal the crack's walls.

"So are you," I told him.

"Eh. You too."

I couldn't see it myself. Sigurd said he couldn't, either. I glanced back. The others glowed too. They became quite bright once they got away from the cavern mouth. It was spooky.

The Harish didn't like it. They were unusually vocal, and what I caught of their gabble made it sound like they were mad because a heresy had been practiced upon them.

The light seemed to come from way down inside the body. I could see Sigurd's bones. And Fetch's, and the others' when I glanced back. But Lord Hammer remained an enigma. An absence. Once more I wondered if he were truly human, or if anything at all inhabited that black clothing.

After a hundred yards the walls became shaped stone set with mortar. That explained the tailings above. The blocks had been shaped *in situ*.

"Why would they do that?" I asked Sigurd

He shrugged. "Don't try to understand a man's religion, Kaveliner. Just drive you crazy."

A hundred yards farther along the masons had narrowed the passage to little more than a foot. A man had to go through sideways.

Fetch stopped us. Lord Hammer started doing something with his fingers.

I told Sigurd, "Looks like the dragon god isn't too popular with the people who worship him."

"Eh?"

"The tunnel. It's zigzagged. And the narrow place looks like it was built to keep the dragon in."

"They don't worship the dragon," Fetch said. "They worship Kammengarn, the Hidden City. Silcroscuar is blocking their path to their shrines. So they blocked him in in hopes he would starve."

"Didn't work, eh?"

"No. Silcroscuar subsists. On visitors. He has guardians. Descendants of the people who lived in Kammengarn. They hunt for him."

"What's happening?"

Lord Hammer had a ball of fire in his hands. It was nearly a foot in diameter. He shifted it to his right hand. He rolled it along the tunnel floor, through the narrow passage.

"Let's go!" Fetch shrieked. "Will! Sigurd! Get in there!"

I charged ahead without thinking. The passage was twenty feet long. I was halfway through when the screams started.

Such pain and terror I hadn't heard since the wars. I froze.

Sigurd plowed into me. "Go, man."

An instant later we broke into a wider tunnel.

A dozen savages awaited us. Half were down, burning like torches. The stench of charred flesh fouled the air. The others flitted about trying to extinguish themselves or their comrades.

We took them before the Harish got through.

Panting, I asked Sigurd, "How did he know?"

Sigurd shrugged. "He always knows. Almost. That first barrow. . . ."

"He smelled their torches," Foud said. The Harish elder wore a sarcastic smile.

"You're killing the mystery."

"There is no mystery to Lord Hammer."

"Maybe not to you." I turned to Sigurd. "Hope he's on his toes. We don't need any surprises down here."

Lord Hammer stepped in. He surveyed the carnage. He seemed satisfied.

Several of the savages still burned.

Fetch lost her breakfast.

I think that startled all of us. Perhaps even Lord Hammer. It seemed so out of character. And yet. . . . What did we know about Fetch? Only what we had seen. And most of that had been show. This might be the first time she had witnessed the grim side of her master's profession.

I don't think, despite her apparent agelessness, that she was much older than Chenyth. Say twenty. She might have missed the Great Eastern Wars too.

We went on, warriors in the lead. The tunnel's slope steepened. Twice we descended spiraling stairs hanging in the sides of wide shafts. Twice we encountered narrow places with ambushes like that we had already faced. We broke through each. Sigurd took our only wound, a slight cut on his forearm.

We left a lot of dead men on our back trail.

The final attack was more cunning. It came from behind, from a side tunnel, and took us by surprise. Even Lord Hammer was taken off guard.

His mystique just cracked a little more, I thought as I whirled.

There was sorcery in it this time.

The hillmen witch-doctors had saved themselves for the final defense. They had used their command of the Power passively, to conceal themselves and their men. Our only warning was a premature war whoop.

Lord Hammer whirled. His hands flew in frenetic passes. The rest of us struggled to interpose ourselves between the attackers and Lord Hammer and Fetch.

Sorceries scarred the tunnel walls. The shamans threw everything they had at the man in black.

Their success was a wan one. They devoured Lord Hammer's complete attention for no more than a minute.

We soldiers fought. Sigurd and I locked shields with Contini-Marcusco and the Itaskian. The Harish, who disdained and reviled shields, remained behind us. They rained scimitar strokes over our heads.

The savages forced us back by sheer weight. But we held the wall even against suicide charges.

They hadn't the training to handle professional soldiers who couldn't be flanked. We crouched behind our shields and let them come to their deaths.

But they did get their licks in before Lord Hammer finished their witch-doctors and turned on them.

It lasted no longer than three minutes. We beat them again. But when the clang and screaming faded, we had little reason to cheer.

Hanneker was mortally wounded. Contini-Marcusco had a spearhead in his thigh. Sigurd had taken a deep cut on his left shoulder.

Fetch was down.

Me and the Harish, we were fine. Tired and drained, but unharmed.

I dropped to my knees beside Fetch's still little form. Tears filled my eyes. She had become one of my favorite people.

She had been last in line, walking behind Lord Hammer. We hadn't been able to get to her.

She was alive. She opened her eyes once, when I touched her, and bravely tried one of her smiles.

Lord Hammer knelt opposite me. He touched her cheeks, her hair, tenderly. The tension in him proclaimed his feeling. His gaze crossed mine. For an instant I could feel his pain.

Lord, I thought, your mystique is dying. You care.

Fetch opened her eyes again. She lifted a feeble hand, clasped Lord Hammer's for an instant. "I'm sorry," she whispered.

"Don't be," he said, and it felt like an order from a god. The fingers of his left hand twitched.

I gasped, so startling was his voice, so suddenly did the Power gather. He did something to Fetch's wounds, then to Sigurd's, then to Contini-Marcusco's. Hanneker was beyond help.

He turned, faced downhill, stared. He started walking.

We who could do so followed.

"What did he do?" I whispered to Sigurd.

The big man shrugged. "It don't hurt anymore."

"Did you hear him? He talked. To Fetch."

"No."

Had I imagined it?

I glanced back. The Harish were two steps behind us. They came with the same self-certainty they always showed. Only a tiny tick at the corner of Aboud's eye betrayed any internal feeling.

Foud smiled his little smile. Once again I wondered what they were doing here.

And I wondered about Lord Hammer, whose long process of creating a mythic image seemed to be unraveling.

A mile down into the earth is one hell of a long way. Ignoring the problem of surviving the dragon, I worried about climbing back out. And about my little brother, up there getting his blooding. . . .

I should have stayed with Chenyth. Somebody had to look out for him. . . .

"I have taken the gold," I muttered, and turned to thoughts of poor Fetch.

Now I would never learn what had brought her here. I was sure we wouldn't find her alive when we returned.

If we returned.

Then I worried about how we would know what Lord Hammer would want of us.

I needn't have.

XI

The home hall of the Father of All Dragons was more vast than any stadium. It was one of the great caverns that, before Silcroscuar's coming, had housed the eldritch city Kammengarn.

The cavern's walls glowed. The ruins of the homes of Kammengarn lay in mounds across the floor. As legends proclaimed, that floor was strewn with gold and jewels. The great dragon snored atop a precious hillock.

The place was just as Rainheart had described. With one exception.

The dragon lived.

We heard the monster's stentorian snores long before we reached his den. Our spines had become jelly before we came to that cavern.

Lord Hammer paused before he got there. He spoke.

"There are guardians."

"I wasn't wrong," I whispered.

The others seemed petrified.

The voice came from everywhere at once. It was in keeping with Lord Hammer's style. Deep. Loud. Terrifying. Like the crash of icebergs breaking off glaciers into arctic seas. Huge. Bottomless. Cold.

Something stepped into the tunnel ahead. It was tall, lean, and awkward in appearance. Its skin had the pallor of death. It glistened with an ichorous fluid. It had the form of a man, but I don't think it was human.

Fetch had said there would be guardians who were the descendants of the people of Kammengarn. Had the Kammengarners been human? I didn't know.

The guardian bore a long, wicked sword.

An identical twin appeared behind it. Then another. And another.

Lord Hammer raised his hands in one of those mystic signs. The things halted. But they would not retreat.

For a moment I feared Lord Hammer had no power over them.

I didn't want to fight. Something told me there would be no contest. I am good. Sigurd was good. The Harish were superb. But I knew they would slaughter us as if we were children.

"Salt," Lord Hammer said.

"What the hell?" Sigurd muttered. "Who carries salt around?. . ."

He shut up. Because Foud had leaned past him to drop a small leather sack into the palm of Lord Hammer's glove.

"Ah!" I murmured. "Sigurd, salt is precious in Hammad al Nakir. It's a measure of wealth. El Murid's true devotees always carry some. Because the Disciple's father was a salt caravaneer."

Foud smiled the smile and nodded at Sigurd. Proving he wasn't ignorant of Itaskian, he added, "El Murid received his revelation after bandits attacked his father's caravan. They left the child Micah al Rhami to die of thirst in the desert. But the love of the Lord descended, a glorious angel, and the child was saved, and made whole, and given to look upon the earth. And, Lo! The womb of the desert brought forth not Death, but the Son of Heaven, El Murid, whom you call the Disciple."

For a moment Foud seemed almost as embarrassed as Sigurd and I. Like sex, faith was a force not to be mocked.

Lord Hammer emptied the bag into his hand.

Foud flinched, but did not protest. Aboud leaned past Sigurd and me, offering his own salt should it be needed.

Lord Hammer said no more. The guardians flinched but did not withdraw.

Hammer flung the salt with quick little jerks of his hand, a few grains this way, a few that.

Liverish, mottled cankers appeared on the slimy skin of the guardians. Their mouths yawned in silent screams.

They melted. Like slugs in a garden, salted.

Like slugs, they had no bones.

It took minutes. We watched in true fascination, unable to look away, while the four puddled, pooled, became lost in one lake of twitching slime.

Foud and Aboud shared out the remaining salt.

Lord Hammer went forward, avoiding the remains of the guardians. We followed.

I looked down once.

Eyes stared back from the lake. Knowledgeable, hating eyes. I shuddered.

They were the final barrier. We went into the Place of the Dragon, the glowing hall that once had been a cavern of the city Kammengarn.

I began to think that, despite the barriers, it was too easy, without Lord Hammer. Mortal men would never have reached Kammengarn.

"Gods preserve us," I muttered.

The Kammengarn Dragon was the hugest living thing I've ever seen. I had seen Shinsan's dragons during the wars. I had seen whales beached on the coast. . . .

The dragons I had seen were like chicks compared to roosters. The flesh of a whale might have made up Silcroscuar's tail. His head alone massed as much as an elephant.

"Reckon he'd miss a cup of blood?" Sigurd whispered.

The northmen and their gallows humor. A strange race.

The dragon kept on snoring.

We had come in winter, according to Fetch, because that was the best time of year. I suppose she meant that dragons were more sluggish then. Or even hibernated.

But at that depth the chill of winter meant nothing. The place was as hot as an August noon in the desert.

We flanked Lord Hammer. Sigurd and I to his right, the Harish to his left. Hammer started toward the dragon.

The monster opened an eye. Its snakelike tongue speared toward Lord Hammer.

I interposed my shield, chopped with my sword. The tongue caromed away. My blade cut nothing but air.

A mighty laugh surrounded us. It came from no detectable source.

"You made it, fugitive. Ah. Yes. I know you, Lord Hammer. I know who you are. I know what you are. I know more than you know. All tidings come to me here. There are no secrets from me. Even the future is mine to behold. And yours is a cosmic jest."

Lord Hammer reacted only by beginning a series of gestures, the first of which was the arm cross he had used at the barrows in the forest.

The dragon chuckled. "You'll have your way. And be the poorer for it." It yawned.

My jaw sagged. The teeth in that cavernous mouth! Like the waving scimitars of a horde of desert tribesmen. . . .

Laughter assailed the air. "I have been intimate with the future, refugee. I know the vanity of the course you have chosen. Your hope is futile. I know the joke the Fates have prepared. But come. Take what you want. I'll not thwart you, nor deny the Fates their amusement."

The dragon closed his eye. He shifted his bulk slightly, as if into a more comfortable position.

Lord Hammer advanced.

We stayed with him.

And again I thought it was too easy. The monster wasn't making even a token attempt to stop us.

That matter about the Fates and a cosmic joke. It reminded me of all those tales in which men achieved their goals only to discover that the price of success was more dear than that of failure.

Lord Hammer clambered up the mound of gold and jewels, boldly seizing a gargantuan canine to maintain his balance.

My stomach flopped.

The dragon snored on.

Sigurd started grabbing things small enough to carry away. I selected a few souvenirs myself. Then I saw the contempt in Foud's eyes.

He seemed to be thinking that there were issues at stake far greater than greed.

It was an unguarded thought, breaking through onto his face. It put me on guard.

"Sigurd," I hissed. "Be ready. It's not over."

"I know," he whispered. "Just grabbing while I can."

Lord Hammer beckoned. I scrambled across the treacherous pile. "Cut here." He tapped the dragon's lip where scaly armor gave way to the soft flesh of the mouth. "Gently."

Terror froze me. He wanted me to cut that monster? When it might wake up? What chance would we have?. . .

"Cut!"

Lord Hammer's command made the cavern walls shudder. I could not deny it. I drew the tip of my blade across dragon flesh.

Blood welled up, dribbled down the monster's jaw.

It was as red as any man's. I saw nothing remarkable about it, save that men had died for it. Slowly, drop by drop, it filled the ebony container Lord Hammer held.

We waited tensely, anticipating an explosion from the monster. Dragons had foul and cunning reputations, and that of the Kammengarn Dragon outstripped them all.

I caught a smile toying with Aboud's lips. It was gone in an instant, but it left me more disturbed, more uncertain than ever.

I searched the cavern, wondering if more guardians might not be creeping our way. I saw nothing.

Sigurd bent to secure one more prize jewel. . . .

And Lord Hammer screwed a top onto his container, satisfied.

Foud and Aboud surged toward him. Silver Harish kill-daggers whined through the air.

I managed to skewer Aboud and kick Foud in one wild movement. Then my impetus carried me down the mountain of treasure to the cavern floor. Golden baubles gnawed at my flesh.

Sigurd roared as he hurled himself at Foud, who was after Lord Hammer again. I regained my feet and charged up the pile.

A gargantuan laughter filled the caverns of Kammengarn.

Foud struck Lord Hammer's left arm, and killed Sigurd, before he perished, strangling in the grip of Lord Hammer's right hand.

Aboud, though dying, regained his feet. Again he tried to plant his kill-dagger in Lord Hammer's back.

I reached him in time. We tumbled back down the pile.

Lord Hammer flung Foud after us.

Aboud sat up. He had lost his dagger. I saw it lying about five feet behind him. Tears filled his eyes as he awaited the doom descending upon him.

"Why?" I asked.

"For the Master. For the blood of the dragon that would have made him immortal, that would have given him time to carry the truth. And for what was done to him during the wars."

"I don't understand, Aboud."

"You wouldn't. You haven't recognized him as your enemy."

Lord Hammer loomed over us. His left arm hung slackly. The kill-dagger had had that much success.

Lord Hammer reached with his right, seizing Aboud's throat.

The Harish fought back. Vainly.

I recovered his dagger during the struggle. Quietly, carefully, I concealed it inside my shirt. Why I don't know, except that the genuine article was more valuable than anything in the dragon's hoard.

"Come," Lord Hammer told me. Almost conversationally, he added, "The dragon will be pleased. He's hungry. These three will repay him for his blood." He strode to the gap where the guardians had perished. Their hating eyes watched us pass.

I had to strain to keep pace with him. By the time we reached Fetch I was exhausted. Hanneker had expired in our absence.

"We rest here," Lord Hammer told me. "We will carry these two, and there may be ambushes." He sat down with his back against one wall. He massaged his lifeless arm.

The image had slipped even more. He seemed quite human at that moment.

"Who are you?" I asked after a while.

The iron mask turned my way. I couldn't meet his gaze. The Power was still there.

"Better that you don't know, soldier. For both our sakes."

"I have taken the gold," I replied.

I expect he understood. Maybe he didn't. He said nothing more till he decided to go.

"It's time. Carry Fetch. Be wary."

I hoisted the little woman. She seemed awfully heavy. My strength had suffered. The mountains. The forest. The fighting. The tension, always. They ground me down.

We met no resistance. Only once did we hear what might have been men. They avoided us.

We rested often. Lord Hammer seemed to be weakening faster than I, though his resources were more vast. Maybe the Harish kill-dagger had bitten more deeply than he let on.

"Stop," he gasped. We were close to the end of the tunnel. I dropped Fetch. Men's voices, muted, echoed along the shaft. "Chenyth." I started on.

"Stay." The command in Hammer's voice was weak, but compelling.

He moved slowly, had trouble keeping his feet. But he negated the spells that made us glow. "We must rest here."

"My brother. . . ."

"We will rest, Willem Potter."

We rested.

XII

Outside ambushed us.

The sun had set. No moon had risen. The stars didn't cast much light. Bellweather had lighted no fires. We were suddenly there, beside Lord Hammer's stallion.

The last dozen yards we had to step over and around the dead and wounded. There were a lot of them. I kept whispering Chenyth's name. The only man I could find was Brandy. The griper had been dead for hours.

"They've killed or captured most of the animals," Bellweather reported. Lord Hammer grunted noncommittally. "We've killed hundreds of them, but they keep coming. They'll finish us in the morning. This is serious business to them."

"Chenyth!" I called.

"Will? Will! Over here."

I hurried over. He was doing sentry duty. His post was an open-topped bunker built of the corpses of savages.

"You all right?" I demanded.

"So far. Brandy and Russ and Aral are dead, Will. I'm sorry I came. I'm tired. So tired, Will."

"Yeah. I know."

"What happened down there?"

"It was bad." I told him the story.

"The other Harish. Will they?. . . "

"I'm sure their daggers are consecrated to the same name."

"Then they'll try again?"

"They made it? Then we'd better warn. . . . "

A shriek ripped the air.

I hurled myself back toward Lord Hammer. I arrived at the same time as the Harish. Blades flashed. Men screamed. Lord Hammer slew one. I took the other. Bellweather and the others watched in dull-eyed disbelief.

Before Jamal died he cursed me. "You have given the Hammer his life," he croaked. "May that haunt you all the ages of earth. May his return be quickened, and fall upon you heavily. I speak it in the Name of the Disciple."

"What did he mean, Will?" Chenyth asked.

"I don't know." I was too tired to think. "They knew him. They knew his mission. They came to abort it. And to capture the dragon's blood for El Murid." I glanced at Lord Hammer. He had begun a sorcery. His voice sounded terribly weak. He seemed the least superhuman of us all. My awe of him had evaporated completely.

He was but a man.

"Maybe they were right," Chenyth suggested. "Maybe the world would be better without him. Without his kind."

"I don't know. His kind are like the dragon. And we have taken the gold, Chenyth. It doesn't matter who or what he is."

Sleep soon ambushed me. The last thing I saw was a ball of blue light drifting into the rocks where the savages lurked. I think there were screams, but they might have come in my dreams.

They took me back to the wars. To the screams of entire kingdoms crushed beneath the boots of legions led by men of Lord Hammer's profession. Those had been brutal, bitter days, and the saddest part of it was that we hadn't won, we had merely stopped it for a while.

My subconscious mind added the clues my conscious mind had overlooked.

I awakened understanding the Harish.

"His name is a joke," Fetch had said.

It wasn't a funny one. It was pure arrogance.

One of the arch-villains of the Great Eastern Wars had been a sorcerer named Ko Feng. He had commanded the legions of the Dread Empire briefly. But his fellow wizards on the Council of Tervola had ousted him because of his unsubtle, straightforward, expensive, pounding military tactics. For reasons no one understood he had been ordered into exile.

His nickname, on both sides of the battle line, had been The Hammer. Aboud had told me he was my enemy. . . .

The savages bothered us no more. Lord Hammer's sorcery had sufficed.

Only a dozen men were fit to travel. Chenyth and I were the only surviving Kaveliners. . . .

Kavelin had borne the brunt of the Great Eastern Wars. The legions of the Dread Empire knew no mercy. The nation might never recover. . . .

I was sitting on a rock, fighting my conscience. Chenyth came to me. "Want something to eat?"

"I don't think so.

"What's the matter, Will?"

"I think I know who he is. What he's doing. Why."

"Who?"

"Lord Hammer."

"I meant, who is he?"

"Lord Ko Feng. The Tervola. The one we called The Hammer during the wars. They banished him from Shinsan when it was over. They took his immortality and drove him onto exile. He came for the dragon's blood to win the immortality back. To get the time he needed to make his return."

"Oh, Gods. Will, we've got to do something."

"What? What's the right thing? I don't *know* that he's really Ko Feng. I do know that we've taken his gold. He's treated us honorably. He even saved my life when there was no demand that he do so. I know that Fetch thinks the world of him, and I think well enough of Fetch for that to matter. So. You see what's eating me."

My life wasn't usually that complicated. A soldier takes his orders, does what he must, and doesn't much worry about tomorrow or vast issues. He takes from life what he can when he can, for there may be no future opportunity. He seldom moralizes, or becomes caught in a crisis of conscience.

"Will, we can't turn an evil like Ko Feng loose on the world again. Not if it's in our power to stop it."

"Chenyth. Chenyth. Who said he was evil? His real sin is that he was the enemy. Some of our own were as violent and bloody."

I glanced back toward the split in the mountain. The giant black stallion stood within a yard of where Lord Hammer had posted him yesterday. Hammer slept on the ground beneath the animal.

Easy pickings, I thought. Walk over, slip the dagger in him, and have done.

If the horse would let me. He was a factor I couldn't fathom. But somehow I knew he would block me.

My own well-being wasn't a matter of concern. Like the Harish, it hadn't occurred to me to worry about whether or not I got out alive.

I saw no way any of us could get home without Lord Hammer's protection.

Fetch dragged herself to a sitting position.

"Come with me," I told Chenyth.

We went to her. She greeted us with a weak smile. "I wasn't good for much down there, was I?"

"How you feeling?" I asked.

"Better."

"Good. I'd hate to think I lugged you all the way up here for nothing."

"It was you?"

"Lord Hammer carried the Scuttarian."

"The others?"

"Still down there, Love."

"It was bad?"

"Worse than anybody expected. Except the dragon."

"You got the blood?"

"We did. Was it worth it?"

She glanced at me sharply. "You knew there would be risks. You were paid to take them."

"I know. I wonder if that's enough."

"What?"

"I know who Lord Hammer is, Fetch. The Harish knew all along. It's why they came. I killed two of them. Lord Hammer slew two. Foud killed Sigurd. That's five of the company gone fighting one another. I want to know what reason there might be for me not to make it six and have the world rid of an old evil."

Fetch wasn't herself. Healthy she would have screeched and argued like a whole flock of hens at feeding time. Instead, she just glanced at Lord Hammer and shrugged. "I'm too tired and sick to care much, Will. But don't. It won't change the past. It won't change the future, either. He's chasing a dead dream. And it won't do you any good now." She leaned back and closed her eyes. "I hated him for a while, too. I lost people in the wars."

"I'm sorry."

"Don't be. He lost people, too, you know. Friends and relatives. All the pain and dying weren't on our side. And he lost everything he had, except his knowledge."

"Oh." I saw what she was trying to say. Lord Hammer was no different than the rest of us leftovers, going on being what he had learned to be.

"Is there anything to eat?"

"Chenyth. See if you can get her something. Fetch, I know all the arguments. I've been wrestling with them all morning. And I can't make up my mind. I was hoping you could help me figure where I've got to stand."

"Don't put it on me, Willem Potter. It's a thing between you and Lord Hammer."

Chenyth brought soup that was mostly mule. He spooned it into Fetch's mouth. She ate it like it was good.

I decided, but on the basis of none of the arguments that had gone before.

I had promised myself that I would take my little brother home to his mother. To do that I needed Lord Hammer's protection.

I often wonder, now, if many of the most fateful decisions aren't made in response to similarly oblique considerations.

XIII

I need not have put myself through the misery. The Fates had their own plans.

When Lord Hammer woke, I went to him. He was weak. He barely had the strength to sit up. I squatted on my hams, facing him, intimidated by the stallion's baleful stare. Carefully, I drew the Harish kill-dagger from within my shirt. I offered it to him atop my open palms.

The earth shook. There was a suggestion of gargantuan mirth in it.

"The Dragon mocks us." Lord Hammer took the dagger. "Thank you, Willem Potter. I'd say there are no debts between us now."

"There are, Lord. Old ones. I lost a father and several brothers in the wars."

"And I lost sons and friends. Will we fight old battles here in the cupped hands of doom? Will we cross swords even as the filed teeth of Fate rip at us? I lost my homeland and more than any non-Tervola could comprehend. I have nothing left but hope, and that too wan to credit. The Dragon laughs with cause, Willem Potter. Summon Bellweather. A journey looms before us."

"As you say, Lord."

I think we left too soon, with too many wounded. Some survived the forest. Some survived the plains. Some survived the snows and precipices of the Dragon's Teeth. But we left men's bones beside the way. Only eight of us lived to see the plains of Shara, west of the mountains, and even then we were a long way from home.

It was in Shara that Lord Hammer's saga ended.

We were riding ponies he had bought from a Sharan tribe. Our faces were south, bent into a spring rain.

Lord Hammer's big stallion stumbled.

The sorcerer fell.

He had been weakening steadily. Fetch claimed only his will was driving him toward the laboratories where he would make use of the dragon's blood. . . .

He lay in the mud and grass of a foreign land, dying, and there was nothing any of us could do. The Harish dagger still gnawed at his soul.

Immortality rested in his saddlebags, in that black jar, and we couldn't do a thing. We didn't know how. Even Fetch was ignorant of the secret.

He was a strong man, Lord Hammer, but in the end no different than any other. He died, and we buried him in alien soil. The once mightiest man on earth had come to no more than the least of the soldiers who had followed him in his prime.

I was sad. It's painful to watch something magnificent and mighty brought low, even when you loath what it stands for.

He went holding Fetch's hand. She removed the iron mask before we put him into the earth. "He should wear his own." She obtained a Tervola mask from his gear. It was golden and hideous, and at one time had terrorized half a world. I'm not sure what it represented. An animal head of some sort. Its eyes were rubies that glowed like the eyes of Lord Hammer's stallion. But their inner light was fading.

A very old man lay behind the iron mask. The last of his mystique perished when I finally saw his wizened face.

And yet I did him honor as we replaced the soil above him.

I had taken his gold. He had been my captain.

"You can come with us, Fetch," Chenyth said. And I agreed. There would be a place for her with the Potters.

Chenyth kept the iron mask. It hangs in my mother's house even now. Nobody believes him when he tells the story of Lord Hammer and the Kammengarn Dragon. They prefer Rainheart's heroics.

No matter. The world goes on whether geared by truth or fiction.

The last shovelful of earth fell on Lord Hammer's resting place. And Chenyth, as always, had a question. "Will, what happened to his horse?"

The great fire-eyed stallion had vanished.

Even Fetch didn't know the answer to that one.

DARKWAR

"Darkwar" was a cover story for Isaac Asimov's Science Fiction Magazine. After it appeared, I just had to write the Darkwar Trilogy to explain the back-story of the novelette.

1

Three figures glided through an empty night street. Moon-light twinkled off the medals and tunic buttons of the tallest. There was a gentle tinkle as she moved. The smaller two made no sound at all. They were silth sisters, sorceresses, trained to the ways of the dark. The tall female, Kerath Hadon, knew that they trailed her only because she had asked them to do so.

A remote flash brightened the quiet street. Kerath glanced up. For a moment she saw only three moons. The smallest had an orbital motion perceptible to the eye.

Razor slashes of coherent light ripped the velvet sky, come and gone so fast she actually saw only afterimages. "Another strike at *Frostflyer* and *Dreamkeeper*," Kerath said.

Her companions said nothing. One may have nodded. These silth wasted no words. Kerath shivered. They spooked her. "Come. Let's get this done while we still have a few ships left."

A series of flashes illuminated the city, revealing crumbling old walls recently whitewashed in defiance of the doom overhanging the Meth homeworld, filling gothic aches with shadows, silhouetting distant onion domes. Kerath snarled, "Suslov is serious tonight. Here." She tapped a sagging door. It opened. A gray-whiskered male poked his muzzle into the rippling light, his eyes flashing golden.

"You?"

"Yes, it's me, Shadar. Wouldn't you know it? Is the High Lord here?"

"Waiting impatiently, Marshall. Off the street before you're seen."

Kerath pushed inside. Her shadows followed, two dark ghosts. Shadar led them through two rooms, to the foot of a stair. "Up there. Kerath? Marshall? Good luck."

"No luck involved, Shadar. Strictly fiat. But thank you." She touched his hand gently.

A moment later she stood in the doorway of a brightly lighted room. A half-dozen males with gray whiskers and ragged fur stared at her with tight eyes and tighter lips. Kerath flashed teeth. Folgar suspected. She stepped inside. "I thought this would be private, High Lord."

The eldest male flexed muscles still powerful despite gnawing age. "The circumstances suggested some unpleasant possibilities. You'll understand my urge to include reliable witnesses, Marshall." His teeth showed mockingly.

Kerath's ears tilted forward and down, the Meth equivalent of a sneer. The presence of his henchmen would do Folgar no good. "You and your packmates have destroyed the Meth, High Lord. The people are sick of alien ways, and even more sick of endless defeat." Kerath gestured toward the doorway. "The Meth might welcome the return of old ways."

A low rumble started deep in a half-dozen throats, an unconscious warning sound from males who saw their territories threatened. "Why are those silth witches here?" one demanded.

"Marshall?" Folgar asked. He concealed his emotions well for a male.

Kerath drew herself to her straightest. She knew she made an imposing figure, a hero of the Meth, well marked with medals and scars. She even wore the white cuff badge of Snow-No-More, a defeat that fewer than a hundred Meth had survived. "For three generations your all-male party has held the power, High Lord. What have you done with it? You have harried the silth. Slain their greatest. And you have made the Meth into bumbling imitations of the humans you admire." She had rehearsed the message often, but her delivery was not going well. She did not *feel* it.

Folgar nodded. "To the point, Marshall. The Command had something in mind when they sent you."

Kerath would not be hurried. "You set aside the old ways, the old truths, the old knowledge. You made mock of millennia of tradition. You made the Meth a reflection of Man. Then you tried to usurp the humans. What has it profited you? What has it gained the Meth?"

Folgar stared stonily. His companions watched the silth warily, frightened, as if faced by something returned from the grave.

"Our worlds are lost. Our greatest warships are debris scattered among the stars. Our best fighters lie in iron coffins far in the bitter cold of the deep. We retain only that speck of space inside Biter's orbit. *Frostflyer* and *Dreamkeeper* are our last heavy ships. We have become prisoners upon our homeworld, awaiting the fall of a monstrous hammer. We are helpless to turn away the asteroid Suslov sends to shatter our world."

"He won't bring it all the way in," Folgar countered.

"He will if he must. I know Pyotr Suslov, High Lord. He doesn't bluff. But, of course, your contention is correct insofar as you know. You have been arranging a secret surrender."

Folgar's ears flicked in surprise.

"The Command knows." Kerath did not conceal her contempt. "Male treachery. It's always with us. You started this war, and now you mean to sell the Meth simply so you can retain power when the fighting stops."

"Now Marshall . . ."

"The Meth would drink your blood if they saw the Command's tapes of your communications with Suslov."

"Are you threatening me, Marshall?"

"This is the message from the Command. There will be no surrender. The Meth will die as they have always lived: without dishonor. If the asteroid cannot be turned, so be it. May the All forfend."

"Marshall—" Folgar's ears were back now, in fighting position.

"The Command will take appropriate steps if you have any further contact with Suslov."

"This is rebellion."

Kerath admitted it. "The Armed Force is the source of all power, Folgar. It no longer supports you. It is assuming direction of the war effort."

"Why are *they* with you?" Loathing and hatred edged Folgar's voice as he indicated the silth.

"We fought your way, the way that imitates humans. We failed. Now we turn to the ways of our foremothers."

The old males growled. A chair overturned. Someone dropped a bottle. The stink of male fear filled the room.

"Darkwar?" Folgar asked.

"Darkwar."

"But the old darkships were scrapped. Nor are there trained silth crews anymore."

Kerath revealed the points of her teeth. "Wrong on both counts. The silth have ships you never found. The legendary Ceremony darkships. And sisters who escaped your hunters. End of message from the Command."

Folgar growled, but there was a touch of fear in his defiance.

Kerath turned away. "Come," she told the silth.

Shadar awaited her at the foot of the stair. "You did well."

Kerath nodded. "I thought so."

"Good luck again, Marshall." Shadar touched her arm.

Kerath paused to hug the Meth who had sired her, before pushing into the street.

The sky was quiet. The orbital skirmish had ended. *Frostflyer* and *Dreamkeeper* still radiated the glow of active energy screens. They had survived again.

2

Kerath was uneasy in the company of the silth, though she concealed it well. Her adult life had run in tracks prescribed by Folgar's ilk. These sorceresses were anachronisms, shadows of ideas long outdated. Facing down Folgar's scruffy pack was one thing; believing that the Command was doing right was another.

She pushed off a bulkhead, floated across the lighter's cabin, checked the harnesses of her companions. "Rendezvous with *Dreamkeeper* in fifteen minutes." They looked at her with fathomless eyes, saying nothing.

They were so young to be so spooky. They never spoke. That was unnerving. But they had to be good. Littermates, they had been chosen Mistresses of the Ships over any others of the surviving silth. It was said they were as filled with the dark strength as the great silth of old, when darkwar decided the destiny of the Meth.

Did the Command want those grim days to return from shadow? Folgar was a fool, yes, but he was right when he claimed the Meth were better off for having shed the yoke of the silth.

Docking alarm sounded. Overhead speakers relayed crisp instructions. The crew was trying to impress the oncoming Marshall.

Kerath needed no impressing. *Dreamkeeper* sprang from the same core of honor as she. The ship was a survivor.

She released her charges. "Follow me."

An honor guard waited aboard the warship. Kerath accepted their accolade but told the ship's commander, "Don't waste any more energy on protocol. My companions are cargo, and I don't need it."

"As you will, Marshall. Let me show you to your quarters."

"Have the other personnel arrived?"

The commander glanced back. The silth stalked them like wicked shadows. The boots of Kerath and the commander rang on the gray-painted steel decks. The two in black seemed to glide a whisker above the plating. "They're here. Have you noticed the quiet?"

"I noted a distinct lack of curiosity."

"The crew is staying out of the way. The first group distressed them. Now you bring Mistresses of the Ships. "They're frightened."

Kerath showed a glimpse of teeth. "They have cause, Commander. *I* wouldn't be here had I not been directed."

"When you were a whelp, did they tell you tales about the grauken?"

"Did they? My older brothers tried to convince our litter that he lived under our bed." The grauken was a shape-changing night monster fond of delicate young flesh, an archetype born during primitive winters, when desperate packs resorted to cannibalism to survive, luring or capturing the young of other packs.

"Seeing the silth aboard my ship gives me the feeling I'd have if I did find the grauken under my bed."

"I know," Kerath said. "How well I know."

"These are our guests' quarters," the commander said, halting before a door. He tapped. The door slid open a crack. "Sisters?" He indicated the two figures in black.

Kerath caught a glimpse of the cabin as the two entered. The darkness was barely broken by red light. Shapes in black sat motionless. A terrible bittersweet odor rolled out, offending Kerath's nostrils.

The door clumped shut.

"The grauken's den," the commander observed. "They're calling it that already. I hope the Command knows what it's doing."

"So do I, Commander. So do I. I don't think I could go on if I thought my efforts would facilitate a silth rebirth."

"Nor I. I suppose we must have faith that the Command can neutralize them once they have served their purpose."

"Are we ready to space?"

"Programmed for jump. *Frostflyer* should be moving up to cover our drive ports. Whenever you give the order, Marshall."

"Then show me my quarters. I'll shift uniforms and join you on the bridge."

3

"Ready on *Frostflyer*, Marshall."

"Ready here, Marshall," the ship's commander said.

Kerath stared into the situation display tank. The humans were shifting their dispositions. Suslov had noted *Frostflyer*'s change of station. "They anticipate a strike at the asteroid."

"As they would say, it's in the cards," the commander replied. "They would see that as our only remaining option."

"A weak one, though. If we reshape the collision orbit, they'll just warp another hunk of rock into the same groove."

"In that light, what we're doing here doesn't make much sense either."

"No. I suspect the Command just wants to scare them into backing off." Kerath studied the proposed track of the warship. It feinted toward the incoming asteroid, then curved out of the system. "It should work. They should be rushing one way while we jump the other."

"And then what?"

"It's hoped they'll assume we've been sent out as commerce raiders. If we shake loose, they'll concentrate on guarding their shipping lanes."

"That's the book?"

Kerath revealed a little tooth. "That's the book. Let's hope Pyotr Suslov buys it. Go when ready, Commander."

It looked book for awhile. But when *Frostflyer* and *Dreamkeeper* turned, human warships responded immediately. Kerath studied the tank. "Two main battles and a heavy chaser. Suslov hedged his bets." She turned suddenly, sensing a difference, a change of energy in the air.

Two silth had come onto the narrow balcony overlooking the fighting bridge: the two she had brought aboard. They remained out of the way, observing, but their chill filled the compartment.

"Coming up to first jump," the commander said. "And two. And one. And jump." The tank blanked. The fringes of the universe folded in. Bulkheads melted and crawled. Meth wavered like dancing flames. Kerath glanced at the silth. *They* remained rocks of blackness.

Real space clicked into place.

The tank began to assemble a portrait from data retrieved by the ship's exterior sensors. "*Frostflyer* is with us, right on station."

Kerath stared into the tank, watching starpoints wink into being, willing it not to show anything red.

"One counter. Two counter. Three counter. They stayed with us, Marshall."

"I see them, Commander. Next jump."

The stars changed thrice more. Three times the human trackers came through behind them. "They're good," Kerath observed. "Really good."

"Suggestions, Marshall?"

"They were ragged that go. The chaser was a half-minute late. Perhaps it's a cumulative error."

"We have only four jumps to shake them, Marshall."

"Continue, Commander."

Next jump the humans translated even more raggedly, arriving over a span of a full minute. Kerath sighed. Time to act. "Commander, Mission Officer to *Frostflyer*. Turn and attack after next drop. Lead them away. Head for home the long way."

The commander stared at her for several seconds before relaying the order.

The ships jumped, and dropped. *Frostflyer* charged toward where the humans were expected to appear. Kerath glared at the tank.

The first human ship appeared directly in *Frostflyer*'s path. The tank showed a great deal of weaponry action.

A second ship dropped. And then the first vanished.

"Ha!" a tech cried. "Got one!"

"Or it jumped out," Kerath whispered to herself, watching *Frostflyer* curve toward the newcomer.

The chaser arrived as the commander ordered the next jump. When translation was complete, Kerath suggested, "Hold the next jump. Let's see if they come through after us. Better to fight them here than around the target."

The commander observed, "It won't much matter now, will it? They've followed long enough to know we're not headed toward any commerce lane. If they bring in a fleet on our line of flight . . ."

"But it'll take days, or even weeks, to find us. That should be time enough."

Nothing appeared on *Dreamkeeper*'s backtrail. After waiting an hour, Kerath ordered the journey resumed.

Much, much later, as the ship cruised that section of space approximating its destination, she directed, "Secure to quarters, Commander. Standard watches. We'll begin searching after we've rested."

"Very well, Marshall."

The silth were at the hatchway when Kerath departed. She thought their eyes looked feverish in the subdued lighting. She nodded greeting and started to slip past.

A hand touched her elbow. She stopped as if she had encountered an iron bar. A whisper said, "The steel ship, *Frostflyer*, is no more. Two alien ships lighted its path into darkness. The third is injured. It limps back to its base. We tell you, that those with kin aboard *Frostflyer* might begin mourning in timely fashion."

"Yes. Thank you." Kerath shook off the staying hand and rushed to her quarters. For half an hour she sat rubbing fingers over her personal sidearm. The action had a calming effect.

She had ordered *Frostflyer*, half the fleet-in-being, half the surviving might of the Meth, to its death.

Her sleep was filled with terrible dreams, haunted by dry, withered old bitches flying on black wings. Last hope of the Meth. The Command had given its trust into the wrong hands.

4

"Coming up now, Commander."

Kerath and the ship's commander leaned over a vidtech's shoulders, peering into her screen. "Searchlights," the commander ordered.

Immediately something flashed out in the darkness. "There," Kerath gasped. "More light."

Several lights concentrated on the target. Gradually, parts became visible.

"Darkship," the commander breathed. "They really still exist. The Ceremony legend is true."

Kerath nodded, unable to avert her gaze from that ghost out of the far past, when disputes between silth sisterhoods were settled by combats between Mistresses of the Ships far in the black heart of space. The darkship didn't look like a ship at all, just a giant titanium girderwork dagger marked with mysterious symbols.

The darkship sprang from an era when sisterhoods formed associations human translators still confused with nations, corporations, and even families. The competition for control of the wealth of the stars had been savage, till silth-run merchanters had encountered humans, with their contagious alien ways and unshakable disbelief. The ensuing confusion among the silth had allowed their overthrow, and hatred of their long tyranny had led to merciless slaughter, witchhunts that persisted yet, and over-reactive tilts toward the new human ideas.

"It needs a lot of repair," the commander observed.

"Supposed to be twelve of them," Kerath replied. "The legend is, they chose to meet and die a ritual death here rather than go home and submit to the will of the new order. We'll choose the best preserved."

The silth had other ideas. They wanted to locate specific ships.

"The spells of our foremothers guard them still," said the one who did the talking. "Only those two will be accessible to us."

Kerath frowned. That might mean troublesome delays. "You're the experts," she said, grudging them every extra minute.

Two days went into locating the right ships. They had drifted apart over the centuries. One of the two had sustained considerable damage.

Kerath worried. Suslov would be on the hunt. She did not want to waste time making repairs. The silth ignored her protests. They led their shadowy sisters out and went to work. There was nothing Kerath could do to hurry or help them, or to alter their perception of the way things should be done.

Kerath was sleeping when an orderly came with the commander's request that she join her on the bridge.

"Thought you'd want to see this, Marshall." The commander indicated a screen. "They've got one moving. There's not a hint of drive, but it's moving."

Kerath surveyed the detection boards. The commander was right. The darkship appeared only on visual and radar. She stared at the titanium dagger. It was receding toward distant stars. A vague glow surrounded it. "She's getting the feel of it. The old stories say they glowed too brightly to look at."

The commander nodded. Then she gasped, "Where did it go? Radar. Where is that target?"

"Gone, Commander. I'm not getting anything . . . Wait. Here it is. Nadir, thirty-five degrees, range fifteen."

Kerath exchanged glances with the commander. "Through the Up-and-Over," she murmured. "She's found her demons."

"So that's true too." The commander looked frightened. "Witches. You know, I didn't really believe this before."

Kerath stared at the empty screen. "I didn't either, Commander. Not down deep in my heart." She began to grow a little frightened too.

5

Fifth day on station. The second darkship had completed repairs. Both crews were outside learning to handle their ships. Kerath thought practice seemed unnecessary. "They appear to have been born to it," she said.

The commander growled, "They are, aren't they?"

Kerath's ears tilted slightly, expressing mild amusement. The silth claimed to possess the memories of all their foremothers. Watching these sisters ride their darkships, she was inclined to discard former doubts.

"Do they have names?" the commander asked.

"The silth? I don't know. I see. You can't keep them straight. Neither can I."

"One is faster than the other. I'd like some way to differentiate before we go into rehearsal."

Kerath's hackles rose slightly. She checked the time. In half an hour she would be out there herself, riding a darkship during the first mock attack. *Dreamkeeper* would play alien, its technicians searching for weaknesses Suslov could exploit.

Kerath was not sure why she was going out. An observer run was not essential to her mission. But she had been invited by the Mistresses of the Ships. Acceptance seemed politic.

Fear stalked her like a shadow that disappeared when she turned, like the grauken sliding out from under the far side of the bed as she bent down to look for it. The silth had reasons for being here that had nothing to do with saving the Meth homeworld. That would be incidental to their accomplishment of their true ambitions.

Seconds and minutes rolled past. Kerath watched the tank and screens and hoped they would forget her. Out there *she* would be the powerless minority, unable to call for help. She turned. "Commander, there's a hole in this thing. Darkships were meant to fight alone, against other darkships. They could smell each other in vacuum. But how will they find a human ship? How will they handle unexpected changes? This is going to be an attack by rote."

The commander nodded. "I was going to suggest we throw some kinks into the later maneuvers, to test their flexibility. Lack of flexibility broke them back when. They couldn't cope with the flood of novel ideas that came after meeting the humans. They couldn't shed roles programmed by their foremothers."

"I'll mention that to the silth."

"In a way, I feel sorry for them. Time has passed them by."

"Perhaps." Kerath glanced at the screen. A darkship was docking. "They didn't forget me. Wish me luck."

The Mistress of the Ship met her in docking bay. She had brought her darkship inside. It floated free, ignoring *Dreamkeeper*'s artificial gravity. Fresh, updated symbols had been painted on the titanium beams. A variety of new mystical hardware had been installed. Overall, the darkship looked new.

Kerath opened a locker to secure an eva suit.

"No, Marshall. No artifacts. You alone, naked."

Kerath bared her teeth. "No."

"We wish you to partake of the silth experience. We wish you to meet those-who-dwell."

"That's your problem. If you really want me to make the fly, do it on my terms."

"No."

"Compromise?" Kerath thought the female's eyes flared for an instant. Silth did not compromise. "I want my clothing and my communicator."

"Clothing is neither dignity nor worth, Marshall."

"Then shed yours, silth."

The female's eyes flared. "Very well. Set your communicator to receive only. We wish you to concentrate on the experience, not what to report."

"Agreed."

The Mistress glided away. Kerath followed. The silth was angry. She stepped heavily enough to be heard.

The Mistress led her to the axis of the titanium dagger. "Stand here. This is the traditional Place of the Mother in combats to determine the fates of sisterhoods in blood feud. Fear not. A dome of power will shield you from the breath of the All." The silth left her and took her own station at the tip of the longest arm of the cross. Riding the point of the dagger, Kerath thought.

"Marshall?" Another silth held out a silver bowl filled with an amber liquid. Kerath had seen the sisters sip from similar bowls before each of their trips outside. Shakily, she took the bowl and drank.

"More," the sister said.

Kerath drank.

"More ... Enough. Yes. I think that's enough."

Kerath felt lightheaded. Her eyeballs felt prickly.

The silth took the bowl to each of the stations, then assumed her own place at the tip of one of the dagger's arms.

Kerath became aware of microscopic points of light around her. She caught hints of similar phenomena surrounding the other females. The phenomena grew more pronounced as *Dreamkeeper* evacuated the atmosphere from the bay.

The bay door opened. Naked stars stared in. Kerath felt only a slight moment of chill; then the golden points redoubled in intensity.

The darkship turned, pointed toward the stars—then stabbed toward them at screaming speed. Kerath felt no inertial drag. She turned and saw the rectangular lighted bay shrink with incredible rapidity. This was impossible. Even more impossible, her fur rippled as if in a strong wind.

Dreamkeeper shrank to a point and vanished.

She was alone among the stars, standing in space. She could not see the darkship. Her companions were golden columns that looked more like distant star clusters than nearby phenomena. She was alone, and frightened as she had never been frightened before. Something burned in her veins. Her head spun. Her eyes would not track. The amber drink? Strange, colored things crawled round the edge of her vision.

Had they poisoned her? No. They had drunk from the same bowl. Suddenly it became clear, a whole different view of the darkful deep between the stars; a view of a chill filled with color and life. Life? Life was impossible out here . . .

A swarm of a million bright little deltoid darts drifted toward her, slowly shifting color from yellow through red and back again, in perfect unison. They sensed the darkship suddenly. As one they turned white, flipped around, and streaked away. They moved almost faster than the eye could track.

There were little things, big things, even bigger things. Some crowded the darkship, curious. Some remained indifferent. Some fled. A few cruised with the ship, seeming to pull it along. Those were the demons of legend, Kerath decided. The demons the silth summoned and commanded to carry their darkships through the Up-and-Over.

In her wonder she forgot her fear. "Oh!" Fear returned a dozenfold. But why? It was nothing. Just a dust cloud obscuring a few stars. Wasn't it?

The stars rotated around her. Vaguely, she sensed the approach of the second darkship. The creatures of color shuddered and made way, slithering over and around one another like a nest of serpents. Four columns of witchfire took station to Kerath's right. The entire second ship began to glow. Ahead of Kerath, her Mistress of the Ship caught fire. The stars began to rock. Moving again, Kerath thought. The things of color—those-who-dwell, in silth parlance—scattered. So fast!

The universe turned inside out. Horrible things clawed and howled at her. "Up-and-Over!" she screamed. The silth had conjured them into the Up-and-Over, where the darkship dagger hurtled faster than light. She screamed again as *Dreamkeeper*'s lights appeared for a second, so close she could almost touch them.

And she screamed once more as the darkship returned to the Up-and-Over.

Drifting. Shaking. *Dreamkeeper* a few light-seconds away. A voice in her ear. It was several seconds before she could concentrate on the message. "Impressive, Marshall, but abort the drill. I say again, abort the drill. We have unfriendly company. Get aboard fast."

Get aboard? How was the Mistress of the Ship to know? No! She couldn't. But she found her feet moving of their own volition, carrying her forward. The commander kept chattering in her ear, telling her how close the enemy was. In half a minute she was at the tip of the dagger. Her shielding melded with that of the silth. "Enemy ship, Mistress," she gasped. "Only a light-minute away, right on a line with our sun. We have to get back aboard *Dreamkeeper*."

The Mistress bobbed her head, asked a few questions. Then she said, "Back to your position."

The return trek seemed far longer. She finished it with a bad feeling gnawing her gut.

6

The darkship began to glow. Round it those-who-dwell scattered. They seemed suddenly two-dimensional, bright paper cutouts imbued with panic, flickering toward silent stars. Only the silth's driver creatures remained, stretching and straining as they dragged the darkship.

Kerath glanced upward. A chill seized her. That dark dust-cloud thing hovered overhead, obscuring different constellations.

The darkships became a pair of fiery daggers hurtling toward nowhere. The universe twisted and folded and opened its evil belly and gave birth to a horde of silently screaming horrors. They had gone into the Up-and-Over. Kerath screamed back. They weren't supposed to do this.

Normal space exploded around her. She caught a half-second glimpse of a human warship, long and lean and deadly, its riders already running free. *Dreamkeeper* had been spotted!

Cold blackness enveloped her. She could not see her sisters on the darkship. She felt their fear, felt the Mistress waver. The stench of death stung her nostrils. Something that felt like the damp at the bottom of a grave crawled over her protective shielding. In her mind she heard the first of a thousand death cries . . .

Twist. Fold. The Up-and-Over. A distinct feeling of hard deceleration a twinge of fear. Something was wrong with the Mistress. The darkship was out of control. *Dreamkeeper* was swelling ahead, docking bay ablaze with light. "Too fast!" Kerath cried. "Slow down!" Her ears folded forward. She sank to all fours, sure she was about to die.

What a waste, to end it all here. *Dreamkeeper* would be crippled, and the Meth could no longer manage major repairs. She had failed, and would not live to see the final consequences.

She was right and she was wrong. The darkship continued its deceleration, lowering its daggertip slowly. In a flicker the warship swelled, rose . . . they were going to make it! They were going to slide beneath it.

The shock of an earthquake hit her. The titanium girderwork ripped, tore, screamed in the silence of the big chill. Kerath clung to the metal. The stars twirled. And then they went out.

She awakened in her quarters. The ship's commander appeared almost immediately, her face grave. "I told you one of them was slow."

"How bad was it?"

"The darkship was a total loss. An arm torn off. One of the silth is dead. *Dreamkeeper* lost a main vent stack. It's not serious as long as we don't have to face heavy particle beam fire."

"One darkship left to complete the mission. Maybe we should abort."

"I don't think so."

"Commander?"

"You'd have to see the human ship to understand." The commander paced, made several false starts before saying, "The old darkwar legends understate. I say send the fast one in and hope the humans get her before she gets all of them. She might have impact enough to encourage a negotiated peace."

"I don't understand, Commander."

"You haven't seen that ship. There may be futures worse than surrender. Would the silth be forgiving if they returned to power?"

"No."

"When you visit the human ship, remember that you're looking at enemies of the silth. The ancient mothers confined darkwar to their high duels in deep space, but it *could* be used against a world. The Command made a grave mistake. The silth offered a straw to grasp, and they grabbed it without looking for the trap. These are new, young Mistresses of the Ships, probably bred and trained for a mission like this. The silth claim to see the future. If they really do, then they would have foreseen desperate times and would have prepared Mistresses like these. If just one survived, with her ship, the silth would win their gamble. They would return."

"You're uncommonly emotional today, Commander."

"I saw the enemy ship. See it yourself. All else will follow."

She had nightmares every time she slept. The human ship had been that grim. The dead had looked as though they had been torn apart from within, or as though they had tortured themselves to death slowly. Just what the silth would wish on their enemies. A lot of Meth would go the same way if the silth had their day.

Kerath studied the rehearsal runs of the surviving darkship. The Mistress of the Ship was superb. She never gave *Dreamkeeper*'s weapons people time to track, train, and fire. And unlike her failed sister, she had no trouble handling the Up-and-Over in rapid sequence. She was a creature without soul, a reflection of the popular view of what silth were.

Kerath studied the silth while they were aboard. They were cold creatures, but her taste of the amber drink, of flying with the darkship, had sensitized her to subtle nuances. Even the failed Mistress was frightened of the other.

Days rolled away. Kerath was tugged this way and that. It would be so simple to abort the mission, equally easy to loose the darkwar and blind herself to the harvest that must follow. Or equally difficult. Either way, she would live in infamy in the legends of the Meth, as she who was afraid to save the race, or as she who had destroyed everything gained in generations free of the silth. She saw no middle road—unless Suslov's gunners got lucky.

Dreamkeeper, last of the great warships of the Meth, was creeping toward home system. Whose dream would it preserve?

7

Kerath turned her back on screens and tank. "Scan on the asteroid?"

"In the groove, Marshall. Three days until it's too late to divert."

She turned to see if the silth had sent an observer. They had: the talker. From a place of power and honor she had fallen to go-between. Kerath almost pitied her. She had suffered that decline herself after Snow-No-More, until the Command had needed her for another suicidal operation.

"Tight beam to the Command. Full report. Request update and instructions." She went to the silth. "Could your people divert the asteroid past the point where it's no longer possible for technology to do so?"

The silth looked at her with empty eyes. "No."

314 — GLEN COOK

"Thank you." So. There was very little time to decide. The darkship strike had to be launched soon if there was to be time left for reshaping the asteroid's orbit. But for now she could only await the Command's reaction to what had happened in the deep.

She fell asleep and dreamed worse nightmares than ever before. The commander awakened her.

"Reply from the Command. Proceed with mission."

"That's all?"

"That's it."

"No shock? Commander, would the silth have collaborators there?"

The commander eyed the screens. "I've wondered about that since I visited the human ship. I think so. I can't picture the Command jumping into anything blind."

"My own impression. That means I'm more a pawn than I thought. Perhaps I was supposed to be converted."

"Have you decided? I'll follow your orders even if they contradict the Command's apparent intent."

"Thank you. I won't be long." Kerath moved away. She wanted to pace, but there wasn't room. She chewed a claw and searched for a middle road.

She had little choice about the strike itself. It had to go on. The question was how to ensure that the silth did not survive. She checked the observer from the corner of her eye. The silth was watching intently. This would be delicate. Timing would be critical. "Commander, are we in enemy detection?"

"I don't believe so, Marshall. They would have reacted."

Of course. Suslov would want to finish *Dreamkeeper*, definitely as a symbolic move, possibly to retaliate for ships recently lost.

She turned slightly and examined enemy positions estimated from data squirted in with Command's message. "Prepare to launch the strike."

The silth turned and glided out.

"Commander, tight beam to Suslov's flagship. I want the Admiral himself. Quickly."

"This will reveal our position, Marshall."

"So be it. Quickly, now. Quickly." Kerath grabbed a young male. "Go stand by the hatch. Watch for the silth." She turned. "I want the docking bay on screen. What's holding that link, Commander?"

"Have to find a target first, Marshall."

"Don't waste time." Kerath faced the screens. Someone had keyed into an eye cell overlooking the entrance to silth quarters. Kerath watched the observer enter.

She could not remain still. Somehow, movement was so soothing.

Ping!

"We have a beam lock on a human ship, Marshall."

"It had better be the right one," Kerath murmured. The silth were leaving their quarters. All seven turned toward the docking bay. Kerath released a long sigh.

". . . Corps Marshall Kerath Hadon for Vice Admiral Pyotr Suslov, personal access only urgent," the commander loudly said as if volume could make up for her difficulty in speaking the alien language.

Suslov's rumpled face appeared with gratifying swiftness. "Kerath. I thought I smelled your touch in that breakout." He exposed his teeth. She reminded herself that humans considered that a pleasantry. "Why haven't they hung you out yet? Calling to surrender? It's almost too late."

"I want to offer you the opportunity you gave me before Snow-No-More. I hope you have more sense than I had."

"Really? You're going to hurt me with one ship?"

"One ship like nothing in human experience, Pyotr Suslov. Conscience forces me to advise you to depart."

The sentry called, "She's coming back, Marshall."

"Pyotr Suslov. Key darkwar your Meth history tapes. Out. Secure, Commander." She faced the screen relaying events in the docking bay. The silth were aboard their darkship. The titanium dagger floated away from the docking grappels. Camera and screen were unable to relay the true intensity of the golden nimbus surrounding the darkship, but Kerath felt its power in some remote recess of being still touched by the amber fluid.

She went to meet the silth. "Darkship ready?"

"Yes." The female's voice was hollow. Failure had emptied her.

"The enemy have a saying, sister. They also serve who stand and wait." The attempt at comfort fell flat. For silth there were no shadow gradients between success and failure. Kerath gestured. "Launch the darkship, Commander."

The commander hit an alarm. It honked throughout the vast warship. "Commencing darkship strike. All personnel take combat stations."

The docking bay screen relayed the cry of klaxons warning of decompression under way. The titanium dagger rotated until its blade faced the bay door.

"Decompression complete, Commander."

"Open the bay door."

Everything went so slowly. Every detail registered on Kerath, even the tiny groan of scraping metal, conducted through the fabric of the ship, as the bay door moved.

It was just a third of the way open when the darkship surged out into the night. On visual, the darkship dwindled rapidly. Such a tiny thing to be so deadly, not a thousandth the mass of *Dreamkeeper*. Kerath faced the tank. Detection had the darkship moving away fast. "She's in a hurry," Kerath whispered to the commander.

"Maybe she enjoys her work."

Four red alien blips were moving toward *Dreamkeeper*. Kerath beckoned the silth observer. "You'll have a better perspective from down here."

She had racked her brain trying to figure how the darkship would locate its targets without radio. She now understood. The Mistress of the Ship had mind-to-mind contact with her unshipped sister on *Dreamkeeper*'s bridge. That was why the silth had taken her into space. They had meant her to become their contact until the slow sister's unshipping made her redundant. Mind to mind. More silth sorcery. No capability surprised Kerath now, not since she had seen the dead ship.

The observer descended to the operations deck. She did nothing to support or refute Kerath's suspicion or to acknowledge her aid.

"Up-and-Over," a tech announced.

8

"Four," the silth whispered.

That was the last of the outbound hunters. *Dreamkeeper* was safe for the moment.

What state was Suslov in, after losing contact with four heavy warships? How would she respond in similar circumstances?

She would get the hell out. But she was Meth, and she knew about darkwar from old legends. Suslov would examine his Meth historical data and scoff. Being human, he was sure to delay too long.

"Up-and-Over."

A moment later, the silth murmured, "Five. She is well named."

"What?" Kerath was startled by the gratuitous remark.

"She Walks in Glory."

"Ah. Commander, it'll be a while. I feel the need to roam. I'm on pager three if I'm needed."

"Very well, Marshall."

She stopped at her quarters briefly, collected her sidearm, then went on to a weapons observation bubble high on *Dreamkeeper*'s humped back. She chased the weaponry technicians out and stood there staring at the stars. A part of her yearned for another darkship experience. A part sobbed for the sentients dying down near the sun of the Meth.

Colored cutouts flickered at the edge of her vision, legacy of the amber drink. The silth sisters must see them all the time. She forgot *Dreamkeeper* and tried to bring those-who-dwell into focus. Success opened her to a trickle of screams from down near the homeworld.

The cutouts faded. She was not silth. She faced the cold, colorless stars, the stars she loved, the stars that would be lost to the Meth if she made one misstep traversing her middle road.

She took one deep breath for courage and started the long walk back to the fighting bridge.

"Status?" she demanded as she entered.

"Fourteen gone, Marshall," the commander replied in a tight voice. "The silth says the darkship suffered slight damage by catching the edge of a particle beam. Suslov seems to have developed an attack profile. He'll get her if she doesn't control her silth arrogance."

"Fifteen."

"Tell her not to underestimate the alien, silth," Kerath said.

"Marshall, here's an anomaly," the commander said.

Kerath stepped over to study the tank. "He's jumping out," she whispered, excited. "Those look like long jump lines. He's running, Commander."

"He'll come back."

Kerath controlled her emotions. "Of course. But maybe he'll be more amenable when he does."

"The High Lord will be pleased."

"Sarcasm, Commander? The High Lord lives numbered days. His clique are walking worm food." Including her sire, she thought. Poor Shadar, doomed though he was but a servant.

"There goes the last squadron, Marshall. Can the silth follow them?"

"No. Commander, in the next few minutes I'll need absolute obedience. Yes?" She turned to the silth's touch.

"She's hit, Marshall. The last attack. One of her bath was killed."

"Bath?"

"The females who help. Bath. She will have difficulty returning."

Bless the All, Kerath thought. "Medical team and damage control people to docking bay, Commander."

"Thank you," the silth said. The words seemed to rip themselves from her hidden self.

"Up-and-Over," a detection technician called.

Kerath drew her handgun and shot the startled silth through the heart. "Order here!" she shouted, as panic hit the bridge. "Order. Full battle alert, Commander. I want that darkship under fire the instant it reappears. Somebody get rid of this body. Send a security party to arrest the other two silth."

The commander executed orders in a daze. "What are you doing, Marshall?"

"Ensuring the failure of the silth design. The All favored us by taking one of her crew. She will have less control. Less ability to resist the vacuum. By firing upon her I prevent her from coming aboard, reaching safety, and finding a replacement bath. Maybe I'll destroy her. Maybe not."

"She'll attack us."

"She can't send the cloud against us. She can't destroy *Dreamkeeper* without destroying herself."

The commander looked puzzled. "Can't she Up-and-Over home and let one of the orbital tugs pick her up?"

"She doesn't know where home is, Commander, not without somebody here to tell her. To reach homeworld she first has to get orbital data from us and translate it into something understandable by those-who-dwell. To survive she has to come here and has to get inside. I don't intend to let her."

The commander nodded. After a few seconds she said, "But you would have done this even if she were returning healthy."

"Yes. I sought a middle road between surrender and a return of the silth. This was the best I could do."

"They'll make a villain of you."

"They would in any case. That's why they sent a loser of battles who always came home a hero. This time they gave me one they thought I couldn't win no matter what."

"Darkship is here, Marshall. Headed for docking bay."

Kerath nodded.

"Commence firing," the commander directed.

9

Swords of fire flailed the dark. The darkship reeled, slid sideways. Something in Kerath's backbrain buzzed. She saw the darkship as a glowing, tumbling cross. One arm flew off, chased by a golden shape grabbing wildly at nothing. The silth bath's deathwail burned through the core of her mind.

You traitor.

Kerath wobbled under the impact of the mental blow.

You have betrayed your sisters.

The Mistress of the Ship! She couldn't be alive. Nothing could come through that fury . . . *I am not silth!* she cried back.

The darkship straightened up and turned its daggertip to *Dreamkeeper*. Bright paper cutouts swirled around it. A black cloud slithered across the stars behind it. Panicky, Kerath shouted, "Commander, destroy that damned ship!"

"I'm trying, Marshall. I'm trying." Terror haunted the commander's eyes.

"Then jump, dammit. It's a short jump to Biter orbit. Leave her out here."

The commander stabbed a finger at the jump operators. "Program it."

Kerath stared at the screens, transfixed. The darkship was coming in, accelerating, a screaming, flaming sword. A skeleton rode its tip, jaws opened wide, blood trailing from its fangs. A hungry darkness coiled behind its hollow eyes. The silth was insane. She meant to board by ramming!

Alarms sounded. Collision alarms, never heard except during drills. "Jump, Commander. Dammit, jump anywhere."

The darkship kept accelerating.

Jump alarms shrilled a five-second warning—just as the darkship reached *Dreamkeeper*'s fat guppy belly.

The warship began to twist with the impact. Torn metal shrieked. Breech alarms wailed. Kerath watched the burning blade drive deeper and deeper into the great vessel's belly. "No," she breathed. The silth had lost control and come in far too hard.

A tendril of the black cloud touched the ship.

Then *Dreamkeeper* finally jumped, carrying the darkship with it, still boring into its guts.

Crew people added their screams to those of the alarms, responding to the instant of cloud-touch. On the fighting bridge they clawed their scalps and smashed their foreheads against their consoles. Below, where the darkship's momentum still drove it deeper into *Dreamkeeper*'s belly, it was worse. They were clawing at their eyes.

Dreamkeeper rolled out of jump. Kerath glanced at the readouts. Orbit around homeworld. Almost perfect . . . Only then did she realize that the blackness had barely caressed her. The silth drink had prepared her for that, too.

The comm boards began lighting up, announcing incoming traffic. Kerath ignored them. She listened. No sound came from below. The darkship had come to rest. "Commander!" She swung hard. "Snap out of it." She exaggerated. "We're in a decaying orbit."

The glaze left the commander's eyes. She scanned the bridge. "Internal pressure is down, but the collision doors have maintained integrity. Help me shake these people out of it. We've got to get moving. The ship is in a bad way." She surveyed the available data again. "We will be lucky to save it."

"We'll save it, Commander. We have no choice. We have to shunt that asteroid."

"That's the Command channel screaming over there."

"To hell with Command. We don't have time for them."

Getting the bridge crew back to work was not difficult, but there was trouble down in the collision area. Half the crew there was dead. The rest had to be restrained for their own protection. Officers culled every department for extra bodies.

Kerath went down, donned an eva suit, and combed the wreckage for the Mistress of the Ship. She refused to be satisfied until she found a mass of torn, raw meat and fur in tatters of black near the head of the column of scrap that had been a darkship.

An hour passed before Kerath was sure that *Dreamkeeper* would survive—if nothing else went sour. She returned to the bridge and collapsed into the first seat she found vacant.

The Command was still trying to get through. By now, they would have studied the damage optically from the surface. They could guess that the darkship had rammed. They would be thinking up cruel replies to her middle-road venture.

Detection showed a number of small vessels closing in—coming to look *Dreamkeeper* over, of course, maybe to put a representative of the Command aboard.

She did not much care now.

"Route that Command call to this board, please," she said. "I might as well face them now."

"Sure you want to deal with them?" the commander asked. "I can . . ."

"There's no getting out of it." Kerath stabbed a button.

A weathered old female appeared on screen, growling and snarling. Kerath allowed the storm to run its course. When it slackened, and she could pull the main thread from the skein of complaints, she decided that the Command was more interested in the fate of the silth than in Kerath Hadon or *Dreamkeeper*.

"Here's our silth insider," Kerath whispered to the commander.

"The Supreme Commander. I suppose it had to be."

Kerath was exhausted, but she had enough anger and outrage left to respond. She depressed the send key and shouted a line spoken by a victorious pup to conclude a popular story told to small Meth. "The grauken is dead."

The Commander revealed her teeth. She was amused. She keyed into the Command net herself. "Command, this is *Dreamkeeper*. Confirm that last from mission officer Kerath. The grauken is dead." Off comm, she added, "They can't court martial everybody."

Kerath leaned back, closed her eyes, and said, "Secure outside comm. Commander, we'll let them wonder what we meant. The grauken is dead. I wriggled away again." She had found the middle road.

But middle roads went nowhere. They just bought time. Suslov would return. The silth would persist. But there was time now, precious time, to buttress the bridge she had begun to build.

ENEMY TERRITORY

Although not a Vietnam veteran, I am a Vietnam Era veteran. I never much liked how military folks were treated, back then.

TUESDAY, 14 APRIL

"They do it after every war. We're not unique." There goes Mickey with the old bullhoolie. Naturally, Tommy powders back a yeahbut.

"Yeah, but not like they done us. They should've saved trouble and gassed us."

So Mickey blazes him with an irrelevancy. "Hell, during the Hundred Years' War the English sometimes didn't even bring their troops home. Just left them in France."

Round the table. "Goddamned company man." "Nah. He's just stupid." "Stuff it, Mickey."

"Whyn't you guys shut up and play cards?" Corky says. He is winning.

Don't think I got no imagination. That's the kind of names they gave us. Mickey. Tommy. Billy. Joey. Nicky. Child names hung on the killers of the 454th Special Commando. We invented our own last names. They don't matter now. We can't get confused anymore. Since the Defile we've only had two doubles: Freddie Hoarfrost and Freddie Lightning, Willie Greensnakes and Willie Fear. Of course, here at Center we mix with the survivors of all the other special commandoes: elephant men, ape men, spider men, frog men, what have you. It's a regular human zoo.

Major Willie Fear says, "I was a goddamned battalion commander. Don't that mean nothing? What're they trying to do to me?" He talks fast when he's mad. I can barely write down what he's saying.

Mickey says, "They locked up Billy Thunderballs again," by way of hinting that Major Willie should tone it down. General Billy commanded the whole Special Commando. He spends more time in Building Four than out. Can't keep his mouth shut. He scares the crap out of the desk jockies up the line.

No matter how you feel, inside the band or out, we got us a real question here. What do you do with us after we finish our job? Take 454 Codo. I mean, we're smart enough, and our parents were human, but how the hell do spider monkeys fit into civilian life? We've got one talent. Soldiering. Anything else we taught ourselves. Half the people outside are scared of us. The other half want to make pets out of us.

Some guys find themselves do-gooder sponsors. They figure anything is better than Center. They go out, and they all come back. A monkey can be a monkey. A man gets his pride up sooner or later.

There aren't no pretty alternatives. We were genetically engineered, raised, and schooled to be soldiers. What else can we be? What a lot of guys can't figure is why they didn't keep us on. The Service didn't fold because the war ended.

They're scared of us, that's why. They put up with us when they needed us, but ... Well, they don't need us any more. They want to sweep us under the rug now. We're different.

Don't get me wrong. It's not something really pushy. Most people don't realize what they're doing. But the fear is there. You can smell it when you're out with the Normals. The quick, surprised rise of the eyebrows when they run into you, the stiffness of speech, the withdrawal ... You can see it if you look. Most of us pretend real hard. Some of us even fool ourselves.

Center isn't a prison. They say. It's a "Readjustment Interface." We can come and go when we want. We can leave forever. And can come back when it gets too rough outside. Center will be here as long as we need it. They promised. After all, without us the war wouldn't be over yet.

So how come the news is full of speeches by guys who want to close Center?

We're dead if the budget cuts start. We don't have a lobby. Anybody who cares about us is right here in Center already.

All the arguing is old stuff. It's been the same so long it's like a liturgy. I should make cards for them. They could hold the right one up at the right time and save their jawbones.

SUNDAY, 19 APRIL

"I'm going to torque over and see Harry. Anybody want to go?" No. Hospital gives them the drooling grey creeps. Hardly anybody goes anymore.

You step off the elevator. To right and left the ward stretches toward infinity. No rooms. No partitions. Just beds as far as you can see, a line against each wall and two down the middle, toe to toe. A few tired, sad-eyed Normal nurses try to keep up. They are good ladies. They believe. They agree we're getting shafted. Some of them have people here. Hospital treats Normal vets too. They come in as beds open up. Every bed is used.

They were racing wheelchairs today. A marathon, apparently. They came from my right, faded to my left. More chairs sped the other direction in the far aisle. The staff ignored them. They ignore anything that helps the guys get by.

There are twenty-eight levels to Hospital, each exactly like all the others.

The unwritten law there is, don't give staff no grief. They're dedicated people. They're about the only Normals who treat Specials like people.

Still . . . Still. Patients are patients. Some are cranky and unreasonable.

A surge of racers whipped past. I ducked into a break in the flow and skipped down the aisle.

"Look out, runt!" An elephant man in a tank-sized chariot came roaring toward me. I dodged, snagged his chair, hitched a ride. He laughed, called me a parasite, slowed a little when we reached the monkey man section.

He wasn't really an elephant, any more than I'm a monkey. He was just engineered big and strong. His kind usually go on all fours because of the weight they carry. I am cat size, with elongated arms, legs, fingers, and toes. Spider monkey without a tail. Big eyes, to see good at night. Extra good hearing and smell. We were engineered to become infiltrators, scouts, snipers, attackers of points inaccessible to Normal troops. Like fastnesses in stony badlands . . . Stony badlands . . .

"Hey, Sammy!" Harry's face lighted up. "How's the boy?"

"Same old shit, Sarge." Harry was my platoon sergeant in the Defile.

Harry stuck out the wrist stump of his one remaining arm. He is in Hospital for life. All he has left is one foot. A man can't do much with that. But Harry tries.

"What's the matter, Sammy? You don't look so good." Nothing gets

Harry down. He's one of those people who's by damned going to enjoy life or die trying.

"Guess it's starting to get to me, Sarge."

"You think too much, Sammy. Always did. Relax. Enjoy."

"Sarge, that's damned hard when you look at this." There are five thousand men just on his floor, all of them permanently disabled. That's why the other guys don't come anymore. It's hard to be cheerful in surroundings so grim.

"You got to censor your outlook, Sammy. Concentrate on the good times. Look at me. I got plenty to cry about if I want to be a whiner."

Yeah. Good old Harry. Sometimes he's so Pollyanna he drives you up the wall.

"Been thinking, Sammy."

"Sounds dangerous, Sarge."

"Yeah, sure. Look. We've got to get the band out of Center."

"There ain't nothing out there for us, Sarge. They should've kept us in Service."

"But they didn't, Sammy. So we go on. We've got to worry about tomorrow, not yesterday's should have beens."

"The future is enemy territory."

"Hum. That's profound, Sammy. Not like you. Enemy territory, eh? And we've seen so much that we're gunshy. So we turn Center into a bunker and sit tight? Sammy, it's not going to go away. You gotta do something besides keep your head down."

"Like what?"

"Like find something we can do better than Normals. You tell Major Willie I said that. Then break up the damned card games and woe-is-me sessions and get to work, same as if you were preparing a mission. Figure out what to do, then by damned do it."

"Like we did in the Defile, eh?"

Harry's face clouded. "Could end that way, Sammy. But even that was better than rotting like an old tree that fell down and nobody cared."

"Sarge . . . Harry . . ."

"Try it, Sammy. For me. Right?"

"For the band, Sarge. All right."

I thought about it going back to barracks. It just depressed me. I told the Major what Harry said. He suggested we sleep on it.

WEDNESDAY, 22 APRIL: TWO YEARS AGO TODAY

It was all slow motion. Shadows drifting among the rocks. Glimpses of monkeylike figures slipping from cover to cover by the light of three moons. Somewhere ahead, a sound, a swelling rumble. Freeze!

An atmosphere fighter streaked overhead, a glowing blue diamond with a needle nose. Its growl faded into the distance. Zoof! Zoof! Zoof! Three more belched from the Defile ahead.

We scrambled forward, froze again. A second flight followed the first. Scramble. A third flight. Scramble. A fourth. There was a brief, blinding flash in the distance behind us. A sky battle was shaping up over the diversionary attack on the Eben pocket.

"Move them up, Sammy," the sergeant said. "That ain't going to last."

It didn't. Their flyers were the best, aces all. They'd been sent to Dorphat to fight a last stand or tide-turning battle. That night they seized the air for their own.

Neither attack from the air or from orbit could silence their subterranean base because it couldn't be properly located. We were headed in to wipe it the hard way.

Rustle, rustle, among the shadows of steeplelike rocks. Even the best of us couldn't avoid making noise.

Never had we fought in stranger, wilder country. It was a grownup cousin of Bryce Canyon, hammered into a hundred kilometer wide gap in a gargantuan cordillera. The Defile. A home for devils. Scorching by day, frosty by night.

Zoof. Zoof. More fighters went up. The sergeant whispered to his throat mike: "Anybody spot their launch gate?" A chorus of negatives on platoon tac. Too far away.

Rustle. Rustle. Four hundred odd little men crept forward . . . Flash! Somebody missed a sentry. We'd been spotted. Flash! Flash!

My earplug speaker went crazy. Everybody asked questions at once. The Major shut them up, demanded proper reports. Forward again, under fire from a hundred weapons.

We were expected.

Mortar bombs fell to the right of my platoon. I waved the squad forward. An enemy position lay dead ahead. Grenades arced through the air. The shooting stopped.

Their first line gave way. The mortars stopped talking while their crews dropped back. Obviously old hands. Probably veterans on a par with the flyers. The ambush was calculated to reveal our mettle.

Boom-boom-boom-zing-whine. Ricocheting shrapnel howled all around us. It was nasty in those rocks.

Thump-Thump-thump. Friendly mortars talked back. One weapons company of ape men were along to support us. We were too small to handle heavy weapons ourselves.

Harry dropped down beside me. "It's rotten, Sammy. The Major's asking if we can pull back." Someone moaned a dozen meters behind us. "How're your boys?"

"Okay. So far."

Sudden radio chatter. A counterattack coming in. A rolling barrage crept past us. The lock spires did a *danse macabre* in the flicker of weapons and explosions. They were delicate structures. Many of them fell. We squeezed into cracks, fired at glimpses of silver-blue shapes. "What was that shit about they've used up all their crack troops?" I asked an unanswering night.

There was a lot of noise to our left. It was hand to hand over there. Harry poked me, said, "We're wheeling left to help Charlie Company."

Mortar bombs rained down. I kept the squad low. "Whoa!" Enemy squad ahead. Massed fire. The opposition vanished. In my ear, "Pull back. Third platoon, pull back. Original positions."

We were too late. Charlie Company was beyond help.

"Where's the air cover?" Harry grumbled. "We're supposed to get air support if we get in a firefight."

It was a great game. Couldn't get air support without clearing the Defile, and couldn't clear the Defile without air support.

"Here they come again!"

Aim-fire. Aim-fire. I froze in a shadow while a big body lumbered past, shot it in the back.

"Tighten it up! Tighten it up!" The Major was on the all-channel. Training and experience overcame dismay. The second attack faded. Platoon leaders and company commanders consulted. I checked the time. Holy! . . . It was almost morning.

The sergeant poked me. "We're pulling out whether Division likes it or not. Major's asking for emergency evac."

I assembled the squad. I had two wounded and one dead. "Have to leave him. Carry those two." We scrambled and trudged a panicky two kilometers.

The sky began to lighten. My earplug squeaked. Harry growled. "Rearguard says they're coming."

A hurricane of mortar bombs. Weapons company didn't answer it. They were scattered all over hell, running away. Senseless rhythm. Aim-fire. Aim-fire. The sun crept over the horizon. We had to hide before it cooked us.

454 Codo was surrounded. The mortar attack let up only because the other side ran out of bombs. I checked the squad. Four more dead. Two missing. Two wounded. One would die without quick evacuation. Willie Hoarfrost and I were the only healthy soldiers left. Willie was trying to help Harry. Harry had caught a bomb in his lap. He had a tourniquet on each arm and one on a leg. "Not much hope there, Willie."

"Don't hurt to try, Corporal."

The sun climbed higher. The temperature soared. Breathing became painful. Even in the shade the heat was maddening. The other side laid low, letting the sun work for them. They had their suits and nearby base.

Stubborn Harry wouldn't die. He came round once, grinned, whispered, "I didn't duck fast enough." I gave him a knockout shot. I couldn't stand his smiling.

High noon. The Major spoke on the all-channel. He sounded crazy. "Everybody gather round me. To my beacon. Forget the perimeter. Boys, the war is over. Belimar surrendered four days ago."

Was there cheering? No. Plenty of cussing and nobody believing, though.

Four days ago? Ours and a hundred simultaneous strikes, all over Dorphat, were a waste? Half a million men, mostly Specials, committed after there was no more point? What the hell? Communications lag? That's the kind of screwup that makes a soldier hate everybody on top.

The Major said, "Lay down your weapons. They're going to give us a hand."

"Like shit," somebody replied.

"Do what you're told, soldier. Or I'll shoot you myself."

That was the day suspicion was born. The rumors started as soon as the fighting stopped.

SUNDAY, 26 APRIL

My thirty-second birthday today. Wish I could share it with Harry, but I just can't stand the hopeless look he gets when I tell him I haven't found anything yet. Damn it, we need a war.

I was in the mine for fourteen years. God knows how long it went on before I arrived. Why did it have to end?

Four hundred men died in those godforsaken rocks . . . For what? Center? Maybe we were on the wrong side. It was those guys that helped after the shooting stopped, not ours. Harry owes them a life.

Screw it. Some birthday. Might as well sack out.

I must have screamed. The Major shook me. I cracked an eyelid. "Dreaming about it again?" he asked.

"Yeah." We all do.

"Been thinking," he said over supper. "Harry has the right idea."

"'Bout time somebody admitted it."

"Sammy . . ."

"But we've been over it a hundred times."

"So we keep on."

"Would they let us go?"

"Hell, why not? Most of them would love to get rid of us."

"By burying us."

"Don't go General Billy on me. They let him out yesterday. He's already stirring the pot again. He's more trouble than any normal. He gives the nuts all the ammo they can use. If he don't stop claiming the Board of Inquiry is a coverup, somebody's going to run out of patience."

"We'd make good burglars." The Major glared at me. "Just a thought."

"Corporals don't think. It's dangerous."

"Security work? Go mercenary?"

"Cram that. It ought to be something where we can stick together. And where we can stay out of the Normals' way. But not no bloody damned freebooting. You sound like one of the General's idiots."

On cue, Mickey stuck his head in the door. "Major? Might be trouble. General did something again. There's a thousand MPs out there looking for him."

"So?"

I said, "Ease up."

"Yeah. I'm just tired of Billy Thunderballs. He's going to kill us, you know."

"Better check it out."

"Yeah."

We went outside. Mickey hadn't exaggerated. The grounds were lousy with MPs. All Normals, and some damned arrogant. The Major was in a mood to turn the General in till he talked to an MP lieutenant. That idiot almost got his head broke.

Back in the barracks, the Major said, "The reactionaries are taking over."

"They aren't all like that."

"One is one too many, Sammy. I'm going to find the General. There's something going on. Ain't no call for a whole police brigade to move in on us."

The invasion wasn't limited to Center. They'd put teams into the city, shutting down transportation and communications. That *was* a little too much effort to spend harassing one pain in the ass General.

We've got to get out of here. Before this kind of crap gets worse.

Wouldn't you know silly Mickey would have an idea? One that sounds only half bad?

"Sammy," he said, softlike, not wanting the others to hear and maybe mock him, "I maybe got something." He showed me a city paper. The classified. Us brains never thought to pick up a hard-print and look through the want ads. He had one circled:

VETERANS: *Combat or Military Police. Major police command has immediate openings in all entry-level police MOS. Excellent salary and fringes. Performance bonuses, hazard pay. Accelerated advancement to qualified personnel. Contact North American Interest Section, Old Earth Chancery, Inglespoort, 31-28-2211*

"Police work? On Old Earth? They won't get a lot of takers?"

"It's the kind of thing we could do, isn't it?"

"Maybe." Funny. Old Earth doesn't intimidate me the way it does most Normals. "Be going back into action, if the stories are true. But would they take Specials?"

"I called. They said come on over and sign up. The guy I talked to sounded excited."

"Read me that number." I called, asked questions Mickey hadn't, wrote down answers. They had a variety of openings and no apparent prejudice against Specials. It sounded too good to be true.

I thought about it a while, decided they would give us duties nobody else would take. Well, we were used to that. That's why we were created. "It might be a ticket out, Mickey. Rough or not. I'm going to talk to Harry before I take it to the Major. He's got a better head for stuff than me."

MONDAY, 27 APRIL

Couldn't see Harry till this morning. MPs kept us buttoned. Couldn't get out. The Major didn't get in. I left right after breakfast, before he came back.

Harry lit up like always. He really gleamed after he took a second look. "You finally got something."

'Yeah. Not great, but maybe the best we'll ever do." I showed him the ad and told him what the Chancery had to say.

"Fits the character of the outfit," he said. "Puts us in an us-against-everybody spot. Like always."

"What I was worrying about was, we'd need to put a team together. Ape men. Elephant men. The works. It'd be like full time war again." They say the safest spot on Old Earth is just a whisker less deadly than the most dangerous. Police there are nothing but moving targets. The whole world is an armed ghetto with a big hatred for anybody who wants to tame it. I added, "I think they'd sign up everybody in Center if they could get them."

"Sign up?"

"They want a six year first contract."

"What's the Major think?"

"I don't know. Curfew caught him outside last night."

"Curfew? The General again? What'd he do now?"

"I don't know. I guess he just won't learn."

"Tell the Major I said give this a good look." The Major trusts Harry's judgment.

Something went bad wrong during Major Willie's visit with the General. He was in a lousy mood. He did agree that the police thing was maybe the best we could do.

"One problem," he said. "General Billy." He handed me a wad of papers.

They unfolded into a three page copy of an official document copied from a copy of a copy. It was a precis of an interim report from the Dorphat Board of Inquiry. It said that, despite a lack of hard evidence, it was probable that high level officers on the scene had conspired to delay the announcement of the armistice. The delay had resulted in almost two hundred thousand friendly casualties. And there was more. Support for some of General Billy's wildest accusations.

The thing was a top-secret bomb and somebody had started it ticking by turning it loose. "How'd he get ahold of this?"

The Major shrugged. "The problem is, he's going to go public."

"That's why we're up to our ears in MPs?"

"They're trying to stop him. Somebody way up is nervous. Somebody with enough clout to deploy a police brigade so he can cover his ass."

"What do we do?"

"Probably too late to do anything, Sammy. We're in for it. A lot of guys are damned mad. One stupid mistake will blow this place apart."

The MPs didn't find General Billy. They didn't keep him from connecting with the media. He hit the evening network news.

There was a little trouble when MPs tried to arrest one of the General's aides. They got too enthusiastic. He came out with bruises, broken ribs, and a concussion. That made the late news.

Center was a neutron short of critical, and hanging there, teetering, waiting for some genius or fool to tilt things. News anchors talked about the chances of a veterans' mutiny. Center isn't the only installation with a lot of unhappy old soldiers. High General Staff officers issued soothing reports. Their faces were twisted, like they couldn't figure out why this was happening to them. Bigots ranted. Spokesmen for veterans' organizations claimed neutrality, but with an obvious lean towards the General. Scared politicians yelled for blood. There are a lot of veterans, and veterans tend to vote.

General Billy dropped his rabble-rousing. He talked about staying calm and investigating. Here at Center he kept the lid on. He sent his own men out with the MP patrols till somebody topside had smarts enough to make the MPs less visible.

TUESDAY, 28 APRIL

"We're talking Sepoy Mutiny," Mickey said. "We're talking *Aurora*, Battleship *Potemkin*, like that. It doesn't have to do with being treated right. It's class struggle." He was going good. And he had an audience. "Those MPs aren't going to shoot us to shut us up. Ain't nothing we could tell anyway. They'll do it to show us who's boss." I don't know about the accuracy of his historical parallels. I do know you can't always trust them. Sometimes he makes them up.

Fiction or not, his theme attracted interest. He was telling us that no hierarchy tolerates rebellion by its working class. The more rigid and militaristic the hierarchy, the more likely it is to respond by choosing a hard option. He was saying that generals capable of the Dorphat betrayal might be blind and arrogant enough to go the hardest way of all with Center.

Mickey is a little cowardly and a lot imaginative. I can't see it going that far. They could play their games on Dorphat because nobody was watching. They don't have that luxury here. This is getting to be a media happening.

General Billy probably holds the key. If he can keep it cool here, if he doesn't let his own prejudices run away with him, we could come out of this better off than we went in . . . I hope Harry hasn't talked me into being a complete head in the clouds fool.

WEDNESDAY, 29 APRIL

We've got trouble. Shots were fired this morning. The General couldn't contain it. His own fault, really. He's been whipping the men up for so long. Some of his vigilantes splintered off and started them a guerrilla campaign.

The MPs showed more restraint than I expected. There were only a couple of firefights when those clowns took over the city. They grabbed the port, communications, the arsenal, and the power station. They made some pretty silly broadcasts.

The rest of us are sitting around wondering what to do. We're specials, and it's always been Specials against everybody else, right or wrong.

Harry says our getting out is dead now. Practically a case of suicide. I could cry about it.

"Look at it this way," somebody said a while ago, "our problems are over. No more worries. No more mystery about tomorrow."

No mysteries . . .

I hope it isn't that bad. I hope it isn't moving so fast cool heads can't tame it.

THURSDAY, 30 APRIL

Maybe there is hope. The Major talked to the Chancery this morning. He says the Old Earth government will try to stop High Command from making a show of force. They're also demanding an investigation from outside the Service. High Command claims we're all in on this, and deserve a good slapping around. Old Earth says we should be given amnesty. We were provoked.

Tempers are pretty hot. Nobody really cares about the facts.

The Major says the Old Earth people must want our help real bad. That's scary. If they're so desperate to beef up their cops, their law enforcement situation has to be worse than anybody guessed. Gives me the feeling I'm going to be gun-fodder in a desperate delaying-action against the forces of chaos.

The news is all guesswork about using force to straighten Center out. All the pros and cons, with generals and politicos getting red in the face arguing their sides. I saw one series of interviews with enlisted men who might be sent here. They said they wouldn't fire on us, orders or not. They aren't stupid. They understand precedent and getting your turn in the barrel.

The politicians smell blood. For the first time in their generation they have the upper hand on the Service. They want "the Butchers of Dorphat" strung up. They don't much care about justice for veterans. They see a chance to grab back some power lost during the war. They're taking it.

All the howling may turn out to be sound and fury signifying nothing. The public don't give a damn. The war is over. They're safe. They don't want to remember what they owe us, and they don't care who holds the hammer in government. Government is one of the trials of life. It has to be endured, and, as much as possible, ignored.

The Major came in. "They arrested the guy who sent in the MPs," he said. "Charged him with abuse of power."

Mickey grumbled, "Abuse of power? Conspiracy to commit murder would be more like it."

"They did it mostly to put the General on the bad side. He foxed them. Did a song and dance for the news people. Told them he'd take full responsibility for the mutiny if there was amnesty for the rest of us. He really hammed it up. They won't be able to turn him down."

"Good old Billy," I sneered. "Didn't know he had a Jesus complex. Going to die for our sins, eh?"

"That's the general idea."

Mickey made a rude noise reinforced by an obscene gesture. "He's just showing off. He'd love to go out a martyr. Despite all his pissing and moaning about justice, he never attacks the real question."

"What would that be?" the Major asked. There was sarcasm in his voice. He can't take Mickey serious.

"What does society do with its veterans? It takes years from their lives, their sanity sometimes, and maybe wrecks their future by taking away their chance to keep up with guys who didn't have to go. Society owes for that. The question is, how much? How much return can a veteran expect for having met *his* obligation?"

"I suppose you're going to tell us," the Major said.

"No. I can't. It's an ancient question. Nobody has ever answered it. Since societies stopped sending everybody to war, most of them have done what ours has. Tried to forget the whole thing as soon as the blood stopped running."

Silly little Mickey. Always so serious. "You're forgetting this war had a new wrinkle," I said. "The laboratory soldier. The soldier who never was a part of society. Who was made, same as tanks and rifles. What about us?"

Mickey, of course, had thoughts on the matter, but I didn't hang around to hear them. I have the same trouble as the public: Too much thinking gets painful.

FRIDAY, 1 MAY

May Day. Famous in the history of insurrections. Looks like ours is over. General Billy hasn't said, but the nets claim he made a deal with High Command. He'll take the rap for the mutiny. They'll ignore the rest of us and throw the book at the Dorphat clique. Those people deserve whatever they get. The latest leaks say they weren't just trying to kill us off, they were trying to rack up enough casualties so public reaction would wreck the armistice. They wanted the war to go on. They wanted a more decisive victory.

No wonder the politicians are mad. Somebody was tromping on their power preserve.

SATURDAY, 2 MAY

Happy faces everywhere I look today. Harry was fizzing when I saw him. The storm has broken. It's over. Senate voted to take the whole thing away from the Service. An investigative team is on its way. And old Earth Chancery says they'll start placement testing Monday. The Major is out rustling up volunteers from the other commandos.

This mutiny thing woke a lot of guys up. They got slammed in the chops with how fragile our situation is. We don't need the General or High Command's reactionaries to get wiped. Politicians could scuttle us quicker than they saved us, for a handful of votes. We're vulnerable as long as we let ourselves be kept here.

MONDAY, 4 MAY

The crowds at the Chancery were impossible. They couldn't handle everybody. Hard to believe how excited everybody is. After two years of doing nothing, any growth of purpose has to run wild.

It's caught on all through Center. A lot of other outfits say they're taking their Harry's along too. A lot, like 454 Codo, are closed bands, almost families.

Mickey is a genius in disguise. This thing could solve most of our problems.

Chancery says they'll move the first shipload the end of this week. They want people so bad they're taking almost anybody who wants to go.

THURSDAY, 7 MAY

The first ship is off. 1200 apemen and elephant men. 454 Codo is scheduled out Sunday. We've made it! We're going to slide out the side door before this mutiny business is really settled. The Senate investigators won't get here till next week.

I can't believe how happy everybody is. After two years of dying inside there's suddenly a future.

FRIDAY, 8 MAY

There's something funny going on. Port traffic is stacked. Chancery is chartering everything. Hauling out all the bruisers they can, like they're racing a deadline.

SATURDAY, 9 MAY

I was right. Two heavy attack transports just made orbit. With a division of Force Marines. Somebody told some big lies. And we get the dirty end again. Late news tells it all. All those encouraging news releases were smokescreen. Only maverick Old Earth really stood with us. Senate's true attitude is that treating us right will cost too much. So the Marines are here to put us in our place. And then what?

Guess I could get me an organ grinder and a tin cup.

The part that rankles is that so many of the real rebels have gotten out, leaving us to face the music. 454 Codo went right on just like every other day, and stayed out of it completely, but will that make a difference? Not bloody likely.

All that's left is a big moral decision. Join the guys who want to shoot it out as a sort of final protest? Or sit tight, try to ride it out, and pray for that ever receding brighter day?

SUNDAY, 10 MAY

There's firing in the northern part of Center. Building Two is burning. Too many men with too little hope, who decided they might as well go out fighting.

Lunatics. I don't care what they do anymore.

The band are sitting round the card tables, eyes vacant, nobody talking. Waiting. Just waiting. Only Mickey fidgets. he wants to fight. The Major made him sit.

Somebody pounds on the door. Nobody moves. More pounding. After a while, the Major sighs and goes over.

It's Harry and a brain-damaged ape man buddy of his named Kenny. Kenny is carrying Harry cuddled in his arms like a newborn. Kenny squats down on the floor. He doesn't say anything. I've never heard him say anything. His eyes are kind of misty.

The Major finally reacts. "What the hell are you doing here, Sergeant?"

"I'm still part of the band, Major." Harry's eyes are wet too. And for the first time since I've known him they hold no humor or hope.

I want to cry.

THE WAITING SEA

"The Waiting Sea" was kind of a touch of Lovecraft, a passing whiff of weird.

1943

The sea was an obsidian plain, hard and glossy, flecked with flashes of silver. The moon was a god's thumbnail clipping riding low in the west, a thin crescent about to hit the water. The air was cool and still. Not a ghost of a cloud marred the nighttime sky. The stars blazed down in their billions, indifferent to one insignificant man standing on the starboard bridge wing of a scab of rusty iron doggedly churning across a mote of cold black water.

The sea whispered along the vessel's side, rolling up faces of pale fire as disturbed plankton luminesced. Below, the boilers groaned and the engines grumbled in their soft deep voices. The ship pushed ahead an unchanging eight knots. The sounds were more felt through the metal than heard on the wing. The deck gently pushed against his feet as the ship turned to a new tack.

Zigging and zagging, he thought. Turtle trying to run like a rabbit, or a halfback in the open field.

Now he could see the ship ahead in column, a fat tanker looming a deeper black in the darkness. A hint of stack smoke touched his nostrils, then a whiff of tobacco. Somebody inside the bridge had lighted a smoke. He ached for a drag of calming nicotine.

He raised the glasses to his eyes and slowly swept the sea. How many times had he done so? Put a buck in the bank for every one and he could live on the interest. Nothing out there. A whole lot of nothing.

The sea whispered along the vessel's side, a steady, barely audible susurrus. It could put you to sleep. Or it started talking to you. You started straining to hear the voices, and forgot to watch . . .

He whipped the glasses to his eyes, searched the night. More nothing.

Those were the real sirens of the deep down there, murmuring and playing in the froth along the hull. Poison, they were. Murderous. Hear them. "Shawn. Shawn. We're coming for you, Shawn. Sleep, Shawn."

Cold sweat stood out on his forehead. He snapped the glasses into position, scanned. Nothing but the wolf-shape of a destroyer across the silvery trace shed by the moon.

He had to get out of this. Those voices again. They were getting to him. This would be his last crossing. It got scary when you started hearing voices.

He stared down at the water rolling from beneath the ship's bows, watched the pale light vanish into the polished stone of the surrounding plain. It was all an illusion. The ship wasn't going anywhere. She was frozen here, like that ship that tried to go to the north pole and got caught in the ice. There was no end to the sea. The sea was eternal and infinite. Tonight's calm was a soft mockery, a taunt thrown at the little mortals who dared challenge it.

He cursed softly. What fool notion had gotten him into this? He hated the ocean. It was a great hungry monster with an appetite that couldn't be appeased. It was sleeping now, or pretending, but soon it would waken or lose patience. The water would turn angry grey and hurl giant's fists against the hull, pounding with an endless, senseless, lunatic rage, till even the Old Man looked grim and green.

He slammed a palm against the rail. Pain obliterated the crazy thoughts. He raised the glasses and looked for the enemy.

A sneer stretched his lips. The enemy. He didn't need binoculars to see the enemy. The enemy was all around him, waiting with the patience of a spider. The ship was caught in its glassy web.

"Shawn. Shawn. Come to us, Shawn." There they were, their faces foaming in and out of focus along the ship's side. They watched with black, bottomless eyes, called with toothless mouths stretched in hungry grins. "Come to us, Shawn."

Their voices were plain now. He didn't misunderstand a word. Before, he hadn't understood. But the voices got plainer and louder every crossing.

Angrily, he spat into their restless, formless faces. "Not me," he murmured. "You're not getting me."

"Come to us, Shawn. Shawn. Shawn."

He glanced at his watch, to see how much longer the watch would run. It seemed he had been on the wing for an eternity. But hardly an hour had passed. Still an hour before he could slip inside for a smoke and coffee while Tony gave him a break. Lord God, why did you make the hours of the night so long?

The moonlight was almost extinct. A few minutes and its danger would no longer exist.

The ship's body continued to relay a soporific rhythm of sound and roll. "Shawn, Shawn," the sea whispered. "Come to us, Shawn." His eyelids slid together. He caught himself, shook his head violently. For an instant he thought he saw mocking grins in the foam. He raised the glasses. His eyelids drooped. He should step to the bridge hatch and ask for coffee. Something off the bottom of the pot, the thick black stuff so terrible the aftertaste stayed with you a week. But he didn't. He wasn't going to be beaten by the sea.

The moon was gone. The stars seemed even more cold and remote, turning their backs one by one. His eyelids drooped again.

A deep, rending boom tore the guts from the night. The sea spawned a terrible flower of orange and yellow light. He stared at the tanker, unable to comprehend.

Again that great deep boom as an explosion ripped the tanker's iron hide. Out across the water, a klaxon shrieked as a destroyer protested this maltreatment of her flock. The horn made a mournful cry of, "Too late. Too late."

"Shawn."

He whirled and stared at the sea. His mouth worked. Nothing came out. The luminescent streak arrowed closer and closer, as if in extremely slow motion. Finally, he croaked, "Torpedo!"

None heard him but the sea. His puny cry vanished in the explosion's roar.

Gentle hands tugged him down, urging him deeper. Champagne bubbles boiled around him, whispering, "Come with us, Shawn."

No! Damn it, no! He fought upward, against the undertow of the sinking ship, toward the orange boundary of his own world.

Metal shrieked beneath the sea. The ship was breaking up. Dull screech and thunder as watertight doors yielded to ever-increasing pressure . . . Was he imagining the screams of the men trapped in the flooding compartments?

He should have seen the torpedo earlier. His woolgathering had killed . . . how many?

"Come with us, Shawn." The caress of the sea was gentle and intimate and seductive. Watery fingers tugged him down.

No! The orange was right above him now. He broke the surface, gasped violently . . . and screamed amidst the burning oil from the tanker. The whole sea was aflame. He went under again, all rationality and hope gone, knowing nothing but the pain and the whisper of the sea.

He came to once, clinging to something in an aisle between lakes of flame. The stern of the tanker remained afloat, metal glowing cherry red in spots. Amazingly, men danced and screamed amongst the flames. Somewhere beyond the tanker, an ammunition ship was tearing its own guts out, shooting off all the fireworks of the Fourth. Out in the darkness there was a whoop of horns and rumble of depth charges as the tin can wolves snarled and snapped at the enemy.

Blackness returned.

Awareness again. A bluishness in the east. The tanker was gone. Only small pools of burning oil remained. The flicker of huge fires defined the horizon. The convoy was miles and miles away, maybe scattering. The sea had him now.

A *chwung-chwung-chwung* came from behind him, growing rapidly louder. Diesels. Feebly, he turned till he saw the lean iron shark shape come out of the dark. He saw the silhouettes of the men on the tower. He tried to raise a hand, tried to shout, did not have the strength. The sub swam on, following the spoor of its prey. Its wake rocked him to sleep.

Fingers plucked at him. Hands dragged him out of the cool, dark sea. He screamed. The pain! He had one glimpse of friendly sailors, of a motor whaleboat, of a grey destroyer bobbing in the background. He sobbed. He was one of the lucky ones.

1955

They finally talked him into going to the seashore. "About time you faced up to it," Gladys told him when the kids were out of hearing. "You can't let it rule you. You're not the only man who had a ship knocked out from under him."

All the old arguments. All irrefutable. He did have to face it, to conquer it.

There was a breeze off the ocean, salt and cool. It brought back that wartime sea. He found himself listening . . . He started shaking. Gladys put both hands on his arm and pushed him forward. The boys put the umbrella up and charged the water, their shouts drifting back like old battlecries fading into the mists of time. "C'mon, Dad. C'mon."

He looked at the plain of blue and the far horizon and froze. He began shaking his head.

"It's all right," Gladys said. "Just sit under the umbrella. I'll ride herd on the monsters.

Umbrella and blanket were too close to the water.

After one gut-wrenching minute of trying to watch his brood, he turned his back, stretched out on his stomach, and tried to escape into sleep.

The surf rolled in behind him, a gentle whoosh, roar, sweep of sand back into the deep. A whisper in the waves, "Shawn, Shawn. Come to us, Shawn."

Shaking, he begged sleep to come.

He wakened to the cold grasp of watery claws on his calves, trying to drag him down the beach. Eager, bubbling whispers. He clamped his eyes shut and clung to the umbrella pole.

Another wave swept in. And another. Oh God. They had him. This time, they had him. They were going to pull him in.

"Shawn-Shawn-Shawn," came in an eager, tumbling babble.

"Shawn! Snap out of it!" A palm hit the side of his face. "I'm sorry, Honey. The boys wanted to go get hot dogs."

1968

A different coast and a different wife, Madelaine. Lean and cool, ten years younger than Gladys. Hip. Almost able to bridge the gap to the boys. The sullen, unpatriotic little bastards. Long hair and pimply faces behind ragged beards, desecrating the flag of the country for which he'd almost died . . . They didn't even try to understand. Called him a fascist. Him! *They* didn't know what fascism was. *They* hadn't seen the wolf packs maul a convoy and kill a thousand men . . .

"Here they are," she said. "Try not to mention the war. Either war. Give them a chance. They'll give you one." Amateur psychiatrist. She was good with words. Gladys hadn't been. The boys liked her well enough. They could talk to her.

But why did she have to try killing two birds? This Marineland outing... He exchanged unenthusiastic greetings with his sons. The tension ... He could think of only one thing to compare. Salt water in burn wounds.

Madelaine chattered brightly in her false, amateur diplomat way. The boys didn't mind, or didn't detect the phoniness. Or maybe they just accepted it as natural. This was the west coast. And, much as they finger-pointed his generation, the foundation of theirs was sand cemented by willful blindness and wishful thinking.

"Stop dragging your feet, Dear," Madelaine whispered. "Do you want these hippie freaks to think you're scared?"

That was a shot. Just because of what he'd called the oldest because he didn't want to go to Viet Nam ... She was right. He couldn't call the boy yellow for not wanting to face enemy fire if *he* couldn't face a little water.

He stared down at the sea and glass-bottom boat. His stomach knotted, but it wasn't as bad as he had anticipated. He seemed to step outside and watch his legs carry him along the pier. Madelaine chattered at him and the boys. They all answered her, but he could not recall what anybody said.

Half an hour out. "Seasick?" his younger boy asked. "I thought you were a sailor, Dad."

He nodded. His stomach was grinding and churning. This was different, somehow. Maybe because the boat was so small. He tried to ignore it, to get into Madelaine's game, to share his knowledge of the deep.

He had to give it up. He closed his eyes and leaned on the gunwale, concentrated on retaining his breakfast. The water whispered past, occasionally licking his fingers.

He was half asleep, one arm extended. A wavetop caught his hand, nearly wrenched his arm away. "Shawn! Shawn! Come to us, Shawn!"

The voices! Still there! Out here. They had him.

He jumped up, yelling, and staggered as the boat climbed a wave. Arms flailing, he went over the side.

He was under for just a few seconds, looking upward, clawing his way toward the sun, a scream locked in his throat by the pressure of the sea. The fire up there ... The burning tanker ... Better to stay down here with them ... His floatation jacket drove him to the surface.

"Shawn. Stay, Shawn." Their fingers tugged at his clothing.

He was back aboard the boat in seconds, sobbing. Far, far away, Madelaine was telling the boys what had happened in '43. He wanted to yell at her to shut up. But she couldn't tell it all. She didn't know it all. Did she?

"It wasn't your fault, Shawn. Don't you understand that? It wasn't your fault. There was no way your ship could have escaped."

He wished he could believe it. Whining, he surged up, pushed her away, threw himself over the side again.

Eager murmurs. Grasping hands. "Shawn. You've come. At last, Shawn. At last."

Yelling and panic above. Salt water in his mouth. The people in the boat were quicker, stronger, and trickier than the sea. They pulled him out again. For a moment he thought he was tumbling into that ill- remembered motor whaleboat.

"Come back, Shawn. Shawn?"

1980

No wife now. Madelaine had died in an encounter with a drunk driver. She would have left by now anyway, he figured.

The younger boy was gone, too. Killed by a mortar bomb outside Khe Sahn. The older boy was in retail sales. Appliances. A college education down the tubes. There were grandchildren. He didn't see them often. There was too much bitterness still.

"Come on down to Florida," the guys said.

"We're taking the company plane. We'll go after the big ones off the outer keys. Remember that marlin Wally hooked last year? That baby has cousins just waiting to jump in the boat."

He had nothing else to do over Christmas, and, somehow, the sea didn't seem scary anymore. He agreed to go.

So there he was, somewhere over the Gulf Coast, staring down at the sharp shadings of color in the shallows, marveling at the clarity of the water. Search as he might, he could find no fear in himself, though there was something there that might have been resignation.

The sea rose to greet them. The plane shivered as its landing gear locked down. "Going to refuel," Wally called back. "Won't take long."

The runway ran straight toward the Gulf. He watched the concrete come up, wondering if the plane would overshoot. But the tires touched and squealed almost before his imagination could slip into gear.

The others wanted to eat while they were down. He wasn't hungry. He walked to the edge of the beach and watched the combers roll in from Mexico. He stood there, the breeze teasing the remnants of his hair, listening.

He couldn't hear the voices. Not a hint, not a whisper. Just the sound of warm tropic waters lazily washing the sand.

It was over. Somehow, he had whipped it. He poked around inside, just to make sure, going deep, prodding the old sore spots. There was no pain, no guilt. While he wasn't watching, he had done what Gladys and Madelaine had demanded a thousand times. He had grown up. Somehow, he had accepted the truth. There was nothing he could have done that night. The ship's number had been up, and that was that.

That was that. One boat had sunk three ships with its first spread. None had had a chance.

He shivered again. So long ago. Two thirds of a lifetime, in a different world. A forgotten age. Most of the people now alive hadn't been born.

"Shawn. Hey, Shawn."

He jumped, then lifted a hand to let the guys know he had heard. He looked out onto the Gulf, a grin stretching his wrinkled face. "I don't know if you're real or not, but, damnit, I know I've beaten you." As he walked toward the plane, he wondered how much he had put together retroactively. A man dying of burns and exposure couldn't help going a little goofy. He really shouldn't have survived.

"Holy shit!" Wally yelled in his ear. "Jesus! You guys, get up here! Shawn's got one. Look at the size of this bastard."

The marlin came up and stood on its tail, dancing on the wavetops. It fell back with a slap audible aboard the boat. "He's going down. He's sounding," one of the guys said. "Watch your line, Shawn. Give him some slack."

"He's not," Wally insisted. "He's going to run in on us. Reel it in, Shawn. Reel it in. Keep the tension on it. Make him work."

He'd never done this before. He didn't know what he was doing. He hadn't had a line in the water since the war, when they had fished for sharks off the fantail. He offered the rod to someone more experienced.

"This is your baby, Shawn," Wally said. "We're not going to take it from you."

346 — GLEN COOK

He began to taste the excitement that drove the others, that sense of a test of endurance and will against something strong and wild . . . One instant of flashback, flame gouting against the night when the first torpedo hit the tanker. Man. There was an opponent to test your limits. The boats tried to catch the fat-bellied freighters and tankers. The destroyers tried to catch the boats. Losers slept forever in the deep.

"Shawn don't daydream, man! Give me that rod if you're going to . . ."

He told Wally he had it under control. Now he wanted to do it himself. His victory would be complete when he brought that big bastard alongside. He would have beaten the sea once and for all.

"What's that?" one of the guys asked.

"Looks like a shark."

"That's all we need. Somebody get the rifle."

He heard the bolt slam a cartridge home. Sweat rolled into his eyes. He asked somebody to do something. He couldn't take his hands off the rod. Wally mopped his face with a handkerchief. "Hang in there, Shawn. He's weakening."

"There it is."

More sweat rolled into his eyes.

Bam!

"Missed him."

"Shit, too. Right through his fin."

"Master gunfighter. Like hell. That slug hit fifty feet the other side of him. Give me that thing." The bolt worked again.

"What's the matter, Shawn?"

He shook his head. He couldn't tell Wally he had seen the shark's fin from the corner of a watery eye and imagined it to be a hand with webbing between its fingers beckoning.

No time to get silly. He had to remember he had it whipped.

"Somebody better help him," one of the guys said. "He don't look so good."

He gritted his teeth and refused to let loose of the rod. This one was his, all his. It wasn't much, but, by damn, this was going to be the victory of his life.

Something clicked. He seemed to have been doing this forever. He played the monster perfectly, with total concentration. The voice of the rifle was barely audible as the others took turns sniping at the shark. Their excitement came from another galaxy. "Go, Shawn." "You got him, fellow." "Hang in there, Shawn. It won't be long now. He's ready to give up."

Tension on his line. Keep that tension on his line. The marlin was barely fighting now. Coming in. Closer and closer.

"Hey, Wally. Shawn really don't look good."

"Leave him alone, will you? There you go, Shawn. He's done now. He'll do whatever you want. Bring him on in. Somebody get the gaff."

Right up next to the hull now. He laughed and told somebody to take the rod. He pried his stiff body out of the chair and staggered to the rail, looked down. Obsidian water, rolling along the side. Black, bottomless eyes staring out of the luminescence. "Shawn. Come to us, Shawn."

He laughed.

"Give him the gaff."

He took the gaff and leaned over the side . . .

The laughter left him. The creature looked back with hollow eyes, and it was no marlin. It had webbed hands. "No! Damnit, no!" He raised the gaff like a throwing spear.

"Shawn? What the hell is the matter?"

Something slammed against his chest. No. It was inside. There had been smaller blows while he was fighting the fish—or whatever it was. This one hurt. Oh, it hurt.

Shouts. Hands grabbing as he dropped the gaff. He staggered. Somehow, despite them, he slipped forward and tipped right over the rail. The thing on his hook grinned.

The yelling faded away, away, far away, even before he hit and the happy laughter surrounded him.

Brine filled his mouth. The bright surface dwindled. Champagne-bubbly chuckling filled his ears. He struggled, but the agony in his chest left him without strength to fight. The gentle hands drew him down, down.

"Shawn. Shawn. You've come. We've been waiting so long." Their caresses and kisses roamed over him. The wrinkly light of the surface receded ever farther away. "We waited so long, Shawn."

But not long in the life of the eternally waiting sea.

The darkness came and took him, and even the happy laughter faded.

SEVERED HEADS

*The following story is one of my favorites of everything that I've done.
Partly, that is, because it was so very successful, having been reprinted
so many times overseas that it earned me more, in its time, than most
of my novels had. Then, too, at its core lie elements of a family legend.*

I

Narriman was ten when the black rider came to Wadi al Hamamah. He
rode tall and arrogant upon a courser as white as his djellaba was black.
He looked neither right nor left as he passed among the tents. Old men
spat at his horse's hooves. Old women made warding signs. Children and
dogs whined and fled. Makram's ass set up a horrible braying.

Narriman was not frightened, just confused. Who was this stranger?
Why were her people frightened? Because he wore black? No tribe she
knew wore black. Black was the color of ifrits and djinn, of the Masters of
Jebal al Alf Dhulquarneni, the high, dark mountains brooding over Wadi
al Hamamah and the holy places of the al Muburak.

Narriman was a bold one. Her elders warned her often, but she would
not behave as fit her sex. The old ones shook their heads and said that
brat of Mowfik's would be no good. Mowfik himself was suspect enough,
what with his having gone to the great wars of the north. What business
were those of the al Muburak?

Narriman stayed and watched the rider.

He reined in before her father's tent, which stood apart, drew a black rod
from his javelin case, breathed upon it. Its tips glowed. He set that glow

against the tent, sketched a symbol. The old folks muttered and cursed and told one another they'd known despair would haunt Mowfik's tent.

Narriman ran after the stranger, who rode down the valley toward the shrine. Old Farida shouted after her. She pretended not to hear. She dodged from shadow to shadow, rock to rock, to the hiding place from which she spied on the rites of her elders.

She watched the rider pass through the Circle with arrogance unconquered. He did not glance at Karkur, let alone make obeisance and offerings. She expected the Great Death to strike him ere he left the Circle, but he rode on, untouched. She watched him out of sight. Narriman stared at the god. Was Karkur, too, a frightened antique? She was shaken. Karkur's anger was a constant. Each task, each pleasure, had to be integrated with his desires. He was an angry god. But he had sat there like a red stone lump while a heathen defiled his Circle.

The sun was in the west when she returned to camp. Old Farida called her immediately. She related what she had seen. The old folks muttered and whispered and made their signs.

"Who was he, Farida? What was he? Why were you afraid?"

Farida spat through the gap in her teeth. "The Evil One's messenger. A shaghûn out of the Jebal." Farida turned her old eyes on the Mountains of a Thousand Sorcerers. She made her magic sign. "It's a mercy your mother didn't live to see this."

"Why?"

But just then the guard horn sounded, ending on a triumphant note. The hunters had returned. Karkur had favored the tribe. Narriman ran to tell her father about the stranger.

II

Mowfik had an antelope behind his saddle, a string of quail, a brace of hares, and even a box terrapin. "A great hunt, Little Fox. Never was it so fine. Even Shukri took his game." Shukri could do nothing right. He was, probably, the man Narriman would wed, because she was her mother's daughter.

Her father was so pleased she did not mention the stranger. The other hunters heard from the old ones. Dour eyes turned Mowfik's way. Narriman was afraid for him till she sensed that they felt pity. There was a lot of nodding. The stranger's visit confirmed their prejudices.

Mowfik stopped outside their tent. "Little Fox, we won't sleep much tonight. I hope you've gathered plenty of wood."

She heard the weariness in his voice. He had worked harder than the others. He had no woman to ride behind and clean game, no woman to help here at home. Only old Farida, his mother's sister, bothered to offer.

Narriman took the quail and hares, arranged them on a mat. She collected her tools, stoked up the fire, settled down to work.

The sun settled westward and slightly south. A finger of fire broke between peaks and stabbed into the wadi, dispelling shadows. Mowfik glanced up.

He turned pale. His mouth opened and closed. Finally, he gurgled, "What?"

She told him about the rider.

He sat with head bent low. "Ah, no. Not my Little Fox." And, in response to an earlier question. "There are those even Karkur dares not offend. The rider serves one greater than he." Then, thoughtfully, "But perhaps he's shown the way. There must be a greater reason than a feast when game runs to the hunter's bow." He rose, walked into the shadows, stared at those dread mountains that no tribe dared invade. Then he said, "Cook only the meat that might spoil before we get it smoked."

"Tell me what it means, Father."

"I suppose you're old enough. You've been Chosen. The Masters sent him to set their mark. It's been a long time since the shaghûn came. The last was in my mother's time."

III

Mowfik had been north and had bathed in alien waters. He could think the unthinkable. He could consider defying the Masters. He dug into his war booty to buy Makram's ass. He loaded all he possessed on two animals and walked away. He looked back only once. "I should never have come back."

They went north over game trails, through the high, rocky places, avoiding other tribes. They spent twelve days in the hills before descending to a large oasis. For the first time Narriman saw people who lived in houses. She remained close to Mowfik. They were strange.

"There. In the east. That is el Aswad, the Wahlig's fortress." Narriman saw a great stone tent crowning a barren hill. "And there, four days' ride, lies

Sebil el Selib, the pass to the sea." He pointed northeast. His arm swung to encompass the west. "Out there lies the great erg called Hammad al Nakir."

Heat shimmered over the Desert of Death. For a moment she thought she saw the fairy towers of fallen Ilkazar, but that was imagination born of stories Mowfik had brought home from his adventures. Ilkazar had been a ruin for four centuries.

"We'll water here, cross the erg, and settle over there. The shaghûn will never find us."

It took eight days, several spent lost, to reach Wadi el Kuf, the only oasis in the erg. It took fourteen more to finish and find a place to settle.

The new life was bewildering. The people spoke the same language, but their preoccupations were different. Narriman thought she would go mad before she learned their ways. But learn she did. She was the bold one, Mowfik's daughter, who could question everything and believe only that which suited her. She and her father remained outsiders, but less so than among their own people. Narriman liked the settled people better. She missed only old Farida and Karkur. Mowfik insisted that Karkur was with them in spirit.

IU

Narriman was twelve when the rider reappeared.

She was in the fields with her friends Ferial and Feras. It was a stony, tired field. Ferial's father had bought it cheap, offering Mowfik a quarter interest if he would help prove it up. That morning, while the children dug stones and piled them into a wall, Mowfik and his partner were elsewhere. Feras had been malingering all morning, and was the scorn of Narriman and his sister. He saw the rider first.

He was barely visible against a background of dark rocks and shadow. He was behind a boulder which masked all but his horse's head. But he was there. Just watching. Narriman shuddered. How had he found them?

He served the Masters. Their necromancy was great. Mowfik had been foolish to think they could escape

"Who is he?" Ferial asked. "Why are you afraid?"

"I'm not afraid," Narriman lied. "He's a shaghûn." Here in the north some lords had shaghûns of their own. She had to add, "He rides for the Masters of the Jebal."

Ferial laughed.

Narriman said, "You'd believe if you had lived in the shadow of the Jebal."

Feras said, "The Little Fox is a bigger liar than her namesake."

Narriman spit at his feet. "You're so brave, huh?"

"He doesn't scare me."

"Then come with me to ask what he wants."

Feras looked at Narriman, at Ferial, and at Narriman again. Male pride would not let him back down.

Narriman had her pride too. I'll go just a little way, she told herself. Just far enough to make Feras turn tail. I won't go near him.

Her heart fluttered. Feras gasped, ran to catch up. Ferial called, "Come back, Feras. I'll tell Father."

Feras groaned. Narriman would have laughed had she not been so frightened. Feras was trapped between pride and punishment.

The certainty of punishment made him stick. He meant to make the whipping worth the trouble. No girl would outbrave him.

They were seventy yards away when Feras ran. Narriman felt the hard touch of the shaghûn's eyes. A few steps more, just to prove Feras was bested.

She took five long, deliberate steps, stopped, looked up. The shaghûn remained immobile. His horse tossed its head, shaking off flies. A different horse, but the same man. . . . She met his eyes.

Something threw a bridle upon her soul. The shaghûn beckoned, a gentle come hither. Her feet moved. Fifty yards. Twenty-five. Ten. Her fear mounted. The shaghûn dismounted, eyes never leaving hers. He took her arm, drew her into the shadow of the boulder. Gently, he pushed her back against the rock.

"What do you want?"

He removed the cloth across his face.

He was just a man! A young man, no more than twenty. He wore the ghost of a smile, and was not unhandsome, but his eyes were cold, without mercy.

His hand came to her, removed the veil she had begun wearing only months ago. She shivered like a captive bird.

"Yes," he whispered. "As beautiful as they promised." He touched her cheek.

She could not escape his eyes. Gently, gently, he tugged here, untied there, lifted another place, and she was more naked than at any moment since birth.

In her heart she called to Karkur. Karkur had ears of stone. She shivered as she recalled Mowfik saying that there were powers before whom Karkur must nod.

The shaghûn piled their clothing into a narrow pallet. She gasped when he stood up, and tried to break his spell by sealing her eyes. It did no good. His hands took her naked flesh and gently forced her down.

He drove a burning brand into her, punishing her for having dared flee. Despite her determination, she whimpered, begged him to stop. There was no mercy in him.

The second time there was less pain. She was numb. She ground her eyelids together and endured. She did not give him the pleasure of begging.

The third time she opened her eyes as he entered her. His gaze caught hers.

The effect was a hundred times what it had been when he had called her. Her soul locked with his. She became part of him. Her pleasure was as great, as all-devouring, as her pain the first time. She begged, but not for mercy.

Then he rose, snatched his clothing, and she cried again, shame redoubled because he had made her enjoy what he was doing.

His movements were no longer languid and assured. He dressed hastily and sloppily. There was fear in his eyes. He leaped onto his mount and dug in his heels.

Narriman rolled into a tight ball of degradation and pain, and wept.

∪

Men shouted. Horses whinnied. "He went that way!"

"There he goes! After him!"

Mowfik swung down and cast his cloak over Narriman. She buried her face in his clothing.

The thunder of hooves, the cries of outrage and the clang of weapons on shields, receded. Mowfik touched her. "Little Fox?"

"Go away. Let me die."

"No. This will pass. This will be forgotten. There's no forgetting death." His voice choked on rage. "They'll catch him. They'll bring him back. I'll give you my own knife."

"They won't catch him. He has the Power. I couldn't fight him. He made me *want* him. Go away. Let me die."

"No." Mowfik had been to the wars in the north. He had seen rape. Women survived. The impact was more savage when the victim was one of one's own, but that part of him that was Man and not outraged father knew that this was not the end.

"You know what they'll say." Narriman wrapped his cloak about her. "Ferial and Feras will tell what they saw. People will think I went willingly. They'll call me whore. And what they call me I'll have to be. What man would have me now?"

Mowfik sighed. He heard truth. When the hunters returned, chastened by losing the man in their own territory, they would seek excuses for failing, would see in a less righteous light. "Get dressed."

"Let me die, Father. Let me take my shame off your shoulders."

"Stop that. Get dressed. We have things to do. We'll sell while people are sympathetic. We started over here. We can start again somewhere else. Up. Into your clothes. Do you want them to see you like this? Time to make the brave show."

All her life he had said that, whenever people hurt her. "Time to make the brave show."

Tears streaming, she dressed. "Did you say that to Mother, too?" Her mother had been brave, a northern girl who had come south out of love. She had been more outsider than Mowfik.

"Yes. Many times. And I should've held my tongue. I should've stayed in the north. None of this would have happened had we stayed with her people."

Mowfik's partner did not try to profit from his distress. He paid generously. Mowfik did not have to waste war booty to get away.

UI

A Captain Al Jahez, who Mowfik had served in the wars, gave him a position as a huntsman. He and Narriman had now fled eight hundred miles from Wadi al Hamamah.

Narriman began to suspect the worst soon after their arrival. She remained silent till it became impossible to deceive herself. She went to Mowfik because there was nowhere else to go.

"Father, I'm with child."

He did not react in the traditional way. "Yes. His purpose was to breed another of his kind."

"What will we do?" She was terrified. Her tribe had been unforgiving. The settled peoples were only slightly less so in these matters.

"There's no need to panic. I discussed this with Al Jahez when we arrived. He's a hard and religious man, but from el Aswad originally. He knows what comes out of the Jebal. His goatherd is old. He'll send us into the hills to replace him. We'll stay away a few years while he stamps your widowhood into everyone's mind. You'll come back looking young for your age. Men will do battle for such a widow."

"Why are you so kind? I've been nothing but trouble since the rider came down the wadi."

"You're my family. All I have. I live by the way of the Disciple, unlike so many who profess his creed only because it's politic."

"And yet you bow to Karkur."

He smiled. "One shouldn't overlook any possibility. I'll speak with Al Jahez. We'll go within the week."

Life in the hills, herding goats, was not unpleasant. The land was hard, reminding Narriman of home. But this was tamer country. Wolves and lions were few. The kids were not often threatened.

As her belly swelled and the inevitable drew near, she grew ever more frightened. "Father, I'm not old enough for this. I'm going to die. I know it."

"No, you won't." He told her that her mother, too, had grown frightened. That all women were afraid. He did not try to convince her that her fears were groundless, only that fear was more dangerous than giving birth. "I'll be with you. I won't let anything happen. And Al Jahez promises he'll send his finest midwife."

"Father, I don't understand why you're so good to me. And I'm baffled as to why he's so good to you. He can't care that much because you rode in his company."

Mowfik shrugged. "Perhaps because I saved his life at the Battle of the Circles. Also, there are more just men than you believe."

"You never talk about the wars. Except about places you saw."

"Those aren't happy memories, Little Fox. Dying and killing and dying. And in the end, nothing gained, either for myself or for the glory of the Lord. Will you tell the young ones about these days when you're old? Those days weren't happy, but I saw more than any al Muburak before or since."

He was the only one of a dozen volunteers who survived. And maybe that, instead of the foreign wife, was why he had become an outcast. The old folks resented him for living when their own sons were dead.

"What will we do with a baby, Father?"

"What? What people always do. Raise him to be a man."

"It'll be a boy, will it?"

"I doubt me not it will, but a girl will be as welcome." He chuckled.

"Will you hate him?"

"We are talking about my daughter's child. I can hate the father, but not the infant. The child is innocent."

"You did travel in strange lands. No wonder the old ones didn't like you."

"Old ones pass on. Ideas are immortal. So says the Disciple."

She felt better afterward, but her fear never evaporated.

VII

"A fine son," the old woman said with a toothless smile. "A fine son. I foretell you now, little mistress, he'll be a great one. See it here, in his hands." She held the tiny, purplish, wrinkled, squalling thing high. "And he came forth with the cap. Only the truly destined, the chosen ones, come forth with that. Aye, you've mothered a mighty one."

Narriman smiled though she heard not a tenth of the babble. She cared only that the struggle was over, that the pain had receded. There was a great warmth in her for the child, but she hadn't the strength to express it.

Mowfik ducked into the tent. "Sadhra. Is everything all right?" His face was pale. Dimly, Narriman realized he had been frightened too.

"Both came through perfectly. Al Jahez has a godson of whom he can be proud." She repeated her predictions.

"Old Mother, you'd better not tell him that. That smacks of superstition. He's strict about religious deviation."

"The decrees of men, be they mere men or Chosen of the Lord, can't change natural law. Omens are omens."

"May be. May be. Shouldn't you give her the child?"

"Aye. So I should. I'm hogging him because one day I'll be able to say I held such a one." She dropped the infant to Narriman's breast. He took the nipple, but without enthusiasm.

"Don't you worry, little mistress. Soon he'll suckle hearty."

"Thank you, Sadhra," Mowfik said. "Al Jahez chose well. I'm in both your debts."

"It was my honor, sir." She left the tent.

"Such a one, eh, Little Fox? Making him the Hammer of God before he draws his first breath."

Narriman stared up at him. He wasn't just tired. He was disturbed. "The rider?"

"He's out there."

"I thought so. I felt him."

"I stalked him, but he eluded me. I didn't dare go far."

"Perhaps tomorrow." As she drifted into sleep, though, she thought, You'll never catch him. He'll deceive you with the Power. No warrior will catch him. Time or trickery will be his death.

She slept. And she dreamed of the rider and the way it had been for her the third time.

She dreamed that often. It was one thing she kept from Mowfik. He would not understand. She did not understand herself.

Maybe she *was* a whore at heart.

VIII

Narriman called the child Misr Sayed bin Hammad al Muburaki, meaning he was Misr Sayed son of the desert, of the al Muburak tribe. Hammad could be a man's name also, so it became that of her missing husband. Misr's grandfather, however, called him Towfik el-Masiri, or Camel's Feet, for reasons only he found amusing.

Misr grew quickly, learned rapidly, and was startlingly healthy. Seldom was he colicky or cranky, even when cutting teeth. He was happy most of the time, and always had a big hug for his grandfather. Narriman remained perpetually amazed that she could feel so much love for one person. "How do women love more than one child?" she asked.

Mowfik shrugged. "It's a mystery to me. I was my mother's only. You're your mother's only."

The first two years were idyllic. The baby and the goats kept them too busy to worry. In the third year, though, Mowfik grew sour. His heart was not in his play with Misr. One day Narriman found him honing his war sword and watching the hills. Then she understood. He expected the rider.

The prospect fired her fantasies. She ached for the shaghûn. She held her left hand near the fire till pain burned the lust away.

Shortly after Misr's third birthday Mowfik said, "I'm going to see Al Jahez. It's time you became Hammad's widow."

"Will we be safer there? Won't the shaghûn just ride in like he did before?"

"Al Jahez thinks not. He thinks the priests can drive him away."

Narriman went to the tent flap, surveyed the unfriendly hills. "Go see him. I'm afraid to go back where people might cry shame, but I'm more scared of the shaghûn."

"I'd hoped you'd feel that way."

She had begun to relax. The night had passed without incident. Mowfik should be back by noon. If she could stay too busy to worry. . . .

It was almost noon when Misr called, "Mama, Grandpa coming." She sighed, put her mending aside, and went to meet him.

"Oh, no. Karkur defend us." Misr could not be blamed for his mistake. He'd seldom seen anyone but Mowfik on horseback.

The shaghûn was far down the valley, coming toward her. He seemed larger than life, like a far city seen through the shimmer over the great erg. He came at an unhurried walk. The rise and fall of his animal's legs was hypnotic. He did not seem to draw any closer.

"Go into the tent, Misr."

"Mama?"

"Do it. And don't come out till I tell you. No matter what."

"Mama, what's wrong?"

"Misr! Go!"

"Mama, you're scaring me."

She gave him her fiercest look. He scooted inside. "And close the flap." She turned. The rider looked twice as big but no nearer. His pace was no faster. The pain in her heart grew with the heat in her loins. She knew he would take her, and her evil side called to him eagerly.

He came closer. She thought of running into the hills. But what good that? He would hunt her down. And Misr would be left alone.

She snatched the bow Mowfik used for hunting, sped an arrow toward the rider. She missed.

She was good with that weapon. Better than her father, who remained perpetually amazed that a woman could do anything better than a man. She should not have missed. She sped a second and third arrow.

Each missed. The fourth plucked at his djellaba, but only because he was so close. There was no fifth. She had seen his eyes.

The bow fell from her hand. He dismounted and walked toward her, reaching.

Only one moment from the next hour stuck with her. Misr came outside, saw the rider thrusting into her, ran over and bit him on the buttocks. That would remain with her forever, in that mixture of amusement and pain such a thing could recall.

Afterward he stared into her eyes. His will beat against her. She dwindled into sleep.

Cursing wakened her. It was the violent cursing of savagery and hatred. She was too lazy to open her eyes.

She recalled the inexorable approach of the man in black coming up the valley on a line as straight as the arrow of time. She recalled his touch, her fevered response. She felt the sun on her naked shame. She flew up, wrapped herself in discarded clothing.

Mowfik belabored a fallen tree with his axe, cursing steadily. He blasphemed both Karkur and the Lord of the Disciple. She scrambled into her clothing, frightened.

Exhaustion stopped Mowfik. He settled on the tree trunk and wept. Narriman went to comfort him.

"It's all right, Father. He didn't hurt me. He shamed me again, but he didn't hurt me." She put her arms around him. "It'll be all right, Father."

"Little Fox, he took Misr. It wasn't you this time."

IX

Narriman changed, hardened, saddened. The Narriman of Wadi al Hamamah would not have recognized her. That Narriman would have been terrified by her.

Mowfik took her to see Al Jahez. The captain was properly outraged. He set his men to scouring the country. He sent an alarm across the kingdom. He appealed to the Most Holy Mrazkim Shrines for a Writ of Anathema, and for prayers for the Lord's intervention.

"And that is all I can do. And it's pointless. He won't be seen. Those who serve the Masters come and go as they please."

"Can't somebody do something?" Narriman demanded. "How long has this been going on? How many women have had to suffer this?"

"It's gone on forever," Al Jahez said. "It went on throughout the age of Empire. It went on before the Empire was born. It'll go on tomorrow, too."

"Why isn't it stopped?"

"Because no one can stop it. One of the Emperors tried. He sent an army into the Jebal. Not one man returned."

She was venting frustration. She knew the futility of battling the Masters. No, this was personal. This was between herself and one shaghûn. The Masters were but shadows beyond the horizon, too nebulous to factor into the emotional equation.

"That man took my son. *My* son. I don't recognize his claim. He did nothing but force me onto my back."

"Narriman?" Mowfik said, baffled.

"I want my son back."

"We can't do anything about that," Al Jahez said. "The shaghûn is who he is, and we're who we are."

"No."

"Narriman?" Again Mowfik was puzzled.

"I thought about this all day, Father. I'm going after Misr."

Al Jahez said, "But you're a child. And a woman."

"I've grown up in the past few years. I'm small, but I'm no child. As to my sex, say what you will. It won't change my mind."

"Narriman!"

"Father, will you stop saying that? You stood by me when I begged you not to. You drowned me in love I did not deserve. Stand by me now. Give me what I need to get Misr back. Teach me what I need to know."

Al Jahez shook his head. "Mowfik, you were right. She *is* remarkable."

"Little Fox. . . . It would take so long. And I'm not rich. I can't afford weapons and mounts and. . . ."

"We have a horse. We have a sword. You were a soldier. I can survive in the wilderness. I was of the al Muburak."

Mowfik sighed. "The sword is too heavy, girl."

Narriman glanced at Al Jahez. The captain tried to disappear amongst his cushions.

"Little Fox, I don't want to lose you too. I couldn't bear that." Mowfik's voice cracked. Narriman glimpsed a tear in the corner of one eye. This would cost him dearly from his beggared emotional purse.

He did not want to see her ride away. His heart said he would not see her again.

That dark rider had stolen her from him as surely as he had stolen Misr. She threw her arms around Mowfik. "Father, I have to do this. Wouldn't you come after me?"

"Yes. Yes. I would. I understand that."

Al Jahez said, "This isn't wise. The impossibility of dealing with the shaghûn and the Jebal aside, what would happen to a young woman alone? Even honest men would consider her fair for a moment's sport. Not to mention slavers and bandits. The Disciple instituted a rule of law, little one, but the Evil One, as ever, rules most of the land."

"Those are problems to face when they arise." What he said was true. She could not deny that. Women had no legal status or protection. When the shaghûn forced her onto her back he injured her father, not her. An unattached woman was not a person.

Her resolve was not shaken. Damned be the problems, and anyone who stood in her way.

✗

When she wanted something badly Narriman got her way. Mowfik surrendered in the end. Once he gave in, Al Jahez grudgingly endorsed her training.

Narriman pursued it with a dogged determination that, in time, compelled the respect of Al Jahez's men. She arrived early and left late, and worked harder than any boy.

She was hard. She ignored bruises and aches. Her instructors called her Vixen and backed away when the deadly fire rose in her eyes.

One day she browbeat Mowfik into taking her to the captain. She told Al Jahez, "I'm ready. I leave tomorrow."

Al Jahez addressed her father. "Will you permit this, Mowfik? A woman under arms. It's against nature."

Mowfik shrugged.

Narriman said, "Don't stall me. Father's done that for weeks. I'll go with or without your blessing."

"Mowfik, forbid this madness."

"Captain, you heard her. Shall I put her in irons?"

Al Jahez looked at her as if he would cage her for her own protection. "Then marry her to me, Mowfik."

Though struck speechless, Narriman understood. Al Jahez wanted the legal rights of marriage. So he could forbid, so he could call upon the law if she persisted. If she rebelled, they would hunt her like a runaway slave.

Pure terror gripped her. She stared at her father, saw him tempted.

"Captain, heart and soul cry for me to accept. But I can't. A stronger voice bids me let her go. No matter how it hurts me."

Al Jahez sighed, defeated. "As you will. Child. Bring your father no sorrow or shame." He scowled at her expression. "No sorrow or shame of your own doing. That which is done by a shaghûn isn't of your doing. They're like the great storms in the erg. A man—or woman—can but bow his head till they pass. Come. The priests will bless your quest."

They waited in their fine ceremonial raiment. Al Jahez's eyes twinkled. "You see? Even the old Captain begins to know you."

"Perhaps." She wondered if she was too predictable.

The ceremony was less important to her than to Mowfik and Al Jahez. She endured it for their sakes. She would ride with Karkur.

"Now then," Al Jahez said. "One more thing and I'll harass you no more. Gamel. The box."

A priest presented a sandalwood box. Al Jahez opened it. Within, on white silk, lay a pendant. It was a small, pale green stone not unlike many she had seen on the ground. Al Jahez said, "Perhaps this will be gift enough to repay you, Mowfik." And to Narriman, "Child, the Disciple teaches that even the acquiescence to sorcery is a sin, but men have to be practical. The Disciple himself has shaghûn advisers.

"The stone is an amulet. It will warn you if you are near one with the Power. It will begin to grow cooler when you're a mile away. When you're very near, it will shed a green light. It's the best weapon I can give you."

Narriman tried to control the shakes. She failed. Tears broke loose. She hugged the captain. He was so startled he jumped away, but his face betrayed his pleasure.

"Go with the Lord, Little Fox. And with Karkur if it pleases you."

"Thank you," she said. "For everything. Especially for being Father's friend."

Ah Jahez snorted. "Ah, child. What are we without friends? Just severed heads rolling across the sands."

XI

Narriman looked back just before Al Jahez's fortress passed out of sight. "That's yesterday." She looked southward, toward the great erg. "There lies tomorrow. Eight hundred miles." She gripped her reins, touched the amulet between her breasts, her weapons, the bag that Mowfik had filled with war booty when he thought she was not looking. He had done everything to dissuade her, and everything to help her.

She looked back again, wondering if their concepts of manhood and womanhood would compel them to send guardians.

"Go, Faithful," she told her mare. The fortress disappeared. Her heart fluttered. She was going. Alone. A severed head, rolling across the sand, cut off from her body—with a little help from the rider.

She pictured him as he had been the day he had taken Misr. She got that warm, moist feeling, but not as powerfully. Hatred had begun to quench that fire.

She wished there was a way a woman could do to a man what he had done to her.

The wilderness was all that she had been warned. It was bitter, unforgiving, and those who dwelt there reflected its harshness. Twice she encountered men who thought her a gift from heaven. The first time she outrode them. The second, cornered, she fought. And was surprised to find herself the victor.

Though she had told herself that she was the equal of any man, she'd never believed it in her heart. Could the wisdom of centuries be wrong? She rode away more mature, more confident.

The great erg was more vast than she remembered. It was hotter and more harrowing. She had no one and nothing to distract her.

"The severed head has to roll without its body." She put her thoughts into words often. Who was to hear?

She had no choice but to enter Wadi el Kuf. They were shocked to see her, a woman in man's wear, hung about with weapons, talking as tough as any wandering freesword. Even the whores were scandalized. Nobody knew what to make of her. She bought water, asked questions, and rode on before they regained their balance.

Someone came after her, but one arrow altered his ambitions.

She rode with dust devils as companions. The al Muburak believed dust devils were ifrits dancing. She called out, but they did not respond. After a few days she began to think oddly, to suspect them of being spies for the Masters. She mocked and taunted them. They ignored her.

Finally, she checked the amulet. Not only did it not shed light, it was not cool. "So much for old stories."

She rode out of the erg and paused at the oasis she had visited coming north. There, as at Wadi el Kuf, she asked about a man in black traveling with a child. There, too, no one had seen such a traveler.

"Of course," she muttered. "And maybe they're telling the truth. But he's human. He *had* to stop at Wadi el Kuf." But he need not have appeared as a shaghûn out of the Jebal, need he?

No matter. She knew his destination.

Fourteen days passed. She rode into Wadi al Hamamah.

The al Muburak were not there. It was the wrong time of year. They were farther west, stalking wild camels in hopes of adding to their herd.

She camped in the usual place. When night fell she went to Karkur.

After the proper greetings and obeisances, she told her story in case Mowfik was wrong about his being able to follow an al Muburak anywhere. Karkur sat and listened, firelight sending shadows dancing across his ugly face.

She said, "Father says you aren't as great as I thought. That others are more powerful so sometimes you don't dare help. But if there's a way you can, help me do what I have to do."

She stared at the image. The image stared back. Time passed. The fire died. The moon rose, filled the Circle with shifting shadows.

"Karkur, there's a man named Al Jahez. He follows the Disciple, but he's a good man. Could you reward him? Could you tell Father I've come here safely?"

She thought, I'm talking to a lump of rock as though it really could do something. "Tell Al Jahez the severed head goes daft after it's separated."

The moon was a great, full thing that inundated the wadi with silver light. She leaned back and stared.

Something startled her. Fool, she thought. You fell asleep. Her dagger filled her hand. She searched the shadows, saw nothing. She listened. Nothing. She sniffed the air. Again nothing.

She shivered. It was getting cold. Colder than she remembered the nights this time of year. She pulled her cloak tighter.

And realized that the cold radiated from one point. The amulet!

She snatched it out. Green! Glowing green. Had the shaghûn come out to meet her?

The stone flared. It crackled. An emerald snake writhed between it and Karkur. A cold wind swirled around the Circle. Dead leaves pattered against her. She glanced up. No. The sky was clear. Stars winked in their myriads. The moon shone benevolently.

The emerald snake turned amber shot with veins of blood. Narriman gasped. That was the combination they mentioned when they talked about the Great Death.

The snake died. The stone grew less cold, became just a small, pale green piece of rock lying in her hand. She stared at Karkur.

"What have you done? What have you given me? Not the power of the Great Death?"

The image stared back, as silent as ever. She was tempted to rant. But Karkur gave short shrift to ingrates. He was more a punitive than a helpful god. "But loyal to his people," she said. "Thank you, Karkur."

She hurried through the parting rituals and returned to camp. She fell asleep still astonished that Karkur had responded.

There were dreams. Vivid dreams. She rode into the Jebal, moving with an absolute certainty of her way. She knew exactly when to expect the first challenge.

The dream ended. The sun had wakened her. She felt fit and rested. She recalled every detail of the dream. She looked down the wadi. A dumb stone god? She examined Al Jahez's stone. It looked no less ordinary this morning.

XII

The trails were faint, but she followed them confidently. Once she noted an overturned stone, darker on the exposed side. Someone had been this way recently. She shrugged. The amulet would warn her.

The mountains were silent. All the world was silent when you rode alone. The great erg had been filled with a stillness as vast as that of death. Here it seemed there should be some sound, if only the call of the red-tailed hawk on the wing. But the only sounds were those of a breeze in scrubby oaks, of water chuckling in one small stream.

She moved higher and higher. Sometimes she looked back across the hills where the wadi lay, to the plains beyond, a distance frosted with haze. The al Muburak might profit from such a view.

Night fell. She made a fireless camp. She drank water, ate smoked meat, turned in as the stars came out.

She wakened once, frightened, but her stone betrayed no danger. The mountains remained still, though the wind made an unfamiliar soughing through nearby pines. She counted more than a dozen meteors before drifting off.

Her dreams were vivid. In one her father told Al Jahez he was sure she had reached Wadi al Hamamah safely

The mountains continued their rise. She rested more often. Come midday she entered terrain scoured by fire. That stark, black expanse was an alien landscape.

The trees changed. Oaks became scarcer, pines more numerous. The mountains became like nothing in her experience. Great looms of rock thrust out of their hips, the layering on end instead of horizontal. Even where soil and grass covered them she could discern the striations. Distant mountainsides looked zebra-striped in the right light.

Higher still. The oaks vanished. And then, in the bottom of one canyon, she encountered trees so huge a half dozen men could not have joined hands around their trunks. Narriman felt insignificant in their shadows.

She spent her fourth day riding up that canyon. Evening came early. She almost missed the landmarks warning her that she was approaching the first guardian. She considered the failing light. This was no time to hurry. She retreated and camped.

Something wakened her. She listened, sniffed, realized that the alarming agent was not external. She had dreamed that she should circle the watch post.

"Come, Faithful," she whispered. She wrapped the reins in her hand and led away.

She knew exactly where to go, and still it was bad. That mountainside was not meant for climbing. The brush was dense and the slope was steep. She advanced a few yards and listened.

The brush gave way to a barren area. The soil was loose and dry. She slipped several times. Then her mare went down, screaming and sliding. She held on stubbornly.

The slide ended. "Easy, girl. Easy. Stay still."

A glow appeared below. She was surprised. She had climbed higher than she had thought. The glow drifted along the canyon.

"I can't fail now. Not at the first hurdle."

Her heart hammered. She felt like screaming against clumsiness, stupidity, and the whim of fate.

The glow drifted down the canyon, climbed the far slope, came back. It crossed to Narriman's side and went down again. It repeated the patrol but never climbed far from the canyon floor. It never came close enough to make her amulet glow. It finally gave up. But Narriman did not trust it because it had disappeared. She waited fifteen minutes.

The sky was lightening before she felt comfortably past. She was exhausted. "Good girl, Faithful. Let's camp."

XIII

A horse's whinny wakened her. She darted to Faithful, clamped her hands over the mare's nostrils.

The sound of hooves on brookside stone came nearer. The amulet became a lump of ice. She saw flickers of black rider through the trees.

This one was stockier than her shaghûn.

Her shaghûn? Had he touched her that deeply? She looked inward, seeking the hatred of rider and love of son that had brought her to the Jebal. And it was there, the hatred untarnished by any positive feeling.

Then the rider was gone, headed down the canyon. Was he going to the guardian?

She had no dream memories of the canyon above the guardian. Why not? Couldn't Karkur reach into the realm of the Masters?

The uncertainty became too much. She dismounted and walked. No need to rush into trouble. Minutes later she heard a rhythmic thumping ahead. Something rumbled and crashed and sent echoes rumbling down the canyon. She advanced more carefully, sliding from cover to cover.

She did not know where they came from. Suddenly, they were there, across the brook. They walked like men but were shaggy and dark and tall. There were four of them. The biggest growled.

"Damn!" She strung her bow as one giant bellowed and charged.

Her arrow split its breastbone. It halted, plucked at the dart. The others boomed and rushed. She sped two quick arrows, missed once, then drew her saber and scampered toward a boulder. If she got on top. . . .

Neither wounded monster went down. Both went for the mare. The others came for her.

Faithful tried to run, stumbled, screamed. The beasts piled on her.

Narriman drew her razor-edged blade across a wide belly. The brute stumbled a few steps, looked down at its wound, began tucking entrails back inside.

Narriman glanced at the mare as she dodged the other beast. The wounded creatures were pounding her with huge stones.

A fist slammed into Narriman's side. She staggered, gasped. Her attacker bellowed and closed in. She tried to raise her saber. It slipped from her hand. She hadn't the strength to grip it.

The thing shook her half senseless. Then it sniffed her and grunted.

It was something out of nightmare. The thing settled with Narriman in its lap, pawed between her thighs. She felt its sex swell against her back.

Was the whole Jebal rape-crazy? "Karkur!"

The thing ripped her clothing. Another grunted and tried to touch. The beast holding Narriman swung at it.

She was free for an instant. She scrambled away. The beast roared and dove after her.

She closed her hand on her amulet. "Karkur, give me the strength to survive this."

The beast snorted weirdly, uttered an odd shriek that tortured the canyon walls. It stumbled away, enveloped by an amber light laced with bloody threads.

Another beast came for her. Its cries joined those of the other.

Narriman scrambled after her saber. The last beast, with an arrow in its chest, watched her with glazed eyes, backed away. She arranged her clothing, ran to Faithful.

"Poor Faithful." What would she do now? How would she escape the Jebal without a horse for Misr?

The beasts in amber kept screaming. The Great Death was a hard death. It twisted their muscles till bones broke.

The screaming finally stopped.

She heard distant voices.

Hurriedly, she made a pack of her possessions, then climbed the canyon wall. She found an outcrop from which she could watch the mess she had fled.

Those things! She recalled their size and smell and was sick.

The investigators were ordinary men armed with tools. They became excited and cautious when they found the beasts. Narriman heard the word shaghûn used several times. "Keep thinking that," she murmured. "Don't get the ideas there's a stranger in the Jebal."

Her shakes faded. She offered thanks to Karkur and started across the mountainside.

What were those beasts? Those men feared them. She moved with saber in hand.

The investigators had come from a lumbering camp. She watched them drag a log up the road, toward the head of the canyon. Why? She shrugged. The Masters must want it done.

She took to that road once she passed the camp.

That afternoon she heard hoof beats. She slipped into the underbrush. "Oh, damn!" The horseman carried two of her arrows and Faithful's saddle. She strung her bow, jumped into the road, shouted, "Hey! Wait a minute!"

The rider reined in, looked back. She waved. He turned.

Her arrow flew true. He sagged backward. His horse surged forward. Narriman caught it as it passed. She dragged the body into the brush, mounted up wondering how soon he would be missed.

The canyon walls closed in. The brook faded away. She reached the summit. The road wound downhill, toward a far haze of smoke. There were a lot of hearth fires down there.

XIV

She traveled for two days. The only people she saw were men working logs down the road. She avoided them. She topped a piney ridge the second day and saw a city.

Thoughts of Misr nagged her. Should she go down now? She was ahead of news from the logging camp. But he might not be there. And she was tired. She was incapable of acting efficiently in a desperate situation. Her judgment might be clouded, too.

She settled down off the road. She would have loved a fire. The mountain nights were chilly. Gnawing dried meat, she grumbled, "I'd sell my soul for a decent meal."

Sleep brought dreams. They showed her the town, including a place where children were kept. She also saw a place where shaghûns lived, and beyond the city a tower that was an emptiness fraught with dark promise.

She wakened knowing exactly what to do. Come nightfall she would slip into the city, break into the nursery, and take Misr. Then she would flee, set an ambush down the trail and hope her shaghûn was the one who came.

Her plan died immediately. Her mount had broken its tether. Its trail led toward the city.

What would they think? Would they investigate? Of course. She'd best move elsewhere.

She trudged southward, circling the city. Time and again she went out of her way to avoid farmsteads. By nightfall she was exhausted again.

It had to be tonight, though. There was no more time.

What would she do for a mount? Her hope of escape hinged on her being able to lead the pursuit to ground of her own choosing.

She settled down near the city's edge. "Karkur, wake me when it's time."

It was a dark night. There was no moon. Clouds obscured the stars. Narriman arose shaking. Her nerves got no better for a long time.

The streets were strange for a girl who'd never walked pavement. Her boot heels kept clicking. Echoes came back off the walls. "Too quiet," she muttered. "Where are the dogs?"

Not a howl went up. Not one dog came to investigate. Her nerves only tautened. She began to imagine something watching her, the town as a box trap waiting for her to trip its trigger. She dried her hands on her hips repeatedly. The moths in her stomach refused to lie still. She kept looking over her shoulder.

She gave the place of the shaghûns a wide berth, closed in on the nursery. Why were the youngsters segregated? Was it a place for children like Misr? The city made no sense. She didn't try to make it do so.

The only warning was a rustle of fabric. Narriman whirled, saber spearing out. It was an automatic move, made without thought. She found herself face to face with a mortally wounded shaghûn.

He raised a gloved hand as he sank toward the pavement. His fingers wobbled. Sorcery! She hacked the offending hand, came back with a neck stroke. She cut him again and again, venting nervous energy and fear.

"What do I do with him?" she wondered. She examined him. He was no older than she. She felt a touch of remorse.

She glanced around. The street remained quiet. A convenient alleyway lay just beyond the body.

She wondered what he had been doing. Her dreams had suggested that no one wandered the streets after dark, save a night watchman with a special dispensation.

Had the horse alerted them? Were there more shaghûns to be faced? Her stomach cramped.

Maybe her father and Al Jahez were right. Maybe a woman *couldn't* do this sort of thing. "And maybe men feel as ragged as I do," she muttered. She dropped the body into shadow. "Give me an hour, Karkur." She went on to the nursery.

Anticipation partially overcame her reaction to the killing. She tried a door. It was barred from within. A second door proved as impenetrable. There was a third on the far side but she assumed it would be sealed, too.

Above, barely visible, were second-story windows, some with open shutters. If she could. . . .

She spun into shadow and balled up, blade ready. A shape loomed out of the night, headed her way. Shaghûn! Were they all on patrol?

He passed just ten feet away. Narriman held her breath. What were they doing? Looking for her? Or was her fear wholly egotistical?

There was a six-foot-wide breezeway between the nursery and the building to its left. A stairway climbed the neighbor. A landing hung opposite a nursery window. Narriman secreted her possessions beneath the stair and crept upward. The stair creaked. She scarcely noticed. She could think of nothing but Misr.

The window was open. It was but a short step from the landing. She straddled the railing.

Someone opened the door to which the stair led. Light flooded the landing. A fat man asked, "Here, you. What's?. . . "

Narriman slashed at him. He grabbed her blade. Off balance, she almost fell. She clung to the railing. It creaked. She jumped for the window.

The fat man staggered, reached for her, ploughed through the railing. Narriman clung to the window's frame and looked down. The man lay twitching below. "Karkur, don't let him raise the alarm."

The room before her was dark. A child mumbled something. Behind Narriman, a woman called a question. Narriman eased into the room.

The child was not Misr.

Someone shrieked. Narriman glanced outside. A woman stood on the landing, looking down.

Narriman slipped into a hallway running past other bedrooms. Which one? Might as well start with the nearest.

She found her son in the fifth room she checked. He was sleeping peacefully. His face looked angelic. He seemed healthy. She threw herself on him, weeping, and remained lost within herself till she realized he was awake.

"Mama! What're you doing here?" Misr hugged her with painful ferocity. He cried too. She was glad. Her most secret fear had been that he would have forgotten her.

"I came to take you home."

"Where's Grandpa?"

"Home. Waiting for us. Come on."

"The man, Mama. The dark man. He won't let us." He started shaking. His body was hale but they had done something to his mind.

"He won't stop us, Misr. I won't let him. Get dressed. Hurry." People were talking in the hall.

Misr did as he was told. Slowly.

Someone shoved through the doorway. "What's going on?. . . "

Narriman's saber pricked his throat. "Over there."

"A woman? Who are you?"

She pressed the sword's tip a quarter inch into his chest. "I'll ask. You answer." He shut up and moved. Small children watched from the doorway. "How many shaghûns in this town?"

He looked strange. He did not want to answer. Narriman pricked him. "Four! But one went to the lumber camp three weeks ago. He hasn't come back. You're the boy's sister?"

"Misr, will you hurry?" Four shaghûns. But one was out of town and another was dead. A third roamed the streets. Was hers the fourth?

"You can't take the boy out of here, woman."

She pricked him again. "You talk too much. Misr!"

"He belongs to the Old Ones."

Misr finished and looked at her expectantly.

Now what? Go out the way she had come? She stepped behind her prisoner and hit him with her pommel. He sagged. Misr's eyes got big. She dragged him toward the hallway. He told the other children, "I'm going home with my mother." He sounded proud.

She was amazed at how he had grown. He acted older, too. No time for that. "Come here." She tossed him across to the landing, jumped, hurried him downstairs. She recovered her belongings.

The fat man's woman howled all the while. "Shut up!" The woman retreated, whimpering.

Narriman looked into the street. People were gathering. "Misr. This way." She withdrew into the breezeway. "A horse," she muttered. "Where do I find a horse?"

She was about to leave the breezeway when she heard someone running. "Get back, Misr. And be quiet." She crouched.

The runner turned into the breezeway. Shaghûn! He tried to stop. Narriman drove her blade into his chest. He staggered back. She struck again. This was the shaghûn who had missed her earlier.

She smiled grimly. Succeed or fail, they would remember her.

"Come on, Misr." People were shouting to her right. She headed left, though that was not the direction she preferred. Misr ran beside her. She searched her dream memories for a stable. She did not find one.

Hope of escape came out of a walking dream that hit like a fist, made her stumble.

Karkur wanted her to go eastward. There was a road through the mountains. They would not expect her to flee that way. If she reached the seacoast she could go north and recross the mountains at Sebil el Selib, where the Masters held no sway.

But this end of that road ran around the dread tower of her dreams. Who knew what the Masters would do? If their shaghûns were but shadows of themselves, how terrible might they be?

She was afraid but she did not stop moving. Karkur had not failed her yet.

And Karkur was right. It *was* the best way. She saw no one, and no one saw her. And the dark tower greeted her with an indifference she found almost disheartening. Was she that far beneath their notice? She had slain two of their shaghûns.

"Keep walking, Misr. We're going to get tired, but we have to keep walking. Otherwise the dark men will catch us."

His face puckered in determination. He stayed with her. The sun was high before she decided to rest.

XU

"Narriman!" The voice boomed through the forest, rang off the mountains. "Narriman!" There was an edge of anger to it, like hers when she was impatient with Misr.

It was him. He had not been deceived.

Misr snuggled closer. "Don't let him take me, Mama."

"I won't," she promised, disentangling herself. "I'll be back in a little while."

"Don't go away, Mama."

"I have to. You stay put. Just remember what happened last time you didn't do what I said." Damn! That was unfair. He would think the whole thing was his fault. She spat, strung her bow. Selected three good arrows, made sure her other weapons were ready. Then she went to hunt.

"Narriman!" He was closer. Why act as if he couldn't find her?

Karkur, of course. That old lump did not dare smash things up in the Jebal. He would not want his hand seen. But he could confuse his enemies.

Brush crackled. Narriman froze. He was close. She sank into a patch of shade, arrow on bowstring.

"Narriman!" His voice boomed. More softly, he talked to himself. "Damned crazy woman. I'll use her hide to bind books." His anger was hard but controlled. Fear wriggled through Narriman's hatred.

Memories flashed. His ride down Wadi al Hamamah. Her rape. The day he had come for Misr. Her knees weakened. He was a shaghûn. He had conquered her easily. She was a fool to challenge him.

Brush crackled ever closer. She saw something white moving among the trees. His horse. That was him. Coming right to her.

There he was. Black rider. Nightmare lover. Misr's father. She pictured Mowfik and Al Jahez. "You!" she breathed. "For what you did to my father."

A twig snapped as she bent her bow. The horse's head snapped up, ears pricking. Her arrow slammed into its throat. It should have struck the shaghûn's heart.

The animal kept rising into a screaming rear, hooves pounding air. The rider went over backward. Narriman heard his breath explode when he hit ground.

Up she sprang. She let fly again. Her shaft passed though his djellaba as he rolled, pinned him for a second. In that second Narriman loosed her last arrow.

It glanced off his hip bone, leaving a bloody gash across his right buttock. He stumbled a step, fell, regained his feet with a groan.

Narriman drew her saber, stalked forward. Her mind boiled with all she wanted to say before she killed him.

He regained control, drew his own blade. A strained smile crossed his lips.

Narriman moved in carefully. I'll attack to his right, she thought. Make him put more strain on his wound. He's battered and bleeding. He'll be slow. I can wear him down.

"Little Fox. Little fool. Why did you come here? Outsiders don't come into the Jebal. Not and leave again."

There'll be a first, then, she thought. But she did not speak. Things she wanted to say rattled through her mind, but not one reached her lips. Her approach was as silent and implacable as his preceding her rapes.

She threw three hard, quick strokes. He turned them, but looked disturbed. She was not supposed to do this, was she? She was supposed to fall under his spell.

"Narriman! Look at me!"

She was caught by the command. She met his eye.

The fire ran through her. She ached for him. And to her surprise, she ignored it. She struck while his guard was loose, opened a gash on his cheek.

He went pale. His eyes grew larger. He could not believe it.

She struck again. He blocked her, thrust back, nearly reached her. He knew he was not dealing with a little girl anymore.

He beat her back, then retreated. A weird keening came from him, though his lips did not move. Leaves stirred. A cold wind rose. The tip of

Narriman's saber drooped like a candle in the sun. She shifted it to her left hand, pulled her dagger and threw it. Mowfik had taught her that.

The dagger struck the shaghûn in the left shoulder, spun him. The cold wind died. Narriman moved in with her odd-looking saber. Fear filled the shaghûn's eyes.

He plucked the dagger from his wound and made those sounds again. His wounds began to close.

Surprise had been Narriman's best weapon. Fate had stolen that. She feared she had more than she could handle now.

She launched a furious attack. He retreated, stumbled, fell. She cut him several times before he rose.

But he had his confidence back. She could not kill him. He smiled. Arrow, saber, and dagger. She had exhausted her options. She did have poison. Would he step up and take it? She had a garrote given her by one of Al Jahez's men, half a love-offering and half a well-wish. But would he hold still while she used it?

Brush crackled. She whirled. "Misr, I told you. . . ."

That shaghûn smashed into her, knocked her saber away. His fingers closed around her chin and forced her to turn toward him.

XUI

Lost! she wailed inside. She should have listened to Al Jahez and Mowfik. The fire was in her again and she could not stop him. He stripped her slowly, taking pleasure in her humiliation.

He pressed her down on the stones and pines needles and stood over her, smiling. He disrobed slowly. And Misr stood there watching, too terrified to move.

Tears streaming, Narriman forced her eyes shut. She had been so close! One broken twig short.

She felt him lower himself, felt him probe, felt him enter. Felt herself respond. Damn, she hated him!

She found enough hatred to shove against his chest. But only for an instant. Then he was down upon her again, forcing her hands back against her breasts. "Karkur," she wept.

The shaghûn moaned softly, stopped bucking. His body stiffened. He pulled away. The spell binding Narriman diminished.

"The Great Death!" she breathed.

It had him, but he was fighting it. Amber wriggled over him, flickering. There were few bloody veins in it. His mouth was open as though to scream, but he was gurgling a form of his earlier keening.

Narriman could not watch.

It did not occur to her that a mere shaghûn, even a shaghûn of the Jebal, could overcome Karkur's Great Death. He was but stalling the inevitable. She crawled to her discarded clothing.

Misr said something. She could not look at him. Her shame was too great.

"Mama. *Do* something."

She finally looked. Misr pointed.

The shaghûn's face was twisted. The muscles of his left arm were knotted. The bone was broken. But there was just one patch of amber left, flickering toward extinction.

He had bested the Great Death!

A silent wail of fear filled her. There was no stopping him! Raging at the injustice, she seized a dead limb and clubbed him. Misr grabbed a stick and started swinging too.

"Misr, stop that."

"Mama, he hurt you."

"You stop. I can do it but you can't." Did that make sense? I can murder him but you can't? No. Some things could not be explained. "Get away."

She swung again. The shaghûn tried to block with his injured arm. He failed. The impact sent him sprawling. The Great Death crept over him. She hit him again.

He looked at her with the eyes of the damned. He did not beg, but he did not want to die. He stared. There was no enchantment in his eyes. They contained nothing but fear, despair, and, maybe, regret. He was no shaghûn now. He was just a man dying before his time.

The club slipped from her fingers. She turned back, collected her clothes. "Misr, let's get our things." For no reason she could appreciate, she recalled Al Jahez's words about severed heads.

She collected the shaghûn's sword, considered momentarily, then gave him the mercy he had denied her.

"You killed him, Mama. You really killed him." Misr was delighted.

"Shut up!"

She could have closed her eyes to his screams, but his dying face would have haunted her forever. It might anyway.

When all else was stripped away, he had been a man. And once a mother had wept for him while a dark rider had carried him toward the rising sun.

Misr Sayed bin Hammad al Muburaki, the Hammer of God, would become a major player in desert politics in the later Dread Empire novels, just as Sadhra prophesied.

WINTER'S DREAMS

"Winter's Dreams" is an odd artifact of my creative career. Strange as it is/as it might be, this story takes place in in a weird corner of the otherwise unique universe of the novel I believe to be my best, The Dragon Never Sleeps. *There is no connection to anyone or anything presented in that novel, whatsoever.*

1

The light of three racing moons drenched the smoky city. Silver shadows schooled lazily amongst crowded spires and steeples and minarets, making the gargoyles appear to stir and stretch. Mist crept through the narrow, torturous alleys and streets, heavy with odors foul and sweet. The air scarcely stirred. Tall black prayer banners rose toward the weary stars, swaying like kelp beneath a gentle sea.

A broad-winged shadow wheeled like a hunting moth, began a circumspect descent that seemed to ignore but never moved out of sight of a certain open window high in the city's tallest tower. The separation dwindled. Then ceased to exist.

An indeterminate form perched on the windowsill, wrapped in its own darkness. The city was silent but a deeper stillness gathered 'till it seemed a clash of cymbals would not dare speak louder than a whisper.

The darkness stole inside. A faint, cracking acetylene light tickled the necks of the grey towers facing the window. The gargoyles stirred uneasily.

2

The room was cramped with gaunt, pallid, hand-wringing men in black, few of whom had any business being there. Functionaries and menials, there was not a fat cell among them. Senior Magician Ymarjon Shredlu thought they resembled nothing so much as a brood of devoutly terrified mantids.

"What's wrong with her?" a reedy voice demanded.

Shredlu glanced at the only fat man present. "I've only just arrived, my lord. But as a preliminary I suggest she be allowed more air."

Lord Everay Sloot shooed retainers. They continued to hold their long, bony hands before them as they retreated, robes flapping like raven's wings. Agitated whispers stirred like the soft rustle of trampled leaves. They sensed trouble.

Lord Everay continued to bluster and throw his weight around. Though not half so imposing a figure himself Shredlu ignored the man. He concentrated on Sloot's daughter.

Everay Ake Winter was a golden child-goddess, a throwback to the Star Walkers, perfectly proportioned, at fifteen summers swiftly approaching the peak of her beauty. The Everays bred stronger by the generation. Already Winter outshone her mother's best.

Master Shredlu hardened the shell round the spark he was amazed to discover still dwelt within him. There was a fierce and alien taint to the air; a smell of something from the Old Times. It troubled him deeply, as though he recognized it down on some near-instinctive level like an almost-forgotten fear-fragrance from early childhood. He rested the tips of the central pair of fingers on his right hand upon Winter's forehead, each an inch above the eye. He shut his own eyes to the gothic splendor surrounding him.

An electric tingle climbed his arm. "Uhm! Tackoo?"

"What?" Everay demanded. "What is it? Is she in danger?" Winter was his beloved and overly indulged daughter. In keeping with tradition, she carried his successor already, conceived within the fortnight, with the Senior and Master Magicians chaperoning the rut to guarantee the quickening of a son. Though he saw it every generation, Shredlu did not enjoy witnessing those couplings. But it was essential to the stability of the domain.

Shredlu paid Lord Everay no mind The man was fatter, but weak. Shredlu turned Winter's head slightly. In profile she resembled her mother more strongly. He beckoned his apprentice. "Shubam. Razor and soap. Quickly."

"Instantly, master."

"What is it?" Everay demanded. He indulged Shredlu's moods. Shredlu had been around a long time.

"A moment more, my lord." Shredlu stepped to the window. The alien scent was stronger. He stared out at the grey towers while brushing the sill with the spatulate fingertips of his left hand. The sensitive cells there picked up more of the musk and a strong, ugly taste.

Perhaps the auguries were overly optimistic. Of the thousand futures foreseen for Winter only a scatter in the far estuaries of probability shone brightly.

Apprentice Shubam announced proudly, "Razor, hot water, towels, and shaving lather, master." Shivering, Shredlu turned. His face betrayed nothing. He considered Shubam. The boy was enthusiastic but sloppy—despite knowing what had befallen his predecessor. He had cut no corners with so weighty a witness present, though. The razor was sharp, the towels and water hot, and the lather were of a precisely calculated temperature and consistency. Shubam did well when he concentrated.

Shredlu turned Winter's head farther. "Hold her there, Shubam. Gently!" He daubed lather. Lord Everay continued to fuss but stayed out of the way. Shredlu did not listen. He was old enough to entertain doubts that weight and condition of birth bestowed divinity.

It took just two small strokes of the straight razor to confirm his fears. "Clean her," he told Shubam, dropping the razor into the water. "My lord, she hasn't fallen into a coma at all. A tackoo came in the night."

"Spare me any witchmaster's obfuscations, Shredlu. Speak only with precision and concision. What might a tackoo be?"

Shredlu maintained his bland exterior. Even an apprentice as raw as Shubam—who had gasped—knew, though no tackoo assault had been reported for generations. Magician's generations.

But the dark reaches of the world still harbored many nightmares from the Old Times. Shredlu summoned one or another himself occasionally.

"Tackoo. One of the Artifact Folk. A vampire of dreams. See the mark on her temple." That was a rusty hourglass an inch tall formerly concealed by Winter's hair. "It took her dreams. Now she is trapped in a sleep where no dreams occur. If she does not dream, she cannot awaken as Everay Ake Winter." Shredlu straightened a strand of golden hair, then thumbed open an eyelid, exposing an empty blue iris. It was not necessary for Sloot to know she could be wakened as something else. "My lord. It's going to be a long siege amongst the books."

Lazy Shubam made a whimpering sound.

3

In private, Lord Everay Sloot seldom betrayed the impatience and petulance so often demonstrated before an audience. Shredlu suspected the public Sloot of being a pose. Indeed, he suspected Lord Everay wore several personas, onionlike; the real man might never be found by peeling. Shredlu did not let Sloot concern him overly much. One day he would be replaced by the yet unborn Vonce. Sloot waited quietly while Shredlu consulted his library. Shredlu instructed Shubam who directed a covey of raven men who made haste to comply, lashed on by Lord Everay's unforgiving gaze.

Shredlu sketched a gesture with his right little finger. The light went out of the book before him. It closed itself.

"Magician?"

"This is a matter best not discussed in every pantry and alleyway, my lord."

"As ever, your advice is without flaw, Shredlu. All of you, leave us."

Shredlu nodded at Shubam, who seemed uncertain if the directive extended to himself. Alone with Sloot, Shredlu announced, "My memory betrayed me only in the details, my lord. Tackoo do, indeed, dote on a relish of stolen dreams. They are among the oldest of the Artifact Folk. Literally. They do not die. Neither do they breed. There cannot be more than three left alive in this late age. Our night-visitor will have been the tackoo Syathbir Tolis."

"You put a name to the demon so swiftly?"

"Of the three tackoo known, at most recent report, to survive, only Syathbir Tolis has the capacity for flight. Tackoo are undoubtedly hardy, but I hesitate to credit that even the most resolute non-flyer could clamber past the wards and gargoyles to reach Winter's window."

"Why would even a flyer visit the child? Can her dreams be so much tastier than easier prey found far nearer the lurking places preferred by Old Time things?"

"A flyer would if it were conjured and constrained and placed under obligation."

"A Magician is responsible?"

"Such a conclusion is inevasible, my lord. Your reasoning is apt, no Old Time demon would descend upon us while easier prey is available closer to home. Someone selected Syathbir Tolis from the literature, then found it and bound it to his will. Tackoo appear to be dull of wit and, once located, easily manipulated."

"Who?" Sloot wondered aloud. "Why? I have no enemies."

"We all have enemies, my lord. Occasionally, our enemies do not declare themselves publicly. Often we find the source of their rancor inaccessible or obscure. I suggest we concentrate instead upon freeing Winter, knowing that quest will certainly expose your enemies."

"There is hope?" Sloot brightened. He did love his daughter in more than a carnal manner, as a vessel for the Everay seed, far more than he ever loved their mother.

"The tackoo is a vampire of dreams but seldom a destroyer or vandal. They cherish and keep them. They can be reclaimed. They can be restored. Unless your enemy is so virulent he has compelled Syathbir Tolis to repudiate his very nature. I choose not to believe this is possible."

"What is accomplished by this blow? Vonce resides in her womb already. The progression cannot be interrupted . . . She will not perish of this, will she?"

"She will go on as one in a coma. For however long her allotted span. The cruel truth, though, is that Vonce will enter the world with no dreams, either. The Everay progression can be maintained but you will be the last to think and rule."

Shredlu saw the suspicion poison Everay's thoughts. Sloot's eyes narrowed. They became evasive as he examined the possibility that his enemy was his own Senior Magician, bent on rule through a progression of empty-minded puppets.

"Not I, my lord," Shredlu said. Not this time.

"What will you do next?"

"Locate Syathbir Tolls. The tackoo is the key."

"Find him. Be not retiring in assessing his chastisement."

"Fear not, my lord. Rue and woe. Rue and woe betide."

Shredlu watched as Lord Everay waddled out of the library. Sloot was lost in thought, perhaps reflecting on the strange circumstances that had made him master of Everay a generation before his time.

He was not deep and persistent. Thought would abandon him once he reached the pleasures of the bath and seraglio.

4

Not all Artifacts and Old Timers were confined to the shadowed reaches of the world. Only those whose aspect offended or whose talents terrified and who were not otherwise useful on a regular basis. And those considered too dangerous to Real People. Shredlu saw several of them as he passed through the domestics' corridors. They did not see him. Not even the guards. He wore an illusion supplementing their natural disinclination to see the thing that did not belong. They felt him. They moved out of his path, puzzledly, though even under torture they would recall with certainty nothing concrete.

Shredlu returned to the principal hallways for the final approach to his destination. Manners forbid making his entrance like a servant. He scratched at the appropriate door, waited patiently. She would come when it became clear he would not go away. Someone might pass and remark upon his presence.

Lady Everay Non Ethan appeared beautifully serene when she opened the door herself, more swiftly than Shredlu anticipated. She had prepared herself to receive company. Elegantly gowned and coifed and bejewelled, she appeared a regal vision of Winter, tall, lithe, blonde, her forty-six summers unbetrayed by cunningly engineered lighting. "Shredlu. Will you stand there gawking 'till some roving band of functionaries tramples you?"

The Magician stepped forward. "You surprised me, Ethan. You were waiting."

"Am I so isolated and deaf that alarums and tumults fail to reach me entirely? I hear Winter's name whispered when they think I cannot hear. What disaster has befallen the child so soon after her cheerless nuptials? Has she been laid low by melancholy, like her mother before her?"

Ethan confused melancholy with bitterness, Shredlu feared. Her bottomless well of bitterness was the principal reason he came visiting so seldom anymore. "She is laid low but wicked magic was the agent. Someone sent a tackoo to steal her dreams." His gaze swept the decadence around him. Ethan certainly made Everay pay for her participation in its progression.

"How could that be? Tackoo and dorado and the gell people . . . They're nightfears you Magicians made up so you can extort a livelihood from the rest of us."

She did not believe that. It was a play-argument from a time when there had been less cool between them.

"This is no game, Ethan. A determined and abiding malice has turned its countenance upon Everay. The weight of its animosity is being born by Winter but it is not she who won the motivating hatred. She's never been out of the tower."

"Perhaps she has an enemy inside. Tuft Yarramal springs to mind. Yarramal hates everyone."

Shredlu examined the proposition from obscure and descant angles. Tuft Yarramal did indeed hate everyone but only as a mannered attitude. Nor did Yarramal hate herself enough to devise her own destruction. "It is a thought, Ethan. I shall consult Yarramal."

"Will you go without so much as touching me?"

"My time is no longer my own. I came as a courtesy, to inform you, to caution you."

"Caution me?"

"Catastrophe has struck once. Forewarned, we need not let it slide into our midst again." Shredlu surveyed his surroundings once more. He turned to the door.

"Don't go."

He steeled himself against her loneliness. "I must. I must reclaim Winter's dreams."

He was gone before she whispered, "And what of Ethan's dreams?"

5

In addition to Senior Magician Ymarjon Shredlu and his varying apprentices, Everay employed Master Magicians Rolo Kintrude and Aleas Dubbing, their several apprentices and Journeyman Magician Tuft Yarramal. Yarramal was the sole female in the magical establishment. She subscribed to none of the purported feminine weaknesses, she considered all soft emotions vices. Shredlu suspected she would become a Master at an early age and a threat to his position, if not his person, soon afterward.

The Magicians and their followings assembled in Shredlu's laboratory in response to his summons. He observed a shadow as they awaited his pleasure, unaware of his presence. Kintrude and Dubbing remained near the entrance, in an area plainly devoid of pitfalls, managing their impatience and that of their companions. They did nothing to temper the curiosities of Tuft Yarramal, however. Yarramal prowled the aisles between Shredlu's worktables and curio cabinets, here picking up an alembic full of gangrenous ichor, there a moldy book with an angel's feather as a bookmark. Never a word of caution crossed the lips of the Masters. Perhaps they hoped Yarramal stumbled into something. They had no love for her.

Shredlu noted carefully which particulars attracted Yarramal most strongly. He had shut down most of his little protections, partly as courtesy, partly to allow Yarramal's overconfidence to build to the point where she would take the one step too many if the impulse seized her.

Shubam made his entrance on cue, fawning obsequious to the Masters and haughty toward their companions. The lad looked like he was gaining weight on a diet little better than bark tea and gravel. He might find that proclivity a greater source of embarrassment than his inclination toward sloppiness.

Yarramal poked a finger into a case displaying several ancient tintinabula, one of which was said to have come from beyond the stars on one of the ships that brought the First Fold before the beginning of the Old Times. Yarramal did not subscribe to the theory that Real People were not native to this world. She believed all evidence supporting extraterrestrial origins to have been manufactured . . .

A distinct *clack* reverberated throughout the laboratory. Yarramal yipped in surprise. She tried to withdraw her hand from the display. The case ignored her desire. Shredlu noted that she neither panicked nor yielded to an impulse to implore aid of Kintrude and Dubbing. With her free hand, she rolled up her sleeves and began to experiment.

Yarramal remained unaware of Shredlu's presence 'till he reached past and probed the case with the elongated digit of his right hand. The catch devil recognized him and accepted his admonition against further restraining nosy journeymen. Shredlu said nothing, words had little impact upon Tuft Yarramal. He joined the Masters. Yarramal followed.

Shredlu spoke straightforwardly. "Winter's state is the result of a predatory visitation by the tackoo Syathbir Tolis. There can be no doubt on this point. The tackoo's present whereabouts must be determined. An expedition must be mounted to collect the miscreant so that we may inquire into the causes of its remarkable behavior. To this end, we will now pool our knowledge and resources, reserving nothing, for we have already staked our reputations upon the welfare of the Everay domain."

Kintrude nodded. Dubbing employed all six fingers of his right hand in a gesture indicating absolute agreement. Only Tuft Yarramal disdained demonstration.

Shredlu issued his instructions, Rolo Kintrude to hunt the craggy wastelands to the west; Aleas Dubbing in all his skill to search the haunted forests to the north. The Senior would employ his own powers seeking Syathbir Tolis in the ugly fens and marshes and swamps to the east, known to be a favorite retreat of the more dark and insane Artifact Folk. Tuft Yarramal would examine the registers of Magicians and associated castes in an effort to determine the most probable villains in the case. She could not handle the south; nothing lay in that quarter but a cold, grey heaving ocean.

"We shall gather here again in four hours," Shredlu announced. "I shall provide a banquet. We will plan our expedition."

6

Nervously, Shubam took down the panels concealing the adonnai orden, each a five foot by seven painting in the neoclassical representationalist mode pioneered by Wensby Strait. Each cast a mythological creature against some well-known attractions outside the city. But for one latecomer by Everay Non Ethan, the paintings reminded himself not to be rigidly intolerant of others' infatuations. Time tended to suppress the inessential and pretentious.

The features of six olive drab faces filled the spaces once covered by the panels, each taller between lip and eye than was Shredlu between head and toe. The adonnai slept, kerchiefs and mist wisps of ectoplasmic matter darting and larking in their breaths, into their nostrils and out again, to buzz out across the world like worker bees, harvesting the pollen of secrets. Shredlu considered them for several minutes. There were no immediately apparent differences between the six. All would be equally testy if awakened. All harbored an unreasonable resentment over being bound to his service. He had provided the ingrates a warm and secure place to sleep.

"Shubam, have you carried out my instructions?"

"Yes, master." Shubam was a lad of few words, unlike the run of apprentices, who seemed to have automated the hinges of their jaws.

"Then take the table to the very end." He would begin with Xyyzyx, the least tractable of the adonnai. If by clever badinage and cunning evasion he compelled Shredlu to waken a second adonnai, more animosity would be directed Xyyzyx's way than Shredlu's. The adonnai resented one another more than any other entity. Shubam positioned the wheeled table. Shredlu stepped up. His apprentice had failed to overlook any items and had positioned all with absolute precision. Shubam had heard rumors about the fate of his disorderly predecessor. Adonnai featured largely in every version. Adonnai did not restrain their irrational rancor when tempted by lax preliminary work.

"Excellent, Shubam. Would you care to cast the invoking incantations?" They were simple enough.

"Master, I would prefer not to enjoy my first exercise with Xyyzyx."

"Very well, I will not insist." Time was passing. Scarcely two hours before the Everay Magicians assembled. As he commenced the awakening, Shredlu asked, "Has anyone approached you about our work here? Particularly about our current course of experiments?"

"No, master." Shubam stirred nervously, warily keeping Shredlu between himself and Xyyzyx.

"Has no one shown any curiosity at all? Tuft Yarramal, perhaps?"

"I have never, to my recollection, spoken directly to the Journeyman."

"Excellent. I urge you to persist in your neglect."

"Thou pestilent Ymarjon," Xyyzyx boomed. "I will not ask thee why thou disturbest mine slumbers. I have anticipated thine importunities. Thou art, in point of fact, tardy in launching them."

The huge olive face opened its eyes. They proved to be the most human of the an's features, being vastly enlarged orbs identical to those of a brown-eyed man—'till ghosts began to wisp in and out of their pupils.

"You understand what moves me to trouble you?"

"Thou wishest to unravel the mysteries surrounding a theft of dreams."

"You know about that?" Shredlu was troubled. The adonnai were seldom so direct. Xyyzyx in particular preferred evasion and misdirection.

"Much escapes me. I spend my life in sleepy reverie."

Shredlu supposed it was too much to expect the adonnai to volunteer anything though it was obvious the Artifact was deeply concerned and quite possibly frightened—if such a creature could make the acquaintance of fear.

"Thou needs must ask the right questions, Ymarjon Shredlu."

It could not shake its nature completely. Shredlu asked questions. Scores upon scores of questions. He studied the huge olive face with every one, taking clue from its swift play of expression whether he pursued the correct will-o'-the wisp. Xyyzyx was doing his best to communicate. This fact continued to impress Shredlu.

In response to a particular inquiry, Xyyzyx replied, "Thou art more intuitive than most would suspect, Ymarjon Shredlu. The call for the tackoo did indeed originate within the Everay domain. Sadly no adonnai can identify the source with precision." Shredlu noted five more pairs of adonnai eyes open and turned his way, though he had done nothing to conjure them forth from their sleep. "The thing was done clumsily, though. As thou hast noted secretly. A lack of skill was revealed both in the summoning itself, and in the concealment of the source and nature of the summons."

The attack originated within the Everay domain and was directed against the Everay domain. If Winter failed to dream, it would be but a few generations till the Everay progression concluded.

"You have placed me deeply into your debt," Shredlu confessed.

"Swift recompense of obligations is urged by all great thinkers. Strike while the mood of generosity is yet upon thee. Let down these prisoning walls."

Shredlu chuckled. "Where is the tackoo Syathbir Tolis? One suspects your reveries might have touched upon this matter."

"Indeed. It was an intriguing task. The tackoo's slow wits reached the inevitable conclusion only after it was too late to desist or recant."

"I presume the tackoo eventually converted to the doctrine that his only hope of salvation lay in hiding. That being what he is, he has long had several refuges prepared."

"Thou art intelligent. For a mere man." The adonnai Xyzzyx's grin exposed hideously deformed teeth. Ghosts fluttered in and out of its sparkling eyes. It was prepared to bargain hard.

7

Master Magician Aleas Dubbing declared, "The tackoo Syathbir Tolls failed to make himself evident in my quarter of the compass. Sources available, however, suggested he might be located by an investigator who turned his eye upon the Dustrake Reach of the Lesser Miasmatic Swamps."

"A suggestion in substantial agreement with my own conclusions," Shredlu said. "Kintrude?"

"I found considerable consternation on all levels Outside. Syathbir Tolis is nowhere amongst the Wastes. Outsider rumor reliably places him within the Lesser Miasmatics."

The tackoo appeared to have confused no one. "Yarramal? Have you contradictory evidence?"

"None such was to be found within the registers, even of a caste so remote and narrow as the Necromancers."

A caste of one, which consisted of Shredlu's cousin the freelance charlatan Ousted Delf. Shredlu was confident Yarramal had made her own locational inquiries. "Did you find a name that can be attached to this dream-theft villainy?"

"None whatsoever, Senior." She frowned thoughtfully, as though taking a last look at a decision already made. "Perhaps it is irrational or unreliable intuition, Senior, but I have arrived at a conviction this crime germinated inside the Everay domain, probably within this very tower, possibly close to the child."

"Substantially my own assessment. Shubam. I see you have returned. Have you extended the invitations?"

"Yes, master."

"And the airmen?"

"They have been alerted; His Lordship expects to launch a spontaneous picnic foray."

"Excellent. You outdo yourself in these times of crisis, Shubam. We shall have to reward you by adding to your duties."

"My gratitude knows no bounds, master."

Shredlu could only suspect that Shubam was being less than honest. "Come, then. Let us be off . . . Shubam. You did send to the kitchen for appropriate provisions?"

"I did, master."

Yarramal asked, "We are going out to the Miasmatics?"

"It will make a wonderful afternoon excursion."

"It occurs to me that your plan puts all the domain's Magicians in the same place at the same time."

"It does indeed. And one of us may be the villain of the piece. The black-guard may be hoping for this eventuality. A grave risk. Which of us should remain behind?" Shredlu chuckled. There was a dearth of volunteers, it being evident that suspicion would surround whoever held back.

It would be an interesting journey as each prepared for the worst while pretending to share a social jaunt. "I think we need not take our apprentices. Come. Time flees." He strode forth, snatching his cloak and staff from Shubam as he passed. He offered the apprentice a sharp look. Winter would be his responsibility in his master's absence. Winter would be a test.

8

The airmen had brought the sky yacht *Vangier*, there would be no sneaking into the Dustrake Reach. In any event, it would have to do. There was no time to cover its gaudy paintwork. Lesser craft could not transport the entire party. Nor could he keep an eye on everyone if they scattered amongst several smaller vessels. And it was a picnic, after all.

The picnickers assembled upon the airmen's promenade, eighty levels up Everay Prime. Rolo Kintrude and Aleas Dubbing stood together, conversing in low tones. Tuft Yarramal stood apart, introspective, as was her wont. Lord Everay Sloot stood between his mother, Everay Non Ethan, and grandmother, Everay Tak Arone. In the cruel light of afternoon it was difficult to distinguish which woman was the younger. They did not chat. The Everays had little to say to one another, ever.

The airmen cursed one another as they wrestled *Vangier* into position for boarding. A breeze made the ship difficult to manage. Nevertheless, they performed their task and the picnickers boarded without a festive face among them. Senior Airman Mug Rusale barely waited 'till the boarding steps cleared. *Vangier* sprang upward; grey towers began to slide away underneath. Mists and smoke concealed the streets way down below.

It was an hour's flight to the Lesser Miasmatics. The picnickers remained disposed as before, a group of three, a pair, two alone. Only Kintrude and Dubbing had a word to share and that quite seldom. No one attempted to probe Shredlu's intentions. Questions might bestir presumptions of guilt.

Xyyzyx and his family had been of incomplete assistance in determining the identity of the person responsible for the attack on Winter. Reason and information gathered argued that the villain had to be aboard the sky yacht. Shredlu was inclined to suspect Tuft Yarramal but could not fathom a motive.

As the yacht approached the Miasmatics, the sky outside filled with bizarre creatures more colorful than the airboat itself. The largest of these was an orange-bellied, blue-backed pseudopteronodon with a wicked and intelligent eye. "Hemmaus?" Yarramal asked from behind Shredlu. "It fits the deamon's description."

"Hemmaus," Shredlu agreed. "We have done business before. A dangerous entity, Hemmaus. Intelligent, unpredictable and occasionally treacherous. In no sense should you ever show him your back. But he is a powerful ally when it suits his humor."

A score of Hemmaus' lesser cousins larked around like flickering confetti.

The sky yacht descended. Mug Rusale regaled himself with imprecations, critiquing his own performance. The swamp began to impinge upon more than the eye; its odor, then sound, penetrated the cabin of the airship. The odor alone sufficed to convince even the slowest wit that the wetlands were appropriately named.

Shredlu directed Mug Rusale to a particular stretch of Dustrake Reach. Several thousand acres of vegetation were of a uniform green so dark it verged upon the black. That sprawl consisted of a single million-trunked nedereyya tree harboring an ecology all its own.

Rusale excoriated the yacht for its sudden inclination to proceeded in a nose-down attitude.

Dubbing and Kintrude had come forward. Dubbing asked, "The tackoo is hiding in the canopy there?"

"So my sources indicate. What of yours?"

Both Master Magicians nodded. Shredlu examined them closely. Neither seemed distressed by the swiftness with which the hunt was closing in on Winter's tormentor, not that either would have given himself away easily. Each *was* a master.

Mug Rusale found a bit of solid ground convenient to the vast tree, brought *Vangier* to earth.

Shredlu attended to his host's duties immediately. With the aid of Mug Resale he set up tables and chairs, put out insect repellers on poles at a distance of fifteen feet. There were no protests and no urgings to get on with it. Great stakes were on the board; caution was indicated. Yarramal and Rusale brought out the picnic baskets. Shredlu served a rare wine from his own stock. Lord Everay commented favorably, the first he had spoken since boarding *Vangier*.

Shredlu cast the occasional glance toward the nedereyya, at Hemmaus wheeling high above. Unless he had been anticipated, something would happen soon.

Shadows were long and purple when the swamp suddenly grew raucous with the approach of Hemmaus' smallest cousins. Their reptilian barks and hisses and squalls swept back and forth behind concealing foliage. Shredlu was pleased. Lord Everay's patience had grown lean. Much longer and he would have demanded an end to the outing.

A black butterfly silhouette sprang up against the rosy lilac sky, fluttering in panic. Hemmaus' cousins darted around it. It shifted directions with greater facility than its tormentors, but they had numbers. Where one was outmaneuvered, another flashed in.

With a line of sight established, Shredlu could now bend his own will upon the tackoo. He drew it in, struggling like a fish reluctant to leap into the pan. Shredlu brought it to a perch upon one of the picnic tables. It quivered in terror, surrounded by Real Men. Above Hemmaus' cousins hastened toward their aeries. Night was falling. Darkness would summon forth creatures less condign than they.

Hemmaus himself called down an admonition for Shredlu to mind his debts faithfully.

Shredlu responded in the tongue favored by the flying Artifacts. He always discharged his obligations. Were that not true, Xyyzyx would not have arranged events so that Syathbir Tolis joined the Everay picnickers.

Rolo Kintrude said, "Senior, we should, perhaps, consider going home. Already the night grows aware of our presence."

Shredlu felt it himself. "Rusale, load the sky yacht. Yarramal, lend a hand." The Senior Magician remained close to Syathbir Tolls. He would not allow it out of his sight. He would remain artfully alert on levels natural and magical till he could isolate the creature within his laboratory. Never had the tackoo had another so concerned for his well-being.

Under other circumstances, an attack would not have been a disappointment. It would have exposed Winter's enemy and, perhaps, have defined what motivated such an evil assault. Under other circumstances, however,

Shredlu would have had a better notion whence trouble might come. At the moment, he trusted only Mug Rusale and, to a lesser extent, Lord Everay. His imagination was fertile: he could conceive of circumstances whereby Winter's bereavement would profit each of the others.

The entire party was so paranoid that not a sigh expired but every eye registered that fact and every brain sorted implications. Tension mounted as *Vangier* approached Everay Tower. Shredlu began to doubt his reasoning. Everyone seemed to be waiting for someone else to crack.

In the end it proved that he had been anticipated. Winter's enemy had no need to indulge in self-betrayal aboard the sky yacht. An ambush was in place at the dock. Its fellowship, however, were understandably apprehensive about the risks inherent in an attack upon the combined Magical masters of Everay. Nerves caused a premature tripping of the trap.

Events thenceforth were foreordained: the air howled with vortices of color, screams of despair were heard, prisoners were taken. Shredlu paused a moment to help Mug Rusale extinguish a scamp cantrip gnawing at a landing claw on the sky yacht.

Aleas Dubbing and Rolo Kintrude appeared a bit tattered. Tuft Yarramal smoldered at left hip and right elbow. Shredlu himself had taken no part once he determined that the others were adequate to squelch the tumult. He merely observed, hoping the behaviors of others would prove instructive.

Tuft Yarramal did not become involved till the ambushers, in despair, hurled their final efforts her way.

9

"I suspected Yarramal from the beginning," Shredlu announced in his laboratory. "Simply because she was most likely, in character. Shubam was a surprise, though. And the motives of all involved remain elusive." He considered his sullen apprentice, in restraints beside Yarramal. Shubam's motives became transparent instantly. Slothful ambition coupled with passion. And Yarramal's self-destructive behavior became less opaque when her glance fell, as it did often, upon Everay Non Ethan.

Rolo Kintrude and Aleas Dubbing were proficient readers of pregnant glances themselves. Not only did they discern the source of Everay dismay, they also read Shredlu's cautioning frown. Lord Everay would not hear a word of accusation against the woman who was both mother and sister, however much he detested her personally.

Particularly unfathomable were Ethan's motives for putting together the broad but inept conspiracy in the first place. What hatred could she possibly bear her own daughter? Successful, the plot would have meant the end of the Everay progression.

Senior Magician Ymarjon Shredlu oversaw the bringing together of mothlike Syathbir Tolis and Everay Ake Winter, resulting in the restoration of Winter's dreams. Then, with Winter her sparkling, cheerful self once more, none the worse for her misadventure and full of helpful suggestions and even lending a playful hand, he oversaw the punishment of the guilty. He thought a great deal about Ethan while he worked. He cherished what had been and now could never be again. He thought about the Everay progression. He worried about where he might find a teachable, tractable apprentice.

He was using them up at an alarming rate.

THE GOOD MAGICIAN

About ten years ago I enjoyed one of the great treats of my writerly life: George R. R. Martin asked me to create a story for inclusion in an anthology tribute to Jack Vance's seminal Dying Earth cycle. I squealed like a kid getting exactly what she wanted for Christmas. Figuring that most contributors would set their works in the age covered by the deservedly most beloved first book, I headed west and chose the time of Rhialto The Marvelous.

1

Alfaro Morag, who, in his own mind, styled himself The Long Shark of Dawn, rode his whirlaway high above a forest. Ahead lay the bloody glimmer of the Scaum and his destination, Boumergarth, where he meant to assume protection of a rare tome currently in the collection of Ildefonse the Preceptor. As a precaution against the likelihood that Ildefonse was not prepared to cooperate in the transfer, Alfaro had surrounded himself with Phandaal's Mantle of Stealth.

His desire was *The Book of Changes*, subtitled *Even the Beautiful Must Die*. All secrets of protracted vitality and unending youth were contained therein. The Preceptor's volume was the last known copy.

Ildefonse was unreasonably narrow about sharing. He would not allow *The Book of Changes* to be borrowed or copied, definitely an unenlightened attitude. Certainly Alfaro Morag had a right to review the spells therein. Surely he should have access to the formulae for puissant potions.

Such were Morag's thoughts as he peddled across the sky, ever more displeased with the Preceptor and his hidebound coterie, some of whom had been around since the sun was yellow, half its current size, and not nearly so far away. Those antiquities considered Alfaro Morag a pup, a whippersnapper, a come-lately interloper enslaved by impatience and lack of subtlety in acquiring properties he desired.

Bah! They just felt threatened by the refugee from somewhere so far south no local map revealed it.

Alfaro drifted right, left, up, down. How best to proceed? He spied a silhouette masking the sun, there so briefly he suspected it must be a time mirage. Yet he felt it was familiar.

He swung back, dancing on the breeze. He found the silhouette again, for seconds only. He had to climb to gain the right angle, up where pelgrane would soon cruise, watching the roads for unwary travelers as the last bloody light faded. Or for other things that flew: gruehawks and spent- owls. And whirlaways too small and primitive to be protected by more than a single spell.

Alfaro's machine could not be seen but made noise thrashing through the air. Morag himself shed odors proclaiming the presence of a delicious bounty.

Alfaro veered off Boumergarth. Shedding altitude, he hastened to his keep in the upper valley of a tributary of the Scaum, the Javellana Cascade. He touched down yards from the turbulent stream, pausing only long enough to assure that his whirlaway was anchored against mischievous breezes, then headed for the ladder to his front door. "Tihomir! I come! Bring my vovoyeur to the salon. Then prepare a suitable repast."

Tihomir appeared at the head of the ladder, a wisp of a man featuring sores and seborrheas wherever his skin could be seen, topped by a few strands of fine white hair. His skull had a dent in back and was flat on the right side. He resembled a sickly doppelganger of Alfaro and was, in fact, his unfortunate twin.

Tihomir assisted Alfaro as he stepped off the ladder. "Shall I pull the ladder up?"

"That might be best. It has the feel of an active night. Then get the vovoyeur."

Tihomir inclined his head. Alfaro often wondered what went on inside. Nothing complex, certainly.

Alfaro's tower was nowhere so grand as the palaces of the elder magicians of Ascolais. But it was inexpensive. It had been abandoned when he found it. He hoped to complete renovations within the year.

His salon on the third level doubled as his library. A library bereft of even one copy of Lutung Kasarung's masterwork, *The Book of Changes*. He took down several volumes uniformly bound in port wine leather, each fourteen inches tall and twenty-two wide, with gold embossing on faces and spines.

Cheap reproductions.

All Alfaro's books, saving a few acquired under questionable circumstance, were reproductions created in sandestin sweat shops far to the east. Those he chose tonight were collections of artwork, volumes I through IV and VI, of the fourteen volume set, *Famous Illustrations of Modern Aeons*. Six volumes were all Alfaro could afford, so far. Volume V never arrived.

He finished a quick search of volumes I and IV before Tihomir brought the vovoyeur. "Are the experiments proceeding correctly?"

"All is perfection. Though the miniscules are asking for more salt."

"They're robbers." Literally, actually. There had been a noticeable decline in the number of wayfarers and highwaymen since Alfaro's advent in Ascolais. He did not boast about it. He doubted that anyone had noticed. "Give them another dram. In the morning."

"They're also asking for brandy"

"As am I. Do we have any? If so, bring a bottle with the meal." Tihomir went. Morag lost himself in illustrations.

The one that fickle recollection insisted existed was in the last place he looked, the final illustration in Volume III.

"I thought so. It would be identical if the sun were behind me. And aeons younger."

He warmed the vovoyeur.

Strokes with a wooden spoon did not spark a response. More vigorous application of an iron ladle enjoyed no more success. Alfaro found himself tempted to suspect that he was being ignored.

Perhaps the Preceptor was too engrossed in his pleasures to respond. Irked, Alfaro selected a silver tuning fork. He struck the face of the far-seeing device a half dozen times while declaiming, "The Lady of the Gently Floating Shadows makes way for the Great Lady of the Night."

The surface of the vovoyeur brightened. A shape appeared. It might have been the face of a normally cheerful but time-worn man. Alfaro could not improve the clarity of his fourth-hand device. "Speak, Morag." Uncharacteristically brusque.

"See this illustration." Morag held the plate from Famous Illustrations to the vovoyeur. "Do you know this place?"

"I know it. To the point, Morag."

"I saw it this evening while enjoying an aerial jaunt above the Scaum."

"Not possible. That place was destroyed aeons ago."

"Even so, I spied it in a place where nothing stands. Where no one goes because of the haunts."

Silence stretched. Then the vovoyeur whispered, "It might be best to discuss this face to face. Tomorrow. I will instruct my staff to permit the approach of your whirlaway, so long as it remains visible."

"I shall follow your instructions precisely, Preceptor." Stated while reflecting that his vision had been a stroke of good fortune.

There were reasons the Ildefonses of these fading times persisted.

He examined the plate he had shown the Preceptor. There was no accompanying text, just a word: Moadel.

Alfaro searched his meager library for references to Moadel. He found none.

2

Alfaro dismounted from his whirlaway, bowed to Ildefonse while noting that his conveyance was neither the first nor even the tenth to grace the broad lawn at Boumergarth. He was surprised to be greeted by the Preceptor himself, but more surprised to find that he had been preceded by so many beings of peculiar aspect, magicians of Almery and Ascolais, all. Panderleou, evidently having arrived only moments ago, was haranguing Barbanikos and Ao of the Opals about his latest acquisition, a tattered copy of *The Day of the Cauldrons*. "Hear this from the second chapter. 'So they killed a thief and gave the best parts to Valmur, to hasten him on his way.'" Others present included Herark the Harbinger, Vermoulian the Dream-walker, Darvilk the Miianther, wearing the inevitable black domino, Gilgad, as always in red, Perdustin, Byzant the Necrope, and Haze of Wheary Water with a new green pelt and fresh willow leaves where others boasted hair. There were others, the quieter ones, and Mune the Mage made his entrance while Alfaro still silently called the roll. Mune the Mage preceded the foppish Rhialto the Marvellous by moments, and Zahoulik-Khuntze was scarcely a step behind the odious Rhialto.

These constituted the bulk of the magicians of Almery and Ascolais. Alfaro felt the oppressive weight of many gazes. He had not tried hard to win friends. Nor had felt any need. Till now, perhaps.

What was this? What had he stumbled across? As a group, these men—applying the collective in its broadest definition—consisted of the most unsociable, cranky, and iconoclastic denizens of the region. Some had not spoken for decades.

The magicians watched one another with a casual wariness equaling what they lavished on the interloper.

Ildefonse stepped up to a podium, raised his hands. The approximation of silence gathered shyly. "I do not believe the others will join us. Let us repair to the solarium. I've had a light buffet set out, with breakfast vintages and a selection of ales and lagers. We shall then consider young Alfaro's news."

The magicians brightened. Elbows flew as they jostled for precedence at the buffet. Ildefonse's pride did not let him stint.

Alfaro reddened. The loathsomely handsome Rhialto was heads together with the Preceptor. They kept glancing his way

Alfaro headed for the buffet, only to find it reduced to bones, rinds, pits, and feathers. Some of the 21st Aeon's finest costumery now featured stains of juice, gravy, grease, and wine.

Clever Ildefonse. Magicians with full bellies and wine in hand soon relaxed. His servants moved among them, keeping their favorite libations topped up.

Ildefonse called for attention. "Young Alfaro, taking the upper airs yester eve, chanced to see something that none of this aeon ought, unless as a time mirage. Amuldar."

Susurrus, not a syllable of which Alfaro caught.

"He did not recognize what he saw. He did know that it did not belong. A clever lad, he has built himself a library of inexpensive reproductions of masterworks. In one of those, he found an illustration of what he had seen. Suspecting this to be of importance, he contacted me by vovoyeur." The Preceptor gestured, left-handed, across, up, fingers folded, then open. The Moadel illustration appeared at the western end of the solarium.

A glance at the collective showed the majority to be unimpressed. "Before my time," grumbled the usually reticent Byzant the Necrope. "And, considering the history, definitely a time mirage."

Haze of Wheary Water, leaves up like an angry cat's fur, demanded, "And if it were purest truth, what would it be to us?"

Questions arose.

Likewise names.

Historical events were enumerated.

Accusations flew.

The image did mean something to several magicians.

Arguments commenced, only to be shut down by the host when the spells supporting them threatened damage to his solarium. The magicians were accustomed to making their points briskly, with enthusiasm.

Rhialto approached Alfaro. In Morag's opinion, he did not deserve his sobriquet. Nor was Rhialto half the supercilious fop of repute. "Alfaro, what moved you to stir all this ferment?"

"I intended nothing of the sort. By chance, I spied an ominous structure where none ought to stand. Amazed, I hurried home, did some research, chanced on the illustration floating yonder. I reported the evil portent to the Preceptor." Alfaro meant to pursue exact clarity in all aspects, unless interrogated as to why he happened to be where he had been when he had spied this Moadel.

Alfaro posed a question of his own. "Why all the excitement? I didn't expect to find the entire brotherhood assembled."

"Assuming you actually saw . . . that . . . many magicians' lives might be impacted." Rhialto stalked off, having forgotten his usual exaggerated manners. He intervened in a dispute between Byzant the Necrope and Nahouerezzm, both of whom had honored Ildefonse's vintages with excessive zeal. Nahouerezzin further suffered from senile dementia and thought he was engaged in some quarrel of his youth.

The mood of the gathering changed as the magicians made inroads into Ildefonse's cellar. The oldest became particularly dour and testy.

Rhialto having demonstrated no interest in further converse, Alfaro slipped off into anonymity. The others preferred to ignore him? He would not fail to enjoy the advantages. He made an especial acquaintance with the buffet once the Preceptor's staff refurbished the board. The long gray coat he affected boasted numerous capacious pockets, inside and out, as a magician's coat should. When those pockets threatened to overflow, he strolled down to the lawn. His whirlaway sagged on its springs as weight accumulated in its cubbies and panniers.

During Alfaro's third taking of the air, he realized that chance had granted him an opportunity he had come near failing to recognize.

He was inside Boumergarth, with a rowdy mob, all of whom would be equally suspect if *The Book of Changes* went missing.

3

Among Alfaro Morag's gifts was a near eidetic memory. First time through Ildefonse's library he touched nothing. He examined spines, read titles where those were in languages he recognized, and, so, had nothing in hand when Ildefonse caught him staring at a set of slim volumes purportedly written by Phandaal of Grand Motholam.

"Morag?"

"Preceptor? I overstepped, surely, but I can't help being awed. I might suspect that there is no other library as extensive as yours. Already I've noted three books my teachers assured me were lost forever."

"You suspect wrong, Morag. As you often do, to no great disadvantage to yourself yet. There are much grander collections, all even more direly protected." Ildefonse was in a bleak mood. "Return to the solarium. Do not roam unescorted. Even I don't remember all the traps set to take an interloper."

Alfaro did not doubt that. Neither did he doubt Alfaro Morag's ability to cope with petty snares.

He followed Ildefonse to the salon, where the older magicians formed ever-changing groups of three or four. Knowing smirks came his way, from faces capable of smirking.

A servant in livery boasting several shades of orange on dark violet blue entered. "Should Your Lordships be interested, an historic solar event appears to be developing. It can be best viewed from the upper veranda."

The magicians topped up their drinks and climbed to the veranda, impelled by the servant's intensity.

The fat old sun had completed a third of its descent toward the western horizon. It revealed a portentous case of acne, a dozen blotches that swirled and scurried around its broad face. Some collided and formed larger blemishes, while new blackheads developed elsewhere. Soon a quarter of the red face was hidden behind a shape-shifting dark mask.

"Is this it?" someone asked. "Has the end finally come?"

The sun flickered, grew by perhaps a tenth, then shuddered and shook it all off. It returned to its usual size. The blotches dispersed. The smallest sank into the dark red fire.

Hours fled while the magicians remained transfixed by the drama.

Ildefonse began to issue orders. His staff unfroze. He announced, "The lower limb of the sun will reach the horizon within the hour. I have ordered my largest whirlaway readied. Let us go. Young Morag will guide us to the point where he spotted his untimely marvel."

Apparently at random, Gilgad remarked, "The sun has developed a green topknot. And tail." An eventuation apparent only to his unique eye. He dropped the matter quickly

4

Ildefonse's largest whirlaway was a palace in itself. Alfaro was hard pressed to conceal his envy.

As yet, he had no clear idea why the magicians were interested in Moadel. They ignored his questions. They were not pleased, that was plain. They were nervous. Some might even be frightened. More than a few sent dark looks Alfaro's way, sure that he was a taunting liar working a confidence scheme.

Only Ildefonse spoke to him, and that with obvious distaste. "The sun will be behind Amuldar shortly. Where do I situate us?"

"Amuldar? I thought it was Moadel."

"Amuldar is the place. Moadel was the artist."

"Oh." Alfaro had spent some energy seeking an alternative to admitting that he had been near Boumergarth. He had come up with nothing. Nor was it likely that any disclaimer would be accepted. Ildefonse had dropped hints enough.

Morag delivered the true ranges and bearings.

He would build an image of honest cooperation. That might prove useful should flexibility be called for later. "It's difficult to judge from so grand a standpoint but I would move a hundred yards back from the Scaum and rise half a dozen."

The palatial conveyance adjusted its position, possibly in response to the Preceptor's thoughts.

"Here. This is almost exactly . . ."

"Excellent." With an undertone suggesting that Alfaro Morag had won a stay.

Alfaro had spent little time with the elder magicians since his advent in Ascolais. Now he suspected that they were deeper than they pretended. And were very clever at making outsiders feel small.

5

The tips of the spires and bulbous towers of Amuldar rose stark black against the sun, seeming to climb it. Beforehand, the magicians had been indifferent. Now they were interested. Some dramatically so.

Ildefonse and Rhialto lined the rail of the promenade. Alfaro leaned against that rail between them. Rhialto mused, "We may have misjudged our new associate."

"Possibly." Ildefonse seemed to doubt that.

"I, for one, am pleased. This could be a splendid opportunity. Alfaro, tell us more."

"There's nothing to tell that hasn't been told."

"Indeed? So. Why go home and contact Ildefonse rather than investigate?"

"I am neither a fast thinker nor particularly courageous in the face of something that should not be."

Ildefonse said, "Any of these, starry old bull erbs would have swarmed straight in, hoping to strike it rich."

Alfaro noted that Zahoulik-Khuntze and Herark the Harbinger, both, had developed a furtive manner. Nor were his immediate companions demonstrating their customary flash and bravura.

Panderleou presented himself. "Ildefonse, I have recalled a critical experiment I left active in my laboratory. Return to Boumergarth. I must get home quickly."

"And thence, whither?" Rhialto inquired.

"This is no time for your superior airs and snide mockeries, Rhialto. Preceptor! I insist."

"Dearest Panderleou, companion of my youth, you are entirely free to come and go as you will."

"A concept exceedingly appealing but one you have rendered impracticable."

The sun declined behind Hazur. The after light revealed no sign of Amuldar. Nothing could be seen but a brace of pelgrane circling.

With little expectation of a useful answer, Alfaro asked, "Will someone tell me something, now? Anything?"

Ildefonse said, "We will honor Panderleou's request. I set course for Boumergarth. After a suitable evening repast, we will repair to the library, research, and consider what actions we should take or should not take tomorrow."

The grand whirlaway soared, leaned, swept away across the dying light. The hundred colorful banners dressing its extremities cracked in the passing air.

6

A scramble commenced as the whirlaway docked. Most of the magicians rushed the buffet, determined to further deplete the Preceptor's larder. A few fled to the lawn and their conveyances. Those returned in a squawking gaggle, righteously outraged.

Ildefonse said, "After protracted soul-searching, I suffered a change of heart. Prudence demands that we remain together and face the future with a uniform plan and resolute purpose."

Mune the Mage, mouth filled with lark's liver croquets, observed, "The most salubrious course would be to continue the exact policy pursued since the incident of Fritjof's Drive. Ignore Amuldar."

A strong minority were swift to agree.

Herark the Harbinger declared, "I put that into the form of a motion. Though it would seem that Amuldar inexplicably survives, it has offered no provocation since the age of Grand Motholam. Let sleeping erbs lie." The Harbinger had not yet recovered his color. Alfaro feared the man might have caught some dread scent drifting in from the future.

Rhialto said, "An admirable strategy, tainted by a single flaw. When Alfaro became aware of Amuldar, Amuldar became aware of Alfaro."

Morag enjoyed a barrage of dark looks. These magicians seldom let reason sweep them away.

"When we went out to learn the truth of Alfaro's sighting, Amuldar sensed us looking. Te Ratje knows we know."

"Unacceptable," Panderleou declared.

And Herark, "I call for a vote of censure against Alfaro Morag, the penalty to include confiscation of all his possessions."

Ildefonse stepped in. "Control yourselves. Alfaro is but the messenger.

In any event, did he possess anything of merit someone would have taken it for safekeeping already."

Alfaro suffered a chill. This might be an ideal time to refill his pockets and hurry home, then move on, perhaps into the wastes beyond the Land of the Falling Wall.

Herark grumbled, "Will no one second either of my motions?"

No. But Haze of Wheary Water, leaves again in a ruff, offered, "I make a motion that Ildefonse, Rhialto, and others with the apposite knowledge, render the rest of us fully cognizant of the truths concerning Amuldar, being candid in all respects and reserving no salient point."

"Hear! Hear!" from a dozen throats. The young insisting on knowing what the old had gotten them into.

Alfaro, having heard no actual second, declared, "I second the motion offered by the esteemed Haze."

The "Hear! Hear!" chorus gave way to protests of Alfaro's audacious conceit. He had no standing.

"Quiet," Ildefonse said. "I have another second from Byzant."

Startled, the Necrope turned his back to the buffet and glared at the Preceptor.

"Panderleou, you were in the front rank at Fritjof's Drive. You have an agile tongue. Tell the tale. Cleave close to the truth. Neither fanciful embellishment nor self-effacing modesty are appropriate."

Sourly, Panderleou suggested, "Let Rhialto tell it. He was nearer the action than I."

Ildefonse demurred. "Rhialto was too near. And, as we well know, Rhialto holds himself too dear to relate any story involving Rhialto with precise accuracy."

Morag smiled. Even Rhialto's closest crony had reservations about his character.

Sullen, Panderleou growled, "All right. Gather round. I'll tell this once, touching only the critical moments."

The magicians gathered. Those with only two hands had difficulty managing their food and wine. And Ildefonse was of that inhospitable breed who did not allow guests to use magic inside his house. Which could explain his continued robust health.

Panderleou said, "At some undetermined point in the 16th Aeon, the first Great Magician rose, Te Ratje of Agagino, who may have been greater than Phandaal himself. Long gone, he is recalled only in footnotes in the most ancient tomes, where his name is inevitably misspelled Shinarump, Vrishakis, or Terawachy."

Panderleou headed for the buffet.

Ildefonse cleared his throat. "Panderleou, that was far too spare for those unacquainted with the name or situation."

Panderleou grumbled, "I blame modern education. Very well. In his day, Te Ratje was known as the Good Magician. All magic, he claimed, was a gift that should be used to benefit mankind as a whole. In his self-righteousness, he was more objectionable than is Rhialto in his egotism. He was smug, he was absolute, he was too much to endure. His fellow magicians concluded that an intervention was necessary. Te Ratje's eyes had to be opened. In consequence, much of the earth was burned clean of life. A wave of emigration took most of the survivors to the stars. Their descendants return occasionally, so changed we fail to see them as human."

Alfaro scanned faces. None of the magicians resented that remark.

"This was in the time of Grand Motholam. Many magicians since have wondered how Valdaran the Just, a mere politician, could have decimated the mages of Grand Motholam. The answer is, Te Ratje, the Good Magician. In the end, though, Te Ratje and his perambulating city were extinguished. Or driven into the demon dimensions. Valdaran succumbed to time's bite. The Earth went back to being what it always was, absent a few hundred million people."

"Until today," Ildefonse observed. He gestured. Amuldar reappeared. "Moadel painted this after Te Ratje disappeared. From a dream, he said. From a time mirage haunting the dreamlands, Vermoulian said at the time."

Vermoulian the Dream-walker pulled a thrush's drumstick out of his mouth. "I did advise you that I had found no trace of any such dream when Moadel made his claim."

"Yes, you did. I was complaisant. Te Ratje was no longer under foot. Evidence sufficient to consider the problem solved."

Alfaro tried to think himself beneath notice. He was at risk of being swept up in a quarrel that harkened to an ancient confrontation between vigorous rectitude and a relaxed attitude toward corruption.

The past might have come back.

Alfaro worried that it might bite him, too.

7

Once Boumergarth was a palace of vast extent. The countless towers and rooms—some in realities not of Earth—were fading with their master. Ildefonse was nearing his dotage, despite the mysteries spun by Lutung Kasarung. Or had lost his taste for the grand show. When guests were not present, he and his staff lived no better than common tradesmen, in a fraction of Boumergarth. Heroic expenditures of effort had been needed to provide for the current infestation.

It was, indeed, tempting misfortune to roam Boumergarth without Ildefonse. Who, occasionally, fell prey to his own forgotten snares.

So Alfaro learned in discourse with Ildefonse's staff, during a night when sleep proved hard to secure. During a night when discontent plagued the full company.

Ildefonse was determined to deal with Amuldar as soon as daylight drove more mundane dangers into forests and caves.

The breakfast buffet was basic. Fuel for a hard day's work.

Why go gourmet for the condemned?

By way of elevating spirits, the Preceptor announced, "I deployed my sandestins during the night. Expect a dead city, if we find anything more than a time mirage. Te Ratje detected would have acted by now. His recollections of us would be less affectionate than ours of him. So. One last sup of wine, and away!"

The magicians arrived on the lawn in a grumbling scrum, only to be disappointed again. Ildefonse did grant leave for individuals to provide their own transport. Woefully, that transport would proceed exclusively to the destination the Preceptor chose.

Most whirlaways used a minor demon called a sandestin to move them about. The Preceptor had suborned those with threats and loose talk of a release of indenture points, which were within his power to award.

He told Rhialto, "Lead the way, with young Alfaro. I will come last, sweeping up stragglers."

Alfaro thought Rhialto approached this morning with no more enthusiasm than did Panderleou or Zahoulik-Khuntze. Both continued to plead a pressing need to attend to business at home.

Ildefonse, from behind, shouted, "Each of you came to Boumergarth armed with several spells. I hope that, collectively, we're armed with a broad variety."

"Spells?" Alfaro gobbled. "I didn't . . . Why would . . ."

Rhialto looked at him with what might have been pity. If not disdain. Assuming that was not just the wind in his eyes.

8

The magicians neared Hazur. Ildefonse relaxed control. They buzzed round the headland like giant gnats. Alfaro remained near Rhialto, keeping that magician between himself and the haunted country the best he could.

Magicians sparking about attracted attention, first from the road hugging the far bank of the Scaum, then from above. Yonder, travelers stopped to gawk. Above, the activity attracted pelgrane, monsters remotely descended of men. Their slow brains understood that all that sweet meat bobbing around Hazur could be deadly. Ao of the Opals underscored the point with his Excellent Prismatic Spray.

The gallery beyond the river roared approval when a hundred scintillant light spears pierced a too daring pelgrane. Sizzling, the monster plunged toward the Scaum.

The magicians closed with the headland, which consisted of rocky ground strewn with deadwood and clusters of stunted brush.

Ildefonse called to Rhialto, "Do you apprehend any cause to avoid the Forthright Option of Absolute Clarity?"

"It costs but a spell to try. Though it is absolute. And unlikely to have a broad impact on a target as grand as Amuldar."

The Preceptor made sure none of the magicians were slinking away. He whispered. His whirlaway plunged toward the forest choking the approaches to Hazur. He curved round above the treetops and hurled his spell.

The Forthright Option was new to Alfaro. Few magicians used it because it banished all illusion, not just what the spell caster wanted brushed aside.

The air coruscated. A patch an acre in extent became the flank of a transparent dome rising from barren rock. A city lay behind that patch.

The orbiting magicians swooped in to look.

The Preceptor preened.

Rhialto told Alfaro, "That took the aeons off. He's a boy again."

Morag was more interested in the city. The not-mirage.

Nothing moved there. There was no obvious decay, but the place had the look of having been abandoned to vermin and dust for ages.

410 — GLEN COOK

For aeons, Alfaro reminded himself. Meaning there were potent sustaining spells at work.

The older magicians, so recently determined to attend interests elsewhere, now chattered brightly of what might be unearthed here.

Terror had been forgotten. Greed reigned. There was much snickering at the certain disappointment soon to grip those who had failed to respond to Ildefonse's summons.

The Preceptor observed, "Once again avarice trumps caution."

Alfaro saw something. "There! Did you see?"

"What?"

"A blue moth. It was huge."

Ildefonse said, "Blue was not Te Ratje's favorite color."

"An understatement," said Rhialto. "Te Ratje appears to be out of patience. He is ready for the test direct."

The Preceptor's whirlaway rose and darted away. Alfaro followed, as did Rhialto. Below, Barbanikos launched a spell with dramatic results.

The spell struck the dome, flashed brilliantly, rebounded, caught Barbanikos before he could dodge. His great dandelion puff of white hair exploded. Down he went, smoldering, whirlaway shedding pieces, its animating sandestin shrieking. Wreckage scattered down the flank of Hazur. Small fires burned out before they could spread.

Rhialto observed, "Barbanikos succeeded."

A black O ring a dozen feet across pulsed in the surface of the dome. Haze of Wheary Water darted through. No instant doom struck him down. Mune the Mage followed. The other magicians wasted no time.

Rhialto remarked, "Our reputations are unlikely to recover if we fail to follow."

Alfaro had a thought about opportunity knocking. Should that slowly shrinking O ring close, a dozen estates would become masterless.

Ildefonse caught his eye. "Learn to think things through."

Alfaro opened his mouth to protest.

"Had you developed that skill early you would have had no need to migrate in haste."

Rhialto observed, "You are a slow learner. Nevertheless, you show promise. And you have youth's sharp eye."

Youth's sharp eye, unable to meet Ildefonse's fierce gaze, wandered to the pelgrane contemplating prospects on the river road, then to the feeble sun. "Gilgad was right. The sun has a green topknot. And maybe a beard or tail." Both discernable when considered from a dozen degrees off direct.

Rhialto and Ildefonse discovered it, too. And Rhialto saw something more. "There is a line, fine as a thread of silk, connecting the earth to the sun." Ildefonse said, "Would that we had Moadel here to sketch it."

Alfaro suggested, "I could get my brother. He has a talent for drawing." Tihomir was immensely blessed in that one way.

"Unnecessary. The sun will persist for a few more days. Our task is more immediate. Rhialto. Lead the way. I will sweep up the rear."

Rhialto tilted his jeweled whirlaway toward the shrinking O ring. Disgruntled, Alfaro followed.

9

"There's no color," Alfaro exclaimed.

"But there is," Rhialto countered. "Te Ratje's gray, in all its thousand shades. Gray is the color of absolute rectitude."

"Unsettling news," Ildefonse said. "Barbanikos's aperture has closed." The hole had become a black circle floating in the air. The acre unveiled by the Forthright Option of Absolute Clarity had dwindled to a patch a dozen yards in its extreme dimension, too.

Rhialto said, "I have not been here before."

Ildefonse confessed, "My visit has become so remote that I might need weeks to exhume the memories. Alfaro was correct. There is a blue moth. I need recover no memories, though, to understand that the street below leads to the heart of Amuldar."

The others had gone that way. Dust hung in the air, stirred by their passage. There was nothing here to seize their attention. This was the most bland of cities. No structure stood taller than three stories, nor wore any shape but that of a gray block, absolutely utilitarian.

"Where are the towers? The minarets? The onion-domed spires?"

Ildefonse said, "The silhouette was what the Good Magician believed he was creating. Now we are inside what actually came of his vision."

"Valdaran the Just destroyed the magicians of Grand Motholam for this?" Rhialto chuckled. Ildefonse did not respond.

Alfaro squeaked, startled by a big blue moth that just missed his face.

The elder magicians slowed. "Time for caution," Rhialto said, indicating a strew of polished wood and wickerwork that had been a whirlaway not long ago.

"Mune the Mage," Ildefonse decided. "I don't see a corpse, so he walked away."

Several large moths, or maybe butterflies, flitted randomly nearby. They ranged in color from dark turquoise to pale royal blue. Alfaro said, "Looks like writing on their wings."

"Those are spells in Te Ratje's own script." The Preceptor evaded a moth as big as his spread hand. "One of his contributions to magic. Even he could encompass no more than four spells at a time. So he made these creatures. He could read a spell if he so chose, or he could arm them so the insects could deliver disaster by fortuitous impact. This would be an instance of the latter." Rhialto prized a small purple stone from its mount on the tiller bar of his whirlaway, whispered to it, pegged it at an especially hefty moth. The moth turned onto its back and wobbled downward.

Ildefonse observed, "That one carried the Dismal Itch."

"They're all nuisance spells." Rhialto's right hand danced. His purple stone zipped from butterfly to moth, trailing ichors and broken wings.

They fell where others had fallen already. Then there was Mune the Mage, clumping onward with inspired determination, his iridescent cape an aurora against the gray. Ghostly, shimmering footprints shone where he trod but faded quickly. Ildefonse observed, "I believe his temper is up. Forward, Mune! Forward, with alacrity!"

Mune the Mage made a rude gesture. Even so, Rhialto swooped down for a few words. He returned to report, "Only his dignity is injured. As you might expect, though, he's already grumbling about restitution."

Alfaro said, "I see something."

All three slowed.

There was a hint of color at the heart of Amuldar, about as lively as that of a plant found lying beneath a rock. It filled the spectrum but every shade was washed out, a ghost of what it might have been.

Thither, too, stood a scatter of structures resembling those seen against the sun. None were the size the silhouette had suggested.

An expansive plaza lay surrounded by those. A squadron of unmanned whirlaways sat there. The Preceptor said, "They're all here but Barbanikos and Mune the Mage."

The three settled to the gray stone surface, which trembled with ribbons of color for an instant after each dismounted.

Alfaro understood. The color here, weak as it might be, existed only because outsiders had tracked it in.

10

Fallen Lepidoptera marked the path into the squarest and grayest square gray structure, where no light lived. Alfaro drew his short sword from beneath his coat. A moonstone in the pommel, properly seduced, shed a brisk light, which illuminated a circle twenty feet in radius. Rhialto and Ildefonse were impressed. "An heirloom," Alafaro explained. The acquisition of which had precipitated the cascade of events that had brought the Morag brothers to Ascolais.

"Amazing," Ildefonse said. "But we need something more."

The hall seemed to have no boundary but the wall through which they had entered. The other magicians were around somewhere, though, as evidenced by remote echoes and flashes.

"What is this place?" Alfaro asked.

The Preceptor said, "Your guess will be as good as any."

There was a deep mechanical clunk. The floor shuddered. Light began to develop, accompanied by a rising hum. The distant voices sounded distraught.

Alfaro damped his moonstone, turned slowly.

The wall behind boasted countless shelves of books, up into darkness and off into the distance to either hand. "Preceptor . . ."

"I did tell you there were libraries superior to my own. Forward!" Ildefonse stepped out. Alfaro followed. He did not want to be alone, now. There was danger in the air. Rhialto felt it, too. He appeared uncharacteristically nervous. Ildefonse followed tracks in dust disturbed by those who had run the gauntlet in the dark.

"Ghosts," Alfaro said as they moved through acres of tables and chairs, all dusty.

Creatures high in the air floated their way. Both were near-naked girls who appeared to have substance. Rhialto murmured approval. He had a reputation concerning which no one had yet produced hard evidence. "Take care," Ildefonse warned. "They'll be more than they seem." Rhialto added, "I suspect a sophisticated twist on the theme of the moths. The one to the left seems vaguely familiar."

The Preceptor said, "She is showing you what the secret Rhialto wants to see. This trap consists of choice. You have to choose to touch. But if you do, you'll have no time for regrets."

"Te Ratje's way. Destroy you by pandering to your weaknesses."

Similar ghosts floated ahead. They formed an aerial guide to other magicians. Not all those ghosts were female or young.

A scream, yonder. A brilliant flash. Then a half minute of utter silence during which the ghosts hung motionless. Then a grinding began, as of hundred ton granite blocks sliding across one another.

Ildefonse stepped out vigorously. Alfaro, perforce, kept up. Rhialto remained close behind, muttering as he wrestled temptation.

11

Perdustin had screamed. Gilgad reported, "He touched a girl. Haze saw it coming. He interceded."

Perdustin was down and singed but alive at the center of an acre of clear floor under the appearance of an open sky

"And the girl?" Ildefonse asked.

"Shattered." A red-gloved hand indicated a scatter that appeared to be bits of torn paper. "Sadly, none of the young ladies are any more real."

"It's all illusion," Haze said, before retailing his version of events.

Ranks of gargantuan, dusty machines surrounded the acre. "Where did that come from?" Alfaro asked. "We saw none of it till we got here."

Gilgad shrugged. "Things work differently inside Amuldar." He was frightened. And, in that, he was not unique.

"What is that?" Morag indicated the sky, where alien constellations roamed. Where fine lines, plainly visible despite being black, waved like the tentacles of a kraken eager to feast on stars.

Someone said, "Ask Te Ratje when he turns up."

A dozen pairs of eyes contemplated the wispy curve of pale green trailed by a sun that had set.

Ildefonse knelt beside Perdustin. Rhialto hovered. The other magicians grumbled because not one worthy souvenir had surfaced.

Alfaro glanced back. What about those books? Then he resumed studying the sky.

Saffron words, written on air, floated over his shoulder. YOU WITNESS THE EVOLUTION OF THE STARS. A MILLION GALACTIC YEARS PASS FOR EACH THREE MINUTES YOU WATCH.

Stricken, Alfaro watched black tentacles for a moment before he turned to face the oldest little old man he had ever seen. Liver spotted, nearly hairless, with a left eyelid that drooped precipitously. The left end of his mouth sagged, too. His wrinkles had wrinkles. He had an arresting nymphet under either arm. His toes dragged when they moved. They were no ghosts. Alfaro felt the heat coming off them. They would bleed, not scatter like bits of torn paper.

Alfaro watched the improbable: self-proclaimed fearless magicians of Almery and Ascolais began to mewl, to wet themselves, and, in the case of Nahourezzin, to faint. Though, to be exactly reasonable, his faint had exhaustion and prolonged stress behind it. Morag noted, too, some who were not obviously intimidated, the Preceptor and Rhialto the Marvellous among them.

12

"Te Ratje?" Rhialto asked.

The old man inclined his head. After a pause. He did not seem quite sure. More girls gathered to support him. Their touch did not inconvenience him.

"Their concern is intriguing," Ildefonse murmured. "They exist at his will. And he isn't healthy."

Rhialto opined, "Even my formidable resources would be taxed were I tasked to entertain so many gems."

Alfaro asked, "Who are they? They're exquisite. Does he create them himself?" His own such efforts always turned ugly.

"No. Long ago he traversed time, harvesting the essences of the finest beauties and most accomplished courtesans, each at her perfect moment of ripeness: firm, unblemished, and a trifle green. He decants their simulacra at will."

Ildefonse added, "Youth's fancy."

Rhialto said, "The girls are not precisely aware of their status, but do understand that they have been fished from time's deep and are dependent on his affection for their immortality."

Alfaro wondered, "Why is he so old?" By which he meant: Why had Te Ratje let himself suffer time's indignities?

According to Rhialto, "His mind never worked like any other. Belike, though, this is just a seeming, like Ildefonse, or Haze, or Zahoulik-Khuntze with his illustrated iron fingernails."

Alfaro examined the Preceptor. As ever, Ildefonse seemed a warm, plump, golden-whiskered grandfather type. Had he a truer aspect?

The Good Magician became someone dramatically less feeble. He stood tall, strong, hard, saturnine, and entirely without humor. But his eyes did not change. They remained ancient and half blind. Nor did he speak.

Te Ratje stabbed the air with his left forefinger. His fingernail glowed. He wrote: WELCOME, ALL. ALPARO MORAG. SCION OF DESTINY. YOU HAVE BEEN A LONG TIME COMING. His lines were thirty characters long, floated upward to fade in tendrils and puffs of yellow-lime vapor.

"Always a showoff!" Herark the Harbinger sneered.

TIME HAS BETRAYED ME. MUST YOU SABOTAGE MY GREAT WORK AGAIN?

Rhialto was skeptical. "I see no sign of work, great, trivial, wicked, or otherwise. I see the dust of abiding neglect."

I HAVE ABANDONED ALL EFFORTS TO IMPROVE MANKIND. THE BEAST IS A SHALLOW, SELFISH, INNATELY WICKED INGRATE. I LEAVE HIM TO HIS SELF-DESTRUCTIVE AMUSEMENTS. I FOCUS SOLEY UPON THE PRESERVATION OF KNOWLEDGE AND MINISTRATION TO THE SUN.

The Good Magician gestured. The air between himself and the magicians resolved into a diorama six feet to a side and three deep. An exact replica of the space they occupied revealed itself, with miniscules of magicians and girls at its center.

Te Ratje's illuminated forefinger extended to become a slim four foot yellow-green pointer. LIBRARY. INCLUDING EVERY BOOK WRITTEN SINCE THE 13TH AEON.

Ildefonse actually winked at Alfaro.

THESE ENGINES DETECT CREATIVE WORK IN PROCESS. WHEN

THE GOOD MAGICIAN — 417

A WORK IS COMPLETED, A SUITE OF SPELLS INTERRUPTS TIME, AN ASSOCIATE TRAVELS TO THE CREATION POINT AND RENDERS AN EXACT DUPLICATE. NO POEM, NO SONG, NO ROMANCE, NO MASTERWORK OF MAGIC OR HISTORY IS EVER LOST, THUS.

Alfaro detected a taint of madness.

The magicians had ignored the books in their haste to find more worldly treasures. But, now, every book written for eight aeons? Including the lost grimoires of Phandaal, the Amberlins, the Vaspurials, and Zinqzin? Three quarters of all magical knowledge had been lost since Grand Motholam.

A blind man could smell the greed beginning to simmer.

Deliberately provoked? Alfaro wondered.

Inside the diorama several engines turned a pale lilac rose. THERE BEATS THE HEART OF AMULDAR. THOSE DO THE GREAT WORK OF TIME. THOSE REACH OUT TO THE STARS AND DRAW THE SUSTENANCE FOR WHICH OUR SUN HUNGERS.

Gesture. A sphere of denominated space appeared overhead, the sun a bloody pea at its center. A scatter of latter age stars blazed at the boundary, true scale of distance ignored. Threads of black touched those and lashed the empty regions between. Every thread pulled something unseen into one of the two green tails spiraling out from the sun's poles.

AS I GIFT MY ANGELS LIFE, SO DO I GIFT LIFE TO ALL THAT GOES UPON THE EARTH. COME.

Alfaro blurted, "Me?"

YOU. YOU ARE THE ONLY INNOCENT HERE.

Morag gulped air. He felt like a small boy caught with his hand in a purse that was not his own. A situation in which he had found himself more than once. A glance round showed him none of the magicians moving, or even aware. "A stasis? One that exempts me, though I'm at a distance and did not initiate it?"

YES. Wicked smile. The Good Magician continued to grow stronger and younger. THERE IS LITTLE TO DO HERE BUT TEND THE ENGINES, STUDY, AND INDULGE IN RESEARCH. He smiled more wickedly as two of his pets slipped under his arms. Another, a sleek black-haired beauty wearing a pageboy cut like a visorless bascinet, who roiled Morag's thoughts from the moment he spied her, sidled up beside Alfaro. Her wicked eyes told him she knew perfectly well that she could make him her slave in an instant.

Te Ratje said, WITH ALL THE GREAT MAGICAL TEXTS AT HAND, AND TIME IN NO SHORT SUPPLY, EVEN A DILETTANTE CAN FIND CLEVER NEW WAYS TO USE MAGIC.

Distracted by the nymph and natural flaws in his character, Alfaro followed Te Ratje s speech only in its broadest concept.

The story Te Ratje told was dubious even to a naive youth just beginning to grasp how far out of his depth he was with the magicians of Almery and Ascolais. Who had begun to understand that he needed, desperately, to rein in his natural inclinations, lest he suffer a fate not unlike that enjoyed by his miniscules.

From glances caught, he knew that Byzant the Necrope had something in mind.

13

The nymph rubbed against Alfaro like an affectionate cat. He asked, "Is this distraction necessary?"

I CANNOT CONTROL THEIR AFFECTIONS.

Alfaro remained unsure of how he had moved from the plaza of the engines to a cozy little library rich with comfort and polished wood. It could not possibly hold all the books created across eight aeons. It was crowded by two magicians and three girls.

WHAT BOOK WOULD YOU LIKE TO SEE?

Because a lust for its possession had brought him to this pass, Alfaro said, "Lutung Kasarung's *The Book of Changes.*"

Te Ratje extended an arm impossibly far, retrieved a volume. He presented it to Alfaro. It was a pristine copy, never opened. Alfaro placed it gently on a small teak table featuring a finish so deep the book seemed to sink. Shaking, he asked, "What are you doing to me?"

I WANT YOU TO BECOME MY APPRENTICE.

"Why?" Morag blurted.

YOU ARE THE FIRST TO FIND AMULDAR IN AEONS. YOU COME BURDENED BY NEITHER PREJUDICE NOR GREEDS FROM THE PAST, ONLY BY PICAYUNE WEAKNESSES EXAGGERATED BY YOUR TALENT.

"Why would Te Ratje want an apprentice?"

EVEN THE BEAUTIFUL MUST DIE.

Alfaro was baffled. He was confused. In moments of honesty, he could admit that he was not a good man, just a man who excelled at self-justification. He was not a man made in the style of the Good Magician.

There was a trap here, somewhere.

COMES THE DAY, COMES THE MAN. THE CHALLENGE CREATES THE MAN. I HAVE STRIVEN, ACROSS AGES, TO PRESERVE KNOWLEDGE AND PROLONG THE HOURS OF THE SUN. THE STRUGGLES OF THE 18TH AEON COST ME MY POWER AND AFFLICTED WOUNDS THAT GNAW ME TODAY.

Could the snare be emotional?

EVEN HIDDEN, UNKNOWN, WITH ALL THE KNOWLEDGE OF THE AGES, I COULD NOT RECLAIM WHAT HAD BEEN RIPPED AWAY. BUT NOW CHANCE OFFERS AN OPPORTUNITY. I CAN PREPARE A REPLACEMENT.

Alfaro concealed all cynicism. He did not believe. He could envision reality only through his own character. Te Ratje must be another Alfaro Morag, ages subtler and craftier.

Even so, Alfaro sustained his resolution to honesty. "I'm not the man you need. The best I can be called is rogue or scoundrel." And he did have obligations elsewhere.

YOUR BROTHER. OF COURSE. YET I HAVE ALL THESE DELICACIES. TEN THOUSAND OF THE SWEETLINGS, WHO LIVE BUT A DAY OF EACH HUNDRED YEARS. I HAVE THE WORLD, WHERE THE SUN'S TIRED OLD LIGHT WOULD BE EXTINGUISHED BUT FOR TE RATJE'S MIRACLE ENGINES.

"You read minds?"

SOME, I DO. YOURS IS OPEN. THOSE OF MY ANCIENT ANTAGONISTS, THOSE PRINCELINGS OF CHAOS AND SELFISHNESS IN THE SQUARE, NO. BUT I KNOW THEM. AND THE ENGINES UNDERSTAND THEM.

IT IS DETERMINED. ALFARO MORAG WILL BEGIN TRAINING TO BECOME THE GOOD MAGICIAN.

Alfaro's companion snuggled close and purred.

14

Ildefonse stepped into the library. The girls squeaked in surprise. The Good Magician shimmered.

The Preceptor asked, "Morag, what is this?"

Alfaro blurted, "What happened? How did? . . ."

"Mune the Mage arrived. He broke the stasis. Only, I'm sure, after making sure there were no loose treasures in need of pocketing. Answers, please."

"Te Ratje would like me to become his assistant."

The Preceptor chuckled wickedly, his mirth echoed by the other magicians, outside. Ildefonse turned to the doorway "I spent my Forthright Option of Absolute Clarity. Does anyone have a spell meant to disperse illusion?"

Vermoulian the Dreamwalker pushed forward. "I have a charm, not a true spell, which will distinguish illusion from waking dream."

"Try it. Young Alfaro needs to see how far in he has been drawn."

"That seems profligate."

"We were all young once."

"Very well. The charm is renewable." The Dreamwalker gestured, said a few words.

Ildefonse asked, "Is it time release? Nothing happened."

"The effect is instantaneous."

"Nothing has changed."

Not strictly true. Nothing he wanted to be illusion had changed. Ildefonse himself reverted to his natural form. The change lacked drama. He developed a paunch and lost some looks, hair, and his avuncular warmth.

A brief disturbance arose outside the library, where the magicians saw one another clearly for the first time.

The library remained precisely unchanged. Likewise, the three beautiful girls. But an odor pervaded the scene.

"Ach!" Alfaro gasped. "Te Ratje!"

The Good Magician's response to the charm was to grow old again, to become the wizened gnome, then to stop moving.

Nearest, Alfaro pronounced, "Dead! A long time dead. A mummy. Have we been dealing with a ghost?"

A shimmer formed about the husk. A voice inside Alfaro's head said, *I am a memory in the same engines that recall the delicate legion. Even the beautiful must die. But an idea, a dream, lives forever in Amuldar. The engines will labor on after the last star gutters.*

"Not a dream," Vermoulian opined. "A nightmare, brought to life."

Ildefonse nodded. Alfaro failed to comprehend. His kitten slithered up him and nipped at his left earlobe. "I lack key information. Te Ratje did not discuss his old feud. He dismissed it as of consequence only insofar as it might interfere here."

"Te Ratje was a zealot, of the narrowest focus, prepared to wreck civilizations to enforce his concept of right. The city outside, the gray, is the gift the Good Magician planned for us all." Ildefonse spoke passionately

"And yet, after the excesses of Grand Motholam, he ceased intercourse with mankind. He focused on sustaining the sun."

"For which we must express gratitude, of course. But . . ."

The nymph had a hand inside Alfaro's coat and shirt. He had trouble concentrating.

The Good Magician—or the machine inside which his ghost still conspired—read his mind.

The truth is the truth, whatever hat it wears.

Alfaro disagreed. "The truth is different for each observer. Even the laws of nature are protean in some circumstances." He eased the hand from beneath his shirt, pushed the girl far enough away that her warmth no longer heightened his blood. "Forces try to enlist me, by seduction or implied threat. Why?"

Ildefonse betrayed a momentary surprise.

"The seducer is easily understood. My wants and fantasies will be fulfilled. The Preceptor, on the other hand . . ."

Ildefonse visibly controlled his tongue.

Truth is truth. The spell has been spun. Henceforth none can lie, save by silence. But truth will fill their thoughts. The Preceptor wishes to plunder Amuldar, then complete its destruction. So much does he loathe the vision of the Good Magician.

"Even to the cost of the sun?"

Even the beautiful must die. There are other suns. The magicians of Ascolais can travel in the palace of Vermoulian the Dreamwalker.

Why did the magicians so hate the Good Magician's vision?

The engines showed him the world Te Ratje would have made, first according to his truth, then according to neutral machines capable of calculating the sum vector of all the stresses presented by the ambitions of the beings within that world. There was little resemblance.

Morag rode the engines' memories, observing incident and fact, absorbing the truths lurking between the biases.

15

Time had fled. Ildefonse had gone into a stasis again, his mouth open to protest. Likewise, the girls and the mummy.

Who had not been the Good Magician. Te Ratje had perished in the ancient conflict. He had been replaced by a follower with a lesser grasp of magic.

And had been replaced himself, in time.

"Relax the stasis."

Ildefonse resumed protesting. The yelp of his stasis alarm interrupted. "What happened?" he demanded.

"The engines shadowed me through history."

Ildefonse had no comment. Neither did the magicians outside. "Preceptor, Te Ratje did fall at Fritjof's Drive. The Good Magician here was a follower who salvaged Amuldar and carried on in secret. He made sure the engines will not fail in the lifetime of this universe. Amuldar is no threat to you. It will tend to the sun. It will care for Te Ratje's beloved daughters. It will protect itself."

Ildefonse absent his normal semblance could not conceal his inner self. Nor could he hide from Amuldar, which did not withhold salient information from Alfaro.

Morag said, "You all need to understand that none of the things you're thinking will work. Content yourselves with the status quo."

"Which is?" Vermoulian demanded.

"We are guests of Amuldar. For so long as Amuldar wishes." Alfaro flung a thought at the engines. "A buffet is being set out. Follow the young women with the lights. Restrain your lusts. Vermoulian, go. Preceptor, stay. Rhialto, join us in here." At a thought from Alfaro, the husk of the Good Magician floated away. Morag did not look. He feared it might be watching him as it went.

The dimensions of the library shifted. There was room for three men in three comfortable chairs attended by three implausibly beautiful young women. Alfaro reviewed his own sour history. One vision plagued him: Tihomir's injury.

Several new girls appeared. They brought wines and delicacies.

Alfaro said, "I've been bitten by the serpent whose venom moved Te Ratje. I'll do as he asked. So, now, the question. What to do about you?"

"Release us," Rhialto said, distracted. He had a princess on either knee.

"The machine considers that dangerous. It knows your minds. You are who you are. Yet returning you to Ascolais would be my preference."

Alfaro was amazed. He was talking like the man in charge.

He asked, "Who among you can be trusted?"

Rhialto and the Preceptor instantly volunteered.

"I see. The engines disagree. I want to send for something. But whoever I send is likely to plunder those who stay behind. Excepting Nahourezzin, who would fail to remember his mission. Yes. An excellent strategy. There. And done."

"What is done?" Ildefonse asked, nervously

"The sandestins from the whirlaways have been enlisted for the task, in return for remission of their indentures."

"In just such manner did Te Ratje become unpopular, making free with the properties of others."

"A paucity of otherworldly servants should make actions against Amuldar less practical. Enjoy the wine. Enjoy the food. Enjoy the company." Alfaro leaned forward to whisper, "I'm doing my best to get you out of here alive."

16

Tihomir stared at the gray city childlike. The sandestins had deposited him, and the contents of the tower beside the Javellana Cascade, in the center of the acre square. Alfaro rushed to greet his brother. Several favorite nymphs followed. He anticipated meeting the others wholeheartedly. Ten thousand of those precious, wondrous gems!

There were no magicians or whirlaways in the square.

After embracing his brother Alfaro commenced the slow process of making Tihomir understand their new situation. He worried overmuch. Tihomir would be comfortable so long as he remained near Alfaro. He had arrived frightened only because they had been separated for a time, then strange demons had come to carry him away.

Alfaro Morag. The bad magicians are escaping.

"How can that be?" Though he had noted the absence of the whirlaways, including his own.

The one called Barbanikos propped the way open when the demons returned. The demons themselves had no confidence in your promise to relax their indentures.

Golden-tongued Rhialto and Ildefonse would have leveraged any demonic doubt to adjust notoriously evanescent sandestin loyalties.

There was a reason they were indentured rather than hired.

Alfaro shrugged. He remained irked that his whirlaway had been appropriated—by Mune the Mage, surely—yet here was a problem solved without his having to offend Amuldar. A prodigy. He was free to be the Good Magician and free to make Tihomir whole.

A dozen more girls arrived to help Alfaro move his possessions into his wondrous new quarters, shaped by Amuldar's engines based on his deepest fantasies.

Not even Ildefonse's Boumergarth could match their opulence.

He had fallen into paradise.

Paradise was a blade with vicious edges.

Across subsequent centuries, individual magicians, or, occasionally, a cabal, attempted to avail themselves of the riches of Amuldar. Every stratagem failed.

Only Vermoulian the Dream-walker penetrated Amuldar's shell—by stalking the nightlands. The Dream-walker traced the nightmare into which the Good Magician descended.

Alfaro Morag, as all the Good Magicians before him had, discovered that only a few millennia of this paradise left him unable to continue to endure the cost. As had they, he began to yearn for the escape of the beautiful.

The better grounded and rounded Tihomir Morag would gain fame as his brother's successor.

AFTERWORD:

I entered the Navy out of high school in 1962, severely afflicted by Ambition Deficit Disorder. Nevertheless, when the Navy offered to send me to college for an additional four years of my life I said "Yo-ho-ho!" and went off to the University of Missouri. As a gangly, uncoordinated freshman I lurched about in the wake of a senior keeper whose name I have forgotten but whose greatest good turn remains with me still.

On learning that I favored science fiction, too, he dragged me into the independent bookstore next door to the tavern where we spent our evenings practicing to become sailors on liberty. There he compelled me to fork over the outrageous sum of, I believe, 75 cents (plus tax!) for the Lancer Limited Edition paperback of Jack Vance's *The Dying Earth*. I was aghast. Paperbacks were 50 cents or, at most, 60 cents at the time. But I got my money's worth, yes I did. That book is gone, along with a couple of subsequent editions, because I have read and read and read, I cannot say how many times.

I was hooked from the first page. This was intellectual meth. I cannot shake the addiction, nor have I ever lost the tyro's longing to create something "just like—" What every author feels about favorites who blazed new roads through the ravines and thickets of literature's Cumberland Gaps. One of the great thrills of my writing career was being invited to participate in this project. So, for the first time in two and a half decades, I wrote a piece of short fiction, to honor one of the greats who lured me into this field.

Events here chronicled occur at the extreme end of the 21st Aeon, in an otherwise dull epoch some centuries after happenings recorded in *Rhialto the Marvellous*.

—Glen Cook

SHADOW THIEVES

*Asked to contribute an urban fantasy to an anthology (*Down These Strange Streets*), I threw a slider, down and away, with a story about my detective character Garrett in his deeply Dickensian home universe. It is a semi-spoof of the movie version of* The Maltese Falcon.

I was half asleep in the broom closet I call an office. Somebody hammered on the front door. Odd that they should. I wasn't home much anymore.

This time I was hiding out from the craziness that comes down on the newly engaged. My future in-laws dished me make-crazy stuff relentlessly.

I began disentangling myself from my desk and chair.

Old Dean, my cook and housekeeper, trundled past my doorway. He was long, lean, slightly bent, gray, and almost eighty, but spry. "I'll get it, Mr. Garrett. I'm expecting a delivery."

That was one impatient deliveryman. He was yelling. He was pounding. I couldn't understand a word. That door was fortress grade.

Dean did not use the peephole. He assumed the noise came from whoever he was expecting. He opened up.

All kinds of tumult rolled on in. Dean shrieked. A deeper, distressed voice bellowed something about getting the frickin' frackin' hell out of the way!

I started moving, snagging an oak nightstick as I went. That gem had two pounds of lead in its kissing end.

More demanding voices joined the confused mix.

I hit the hall fast but my ratgirl assistant, Pular Singe, was out of her office faster. At five feet Singe was tall for her tribe. Her fine brown fur gleamed.

She slumped a bit more than usual. Her tail lashed like an angry cat's but she emptied a one-hand crossbow as calm as sniping at the practice range. Her bolt hit the forehead of a thing whose ancestors all married ugly. It was a repugnant shade of olive green, wide like a troll, and wore an ogre's charming face. It smelled worse than it looked. It filled half the hallway. Its forehead looked troll solid but Singe's quarrel was unimpressed.

What kind of toy had she found herself now?

She stepped out of my way, whiskers dancing.

Big Ugly finished collapsing. Two of his friends clamored right behind him. One tried to get hold of a very large, equally ugly human being who was down and squashing Dean because Singe's victim had fallen forward onto him. The guy was still breathing but wouldn't stick with it long. He had several serious leaks.

I laid into the hands trying to drag him. Bones crunched. Somewhere beneath it all Dean groaned piteously. I gave the final villain a solid bop between snakish yellow eyes. He took a knee after gifting me with a straight jab that flung me two-thirds of the way back toward the door to Dean's kitchen kingdom. From her office Singe called, "I was counting on you to last a little longer."

Females.

I glanced in as I headed back for more. Singe was cranking a device that would span her little crossbow, which apparently had the pull to drive steel quarrels through brick walls.

One ugly was just plain determined to take the big man home with him. The other scrabbled after a wooden box said fellow must have dropped. I made sure my feet were solidly arranged on my downhill end and waded in.

I gagged. The guy on top of Dean, though breathing, had begun to rot.

My partner quit daydreaming and got into the game at last.

One ugly responded by voiding his bowels. He grabbed Singe's victim by an ankle and headed out. I whapped his pal till he gave up on the box, then stomped on the ally his buddy had given up dragging as he went through the doorway. Despite the bolt in his forehead, that one retained the ability to groan.

With generous assistance from a wall I launched my pursuit, but ended it leaning on the rail of the stoop.

Singe bustled out beside me, anger smoking off her. She pointed her weapon. Her bolt ripped right through one creature's shoulder. The impact spun him and knocked him down. "Whoa! This sumbitch has some kick! I think I just sprained my wrist." She watched the uglies trundle up Macunado Street. "I will go reload, then we can get after them."

Besides her genius for figures and finance, Pular Singe is the best damned tracker in TunFaire.

"The Dead Man couldn't control those guys."

"You are correct. That is not good." Singe eyed the fetid mess blanketing Dean. The big man had ceased to resemble a human being. His sailor's rags had begun to drift out of the mess.

Nothing mortal ought to decay that fast.

"I'm sure the Dead Man will tell us all about it." Which was a subtle test to see if my partner was paying attention.

A little blonde watched us from across the street, so motionless she didn't seem to be breathing. She clutched the string handles of a small yellow bag in front of her. She wore a floppy blue hat somewhere between a beret and a chef's cap. Her hair hung to just above her shoulders, cut evenly all the way round. A wisp of bang peeped out from under the hat. She wore an unseasonably heavy coat made up of sizable patches in various shades of red, gold, and brown. Its hem hovered at her knees. Quite daring, that, as her legs were bare. Her eyes were big, blue, and solemn. She met my gaze briefly, then turned and walked uphill slowly, goose-stepping, never moving her hands.

I guessed her to be in the age range large nine to small eleven.

Singe said, "She has no scent."

Nor any presence except in the eyes of you two. Most unnatural.

That was my partner, the Dead Man.

A sleepy voice said, "I see her, too. I'll follow her."

Penny Dreadful, human, girl, teenager (a terrible combination), the Dead Man's pet, and the final member of this strange household, had decided to drag herself out of bed and see what the racket was all about.

As Penny pushed in between us, Singe turned a blank face my way that was all too expressive. I was in no position to grumble about anyone lying in bed since it usually takes divine intervention to roust me out before the crack of noon.

Penny is fourteen, shy around me but brash toward everyone else. She used to be the last priestess of a screwball rural cult. She lives with us because we stashed her once for her protection and she never got around to leaving. The Dead Man is fond of her inquiring mind.

"Let's deal with this mess before we do anything else. Penny, get the field cot set up in my office. We'll put Dean in there."

She grumbled. That's what teens do when they're told to do something. All life is an imposition. But she went. She liked Dean.

Singe said, "Let us shut the door before the second wave shows up."

She helped drag the injured raider. The door needed no major repairs. The damage was all cosmetic. I was pleased.

Dean and Singe's victim were less encouraging. Dean was unconscious and covered with yuck. I worried that he had internal injuries. "I'll get Dr. Harmer in a few minutes."

No need, my partner sent. *The solution to several problems is at hand.*

I stood up, bemused, though this was not the first time my stoop had hosted a raff of violent idiots. I was bemused because my telepathic side-kick was bemused. He was bemused because he had been unable to get past the surface thoughts of the raiders.

The door resounded to a tap.

Singe's head whipped round. She pushed me out of her way, cracked the peephole for form's sake, then opened up for her half-brother, the ratman gangster John Stretch. Behind him loomed his lieutenant, Dollar Dan Justice, the biggest ratman in town. All five feet three of him. More henchrat types lurked in the street.

John Stretch said, "We heard there was trouble." His whiskers wiggled as he sniffed out the story. He was a colorful dresser, wearing a yellow shirt, striped red-and-white trousers, and high-top black boots. Dollar Dan, though, was clad plain as dirt.

Singe babbled.

John Stretch patted her shoulder. "Two of them? With poisoned bolts? No? Too bad. What can we do?"

The Dead Man asked for someone to hustle a message to Dr. Harmer. And could someone please track the ones that got away? The wounded one had left a generous blood trail. I said, "I could use some help moving Dean. And some cleaning specialists to clear the mess." Meaning the rotting remains.

John Stretch said, "I hope my women can stand that."

Which said a lot about the pong. Ratfolks find most smells I don't like to be lovely fragrances.

Dollar Dan got busy lieutenanting while his boss and I chewed the fat. The crowd in the street broke up. One ratman headed downhill to get the doctor. The nastiest bunch headed the other direction, never asking what they should do if they caught up. Two more sniffed around the spot whence the blonde had watched. They couldn't find a scent.

Singe said, "I will take that once we finish here."

Her brother didn't argue so I didn't. He said, "I will ask Dollar Dan to go along. No one will look out for you better, Singe," he added when she gave him the fisheye. "So let me be selfish."

Garrett. Please bring that box in to me.

"Box?" What box?

The box that may be the reason for all the excitement.

"Oh. That box."

That bit of art in cherrywood, coated with mush, lay snuggled up to the wall beside the umbrella stand.

"It's all nasty."

Limit your contact with the filth.

"Crap. Not good. We might have to redo the floor." I scooted into the kitchen, filled a bucket with water, rounded up some cleaning rags, got back out into the hall. I found brother and sister rat people in a heated debate about Dollar Dan.

I said, "Singe, let them look out for you. It won't hurt. It's not a sign of weakness. And it'll keep your brother and Dan and me all happy."

She gave me an exasperated look but abandoned the argument.

Do not be an idiot, Garrett!

"What?" I have an old reputation as a master of repartee.

Do not open the box!

Oh. Yeah. Might be demons were willing to kill for it. It must contain something special. Maybe something dangerous.

"Right. I was distracted. Wondering why we haven't heard from the tin whistles yet."

An excellent question.

The red tops, the tin whistles, the Civil Guard, jump onto any excitement like a cat onto a herd of mice.

Be confident we will hear from them soon. Meantime, please bring the box so that I may make a more intimate examination.

Singe said, "Put it where they won't think that it might have something to do with the attack."

Yes. Of course.

"I should start my track before they get here. Otherwise, it could be tomorrow before I can get away."

Good point. The red tops, with the Specials even worse, can be intrusive and obstructive.

John Stretch said, "Hide your weapon. They see that, they will lock everyone up."

For sure. Our protectors don't want us able to fight back.

Singe and Dollar Dan, with Penny tagging along, did get gone before the Civil Guard arrived. I wasn't thrilled about Penny going, but the Dead Man backed her up. I couldn't argue with that.

John Stretch and I made tea, hovered over Dean, and waited. I asked, "How come you turned up so fast?"

"We keep an eye on the place."

"You do?"

"Dollar Dan does, mostly. But there is always someone."

"He's wasting the emotion."

"You know. I know. Even Dan knows. But I will not stick my nose in."

"Probably best we don't."

"So Dan was watching when you showed up, which was a sure sign that something was about to happen."

"Hey!"

"Does anything happen when you are not here?"

"Purely circumstantial."

"No. Purely Singe. She sensibly sticks to high-margin, nontoxic projects like looking for lost pets and missing wives, and forensic accounting. She does not get tangled up with the undead, mad gods, or crazed sorcerers until you come around."

He might have some basis for his argument. But it's not like I go looking for weird. Bizarro comes looking for me.

The Guard are here and Doctor Harmer is approaching.

"And there you go," the ratman said. "You picked a family physician named Harmer."

"I did not. Singe did because he'll treat rat people, too."

"I will wait in the kitchen while you handle the Guard."

"Thank you."

The minions of the law would be excessively intrigued by the presence of a senior crime boss.

Be polite.

I was headed for the door. "I'm always polite."

You are always confrontational.

"They start it."

I do not deal well with authority. The Civil Guard is self-righteously authoritarian in the extreme.

I will spank you if you are rude.

Wow! He sounded like my mother when I was eight.

There were two tin whistles on the stoop and a platoon in the street. John Stretch's henchrats had turned invisible.

Dr. Harmer was just dismounting from his pretty little buggy. His driver, his gorgeous half-elf wife, stuck with the rig in case somebody tried to kype it among all the red tops.

"Lieutenant Scithe. How are you? How's the missus? Have you lost weight?"

"I *was* living a good, boring life in a tame district. Then you swooped down off the Hill."

Scithe was a tall, thin man in a big, bad mood and an ill-fitting blue uniform to match. He didn't talk about his wife. He didn't ask about my fiancée.

My whole damned life works this way. Anything happens, whatever it is, it gets blamed on Ma Garrett's oldest boy.

My partner gave me a mental head slap before my mouth started running.

Dr. Harmer shoved through the press, a thin, dark character with merry brown eyes, unnaturally white teeth, and a devilish goatee. "Show me what you've got."

"Dean is in my office. He got smushed under this thing and a guy even bigger who turned into that pile of goop."

That pile was getting smaller. Some was evaporating. Some was seeping through the floor, where it could lie in the cellar and make the house stink forever.

The doctor snorted. "I'll look at Dean first." He eased along the hallway, stepping carefully.

Scithe said, "We should have been here sooner. If we'd known you were back we'd have had somebody watching. And I had to ask the Al-Khar about special instructions." The Al-Khar being Guard headquarters.

The Dead Man laid a mental hand on my shoulder.

"The Director said we didn't need the Specials."

Oh, good. The secret police would let me skate. For now. They're so nice.

"How thoughtful."

The Dead Man squeezed, just hard enough.

Scithe asked, "So what's the story?"

"Same old, same old."

"Meaning you'll claim you don't know a thing."

"Not quite." I told it like it happened, every detail, forgetting only the cherrywood box, Singe's artillery, and John Stretch, who was probably devouring everything in my larder while he waited.

Scithe squatted beside the thing with the bolt in its forehead. "Still breathing, here." He tapped the nock of the quarrel. "I could use a better light."

The tin whistle who had come in with him said, "The wagon just rolled up, boss. I'll get a lantern."

A big brown box had pulled in behind the doctor's rig. It had crowns, keys, nooses, and whatnots painted on to proclaim it a property of the Civil Guard supported by a royal subsidy.

Scithe asked, "Any theories, Garrett?"

"Only what's obvious. He probably wanted to see the Dead Man. Somebody didn't think he should."

"They got their wish. What does the Dead Man think?"

The Dead Man is frustrated. He could not penetrate the minds of any of the attackers. Not even that one who is wounded and unconscious. Yet. That is a him, is it not?

I replied, "More or less." Mostly a whole lot more.

Scithe said, "I see ogre and troll and bits of other races."

"Trolls and ogres don't mix."

Scithe shrugged. "I see what I see. Which is that somebody with a huge ugly stick whaled on all his ancestors for five generations back. Then he fell in a barrel of ugly and drank his way back to the top."

Trolls will cross with pygmy giants on occasion. However, a more likely explanation would involve rogue researchers and illegal experiments.

The three strains of rat people exist because of old-time experimental sorcery. That stuff is worse than murder. You can get away with murder if you make a good case for the son of a bitch needing killing.

Scithe's man came back. His lantern flung out a blinding blue-white light. Scithe got busy. He used chopsticks to poke, prod, probe, and dig into pockets. Nothing useful surfaced. He moved on to the stench pile. "Check this out."

He held up what looked like a two-inch lead slug three-eighths of an inch in diameter, pointed at one end. It had four lengthwise channels beginning just behind the ogive. The channels contained traces of brown.

"A missile?"

"Maybe. Definitely poisonous. But delivered how?" By whom, and why, were out there floating, too.

Dean's delivery has arrived.

I stepped outside.

Jerry the beer guy had pulled up in front of the doctor's rig. He was making conversation with the delectable Mrs. Harmer. He noticed me, said something to a couple red tops hating him for knowing the beautiful lady well enough to gossip with, and got them to volunteer to show off by helping carry kegs.

They brought in three ponies of froufrou girlie beers. Jerry indicated the crowd outside and the mess in the hallway. "You're back."

"What does that mean? Never mind. Just drop those by the kitchen door." I didn't want anyone to see John Stretch.

"They keep better if they stay cool."

"Put them in with the Dead Man, then."

Jerry and his helpers tiptoed around the mess and entered the demesne of the Dead Man.

I said, "Anywhere out of the way." I glanced at the cherrywood box, on a shelf with mementos from old cases. "What're they for, anyway?"

"Dean wanted to test some varietals for your reception."

"Well. That sneaky old fart."

A tin whistle pointed. "Is that him?" He'd gone as pale as paper.

My partner is a quarter ton of defunct nonhuman permanently established in a custom-built oak chair. First thing you notice, after his sheer bulk, is his resemblance to a baby mammoth with a midget trunk only a quarter the length you might expect.

Most visitors don't look close. They're petrified by the fact that he can read minds.

One red top fingered the whistle on the cord around his neck. The talisman didn't help. "Too cold in here, brothers." He beat a retreat. His pal trampled on his heels.

Jerry didn't get left behind.

The Dead Man is a Loghyr. They are exceedingly rare and exceedingly deliberate about giving up the ghost. This one has been procrastinating since he was murdered more than four hundred years ago.

Dr. Harmer tried smelling salts. The character in the hallway didn't respond. Scithe finally had a flatbed haul him off to Guard headquarters after Harmer slapped a patch on his forehead leak. The bolt stayed where it was.

Scithe left us a promise to share information, worth the paper he never wrote it on. Jerry left a real receipt. I found it a home on Singe's desk, snuggled up with Dr. Harmer's bill.

The doctor went away, too, leaving Dean in a drugged sleep.

I let John Stretch know it was safe to come out.

Ratwomen cleaning specialists turned up fast. They had been waiting on the tin whistles. They had nothing flattering to say about the mess. They wrapped their faces with damp cloth and misted the fetid air with something that smelled like the spice in hot peppers. They used garden tools to scoop goop into pails they covered securely before sending them to be chunked in the river. They avoided contact with the goop.

John Stretch and I visited the Dead Man.

"Too cold in here," the ratman complained.

"Singe's fault. She claims the colder we keep him the longer he'll last. And he don't feel it."

"I am sure she knows what she is talking about."

"She knows everything about everything. So, what's in the precious box?"

Air.

"Excuse me? Nothing? A guy died. Two more got hurt."

It is a red herring. The real box is somewhere else.

"You came up with that, how?"

With great effort and stubborn determination, reasoned out from what little I retrieved from the creature Lieutenant Scithe took away.

The Dead Man likes his strokes. "That was some good work, then."

The ladies are returning. It would appear that they enjoyed a limited success.

I let them in. Penny scooted past me and the cleaning women. Singe joined me in the chill.

"I hear you got lucky." I flipped a thumb at the Dead Man.

"The gods smiled. Just barely. There was no trail for the girl. That means sorcery. We followed the wounded creature. Those things were not with her. We were tracking them when we saw her come out of the Benbow." The Benbow is a staid old inn in the shadow of the Hill, used by out-of-town-ers who have business with the sorcerers infesting that neighborhood. "I sent Penny in. She oozed some girl charm and found out that she had just missed her pal Kelly, who calls herself Eliza now. Eliza shares a third-floor suite with her aunt, Miss Grunstrasse. They arrived in TunFaire yesterday."

Penny joined us. "I had to check on Dean."

"Doctor says he'll be fine. Anything to add?"

"The manager is a little guy who looks like a squirrel. I put on some cute. He let me talk to people. Eliza came from Liefmold. There's something not right about her. She doesn't talk. Her aunt has a fierce accent. That's when the squirrel got that I wasn't really their friend. He sent somebody upstairs, probably with a warning, so I cleared out."

The Dead Man touched me lightly to let me know I had no need to know about how she had charmed the Benbow staff. He didn't want me going all dad.

"I pretended I didn't know Singe or Dollar Dan when I left so they could see if anybody followed me."

"Good thinking."

Singe said, "A kitchen boy tried. Dollar Dan scared him so bad he wet himself."

"He's not useless after all."

Singe glowered. She wasn't ready to concede that. And Penny . . .

Aha! The kitchen boy's interest hadn't been his employer's idea.

Come here. All of you.

The Dead Man can tease out memories you don't know you have. He'll put his several minds to work sniffing along several distinct trails and tie everything together in startling ways.

There is nothing beyond the obvious. Our victim, Recide Skedrin, interested at least two parties enough to involve them in murder. It is likely that he was a red herring himself.

How did he know all that, suddenly?

Penny, please stand in for Dean while he recovers. Garrett and Singe will assist where necessary.

Someone had forgotten who was senior executive.

Go open the door, Garrett.

The man on the stoop was short, flabby, and nervous. He had large, wet, brown doggie eyes. He felt like a guy who had lived a life of sorrow. His clothing was threadbare and dated, twenty-years-ago chic. My appearance startled him.

He had been trying to decide whether to knock. He squeaked, "Who are you?" He had a lazy, girly voice and an accent so heavy you needed a machete to cut through it.

To Singe's office, please.

The newbie did not know about the Dead Man, who reeked of wicked glee. This twitch must be an easy read.

"How come you're camped on my stoop, little fellow?"

"Uh . . ."

He would be the source of the Dead Man's unexpected knowledge.

He invested a few seconds in wondering if he should go with the lies he had rehearsed. While he strategized, Singe arranged papers so she could take notes. She was amused.

I don't care if they lie. The Dead Man can burgle their minds while they're exercising their capacity for invention.

Our visitor asked, "With whom am I speaking?"

He came without knowing? "Name's Garrett. The most handsome blue-eyed ex-Marine you're ever likely to meet. This is my place. You sure you got the right one?"

He is, in the sense that he believes this is where he may find the object of his quest.

"Mr. Garrett, I represent the Council of Ryzna." He spoke Karentine like he had a mouth full of pudding and acorns. Lucky me, I had a partner who could pass on not only what the man wanted me to know but also what he was thinking.

He realized recently that he is mostly under his own supervision. He has developed personal ambitions as a consequence.

Little man clicked his heels and bowed slightly, a habit they have in his part of the world. "Rock Truck, Rose Purple, at your command, sir," is what I heard. I shrugged. I'd heard stranger names. He made sure I knew his father was a player back in the old country. His family had been exploiting the masses for centuries.

I listened. If the silence lasted long enough he might fill it with something interesting.

"Recide Skedrin came to see you." He pronounced it *Ray-see-day Skaydrene.* Very Venageti.

The one who died.

I knew that. I am a trained observer. "I don't know that name."

"That does not surprise me. He was no one. Mate on a tramp freight carrier trafficking between TunFaire and Liefmold. A wicked young woman, Ingra Mah, recently deceased, seduced him and persuaded him to smuggle a Ryznan national treasure from Liefmold here for her. She hoped to auction the item on your Hill."

Well. That would make it a sorcerer's toy, likely with major oomph. People wouldn't be dying, elsewise.

He is telling the truth and your reasoning is sound. However, the full story also has a political aspect. The Dead Man added some visuals he had shoplifted.

I'd have to work out the man's name later. They don't put them together our way, down south. It sounded like he had done some translating. There might be a job title in there, too.

Little man produced a dagger. He said, "I am going to search . . ."

Singe said, "Really, Mr. Rock. Such bad manners."

He seemed startled to see her. The Dead Man had blinded him.

I took his dagger, careful not to touch the blade. That bore streaks in several colors, none obviously dried blood.

It went briskly. The Dead Man did not reveal himself. Singe did not leave her desk. Rock squeaked when I put him in a chair. He pouted and massaged his twisted wrist. He had extra water in his eyes.

"We'll have no more of that. Why are you haunting us?"

"I am here, at the behest of the Council, to recover the Shadow."

"The Shadow." You could pick up the capital without a hint from the Dead Man.

"What do you know about Ryzna, Mr. Garrett?"

"It's a town in Venageta with a nasty reputation."

"Sir! Ryzna is Venageti by compulsion, only because someone let besiegers into the city under cover of a bright, cloudless noonday sun, whilst all men of substance were . . ." He burbled history more than a century old.

His ancestors were the traitors. The Venageti failed to reward them to their satisfaction. They see an opportunity to turn the tables in the theft of this Shadow.

All right. I never let the fact that I don't know what's going on get in the way of getting on with getting on. "What's this Shadow gimcrack? And why look for it here?"

Any chance there was something in that box after all?

No. This would be something so powerful that any of us would have sensed it. The genuine box is lined with iron, lead, and silver. The Shadow is an aggregation of the souls of Ryzna's departed sorcerers. Their powers combined, without the personalities. Its importance to Ryzna and Mr. Rock is narrowly envisioned. The universal ambition there is to use it to control Ryzna. The deceased thief, however, realized that it could be a potent tool useful to any sorcerer anywhere.

She must have lacked wizardly talents herself. She would be busy trying to take over the world if she had some.

Exactly. Mr. Rock sees the Shadow as something abidingly dark and strong. He is in love with the potential.

So. To review. A freelance socialist decided to redistribute the wealth by purloining the Shadow of Ryzna. Rock got conscripted to bring it back because he was considered too dumb to see the personal opportunities. He'd been sandbagging. He'd decided that no one deserved to use that toy more than sweet old Rock Truck, Rose Purple, his own self.

Rock wasn't my kind of guy but he was, for sure, a type I run into a lot.

"The Shadow is ... No. To you what it is matters not. What does matter is that it belongs to the people of Ryzna and we must have it back. I am prepared to pay four thousand silver nobles for its return."

That got my attention. And Singe would have grinned if rat people had something to grin with.

I said, "That's good." Four thousand would make me a nice dowry.

"That is very good." Then he went stupid, like I might have forgotten the original thief's reason for sending her plunder to TunFaire. "The Shadow is no good to anyone outside the Ryzna Council."

Not even true in Ryzna. The Venageti held Ryzna down with the Shadow until a sloppy guard too young to think with his head let the Ingra woman get to it.

Ingra Mah sounded like a talent. Too bad she let somebody get behind her.

"Let us be exact, Mr. Rock. What do you want? We don't have your Shadow. But we could look for it. That's what we do here."

"Recide brought you a box."

"It was empty. And he didn't live long enough to explain."

The creatures pursuing Mr. Recide were associated with Mr. Rock. There were five, assigned by the Ryzna Council to assist Mr. Rock and to keep him walking the line. They were not responsible for Mr. Recide's death.

Five. Two hurt. One of those in the hoosegow. Rock's keepers as well as consorts. Good to know. And the original thief? Was she really dead? Had she been slick enough to break her trail by faking her own demise?

"Oddly enough, I believe you, Mr. Garrett."

At the same time, Old Bones sent, *He believes she is dead.* He sent a picture from the little man's mind.

Ingra Mah had gone the way of Recide Skedrin. Rock had arrived on scene soon after the process began. The Dead Man assured me that, though Rock was a thorough villain and fully capable, he was not responsible.

Truck continued, "Recide and his ships master moonlighted as transporters of questionable goods."

"They were smugglers."

"Bluntly put, yes."

"Why come to my house?"

"I can only guess, Mr. Garrett. Either he was directed to do so before he left Liefmold or he made inquiries on arriving and thought you met his requirements. My inquiries suggest that you have important contacts on the Hill. On the other hand—and this is the way I see it—he may just have wanted to lay down a false trail while his ship's master delivered the actual Shadow elsewhere."

"Say I find your gimcrack. How do I collect my four thousand?"

"I have taken rooms at the Falcons Roost. You may contact me there." Ugh. The Roost is a downscale sleaze pit not far from the Benbow. You don't have to fight off the hookers and grifters to get in or out, but its main clientele are ticks on the belly of society who perform unsavory services for those who shine from the Hill.

A man with more than four thousand nobles would be able to afford better.

Rock indicated his dagger, now resident on the edge of Singe's desk. "May I?"

"Knock yourself out."

He collected the blade, moved past me as though to leave, then turned and said, "I am going to search . . ."

Penny hit him from behind with a pot. "Supper's ready, guys."

I told her, "Keep your wrists a little looser. You don't want to end up with a serious sprain."

She gave me the fisheye but joined Singe in helping me go through Rock's pockets. We didn't find anything, so we chunked him out on the stoop, minus one deadly knife.

That became a trophy on the same shelf as the cherrywood box.

Then we convened in the kitchen.

I settled at the table again. Singe asked, "who was at the door?"

"Scithe. He thought we should know the prisoner died without talking. And wondered a lot about how a home invader ended up with a quarrel in his forehead."

"A good man. Has a sense of justice. Are you surprised about that thing dying?"

"He was lucky to hang on as long as he did."

Penny asked, "What next? How about we go back to the Benbow? After Dan scared Bottle . . ."

"You got his name?"

"He was cute."

"Don't I have worries enough?"

Singe snickered. Penny ignored all annoying parentish behavior. "How's the soup, old man?"

A little spicy. "Excellent. You paid attention when Dean showed you how."

"Thank you." She managed to sound surly while looking pleased.

Singe said, "My turn," and pushed back from the table.

Penny grumbled, "That's just sick spooky, the way she hears and smells stuff."

Singe came back with a folded letter closed with wax and a Benbow seal. "That was the blond child. Still with very little scent."

Nor any detectable presence. Though I felt unsettled. Vertiginous. Almost nauseated.

The letter was addressed to **Mr. Garrett** in a bold hand. "What did she say?" "Nothing. She handed that over and walked. She can't be human."

I chewed some air, thinking. "Was there a clay smell? Anything like that?"

"No. But I will consider the implications."

"What is it?" Penny asked, being the only one who couldn't read over my shoulder.

"A request that I join a Miss Grünstrasse for a late dinner and a bottle of TunFaire Gold." Which is the city's finest vintage.

Penny asked, "Do I have time to clean up?"

I didn't get to explain that the invitation was just for me.

Penny, this is one of those times when you should have Garrett and Singe assist you.

There was going to be a revolution around here. Or maybe a counter-revolution.

Sailor Recide Skedrin had been a junior partner in a vessel rumored to be a smuggler. His ship and crew deserved a look. But, "I was too honest with Scithe. He'll have Specials poking every shadow on the waterfront."

Your appointment at the Benbow is of more immediate import. Lieutenant Scithe will begin making rounds of the public houses soon.

We were about to go, even Penny surreptitiously armed. She suddenly decided to head upstairs.

Singe dealt with the waterfront angle already.

She said, "My brother let me send Dollar Dan. Dan won't be noticed down there."

A rat on the wharves? Not hardly. He wouldn't draw a second glance.

"We set? Penny! Come on!"

Do find out why people feel free to commit murder inside our house.

"Gah! I just came here to relax!"

Singe swung the door open but didn't step out.

It was raining. Hard.

Penny thundered downstairs with umbrellas, hats, and canvas coats.

The Benbow has been there for ages. It put me in mind of a cherrycheeked, dumpy little grandmother of a sort I'd once had myself. It was warm, smelled of hardwood smoke and ages of cookery in which somebody particularly favored garlic. It had settled comfortably into itself. It was a good place occasionally disgraced by the custom of a bad person.

The right side, coming in from the street, was a dining area, not large, empty now. Most guests preferred taking their meals in their rooms. To the left stood a fleet of saggy, comfortable old chairs and divans escorted by shopworn side tables. Three old men took up space on three sides of a table there, two playing chess while the third grunted unwanted advice. There was no bar. Management preferred not to draw custom from the street.

The stair to the guest rooms lay straight ahead, guarded by a persnickety-looking little man with rodentlike front teeth. His hair had migrated to the sides of his head. His appearance begged for him to be called Bunny or Squirrel.

He rose from beside a small, cluttered table, gulping when Penny took off through the dining area.

His voice proved to be a high squeak.

Penny paid no attention.

Bunny sputtered. Then he recognized Singe for what she was. His sputter went liquid.

I presented my invitation.

"Oh. Of course. I didn't actually expect you." He threw a despairing glance after Penny, then another at Singe. It pained him to say, "Please come with me." There is a lot of prejudice against ratfolk.

Miss Grünstrasse occupied a suite taking up the west half of the third floor. I huffed and puffed and wondered if I was too old to start exercising. Bunny got his workout by knocking.

The blonde opened up. She stepped aside. For all the warmth she showed she could have been baked from clay. Her eyes seemed infinitely empty.

Singe went first. I followed. The door shut in Bunny's face. The girl threw the bolt, moved to the left side of the sitting room. She stood at parade rest, but with hands folded in front. She wore a different outfit without the coat. Her sense of style had not changed.

"Ah. Mr. Garrett. I was not sure you would respond. I do appreciate the courtesy. Indeed, I do."

I did a double take.

"Sir? Is something wrong?" Fury smoldered in the glance she cast Singe's way.

"Sorry. Just startled." In low light she resembled my prospective grand-mother-in-law, one of the most unpleasant women alive.

This one was huge and ugly and smelled bad, too.

The smell was a result of diet and questionable personal habits.

Her accent was heavier than Rock's, with a different meter.

"Come, Mr. Garrett. Be comfortable. Let us chat while Squattle prepares dinner." She spoke slowly. Each word, though individually mangled, could be understood from context.

I sat. Singe remained standing. There were no suitable chairs. Neither did she shed her coat, which was psychological warfare directed at the niece. The blonde adjusted her position after I settled.

"Now, then, Mr. Garrett. The Rock Truck, Rose Purple, visited you today. He was, without doubt, a fount of fabrication. He will have laid his own crimes off on others."

Rock was my client, in his own mind. I volunteered nothing.

"So. Very well, then, sir. Very well. Eliza and I have come to your marvelous city to reclaim a precious relic."

"The Shadow."

"Indeed. Exactly. The Rose Purple did not misinform you completely, then. Remarkable. Yes. The Shadow. Of negligible intrinsic worth, it nevertheless has substantial moral value among folk of a certain sort. We are here, at the behest of the Venageti Crown, to recover the royal property." She studied me from narrowed, piggy eyes, vast and truly ugly. "That would not be a problem, would it, sir? You won't judge me simply for being Venageti?"

"No. We won the war."

"Excellent. Excellent. I endured my own sorrows during those bleak seasons, I assure you. As did we all. Well, sir. Can I count upon you, then?"

I frowned. That didn't make sense. I confessed, "I don't get what you're asking."

"In the spirit of the new friendship between our peoples, you will return the Shadow to me, the Hand of Begbeg."

All Venageti rulers have Beg in their name. The one who quit fighting called himself Begbeg, which means King of Kings or King of the World.

"I don't have your doohickey. I don't know where it is. I don't know what it is. I wouldn't recognize it if it bit me on the ankle. And I don't much care."

"Sir!"

"I do know that somebody tried to bust into my place, somebody else made him dead, and one of those somebodies got dead himself, later on. Cutie-pie there watched everything from across the street. You probably know more than I do."

"But Recide brought you a box."

"He did? Singe, did you see a box?"

"I did not." She was distracted. Beyond Miss Grünstrasse's pong, the suite was replete with unusual odors.

"Really, Mr. Garrett. You dissemble. Eliza saw the box."

I looked at the blonde, as still and perfect as ornamental porcelain. Had she, indeed? Unlikely. Why say so, then? "She has magic eyes, she could see inside my place from where she was standing."

"You waste your time trying to provoke her."

Little bits was not my target.

Someone thumped the door with grand enthusiasm.

Bunny led the dinner delivery. He was in a black mood. His principal assistants were a boy and girl in their early teens. Penny was the girl. The boy, presumably Bottle, was more damned dangerously good-looking than she had hinted. He was blessed with way too damned much selfconfidence, too.

Two more staffers brought folding tables, one at which to dine and another whence the kids could serve.

A sad old frail who might be Bunny's mate bustled in. "Found it!" She unfolded a chair designed to fit someone equipped with a tail.

The crew set four places atop clean linen. Eliza sat down but did not seem pleased.

We ate, mostly in silence, duck and some other stuff, none of it memorable. Neither was the wine, though it was a TunFaire Gold. Singe was the only one who knew what to do with the arsenal of tools.

Eliza ate just enough to claim participation. She never spoke. Her eyes were not shy, however.

Finally, over the bones, Miss Grünstrasse observed, "I will miss the food here. So. Mr. Garrett. You hope to gain some advantage from holding out on the Shadow. How can I change your mind?"

"You can't. I don't have the damned thing."

The woman laughed. Tremors surged through her flab. "Very well, then. Very well. What will it take to encourage you to find it?"

"I don't know what to look for. But Rock offered four thousand silver nobles for it."

Miss Grünstrasse began to quake all over. "The Rose Purple? Four thousand? That prince of liars! That latest in an endless procession of thieves! He will abscond on his account, wherever he is staying."

Odd thing to say. Silence followed. Eliza seemed especially interested.

Miss Grünstrasse changed approach. "You have barely touched your wine, Mr. Garrett. Is there a problem? The publican assured me that it is the finest vintage TunFaire offers."

"He would be correct, too, but I'm a beer snob." The modern obsession with spoiled grape juice is inexplicable. As someone once observed, beer is proof that the gods don't always get off on tormenting us.

"Beer, sir? I understand that TunFaire is famed for the variety and quality of its brews. Have you a favorite?"

Why not be difficult? "Weider Wheat with a blackberry finish."

"Eliza, see what Squattle has available."

The blonde inclined her head, rose, and left the suite as though driven by clockwork. I asked, "What's the story with her? Is she even human?"

"Oh, yes. She is, sir. Yes, indeed. Just quite serious. My niece. My intern, as well. Completing her elementary training. A remarkable child. Brilliant beyond her years. She will become one of the greats." Aside, "What is this, girl?"

Penny had set a plate in front of her. "A pumpkin spice turnover, ma'am.

Specialty of the Benbow." She served me and Singe. Bottle followed with a cloth bag from which he squeezed a rum-based syrup.

Penny asked, "Should we ready one for the young miss, ma'am?"

Miss Grünstrasse was disgruntled. She was not accustomed to being a common "ma'am." "Keep it in the warmer. She may not want it. She doesn't eat many sweets."

I asked about Ryzna, Venageta, and the Shadow. Miss Grünstrasse evaded or tried to sell me on the sheer marvel of helping reclaim her missing gimcrack.

"Do we have an understanding, Mr. Garrett?"

"I haven't heard a word about potential benefits to me and mine. Other than this fine dinner."

She was not pleased. That was not the response that was her due. "Very well, sir. Very well. I do have to remember that I am outside that realm where my wishes have the weight of law. Very well. Bring me the Shadow and I will pay you an eight-hundred-noble finder's fee." She raised a hand to forestall the remark she expected. "Genuine Full Harbor trade nobles, not the fairy gold of the Rose Purple's will-o'-the-wisp promise."

I remained unconvinced. I looked unconvinced.

"Come with me, then, sir. Come with me." She got up, beckoned like someone Eliza's age eager to show a friend a secret.

I followed reluctantly, and got more reluctant when she headed into an unlighted bedroom. A light did come up momentarily, though. I glanced back. Boy, girl, and ratwoman looked puzzled but alert.

"Come along, Mr. Garrett. I promise not to test your virtue."

She had a sense of humor?

I relaxed a little.

"Do close the door, though. In case my niece returns. I would rather she remained unaware of this."

"Does she speak or understand Karentine?" Lacking a knowledge of the language might explain her disinterest in communication.

"Not that I am aware of, sir. But the child is full of surprises. Lend a hand, will you?"

She wanted a trunk dragged out from under the unmade bed. The bedding smelled like Miss Grünstrasse, only worse. I couldn't help wondering if she wasn't suffering from something malignant.

We swung the trunk onto the bed. She said, "Step away while I work the combination."

The latch of the trunk glimmered with a tangle of lethal spells.

I wondered if those who mattered knew we had a foreign heavyweight among us. A Venageti heavyweight who, likely, had survived our Hill folk in the Cantard.

"The war is over, Mr. Garrett. And my mission now is more important than any vengeance." She opened the trunk and removed a tray filling two-thirds of the trunk's depth. Beneath lay silver coins, rank against rank, side to side, standing on edge. Hundreds and hundreds. There was gold, too, but she hadn't offered me gold.

Eight hundred nobles is a lot of money. And this was the real magilla.

"Take a coin. Any coin. Test it."

"I can see they're real." They had the Full Harbor reeding that discourages counterfeiters.

"Even so, take one. Have it examined." She waited while I helped myself. "Eight hundred nobles, Mr. Garrett, and the rest for expenses and a shopping spree before we go back to the gloom of Venageta."

I hate it when bespoke villains show a human side.

"Come, Mr. Garrett. Let us return to the sitting room before your assistant loses her composure . . . First, though, assist me with the chest." She reinstalled the tray. She reset the locking spells, which smelled of death. I helped swing the trunk down. She positioned it with exact care.

Being in front, I missed the smug look she swept across Singe, Penny, and Bottle.

We settled at the table.

Miss Grünstrasse began to frown and fret and smell worse, which troubled Singe. The woman started muttering. "Where *is* that girl? Why does she *do* this?"

I'd picked up enough Venageti in the war zone to puzzle that out. Miss Grünstrasse was not pleased with her wonder apprentice.

She said, "I apologize, Mr. Garrett. Eliza gets distracted."

Eliza finally did turn up, carrying a tray with eight mugs aboard, in precise formation. She set the tray beside me. I said, "You are a treasure, Eliza."

I might have been furniture.

I noted moisture on her shoes. Singe's nostrils and whiskers twitched. She smelled something that hadn't been there before.

I sniffed the beers, evidently one each of what Bunny had available. Two I passed to Singe.

Penny delivered Eliza's pumpkin turnover. Bottle did the sauce. The girl fiddled, frowned, sniffed, tasted, then damned near smiled. She devoured the whole thing, taking dainty bites. Miss Grünstrasse was impressed. "We'll be seeing more of those."

Penny and Bottle began clearing away. Penny sensed a change and wanted to get a head start.

Singe began complimenting the house's selection of drafts, pretending to get tipsy. Foreigners wouldn't know that some ratfolk can suck it down by the barrel.

Once the kids were away, Singe began babbling about needing to get back to the house fast. We had a garderobe that a ratgirl could use. She didn't want to embarrass herself.

Miss Grünstrasse smiled indulgently. "Please consider my offer, Mr. Garrett."

"That's guaranteed. I'm getting married. I could use the cash."

"I'll be here till the Shadow turns up."

"I'll have a confab with my partners as soon as we get back to the house."

That sparked a big smile. Then, "I will be here."

Something was happening in an alley just yards from the Benbow. Senior Lieutenant Scithe was there, up late buzzing like the mother of all flies.

I stuck my nose in. That cost us a half hour spent answering pointless questions about how Singe, Penny, and I could possibly be found in the same city as a spanking new double homicide.

The victims were creatures like those who had invaded my house. The thing that had gotten Recide Skedrin got them, but they were melting slower. Similar lead pieces had gone in where the rot began.

Singe pointed with her folded umbrella.

I asked, "Lieutenant, might that busted box have something to do with this?" Said box was a ringer for the one recently added to the Dead Man's collection, but lined with layers of metal. It had been ripped open.

"It's got a weird feel. We'll let the forensics wonks have a sniff."

Singe got a sniff of her own.

Scithe turned us loose. Out of earshot, Singe said, "It stopped raining while we were inside, but the pavement is still wet. The girl smelled damp when she brought the beer."

"And that box was dry inside."

"She said nothing to her aunt."

"She didn't. I feel like running all the way home."

Singe and I were rattled, but Penny had other things on her mind. She said she would catch up at the house. She and Bottle were going to meet up for an egg cream.

Singe wouldn't let me get stupid.

"Here." I fished out the coin the fat woman made me take. "I want to see some change. And be careful."

Penny laughed, waved the noble in the air, and then dashed away.

Singe promised, "She will not spend it all."

The Dead Man sensed our agitation while we were getting the door unlocked. *Come straight to me. Dean is fine.*

He asked no questions. He dived straight into our minds, slithered through the muck. He expressed no concern about Penny.

I asked, "Am I off? Or is that Eliza kid a killer?"

Given what you brought, what I got from Rock Truck, and subject to what I may get from Penny, yes. She is not what she seems. Give me a minute to digest.

He took five.

Why did the woman send the child out? Being distracted enough to have done so in Karentine?

I had overlooked that.

The answer might be implied from her lack of scent, her absence of presence, and the deep nausea I felt when she came to the door.

"Grünstrasse wanted her out because she interferes with mind stuff."

Excellent.

"And she wanted a peek inside my head."

Which she got. Clearly, though, her talent holds no candle to mine. She could not discern details or specific thoughts but did see that you truly do not have the Shadow. She saw that Penny was with you. She may have been alerted to my existence.

That might not be a bad thing. She would want to stay away.

Did she develop suspicions of the girl? Did she note the evidence you did when the child returned? If Eliza fails to volunteer a satisfactory explanation, the aunt should become extremely nervous. If she learns of the incident outside, she might suspect a sudden alliance between Eliza and Rock Truck.

I do wish I could have her in for a consultation.

I wasn't sure how he might connect Rock and Eliza but wouldn't bet against it. He conjures correct answers from gossamer and fairy dust, drawing on centuries of observing how human bad behavior takes shape.

Proof of that hypothesis will be Mr. Rock returning here.

"You think he'll panic and come to us because he doesn't know anyone else."

Yes.

"He's lethally stupid."

That was obvious from the beginning.

"What was in the box in that alley?"

Singe opined, "The same thing that was in our box here."

Air. Yes. Almost certainly. Somewhere a ship's master lies dead, murdered for nothing. Rock Truck and Miss Grünstrasse are chasing a phantom. The Shadow never came to TunFaire.

"Is Ingra Mah dead?"

Whether she tricked the child into killing someone in her place or she was killed herself after being robbed by a third party does not matter here. I do, however, fear that dreadful times will soon commence somewhere between Ryzna and Liefmold. Someone will try to use the Shadow and it will begin using him. Or her.

You may turn in, Garrett. We are done for the day.

"Not till Penny gets home, we aren't."

Diffuse amusement.

The Dead Man began to commune with Singe. I visited Dean. That old boy was sleeping normally. He had a magnificent shiner but looked likely to be back in the saddle tomorrow.

Penny turned up sooner than I expected. She was livid. "I want you to stomp that Bottle into meat jam!" she snarled. "That...! That...!" Her language failed the gentility test.

"What happened?"

"We got to the place he wanted to go, and suddenly he didn't have no money! Suddenly he did have four hungry friends, one of them a bimbo named Tami."

"Life's a bitch."

"You think it's funny."

I did. But she wouldn't get the joke. Hell, I wouldn't hear the real punch line for eight more hours.

"Go see the Dead Man."

"He already sucked everything out of my head. I'm gonna go cry myself to sleep."

Rock Truck turned up so early that nobody but Singe and the Dead Man were awake. The Rose Purple was on the run. He was wet, filthy, terrified, and exhausted. Singe let him in, planted him in a chair, and told him, "Don't move." She went back to the front door, went outside, and waved.

Dollar Dan wasn't there but another ratman did ooze out of a shadow. She gave him instructions. Then she came upstairs to roust me, like the whole thing couldn't wait till a civilized hour.

While she was charging back and forth, up and down, Rock from Ryzna learned that her word was law. Hard as he tried, he could not get out of that chair.

Singe had heavy black tea steeping when I got to the kitchen, still cross-eyed sleepy. "Not ready, Garrett. My office. See the man. I'll bring it."

I was still trundling those hallway miles when the Dead Man sent, *Answer the door.* Disconcerted.

The knock happened as I freed the first bolt. I opened. Scithe boggled. I said, "You got here fast."

"Huh?"

He did not get our message.

"Serendipity?"

Scithe stepped back. Big word. Might be dangerous.

"Singe sent a runner. We caught a bad guy."

That just baffled him more. I stepped aside. Scithe and his henchman entered. Singe came out of the kitchen with a tray, half a dozen cups and tea still steeping. Scithe said, "We came about . . ." His eyes glazed.

I got a message myself, as did Singe, who nearly fumbled her tray.

Scithe closed in on Rock and rested a hand on his right shoulder. "This is the devil? Four counts of murder? He don't look the type." He bent down to whisper, "You're in the shit deep, sweetheart."

Rock squirmed. His big brown eyes ached with appeal.

I said, "Bad news, Rock. It was all for naught. The Shadow never came to TunFaire."

The Rose Purple made noises like a man trying to shout with a gag in his mouth. I think he was upset.

Scithe asked, "He's not going anywhere, is he?"

"Only if the other villains rescue him."

Chuckles all around. The other villains were about to have troubles of their own.

Scithe said, "I got to get moving on this. Ah!"

Penny had come down. She looked grimmer than I usually feel at such an absurd hour. She grabbed a cup. Singe poured. Penny added lots of sugar. "'S goin' on? Cha' wan' me for?"

Scithe said, "You were in Torah's Sweetness last night. Got rowdy."

"So? Wanna make sumpin' of it?"

"I do."

I said, "He does, Penny. Everybody there ended up a drooling moron after you left."

"Huh? Crap. You ain't gonna put that on me."

Her eyes glazed.

She settled on the nearest chair afterward. "There must've been twenty kids in there. They didn't have nothing to do with any of this. Why would somebody do something like that?"

"She wasn't after them. She expected me to bring that coin home. When her curse homed in on it, Old Bones and I would stop being the threat we turned into when she found out that we didn't have the Shadow."

"She would've got Singe and Dean and me, too."

"Yes."

"Aren't you glad you didn't get all hard-ass about me going with Bottle?" Her heart wasn't in that, though.

"I am. That worked out nicely." Neither I nor the Dead Man chalked that up to luck, though. We believe in intuition. Something down deep had moved me to shed that coin.

454 — GLEN COOK

I could have done a better job than I did, though.

Scithe asked, "You coming with, Garrett?"

"You inviting?"

"If you don't get underfoot and don't run your mouth."

"I agree for him," Singe said. "I will smack him if he gets out of line." Scithe considered her with eyebrow arched.

"I'm coming, too."

"Me three," Penny added.

Scithe sighed. Civilians.

We got started after the Specials arrived. Three took charge of Rock Truck. The rest went to the Benbow with us.

Bunny was unhappy. Miss Grünstrasse had decamped during the night. Her tab was not in arrears but she had left her suite a wreck. It looked like a fight had taken place.

Singe reported, "The fat woman had words with her niece."

I asked, "Can you track her?"

"Under water. She was extremely distressed. It did not go well for her."

The trail led first to where the fat woman had intercepted the Specials taking Rock to headquarters. That resulted in a kidnapping, not a rescue. Witnesses said she made it quick and ugly, with no assistance from children. Her trail ran on to the waterfront, ended on an empty wharf. The ship that had been tied up there was out of sight, current carrying it out of the Guard's legal jurisdiction.

It began to rain again.

"They get away too often." Scithe hunched to keep the drizzle from running down his neck.

"They'll cut each other's throats." Unless the Specials caught up first. They recognize no limitations in times of murder.

"Maybe."

"My first platoon sergeant used to say, some days you eat the croc and some days the croc eats you."

"Yeah." He smiled grimly. "The bitch left the kid to face the music. Let's go find her and play a few bars."

SHAGGY DOG BRIDGE
A BLACK COMPANY STORY

*Commencing about 2012 there was a small storm of original Sword
& Sorcery and Military Fantasy anthologies. Upon request I produced
a flurry of Black Company short fiction for those, much of which
became parts of my recent novel,* Port of Shadows. *I also did three
pieces set in the interim between events chronicled in* Shadows Linger
and in The White Rose. *"Shaggy Dog Bridge" was the first of those.
The thinking, if in time there became enough of these they could be
gathered into a collection entitled* On The Long Run. *However, the
thirst for such stories seems to have been slaked.*

To paraphrase a bit player named Rusty, "Shit happens. Sometimes no
matter how much you dog-gnaw the bone you don't get it to make no
sense, 'specially the who done what why."

So it was with the shaggy dog bridge.

The greens and grays around and below me had become perilously hypnotic. Then a buccaneer deer fly snagged a big-ass bite just west of my
Adam's apple.

I let go the rope to take a swipe. Naturally, I missed the agile little buzzard.

Better lucky than smart, sometimes. My lifeline caught me. I stood on
my head on a hundred feet of air while the guys up top lowered away. The
dickheads on the stone shelf below grinned but tucked the needle in the
trick bag for later.

I lack the born-again haughtier of a cat. No way could I manage a pretense of deliberate intent.

"Hold still." One-Eye smeared something stinky on the bug bite. "That will kill any eggs."

"Admirable caution," I grumbled. We had yet to see the botfly horror in these parts, but the people hunting us would deploy them gleefully if they had some and could get them to bite Black Company guys exclusively.

Eight men crowded the ledge. More would follow me down. At the narrow end Rusty told Robin, "I ain't carrying that dumbass crab catcher out'n here, he gets hisself hurt."

Rusty was a FNG, with us only six months. He had no hope of becoming a Fucking Old Guy. He was an asshole and a bully. His type never prospers with us.

First aid complete, One-Eye faced the view.

"Sure is something. So much green." The Rip. To the left it was a thousand feet more to the bottom. To the right, cliff collapses had choked the canyon partially, so long ago that heavy forest cloaked the fill.

One-Eye gave his filthy black hat a quarter turn, 'To confuse the enemy,' and said, "Something ain't right, Croaker. I smell something gone off."

His wizard's sniffer was why Elmo had brought him along.

Before humanity began counting time, and maybe before there was any humanity to count it, something weird smacked the living shit out of this end of the world. Maybe a god swung a cosmic cleaver. Maybe some natural force acted up. Whatever, a knife-edge wound slashed the earth for seven hundred miles, across the grain, through mountains and forests, swamps and plains, often more than a thousand feet deep, never more than an eighth of a mile wide. It drained lakes and shifted rivers. Our side, the west, boasted hundreds of square miles of dense hardwood forest on rounded mountains with deep valleys between. Tough traveling. From what I could see the east side was exactly the same.

We were on the run. Bad people were after us, in no special hurry. We were nuisances. They had bigger fish in the pan, like overrunning the unconquered civilized world. They pushed just hard enough to keep us from wriggling loose.

We had been herded here, to be pinned against the Rip. We would cross only if we abandoned our wagons, animals, equipment, our crippled and sick. First, though, we had to find a way down this side, then up the other.

Rusty belonged to a faction disgruntled because the feeble and dying were sucking up resources that could be better used to keep him chubby.

Whittle said, "I gettin' weak-kneed in the 'membrance, some, but seems like dere was you all graveyard sick jes' las' spring. De buzzards was roostin' on your shoulders." Whittle whittled while he talked. He could lure some peculiar folk art out of plain dead wood.

Robin caught Rusty's wrist. Whittle was not just a master at finding hideous things hidden inside chunks of wood. He was a master at letting out the ugly stuff inside people.

Elmo declaimed, "Gentlemen, save it for our enemies."

We had plenty, including several Taken.

One-Eye went into a trance, for sure smelling something not right.

I exchanged looks with Robin. The boy was Rusty's favorite victim . . . and his only excuse for a friend.

Some relationships answer only to their own secret logic.

Robin showed a flash of private pain. He knew there was a pool. How long would Rusty last?

Rusty shook him off.

Whittle rose from his couch of broken granite. "First news you know, you goin' to be blessed to fine out what pain an' sufferin' is all about."

Elmo interposed himself. "That's it. Knock it off."

Whittle leaned around him. "First time you wink loud." He jerked a thumb toward some crows above the far side of the gorge.

One-Eye blurted, "It's all illusion!"

Elmo snapped, "What is?" He was on edge. If we did not find an out soon our next all-Company assembly would happen at the bottom of a shallow mass grave. The Rip left no room to run. Unless . . .

Elmo was convinced that the 'unless' was his to create.

Escape was sure to be expensive. We would take nothing but personal weapons and what we could carry or wear. It would become pure march or die.

Whisper, the Taken managing the hunters, was enjoying the cat and mouse. We had messed her up for years. But she had us now.

One-Eye, always drowning in showers of self-delusion, suddenly wanted to call shenanigans.

Elmo loomed fierce, as only a natural born first sergeant can. "Talk, runt. Straight. I'm fresh out of patience for witch-man talk-around."

He was displacing his irritation with Rusty, but scapegoating a sorcerer can become a less than profitable exercise.

One-Eye had looked past the moment. He had seen something to make him nervous. "That woods mostly isn't real. It's the most persistent daylight illusion I've ever seen but from up close you can tell." His old black face twisted. He was puzzled.

The troops stayed quiet. Sorcery encountered in strange country never bodes well. It is a definite conversation stopper.

One-Eye scowled at the Rip some more.

Elmo prodded, "Any day now."

"Sometimes even sergeants need to be patient."

Certainly not their nature but this one let a few minutes glide. Then One-Eye sighed, sagged under the weight of the world. "I'm not strong enough to see inside. We have to go look."

Rusty barked, "We ain't out here to go poking sticks in no hornet nests."

Elmo glowered. "That's exactly why we're here, moron. The name says it. Recon. We look. We poke. We find out."

And we might ought to get on with looking for our latest way out.

For centuries the Company has found one. Always.

This was the twentieth-something search but my first. I was 'too valuable' for grunt work. I had invited myself on the sneak and had stayed out of sight till it was too late for Elmo to send me back . . . and too late for me to admit that I had made a mistake.

The view of the Rip, though, was amazing.

Nervously, the squad helped One-Eye study the landscape. He became fixated on the Rip to our right. We stayed quiet. Nature did not. The crow posse across the way kept getting louder. The birds had a lot to debate. Closer by, buzzing insects scouted our potential as fodder.

One-Eye announced, "I'm going to mess with the old girl's wig and makeup."

"Meaning? Try some plain language."

"All right. What a grouch." He frustrated Elmo by taking time to loose a curse that crisped every bloodsucker within fifty yards. Though selfishly motivated, that did move him a few slots down the communal shit list.

"All them five hundred year oaks and ashes and chestnuts, hardly any of them are real."

Elmo cut to it. "Means somebody has something to hide. Saddle up, troops. We're gonna take a peek."

We worked more sideways than down. Come mid-afternoon we busted through some thorns and found a fine place to rest, a flat, wide, descending ledge that ran in the direction we were headed.

Super genius Rusty announced, "It's almost like a road."

Even the parliament of crows seemed to go quiet.

One-Eye butchered the silence. "You don't see what you don't expect."

It was obvious once someone said it. This was a road cut into the wall of the Rip. It had been there for ages. It showed signs of use, though not recently.

Elmo split the band. Rusty, Robin, and two others he sent upslope, to find a way back to camp. The rest of us went the other direction.

I got everybody scowling by asking, "Who could be using this? Where could it go?"

Elmo suggested, "How about you shut the fuck up?" He indicated the caucusing crows. "One of them just asked a dumbass question, too."

'Dumbass' was the Croaker referent of the day.

I am nothing if not unable to take a hint. "One-Eye, you saying all this nature is fake? The bug bites sure feel real."

"Seventy per cent. Just to hide the road."

Elmo signaled a halt.

One tight turn under leaves turning golden had us facing an unexpected phantom bridge. It spanned the Rip where the massive collapses had filled the gap two thirds of the way.

"Nobody do anything till I say it's all right," One-Eye ordered. "Including you, Croaker." He babbled about lethal residual magic, the half-lives of curses, and the magnitude of the sorcery needed to drop the walls of the gorge.

The more I stared the more real that bridge became.

The top hundred feet was a complex of mutually supporting wooden beams perched on two massive stone piers. The taller pier rose two hundred feet from the scree. The worked blocks making it up fit so finely that mortar had not been necessary.

Serious sorcery helped, surely, or time would have taken considerably bigger bites.

One-Eye said, "There are no booby trap spells."

Elmo said, "I don't like it. It's too damned convenient."

I grumbled, "So some villain four hundred years back built a bridge just to lure the Black Company into a trap?"

One-Eye argued, "If it was convenient we would've found it a long time ago. We'd be five hundred miles east of here, now."

Whittle volunteered to go over first. If he found no trouble we would set a cold camp on the other side.

We meant to give Whittle a forty yard lead, keeping him within bowshot, but at twenty yards he began to fade.

The crows got all raucous again.

"The illusion is old," One-Eye said. "It's getting patchy."

We found a shack twenty yards beyond the end of the bridge. Inside there was firewood cut for cooking and split for heating, with tinder and kindling. Elmo nixed a fire. Grumble grumble. Mountain nights got chilly, but no need to attract the attention of the people who stored the wood.

It rained enthusiastically all night. The roof leaked only a little.

Come morning Elmo sent three guys back to report. I made myself scarce and deaf so none of them would be me.

Elmo told me later, "You are so lucky you count as an officer. I'd beat you bloody if you were a grunt."

We ate a nasty cold breakfast. One-Eye gave the shack a going-over. All he found was a coin so corroded its provenance could not be determined. Elmo announced, "Now we scout. Croaker, how about you wait here for whoever the lieutenant sends." Phrasing a suggestion but sounding all officious. One-Eye, Whittle, and Zeb the archer nodded.

Selfish bastards. They just wanted to make sure I did not get killed and leave them to self-medicate when they caught the crabs or came up with a dose of the clap.

One-Eye grumbled, "There's that stubborn look, Elmo. He gets that look, somebody is about to come down with the drizzling shits."

"Screw it, then," Elmo said.

I smirked. I got my way, I did, without a word of argument.

We walked a ways. The road was hidden by leaves and brush and faded spells. While you were on it, though, there was no missing it.

Some of the crows stuck with us. They never shut up.

"A secret bridge and a secret road," I mused. "Used, but not much."

"It's old," One-Eye said. "*Way* old."

The world is filthy with old things. Many of them are deadly.

The road did not have that smell.

It was on no modern map. Were it, we would have been long gone.

The road inclined upward for a mile, then began a gentle descent. We encountered our first obstacle after eight or nine miles. Deadwood had clogged a culvert during the night. Run-off had overtopped the road and washed away some fill.

Elmo said, "This won't be hard to fix. Pray there's nothing worse."

The road was wide enough to carry everything we had.

The crows shrieked, scattered. I jumped like somebody had slammed me with a hot iron spike. I squawked, "Spread out! Get down! Get under something and don't move. Don't even breathe."

I took my own advice.

I had just stopped twitching when I heard the scream that had set me off repeated.

It was not audible. It was inside my head, a paean of agony, rage and hatred. It approached unsteadily but should pass to the south.

"Taken!" I breathed. One of the Lady's enslaved sorcerers. Whisper has been after us forever, carrying a bushel of grudges. This airborne sack of pain, grief, and hate, though, was not one I recognized.

Taken are hard to kill. Whisper was harder than most. Yet death is the only escape for the Taken.

Each was once a massively wicked sorcerer who fell prey to the Lady. They never forgot who and what they were but could do little to resist. They were the most damned of the damned.

This latest reeked of aggravated despair and self-loathing.

The scream faded. One-Eye called, "Allee-allee-in-free!"

Elmo observed, "Must be a new one."

One-Eye bobbed his head. That stupid black hat flopped off. I said, "She wasn't hunting."

"She?"

"Felt that way. It don't matter. Taken is Taken. Elmo, we've hiked far enough." I was not used to all this walking. And the farther we went the farther I would have to walk back, uphill all the way.

"We'll stay here. We'll work on the road while we wait."

Whittle reserved his opinion, as did Zeb. One-Eye did not. Elmo paid no attention. One-Eye is always whining about something.

A few riders caught up next morning. They said the Company was on the move. The enemy had not yet noticed.

Elmo told the riders to take over fixing the road. He and his crack team would go find the next obstacle.

The dick.

Our corvine escort never rematerialized. We heard nary a caw.

The moon was near full in a cloudless sky. The screaming Taken passed again, unseen but strongly felt. I could not get back to sleep. I imagined ghosts slinking through the moonlight. I heard things not there sneaking toward me. I had caught more from that Taken than just a scream.

We found another little bridge next morning. It spanned a steep run where the rushing water was barely a yard wide. One rough-hewn replacement plank had not yet begun to gray.

We smelled smoke soon afterward. Lots of smoke, wood and something with a sulfurous note.

I guessed, "There's a village ahead."

Whittle volunteered to scout. Elmo sent One-Eye instead. One-Eye could make himself invisible. He could use birds and animals to spy, given time to prepare them. No breeze stirred a leaf while he was gone, which explained why the smoke hung around.

One-Eye reported. "There are a hundred homesteads scattered around a valley. Motte and timber bailey, in the middle, town around it. Wooden blockhouse where the road leaves the woods. It isn't manned. People are in the fields but they're not working. They're watching the sky."

A farming community hidden in the mountains? Sketchy. Whittle guessed, "Dey's maybe bein' religious crazies."

The cleared ground was a mile wide and several long. The road dropped in near the north end. It wandered the open ground beside a modest river. The river had been dammed in three places, creating one large and two small pools. The large one served watermills on either bank, a flour mill and another, its purpose less obvious. As reported, a blockhouse guarded our approach.

Elmo pointed. "There. In the woods. Tailings piles."

He might know. He supposedly ran away from some mines when he was thirteen. But we all lie about who we used to be.

One-Eye was right about the people. They were bothered.

Elmo suggested, "Let's don't let them know we're here."

We kept a rotating one-man watch.

The moon was full. I had the watch. Whittle would relieve me. Shifting moon shadows had me spooked. I squeaked like a little girl when Whittle got there.

"Gods damn! Do you have to sneak?"

"Yes." Of course he did. The locals had sent four youths to the block-house come sunset.

I had eavesdropped and had learned two things. The boys were not alert and I could not understand a word they said.

I whispered, "Other than those kids coming out nothing's . . . Shit!" The Taken was coming. I sprawled on my belly, bit my lip, wrestled my dread. All that pain and hatred passed directly overhead, fifty feet up, illuminated by the moon.

"Weird," I breathed once it was gone. "I didn't see a carpet, just a lot of flapping cloth." Maybe scarlet cloth. Hard to tell colors by moonlight.

"No carpet," Whittle agreed. Taken use flying carpets.

Petals of cloth whipping in a violent updraft, like leaping black flames, crowned the bailey in the moonlight.

The boys in the blockhouse wailed.

I whispered, "Think they know something they don't like?"

Screaming came from the valley.

"Gots me a 'spicion."

The night puked One-Eye, shaking. He said nothing. Not much needed saying. Something ugly was going on yonder.

The bailey produced what sounded like a god's liquid fart, then violet and darker lightning. We missed some of the show because it was in indigos too dark to see.

"Something awful is happening," I blurted.

Whittle chuckled. "Mought be blessed to spell him quiet."

One-Eye tapped my lips. "Shut the fuck up."

I bobbed my head. I was now inspired. My precious ass's fine health could benefit from an extended silence.

Purple lightning pranced among the rooftops of the town skirting the motte. Something did something weird to something. There was a flash and a roar that left us too deaf to hear one another whine, "What the hell?"

Elmo arrived. Whittle used sign to explain the nothing we knew. Elmo grunted. He waited. We waited. Hearing returned. The boys in the blockhouse caterwauled. The night reeked of Taken rage and despair.

"Overturned anthill over there," Zeb explained. There was just enough light to show it.

The kids from the blockhouse headed home at an uninspired pace.

There was no sign of the Taken.

Elmo looked rough. He had not gotten much sleep. "Damn! There's a thousand people out there. Maybe even two thousand. And half of them got split tails. That's gonna mean trouble."

Few of our not-so-nice brothers had seen a woman lately. Though Elmo did not favour men he did own an abiding conviction of the innate wickedness of women. He *knew* all the ills of the world could be traced to the ear-whisperings of evil-minded females.

I sometimes remind him that his mother was probably a woman. He says that proves his point.

"What's that?" Zeb asked. "What the hell *is* that?"

'That' was the Taken blossoming atop the bailey.

I was right about the scarlet, only it was a deeper red still, like cardinal. Once the bloody petals settled I could not distinguish her from the other figures on the stronghold's catwalk lookout.

The internal screams had been nominal before the bloom. Now they promised headaches.

A long column of mules began to emerge from the town around the artificial hill. They headed our way.

Elmo decided, "Time to go, troops!"

It was. Oh, it was.

The Taken blossomed again, took to the air. How did the mules endure her?

So. We had a Taken headed west on a road where the Company was strung out for miles, supposedly making a miracle escape.

"We need to warn them," Elmo announced, like that was something only he would realize. "Move faster!" He set a ferocious pace. It was soon evident that the Company doctor could not keep up.

Elmo and I went back a long way. He did not let sentiment hamstring him. "You're still moving faster than she is. Keep plugging." Smug ass saw a teachable moment. Croaker would learn about pushing in where he was neither wanted nor needed.

I dawdled, alone, revisiting my arsenal of obscenities, till I felt the Taken gaining.

Snapper's patrol picked me up. Seven riders with eight horses. Timely. The strain of trying to keep the Taken out had exhausted me.

Her sad history kept leaking over. I had my time as a prisoner of the Lady to thank. That lovely horror had burrowed never healed channels into my mind. To the grand good fortune of the world she never found anything useful there.

I observed, "Elmo isn't a complete dickhead."

The nearest horseman snorted. Elmo was a sergeant. That made him a dick by definition.

Soon we ran into other Company people. They were not withdrawing. They were preparing hiding places.

The hell? What about the wagons and artillery and animals? Even if you hid up every other trace you would still have the reek of animals and unwashed men hanging in air that would not stir.

I asked. My companions shrugged. Nobody cared but me.

The shack had become a clinic. My medicine wagon was cunningly hidden in the woods behind. I had patients waiting, and the lieutenant. He did not care that I was tired and hungry.

"I'm considering lopping off one of your feet so you can't pull this shit. You pick."

"There wasn't anybody who couldn't get along without me . . ." Dumbass Croaker, arguing with the boss.

"There are now. See me when you're caught up."

Little actually required my attention. Ticks were the big issue. That was an educational matter, really. The same for blisters, common because nobody had decent footwear anymore.

I wrapped up, washed up, went to see the lieutenant for my reaming.

He and his staff were watching limping men appear over the Rip, on the bridge. This Company flight was no precision manoeuvre.

He will let slide lesser things situationally. His recollection of them is eidetic, however. They ripen. They come back. He looked at me like he was reviewing every indiscretion of mine across the last two decades. "Are the Annals up to date?"

I am Company historian as well as lead physician.

"Up to the day before I went on patrol."

"There's a shitstorm coming. We'll talk job obligation afterward."

"I reckon. We are in a narrow passage. Whisper behind us and this new Taken on the road ahead."

"Not a Taken, Croaker. But definitely new to us."

"Sir?"

"The road."

Oh, the laconic treatment! "What about it?"

"It runs two directions."

"That's kind of in the rules for roads."

That crack brought in a crop of dark looks. Some folks do not appreciate Croaker the Annalist. He has a nasty habit of recording flaws and fuckups as well as triumphs. Plus, as he ages he speaks his mind more.

The lieutenant made a mark in the notebook of his mind. "This road could go back to before the Domination. You went east. We went west. We found a ruined fortress that was the nightmare of someone worse than the Dominator."

So. Once he knew there was a secret bridge and hidden road he went to see where it started.

"The new Taken hails from there?"

"She does. Reminding you, she isn't Taken. Yes. It's only eight miles. It was uglier than that place in Juniper was. Bones everywhere, some of them human."

I was not overwhelmed. Some of that had leaked across from the Taken. "There's more?"

"We found people there, living in squalor you wouldn't believe. Servants, sort of, and livestock in lean times. They don't speak a modern language. We couldn't have communicated without Goblin and Silent." Those two being senior Company wizards.

"Your new Taken is Blind Emon. She *is* blind. She's the slave of something called the Master, which sounds more intimidating in their language. He was human once. He made himself immortal. Now he just lays around and eats, too bloated to move. No one has seen him for ages except Blind Emon. Anyone else gets that close, they end up on the menu."

Ours is an ugly and challenging world.

"So Blind Emon *is* a Taken, just not the Lady's Taken."

Much that had leaked to me from her to me now made more sense.

"If that's how you want to see it. It doesn't matter. What does is, we need her not to notice us."

Hmm. The hiding off the road now made sense. He wanted Blind Emon's caravan to slide by rather than us falling back toward Whisper.

He said, "You know what you need to do. Go do it."

Blind Emon's mules would not be long arriving. Time to get the clinic hidden inside a glamour.

Likely the bridge and road had been built to connect the settlement and the Master's hangout. I could not imagine why, though.

Everybody hid in the best glamour.

Warning came. The mule train was close. I needed no word of mouth. I felt Blind Emon's pain. I was more sensitive to her than was anyone else. Bless my happy days as a prisoner in the Tower!

This contact was the worst yet. It wormed inside more deeply. I became disoriented and distraught. I suffered fifteen minutes of condensed torment, reliving Blind Emon's Taking.

There had been others like Emon, once. She was the sole survivor of the Master's ancient collision with the Domination. He actually antedated the Domination era. He had repulsed the bilious sorcerer-tyrant known as the Dominator, at the cost of becoming the darkness-bound buried horror that he was now.

Emon had started out as a brilliant mage known for her clever mining of ancient mysteries. She was beautiful, she was young, she was in love . . . Then she unearthed something foul that had faded to a dreadful rumour and should have been left to fade even further.

Blinding was the first of a thousand atrocities she suffered.

Too much of her torment leaked over. I was so bowels-voiding scared that I was leaking back.

She was past. She had become an intermittently visible scarlet lily blossoming over the improbable bridge. Countless mules and men crossed that dispiritedly, making an art of their absence of enthusiasm. Blind Emon barely kept them moving.

Shit. Toss it in a hot iron skillet and fry it up, shit!

Distracted, I thoughtlessly moved to get a better look at Blind Emon. Now I had a frozen muleteer staring at me, mouth agape.

I froze, too, hoping to disappear into the glamour.

He dropped his mule's lead tether and oozed away, never breaking eye contact and never showing expression. As I began to have trouble keeping him in focus he stepped out briskly toward home. He never said a word to the mule driver behind him.

Him just taking off was as good as doing some yelling. He was too near Blind Emon to exit unnoticed.

Emon was a ruddy shimmer amidst the high foliage of illusory trees when the muleskinner began his heel and toe dance toward home. She solidified as she moved my way.

I tried becoming one with the forest. That worked, some. She failed to pick me out of the mast but she for sure did sense someone who could be touched, mind to mind.

She searched but never pinned me down.

Kill me!

She knew I would hear her.

Kill me, I beg you!

Her dash round the sky turned frantic. My head felt ready to explode, Normal men ground their knuckles into their temples. Mules brayed.

The plea for surcease from pain, *Kill me!* eventually knocked me out.

Elmo and the original patrol, with my apprentices, surrounded me. I mumbled, "Shouldn't have tapped that last keg." My head throbbed, worst hangover ever. There was a foul taste in my mouth. "I puked?"

"You did, sir," my apprentice Joro admitted. "In record fashion."

I was dizzy. The dizzy was getting worse.

Elmo added, "You yelled a lot, too, in some language nobody knows."

"That was only for a minute," Joro added. "Then you were out and the thing in the sky shrieked in tongues."

Dizziness morphed into disorientation. I fought to focus. "What about her?"

Elmo said, "She went away. She gave up looking for you."

No. Even unconscious she had left me with news enough to know that she had been summoned by the Master.

The Lieutenant appeared. "He going to make it?"

"Yes sir," Joro replied. "The problem is mostly in his head."

"Always the case with him, isn't it? Move out now, Elmo. Let him get his shit together on the road."

They planted me on a captured mule. The old jenny had been loaded with produce that was in Company bellies now. Other captured mules had carried kegs of salt pork, salt and pepper color granules, or sacks of what looked like copper beads. Elmo thought the beads were ore. Others said it was too light. I felt too lousy to work up a good case of give a shit.

Prisoners had been taken but were almost useless. Nobody understood their turkey gobble.

"What the hell?" I blurted when I realized Elmo was headed across the bridge.

"Super shitstorm about to hit. Our guys will be in it. They need you there."

A fight? I was headed for a fight? Feeling like this?

A lone crow, notably ragged watched us pass from a perch on the rail of the bridge. It offered no comment.

The earth trembled. My mule shied. She had been skittish for a while, now.

We were two hours west of the bridge, near where our guys were operating. Twice we heard distant horns.

I was lost. Nobody else had a clue, either. Some thought that the lieutenant hoped to engineer a collision between Whisper and the Master. If that happened Whisper would have to consult the Lady, who might recall the Master from back when she was the Dominator's wife. She might want to get in the game herself. All that would cost time. The lieutenant could build a bigger head start.

The road west of the bridge was better hidden. The farther we went the healthier the glamours became. The earth trembled again. There was noise ahead, muted by the forest and the hill we were climbing.

We found a gang of mules and mule drivers hiding beside the road, just short of the crest. They were unarmed and disinclined to resist. They were terrified. I did not blame them. Blind Emon was not happy.

Some heavy-duty shit was shaking beyond that ridge.

I urged my mule forward. I had friends involved. Some might need help.

Came an epic flash. An invisible scythe topped every tree rising above the ridgeline. Whittle observed, "First news you know, de weader be gettin' parlous roun' dese parts."

Rusty did a credible job of managing his fear. This would be his first experience with battlefield sorcery. A little real terror might be just the specific to purge his soul.

We clambered through fallen limbs that had been shredded like cabbage for kraut, reached a tree line, looked out on a bowl-shaped clearing more than a mile across. It had been farmland once but most was going to scrub, now. A natural rock up-thrust centered it. Ruins topped that. They were ugly and, though it sounds ridiculous, they felt abidingly evil . . . probably because Emon had prejudiced me.

Emon was a roiling storm of cardinal strands above the ruin, filling far more sky than she had over the bridge. Three Taken on flying carpets circled at a respectful distance. A fourth carpet lay mangled in a field, smoldering while someone dragging a damaged leg crawled away.

Imperial soldiers crept toward the downed Taken. Local people were fleeing the invaders.

Elmo nudged me. "Whisper," indicating one of the airborne Taken.

"Where are our guys?" They were nowhere to be seen.

Mule drivers gobbled and pointed.

Some of their gang had reached the ruins before the excitement started.

Elmo said, "We're exposed here. We need to take cover." And that was the moment when ill fortune noticed its opportunity

Whisper sensed me . . . for the same reason that Blind Emon had: my one-time exposure to the Lady's Eye.

Meantime, Emon grew inside my head, trying to gain control of my eyes. She knew who I was, now. She could pull on me as strongly as I could read her. She was more powerful here, near the Master.

She riffled through my memories, trying to gain a better handle on a situation for which she and the Master had been preparing for weeks.

Whisper probed. One sniff of Croaker had her convinced that this incident had been crafted by the Company to inconvenience her personally.

I felt both Taken. Blind Emon had a fine read on my emotions. She pilfered random thoughts while depositing disturbing notions. Whisper drifted our way. Meantime men, mules, and that sentinel crow all oozed into concealment. I refused to give up my view completely.

A keg of the sort that had been aboard so many mules flew up out of the ruin. Blind Emon jinked, did something to shift its course and add velocity. Wisps of smoke trailed it. It exploded thirty feet from Whisper. The fireball enveloped her.

Elmo offered up a soft prayer. "Holy shit. That's gotta hurt."

Whisper wobbled out, trailing flames. She headed down toward someplace where she would not have to fall any farther.

"It was stupid to come here," Rusty grumped. "Ain't our fight."

Even Robin glowered at that. Still, the man was close to making a point. He told Elmo, "We should get the hell gone while that bitch is cleaning the crap out of her drawers."

"Right." Elmo stared past where Whisper had hit hard enough to fling smoking chunks of everything but her fifty yards in a dozen directions. A second keg had sailed out of the ruin.

Blind Emon repeated her manoeuvre, her aim direly precise. A Taken distracted by Whisper's calamity took a direct hit, but this keg did not explode. It fell, shattered, ignited belatedly, created a foul gray miasma.

The impact did overturn the Taken's carpet and left that dread entity hanging on desperately with one hand.

My companions were more interested in travel than observing sorcery spectaculars. Rusty poked me with the dull end of a javelin. "What part of we need to get the fuck out of here are you not getting?" He added, sarcastically, "Sir."

Elmo barked foul agreement from the shredded woods. I moved reluctantly. Our crow friend watched from an oak stump, head cocked.

I felt a sudden urge to put distance between me and what was bound to turn uglier than I could imagine. Emon guaranteed it.

I cannot deliver an account of the evil versus evil sorcery duel of the decade. The desire to see the sun rise again quashed the compulsion to watch. But I do have to report that Emon and the Master engaged in an action they had been preparing for since soon after we invaded their forest.

We clotted up getting out of there, our patrol, mules, gobbling foreigners, local refugees, and the troops and wizards the lieutenant had sent to stir the pot before.

The mob kept moving, less panicked but jockeying and jostling. Everybody wanted across the bridge. Our wizards tried to nurse information out of the gaunt serfs but they were little help.

The road was about to tilt down into the Rip. There would be no leaving it then. A demand of nature haunted me. I would not last till we crossed the bridge. I flitted into the woods, found a useful log, dropped my trousers, began my business buzzed by flies, plagued by mosquitoes, and watched by a curious crow.

I heard a rustle. I looked down. A rattlesnake looked back, equally surprised. I froze. It coiled but reserved its warning rattle.

The crow made a leap and single flap, took station behind the snake. It's eyes shone oddly golden. One began to glow. The glow expanded into a ball an inch in diameter, a foot, a yard. The rattler decided to take its business elsewhere. It took off at maximum snake speed.

My bowels released, explosively and rankly, as I saw exactly what I dreaded: the Lady in the golden light, sweetly beautiful, the most alluring, lovely evil ever. She had not aged a moment in a decade.

The air all round whispered, "There you are. I was afraid I'd lost you. Come home."

Gods! Temptation, Lady is thy name! Suddenly, treason seemed entirely reasonable. I forgot most of what made me *me*, including recollections of suffering in the Tower. She infiltrated channels into my soul already chafed by Blind Emon, scraping up informational residue left by Emon while she explored.

Lady was not pleased.

She abandoned me suddenly, no explanation, leaving me convinced that she regretted not being able to linger.

I tried pretending that I was not disappointed. It gets harder to fool myself as I get older.

One-Eye asked, "You see a ghost?" He was repairing that ugly hat.

"Worse." I told him.

The Lieutenant arrived before I finished. He had a special assignment for Elmo's patrol. We had impressed him that much. Goblin got to join us.

Heads together with the boss, Elmo looked less happy by the second. Meantime, the lieutenant's staff cut mules out of the passing mob. Each carried kegs or sacks of coppery beads.

Elmo rejoined us. "Great news. We've been entrusted with cutting the bridge once everybody gets across. And you get to help, Goblin."

That little wizard's toad face twisted up nasty. He had come around just to check on how we were. Elmo thumped him atop the head before he started bitching. "And we get to do it in the dark, using those kegs that go boom when sorcerers toss them around."

One-Eye got all positive, told Goblin, "There'll be plenty of moonlight later." He grinned wickedly.

"Dey's still light now, some," Whittle noted.

"Yeah. I can still see my wife if I squint," Rusty countered, waving his hand in front of his face.

"We got to do it so let's get doing," Elmo said. "No farting around. Whisper's gang shows before we're done, the lieutenant blows it with us still out there."

A true motivator, our Elmo.

He said, "Robin, you head back up to that last straight stretch and keep a lookout. Somebody comes, you get your ass down here fast."

The complaining commenced.

"Did somebody declare this a democracy?"

One-Eye grumbled, "You can rob a soldier of his choices but you can't take his right to bitch."

Goblin giggled.

Elmo told Robin, "Grab your gear and get. And be careful."

Rusty started getting his stuff together, too.

Elmo shook his head, pointed at the bridge.

So there we were, clambering through the trestlework, operating on guesses based on what we thought we had gotten from the mule people, plus what we saw happen between Blind Emon and the Taken. If it went the lieutenant's way he would look like an improv genius. If not, he could become the fabled Commander Dumbass.

It did not start well.

Rusty fell. He survived only because Elmo had bullied him into wearing a rope safety harness. I dropped a keg, almost fell trying to save it. It rattled around in the rocks below, never breaking up. A keg Goblin was wrestling came apart. Its contents caught fire, sparked by his gear clanking together. For a while we were enveloped by ghastly sulfurous smoke.

There were lesser mishaps too numerous to recount. We accumulated bruises, bloody abrasions, splinters, and mashed fingers. The moon was no help when it rose. We were down in the Rip, under the bridge deck. We did catch a break when a cold breeze rose and dispersed the smoke.

Robin swung over the rail and came down. "Blind Emon is coming." Somewhere, a mule brayed.

Soon we heard chatter and clatter approaching. Blind Emon began to leak over.

Had she won? No. No final winner yet. Whisper and the Taken had gotten mauled, bad. But they had broken the command link between the Master and Emon. A tactical success for them. Emon ran the moment the connection went. No loyalty at all, that gal. She was wiped out, now, barely able to keep up with the people she was trying to protect.

All of the Lady's Taken had suffered grievously.

Emon seemed unaware that the Lady had become interested herself.

The Lady, I was sure, would deal with the Master permanently.

I knew the exact instant that Blind Emon sensed my proximity.

Right away she wanted me to know things. I needed the information. She was hurt bad. She did not expect to see the dawn.

I monkeyed through the trestlework, reported to Elmo. He asked, "You able to communicate?"

"Sort of. She's getting most of my thoughts, now. I think."

"You being a wiseass?"

"No. I feel her emotions. She's excited about being free, down on herself about not being strong enough to refuse to do the evil he made her do, and open about how they planned to use us the way we meant to use them."

"What?"

"They knew we were in the forest from the start. They knew they couldn't avoid a collision with the Taken. There's bad blood from olden times. The mule people serve them, raising most of the food for the people at the ruin. They have been making bang stuff for over a month. They never thought we'd find the road and the bridge. They thought those were hidden too well. They didn't know we had One-Eye in our trick bag."

Elmo muttered something about adding a hundred bricks and chunking that bag into a handy river. Then, "Am I wrong, guessing your new girlfriend wouldn't be running loose if the Lady hadn't been interested?"

I had abandoned all hope of ever clarifying my relationship with the Lady. "Probably."

"So even if Whisper and them are dead and half their troops besides, them that survived will come after us as fast as they can stagger. This shit ain't going near as fast as I hoped. See if you can get her to help."

"How? Doing what?"

"How the fuck do I know? Somehow. Anything. Don't look at me. I'm day labor. I don't get paid to think. I been told that plenty."

A way to make kegs bang bigger slithered into my head. I told Elmo. One-Eye disagreed. "One of them gobble jockeys told me, knock a hole . . ."

"I got it from Blind Emon. The inventor. We pack those sacks of beads around each keg. She sends a curse and the *Bam!* is way bigger."

Blind Emon was feeling vindictive. She hoped people would be on the bridge when she made her wish. She did not much care who.

One-Eye wanted to use burning rope fuses. I wondered where he would get them. Elmo said, "They'd smell the smoke."

"If we do it like Croaker and his new honey want, we have to start all over to pack the stuff the way she wants."

"Then you better not waste time complaining."

I demonstrated the way Emon wanted the bead sacks installed. "And stop asking why. I just know there'll be more bang."

Later, One-Eye announced, "Time to get quiet. Company is coming."

For sure. The enemy, neither sneaking nor hurrying. They had no one pushing them. Their command authority remained engaged with the Master. Chatter suggested that two Taken were gone forever.

I hoped Whisper was one. She had been a pain in the ass for ages.

The Imperials reached the bridge. In moonlight it seemed ephemeral. It caused a lot of awed chatter. Underneath, there was angry muttering bearing on the name of Blind Emon's new boyfriend.

The Imperials were not looking for us. They had been sent to secure a bridge they had not believed existed. They did mention a bounty that had been offered for me.

Some of my brethren probably wondered how they could collect.

The bridge became crowded. The Lady had sent a lot of men. We kept on working underneath, slowly and quietly, me enduring a drizzle of catty whispers. We would have been long gone if that asshole Croaker had not insisted that the kegs and sacks be rearranged.

Even Elmo had an unhappy remark or seven.

The lieutenant did not blow us up, possibly only because he lacked the means.

We were about done. Only Whittle, One-Eye, and I were still under the bridge. Clever Goblin had charted a pearl string of potent glamours that could be used to slink off to the forest unnoticed. Whittle was shaving a bit off a last keg so it would fit where Emon wanted it. One-Eye was doing a whole lot of nothing but being disgruntled. I was trying to manage two sacks of beads while trying not to be distracted by Emon nagging me to hurry. The bridge creaked and rattled as a heavy infantry battalion crossed leisurely. Those not troubled by heights paused to gawk at the spectacular moonlit Rip, where exposed granite looked like splotches of silver.

One-Eye muttered, "Marvelous! And now it's raining!"

Whittle was quickest. He cursed so loud a couple guys up top wondered what they had heard. We were, for once, blessed by Whittle's fierce dialect.

What it was, was, those guys were pissing off the bridge to watch the liquid fall. The breeze broke that up and pushed it under the deck.

Naturally, them amusing themselves that way was all my fault.

One-Eye offered to throw me overboard. He did not do so only because he figured I would glom on and take him with me. All the screaming during the fall might alert the Imperials that something was up.

Finished work, we weaseled carefully out of the trestle into a glamour patch just yards from a clutch of officers debating what to do next. A break for supper and sleep was the more popular proposition. The bridge was secure. The old bitch was busy elsewhere. She would never notice.

A crow squawked angrily.

Crows do not, usually, jabber much after nightfall.

I was behind some brush, inside a glamour reinforced by Blind Emon. She lurked beside me, like a heap of dirty rags, emotion and agony held in check. Most of Elmo's patrol were close, plus the Lieutenant and some henchmen. One-Eye never stopped muttering. He could not let the golden rain go. He would have to take a bath. He had not suffered through one for years. Baths were not healthy. Everyone knew that.

One nocturnal crow nagged on, almost conversationally. Hell! It *was* conversational. One-sided conversational. Listening closely, I could make out most of it.

A generous ass-chewing was in progress. The Lady was not pleased with the day's outcome. She was almost displeased enough to come out her own physical self instead of just relying on a spiritual messenger.

Commanders fell over one another assuring her that a personal visit would be unnecessary.

The lieutenant asked, "What now, Croaker?" He, Elmo, One-Eye, and a dozen others looked at me like the future was mine to design.

Blind Emon sent, *There is only one way.* To her surprise and mine, she had been regaining strength, probably at my expense.

"Huh?" A rejoinder scintillating in its Croakeresqueness.

The conversation between the Imperials and crow drifted our way. I had not paid close attention for several seconds.

"They are here!" the crow insisted. "I smell them!"

"Oh, shit! Get the hell out of here!" I said, having a hard time keeping my voice down. "Run!"

Most of the gawkers had recognized the wisdom of that action already. The lieutenant said, "Whatever the hell the plan is, Croaker, it's time to do it."

"Run."

Then there was just Emon and me, with a hostile horde bearing down and me unable to get my feet to move. Then Blind Emon bloomed.

Petals waving like tentacles, she rose and swept toward our enemies. They produced squeals of awe and fear. Dumbass Croaker got his feet unstuck. He stumbled along after Emon.

Several petals extended. One thirty yards long snapped a fleeing crow from the air with a vicious *crack!* Others snatched at officers' throats.

Get down. Cling to the earth like it is your mother's teat if you want to live.

I did so. That Blind Emon was one smooth talker.

I could still see her and the bridge. She soared over the Rip. Petals reached into the trestlework.

Flash! And then a parade of flashes, with rolling thunder. The middle of the bridge humped up eight feet like the back of a sea serpent surfacing. The rest of the deck rose off its supports. The roar deafened me. I did not hear the screams of the hundreds falling into the gorge.

Nasty smoke masked everything. It swallowed Blind Emon. I never saw her again. She sent no farewells.

In time the breeze pushed the smoke away.

And there stood that gods-be-damned bridge, singed, but ... The gods-be-damned deck had dropped back exactly where it was before it flew up. Imperials lighted torches and started checking its stability.

Shee-it! Oh holy fecal fall!

Time to run!

Run, Croaker, run. Run like hell is on your ass, because it is for sure going to be, real soon now, and it will be very, very hungry.

The miracle in this latest miracle escape had just turned out to have a great big old hairy-assed shaggy dog story ending.

BONE EATERS
THE BLACK COMPANY ON THE LONG RUN

"The Bone Eaters" follows on some time after "Shaggy Dog," when bandits try to ambush the Company vanguard. That does not turn out well for them. Then shenanigans involving Hungry Ghosts ensue.

Whittle and Fall Woo led the trigger gang: four unreliable brothers with a decrepit, covered goat cart, two broke-down mules, a moth-eaten burro dragging an open cart, plus some refugee slatterns and associated brats.

Out of sight behind, the Company stretched for miles along a track locals called a road, crossing stony hills whiskered with brush and scraggly young pines. Wildfire had passed through, years back. Charred adult tree corpses still tilted drunkenly.

I rode with the hidden guard posse supporting the scouts.

The brigands were new to the trade. Only one was mounted, aboard a nag that might not last another month. The rest were kids armed with rusty knives and farm tools.

The barefoot boy on horseback gobbled a stanza of "Stand and deliver!" in the local dialect. Another waved a sharp-ended stick and pranced. The rest approved with less enthusiasm.

A brown something materialized beside the rider's ear. He squealed. The thing looked like a monkey with too many legs, each tipped with a claw like a pruning knife. It had too many yellow eyes, too.

Hiding in the goat cart was that nasty toad of a wizard, Goblin, who loved crafting revolting illusions.

Whittle disarmed six youngsters, injuring two. The boy on the horse galloped off, squalling.

Ranging ahead, I caught up first—and saw nothing to elevate my esteem for humanity.

Whittle had left the captives with Rusty and Robin. Rusty was a waste of meat, a coward, a bully, a shirker, and a scrounge. Only Robin liked him. Everybody thought somebody ought to put Rusty down.

Whittle left Rusty in charge because he wanted to be rid of dead weight. He lacked the imagination to see a potential problem in leaving Rusty self-supervised.

Rusty had a bandit bent over a boulder. Both had their trousers down. Rusty was having no joy. Little Rusty was not interested. Robin sprawled nearby, aching in body and soul, tangled up with a couple of bound, gagged, and extremely agitated male captives. He had tried to interfere. He met my eye, gasped, "Croaker! Please! Help her."

I spurred my mount.

Rusty stayed lucky. A low branch ambushed me as my valiant steed lunged forward. Over her tail I went.

Pants held up left-handed, Rusty gave me a case of boot rash while letting the world know that he had had it with my holier-than-thou, candy-ass whining. "Croaker, grow a set! Act like a godsdamned real soldier."

Hoofbeats approached.

Rusty went white behind his freckles.

His victim moaned and tried to crawl away.

Darling and the sorcerer Silent dismounted. Silent fixed Rusty with a venomous glare. Rusty saved the excuses. He always had some but knew they would be wasted today. Darling always knew the smell of bullshit. Rusty would fool himself before he fooled her.

Darling's sad disdain was palpable. Rusty wilted. Darling was no longer younger, was never pretty and never available, was ice hard outside but suffered from a soft heart. We all love her. And her good regard is precious even to the worst of us.

Was Rusty smart enough to realize how lucky he was, having Darling show up before anyone else? Even in a situation so similar to her own first brush with the Company, back in another age? Death had stalked him for months already. Only Hell's luck and Darling's grace had kept him on the weather side of the grass this long.

Silent's evil eyes said he would happily give Rusty a painful nudge along the downward road, were Darling not there to stay him. His sorcery will not work around Darling. No sorcery will. The Lady herself would have no recourse but mind and muscle in Darling's presence.

Darling set me on the girl. I brushed auburn hair aside. The kid was pretty under the grunge. I saw no physical damage. Darling tapped her own forehead, belly, and signed. Silent shrugged. He could not tell from inside the magical null.

Darling feared the girl might be pregnant, not thanks to Rusty, who had suffered another of his life's numerous disappointments.

She had me check Robin and the male prisoners next.

Robin would heal. That idiot kid was more worried about Rusty than about himself. Some friendships just never make sense.

Rusty now had his arms wrapped around his knees, his head tucked. He rocked slowly, knowing he was well and truly screwed—and probably did not understand why.

No captive was smart enough to speak a language any of us knew. Talking loud or slow did not help.

More Company men arrived. Rusty rocked faster.

His behavior had not been extreme. Rape was weather. War weather. And good men do not join the Company. His big problem was, he was "that asshole Rusty" that everybody loved to hate.

Darling held Robin's hand briefly. The kid took that as a divine dispensation. Then she made a round of the prisoners. One boy met her eye stubbornly, not defiant but definitely determined. He kept an eye on the pretty girl always.

They would be siblings. Maybe twins. They were of a size and looked enough alike.

His glances toward Rusty were not kind.

Rusty rocked.

Robin moved the bandit girl without touching her, distancing her from the scene of her embarrassment. I stayed close. She was scared but neither defiant nor resigned. She observed, calculated, abided her time.

Then she groaned, clutched herself as though kicked in the gut, and puked.

Darling had come close enough to touch her.

Bandit girl was not knocked up despite having run with an all-male gang.

Sporadically, randomly, unpredictably, I am intuitive. She was a witch. A menarche-onset wild talent who did not yet understand what she was. She would not respond to Darling so violently, otherwise.

Wild talents seldom prosper. They scare the mud out of people. Evil sorcerers begin as local nuisances who grow to become regional afflictions. The worst then begin raising wicked armies and putting up dark towers. So why not burn them before they set the earth to shaking?

Me, I reckon any pretty young sociopath can create chaos without injecting magic into the mix.

Darling flurried signs at Silent, telling him to teach and protect the girl and make her keep her distance. When the girl hurt because Darling was close Darling hurt because the girl was close. Darling had me spread the word that the girl was not to be touched even if she sprinted through camp bare-ass begging for male attention.

The girl and her friends became not quite prisoners who were not quite guests. Silent sloughed their care and feeding off onto Robin. The girl seemed comfortable with him.

Rusty got busy being an invisible man. He stayed far away from the girl.

Some of our tagalong refugees spoke a dialect related to that of the bandits. Darling offered the bandits an opportunity to participate in our great adventure. They would be expected to pull their weight, of course.

They owed us for several meals before they fully understood the peril they had put themselves into. Our one-time employer, now our great enemy, the near-goddess the Lady, was a traveler's tale in these parts. Her hunting dog sorceress, the Taken Whisper, was a complete unknown. Too late the newcomers learned that our pursuers were determined to convert us all into acres of feasts for ravens, flies, and scavengers.

The girl's name was Chasing Midnight. She was scary smart. She picked up enough language to get by in just a week. Though officially Silent's

problem, she stuck to Robin till she learned that I was educated enough
to be Company physician and Annalist. Literacy is sorcery itself in the
hinterland. Plus, smelly old Croaker looked easy prey for pretty girl
manipulation.

She definitely had an unconscious talent, proven by her having run
untouched with that gang of boys. It explained Rusty's disappointment,
too. Males who got close could not sustain an interest.

Darling had a similar aura.

Midnight's twin brother was Chasing Moonlight, not so bright but loyal
to a lethal fault. She was twelve minutes older. Their story was familiar.
Bad weather, pests, poor crops, relentless tax collectors. Many of us played
a turn in a similar drama once upon a time.

"They fear me," Midnight complained. She was underfoot all the time,
now, two weeks on. She meant the refugees traveling with us.

"They think you're a witch. They lost everything because of a witch."

"Stupid thinking."

"Never any shortage of stupid, girl."

She muttered something in her own language, which I was having trouble
picking up. She was no help, of course. As long as only she and her boys
spoke the tongue, they could share secrets. She was their leader now.

The cavalier who ran from Goblin's devil was an older brother, now
first on her contemptibles list. He had wakened her keep-off-me talent.
His fierce cowardice was sugar on the biscuit. She only hinted at the ugly.
I did not pursue it. That is not done in this tribe.

I did press her on her personal habits. I want clean, neat, healthy people
around me. She considered the pressure absurdist humor. "Why bother?
You do not expect to escape your Whispering Doom." She meant Whisper,
who certainly planned to be our doom.

"The Company has faith in Darling."

"The black man that does not talk. He is dangerous?"

"Only if you're a threat to Darling."

"Not I."

I shrugged. She could be the Lady's plant. The old terror would not
scruple against using a child. "He's our strongest wizard." She had not
yet met Goblin or One-Eye. One-Eye had been missing for more than a
month. "Just don't make him worry about Darling."

Moonlight and pals rolled up. They were FNGs with attitude now. No longer hungry, they objected to having to do shit jobs just because they were new. They wanted Midnight to wiggle her ass and get them easier jobs.

People. Saints and philosophers tell us to love them. No doubt anchorites who never suffered the everyday mob. I seldom see anyone actually deserving of brotherly love.

But I have been here in the Company most of my adult life.

I do hope that karma is the keystone of the universe—even if I have to come back as a banana slug myself.

Nerves frayed. This was the Company on the long run, a flight already years in duration. We had luck out the wazoo, every day, like it was going out of style, and most of it was bad. Which we expected.

Only . . . Whisper's scouts faded away, which made no sense. They ought to be pressing harder than ever, to repay the hurt we had done them not so long ago. But they lost interest instead. Or they lost the trail.

Our flight slowed. Some days we moved only a mile or three. Other days we did not move at all.

The villages we skirted became less bristly. We paid for supplies rather than make new enemies. Some villages adopted the less repugnant of our female hangers-on. I did not mind. I would not miss having all those children underfoot.

My apprentices were exasperating. They were competing to see who was laziest.

"One of you is going back to the ranks at the end of the week." That got their attention. "Midnight, who is showing some actual interest, will take his place."

She had overtaken them in the last month. She did not evade fatigue details. She worked hard, wanted to learn, never complained. And she was killer cute, a skill with which no boy can compete.

I looked Joro in the eye, he being the most useless. "Since Moonlight and his gang left us there are openings in human-waste management." Of which I was lord and arbiter. I do not get my own paws dirty. I do decide who does.

Midnight's friends had vanished one night, several back. Nobody missed their whining. Only Midnight's feelings were hurt. I wondered why they had not taken her along.

I wondered to Darling, the Lieutenant, Silent, and Elmo. Elmo and the Lieutenant did not care. Darling would see no evil till it bit her. Cynical Silent figured Midnight was behind the desertion even though she stuck with us herself.

By being helpful and pliable she became increasingly suspect to Silent. His reasoning was impossible to follow.

Then One-Eye turned up, which complicated things considerably.

"The Lady called them off," One-Eye reported. "For their own safety." He was tired and hungry. The rest of us thought he needed a bath, something he would not undertake voluntarily. "Two Taken were killed when Whisper attacked that castle. She and the other Taken got hurt, too, but our luck held. She didn't die. She's *almost* dead, but we'll eventually see her back with the last ounce of mercy boiled out. Her troops, after fighting us and suffering what I've been putting them through, are used up."

He meant their fighting spirit was gone, not that their number had been exhausted. There is never any shortage of men willing to take the Lady's coin. She is a reliable paymaster—who purchases your soul and conscience as well as your time.

So with the surviving Imperial sorcerers concentrating on staying above ground, our less potent wizards could serve their minions misery in epic portions.

"You shoulda been with me," One-Eye told Silent. "I ain't never had so much fun since . . . Since before buzzkill Croaker signed up! Mice in a barrel!" He grinned, flashing terrible teeth, trying to flirt with Midnight, who had come along to get a look at a living legend. Said legend was older than dirt, often hard to distinguish from dirt, and when not engaged in criminal activities, about as ambitious as dirt. It was a certainty that he had lined his pockets somehow during his independent venture.

He held a cherished position on every brother's shit list but never soared up where he might be at risk like Rusty. He did occasionally make himself useful. He could do amazing things if the notion took him.

Midnight hunched deeper into my shadow, pressed her fists against my back like she was terrified and needed protection. All contrived. She was raw but definitely an actress, all the world her stage.

Nothing like a hundred-and-some-year-old, shriveled-up little black wizard making eyes at a pubescent girl to get the boys sneering.

One-Eye was calculating himself, of course. His world is a stage, too, his life performance art.

He gave the remnants of his disgusting old black hat a quarter turn, winked again. "I'm in love. You want to sell me that one, Croaker?"

Midnight's squeak might have indicated real concern.

Darling signed almost too fast to follow. Had One-Eye not been as dark and wrinkled as a worn out-boot, he might have turned pale.

Ages have flown since the Company rescued child Darling from some Rebel Rustys when she was years younger than Midnight now. Many who were with us then have gone on to darker worlds. But Darling remembers. Darling does not suffer anyone making light of horrors she endured herself.

She was grimly uncomfortable, anyway, with so many sorcerers so close by.

Midnight was uncomfortable, herself, but stubbornly insisted on slaking her curiosity.

One-Eye said, "Here's the story. The Lady told them to back off, rest up, and get healthy. She'll keep the Eye on us. She'll send new Taken if Whisper can't get healthy. She'll come out here herself if she has to." He winked at me, pumped his left thumb between the first two fingers of that hand.

I was once a captive in the Tower, while the Company was in the Lady's service. She turned me loose eventually. I have been taunted about being the old horror's bed buddy ever since.

Customers awaited me at the clinic. "Twiller, my man, tell me, how does a guy get the clap in the middle of a godsdamn desert?"

True desert it was not, just dry scrubland that went on and on and on.

"Never mind. I know. You got it from some woman who got it from Swain who got it from some other woman who got it from you the last time you had it."

Twiller had the grace to look sheepish. His behavior would not change, though. He was still that young, and none too bright.

Robin was my other customer. His ailment was one no physician has ever cured. Sometimes Midnight seemed interested back. Her stay-off-me aura weakened when he was around.

The kid was the gentle soul that Rusty could never be, which did not serve him well with a girl. He needed more push.

Midnight mused, "The old black man did not tell us everything."

"No." I had seen the tells. One-Eye was shifty. If a potential score was out there we might hear nothing solid till the fallout set in. If it touched on the safety of the Company, though, he would be whispering with Darling and the Lieutenant now.

I asked, "You know anything about what's ahead of us?" I had a suspicion about why the Lady had leashed her hounds.

"We approach the bounds of fable already."

We had covered little more than a hundred miles since her ambush. With no pressure on we slowed despite a consensus that we ought to grab all the separation we could.

"You can't be that ignorant. The bounds of fable sounds like something somebody avoiding the subject would blat. Meaning somebody had something she didn't want to talk about. But that wouldn't make sense. She'd be strutting into the shit storm with the rest of us."

"I know fairy tales. Only fairy tales. I never heard of anybody who ever actually saw the Village of Hungry Ghosts." She paused. I said nothing. The vacuum moved her to fill it. "My da would say that was because nobody who did ever came back."

Her words for Village of Hungry Ghosts were unfamiliar, but the concept was not. I had encountered it long ago, while we served the Lady in the east reaches of the Empire.

Hungry ghosts are not regular spooks, the spirits of dead folks that cannot move on. Legend described hungry ghosts as being more like vampire phantoms. They would possess the living and consume them slowly from within. They would never move on to heaven or hell or wherever because their earthly business was never done. They would migrate from host to host till something somehow annihilated them.

Where did they come from? The stories do not explain. Like monkeys and crows, they are. Likely an ancient sorcerer was involved, or a cruel, mischievous dawn-time god.

Great communal sorcery was required to effect a migration from a dying body to a fresh one, at least in the hungry ghost stories I had heard.

I told Midnight. She shrugged. She had nothing to add. My information fit with what she knew.

I left her to Robin, went to talk it over with those in charge.

Fantastic as a village of hungry ghosts seemed, the behavior of our enemies made more sense in that context.

We should expect an occasional Imperial nudge intended to keep us hopping toward disaster.

I am destined to be in the wrong place at the wrong time when shit happens. I turned up while Rusty was trying to plug Midnight. Then . . .

I was two rods from the latrine when someone inside squealed in surprise, pain, and terror. The moon's light showed me nothing because Darling insisted that the pits be masked by canvas to preserve the modesty of the females among us.

I hollered as I charged.

Two kids came out to see about the noise. Both had deserted with Chasing Moonlight. They owned no combat skills. I laid them out as quick as it takes to tell it.

Canvas did not mask the latrine from the eye of the sky. The half moon shed light enough to show me what I expected: Midnight's brother and friends swarming Rusty, who was in serious trouble, having been caught seated on logs with his trousers down.

Punch! Grab! Sling! Prod, poke, and jab! Punch! I am no master infighter, but I have stayed in one piece for years. And the idiot kids had not posted a lookout, or said lookout had been unable to resist joining in on the fun.

Give them this: they hit their man at the exact perfect moment. But we need to knock off points for not having brought the tools to make quick work of the job.

My yells brought help fast. Quick response is something we do well, our lessons learned in a brutal school. There is still a Company.

Nobody got dead. Not even Rusty, though he might wish for worse luck when he woke up and began to enjoy the pain. His chances would be iffy for a while. He lost a lot of blood, one weeping shallow wound at a time. The boys cut him a lot, inside a shithouse. Sepsis was almost certain. Also, in time, a spider's web collection of thin new scars.

Only a double handful of cuts needed stitching. The rest I cleaned with alcohol and swabbed with an astringent. I made Midnight assist though I was sure she had had nothing to do with the attack. The lesson was that medicine and surgery leave no space for personal feelings.

I know. I make exceptions. I am dumb enough to have recorded a few in these Annals. Sic a lawyer on me. I will borrow some black on his hair-splitting ass, too.

So. Do as I say, child, not as I do.

She amazed me. Rusty naked and painted with dried or jellied blood troubled her very little. She did not interfere with his hunger for breath. She might have considered elevating him to eunuch status but let that go, too. She followed instructions precisely. Scary, a kid her age having that much control. What next? Conquering armies and new dark towers?

I was halfway in love when we finished, not with the girly girl but with the unflappable surgeon's assistant.

All the others did was keep Robin away while Midnight and I fixed Rusty. Then, tired as she was, she took over wrangling Rusty's only living friend.

During that was when Chasing Midnight finally admitted to herself that she might be the wild talent the rest of us said. She began flirting with all of our wizards. They all, Silent included, took her on as a kind of smart, pretty pet.

She started winning the hearts and minds of the soldiers, too. She recruited herself a platoon's worth of adopted, protective big brothers.

Definitely a menace to tomorrow, this Chasing Midnight.

Darling got a little jealous.

She never had any competition before.

I stretched out aboard a cot a parallel yard from Rusty's and fell asleep halfway hoping I had not gotten every wound completely clean. The regular guy suppressed by the physician wished "that asshole Rusty" all the joys and complications of protracted gangrene.

Darling's judgments were neither harsh nor unpopular. Moonlight's boys got extra duty. Moonlight himself got extra extra for fomenting. Darling overlooked their desertion completely.

Oh. The boys had to carry Rusty's litter when we were on the move. That pained them more than any other punishment could.

"We have a problem," the Lieutenant told the assembled officers. Darling sat to one side, leaving it all to him. She washed me in disapproval. I had brought Midnight. She wondered if something untoward was going on with us. Croaker might be a good man, generally, but he *was* a man.

My thinking was, the kid ought to start learning now because she could end up running the show someday. She had that much going on.

Silent disapproved, too, but only because Darling was hurting. He agreed with my long-range assessment despite what having a sorceress in charge might mean.

"We have fallen under a glamour," the Lieutenant told us. "It keeps us from going the direction we want." No secret, that. Whatever we tried, come sundown the sun would be directly ahead. Come sunrise it would be directly behind. Darling's talent was too localized to resist any sorcery beyond a hundred feet. Those she could not shield shambled on like zombies.

Our wizards would fight it but still had to trudge on along with the other hundreds.

So there it was. The Village of Hungry Ghosts, where immortal souls, perhaps once human, lived on in old but epic squalor. I was reminded of a bat cave occupied for ten thousand years. The immortality of the hungry ghosts produced neither prosperity nor any form of sanitation. A commentary on the essential wickedness of willful circumvention of natural order.

Our wizards sat in a row, inches separating their shoulders. They stared at ruins so ancient they were barely recognizable as recollections of human construction. Midnight rested on her knees behind the gap between Goblin and One-Eye, determined to observe and learn. The rest of the Company were supposed to be setting camp a half mile away, beyond a narrow defile of a dry wash, beside a bitter pool fed by a marginally less bitter spring that once must have served the village. Remnants of an aqueduct ran to the memory of a town. Darling made herself an anti-magic plug in the defile, at a point where she could both watch and protect the handful of us who had assistants who could set up our part of the camp for us while we did something we found more interesting.

I was inside Darling's null, barely, feeling the siren call of the village, which was as relentless as gravity itself. Whatever our efforts, sooner or later somebody was going to break down and go sprinting in.

Goblin said, "They're bound here. They can't leave without a body to carry them. But if they do leave and their host dies, they'll die, too."

One-Eye said, "They do generate one hell of a siren call, don't they? We can barely handle it."

"The Lady knew," I told the Lieutenant, who relayed my comment to Darling.

She nodded. She seemed unconcerned, there inside her null, keeping scores from marching toward personality death. Did she not get the horror?

Of course she did. She was Darling. Darling always understood, better than any of us.

Silent signed that he sensed six hungry ghosts but thought there might be more so long separated from flesh that they had become undetectable. He warned that those would be more dangerous than those that he could sense. They would be the hungriest. They would be able to seize living flesh. Elaborate ceremonies were necessary only for abandoning used-up flesh, not for taking new bone.

Silent seemed remarkably well informed. I did not ask. He would tell us if he thought we needed to know.

Goblin and One-Eye muttered. Silent signed. Midnight watched and listened. She read sign well enough now to eavesdrop on Silent's dancing fingers. She was not good at signing herself, yet, though.

She would learn. You have to sign to deal with Darling or Silent. Darling is deaf and dumb. Silent is bone stubborn about not talking. And signing is handy when we are sneaking around on people we mean to hurt or who plan on hurting us.

Darling beckoned. I needed to fall back to where she blocked the defile, restraining glassy-eyed, confused shamblers who wanted to go make love with the hungry ghosts.

Sometimes our most potent resources conflict. Darling's null, though, never spread out enough for general use in battle. We employed her in ambushes and where sorcery-capable antagonists were unaware of what they faced.

Our antagonist here was hunger incarnate, or would-be incarnate. The hungry ghosts had no other drive. Normally they did not need to be anything else. Lure a victim with the siren call, devour him from within, slowly, while the flesh withered, then find another host, always where there were fellow incarnates to help with timely migrations.

Speaking of. If these ghosts snagged enough Company people they could migrate physically, collectively, the lot of them, somewhere with a rich supply of replacement flesh.

Did anyone else realize that? "Are any of them still incarnate?"

Silent raised three fingers and flurried signs that said something about asses.

Goblin translated. "There is one old woman and two wild asses."

"They possess animals, too?" I conjured an image of possessed killer box tortoises. Tortoises were common in this almost desert.

"Higher order vertebrates."

"What do we do now?" Midnight asked. Very young, untrained, yet confident that she belonged to a "we" that included only her and the men she knelt behind, not our broader gang.

Chasing Midnight never lacked confidence or self-esteem. Neither did she own an inflated notion of who and what she might be.

No one but the Annalist, who worries about secret meanings hidden within words, studied her question. The Annalist relayed his curiosity to Darling. Darling was in a mood because people kept piling up and jostling her as they tried to see what was going on out front. She signed back, "Is it possible to kill the hungry ghosts?"

Unsentimental and pragmatic, our Darling, in the hard places—especially where somebody was preying on weaker folks. She disdained painful revenge but lacked all qualms about cutting throats she deemed in need of cutting.

Rusty had that in mind back when he was doing all that rocking. He had it in mind, still. He was putting in his longest streak of good behavior ever.

I relayed Darling's question aloud. Maybe because of the "first do no harm" oath from when I was too young not to have a caul of idealism across my eyes, I do have one of the softer hearts in the Company.

They tell me it will get me killed. No doubt they are right.

Once again Silent had the answer. "Yes."

Darling signed, "Then get killing. I cannot block this path forever."

The null is part of her, always. When it goes active against sorcery it sucks the energy out of her the same as the sorcery sucks it out of the sorcerer.

It was obvious immediately that there was a sad gap between knowing that a hungry ghost could be killed and knowing how the killing could be managed. Even Silent had no suggestions.

"Oh, Sweet Billi Afi!" One-Eye blurted, in a flat voice. "I guess it had to happen."

Four people oozed toward the Village of Hungry Ghosts. They had circumvented Darling by clambering over a ferociously rocky barrier hill between the ruins and the bitter oasis. All four had bloodied themselves during the crossing. Two were refugee kids. One was a mildly retarded cook's helper named Thorodd Asgeir who had been with the Company for years without capturing the attention of the Annalist. The last was one of the Chasings' boy bandits.

I shouted. Goblin and One-Eye shouted. Silent gripped Midnight's arm and kept her from charging her doomed cousin. None of the four heard a word. They walked faster as they got closer to the village. Their expressions said they were marching straight on into heaven.

Goblin and One-Eye groaned. One-Eye began a muttered countdown. Silent shivered, angered by all the stupid. Midnight mostly looked puzzled. Unlike the old men she had no idea what was about to happen.

She had not yet seen the true bleakness of the world. Hunger, cold, and human bad behavior were the only ugliness she knew.

"Two, one, and . . ." Seconds passed. One-Eye was not quite in rhythm today. "And there she goes."

The screaming started as a dense and intense shimmer enveloped the four. One refugee kid's head exploded. All four came apart in tiny, bloody fragments. The insanely hungry ghosts knew no restraint.

The shimmer intensified as ropes of twisted light streaked into the bloody scrum.

One-Eye told Silent, "There were more dormant ones than you thought."

Silent grunted, which proved how rattled he was.

Midnight gasped once, then just watched. Her face lapsed into the grim hostility that had shone there whenever she looked at Rusty back on that first day. She was scary, there, for a while.

Meantime, One-Eye declared this shit to be all Croaker's fault because he disappointed his honey in the Tower so bad that she wanted him and his friends hooked up with horrible deaths.

I called across, "I would sincerely appreciate you giving that crap a rest."

He grinned a grin full of nasty teeth and gave that foul hat of his a full half turn. He was thrilled. He had gotten under unflappable Croaker's skin.

I said, "I guess we can assume we were pushed to these hungry ghosts. But might there be more to it than just trying to put the hurt on us?"

The wizard crew looked up in militarily precise cadence as a shadow rippled across the ground. I looked up, too, in time to see a smaller vulture join a pair already circling. A young one, not long out of the nest, now an apprentice to mom and dad in the carrion clean-up business.

"Suppose the Lady can control hungry ghosts once they occupy somebody's body?"

"She might see this as a kind of Taking?" Goblin asked. "She could get control of the Company?"

"Just thinking out loud."

"It would friggin' fit!" One-Eye bellowed. "For the gods' sake, Croaker, you sure can pick them!"

I had some trouble keeping my temper. "What happened to those four idiots maybe says I'm all wet, but she *is* a long ways away. Maybe she don't know how starved these hungry ghosts are."

Darling's hands danced. I relayed. "The call is getting weaker and confused. The feeding frenzy broke their concentration."

Chasing Midnight now sat between Silent and One-Eye, with Goblin moved to the apex of a triangle. The girl did all the talking. Filthy old gray heads bobbed. Then Silent headed my way.

Silent and Darling may be soul mates at the heart of the romantic tragedy of our age. They are what they are, doomed never to touch, but all their years of yearning have narrowed the distance they have to keep between them. They can stay close for hours sometimes, so long as they do not touch or make eye contact.

They manage, however painful that must be. To quote our fallen Captain, "You do what you got to do."

Darling and Silent would cuddle up as much as nature allowed. They denied that any such thing was going on, of course, but even dim thug Rusty saw the untruth in that.

Which signified only because Silent approached Darling close and signed in a blur, presenting a suggestion on behalf of Chasing Midnight. At the same time he offered arguments against Darling subjecting herself to the risks.

Darling entered the Village of Hungry Ghosts in measured steps, that dumb-ass Company Annalist Croaker beside her on her right. He carried a seldom-seen bow that had been a gift from the Lady on his release from the Tower. He was pretty good with that bow.

Along for the stroll was my favorite sergeant, Elmo, and two old soldiers named Otto and Hagop. Also with us, at Darling's behest, speaking in tongues with terror, was Rusty.

There was no popular support for his presence, but Darling insisted. He needed a chance for redemption. Even he understood, but, still, he looked like hammered shit as we headed into the ruins.

We were about to execute a scheme bought instantly by Darling when Midnight proposed it. Darling had us drafted and rolling as quick as it took the buzzard family to complete a couple circles around the sky.

Darling eased through the ruins, each step careful. We saw some dressed stones still topping other dressed stones, but I suspected that the original structures would have been mostly mud brick. Rain would not be a frequent problem here.

We smelled decay and saw some bones, but nothing like what I had worked myself up to expect.

Hagop grumbled, "This reminds me of someplace we used to be."

Otto bobbed his head. "Aloe, five, six years ago."

I recalled, "That country was flatter. And civilized. There were people. Mostly nice people."

Hagop said, "It had the same feel, though. All the time like the shit was gonna come down any minute."

Yes. True. There was a sense of imminence. I became shakier. Hard not to suffer the heebie-jeebies when what looked like snakes of water slithered and splashed in the air on all the fringes of Darling's tightened null. They would strike instantly if any crack opened.

She grew more bold. That crack would not develop. She *was* the null. It did not turn on and off, though she could control its range and intensity a little. A very little.

Looked like she knew where she wanted to go.

The advancing null scared up a skeleton ass draped in mangy, saggy hide. It shambled out of a dark place, set out to put distance between us and it.

Darling made an impatient gesture my way. Why was I just standing there, gawking?

"Hungry ghosts," I reminded myself. There was no moral ambiguity.

The black arrow hit the air immediately. The frightened animal inside this being with a capacity for moral anxiety *could* get things done. Better to be alive tomorrow to whimper about what got done today.

The arrow wobbled through the fuzzy bounds of the null. The spells on it took life. It struck behind the animal's head, skipped off bone into brain. Rusty charged. Otto and Elmo yelled at him to hold up, it was too dangerous to get so far ahead. But nothing happened. When we got there Rusty was jabbing his spear into the carcass repeatedly.

Otto stepped up with his big ax and removed the wild ass's head, after which good buddy Hagop began trying to recover my arrow for me.

Darling signed, "The brat was right." Not entirely pleased to admit that. "That was a crippling shock to the monsters. Let us move on quickly while they are panicked." She walked on, again looking like she knew where she wanted to go.

We took our places, Rusty now seeming all twitchy. There was a long difference between bullying and cold killing.

The watery ropes around us were fewer and more randomly behaved. They stuck with us out of inertia, not purpose.

Darling's confidence soared. Her step quickened. Thirty yards onward a long, sad moan of despair from under a stone slab brought us to a halt. Shaking, Rusty took a knee, looked underneath. "It's hollowed out under here. Somebody is in here."

Elmo, Hagop, and Otto took hold of the slab and heaved. Three men were not enough. Rusty and I joined them. Darling stood by, shielding us from the raging mad terror of the discorporate hungry ghosts.

The hidden woman had been unable to keep quiet when the null touched her. She was not old in years lived, she was just starved to where her bones were brittle and her weight had shrunk to nothing. Were she not possessed, she would be dead already.

We looked to Darling. Somebody had to act. She should pick.

Ticking and twitching, Rusty started to step up but then thought better. Darling might figure he was sucking up.

Darling used Otto's ax to do it herself. She was muscular, but that ax was heavy. She damaged the blade badly.

Was I alone in seeing the moment of human terror and pleading in the woman's eyes as the ax fell? I did not ask. Something else we do not talk about with our brothers.

The head rolled away. The body jerked once and stopped moving forever. Not much blood got loose. What did smelled diseased.

The impact was instant. Insanely despairing emotion soaked into the null. The siren call collapsed completely. The rest of the Company picked up the next phase of Midnight's plan, which began slowly because people had to shake the wool out of their heads before they could understand.

Our intrepid band pressed on, looking for the wild ass being worn by the last incarnate hungry ghost.

That hungry ghost did not want to get caught. It wanted to stay out of sight till we messed up and exposed some of our people to seizure.

A few of our idiots tried, but Midnight, with stubborn help from Goblin, One-Eye, and Silent, kept the suicidal stupidity in check.

The discorporate hungry ghosts never recovered enough to regenerate their call. Midnight kept their madness boiling by having livestock paraded outside the confining boundary. All reason fled the ghosts. Midnight and the wizards began to expose livestock carefully. The animals fought, futilely. They calmed instantly once a hungry ghost got inside.

I asked Silent, "Can you keep track of which ones are infected?"

Staring into nothing, in the general direction of where Robin and Rusty were watching, he signed, "I can. We can."

Those animals would be slaughtered and eaten first.

Practical, pragmatic Darling and Chasing Midnight! Darling's harshness did not trouble me. I had seen it for years. I was comfortable with how her head worked. Chasing Midnight, though, did worry me. She had so much potential and was still so young. She might make bad decisions. She might be nudged onto the shadowed path by another's bad behavior. She could end up a victim of her own adolescent humors.

Darling smirked when I mentioned that. "Smitten, are we?"

"No! Not that way. But I do like the kid. In a fatherly way. She's brilliant. I don't want to see that wasted."

Darling nodded, reflected, most likely the only member of the Company who would not serve me a ration of shit about incest. She signed, "You fuss too much. She is fourteen. She is already who she is going to be. All you can do is set an example that she will want to follow."

Parenting advice from somebody twenty years my junior.

"All right. I'll try." But I had my reservations. I feared that there was a shadow inside Midnight that she had kept well hidden.

I went walking in the ruins, thinking they would be choked with loneliness and silence. I reexamined recent events repeatedly, sure that I was missing something.

The ruins were neither quiet nor lonely. The hungry ghosts had been replaced by every vulture and carrion eater in nearby creation, all squabbling over the remains of two wild asses and one old woman whose dying eyes I could not get out of my head.

It did not come together for weeks, during our talks with the Magistrates of Rue, who wanted to pay us to discourage the predatory behavior of their neighbors, the Dank. Both sides had heard wildly exaggerated tales of our work for the Lady, years ago.

What I finally noticed, like a sudden slap to the back of my head, was that now always twitchy Rusty hung around Midnight more than Robin did. And Midnight put up with that dickhead.

The last piece clicked. Rusty was no longer an asshole. Since the Village of Hungry Ghosts he had stopped being true to his nature. He had become, in fact, almost Chasing Midnight's dog. And Midnight appeared to have no problems with him anymore.

The same could not be said for her brother and the other surviving bandits. Moonlight still got that look when his gaze chanced upon Rusty.

The Magistrates argued almost not at all before they made a deal. That guaranteed that they would double-cross us as soon as they felt safe from the Dank. We understood. It was nothing new. Evil in its own time. Meanwhile, we could take a break from traveling, in a place where people did not know us.

I set up my clinic inside an actual building. We handled a few cuts, scrapes, and malingerers looking to get out of work. Caught up, I told Midnight, "Go fetch Rusty for me. I want to take a look at him."

She pouted prettily, not pleased. "Robin says he has been having stomach troubles. So, I guess, yes. You should check him out." She left.

I waited, appreciating my new digs. They were part of a small barracks. I might stay warm and well-fed all winter. Fingers crossed. Let us stretch out the war with the Dank.

Rusty arrived. Twitchy, pale, watery-eyed Rusty, not at all pleased to be so close to the Company sawbones. I said, "Have a seat here."

"What's up?"

"I've noticed . . ." and I explained my professional interest.

Where was Midnight? I heard Robin talking in the waiting area. Maybe she was out there with him.

Rusty began to relax. This was all routine. Yeah. He was having trouble with his guts. Maybe he got himself a ulcer. He had an uncle once; he got him a ulcer. Uncle used to puke up blood sometimes.

I got behind Rusty, rested my hands on his shoulders, leaned, whispered, "I know you're in there. And everyone else knows, too."

Rusty lapsed into the worst twitches, ticks, and shakes yet.

The hungry ghost had him only under partial control.

I would start checking local sources right away. There might be an exorcism that could save the man—even though haunted Rusty was better liked than Rusty his own self ever was before.

I never saw Chasing Midnight again. She, Moonlight, and their friends stepped off the face of the earth. Not so difficult in a city. Darling would not let me waste time and energy looking for someone who did not want to be found. Darling wanted to be our unchallenged princess. Moreover, we had soldier business to handle.

The skirmishes with the Dank all ended badly for them. Local fighters on both sides were amateurs of abysmal quality led by fat old men who got their jobs because they were the sons of privilege. And we had Silent, Goblin, and One-Eye to give us that extra edge.

Rusty disappeared a week after Midnight did. Robin did not vanish with him. That boy went half crazy with worry. Nobody else cared. Rusty carried a hungry ghost that could not migrate unless he found another colony. The tacit popular choice was to let nature run its course.

One winter night a partially recovered Whisper slipped into Rue to hand the senior Magistrates a plain directive from the Lady concerning the Black

Company. The Magistrates agreed to her terms but failed to execute their promised treachery because clever One-Eye had rat spies keeping watch on all of Rue's most important men.

We did considerable selective damage before we left town with pockets sagging.

I got the final word on Rusty as we cleared Rue's eastern gate. His mutilated corpse had been found in the mud and water along the edge of the river that ran through Rue. The rats and crayfish had been at him, but they had not done a tenth of the damage that he suffered at human hands before what was left of him was dumped.

I knew then, for sure, why I had grown ever more uneasy with sweet, pretty little Chasing Midnight.

Maybe there will be those new grim armies and fresh dark towers someday, after all.

CHASING MIDNIGHT
THE DARK LORD AS A TEEN

"Chasing Midnight" is original here. Midnight is a girl with serious ambitions. Somewhat darker than the usual light-hearted Black Company tale, this one involves the Company only peripherally. When originally commissioned for an anthology that soon took a stake through its heart, it included the subtitle "The Dark Lord as a Teen."

"Midnight!"

Midnight withdrew her attention from the thing in the black shroud, two hundred feet to her left, that no one else seemed to notice. Her companion, Chick, pointed out something uglier. "Crap. Monkey Butt." With a brace of lesser thugs.

Chick eyed the tavern they were watching. "Don't start anything."

"That's up to him." What the hell was that black shroud thing? *Where* was it? Oh. There. This side of the street now, inside a shadow a hundred feet closer. When did it move? How come . . . ? Never mind. No time for black wrapped spooks or Monkey Butt Face.

A drunk about to lose his fortune exited the Silent Owl. His companion whore did not shine nearly so bright in the sunshine. Crap again. He was not that asshole Rusty.

Midnight saw movement on the tavern roof, Fade letting her know he was paying attention.

Why would that asshole Rusty not come out? Her eyes narrowed, hardened, became too flinty for a kid her age.

Cold killer eyes looked for the black shroud thing, an unknown more disturbing than an approaching villain only slightly brighter than a snail.

The spook had shifted again.

Chick said, "Cold out here."

"Yeah. I should've stuck with the Company till winter was over."

"Maybe they'd let us come back. They let Haru."

"Maybe." Not a problem for her, but for Chick and Fade it might be problematic. "They never even looked for us after we left."

"You think? I bet them wizards know exactly where we are."

"Maybe. But . . ." Where was that damned black shroud thing? Plus, Monkey Butt was definitely headed her way. And, now, two drunks were trying to get out of the Silent Owl at the same time, neither one Rusty.

Chick said, "I'm not liking this, Midnight."

"Keep calm." Monkey Butt would not know what to do if people refused to be frightened.

"I wish Moonlight was here."

Midnight wished her twin was handy, too. Moonlight had his own grudge against that asshole Rusty, and his own magic. But Moonlight was off working a girlie-boy scam.

"Midnight." Chick could barely get it out.

Monkey Butt was almost close enough to smell. Normal people *had* to be afraid of Monkey Butt. Monkey Butt was malice incarnate, with a wine stain birthmark covering most of his face.

Chasing Midnight was a freak. Chasing Midnight was not afraid. Chasing Midnight seldom knew fear. That could become a liability when fear was singularly appropriate.

Anyway, she was busy nursing bruised feelings because nobody looked for her after she and her boys deserted. Plus, she had lost all sense of that thing in black.

Then the gang enforcer was in her face, three times her size, breath foul, birthmark scarlet. His anger was not feigned.

He leaned in to tell her why.

She raised a hand to push him back.

Where is the Shine?

He leaned harder. "Where is the Shine?"

"What?" She smelled something that stank like death itself.

A sound like thumping a watermelon.

Six inches of gory iron-tipped hardwood emerged from Monkey Butt's forehead. He donned a goofy, startled expression, mugging for his audience as he went down.

Whirr! Wham! A second bolt buried itself in a wooden doorframe close by, having clipped the bicep of one of Monkey Butt's companions. The other yanked out a knife that wanted to be a sword when it grew up but he took off, waving it instead of using it, his pal just a step behind.

Panting, Midnight shifted a step sideways. She looked for the shroud thing.

It was gone. Or had turned invisible. Only . . . Just past Chick, who was on one knee, upchucking, a yard of black gauze hung from the crossbow bolt embedded in the doorframe.

"Midnight! We got to get out of here!"

Oh, yes. For sure. People were becoming interested. Killings were not uncommon in Rue but they did not happen in the afternoon, on a busy street. "Hide your face while I get small." "Get small" was a minor sorcery she had invented. It had no real physical effect, it just addled the perceptions of observers. It made her harder to notice and remember.

She snagged the black gauze strip and took off. Chick would keep up. Or not.

He knew where to meet up.

Naturally, once she started to run that asshole Rusty came out of the Owl to see what the excitement was all about.

Crap! She could not go stick a knife in with the whole street watching.

Fade asked, "Did I screw up?"

"No. It was my fault," Midnight said. She stared hard into their little fire. She might find some secret there if she studied long enough. "I gave the sign." Not intentionally, not exactly, but close enough. It was Monkey Butt's fault, anyway. "Don't ask me again." He had done so twice already. "What about the crossbow?"

"Broke down, wrapped in oilskin, and back inside the chimney."

Chick came in, shaking, not from the cold. "I got lost." This was his first up close personal encounter with violent death, too. Even time with the Black Company had not prepared them for the intensity.

Midnight ran the black gauze through her fingers like prayer beads.

Chick settled as near the fire as he could, said nothing more.

Midnight finally asked, "What's the matter? What we did?"

"A little. Though Monkey Butt needed it as bad as Rusty."

"Something else?"

A grunt not followed by any explanation.

What? These boys were like puppies usually, all eager to please Chasing Midnight. "Spill it, Chick."

"I didn't get lost. Not exactly. I just wanted to, on account of what I heard."

"And that would be?" Beginning to lose patience, of which she seldom had much.

"Songo Songaghi is dead. They don't know who hit him but he probably wasn't alone when they got him."

Songo Songaghi would be the high lord gangster in their part of Rue, Monkey Butt's boss. Moonlight's mark. Did Monkey Butt making a run at her have something to do with this?

Songo Songaghi enjoyed the company of younger boys. Not little boys. Boys thirteen, fourteen, fifteen, full of . . . vigor. Like Moonlight. Moonlight wanted to lead the man on while his sister and cousins swarmed round and appropriated whatever they could.

The full import sank in.

Songo Songaghi had not been alone.

"Moonlight?"

"Maybe, the way people talked."

"When?"

"This morning. Moonlight couldn't have more than just got there. Maybe he walked in on something."

Moonlight had left on his private mission an hour before a street kid brought word that that asshole Rusty had been seen at the Owl.

Midnight took a calming breath. Croaker, her mentor within the Company, had warned her that revenge could be like juggling adders. If that news had not come . . . If they had rounded up Moonlight before they headed out . . .

She considered the fabric between her fingers. What was that about? That thing in the shroud? A harbinger? An avatar? No. Could not be. No death spirit would leave bits of its costume behind.

Whatever, whoever, it was real but a total unknown. And probably not related.

Another breath preceded a long sigh. "So let's pull our boots on and go see."

Midnight passed within yards of Monkey Butt's wounded associate. The man did not recognize her. He was distracted, though. Songo's place looked like a god with iron hands had pounded it down. Songaghi's gang were digging through the rubble.

Three bodies had been found, none of them Moonlight. Songo had not yet surfaced, either.

The diggers found the crime lord soon after Midnight's arrival, in no better condition than his house. Chasing Moonlight was not with him.

Midnight began to attract attention despite being small. She got out of there, now really worried.

"He's still alive."

"How do you know?" Fade asked

"We're twins."

"But not identical. You're just brother and sister, born at the same time, from the same mom."

"We can feel each other when we concentrate."

"Even dead?" Not holding back. Everyone had done things Midnight's way for months, now. Look where that got them.

"I'm not a hundred percent but I'm plenty sure he wasn't there when the shit went down."

"Songo's people think he was."

Chick and Fade had worked the crowd while she brooded, being nosy kids who wanted to know all about what happened.

Fade said, "Nobody saw him leave."

"Were they watching for him? Did they see him arrive?"

"No. And no. You really do sense him?"

"No. I just told you."

Chick said, "Let's don't get all upset and take it out on each other. Maybe Moonlight never was there."

So why had he not turned up yet?

Fade slipped into the hideout. "I found some apples."

Midnight rocked beside the fire, no longer convinced that Moonlight had survived. There had been no news in days. Fade folded her fingers around an apple, then settled on the other side of the fire. "Songo's men are looking for Moonlight, too. They think he was in on it."

More bad news. "They figure out who was behind it yet?"

"Some think Chops." Songaghi's cousin and rival, Cotton Pots, went by Chops. "Songo took a run at Chops around when we got to Rue. Hurt him bad. Only . . ."

"Only?"

"On account of what happened with Monkey Butt, and on account of Moonlight still being missing, there's some what think we was the ones that did it."

"Maybe."

"Maybe? What?"

"Maybe Moonlight *was* in on it."

"Girl! Your brother was my best friend but you got to admit he was too damned dumb for anything as complicated . . ."

"Really?" Moonlight was all show boy, sure, but he hid some smart behind that. Midnight mused, "Sorcery."

"What?"

"What about the sorcerer who knocked the place down?"

"Lots of people wonder about that, what with Cotton Pots swearing by two hundred gods that he didn't have nothing to do with it."

Chick settled to Midnight's left, armed with a loaf of hard bread. "Chops is after Moonlight now, too."

"Because?"

"Because Moonlight isn't all that's missing."

Chick stared into the fire. Midnight stared at him. He said, "Those stories about Songo sitting on a treasure like some kind of dragon? They didn't find no treasure in the rubble but cheap flatware and junk jewelry."

"Oh, my."

"Yeah." Chick.

"We're dead." Fade.

Chick asked, "Can we head for the Company barracks, now?"

Fade agreed. "You smile and jiggle, old Croaker will let us come home. He let Haru . . ."

"Stop whistling in the dark! Yeah, he might. Because he thinks I'm smart and I ought to be saved, not because he thinks I might put out. We wanted to be on our own. So now we are. We have to live with whatever stupid . . . All right. I give. If going back looks like the only way, we'll try it. But let's don't leave Moonlight behind."

Where *was* that idiot? Was he ever even at Songo's?

For no cause that she could articulate she began playing with that scrap of shroud cloth again.

Midnight disguised herself as a boy, hair up inside an ugly green hat borrowed from a handy drunk. Fade became a bullish girl inclined to argue. Chick turned into an incompetent holy mendicant. Midnight added dirt highlights that made his natural gauntness look like starvation.

They had to exercise the utmost caution. Gangs of unpleasant gentlemen kept hunting foreign kids. Ever less confidently, Midnight insisted that her twin was still alive.

Songo's successors put a bounty on Moonlight. Rumor daily fattened Songo's fabled treasure.

Time passed. The search for Moonlight faded. He and his gang must have had left Rue with Songo's treasure.

The beginning of a war with the Dank distracted the popular imagination.

Midnight and her boys holed up in the cellar of an abandoned shop. One afternoon Chick showed up lugging a sack of turnips and panting. "Old guy had staying power. Thought he'd never give up." He spilled his treasure, then moved in creepy close to Midnight. "I found out some stuff. One is, Rusty deserted too, only a week after we did. They ain't been looking for him, neither."

"How do you know that?"

"I talked to Haru."

Midnight stifled an irrational rage. Haru had abandoned her for the security of the Company. In the natural course, had a wicked fate not intervened, Haru would have become her husband.

Then old hints tumbled into place. Chick always came up with something to eat when they were desperate. And Chick was seeing Haru. Haru had gone back to the Company . . . to look out for her?

She hated Haru then but loathed Chasing Midnight even more.

Little Miss Sorceress-to-be was making her own way boldly because her boys were looking out for her behind her back.

Chick said, "Haru saw Moonlight. But Moonlight acted like he didn't know who Haru was."

Midnight snuggled closer. "Tell me."

"I ran into Haru and that Robin guy with the bad case of the Midnights, over by the Company barracks."

She winced. Robin was sweet. "Tell me about Moonlight."

"Haru saw him."

"Chick, I'm going to hurt you."

"What do you want?"

"What was he doing? Was he all right? What did he say? Why haven't we heard from him? That kind of crap, dumbass."

"Haru said he was just standing on the side of the street, looking lost. He didn't look hurt but he did act retarded. When Haru tried to talk to him he just looked like he didn't get how come Haru was bothering him. Then he got all scared and took off. Haru says he don't think that was because of him. He didn't see nothing but he thought Moonlight must have."

Midnight wanted to slug Chick. He was *not* telling her what she wanted to know. She took deep breaths. During her brief apprenticeship that geezer Croaker never stopped nagging about learning patience.

"Anyone else see him? Or Haru? Or you guys when you were talking? Like somebody who might recognize you?" Some Company guys might be tempted to claim a bounty. Only . . . They had not, had they? And the hunt would not have been difficult had they begun with Haru.

Midnight said, "There are rumors, now, that Songo's fabulous treasure maybe was just a fable. We'll go poke around where Haru saw Moonlight tomorrow."

Haru had run into Moonlight less than two hundred yards from the Company barracks. How did that add up? Songo's patch was on the other side of town. "Chick, did Haru try to track Moonlight?"

"Yes, my love. None of us is nearly as brilliant as Chasing Midnight but even Haru is smart enough to do that."

Midnight let the attitude slide. "And?"

"Haru said he headed off that way. Then he looked back and maybe because Haru was following him, he ran." Chick pointed. He had walked through the episode with Haru. Of course. "He like stirred up a breeze. Haru said trash and stuff flew around."

"And?"

"He went around that corner, into that breezeway, and totally disappeared."

"More sorcery."

"Does Moonlight have it more than you, he just never let us know?"

"No." Moonlight had a talent for making people like him but that was all. "Let's walk through it. Maybe I can feel something. Hug me! Kiss me. On the cheek, you retard!"

Chick sniggered as a pair of mercenaries ambled past.

"And watch the hands, cousin."

Chick slapped a big grin on each time Midnight looked at him directly. It was a great day for him.

"Bastard!"

"Ha ha ha! You never used the keep-off-me spell. I'll definitely remember that."

Keep-off-me was the first spell Midnight had crafted, essential for sanity and survival for the only girl in a pack of teenage bandits.

"I was distracted! I'll make you eat those hands. Now be quiet!" She rested her own hands on old, old brick. A minute passed. Then she hugged Chick.

"Mixed messages, Midnight." He had no chance but it was fun to tease her.

"I could almost give you what you want, right now. Moonlight is in there, somewhere."

"For sure?" All serious now.

"Yes. But something's wrong. I feel him but he doesn't feel me."

"Let's find a way in."

"Sure. But carefully. There's live sorcery in there."

Chick's excitement faded. He did not like any sorcery, especially hers, feeble though it was.

Chasing Midnight was attractive and desirable. That was another sorcery she used to manipulate those around her. Males would do anything if she got them imagining there was some remote chance she might let them have what they thought they wanted.

The breezeway ended in an alleyway only slightly wider, the breezeway wall having revealed no obvious openings. Nor did the alleyway side, though several that were there once had been bricked up. Chick grumbled, "This doesn't look promising."

"No." The sense of potent sorcery remained but it felt like sorcery long since worked, not sorcery in progress. "How did Moonlight vanish when he was only out of sight for a few seconds?"

They reached the third side of the structure, a street just wide enough for two goat carts to pass. This face boasted one entrance and several windows, all also bricked up.

There had been no visible entrances from the street on which they had approached, either.

"We missed something."

Generous Chick. *She* had missed something. She was the leader. She was the brains. She was the wise woman. She was the sorceress, though not much of a threat yet, she had to admit.

Someday, though . . .

This was today. And her twin was trapped behind walls offering no obvious way through. A prisoner? Perhaps, though maybe just of the mind. There was for sure *something* wrong. He remained deaf to her touch.

"Let's start over."

"Feel everything, high and low." She would cover every reachable inch of brickwork herself, seeking the physical and the magical.

Nine steps in Chick discovered parallel discontinuities in the vertical alignment of the bricks invisible in the available light.

Midnight traced the misalignments, a quarter inch in on the left, a quarter out on the right, twenty-two inches apart. A door, of sorts, which opened easily to Chick's vigorous shove.

Chemical and carrion smells rolled out. Chick gagged. "There's no light inside."

No Moonlight, either. He had to be farther in.

Chick grabbed her arm. "Don't. Let's get some light. Be patient. You aren't big enough to just jump in."

"Yet."

"Let's just close this back up. I'll go get a lantern while you keep watch."

"All right."

Something ugly was going on inside that building. She doubted that Moonlight had become involved voluntarily.

Midnight got small in a shadow that let her monitor the breezeway. There was almost no street traffic. She layered keep-off-me onto the getting small. She threaded black gauze between her fingers while reflecting on the choices that had brought her here.

She was almost ashamed of Chasing Midnight.

A black mist filled the breezeway mouth. A figure shrouded in black emerged. Midnight rested her forehead on her knees and relaxed her spells lest they be noticed.

Black shroud thing stayed vaporous and kept moving. Midnight could make out the shape inside the mist by concentrating. She shivered, glad that it had not noticed her. That might not have gone well.

"What's wrong with you?"

She jumped. She squeaked. Terror hit her hard.

Chick wrapped her in a hug, murmuring, "Hey, it'll be all right. What's wrong? What happened?"

She let the shakes settle till she regained control enough to note that Haru had come back with Chick, lugging a couple of lanterns. Haru looked jealous. Maybe Chick had been telling tall tales.

"You're lucky," Chick told Midnight. "But you generally do stuff right at the right time, so things work out."

Not the first time someone said that, maybe hinting that some divinity or devil must be protecting their beloved Midnight. Sometimes she wondered herself, though the Company wizards had checked. "Some folks are just born lucky," the one called Goblin had told her.

Haru told his story. Midnight rewarded him with a gentle kiss. "You better get back before they miss you."

Breath catching, Haru replied, "Yeah, well. Yeah. You need to get them lanterns back as soon as you can."

"Later today," she promised. Chick nodded. Haru took off, fingers touching his lips.

Chick told her, "You truly are wicked."

Most times she would have snarled, would have whittled him down, but right now she lacked her customary cynical confidence. "Yeah. I probably am. Are you ready to do this?"

Chick grunted, not at all happy.

Midnight told him, "I really need your support, Chick. Please? Because I'm scared half to death."

"I'm doing it. Just don't expect me to break out singing."

The door tried to hide. It was no longer misaligned. Chick shoved brick till a fraction of wall finally gave.

Foul odors rolled out again. Chick gagged. Midnight did the same but still managed to light the lanterns.

She never stopped shaking.

The black shroud thing scared her. Terrified her. Nothing before it ever made her more than mildly nervous.

Even it had done no more than that the day Monkey Butt's luck ran out.

Chick took a lantern. "You all right?"

"Sparkling. Let's do it. Before that thing comes back." Shakes would not stop Chasing Midnight. Chasing Midnight refused to be ruled by her flesh, she told herself as she went into the stench, quaking.

The space behind the brick door was empty. Dust on a rough wooden floor had been disturbed only along a path to a crude wooden door through the opposite wall.

"A storage room," Chick guessed. "It's dark on the other side of that door, too."

Midnight saw. That door consisted of rough planks that passed foul air easily and would do the same with light.

That door was not latched. It scraped the floor when Chick opened it.

Midnight shut the door to the breezeway, making sure its edges aligned. Chick did the same with the inner door after she passed him. That door accessed a space with no discernable bounds. Chick lifted and extended his lantern "Yonder."

Distant points of light shone fifty degrees to their right.

Midnight advanced through what was once a fabric mill, rounding decrepit, abandoned giant looms, as she headed for the lights.

Chick whispered, "We should've brought Fade."

Midnight grunted uncertain agreement. Might be better that Fade was not here. Only, how would he know where to look if she and Chick did not get out?

The smell grew stronger. Another crude door opened on a space less vast than the one just crossed, lighted by batteries of oil lamps. Old machinery had been shoved against the walls. Twelve low tables scattered the middle of the space. Six had coffin-size glass tanks atop them. Five tanks held bodies immersed in fluid the color of pale tea.

Naked corpses lay on two tables lacking tanks.

None of the corpses had entered the putrefaction stage.

Chick whispered, "This is not a good place."

Moonlight entered through a doorway in the far wall, shuffling as though in an opium dream. He carried a pail and a paintbrush.

Chick snagged Midnight's arm. "Hold on. He isn't right."

Yes. Her brother was moving with eyes downcast, unaware of their presence. He was even less Chasing Moonlight than Haru's report had made out. "Is he blind and deaf?"

Moonlight began brushing a syrupy something onto one of the tabletop corpses, his movements unnaturally slow.

Chick released Midnight's arm. "This is hell. Let's get him and go before the monster comes back."

Too late already, children. Where is the Shine?

That came from everywhere and nowhere, not as a sound at all. Midnight began to turn as Chick moaned and sank toward the floor. The black shroud thing had a hold on his shoulder.

Midnight added a kick to her turn, trying to drive her boot right through this fool who thought the boy was the bigger threat. Her body shuddered with the impact.

Black shroud thing was male and alive. He screeched, folded, fell, tightened into a fetal ball, fetched up noises like someone being strangled. Midnight helped Chick up while her victim vomited inside the cloth concealing his face. "Get Moonlight." Moonlight was painting a corpse, oblivious. Midnight eyed the fallen sorcerer. Finish him while he was vulnerable? "Chick, will you get him and go?" Slashing the sorcerer's throat seemed the rational course, but she could not. There was only one man she could send to hell that way, that asshole rapist Rusty.

Chick headed out dragging a baffled and frightened Moonlight, who did not recognize him. He did not recognize his sister, either.

Black shroud thing began to uncurl.

"Faster, Chick!" while checking in with her conscience again.

Black shroud thing ripped the gauze off its face, fought for air and had a hard time getting it, having aspirated some vomit. The face revealed inclined Midnight to upchuck herself. It appeared to have been burned badly, then rotted. Must be rotting still. The stink was there, behind that of vomit and the ambient fetor.

The sorcerer expelled the matter threatening to asphyxiate him. He pushed up on one hand. *You cannot take him. He won't survive. He needs the Shine.* He collapsed, one hand extended toward Midnight as though beseeching favor.

"If ever I see you again I will kill you."

Fade was scared of Moonlight. "He's gone way too godsdamned creepy."

Midnight feared that he was right. Moonlight had gone exceeding weird. And he smelled like the place where she had found him. Bathing did not help.

Moonlight did not talk. Maybe he could not. He did respond to simple instructions frequently repeated. He reacted to no one personally. Midnight, Chick, and Fade might all have been strangers.

One day Chick said, "I don't think he's even alive."

Midnight had begun to entertain that exact notion herself.

What happened after he went off to work on Songo? She failed utterly to get an explanation. Near as she could tell, Moonlight was unaware that he had existed earlier than several days after Songo's house fell down.

"Fade. Songo's gang ever figure out who smashed his house?"

"No. Still the biggest mystery going."

Midnight and Chick exchanged looks. Everybody knew a sorcerer must have been involved. Could it be . . . ?

Fade said, "I don't know how you got Moonlight home, but some of Songo's men saw you. They're after us again."

Chick said, "It's time we swallowed Midnight's pride and found out if the Company will take us back."

So. Chick was in full rebellion. Chasing Midnight's schemes never worked out. Why expect that to change?

Fade reddened. He was not ready to take sides. "This is getting stupid. Both of you."

Midnight stifled her ire. Fade was not interested in her designs. Fade wanted to go home. Never mind that home was no longer there. They would not have left if it was.

"Whatever," Chick said, resigned. Nobody would get what they wanted but nobody dared walk away. "We need to worry about Moonlight now."

Moonlight whimpered like a puppy suffering a bad dream. Midnight put an arm around him. Chick did the same from the other side. That calmed Moonlight.

Chick said, "I thought I'd get used to the smell. But I can't."

Neither could Midnight. It was worsening, too.

Fade settled on his knees in front of Moonlight. They had been best friends. "Remember the time when . . ." Moonlight appeared to listen. After minutes of no other response, Fade announced, "Today I went around hinting that your sorcerer was the one who did for Songo."

Midnight arched an eyebrow. "Clever, cousin."

"I said I heard it from one of Monkey Butt's guys who had too much to drink and was pissed off on account of Monkey Butt got himself dead before anybody who was in on it with him heard how it was supposed to play after Songo went down, so now everybody was getting shut out."

Midnight goggled. Awed, Chick said, "Oh, you are a nasty boy!"

Rue loved a conspiracy.

Fade said, "I wonder how come nobody thought of that before."

Midnight asked, "You think maybe you tripped over the truth with that one?" She felt her age and inexperience then. Songo Songaghi, Monkey Butt Face, Chasing Moonlight, black shroud sorcerer, and her, paths crossing, a sorcerous explosion, deaths, Moonlight lost . . .

"God of Darkness, Midnight, maybe I did! You calculate everything and fill a couple gaps with lucky guesses . . . How come the sorcerer was after you when we had that asshole Rusty staked out? Just when Monkey Butt decided to come at you?"

Right after Songo's place blew up. Because of Moonlight, somehow?

Moonlight was shaking now. They all pressed in. Their bodies ought to warm him.

He *was* cold. So very cold.

Fade said, "We need a fire."

Midnight said, "Maybe the sorcerer already had Moonlight and wanted me, too, because we're twins."

Fade built the fire. Midnight and Chick crowded Moonlight. Chick hummed a lullaby. Fade and Midnight joined in. Moonlight gradually relaxed, then made noises like a happy infant. They had touched him at last.

Midnight knew the truth. Someday, behind whatever mask she wore, Chasing Midnight would be one of the great powers, almost a goddess. Mistress of mistresses, like the Lady, beloved of her Company mentor. Only . . .

Only not once had she foreseen anything like the life that had claimed her this last half year. She dreamed of far tomorrows, not the story of how she would get there.

She was not in a good mood. She could not ignore the probability that she was not yet mature enough to handle the roles she wanted. How could she become a goddess if she could not handle the turbulence besieging her in this backwater town?

"Midnight!"

She returned to the moment, in a chilly new hideout, fiercely hungry because she dared not go out into Rue's streets even in disguise.

Songo's gang *badly* wanted to learn the fate of their boss's fortune, and were, again, sure that those who could reveal it were still in Rue.

Brave Haru was their angel, daring all to deliver onions and turnips and table scraps.

There was no air movement in the new hideout. The stench . . . Moonlight seemed to putrefy even as his mind slowly gained . . . Without memories. While every little noise or flash of motion spooked him. He had the mental acuity of a dim two-year-old. His vocabulary included fewer than two dozen words having to do with hunger, fear, or his need to be changed.

Midnight had found nothing obviously wrong with him, though he was puffy despite an inadequate diet. He looked like he might pop if you poked him with something sharp.

Haru arrived with several leather bags. "I got some good stuff this time. Food and news, both."

Food first was the consensus. One bag contained scraps of rabbit, lamb, chicken, pork, and maybe a bit of horse. Chick, Fade, Midnight and Moonlight indulged in a feeding frenzy.

A second bag held stale bread, crumbs, crusts, chunks, and even a couple of small rye loaves. A third held water. "Good water," Haru promised, without explaining why he dared guarantee that. "There was an attack on the place where you found Moonlight." He offered Fade a sloppy salute. "It involved almost every guy who ever was part of Songo's gang."

Midnight grunted, gobbled, used a hand momentarily free to give Fade a congratulatory pat.

"They showed up with wagons full of tools," Haru said. "They busted in through one of the old bricked up street entrances."

Midnight gnawed on what might have been a partially eaten rabbit's hindquarter. "And then?"

"And then it got exciting. The sorcerer was home. He didn't want company. There was thunder and lightning and screams we heard all the way over to the barracks. Then there was a giant-ass rumble that was half the building falling down. The Lieutenant called out the seventh century and the wizards and took us over there."

The "seventh century" would be the mercenary, sick and lame, unable to participate in the campaign against the Dank.

"They found one truly ugly mess. What you described didn't touch it. He was experimenting on boys our age. Goblin said he must've been trying to steal their life and youth. And he had him some serious sorcery skills. He wouldn't have gotten whipped at all if he hadn't gotten totally swarmed. And he maybe got away anyhow. They don't think he was one of the dead people they cleaned up after it was over.

"Songo's guys ended up two-thirds wiped out. We arrested the rest. The wizards say the sorcerer was definitely the one that blasted Songo's place. Must have been a falling out. Him and Songo were partners. Goblin thinks Songo was passing on his boy toys when he got tired of them."

Chick asked, "Any of that mean we're off the hook?" Oblivious to the implications of what Fade had said. Or indifferent.

Midnight did not catch it herself. "There were only boys there?" She recalled that all the bodies had been young but had not noted their gender.

Had black shroud thing wanted her as a different sort of subject because she was the twin of one he had in hand?

Haru opined, "You're probably safe. There's nobody to pay any bounty. Besides, there are rumors that Songo used up his whole fortune financing the sorcerer. He bought that building two years ago. Which is right about when the toy soldiers started going missing."

Midnight asked, "Toy soldiers?"

"Homosexual prostitutes. Young ones. The kind Songo liked."

Midnight heard it this time. She might not know her brother as well as she thought.

Might Moonlight have chosen self-sacrifice as a way to support a particularly selfish and ambitious sister?

She eyed the mindless thing that Moonlight had become. He was still eager to please though perhaps already dead inside. She glanced at Haru, who worshipped her despite the fact that his own brother, Yuko, had died on the road to Rue. She considered Fade, who just wanted to go home, then Chick, who seemed to know what went on inside her head. Who believed that she would be the death of them but would still stick till her ambition did consume him.

She said, "Haru, go back before you get into trouble. They'll need every man to keep order."

There would be considerable excitement while the horrors remained news but the sensation should not last.

"I'll go," Fade said, volunteering to scout. "I'm least likely to stand out." True. He resembled the locals physically and his accent was thin.

Midnight sighed. "Be careful. Please. I mean, really careful. Anything looks hinky, get away fast." She touched Fade's arm like she was making a promise.

Manipulative, yes, but for the best of reasons: she did not want to lose any more of her boys.

Fade left. Chick said, "Someday you'll try that on somebody who won't let you work them."

Midnight shrugged but her indifference was pretense.

Chasing Midnight had to get stronger. Fast. Bad men guaranteed that, the kind of men who discarded the used up husks of girls her age.

Fade weaseled his way back into the ruin. "Big excitement today. The city fathers put a bounty on our sorcerer. Those dead boys included kids from some important families."

Had black shroud been that stupid? And would Chasing Midnight sometimes be as arrogantly overconfident? "He did survive?"

"They think so, but with fewer friends than we ever had."

But he had immortality to offer!

Then Fade said, "And I found out where that asshole Rusty stays."

"How did you do that?"

"I saw him come out of the Owl. He didn't see me. I followed him."

Midnight produced the happiest face she had shown in ages. Chick turned more sour.

"He won't wake up!" Moonlight had to respond soon or Midnight would have to cry. And she should not to let her boys see her shed tears.

Chick said, "We're safe in the world now. Let's find a place where the air moves. I can't take this stink anymore."

Midnight wanted to snarl at him. Wanted to hurt him. Wanted to hate him. But she did not want to lose him. She was near the brink already.

He was thinking about joining Haru. Fade would follow, sure she would have to toddle on after.

She had heard them whispering when they thought she was asleep.

Fade was close to lost, too. He stayed away more, now, his excuses his scouting and surveillance of that asshole Rusty, but what he really wanted was to be away from Moonlight. He did not want to watch his friend die.

Midnight gave up on Moonlight. She just played with that strip of black cloth, which was little more than bits of tangled thread, now.

Chick said, "I've got to get some fresh air."

Midnight muttered, "Be careful. I don't want to lose you too."

That startled Chick but did not change his mind.

Lacking witnesses, Midnight allowed herself some tears.

Cried out, Midnight eyed the black cloth as though only just now noticing it. Which was true, in a way. She had not thought about it before. It just was. "Hang in there for me, brother. I have an idea." She patted his swollen cheek.

The pus color surface cracked like the skin of an overripe plum but did not bleed. It produced a yellowish ooze. The stench in the hideout redoubled. Moonlight seemed unaware that anything had happened.

Midnight had to get away herself. The stink added incentive and piled on another layer of guilt.

People shied away from Midnight, disgusted, more than one suggesting that she visit a bathhouse and burn her clothing.

Several bathes refused her entrance even when she displayed real coins her boys had scrounged.

But that was only inconvenience. The real challenge would be finding the black shroud thing so she could make him undo what he had done to Moonlight.

"You won't find him," Fade told her. "The Company wizards can't and they want that reward bad."

The official bounty was huge. The oligarchs were not amused by the losses of their sons. Greed and fear had pulled most of Rue into the hunt.

Fear of sorcery ran deep. And black shroud had done his damnedest to prove that the fear was justified.

"What he said," Chick said. "He probably got out of town."

"He couldn't go far. All his work is here."

Fade said, "And the wizards know that. And they're waiting."

Chick added, "Even Songo's dimwit gang, the three or four still breathing and running loose, are set to grab him if he turns up, too. Face it, cousin. There isn't any hope." He choked on the words.

Fade said, "You got to look at Moonlight with your eyes, not your heart. No way will it be much longer."

She treated him to her darkest look.

He suggested, "Why don't I go check on that asshole Rusty."

Chick said, "Wishful thinking never made anything good happen, Midnight. I'm out of here, too."

"I'm sorry I upset you," Fade said when Midnight joined across from the Silent Owl.

"It's all right. I'm all right. You were right. Is he in there?"

"Yes. You hit the public bath again."

"Had to. I couldn't stand myself." But some things soap and water could not wash away.

"New clothes, too."

Not literally. They were secondhand. But they did not smell of death.

"Yeah. I'll change before I go back in there with him." Fighting guilt over not being with Moonlight now. "You checked on the crossbow lately?"

"Last week. Still where I hid it, wrapped in oilskins."

"What do you think about me cutting off my hair? It's hard to get the smell out of it."

Fade's dismay was obvious. Midnight's hair, when she bothered to be a girl, was her best feature.

She sighed. "All right. I'll gut it out." It would not be long. Moonlight had stopped taking nourishment. "Go put it together. Make sure it will work."

Fade considered her with one eyebrow raised.

"I can't keep Moonlight from leaving me. I *can* put that asshole Rusty out there to break trail on his journey to hell."

Fade leaned in, sniffed her hair. "Thought so. All right. I'm on it." He ambled across the street.

Midnight pulled a handful of hair round to sniff herself.

The death smell was there behind the soap and lavender.

Fade appeared atop the tavern, thumb up. He held the reassembled cross-bow up for her to see. "Idiot!" Somebody might see him . . .

That asshole Rusty left the Owl. He did not look good. Times must be tough for him, too.

Midnight tried making discreet signals to Fade to get out of sight. That caught Rusty's eye, just as some butthead on the top floor of the tavern structure leaned out a window to yell, "Who the hell is on my roof?" He could not see Fade from the window.

Rusty, though, was far enough out into the street to spot a kid brandishing a crossbow. And he was sober enough to recognize that kid and the waving girl, both. He lit out, leaving pedestrians cursing in his wake.

"Crap!" Not good. Now he would be alert.

Midnight sniffed her hair again. The smell of death was getting stronger. *Where is the Shine?*

Midnight whirled. A black fog collapsed just three yards away. She gagged. The sorcerer stank worse than Moonlight.

Mad hope died quickly. This monster could not help Moonlight. He could not help himself.

Come. Show me where. He stepped toward Midnight, black-gloved hand reaching. And she could not move herself.

Then he faced the Owl hastily. The excitement there had eluded him till there was a quarrel in the air.

The reaching hand shifted. Black mist formed. Black shroud avoided Monkey Butt's fate, barely. The bolt did smash through his wrist. He squeaked like a stomped mouse. The mist collapsed again.

He leaked yellowish fluid. Its stench was so strong Midnight lost her lunch. Black shroud folded over his damaged wrist. *I have failed.* With so much sorrow. It took him a dozen seconds to recall that he was still exposed, not just to a sniper but to everyone in the street.

Black fog formed. Hunched, black shroud thing turned on Midnight.

Fade's second bolt arrived.

Black shroud slammed against the building, rebounded several steps and collapsed. Midnight took off when onlookers began a lively debate as to who would get to turn Rue's most wanted man into a bag of silver.

Chick cut Midnight off. "Don't go in."

"He's gone?"

"He fell apart. Literally."

Midnight pictured rotting meat and naked bones. She tried to go around Chick anyway. He blocked her again. "Don't."

Fade came limping up. "Sorry, Midnight. I couldn't save the crossbow this time. And I twisted my ankle getting away. Oh." He noticed their grim faces. "Moonlight?"

Chick nodded.

"Oh," again. And, "I don't know what to say."

Midnight said, "There isn't anything. It's all been said. Except for me confessing that it's all my fault."

She was not fishing for an argument and she did not get one.

Haru said, "Here's what happened. Songo and Black Shroud was partners. Songo did finance and subject acquisition. Black Shroud tried to figure out how to make them immortal. They butted heads about something. Songo snatched the Shine, which we don't know what that was and we probably never will, except we know that the sorcerer needed it to stay alive. So Moonlight shows up at Songo's just when the sorcerer comes to take his treasure back. Moonlight sees the shit about to rain, realizes that the Shine is valuable, grabs it and runs.

"Now Monkey Butt knows, or at least suspects, about the Shine. Him and the sorcerer both know that Chasing Moonlight is just an extension of Chasing Midnight. They both go looking. Monkey Butt gets himself dead for his trouble. Black Shroud has a close call and bugs it to keep from getting noticed by the crowd. He lucks out because he runs into Moonlight, which means he gets the Shine back and a new boy besides. Then everything stays quiet until Moonlights gets out of the sorcerer's hideout with the Shine, which he must have ditched somewhere because he didn't have anything weird with him when I found him."

Midnight suspected that Haru's story had been cooked up based on speculations by the Company's wizards. "He was healthy then, too, wasn't he?"

"He looked healthy but he smelled awful. Anyway, he probably left me because he saw the sorcerer. I maybe dodged one there. So, anyhow, with the Shine gone him and Moonlight started going downhill. Then you and Chick took Moonlight out and Fade's rumors brought down the thunder. He was cut off from his resources and he was being hunted so he didn't have much left for looking for us."

"But he still found me."

"Accidentally, probably, and at exactly the perfectly wrong time."

Chick said, "So all the ugly is over. So how about we do right by Moonlight, then go see if they'll take us back?"

"No!" Midnight snapped. "Not while that asshole Rusty is still walking around."

Fade and Chick stared at her hard, expressions cold and blank. And she knew that they knew what she really wanted was to find the Shine and figure out how to make it work for herself.

Her boys. How much longer could she hope to keep them leashed?

PUBLICATION CREDITS

ALSO FROM GLEN COOK
AND NIGHT SHADE BOOKS

The Starfishers Trilogy

"[Cook's] work is unrelentingly real, complex, and honest."
— *NEW YORK TIMES* BESTSELLING AUTHOR Jeff VanderMeer

GLEN COOK

THE
STARFISHERS
TRILOGY

978-1-59780-900-9 / Trade Paperback / $24.99

Centuries ago, a private army's deadly strike freed human slaves from their cruel Sangaree masters. A single Sangaree alien survived—and swore vengeance on the Storm family and their soldiers. Generations later, his carefully mapped revenge scheme explodes as the armies of the galaxies collide.

From Glen Cook comes an omnibus edition of his landmark space opera, trilogy, collecting the novels *Shadowline*, *Starfishers*, and *Stars' End* in a seamless blend of ancient myth, political intrigue, and scintillating space combat.

**Find this Night Shade title and many others online
at http://www.nightshadebooks.com
or wherever books are sold.**

Passage at Arms

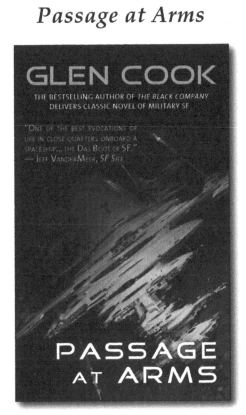

978-1-59780-0679 / Trade Paperback / $14.95

The ongoing war between Humanity and the Ulant is a battle of attrition that Humanity is losing. Humans do, however, have one technological advantage—trans-hyperdrive technology. Using this technology, specially designed and outfitted spaceships— Humanity's Climber Fleet—can, under very narrow and strenuous conditions, pass through space undetected.

Passage at Arms tells the intimate, detailed, and harrowing story of a Climber crew and its captain during a critical juncture of the war. Glen Cook combines speculative technology with a canny and realistic portrait of men at war and the stresses they face in combat. *Passage at Arms* is one of the classic novels of military SF.

Find this Night Shade title and many others online
at http://www.nightshadebooks.com
or wherever books are sold.

A Matter of Time

978-1-59780-279-6 / Trade Paperback / $14.99

Originally published in 1985, this classic science fiction novel is equal parts spy thriller, murder mystery, and time-travel mind-bender.

May 1975. St. Louis. In a snow-swept street, a cop finds the body of a man who died fifty years ago. It's still warm. July 1866, Lidice, Bohemia: A teenage girl calmly watches her parents die as another being takes control of her body. August 2058, Prague: Three political rebels flee in to the past, taking with them a terrible secret. As past, present, and future collide, one man holds the key to the puzzle. And if he doesn't fit it together, the world he knows will fall to pieces. It's just *A Matter of Time*!

Darkwar

978-1-59780-2017 / Trade Paperback / $16.99

As the world grows colder with each passing year, the longer winters and deepening snows awaken ancient fears within the Degnan Packstead: fears of invasion by desperate nomads, of attack by the witchlike Silth, who kill with their minds, and of the Grauken, a desperate time when intellect gives way to cannibalistic instinct.

For Marika, a loyal young pup, times are dark indeed, for the Packstead cannot prevail against these foes. But stirring within Marika is a power unmatched in all the world, one that may not just save her world, but allow her to grasp the stars themselves . . .

Darkwar collects the epic science fantasy novels that originally appeared as *Doomstalker*, *Warlock*, and *Ceremony*.

**Find this Night Shade title and many others online
at http://www.nightshadebooks.com
or wherever books are sold.**

A Cruel Wind

978-1-59780-1041 / Trade Paperback / $16.95

Across the Dragon's Teeth mountains, beyond the reach of the Werewind and the fires of the world's beginning, above the walls of Fangdred castle, stands Wind Tower, from which the Star Rider summons the war that even wizards dread — one fought for the love of Nepanthe, princess to the Storm Kings . . .

Before the Black Company . . . there was the Dread Empire, Glen Cook's enormously influential first foray in fantasy worldbuilding. *A Cruel Wind: A Chronicle of the Dread Empire* is an omnibus collection of the first three Dread Empire novels: *A Shadow of All Night's Falling*, *October's Baby*, and *All Darkness Met*, and features an introduction by Jeff VanderMeer.

A Fortress in Shadow

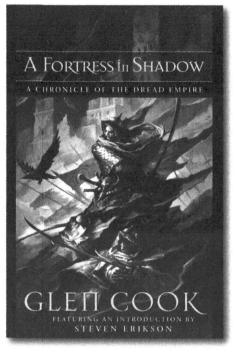

978-1-59780-1003 / Trade Paperback / $15.95

In the vast desert, a young heretic escapes death and embarks on a mission of madness and glory. He is El Murid—the Disciple— the savior destined to build a new empire from the blood of his enemies, who vows to bring order, prosperity, and righteousness to the desert people.

But all is not as it seems, and the sinister forces pulling the strings of empire come into the light. Who or what lies behind El Murid's vision of a desert empire?

A Fortress in Shadow collects *The Fire in His Hands* and *With Mercy Toward None*, which together make up the prequel series to the Dread Empire, and features an introduction by Steven Erikson.

Wrath of Kings

978-1-59780-938-2 / Hardback / $34.99

The Dread Empire spans a continent: from the highest peaks of the Dragon's Teeth to the endless desert lands of Hammad al Nakir; from besieged Kavelin to mighty Shinsan . . .

The time of the wrath of kings is close at hand. Bragi Ragnarson, now the king of Kavelin, has decided to join forces with Chatelain Mist, the exiled princess of Shinshan looking to usurp her throne. But in the deserts on the outskirts of the empire, a young victim of the Great Eastern Wars becomes the Deliverer of an eons-forgotten god, chosen to lead the legions of the dead.

Wrath of Kings collects the final Dread Empire trilogy (*Reap the East Wind*, *An Ill Fate Marshalling*, and *A Path to Coldness of Heart*) into a single volume.

An Empire Unacquainted with Defeat

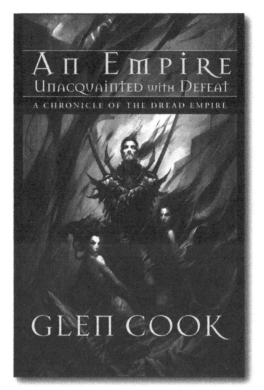

978-1-59780-1881 / Trade Paperback / $14.95

An Empire Unacquainted with Defeat collects all of Glen Cook's short fiction set in the vast world of the Dread Empire. With stories ranging from "The Nights of Dreadful Silence", featuring the first appearance of Bragi Ragnarson, Mocker, and Haroun bin Yousif, to the culture-clashing novella "Soldier of an Empire Unacquainted with Defeat"; from "Silverheels", Cook's first published work of fiction, to "Hell's Forge", a haunting tale of cursed pirates and strange lands, which appeared here for the first time, and also including a detailed introduction and extensive story notes by Glen Cook, *An Empire Unacquainted with Defeat* charts the development of this influential American author and the massive, multifaceted world that he created.

The Swordbearer

978-1-59780-1508 / Trade Paperback / $14.95

A young boy's dreams of glory and war turn into a bitter nightmare as his father's kingdom is overrun by an invading army, led by the Dark Champion Nevenka Nieroda and his twelve Dead Captains, the Toal.

Lost and alone in the woods, with his family slaughtered — or worse — Gathrid finds Daubendiek, the Great Sword of Suchara, a restless and thirsty ancient weapon that promises him the ability to claim his vengeance. But as Gathrid begins to take that vengeance, he comes to realize the terrible price that the sword will demand of him. Enemies soon become allies and strange bedfellows abound as the prophesies of an age swirl into chaos.